MODERN HUMANITIES RESEARCH ASSOCIATION
CRITICAL TEXTS
VOLUME 53

EDITOR
JUSTIN D. EDWARDS
(ENGLISH)

JEWELLED TORTOISE
VOLUME 4

EDITORS
STEFANO EVANGELISTA
CATHERINE MAXWELL

DECADENT AND OCCULT WORKS

ARTHUR MACHEN

EDITED BY
DENNIS DENISOFF

Decadent and Occult Works

by

Arthur Machen

Edited with an Introduction and Notes by
Dennis Denisoff

Modern Humanities Research Association
2018

Published by

The Modern Humanities Research Association
Salisbury House
Station Road
Cambridge CB1 2LA
United Kingdom

First published 2018

ISBN 978-1-78188-216-0 (paperback)
ISBN 978-1-78188-217-7 (hardback)

Copies may be ordered from www.tortoise.mhra.org.uk

CONTENTS

Illustrations   vii
Acknowledgements   viii
Introduction: Arthur Machen's Chamber of Decadence   1
    A Decadent Chronology of Arthur Machen's Life   29
    A Note on the Texts and Editorial Decisions   33

PART I: FICTION

1   The Lost Club (1890)   36
2   The Great God Pan (1894)   43
3   The Recluse of Bayswater (1895)   89
4   The Hill of Dreams (1907)   110
5   The Bowmen (1914)   251
6   The Rose Garden (1924)   256
7   The Turanians (1924)   259
8   The Idealist (1924)   262
9   The Ceremony (1924)   266
10 Ritual (1937)   269

PART II: NON-FICTION

11 The Literature of Occultism (1899)   276
12 Excerpts from *Hieroglyphics: A Note upon Ecstasy in Literature* (1902)   283
13 Introduction to *The Angels of Mons: The Bowmen and Other Legends
     of the War* (1915)   292
14 Introduction to *The Great God Pan* (1916)   300

PART III: CRITICAL CONTEXTS

15 Arthur Edward Waite: Excerpts from *The Occult Sciences* (1891)   310
16 Florence Marryat: Chapter XI, A Chance Séance with a Stranger, from
     The Spirit World (1894)   316
17 William Leonard Courtney: Novels and Nerves (1895)   321
18 Arthur Sykes: The Great Pan-Demon: An Unspeakable Story (1895)   326
19 Review of *The Three Impostors* (1896)   331
20 Alfred Egmont Hake: Chapter IX: The Religion of Self, from
     Regeneration: A Reply to Max Nordau (1896)   332
21 Review of *The Hill of Dreams* (1907)   338

ILLUSTRATIONS

Cover: Aubrey Beardsley, detail of the cover of the first edition of Arthur Machen's *The Great God Pan and The Inmost Light* (1894). Special Collections. McFarlin Library, University of Tulsa.

Page x: Unknown. Photograph of Arthur Machen. Photography Collection. Harry Ransom Center. The University of Texas at Austin.

ACKNOWLEDGEMENTS

I sincerely thank the series editors Stefano Evangelista and Catherine Maxwell, who supported this project from its earliest conception and then, with the altruism of dear friends, encouraged new work as the edition developed both in coverage and conceptual scope. Together we discovered in this project a purpose and potential that none of us had wholly realized at the start. During this process, the community of scholars invested in Decadence, the occult, eco-paganism, and Machen has grown considerably as has their collective contribution to the edition. Decadent authors of the nineteenth century are famous for having written entire chapters of lists — of mesmerizing scents, of rare books, of precious jewels. I don't dare compete, but will attempt instead a list of friends and colleagues whose analyses, conversations, recommendations, and editorial guidance are precious to me: Laurel Brake, Joseph Bristow, Liz Constable, Bénédicte Coste, Richard Dellamora, Catherine Delyfer, Christine Ferguson, Kate Foster-Wallace, Hilary Fraser, Regenia Gagnier, Jason Hall, Sue Hamilton, Lesley Higgins, Morgan Holmes, Linda K. Hughes, Neil Hultgren, Lorraine Janzen-Kooistra, Frederick King, James Machin, Kristen Mahoney, Diana Maltz, Alex Murray, Lene Østermark-Johansen, Ana Parejo Vadillo, Wendy Parkins, Matthew Potolsky, Patricia Pulham, Andrew Radford, Charlotte Ribeyrol, Mark Samuels Lasner, Talia Schaffer, Elaine Showalter, Dale M. Smith, Margaret Stetz, Carolyn Williams, Susan Zieger, and so many others. Simon Davies and Gerard Lowe were frighteningly scrupulous in copy-editing for all things archaic, occult, and obscure, including MHRA formatting; I could not ask for better editors. I am also grateful to my graduate students at the University of Tulsa, Ryerson University, and the Middlebury College Bread Loaf program, and especially to my research assistants and those students who chose to work on Machen in their own scholarship — Dennis Hogan, Colleen McDonell, Steven Maulden, Leila Meshgini, and Rebecca Thursten. I am particularly indebted to the Friends of Arthur Machen; their lively intellect and their publication *Faunus* have served not only as an aid but as an inspiration for my own efforts.

My deepest thanks are reserved for Morgan Holmes, who helped me extensively with the research and editing of this project. Delving deep into the dangerous knowledge of occult alchemy, he so often took the mess of slag I tried to pawn off as a solid draft and transmuted it into something closer to worthy scholarly metal. His investment in details and the thoroughness of his research added to my own keen interests, turning at times our Oklahoma home into the sort of cabinet of obsessions that some friends found worrisome but that Machen himself, I like to think, would have found inviting.

Figure 1. Anonymous, Arthur Machen (photograph)
Photography Collection, Harry Ransom Center,
The University of Texas at Austin.

INTRODUCTION

Arthur Machen's Chamber of Decadence

In his prefatory remarks to *The Angels of Mons: The Bowmen and Other Legends of the War* (1915), Arthur Machen (Arthur Llewelyn Jones Machen, 1863–1947[1]) recommends that an editor 'write an introduction justifying his principle of selection, pointing out here and there, as the spirit moves him, high beauties and supreme excellencies, discoursing of the magnates and lords and princes of literature, whom he is merely serving as groom of the chamber' (Fig. 1).[2] With some editorial licence, this is indeed the main aim of my own introduction — to represent the philosophical interests and bejewelled style that resulted in Machen's utterly original contribution to British Decadence. Doing so requires an explication of his actual connections to the British Decadent movement, as well as a consideration of the unique aspects and origins of his Decadent writing. Who would not relish the image of oneself as the groom to such a Machenian chamber, recognizing that his spiritual and aesthetic interests were premised on a sincere belief in an otherworldly reality beyond the grasp not only of one's modern, materialist society, but also that of contemporary occulture and the arts, including his own literary production? Machen's ongoing investment in a symbolic correspondence between literature and a domain beyond the mystic veil — what in 'The Literature of Occultism' (1899) he describes as 'the knowledge of the secret workings of the universe' — is one of the main qualities that brought his writing within the orbit of other Decadent authors of the period, as literary critics of the 1890s repeatedly pointed out, much to his chagrin.

In the 1922 introduction to his short-story collection *The House of Souls* (1906), Machen brings up reviews over a quarter century old in order to remind readers, yet again, that he is not to be affiliated with Decadence: 'Several papers, I remember, declared that "The Great God Pan" was simply a stupid

---

[1] Upon marriage to Janet Machen, Machen's father, John Edward Jones, changed the family name to Jones Machen in accordance with a request in the will of one of his wife's relatives. Arthur Machen later dropped Jones from his name.

[2] As in this instance, quotations from works included in this edition are not given citations.

and incompetent rehash of Huysmans' "Là-Bas" and "A Rebours." I had not read these books so I got them both. Thereon, I perceived that my critics had not read them either'.[3] Other than his early efforts to develop a style akin to Robert Louis Stevenson's (1850–1894) (which he readily acknowledged), Machen was accurate in declaring that his writing was not notably derivative of other authors' works. Rather, as this edition of his selected writing suggests, while his pieces circulated within the gyre of British Decadent culture, Machen also maintained unique channels of aesthetic and spiritual exploration that resulted in the originality and independent spirit of his voice. It has been only in hindsight, after the movement attained a more solid cultural identity, that his approach to literature and life could be understood as a fresh and innovative form of Decadence marked by a fusion of a symbolism influenced by the occult and the French Symbolists with pagan and Christian myths, ultimately comprising records of both a transhistorical spirituality and the zeitgeist of his time.[4]

It is correct to see Machen as a key originator of modern genres such as weird and horror fiction, but this emphasis has also led many editors of his work to characterize it as primarily populist entertainment, even when they acknowledge that the author himself saw it as more than that. Most editions of Machen to date have framed his work as horror literature, and have provided relatively few scholarly annotations. My current edition has the somewhat different intent of presenting the student of Machen with extensive literary, aesthetic, and philosophical annotations as well as a rich historical contextualization of a wide array of his works. This edition contains not only *The Great God Pan* but also *The Hill of Dreams*, because many Machen experts see the latter as his greatest achievement in literature. I also offer a cornucopia of shorter works that flesh out in particular the diversity of his engagements with Decadent styles, tropes, and authors. I have abetted these materials by also including samples of Machen's nonfiction writings as well as a selection of texts by other authors who engaged in related Decadent, occult, and spiritualist fields of interest. And so perhaps this edition's most original aspect is its extension of our understanding of Machen's innovations in weird and horror literature by focussing on the ways in which his lifelong interests in the occult and supernatural shaped his unique contribution to Decadence.

---

[3]   Arthur Machen, Introduction to *The House of Souls* (New York: Alfred A. Knopf, 1923), pp. 7–17 (p. 17).
[4]   In this edition, I capitalize 'Symbolism' when referring to the historical movement in literature and art, and keep it lower-case when referring to Machen's own symbolism, which was more deeply rooted in his detailed, personal occult studies.

1. Those 'Nineties

The passage of Machen's writing that recent scholars have probably most often quoted is from his introduction to the 1916 edition of *The Great God Pan* (1894), in which he attempts to disassociate himself from 'those 'nineties of which I was not even a small part, but no part at all'. Despite the seeming vehemence of this declaration, it remains that he attained his first notable attention as an author precisely because of what was seen as his close association with 1890s Decadence. In his statement, Machen himself is not addressing Decadence as a poetics or a belief system, but is referring to the most notorious period of the British literary movement that began roughly in the mid-nineteenth century with the works and observations of individuals such as Walter Pater (1839–1894) and Algernon Charles Swinburne (1837–1909). By the *fin de siècle*, this movement was recognized as championing an aesthetic undermining of bourgeois social values and normative cultural assumptions by developing new formal innovations in prose and poetry, as well as in periodical design with works such as *The Pageant* (1896–1897), *The Savoy* (1896), and the *Yellow Book* (1894–1897). During this period, British Decadence gradually became enmeshed with Pre-Raphaelitism, neo-paganism, the new woman movement, Symbolism, scientific theories of degeneracy and eugenics, and especially Aestheticism. As a cultural, philosophical, and artistic movement, Aestheticism began in the second half of the nineteenth century, primarily under the influence of Pater. Not wholly in accord with Pater's position, Aestheticism came to be recognized as regarding devotion to artistic expression as more important than concern with practical matters. Machen's 1916 comments on the closing decade of the previous century were a rather late contribution to the general disapprobation of what had become inaccurately but effectively characterized in the popular consciousness as a coterie of authors and artists — led by Aubrey Beardsley (1872–1898) and Oscar Wilde (1854–1900) — who celebrated deviance simply for its ability to shock the middle-class.

As early as 1893 Arthur Symons (1865–1945) was already arguing that the term 'decadence' had never been adopted by notable authors but, rather, was worn 'as the badge of little separate cliques, noisy, brainsick young people who haunt the brasseries of the Boulevard Saint-Michel, and exhaust their ingenuities in theorizing over the works they cannot write'.[5] Four years later, he observed that the term had 'been narrowed, in France and in England, to a mere label upon a particular school of very recent writers' and was no longer seen as referring to the manipulation of style in 'pursuit of some new expressiveness or beauty, deliberately abnormal'.[6] And yet, as Jason Hall and Alex Murray have argued,

---

[5] Arthur Symons, 'The Decadent Movement in Literature', *Harper's New Monthly Magazine* (November 1893), pp. 858–67 (p. 858).
[6] Arthur Symons, 'A Note on George Meredith', *Fortnightly Review* (November 1897); repr. Arthur Symons, *Studies in Prose and Verse*, 1904 (New York: E. P. Dutton, 1922), pp. 143–51 (p. 149).

the self-aware, anti-realist Decadent style of writing was 'a critique of the nineteenth-century idea of "decadence"[...], a challenge to the materialism of modernity, a counterpointing to its deadening conformity and complacency'.[7] This Decadent literature was, in other words, undermining the very same notions of degeneracy and atavism that later critics of the 1890s would come to rely on to portray Decadent culture as a biological and evolutionary threat.

In his 1916 distancing from 'those 'nineties', Machen never actually mentions Decadence at all. More precisely, he reproaches certain literary aspects of the British *fin de siècle* — such as Grant Allen's (1848–1899) novel *The Woman Who Did* (1895) and the *Yellow Book*, the quarterly known for publishing many of the avant-garde writers and artists of the day. Illustrator, author, and the *Yellow Book*'s art director until 1896, Aubrey Beardsley did much to codify the visual and, to a lesser extent, literary aesthetics of *fin-de-siècle* Decadence. The quarterly's publisher — the Bodley Head (run first by John Lane (1854–1925) and Charles Elkin Mathews (1851–1921) and then by Lane alone) — also published the Keynote series of texts that for many defined British Decadence at its peak. Despite *The Great God Pan* being one of the publications in Lane's series, Machen declares that his novella was not a product of this 1890s zeitgeist but, rather, arose from 'the visions that a little boy saw in the late 'sixties and early 'seventies'. Indeed, the conceptual heart of *The Great God Pan* is its opening chapter, which was published outside what Machen calls, in his introduction to the work, 'the ferment of the 'nineties'; it first appeared as the story 'The Experiment' in the December 1890 issue of a short-lived periodical called the *Whirlwind* that had begun publishing in the summer of that year and had no explicit affiliation with Decadence or Aestheticism. The five years following the novella's appearance in 1894 saw Machen write what most scholars agree is much of his best material, including *The Three Impostors, or the Transmutations* (1895), as well as the short-fiction collection *Ornaments in Jade* (1924) and the novella *The Hill of Dreams* (1907), which many consider his masterpiece. His works written during the 1890s are also his most Decadent. *The Great God Pan*, for example, contains most of the major themes and tropes that have come to be associated with the movement, including occultism, paganism, non-mainstream eroticism, sexual diversity, the femme fatale, violent and strange deaths, and the simultaneous investment in and disavowal of bourgeois identities. In a discussion of Machen's 1890s fiction, Kirsten MacLeod notes that his 'dilettantes valorize the anti-bourgeois and anti-professional values of the Decadents who aimed to escape their class origins'.[8] The characters'

---

[7] Jason David Hall and Alex Murray, 'Introduction: Decadent Poetics', *Decadent Poetics: Literature and Form at the British Fin de Siècle* (New York: Palgrave Macmillan, 2013), pp. 1–25 (p. 2).

[8] Kirsten MacLeod, *Fictions of British Decadence: High Art, Popular Writing, and the Fin de Siècle* (New York: Palgrave Macmillan, 2006), p. 122.

interest in the esoteric, she argues, reflects an effort to shed their professional identities. Such figures riddle *The Great God Pan*, which also offers many examples of Decadent formal techniques, with passages marked by languorous detachment and extensive, detailed description. Moreover, the work's plot is characteristically undirected, with its abundance of flat male characters tag-teaming along diverse channels of action that at times barely maintain narrative momentum.

It appears that, when Machen published the novella in 1894, he had not seen its placement within the Keynotes series as being a risk to the public shaping of his authorial persona; if he had, he would not have allowed the same line just one year later to publish his second book, *The Three Impostors* (1895), thereby making him one of only four authors to place two books in the series. It was, in fact, upon the publication of these two works that Machen claims he 'was at length certain, or almost certain, that [he] was a man of letters'.[9] Having the covers of both books designed by Beardsley, already well known for his explicit portrayal of nightmarish figures and non-normative sexual desires, only further affirmed Machen as a contributor to the Decadent movement. *The Great God Pan* is an earnest, terrifying exploration of psychological and spiritual boundaries marked by sexual violence and abuse; Beardsley's illustration for the publication (repeated on the cover to this edition), however, aestheticizes the hooved demi-god as a gender-ambiguous youth who, among sinuous vines, coyly invites readers to enter into the sexually inflected pleasures of the text.

Beardsley's image is appropriate in so much as *The Great God Pan* and Machen's oeuvre in general do explore issues of sexual power and the gender politics of cultural agency. In his rendering of a sexually alluring Pan figure, Beardsley follows Machen's own conflation of the ecstasy of desire with the terror that had come to characterize the pagan deity. That said, Machen never wrote any extensive nonfictional considerations of pansexual desire or gender politics, and his fiction does not explicitly contribute to the feminist debates of the new woman movement. In a discussion of *Jude the Obscure* (1895), he bemoans the fact that Thomas Hardy (1840–1928) took a 'curious' and 'beautiful' aspect of women's nature embodied in the character of Sue Bridehead and buried it beneath an image of the heroine as 'the prophetess of the "woman question," or whatever the contemporary twaddle on the subject was called'.[10] In the same work, he compliments George Egerton's (1859–1945) short-story collection *Keynotes* as high literature for its portrayal

---

[9] Arthur Machen, Introduction to *The Hill of Dreams* (New York: Alfred A. Knopf, 1923), p. v.

[10] Arthur Machen, *Hieroglyphics: A Note upon Ecstasy in Literature* (London: Grant Richards, 1902), p. 135.

of an essential element of 'real womanhood', but then critiques its engagement with contemporary gender politics as 'preaching'.[11] Of his male characters who display sexual interests, most are presented as either normative or ambiguous but nonthreatening. Female characters that demonstrate agency, conversely, are often portrayed as sexually monstrous, although some (as in certain stories in *Ornaments in Jade*) are not vilified for their desires. The fact that Machen not only avoided the subject of women's rights but criticized others for taking it up suggests a sustained misogynistic strain in his attitude. The hero's critique, in *The Hill of Dreams*, of George Eliot's (1819–1880) *Romola* (1862–1863) as an unjustly celebrated re-writing of Charles Reade's (1814–1884) *The Cloister and the Hearth* (1861) reinforces this tendency to undermine women whom he perceived as strong forces in contemporary British culture and politics.

This aspect of Machen's work must not be ignored, but nor should it be allowed to over-simplify his explorations of desire. His arguably most wicked female character, Helen Vaughan in *The Great God Pan*, is not simply an amorphous embodiment of evil. The representations of her in this form are, after all, offered by a pack of bumbling, self-confident males overwhelmed by the slightest challenge to their assumed social privilege. Helen is herself a product of this same privilege, the result of vivisection performed on her innocent mother, Mary. Justifying his work, the male scientist explains, 'I rescued Mary from the gutter, and from almost certain starvation, when she was a child; I think her life is mine, to use as I see fit'. The name of Mary's daughter, however, suggests Machen's wish to imbue her with a degree of self-respect; it takes an allusion to Helen of Troy, the daughter of Zeus, and combines it with 'vaughan' (Welsh for 'small'), the surname of the early modern Welsh alchemist Thomas Vaughan (1621–1666), whose work Machen began reading in the 1880s. The offspring of a Welsh woman and a demi-god, Helen Vaughan parallels Machen's own authorial self-identity as one arising from not only his Welsh ancestry but also pagan myth. Machen and his heroine are even from the same town of Caerleon (called Caermaen in the novella), which *The Great God Pan* accurately describes as 'a village on the borders of Wales, a place of some importance in the time of the Roman occupation, but now a scattered hamlet, of not more than five hundred souls'. In addition to these suggestions of Machen's empathy for Helen, his view of women is further complicated by his relationships with his two wives, Amelia (Amy) Hogg (*c*. 1850–1899) and Dorothie Purefoy Hudleston (1878–1947), both strong, independent individuals whom he respected greatly. Meanwhile, Lucian Taylor, the hero of his other major novella, *The Hill of Dreams*, displays both feminine and masculine traits. In fact, he embodies a Decadent aesthetic that is permeated by a fluid eroticism of not only diverse genders but diverse species. This bold vision accords with

---

[11]   Machen, *Hieroglyphics*, p. 141.

the fact that Machen completed *The Hill of Dreams* in 1897, notably after the notoriety of Wilde's trials, Lane's firing of Beardsley based on his reputation for sexually deviant artworks, and the *Yellow Book*'s peak in popularity. Machen's sustained thematic interest in non-normative and generally unaccepted models of desire and identity demonstrates not simply his tolerance of *fin-de-siècle* Decadence despite its sensationalist publicity but, more accurately, his commitment to a personal aesthetic philosophy that included the exploration of a sexual and gender amorphousness that, at the time, was also strongly associated with Decadence.

Beardsley's invitation in his illustration for *The Great God Pan* to a populist Decadent reading of Machen's texts was readily accepted by reviewers and parodists alike. Addressing Arthur Rickett's (1869–1937) and Arthur Sykes's (dates unknown) parodies, 'A Yellow Creeper' (1895) and 'The Great Pan-Demon' (1895) respectively, Susan J. Navarette suggests that the former picks up on the enigmatic descriptions and elliptical style that are, for Machen, a 'decompositive strategy' that induces 'the emotional and intellectual short-circuits in which reason gives way to elemental human emotions — to fear, anxiety, and shame'.[12] Both Rickett and Sykes imply that these gaps in information and allusive style are not a critique of rational thought and scientific materialism but, rather, proof of Machen's limited imagination. Sykes's text (included in this edition) also captures the influence of the literary scene on Machen's own authorial identity. A spoof of *The Great God Pan*, 'The Great Pan-Demon' portrays a scientist who embeds a pineal brain cell from a 'hydrocephalous female subject' into the corpse of a 'full-grown male idiot', resulting in a mysterious, evil being that embodies a slew of clichéd allusions to Charles Baudelaire (1821–1867), Gustave Doré (*c.* 1832–1883), George Egerton, and George Meredith (1828–1909), as well as androgyny, diabolism, satyrs, sphinxes, she-centaurs, Satan, and Symbolism, while inaccurately forecasting that Machen's work marked the demise of Lane's press ('BODLEIANUM.CAPUT.'), punning on 'caput' (Latin: head, as in Bodley Head) and 'kaput' (German for 'finished' or 'worn out', and first used as such in English in the 1890s). Sykes's parody suggests not just that Machen was associated with Decadence, but that *The Great God Pan* was no less than the quintessential storehouse of 1890s Decadence itself. By extension, the parodist casts the novella's author in the role of an egocentric scientist, letting loose upon London and an unsuspecting middle-class readership a veritable plague of degeneracy.

Machen was well aware that, just because one's literary efforts may have arisen independent of a particular movement's influences and cultural debates,

---

[12]   Arthur Rickett, 'A Yellow Creeper', *Lost Chords: Some Emotions without Morals* (London: A. D. Innes, 1895), pp. 17–23. Arthur Sykes, 'The Great Pan-Demon: An Unspeakable Story', *National Observer* (4 May 1895); repr. *Faunus*, 31 (Spring 2015), pp. 32–35. Susan J. Navarette, *The Shape of Fear: Horror and the Fin de Siècle Culture of Decadence* (Lexington: University Press of Kentucky, 1998), p. 201.

the published product could nevertheless become a contributor to its canon. Thus, in the same 1916 introduction to *The Great God Pan* in which he distances himself from those 1890s of the Bodley Head, he readily acknowledges that it was Wilde who first inspired him to begin writing short stories. Machen's brief description of the *fin de siècle* was not an attempt to erase his connections to everything and everyone associated with Decadent aesthetics; rather, he hoped to distance himself from the caricature of Decadence developed by critics and parodists of the period and then extended by authors and artists of the historical avant-garde who tried to use it as a strawman against which to demonstrate their own superior aesthetic virility.

II. The Spirit and Style of Machen's Decadence

Nineteenth-century theorists and critics of Decadence attempted to explain into submission something that had already characterized itself as indefinable. As early as Théophile Gautier's (1811–1872) discussion of Baudelaire in 1868, one finds an example of the way in which analyses of Decadent form often found themselves readily morphing into discussions of the ambiguity and formlessness of the spirit driving the work. Baudelaire's is 'an ingenious, complicated, learned style', Gautier proposes, 'taking colour from all palettes, notes from all keyboards, striving to render what in thought is most inexpressible, what in the contours of form is vague and most elusive'.[13] Anatole Baju's (1861–1903) *L'École décadente* (1887) offers one of the first extended articulations of this aspect of Decadence. Appearing 20 years after Gautier's piece, it describes the concept by conflating writing with imagination, presenting it as 'written thought' — something that 'embraces an entire era, giving an overview of all the trends, and is the only source of that true, living, panting life that we love, and that shakes us right to the base of our being through electric and vibrating upheavals'.[14] For Baju, 'this era in which we seem to have acquired the dark and terrible certainty of Nothingness' is characterized by a hopelessness that, curiously, results in 'a thirst for life'.[15] 'Eternity, the Heart and the Infinite', he tells us, 'are three things that will never be given to man to understand fully, three mysteries that will eternally defy Science and that are the indisputable

---

[13] 'style ingénieux, compliqué, savant, [...] pregnant des couleurs à toutes les palettes, des notes à tous les claviers, s'efforçant à rendre la pensée dans ce qu'elle a de plus ineffable, et la forme en ses contours les plus vagues et les plus fuyants'. Théophile Gautier, 'Charles Baudelaire', in Charles Baudelaire, *Le fleurs du mal* (Paris: Calmann-Lévy, 1868), p. 17.

[14] 'La pensée écrite embrasse toute une époque, en résume toutes les tendances et est la source unique de cette vie vécue, vivante, pantelante que nous aimons, et que nous secoue jusqu'au fond de l'être par d'électriques et vibrantes commotions'. Anatole Baju, *L'École décadente*, 3rd edn (Paris: Leon Vanier, 1887), p. 6.

[15] 'cette époque où on semble avoir acquis la sombre et épouvantable certitude du Néant'; 'le besoin de vivre'. Ibid., p. 10.

proof of human powerlessness'.[16] The same emphasis appears in Symons's 1893 essay 'The Decadent Movement in Literature', later included in his 1899 collection *The Symbolist Movement in Literature*. The two main strands of Decadence, Symons proposes, are Impressionism and Symbolism, which work 'on the same hypothesis, applied in different directions'.[17] While the former aims to capture what is seen just as it is seen, the latter aims to

> flash upon you the "soul" of that which can be apprehended only by the soul — the finer sense of things unseen, the deeper meaning of things evident. And naturally, necessarily, this endeavor after a perfect truth to one's impression, to one's intuition — perhaps an impossible endeavor — has brought with it, in its revolt from ready-made impressions and conclusions, a revolt from the ready-made of language, from the bondage of traditional form, of a form become rigid.[18]

This sort of literature, Symons argues, reflects a sense of the inability, from a materialist standpoint, to confirm the existence of a reality beyond our regular sensory engagement with the world. It is the very absence of a solid connection with the mysteries that drives the Decadent author who, unable to capture the life spirit, turns instead to recording *the compulsion* to capture it.

Decadence is, in this context, a reaction against literature as rigid form, language as corpse. The aesthetic engagement with a reality beyond immediate experience, and beyond the conventions of realism, requires an especially flexible imagination. Machen had such an imagination, and his own faith in and commitment to exploring through writing a state of being sensed only through nonmaterial avenues went all the way back to the fantastic visions of his childhood. The town of Caerleon on Usk in southeast Wales, where Machen was born on 3 March 1863, offered a slew of pagan, mystical, and historical allusions that he later appreciated as shaping his imagination. He lived there until 1881, during which time he availed himself of the materials in the library of his father, John Edward Jones, an Anglican vicar in Llandewi, near Caerleon. To these Machen added works borrowed from acquaintances or purchased at the Pontypool Road Railway Station. He familiarized himself with a range of canonical authors, including — as he mentions in his first volume of autobiography, *Far Off Things* (1922) — Charlotte Brontë (1816–1855), Charles Dickens (1812–1870), Sir Walter Scott (1771–1832), Robert Louis Stevenson, and Alfred Tennyson (1809–1892). Here, he notes, he was also introduced to occult topics, finding an article on alchemy in his father's copy of *Household Words*, of

---

[16] 'L'Éternité, le Cœur et l'Infini sont trois choses qu'il ne sera jamais donné à l'homme d'approfondir complètement, trois mystères qui défieront éternellement la Science et qui sont la preuve irréfragable de l'impuissance humaine'. Ibid., p. 11.

[17] Symons, 'The Decadent Movement in Literature', p. 859.

[18] Ibid.

which Dickens was editor.[19] These readings were complemented by his studies of Classics at Hereford Cathedral School (about 40 miles north of his hometown), where he boarded from the age of 11 to 17, as well as by his reading of works such as James Boswell's (1740–1795) *The Life of Samuel Johnson, L.L.D.* (1791), Robert Burton's (1577–1640) *Anatomy of Melancholy* (1621), and the *Mabinogion* (a collection of Celtic-influenced tales from the Middle Ages).[20] The impact on Machen's writing of Burton, Dickens, Edgar Allan Poe (1809–1849), and especially Stevenson has often been observed, while the author himself notes his early efforts to imitate William Morris (1834–1896) and Swinburne.[21] 'I began to write', Machen acknowledges, 'because I bought a copy of Swinburne's *Songs Before Sunrise*'.[22] He found this work of British Decadence 'wholly strange and new and wonderful', admiring it for its 'tremendous boldness' and 'denial of everything that I had been brought up to believe most sure and sacred; the book was positively strewn with the fragments of shattered altars and the torn limbs of kings and priests'.

At the same time, Caerleon's own history — mythic and real — gained added import for Machen when Tennyson came to town to write much of the cycle of twelve narrative poems entitled *Idylls of the King* (1859; revised and expanded, 1869, 1872, 1885). The mythology and mystical aura that Tennyson built around King Arthur's court and interwove with descriptions of the region's natural landscape would have stimulated the imagination of the young Arthur. He would have found in Tennyson's mythologizing of his hometown affirmation that it embodied an eco-spiritual mysticism distinctly its own. One often finds the unique model of ecology, and especially of the natural environment, which arose from Machen's strong childhood sense of place at the heart of his Decadent writing; sometimes figuring — as in 'The Turanians' — as the context in which ancient races and spiritual practices still survive; sometimes — as in *The Hill of Dreams* — as the living, breathing essence of the otherworldly force he venerated. As he declares in *Far Off Things*:

> the older I grow the more firmly am I convinced that anything which I may have accomplished in literature is due to the fact that when my eyes were first opened in earliest childhood they had before them the vision of an enchanted land. As soon as I saw anything I saw Twyn Barlwm, that mystic tumulus, the memorial of peoples that dwelt in the region before the Celts left the Land of Summer.[23]

Machen attempted to capture his devotion to the *genius loci* through his art,

---

[19]   Arthur Machen, *Far Off Things* (London: Martin Secker, 1922).

[20]   Mark Valentine, *Arthur Machen* (Bridgend: Poetry Wales Press, 1995), p. 14.

[21]   Arthur Machen, 'The Young Man in the Blue Suit', *Evening News*, 29 December 1913; repr. *Faunus*, 2 (Autumn 1998), pp. 2–5 (p. 4).

[22]   Machen, *Far Off Things*, p. 92.

[23]   Machen, *Far Off Things*, pp. 8–9.

using writing not to recreate but to access, however evanescently, the reality of the supernatural.

In 'Supernatural Horror in Literature' (1927), H. P. Lovecraft (1890–1937) lauds a variety of Machen's writings, and 'above all his memorable epic of the sensitive æsthetic mind, *The Hill of Dreams*'; Lovecraft's emphasis is on the author's 'exquisitely lyrical and expressive prose style', with its 'almost incomparable substance and realistic acuteness'.[24] Despite a reference to the conventions of realism, Lovecraft's description belies if not a Decadent attention to detail, then a notable control in Machen's aesthetic approach to writing. In his review of the novella, Alfred Douglas (1870–1945) gives this element greater emphasis, concluding that

> Machen's prose has the rhythmic beat of some dreadful Oriental instrument, insistent, monotonous, haunting; and still the soft tone of one careful flute sounds on, and keeps the nerves alive to the slow and growing pain of the rhythmic beat [...]. It is like some dreadful liturgy of self-inflicted pain, set to measured music: and the cadence of that music becomes intolerable by the suave phrasing and perfect modulation.[25]

In 1922, R. Ellis Roberts (1879–1953) celebrated the 'muscular, sinewy narrative style' of *The Great God Pan* and 'The Terror', as well as the more 'elaborate, descriptive prose' of other works by Machen.[26] Tellingly, Roberts is paraphrasing Jean Des Esseintes, the hero of French author Joris-Karl Huysmans's (1848–1907) *A Rebours* (1884). In that classic novel of Decadence, Des Esseintes finds immense gratification in opening his collection of Baudelaire's works bound in flesh-coloured pig-skin to read the works of one who — as Havelock Ellis (1859–1939) translates Huysmans in *Affirmations* (1915) — 'had succeeded in expressing the inexpressible, by virtue of a muscular and sinewy speech which more than any other possessed the marvellous power of fixing with strange sanity of expression the most morbid, fleeting, tremulous states of weary brains and sorrowful souls'.[27]

Although it is common among Machen's admirers to note the versatility of his writing, much of his material does adopt what scholars have recognized as Decadent formal qualities. Moreover, the author's own words on the importance of style reflect a set of philosophical and aesthetic values aligned with those of Decadence. He once declared that 'a good style is always a perfectly clear

---

[24] H. P. Lovecraft, 'Supernatural Horror in Literature', Project Gutenberg Australia <http://gutenberg.net.au/ebooks06/0601181h.html> [accessed 3 March 2016].
[25] Alfred Douglas, Review of *The Hill of Dreams*, *The Academy* (16 March 1907), pp. 273–74 (p. 273).
[26] R. Ellis Roberts, 'Arthur Machen', *The Bookman* (September 1922); repr. *Faunus*, 31 (Spring 2015), pp. 36–40 (p. 40).
[27] Havelock Ellis, 'Huysmans', *Affirmations* (London: Constable, 1929), pp. 158–211 (p. 184).

and lucid style. [...] Affectation is the devil'.[28] A look at his fiction, however, clarifies that he was not condoning a curt, modernist simplicity of form, but a need to focus on the symbolic function of the art form. In *Hieroglyphics: A Note Upon Ecstasy in Literature* (1902), Machen places particular emphasis on the importance of style in the creation of what he calls 'fine' literature. It is through style, he argues, that 'the ear and the soul through the ear receive an impression of subtle but most beautiful music', where 'the sense and sound and colour of the words affect us with an almost inexplicable delight'. Style is no less than 'the glorified body of the very highest literary art. Style is, in short, the last perfection of the very best in literature, it is the outward sign of the burning grace within'. The description brings to mind Decadent interests in Symbolism, synaesthesia, impressionism, and Aestheticism, but one could never admire Machen's Decadence fully without appreciating the particularly unique influences that shaped his aesthetics and subject matter.

III. Machen's Occult Aesthetics and the Tendrils of Decadence

Machen's interest in ceremony, symbol, and mysticism suggested by works such as *The Great God Pan* and *The Hill of Dreams* arose, in large part, from the occult studies he conducted when the publisher George Redway (1859–1934) hired him in 1885 as a sub-editor and later a cataloguer. Redway was a major early supporter of and influence on Machen, even publishing his first book *The Anatomy of Tobacco* (1884), as well as others. Various important occult works were produced by Redway's company during Machen's employ. These included *The Mysteries of Magic: A Digest of the Writings of Eliphas Levi* (1886), edited by A. E. Waite (1857–1942), a renowned occult scholar who would become one of Machen's best friends.[29] Redway also published works by Machen's acquaintance Samuel Liddell MacGregor Mathers (1854–1918),[30] one of the three men who founded the Hermetic Order of the Golden Dawn; these include *Fortune-Telling Cards: The Tarot, its Occult Significance and Methods of Play* (1888) and his translations of *The Kabbalah Unveiled* (1887) and *The Key of Solomon the King* (1889).[31] Redway had Machen create *The Literature of Occultism and Archaeology*, an annotated catalogue of Redway's collection of

---

[28] Arthur Machen, *A Receipt for Fine Prose* (New York: Postprandial Press, 1956); repr. *Faunus*, 1 (September 1998), p. 54. Thomas Horan explains the source of this brief work in the same issue of the journal.

[29] On Waite and Machen's notion of the occult in relation to the art of fiction, see Christine Ferguson, 'Reading with the Occultists: Arthur Machen, A. E. Waite, and the Ecstasies of Popular Fiction', *Journal of Victorian Culture*, 21:1 (2016), pp. 40–55.

[30] Arthur Machen, *Arthur Machen: Selected Letters*, ed. by Roger Dobson, Godfrey Brangham, and R. A. Gilbert (Wellingborough, UK: Aquarian, 1988), p. 77.

[31] Ellic Howe, *The Magicians of the Golden Dawn: A Documentary History of a Magical Order 1887–1923* (London: Routledge and Kegan Paul, 1972).

works on, among other topics, hermeticism, Swedenborgianism, freemasonry, witchcraft, alchemy, psychic research, and the Kabbalah.[32] Machen also began writing reviews under Redway, and Mark Valentine observes that the reviews Machen wrote after leaving the publisher continued to reflect an interest in occult materials.[33]

Machen eventually became a member of the Golden Dawn. Founded in 1888, the society developed from freemasonry by introducing elements of the Kabbalah, Rosicrucianism, Theosophy, and other esoteric systems. According to the Order, magic was a natural set of practices that helped individuals attain a state of self-realization within the psychic plane of being. It has been argued that Machen's fiction of the 1890s was not notably influenced by the Order.[34] After all, he did not become a member until November 1899, possibly spurred by his wife Amy's death four months earlier. Moreover, he was not a particularly devoted member. However, he had already been engaged with occult interests in the 1880s, before the Order even formed, and early works such as *The Great God Pan* reflect this. The novella is not an artistic envisioning of the Order's belief system, but more broadly a conceptualization of reality that explores spiritual and ethical conundrums arising from occult principles and practices.

Although Machen acknowledges in the second volume of his autobiography that the Golden Dawn 'did me a great deal of good — for the time', he is quick to add that, 'as for anything vital in the secret order, for anything that mattered two straws to any reasonable being, there was nothing of it, and less than nothing'.[35] His occult interests did not comfortably mesh with those of the Order's other members or the many other late-Victorians — including Decadents — who were caught up in the period's fervour around supernaturalism, neo-paganism, and spiritualism. This was in large part due to the earnestness with which Machen invested himself and his work in these subjects. He was often frustrated with populist spiritualism and especially with claims, such as those attached to spirit photography and automatic writing, declaring direct communication with a separate reality. He lamented the fact that 'the unseen world, and superstition [...] is now thoroughly "democratised"'.[36] In *The Three Impostors*, one of Machen's narrators boldly condemns 'the "occult" follies of the day, disguised under various names — the mesmerisms, spiritualisms, materialisations,

---

[32] Arthur Machen, *Things Near and Far* (London: Martin Secker, 1923), pp. 20–21.

[33] Valentine, *Arthur Machen*, p. 19.

[34] Susan Johnston Graf, *Talking to the Gods: Occultism in the Work of W. B. Yeats, Arthur Machen, Algernon Blackwood, and Dion Fortune* (Albany: State University of New York Press, 2015), p. 77.

[35] Arthur Machen, *Things Near and Far* (London: Martin Secker, 1923), pp. 149–50.

[36] Arthur Machen, 'Science and the Ghost Story', *Literature*, 48 (17 September 1898), pp. 250–52 (p. 251). See also Arthur Machen, 'Has Spiritualism Come to Stay', *John O'London's Weekly* (12 April 1919), p. 4.

theosophies, all the rabble rant of imposture, with their machinery of poor tricks and feeble conjuring, the true back-parlour magic of shabby London streets'. The same language appears in his article 'The Literature of Occultism', included in this edition. His dismissiveness arose from an earnest belief that the occult was an engagement with the mysteries, which were not phenomena humans could conjure up, let alone prove through modern scientific methods. In a letter to his publisher John Lane in March 1894, Machen points out:

> If I were writing in the Middle Ages I should need no scientific basis for the reason that in those days the supernatural *per se* was entirely credible. In these days the supernatural *per se* is entirely *in*credible; to believe, we must link our wonders to some scientific or pseudo-scientific fact, or basis, or method. Thus we do not believe in "ghosts", but in *telepathy*, not in "witchcraft", but in *hypnotism*.[37]

In his article 'Science and the Ghost Story', he bewails the fact that 'there are few steps between the laboratory and the séance'.[38] The obsession with proving the scientific veracity of magic and occult practices, Alison Butler has noted, is 'characteristic of Victorian occultists and is a key feature in the nineteenth-century revival of magic'.[39] In 1897, W. T. Stead (1849–1912), as editor of the 'psychical' periodical *Borderland*, chided other spiritualists for being 'sublimely indifferent to the duty of supplying evidence or convincing other people' of their views.[40] A critic of Stead's occult writings, Machen felt not only that magic and occult symbology could not be contained by the limited logic of science, but that the dominant sciences themselves were the products of occult methods, as explained by a character in his story 'The Recluse of Bayswater', included in this edition.

Ultimately, for his exploration into modes of communication with other levels of reality and for what became his unique occult symbolism, Machen turned his attention to a range of sources, an inquisitive adventurousness that brought him into the sphere of the Decadent movement. Albeit a secretive society, even the Golden Dawn was a vibrant force within the popular cultural networks of the period, and especially that of the Decadents. To give an indication of the intricate network of associations traversing the British Decadent and occult communities at this time, it is useful to note some informative links among the members of Machen's cultural communities. In 1890, he had sent Wilde

---

[37] Machen, *Selected Letters*, p. 218. The last line of this quotation is also spoken, with somewhat different wording, by a character in 'The Recluse of Bayswater', included in this edition.
[38] Machen, 'Science and the Ghost Story', p. 251.
[39] Alison Butler, *Victorian Occultism and the Making of Modern Magic: Invoking Tradition* (Basingstoke: Palgrave Macmillan, 2011), p. xiii.
[40] W. T. Stead, Introduction, 'Chronique of the Quarter', *Borderland: A Psychical Quarterly*, 4:1 (January 1897), pp. 3–5 (p. 3).

some writing, and upon receiving encouragement, Machen met with him a number of times. Wilde's wife, Constance (1859–1898), had by this time already become a member of the Order and probably shared some of its secret rituals with her husband during her short period of involvement.[41] The first English production of Wilde's play *Salome* (1893), in 1905, was directed by Florence Farr (1860–1917) — an acquaintance of Constance's who had been initiated into the Golden Dawn by W. B. Yeats (1865–1939) in 1890 and became Chief Adept in England in 1897. Like Machen and Golden Dawn members Edith Nesbit (1858–1924) and William Sharp (1855–1905), Farr was published in Lane's Keynote series, although later in life Machen would disparage her occultism.[42] In his 1944 *Pleasant Land of Gwent*, which Machen admired, Fred J. Hando selects as Machen's contemporaries the Golden Dawn members Sharp and Yeats.[43] When Machen himself joined the Order in 1899, Farr was the leader of the English lodges. In addition to the novel published by Lane, Farr also co-authored two occult dramas — *The Beloved of Hathor* and *Shrine of the Golden Hawk* (publication dates uncertain) — with Olivia Shakespear (1863–1938), who herself was a guest at Machen's home in the 1890s. Shakespear was a contributor to the Decadent 1890s periodical *The Savoy*, edited by Symons, with Beardsley as art director. Another guest, the Aestheticist poet A. Mary F. Robinson (1857–1944), edited and wrote the introduction to an edition of Machen's translation of *The Heptaméron* (1886), published by Redway. At this time, Robinson lived only four doors down from Pater, whom she knew well.[44] Robinson was also for a time the partner of Vernon Lee (1856–1935), the author and aesthetic scholar who, during the 1890s, popularized the pagan notion of the *genius loci*, a concept that was central to Machen's writings of the period. Lee gained notoriety for her attack, in her novel *Miss Brown* (1884), on the Decadent aesthetes.

Throughout these last two decades of the century, Machen of course also maintained his occult interests. When the Hermetic Order of the Golden Dawn disbanded at the turn of the century due to internal rifts, Waite initiated a splinter group rooted in mystic Christianity; it was called the Independent and Rectified Rite of the Golden Dawn (1903–1914) and Machen was a member for some time from its inception.

These interweavings through British Aestheticist, Decadent, and occult culture show that the tendrils of Decadence did not have to rely on Machen's conscious veneration and adaptation in order for them to insinuate themselves into his

---

[41] Franny Moyle offers a summary of Constance's investment in the Golden Dawn and the Society for Psychical Research in her biography; see *Constance: The Tragic and Scandalous Life of Mrs Oscar Wilde* (London: John Murray, 2011).

[42] Machen, *Selected Letters*, p. 35.

[43] Fred J. Hando, *The Pleasant Land of Gwent* (Newport, Wales: R. H. Johns, 1945), p. 53.

[44] R. M. Seiler, 'Introduction', in *Walter Pater: The Critical Heritage* (London: Routledge, 1980), pp. 1–45 (p. 2).

literary career; they also influenced his writing through practical publishing arrangements and opportunities, overlapping cultural interpretations, avant-garde literary interests, and extended networks of personal relations. Although Machen was not wholly committed to the visions of influential individuals such as Pater and Wilde, his writing and aesthetics both absorbed elements of the British Decadent movement and made original contributions to it.

iv. Hieroglyphics, the Art of Fine Literature

In 1889, Havelock Ellis translated into English the French author Paul Bourget's (1852–1935) famous description of Decadent style as arising when the unity of the book (generally speaking) is lost to the independence of the page, that of the page to the independence of the phrase, and that of the phrase to the independence of the word.[45] In Bourget's view, this style was a symptom of a parallel degenerate shift in society. The cohesion of social networks, he believed, gave way to increasingly individualistic attitudes that were undermining and destroying civilization. The result was a society in which only a few privileged people were able to realize their hyper-refined experiences. Yet, even as they reached this summit, they discovered that nobody among the barbaric majority had the aesthetic or intellectual refinement necessary to recognize, let alone appreciate, the occasion. Machen himself adopted Bourget's model in his introduction to *The Ghost Ship and Other Stories* (1912) by Richard Middleton (1882–1911), whom Machen knew through their membership in the casual debating group the New Bohemians. Machen compliments *The Ghost Ship*'s alchemical ability to offer 'something formless transmuted into form', to reveal that 'the universe is a great mystery'.[46] 'The consciousness of this mystery', he explains, 'resolved into the form of art, expresses itself usually (or always) by symbols, by the part put for the whole'.[47] Transmutability is central both to Machen's literary aesthetic and his conception of a spiritual symbolism in some ways distinct from the aesthetics of the Symbolist movement in France. The subject of transmutation appears in *The Three Impostors* and *Hieroglyphics*, and the phenomenon is explored in *The Great God Pan*, but it is most explicitly addressed in *The Hill of Dreams*. In this novella, the hero Lucian considers transmutation not only as an alchemical process, but also as a form of occult magic, an approach to social engagement, and the unique means of writing the best literature.

---

[45] Havelock Ellis, 'A Note on Paul Bourget', *Pioneer* (October 1889); repr. *Views and Reviews: A Selection of Uncollected Articles 1884–1932* (London: Desmond Harmsworth, 1932), pp. 48–60.

[46] Arthur Machen, 'Introduction', in Richard Middleton, *The Ghost-Ship and Other Stories* (London: T. Fisher Unwin, 1912), pp. vii–xiv (pp. ix, xi).

[47] Ibid., p. xii.

Middleton himself explores the last of these in his 'The Story of a Book', in *A Ghost Ship*. In that piece, a frustrated writer complains that, 'in spite of his effort to bear in mind that the whole should be greater than any part, his chapters broke up into sentences and his sentences into forlorn and ungregarious words'.[48] Paralleling Bourget's association of Decadent stylistics to society in general, Machen emphasizes the way Middleton extends his ideas about the art of writing to an understanding of the urban landscape — the streets as more than an assemblage of houses, London as more than an assemblage of streets. Machen engaged repeatedly with these aesthetic and philosophical concerns, lamenting the fact that his own writing, like literature in general, could only offer an inadequate rendering of mystic reality:

> nothing is capable of rational demonstration in the true and final sense of those two words [i.e. rational demonstration]: we speculate as to the nature of God, and we speculate as to the nature of gold; and the veil of the everlasting mysteries hides the real and essential nature of each from our eyes.[49]

Middleton responded to this lack of proof with utter frustration, while, as Barbara Spackman argues, Decadent authors generally celebrated (or depicted the celebration of) the inevitability of artifice.[50] Machen, meanwhile, focussed his efforts on exploring affective supernatural experiences that might arise through such things as a devotion to spiritual mystery, an investment in occult and Christian symbology, and a psycho-geographical engagement with one's surroundings. Machen's most extensive articulation of the symbolism at the heart of his Decadent aesthetics appears in *Hieroglyphics*, which he wrote in 1899 and published in 1902. In his prefatory note to the text, he sets up the mind behind *Hieroglyphics* as that of a typical Decadent. Although the work is an articulation of ideas that Machen elsewhere presents as his own, here he declares that *Hieroglyphics* is the record by an unnamed narrator of conversations with an 'obscure literary hermit' who lived in two ground-floor rooms in an unassuming house in Barnsbury. The sitting room in which the conversations occurred contained 'decaying beams' and a 'crypt-like odour';[51] it was a 'hollow, echoing room, the atmosphere with its subtle suggestion of incense sweetening the dank odours of the cellar, and the tone of the voice speaking to me'.[52] Eventually acknowledging the similarities between his

---

[48] Middleton, 'The Story of a Book', in *The Ghost-Ship and Other Stories*, p. 145.
[49] Arthur Machen, 'By the Way', *The Academy* (11 May 1912); repr. *Faunus*, 32 (Autumn 2015), pp. 52–56 (pp. 55–56).
[50] Barbara Spackman, 'Interversions', in *Perennial Decay: On the Aesthetics and Politics of Decadence*, ed. by Liz Constable, Dennis Denisoff, and Matthew Potolsky (Philadelphia: University of Pennsylvania Press, 1999), pp. 35–49.
[51] Machen, *Hieroglyphics*, p. 10.
[52] Ibid., p. 11.

character and that of the 'obscure literary hermit', the narrator observes that 'I believe that once or twice we both saw visions, and some glimpse at least of certain eternal, ineffable Shapes'.

In a section of *Hieroglyphics* included in the current edition, Machen declares that the highest form of writing, what the hermit refers to as 'fine literature', is 'the expression of the eternal things that are in man, that it is beauty clothed in words, that it is always ecstasy, that it always draws itself away, and goes apart into lonely places, far from the common course of life'. Although ecstasy is central to the aesthetic vision of this work, the concept ultimately proves so expansive as to be practically indefinable: 'Substitute, if you like, rapture, beauty, adoration, wonder, awe, mystery, sense of the unknown, desire for the unknown'. In accord with Gautier's defence of *l'art pour l'art*, which proved a cornerstone of Decadent aesthetic theory, Machen explicitly argues for a symbolist, rather than realist, approach to the creation of fine literature. As he writes elsewhere in *Hieroglyphics*: 'Art and Life are two different spheres, and [...] the Artist with a capital A is not a clever photographer who understands selection in a greater or less degree'.[53] Rather than developing a style struggling impossibly for verisimilitude, an artist must foster a deep and sincere connection to nature that allows one to tap into the eternal realm of ecstasy.

Machen's conception of this experience is original but, as the hermit notes, it is also rooted in the model of imagination found in 'Ode: Intimations of Immortality from Recollections of Early Childhood' (1807) by William Wordsworth (1770–1850). In his introduction to *The Great God Pan*, Machen credits Wordsworth's 'supreme and magistral ode' in marking youth as most free from 'the house of prudent artifice'. 'When men are young', he argues in the excerpt from *Hieroglyphics* included here, ecstasy is

> of such efficacy and virtue that the grossest and vilest matter is transmuted for them into pure gold, glistering and glorious as the sun. The child (and with him you may link all primitive and childlike people) approaches books and pictures just as he approaches nature itself and life; and a wonderful vision appears where many of us can only see the common and insignificant.

This model reflects what Alex Murray describes as Machen's shift in emphasis away from attempting 'to solve the riddle of nature through the projection on to it of human reason, to the quest for the enigmatic word within nature, a hieroglyphics of nature'.[54] Acknowledging the limits of his anthropological knowledge, Machen readily adopts a Romantic vision of young or 'primitive' humans as uniquely linked to the state of wonder to which fine literature

[53] Machen, *Hieroglyphics*, p. 34.
[54] Alex Murray, *Landscapes of Decadence: Literature and Place at the Fin de Siècle* (Cambridge: Cambridge University Press, 2016), p. 139.

aspires. Writing prior to the birth of his own daughter and son, he argues in *Hieroglyphics* that 'children before they have been defiled by the horrors of "education" possess the artistic emotion in remarkable purity, that they reproduce, in a measure, the primitive man before he was defiled, artistically, by the horrors of civilisation'. For Machen, fine literature is simply 'a recollection, a remnant' of this childhood vision. He thus declares that *The Great God Pan* was itself first and foremost a product of his childhood, and many of his works, including 'The Turanians' and 'The Ceremony', centre on the mystical vision of the young and naive, with the latter work in particular re-envisioning Wordsworth's formulation. In accord with *The Great God Pan*'s own emphasis, scholars have usually read the novella as portraying the concerns of late-Victorian urban adults regarding such issues as the ignorant egotism of modern science, the frighteningly awesome potential of the spiritual, or the disastrous state of current systems of order such as the law, the police, and the culture of bourgeois, male authority. If one considers the perspective of the work's male characters to be that of a child in a state of wonder, however, *The Great God Pan* becomes not only a fantastic story of men's anxieties around issues of authority, agency, and desire, but the rendering of an innocent's intense, visceral experience of both the modern, urban sphere and the transhistorical mysticism of the countryside.

There is a general tendency to observe among the authors and other contributors to the British Decadent movement a disregard of the countryside as provincial, conservative, and uninspiring, and a focus, instead, on the city, which was seen to offer a combination of cosmopolitanism, excitement, and secrecy. The actual works of most Decadent authors of the period do not fit comfortably within this simple binary. In Machen's case, his investment in the pagan mystery and Celtic spirituality arising from his Welsh roots fosters an aesthetics and philosophy of life that has the natural landscape at its core. And yet paganism, occultism, and ritual also appear in most of his depictions of the metropolis. In *The Great God Pan*, we see these elements move from the dappled countryside to the narrow, night-time streets of London, much as Machen himself brought his Welsh spirituality with him when he moved to the capital's suburbs. Similarly, while the countryside is marked in his work as territory in which the individual is at risk of losing agency to the frightful machinations of otherworldly supernatural forces — including satyrs, fauns, and Turanians — the metropolis consists of nightmarish, suburban mazes strewn with morally vacuous denizens, as in the climactic hallucination of *The Hill of Dreams*. In *Far Off Things*, Machen describes his first views of the British capital: 'I judged of London purely by its exterior aspects, as one may judge of a passing stranger in the street, and decide that he goes to an expensive tailor, without knowing

anything of the condition of his banking account'.[55] While the description
seems to suggest that, for him, British Decadent society at its most popular was
both superficial and inconsequential, he later notes his admiration for a city
of mystery much like that found in *Great God Pan*: 'Holywell Street and Wych
Street were all in their glory in 1885, a glory compounded of sixteenth-century
gables, bawdy books and matters congruous therewith, parchment Elzevirs,
dark courts and archways, hidden taverns, and ancient slumminess'.[56] This
London is not a metropolis of internationalist *flâneurs* tossing about witticisms
while frequenting art galleries, theatres, and Decadent soirées. Nor is it the
suburban purgatory portrayed in *The Hill of Dreams*, 'a city that had suffered
some inconceivable doom, [...] a town great as Babylon, terrible as Rome,
marvellous as Lost Atlantis, set in the midst of a white wilderness surrounded
by waste places'. Not atypical for Decadent authors, the London Machen
admires is, rather, a land of esoteric knowledge, dangerous mystery, solitary
exploration, and self-discovery.

Machen's depictions of London as a maze are thus not simply critiques of
either suburban sprawl or urban Decadence. He more than once coordinates
the urban image with his own narrative form, which he also maps onto the
complex meanderings of the human mind. *The Great God Pan*, for example,
is known for its convoluted narrative and lack of a clear revelation common to
such popular genres as the gothic, sensation literature, and detective literature
with which Machen's work overlaps. The characters' own confusion regarding
the inexplicable deaths of various established London gentlemen conflates the
possibility of scandal or 'suicidal mania' with 'the labyrinth of Daedalus'. Similarly, *The Hill of Dreams* describes the hero in the London suburbs with their

> labyrinth of streets more or less squalid, but all grey and dull, and behind
> were the mud pits and the steaming heaps of yellowish bricks, and to the
> north was a great wide cold waste, treeless, desolate, swept by bitter wind.
> It was all like his own life, he said again to himself, a maze of unprofitable
> dreariness and desolation, and his mind grew as black and hopeless as the
> winter sky.

Machen's metropolis accords with the Decadent London and Paris that late-
Victorian society commonly envisaged and feared as graphic, often terrifying
evidence of human and cultural degeneracy. For the author and his readers,
the cityscape served as a metaphor for the convolutions of the human mind
both maniac and depressing. But overriding this reading of the city, Machen
repeatedly appreciated the ways in which the urban experience is also as
engaging and as mysteriously spiritual as the *genius loci* that permeated the
Welsh countryside.

---

[55] Machen, *Far Off Things*, p. 75
[56] Machen, *Things Near and Far*, 33.

v. The Contents of the Edition

This edition of a selection of Machen's writing is intended to reflect the variety of his Decadent works and to consider some of his key terms and concepts — such as ecstasy, symbolism, and transmutation — in relation to Decadence and its own main interests. *The Great God Pan* and *The Hill of Dreams* are at the heart of this collection, offering particularly complex arrangements of Machen's style, aesthetics, and worldview during his most Decadent period of writing. A comparison of the two novellas signals a shift in perspective from that of an author, in the earlier work, filtering his range of occult interests through a particularly British literary legacy and an interest in populist formal techniques, to one, in the later piece, heavily inspired by his faith in, and desire to engage with, a natural symbology. *The Great God Pan* is also of interest to the scholar of Decadence, as are the short story 'The Lost Club' and the chapter of *The Three Impostors* entitled 'The Recluse of Bayswater' (both included in this edition), for their portrayals of London as a Decadent urban ecology defying coherence and logic. This environment can also be found in writing by late-Victorian authors such as Stevenson, Bram Stoker (1847–1912), and Richard Marsh (1857–1915). These works offer sustained considerations of the dominant male homosocial networks as, in fact, clandestine systems often acting against official institutions of law and order that are generally understood to operate for their privileged benefit. Machen's use of the Decadent urban landscape is unique, however, in being fundamental to his earnest conception of the *genius loci* as a force in human experience. The semi-autobiographical *The Hill of Dreams*, meanwhile, is an articulation of the artist whose aesthetic worldview is rooted in a symbolist faith. There is a greater psychological depth to the central character, the Decadent Lucian Taylor, than there is to any character in the earlier novella, as well as a shift of emphasis from a male team-effort to dominate and suppress that which they cannot comprehend to an individual's struggle to engage with an amorphous force he respects.

I have included 'The Lost Club' as a particularly early rendering of urban Decadence that reflects the influence of both Stevenson and Wilde; the story fits admirably within the dominant trajectory of the British Decadent movement, and its allusions to London haunts speak to a readership keenly aware of the Aestheticist community of the moment. 'The Recluse of Bayswater', meanwhile, offers a curt depiction of an otherworldly reality as both awe-inspiring and horrific. The narrative of drug-induced metamorphosis ends with a succinct critique of scientific materialism and fashionable occult practices, as opposed to the transcendental panpsychism in which Machen was seriously invested. Most editions of Machen that include this work excerpt 'Novel of the White Powder', which is embedded within 'The Recluse of Bayswater'; I have chosen to include the full chapter because the added information regarding the narrator transforms the perspective as well as the implications of the embedded story. It also suggests why we might be wise not to trust Machen's narrators too readily, a warning that is helpful in interpreting many of his texts, from *The Great God Pan* to *Hieroglyphics*. From *Ornaments in Jade*, I have included 'The Rose Garden', 'The Turanians', 'The Idealist', and 'The Ceremony'. The book's name brings to mind Gautier's poetry collection *Émaux et Camées* (*Enamels and Cameos*, 1852), which influenced Baudelaire and which Wilde depicts as an Aestheticist distraction for Dorian after he has committed murder. Indeed, the formal qualities of Machen's *Ornaments* have been compared to the prose poetry of Baudelaire and other Decadents. The works are equally valuable for this edition in capturing Machen's interests in rites and rituals, the connection of innocence to mystical vision, and the presence of ancient cultures in both the occult and everyday modern society. 'Ritual' (1937) is one of Machen's last works. It demonstrates his continued skill as a stylist and story teller, while also confirming his sustained interest in mystery and non-normative spiritualities throughout his life. The story depicts two men, friends, who get lost in London's streets and come upon a group of young males acting out a curious ritual, the end result being the death of one of the participants. This is also the basic plot of 'The Lost Club', published almost 50 years earlier. In 'Ritual', however, Machen makes a very explicit gesture away from the Decadent realms of London's underground, while retaining his earliest investments in pagan spirituality. By taking the idea for the central performance in the story from an adventure novel, *The Yellow God* (1908) by H. Rider Haggard (1856–1925), Machen evokes the way in which literature can operate as a spiritual medium, recording ceremonies and rituals that can then be adopted and adapted in real life, as it is by the boys in his story. In this sense, Machen's work meshes with the field of comparative, cross-cultural anthropology and folklore made famous particularly by James George Frazer's (1854–1941) *The Golden Bough* (1890), published the same year as 'The Lost Club'.

The remaining piece of fiction included in this edition is 'The Bowmen' (1914), a story Machen published in the *Evening News*, for which he worked as a journalist. It is perhaps the least Decadent of the lot in style or occult interests. And yet it too creates a spiritual mystery out of an everyday London experience, with a nondescript meal at a vegetarian restaurant surprisingly offering the symbolic language for the reversal of the outcome of a First World War battle. More astoundingly, as Machen explains in the introduction to the 1915 publication of a collection that contains the story, it itself is a piece of fabulation that hundreds of readers took as fact, offering a rare, public example of the potential for literature to have a mystic influence.

Examples of Machen's nonfiction, such as 'The Literature of Occultism' and excerpts from *Hieroglyphics*, present insightful angles crucial to gaining an understanding of his philosophical and literary views, while his introductions to editions of *The Great God Pan* and *The Angels of Mons: The Bowmen and Other Legends of the War* offer some sense of Machen's own view of the place of his works within the culture of his time. The two reviews and Arthur Sykes's parody 'The Great Pan-Demon' (1895) contextualize these materials by speaking to the reception of Machen's Decadent writing during the 1890s, while works by Alfred Egmont Hake (1849–1916), Florence Marryat (1833–1899), and A. E. Waite suggest the period's larger cultural interest in folklore, spiritualism, and the occult. Taking to heart the vision of the Jewelled Tortoise series, my principal aim has been to establish Machen's considerable and, to date, under-analyzed contribution to British Decadence. In the process, I aim to shift dominant scholarly notions of the content of the Decadent movement by placing greater emphasis, through Machen, on symbolism and ritual as elements of aesthetic faith and practice, as well as on the occulture and eco-spirituality that were popular internationally at the time.

Machen has influenced recent writers such as Clive Barker and Stephen King, as well as the film director Guillermo del Toro. In 2009, King described *The Great God Pan* as 'one of the best horror stories ever written. Maybe the best in the English language'.[57] Nevertheless, *The Guardian* (2009) and the influential horror journal *Rue Morgue* (2013) both recently concluded that Machen remains 'the forgotten father of weird fiction' and 'the unsung granddaddy of weird fiction', respectively.[58] While Machen received a notable increase in interest for some years in the 1960s and again in the 1980s, he has never been recognized as part of the main British literary canon or even the gothic canon (despite repeated comparisons to Poe and Stevenson). The year 2013 saw the 150th anniversary of Machen's birth, and 2015 marked the 125th anniversary of the publication of *The Great God Pan*, his most famous work. These historic moments were recognized by a Machen exhibition at the Newport Museum (2013), the BBC Radio 4 documentary *Arthur in the Underworld*, and a series of articles in *Rue Morgue*, but the moment has passed without yet fostering any major signs of enhanced popular attention.

Among academics, the situation is somewhat different. Since the 1980s, the Friends of Arthur Machen (which began as the Arthur Machen Society) have maintained scholarly interest in the author, most notably through their periodical *Faunus* (1998–present), which combines historical analyses and

---

[57] Stephen King, 'Self-Interview', 4 September 2008 <http://stephenking.com/stephens_messages.html> [accessed 3 April 2017].
[58] Damien G. Walter, 'Machen is the Forgotten Father of Weird Fiction', *Guardian*, 29 September 2009, Books section <www.theguardian.com/books/booksblog/2009/sep/29/arthur-machen-tartarus-press> [accessed 5 May 2017]. Cover, *Rue Morgue*, 131 (March 2013) <www.rue-morgue.com/online-store/Rue-Morgue-131-March-2013-p45607529> [accessed 5 May 2017].

academic articles with re-publications of often more obscure works by and about the author. Over roughly the past two decades, the Friends have been joined by a growing community of researchers interested in occulture, Victorian and twentieth-century spiritualities, and under-studied strains of Decadence. The range of theoretical methodologies these scholars have deployed has opened Machen up to fresh perspectives and nuanced re-interpretations. He may have jeopardized his canonization as a Decadent by steadfastly ignoring, if not denying, the literary movement as one in which he participated. But it is also true that his original contribution to Decadence arose not only because of the eclectic mix of works that influenced his thinking, and the mystical realm of his homeland, but also because of the stubbornly independent spirit with which he pursued his personal interests and values regardless of whether they were seen as fashionable, consistent, or, indeed, Decadent. Had he chosen to perform the role of the Decadent author of the British *fin de siècle* and adopted a self-image, community, and writing style based on this aim, it is less likely he would be recognized as a Decadent today.

Selected Critical Bibliography

Collected Works

MACHEN, ARTHUR, *The Best Weird Tales of Arthur Machen*, ed. by S. T. Joshi, 3 vols (US: Chaosium, 2001, 2003, 2005)
—— *The Collected Arthur Machen*, ed. by Christopher Palmer (London: Duckworth, 1988)
—— *The Great God Pan and Other Horror Stories*, ed. by Aaron Worth (Oxford: Oxford University Press, 2018)
—— *Holy Terrors* (London: Penguin, 1946)
—— *Tales of Horror and the Supernatural* (London: The Richards Press, 1949)
—— *The Works of Arthur Machen*, 9 vols, The Caerleon Edition (London: Martin Secker, 1923)

Bibliographies

DANIELSON, HENRY, *Arthur Machen: A Bibliography* (London: Henry Danielson, 1923)
GOLDSTONE, ADRIAN, and WESLEY SWEETSER, *A Bibliography of Arthur Machen* (Austin: University of Texas Press, 1965)

Autobiography and Biographies

GAWSWORTH, JOHN, *The Life of Arthur Machen* (Leyburn: Friends of Arthur Machen and Tartarus Press, 2005)
GEKLE, WILLIAM F., *Arthur Machen: Weaver of Fantasy* (Millbrook, NY: Round Table Press, 1949)

MACHEN, ARTHUR, *Far Off Things* (London: Martin Secker, 1922)

—— *The London Adventure: An Essay in Wandering* (London: Martin Secker, 1924)

—— *Things Near and Far* (London: Martin Secker, 1923)

MICHAEL, D. P. M., *Arthur Machen* (Cardiff: University of Wales Press for the Welsh Arts Council, 1971)

REYNOLDS, ADIAN, and WILLIAM CHARLTON, *Arthur Machen* (London: John Baker, 1963)

STARRETT, VINCENT, *Arthur Machen: A Novelist of Ecstasy and Sin* (Chicago: Walter M. Mill, 1918)

SWEETSER, WESLEY D., *Arthur Machen* (New York: Twayne Publishers, 1964)

VALENTINE, MARK, *Arthur Machen* (Bridgend: Seren Poetry Wales Press, 1995)

—— and ROGER DOBSON, *Arthur Machen: Artist and Mystic* (Oxford: Caermaen, 1986)

Secondary Critical Works

ABOLAFIA, MICHAEL J., ' "Immortal Groves through which his Spirit Wandered": Some Notes on Arthur Machen's "A Note on Asceticism" ', *Faunus*, 35 (Spring 2017), pp. 26–32

BLOOM, HAROLD, 'Arthur Machen', in *Modern Horror Writers* (New York: Chelsea House, 1995), pp. 155–70

BOSKY, BERNADETTE L., 'Slime and Sublime: Transcendence and De-Evolution in Peter Straub's and Arthur Machen's Fictions', in *Fantastic Odysseys: Selected Essays from the Twenty-Second International Conference on the Fantastic in the Arts*, ed. by Mary Pharr (Westport, CT: Praeger, 2003), pp. 105–14

BOYIOPOULOS, KOSTAS, ' "Esoteric Elements": The Judeo-Christian Scheme in Arthur Machen's *The Great God Pan*', *Neophilologus*, 94:2 (2010), pp. 363–74

BRIDLE, DEBORAH, 'Symbolism and Dissidence: Social Criticism through the Prism of the Golden Dawn in Machen's *The Hill of Dreams*', *Faunus*, 33 (Spring 2016), pp. 2–18

BURLESON, DONALD R., 'Arthur Machen's "N" as Allegory of Reading', *Studies in Weird Fiction*, 7 (Spring 1990), pp. 8–11

CALEB, AMANDA MORDAVSKY, ' "A City of Nightmares": Suburban Anxiety in Arthur Machen's London Gothic', in *London Gothic: Place, Space and the Gothic Imagination*, ed. by Lawrence Phillips and Anne Witchard (London: Continuum, 2010), pp. 41–49

CAMARA, ANTHONY, 'Abominable Transformations: Becoming Fungus in Arthur Machen's The Hill of Dreams', *Gothic Studies*, 16:1 (2014), pp. 9–23

CLAVERIA, ALESAH, 'The Great God Pan/Brown: Shared Origins and Theme of a Victorian Horror Classic and Eugene O'Neill's Masked Play', *Eugene O'Neill Review*, 36:2 (2015), pp. 212–25

CRONIN, BARRY, 'Arthur Machen: The Fourth Impostor', *Faunus*, 1 (Spring 1998), pp. 48–53

DE CICCO, MARK, ' "More Than Human": The Queer Occult Explorer of the Fin-de-Siècle', *Journal of the Fantastic in the Arts*, 23:1 (84) (2012), pp. 4–24

DENISOFF, DENNIS, ' "A Disembodied Voice": The Posthuman Formlessness of Decadence', in *Decadent Poetics: Literature and Forma the British Fin de Siècle*, ed. by Jason David Hall and Alex Murray (Houndmills: Palgrave Macmillan, 2013), pp. 181–200

ECKERSLEY, ADRIAN, 'A Theme in the Early Work of Arthur Machen: "Degeneration"', *English Literature in Transition, 1880–1920*, 35:3 (1992), pp. 276–87

FERGUS, EMILY, '"A Wilder Reality": Euhemerism and Arthur Machen's "Little People"', *Faunus*, 32 (Autumn 2015), pp. 3–17

FERGUSON, CHRISTINE, 'Reading with the Occultists: Arthur Machen, A. E. Waite, and the Ecstasies of Popular Fiction', *Journal of Victorian Culture*, 21:1 (2016), pp. 40–55

FORLINI, STEFANIA, 'Modern Narratives and Decadent Things in Arthur Machen's *The Three Impostors*', *English Literature in Transition, 1880–1920*, 55:4 (2012), pp. 479–98

FOX, PAUL, 'Eureka in Yellow: The Art of Detection in Arthur Machen's Keynote Mysteries', *CLUES: A Journal of Detection*, 25:1 (2006), pp. 58–69

FREEMAN, N., 'Arthur Machen: Ecstasy and Epiphany', *Literature and Theology*, 24:3 (2010), pp. 242–55

GAMES, GWILYM, '*The Great Return*, the Great War, and the Great Revival', *Faunus*, 11 (Winter 2004), pp. 26–54

GRAF, SUSAN JOHNSTON, 'Arthur Machen', in *Talking to the Gods: Occultism in the Works of W. B. Yeats, Arthur Machen, Algernon Blackwood, and Dion Fortune* (Albany: State University of New York Press, 2015), pp. 57–78

HASSLER, DONALD M., 'Arthur Machen and Genre: Filial and Fannish Alternatives', *Extrapolation*, 33:2 (1992), pp. 115–27

—— 'Machen, Williams, and Autobiography: Fantasy and Decadence', in *Imaginative Futures: Proceedings of the 1993 Science Fiction Research Association Conference*, ed. by Milton T. Wolf and Darryl F. Mallett (San Bernardino: Jacob's Ladder Books, 1995), pp. 319–28

HOWARD, JOHN, 'Impossible Histories: Arthur Machen's *A Fragment of Life*', *Faunus*, 35 (Spring 2017), pp. 4–19

HURLEY, KELLY, 'British Gothic Fiction, 1885–1930', in *The Cambridge Companion to Gothic Fiction*, ed. by Jerrold E. Hogle (Cambridge: Cambridge University Press, 2002), pp. 189–207

—— '*The Three Imposters*: Arthur Machen's Urban *Chaosmos*', in *The Gothic Body: Sexuality, Materialism and Degeneration at the Fin de Siècle* (Cambridge: Cambridge University Press, 1996), pp. 159–67

JACKSON, KIMBERLEY, 'Non-Evolutionary Degeneration in Arthur Machen's Supernatural Tales', *Victorian Literature and Culture*, 41:1 (2013), pp. 125–35

JONES, DARRYL, 'Borderlands: Spiritualism and the Occult in *Fin de Siècle* and Edwardian Welsh and Irish Horror', *Irish Studies Review*, 17:1 (2009), pp. 31–44

JOSHI, S. T., *The Weird Tale* (Austin: University of Texas Press, 1990)

—— 'Arthur Machen', in *Supernatural Literature of the World: An Encyclopedia*, ed. by S. T. Joshi and Stegan Dziemianowicz (Westport, CT: Greenwood Press, 2005)

KANDOLA, SONDEEP, 'Celtic Occultism and the Symbolist Mode in the Fin-de-Siecle Writings of Arthur Machen and W.B. Yeats', *English Literature in Transition, 1880–1920*, 56:4 (2013), 497–518

KARSCHAY, STEPHAN, 'Detecting the Degenerate: Robert Louis Stevenson's *Strange Case of Dr Jekyll and Mr Hyde* and Arthur Machen's *The Great God Pan*', in *Degeneration, Normativity and the Gothic at the Fin de Siècle* (Basingstoke: Palgrave Macmillan, 2015), pp. 85–123

LELUAN-PINKER, ANNE-SOPHIE, '"*A unique aura of ancient, elemental evil*": les migrations du feu dans *The Great God Pan* (1894) d'Arthur Machen', *Cahiers victoriens et édouardiens*, 71 (April 2010), pp. 127–37

LESLIE-MCCARTHY, SAGE, 'Re-Vitalising the Little People: Arthur Machen's Tales of the Remnant Races', *Australasian Victorian Studies Journal*, 11 (2005), pp. 65–78

—— 'Chance Encounters: The Detective as "Expert" in Arthur Machen's *The Great God Pan*', *Australasian Journal of Victorian Studies*, 13:1 (2008), pp. 35–45

LUCKHURST, ROGER, 'The Contemporary London Gothic and the Limits of the "Spectral Turn"', *Textual Practice*, 16:3 (2002), pp. 527–46

MACHIN, JAMES, 'Weird Fiction and the Virtues of Obscurity: Machen, Stenbock, and the Weird Connoisseurs', *Textual Practice*, 31:6 (2017), pp. 1063–81

MACLEOD, KIRSTEN, *Fictions of British Decadence: High Art, Popular Writing, and the Fin de Siècle* (New York: Palgrave Macmillan, 2006)

MANTRANT, SOPHIE, '"All London was one grey temple of an awful rite": Londres dans *The Hill of Dreams* d'Arthur Machen (1907)', *Cahiers victoriens et édouardiens*, 77 (Spring 2013) <https://cve.revues.org/344?lang=en#text> [accessed: 20 October 2017]

—— 'La Dissolution du corps dans *The Great God Pan* by Arthur Machen', in *Colloque de Cerli: L'imaginaire medical dans le fantastique et le science-fiction*, ed. by Jerome Goffette and Laurice Guillaud (Paris: Bragelonne, 2011), pp. 77–289

—— 'Pagan Revenants in Arthur Machen's Supernatural Tales of the Nineties', *Cahiers victoriens et édouardiens*, 80 (Autumn 2014) <https://cve.revues.org/1466#text> [accessed: 20 October 2017]

MCCANN, ANDREW, *Popular Literature, Authorship and the Occult in Late-Victorian Britain* (Cambridge: Cambridge University Press, 2014)

MILLER, THOMAS KENT, 'Be Reminded: The Absurdities Depended on the Papers for Wide Dissemination', *Faunus*, 32 (Autumn 2015), pp. 19–27

MURRAY, ALEX, *Landscapes of Decadence: Literature and Place at the Fin de Siècle* (Cambridge: Cambridge University Press, 2016)

NAVARETTE, SUSAN JENNIFER, 'The Word Made Flesh: Protoplasmic Predications in Arthur Machen's "The Great God Pan"', in *The Shape of Fear: Horror and the Fin de Siècle Culture of Decadence* (Lexington: University Press of Kentucky, 1998), pp. 178–201

OWENS, JILL TEDFORD, 'Arthur Machen's Supernaturalism: The Decadent Variety', *University of Mississippi Studies in English*, 8 (1990), pp. 117–26

PASI, MARIO, 'Arthur Machen's Panic Fears: Western Esotericism and the Irruption of Negative Epistemology', *Aries*, 7:1 (2007), pp. 63–83

POLLER, JAKE, 'The Transmutations of Arthur Machen: Alchemy in "The Great God Pan" and *The Three Impostors*', *Literature and Theology*, 29:1 (March 2015), pp. 18–32

PROBERT, JOHN LLEWELLYN, 'Picnic at the Hill of Dreams: Machenesque Moments in Cinema: Part 1', *Faunus*, 30 (Autumn 2014), pp. 3–10

—— 'Waving at the White People: Machenesque Moments in Cinema: Part 2', *Faunus*, 34 (Autumn 2016), pp. 17–24

REBRY, NATASHA, '"A slight lesion in the grey matter": The Gothic Brain in Arthur Machen's *The Great God Pan*', *Horror Studies*, 7:1 (2016), pp. 9–24

REITER, GEOFFREY, '"An Age-Old Memory": Arthur Machen's Celtic Redaction of the Welsh Revival in *The Great Return*', in *Welsh Mythology and Folklore in Popular Culture*, ed. by Audrey L. Becker and Kristin Noone (Jefferson, NC: McFarland & Company, 2011), pp. 61–80

RUSSELL, R. B. (ed.), *Machenalia*, 2 vols (Lewes: Tartarus Press, 1990)

SIMONS, JOHN, 'Horror in the 1890s: The Case of Arthur Machen', in *Creepers: British Horror and Fantasy in the Twentieth Century*, ed. by Clive Bloom (London: Pluto Press, 1993), pp. 35–46

SMITH, ANDREW, *Victorian Demons: Medicine, Masculinity and the Gothic at the Fin-de-Siècle* (Manchester: Manchester University Press, 2004)

SPARKS, TABITHA, 'New Women, Avenging Doctors: Gothic Medicine in Bram Stoker and Arthur Machen', in *The Doctor in the Victorian Novel: Family Practices* (2009; London: Routledge, 2016), pp. 111–31

SPEEDIE, JULIE, *Arthur Machen and the "Sphinx"* (Lewes: Tartarus, 1992)

SUSTER, GERALD, 'Arthur Machen: Satanist?', *Faunus*, 2 (Autumn 1998), pp. 6–13

TEARLE, OLIVER, 'Insectial: Arthur Machen's Phantasmagoria', in *Bewilderments of Vision: Hallucination and Literature 1880–1914* (Eastbourne: Sussex Academic Press, 2014), pp. 108–40

WAGSTAFF, NICK, 'Reflections on Machen's Introduction to *The Ghost Ship* (1912)', *Faunus*, 33 (Spring 2016), pp. 19–28

WARWICK, ALEX, '"The City of Resurrections": Arthur Machen and the Archaeological Imagination', in *The Victorians and the Ancient World: Archaeology and Classicism in Nineteenth-Century Culture*, ed. by Richard Pearson (Newcastle: Cambridge Scholars Press, 2006), pp. 124–38

WILLIS, MARTIN T., 'Scientific Portraits in Magical Frames: The Construction of Preternatural Narrative in the Work of E.T.A. Hoffmann and Arthur Machen', *Extrapolation*, 35:3 (Autumn 1994), pp.186–200

WORTH, AARON, 'Arthur Machen and the Horrors of Deep History', *Victorian Literature and Culture*, 40 (2012), pp. 215–27

WROBEL, C., 'Un roman neo-gothique: The Three Impostors d'Arthur Machen (1895)', *Cahiers Victoriens et Edouardiens*, 67 (2008), pp. 337–48

A Decadent Chronology of Arthur Machen's Life

1862   Algernon Charles Swinburne publishes a keenly supportive review of Charles Baudelaire's *Les fleurs du mal* (1857) in *The Spectator*, triggering the strong influence of French Decadence on British literature.

1863   3 March: Arthur Llewelyn Jones Machen is born in Caerleon on Usk, in the county of Gwent in Wales. He is the only child of Janet Machen and John Edward Jones; his father added 'Machen' to his name to comply with the terms of a will from his wife's side of the family. While Arthur would later drop 'Jones', it was not due to any conflict with his father, an Anglican priest who became vicar of the parish of Llandewi Fach, near Caerleon, soon after Machen was born.

1868   Swinburne publishes 'Ave atque Vale', an elegy for Baudelaire that would become recognized as one of the greatest English elegies of the century.

1870s   Various archaeological digs take place near Caerleon, including excavation work on a temple to the Celtic deity Nodens at Lydney Park, Gloucestershire. Machen describes a pillar dedicated to Nodens at the end of *The Great God Pan*.

1871   Swinburne publishes *Songs before Sunrise*, a collection of poems on Italy's nineteenth-century unification into a single state. In *Far Off Things*, Machen cites his encounter with this work as the reason he began to write.

1873   Walter Pater's *Studies in the History of the Renaissance* published, with its influence on literature and aesthetics marking the start of British Decadence as a movement. At the age of 11, Machen becomes a boarder at Hereford Cathedral School until he is 17, where he focuses on Classics and Divinity. The family could not afford to have him follow his father with studies at Oxford.

1875   The Theosophical Society is founded in New York by Helena Blavatsky, William Quan Judge, and Henry Steel Olcott.

1878   In this year or the next, Machen sees a production of Gilbert and Sullivan's *HMS Pinafore* at Hereford, which he credits in *Far Off Things* for igniting his love of theatre.

1880   Makes his first visit to London, where he and his father see Gilbert and Sullivan's *Pirates of Penzance* at the Opera Comique. He purchases Swinburne's *Songs before Sunrise* at Denny's bookshop, Hollywell Street, London. His father declares bankruptcy.

1881   Privately prints 100 copies of *Eleusinia*, a poem about the Eleusinian mysteries. This anonymous work is his first publication. He moves to the suburbs of London, envisioning a career as a writer or journalist.

1884   First book, *The Anatomy of Tobacco*, is published by George Redway. It is an imitation of Robert Burton's *Anatomy of Melancholy* (1621), addressing the pleasure of smoking.

1885   Begins working for Redway, publisher of occult authors such as MacGregor Mathers and A. E. Waite. Machen's work includes editing, translating, and eventually writing review articles. On Redway's request, he compiles a catalogue published as *The Literature of Occultism and Archaeology*. Machen's mother passes away on 10 November.

1886   Redway publishes Machen's translation of *The Heptaméron*, credited to Marguerite, Queen of Navarre.

1887   31 August: marries Amelia (Amy) Hogg, his first wife. She is about 13 years older than Machen and already part of the London literary scene. His father passes away on 29 September.

1888   Publishes the occult *Thesaurus Incantatus. The Enchanted Treasure; or, the Spagyric Quest of Beroaldus Cosmopolita*. He also publishes *The Chronicle of Clemendy* (his first piece of pure fiction), a collection of linked tales he wrote while back in Wales after his mother's death in 1885. The Hermetic Order of the Golden Dawn is formed. Over the next decade it became the most influential occult order of the century. Mathers (one of Redway's authors) was a co-founder.

1890   Oscar Wilde publishes *The Picture of Dorian Gray* in the July issue of *Lippincott's Weekly Magazine*. The novel version appears the following year. Wilde gains notoriety both through reviewers' critiques of the novel's immorality and through his responses to the accusations.

        Travels to the Touraine region of France. That summer, he contacts Wilde and the two meet for dinner, where Wilde encourages the other to write short stories. In July, Machen begins publishing short stories, including the Decadent 'The Lost Club' and 'The Experiment' (the first chapter of *The Great God Pan*) in *The Whirlwind*. The works evoke the urban gothic literature of the period.

1893   John Lane publishes George Egerton's *Keynotes*. The success of that short-story collection leads to Lane's Keynote Series, the second book being *The Dancing Faun* (1894) by Florence Farr, who had been initiated into the Hermetic Order of the Golden Dawn in 1890.

1894   Lane begins publishing the *Yellow Book*, a periodical considered a central vehicle for British Decadent literature. It attains notoriety primarily through the drawings of its first art director, Aubrey Beardsley. December: Machen publishes *The Great God Pan* and *The Inmost Light* as one book, the fifth work in Lane's Keynote Series, with the cover illustrated by Beardsley. Later, in *Things Near and Far*, Machen describes the moment as that 'when yellow bookery was at its yellowest'.

1895   April: the English translation of Max Nordau's *Degeneration* (1892) is published. The work attacks Decadent art and literature, including influences on Machen such as 'Decadents and Æsthetes', mysticism, Symbolism, Pre-Raphaelitism, and individuals such as Swinburne and Wilde. May: Wilde's trials take place and he is convicted of 'gross indecency'. November: publishes *The Three Impostors: or, the Transmutations*, also in Lane's Keynote Series (having first been rejected by Heinemann). Alluding to the Wilde trials, Machen blamed the weak reception of his book to 'some ugly scandals in the summer of '95, which had made people impatient with reading matter that was not obviously and obtrusively "healthy"'.

1897   Finishes writing *The Hill of Dreams* and *Ornaments in Jade*.

1899   31 July: wife, Amy, dies of cancer. Machen is devastated and begins soul-searching. His friend Waite invites him to join the Hermetic Order of the Golden Dawn. This year, Machen publishes 'The Literature of Occultism'. 21 November: Machen is initiated into the Isis-Urania Temple of the Golden Dawn. He chooses the name Frater Avallaunius and is an active member for roughly one year.

1901   Joins Frederick Benson's theatre company, and is involved in acting on and off until 1907.

1902   Publishes *Hieroglyphics: A Note upon Ecstasy in Literature*, which he finished writing in 1899.

1903   25 June: marries Dorothie Purefoy Hudleston, a strong, artistic individual. Waite starts the Christianity-inflected Independent and Rectified Rite of the Golden Dawn, an offshoot of the Hermetic Order of the Golden Dawn. Machen joins the new order, remaining a member for a number of years. His spiritual interests shift more fully to High Church Anglicanism. In 1903–1904, Machen and Waite work together on a verse drama, *The Hidden Sacrament of the Holy Graal*, which appears in 1906 in Waite's *Strange Houses of Sleep* with Machen credited anonymously as 'a friend and fellow-worker in the mysteries'.

1907   *The Hill of Dreams* published by Grant Richards, having previously been serialized as *The Garden of Avallaunius* in *Horlick's Magazine* (v. II, July–December 1904), edited by Waite. Richards, Lane, and other publishers had earlier rejected the manuscript. Machen finishes writing *The Secret Glory* (1922), reflecting his strong interest in the Celtic influence on legends of the Holy Grail. Around this time, he begins working as a literary journalist for *The Academy*, edited by Alfred Douglas, Wilde's former lover. By 1910, he is also writing for other journals, work he does for the income rather than pleasure.

1912   Son Hilary is born.

1914   29 September: publishes 'The Bowmen' in the *Evening News*, for which
        he worked as a journalist. The story proves a massive success, in large
        part because it is mistaken for a nonfictional report on the Battle of
        Mons.

1916   Publishes introduction to a new edition of *The Great God Pan*, in which
        he explicitly distances himself from the British Decadent movement of
        the 1890s. He also publishes *The Terror* in serialized form, and then
        in book form the following year. The work is a major contribution to
        Machen's ongoing interest in the strategizing potential and agency of
        nonhuman animals (echoing elements of *The Great God Pan*).

1917   Daughter Janet is born.

1918   Vincent Starrett publishes *Arthur Machen: Novelist of Ecstasy and Sin*,
        the first major study of Machen's writing.

1920   Over the next five years, Machen gains popularity in the United States
        (and the UK to a lesser degree), fostered by the advocacy of Starrett,
        James Branch Cabell, and Carl Van Vechten. During this period,
        Machen sees many works published or re-published.

1921   November: stops working for the *Evening News*, after prematurely
        publishing an obituary of Douglas. Douglas sues.

1922   *Far Off Things*, the first volume of his autobiography, is published. It
        consists of memoir pieces he had published in the *Evening News* from
        March to July of 1915.

1923   *Things Near and Far*, the second volume of his autobiography, is
        published.

1924   *The London Adventure, or The Art of Wandering*, the third and final
        volume of his autobiography, is published. Machen also publishes
        Ornaments in Jade, a collection of Decadent works akin to prose poems
        that he had written in 1897.

1929   Moves to Amersham, Buckinghamshire, where he and Purefoy live the
        rest of their lives.

1933   *The Green Round*, Machen's last novel, is published. Machen does
        not care much for the work, which he had written on an advance. It
        addresses many of the author's previous subjects, including mysticism,
        alchemy, horror, little people, and engagement with an otherworldly
        realm.

1937   Publishes 'Ritual'.

1947   Purefoy dies on 30 March, followed by Machen on 15 December. They
        are buried at St Mary Churchyard, Amersham, Buckinghamshire,
        England.

A Note on the Texts and Editorial Decisions

The aim of this publication is to develop a clearer sense of Arthur Machen's place within and contributions to the British Decadent movement, with both the author and the movement attaining their greatest popular recognition during the *fin de siècle*. By reproducing the first publications of each of the works included here, I hope that the edition will enhance a presentation of Machen in conversation with others in the historical moment. Using the first editions may also offer a subtler sense of his shifts in tone, language, and attitude in relation to the changing Decadent movement, although Machen's revisions to the selected pieces were never major and I have addressed a few occasions where I felt revisions were notable. The first editions also help bring forward the vitality of Machen's place at the time within not only British Decadence, but also popular occultism and the burgeoning genre of weird fiction.

All translations are my own, unless otherwise indicated. In developing editorial footnotes, I have tried to engage with more than one audience. Students and others who are discovering Machen and his era for the first time were my first consideration. I have also emphasized those aspects of Machen's work that would be of particular interest to scholars wishing to explore more fully his familiarity with, contribution to, and distinctiveness within the Decadent movement. I have, for example, noted a number of instances where Machen's writing echoes Walter Pater's *The Renaissance*. Machen stated that he had not read much of Pater and was not particularly inspired by his work, but he also acknowledged that Pater's conception of the relationship between art and spirit 'had the root of the matter'.[59] Lastly, I hope that this edition will offer to the many devoted admirers of Machen's work who have studied and explored his writings for many years a few new bits of information regarding the author's extensive studies.

This edition is divided into three sections. Selections of Machen's fiction are followed by related nonfiction, and then works by individuals other than Machen himself that help contextualize his writings within their time period. Works are presented in the order of first publication, although it is important to recognize that *The Hill of Dreams* (1907) and the stories from *Ornaments in Jade* (1924) were written almost simultaneously (the former from 1895 to 1897 and the latter in 1897). While retaining the original punctuation, grammar, and spelling throughout, a few minor corrections have been made invisibly. Some first editions used double quotation marks while others used single quotation marks; I have stayed true to the actual publications in this regard. Citation information is not given for quotations of materials included in this edition. I give birth and death dates when each individual is first mentioned.

---

[59] Arthur Machen, *A Few Letters from Arthur Machen* (Cleveland: The Rowfant Club, 1932). Quoted in Valentine, *Arthur Machen*, p. 50.

The publication information for the items in the three sections of this edition, in the order of their first publication dates, is as follows:

Fiction by Arthur Machen

'The Lost Club', *The Whirlwind* (20 December 1890), pp. 182–84

The Great God Pan. The Great God Pan and The Inmost Light (London: John Lane, 1894), pp. 7–156

'The Recluse of Bayswater', *The Three Impostors* (London: John Lane, 1895), pp. 197–243

The Hill of Dreams (London: Grant Richards, 1907)

'The Bowmen', *Evening News* (29 September 1914), p. 3

'The Rose Garden', *Ornaments in Jade* (New York: Alfred A. Knopf, 1924), pp. 3–5

'The Turanians', *Ornaments in Jade* (New York: Alfred A. Knopf, 1924), pp. 6–9

'The Idealist', *Ornaments in Jade* (New York: Alfred A. Knopf, 1924), pp. 10–15

'The Ceremony', *Ornaments in Jade* (New York: Alfred A. Knopf, 1924), pp. 20–23

'Ritual', *Path and Pavement: Twenty New Tales of Britain*, ed. by John Rowland (London: Eric Grant, 1937), pp. 143–51

Nonfiction by Arthur Machen

'The Literature of Occultism', *Literature: An International Gazette of Criticism*, New Series: 2 (17 January 1899), pp. 34–36

Excerpts from *Hieroglyphics: A Note upon Ecstasy in Literature* (London: Grant Richards, 1902), pp. 11–12, 38–41, 71–75, and 77–85

Introduction to *The Angels of Mons: The Bowmen and Other Legends of the War* (London: Simpkin, Marshall, Hamilton, Kent, 1915), pp. 5–27

Introduction to *The Great God Pan* (London: Simpkin, Marshall, Hamilton, Kent, 1916), pp. vii–xxiii

Critical Contexts

Arthur Edward Waite, Excerpts from *The Occult Sciences: A Compendium of Transcendental Doctrine and Experiment* (London: Kegan Paul, 1891), pp. 1–4, 9–12

Florence Marryat, 'Chapter XI. A Chance Séance with a Stranger', *The Spirit World* (London: F. V. White, 1894), pp. 253–61

W. L. Courtney, 'Novels and Nerves', *Daily Telegraph* (1 February 1895), p. 7

Arthur Sykes, 'The Great Pan-Demon: An Unspeakable Story', *National Observer* (4 May 1895), pp. 669–70

Anonymous, Review of *The Three Impostors*, *The Bookman* (January 1896), p. 131

Alfred Egmont Hake, 'Chapter IX: Religion of the Self', *Regeneration: A Reply to Max Nordau* (New York: G. P. Putnam's Sons, 1896), pp. 230–40

Anonymous, Review of *The Hill of Dreams*, *The Bookman* (September 1907), p. 212

PART I

Fiction

1

The Lost Club (1890)

One hot afternoon in August a gorgeous young gentleman, one would say the last of his race in London, set out from the Circus end, and proceeded to stroll along the lonely expanse of Piccadilly Deserta.[1] True to the traditions of his race, faithful even in the wilderness, he had not bated one jot or tittle of the regulation equipage; a glorious red and yellow blossom in his woolly and exquisitely-cut frock-coat proclaimed him a true son of the carnation, hat, and boots and chin were all polished to the highest pitch;[2] though there had not been rain for many weeks his trouser-ends were duly turned up, and the poise of the gold-headed cane was in itself a liberal education. But ah! the heavy change since June, when the leaves glanced green in the sunlit air, and the club windows were filled, and the hansoms flashed in long processions through the streets, and girls smiled from every carriage.[3] The young man sighed; he thought of the quiet little evenings at the Phœnix, of encounters of the Row, of the drive to Hurlingham, and many pleasant dinners in joyous company.[4] Then he glanced up and saw a bus, half-empty, slowly lumbering along the middle of

---

[1]   Piccadilly Circus is a traffic circle and open square in the West End of London. Just as today, in Machen's time, the road Piccadilly extending from the circle boasted many shops, taverns, inns, and restaurants. Piccadilly was also part of clubland, an area of many gentleman's clubs. The narrator's descriptor 'Deserta' indicates that the area is not its usual bustle of humanity.

[2]   Equipage are articles worn on one's person or clothing for decoration. By the last decade of the nineteenth century, the carnation had become recognized as a symbol of the British Decadents and aesthetes. Robert Hichens's (1882–1940) satire *The Green Carnation* (1894; published anonymously) attained notoriety for bringing together the carnation, Wilde, his lover Alfred Douglas, and same-sex male desire. On the page immediately following 'The Lost Club' in the *Whirlwind*, one finds a mock prize competition for imitations of famous authors, including Wilde, suggesting an editorial aim of situating the journal's contents in the context of the Decadent movement.

[3]   Hansoms are two-wheeled covered carriages, drawn by one horse, with room for two passengers. The driver sat mounted behind on an elevated seat.

[4]   The name 'Phœnix' has been common for such things as clubs, societies, and theatres, but there did exist a Victorian gentleman's club by that name, located at 17 St James Place. A short walk away was Rotten Row (originally *Route de Roi*), or 'the Row', which in Machen's time was a fashionable thoroughfare running along the south side of Hyde Park in West London. Hurlingham was (and continues to be) a private club in Fulham, London.

the street, and in front of the "White Horse Cellars" a four-wheeler had stopped still (the driver was asleep on his seat), and in the "Badminton" the blinds were down.[5] He half expected to see the Briar Rose trailing gracefully over the Hotel Cosmopole; certainly the Beauty, if such a thing were left in Piccadilly, was fast asleep.[6]

Absorbed in these mournful reflections the hapless Johnny strolled on without observing that an exact duplicate of himself was advancing on the same pavement from the opposite direction; save that the inevitable carnation was salmon colour, and the cane a silver-headed one, instruments of great magnifying power would have been required to discriminate between them.[7] The two met: each raised his eyes simultaneously at the strange sight of a well-dressed man, and each adjured the same old world deity:

"By Jove! old man, what the deuce are you doing here?"

The gentleman who had advanced from the direction of Hyde Park Corner was the first to answer.[8]

"Well, to tell the truth, Austin, I am detained in town on — ah — legal business. But how is it you are not in Scotland?"

"Well, it's curious; but the fact is, I have legal business in town also."

"You don't say so? Great nuisance, ain't it? But these things must be seen to, or a fellow finds himself in no end of a mess, don't you know?"

"He does, by Jove! That's what I thought."

Mr. Austin relapsed into silence for a few moments.

"And where are you off to, Phillipps?"

The conversation had passed with the utmost gravity on both sides; at the joint mention of legal business, it was true, a slight twinkle had passed across their eyes, but the ordinary observer would have said that the weight of ages rested on those unruffled brows.

"I really couldn't say. I thought of having a quiet dinner at Azario's.[9] The

---

[5]   The White Horse Cellars is an old inn and tavern on Piccadilly. A four-wheeler is a horse-drawn carriage for hire. Four-wheel hackney cabs usually accommodated up to six people. The Badminton Club was a gentleman's riding club located in the 1880s and 1890s at 98, 99, and 100 Piccadilly.

[6]   The briar rose is a trailing, thorny rose associated with the story of Sleeping Beauty and famously depicted by the Pre-Raphaelite artist Edward Burne-Jones (1833–1898) in his series of paintings The Legend of the Briar Rose.

[7]   'Johnny' is a familiar, slang term for a man or boy.

[8]   Hyde Park Corner is where six roads converge at the south-east corner of London's Hyde Park. From Hyde Park Circle it takes about 20 minutes to walk along Piccadilly to Piccadilly Circus.

[9]   Proprietor Luigi Azario ran the Florence Restaurant at 17 Rupert Street in the nearby neighbourhood of Soho, which had an economy, during Machen's time, based in large part on music halls and theatres, as well as prostitution and other crimes. The area was also recognized for its high level of overcrowding and disease. In Stevenson's Strange Case of Dr

"Badminton" is closed, you know, for repairs or somethin', and I can't stand the Junior Wilton.[10] Come along with me, and let's dine together."

"By Jove! I think I will. I thought of calling on my solicitor, but I daresay he can wait."

"Ah! I should think he could. We'll have some of that Italian wine — stuff in salad-oil flasks — you know what I mean."

The pair solemnly wheeled round, and solemnly paced towards the Circus, meditating, doubtless, on many things. The dinner in the little restaurant pleased them with a grave pleasure, as did the Chianti, of which they drank a great deal too much; "quite a light wine, you know," said Phillipps, and Austin agreed with him, so they emptied a quart flask between them, and finished up with a couple of glasses apiece of Green Chartreuse.[11] As they came out into the quiet street, smoking vast cigars, the two slaves to duty and "legal business" felt a dreamy delight in all things, the street seemed full of fantasy in the dim light of the lamps, and a single star shining in the clear sky above seemed to Austin exactly of the same colour as Green Chartreuse. Phillipps agreed with him. "You know, old fellow," he said, "there are times when a fellow feels all sorts of strange things — you know, the sort of things they put in the magazines, don't you know, and novels. By Jove, Austin, old man, I feel as if I could write a novel myself."

The pair wandered aimlessly on, not quite knowing where they were going, turning from one street to another, and discoursing in a maudlin strain. A great cloud had been slowly moving up from the south, darkening the sky, and

---

Jekyll and Mr Hyde (1886), the doctor rents a place in Soho for Hyde. After the publication of this story, Machen and Wilde dined together at Azario's restaurant. Wilde frequented the restaurant, which is mentioned during his court trials as a place he would dine with young men, sometimes in private rooms.

[10]   There were many 'junior' clubs to which younger, less established men would apply for membership before attempting to join the more prestigious ones. At this time, a notable restaurant named Wiltons (est. 1742) existed on Duke Street, not far from Piccadilly.

[11]   Chianti is a wine from the Chianti area of Tuscany. In this story, the intoxicating qualities of the wine are crucial to the narrative. While it is also consumed in *The Great God Pan* and *The Hill of Dreams*, no mention is made in those works of it affecting characters' mental capacities. Chartreuse is a green liqueur made by French Carthusian monks since the eighteenth century. In his Decadent classic *A Rebours*, Huysmans has his hero construct a 'mouth organ' with which he explores synaesthetic connections between music and liquor (or sound and taste), citing green Chartreuse as an example. The colour green itself became associated with the Decadents, in part through the drink absinthe, also known as the green fairy and the green witch. In the essay 'Pen, Pencil, and Poison — A Study in Green' (1891), Wilde portrays the murdering aesthete Thomas Griffith Wainewright as having 'that curious love of green which in individuals is always a sign of a subtle, artistic temperament, and in nations is said to denote a laxity, if not a decadence of morals' (*Intentions* (London: Methuen, 1921), p. 64). Wilde encouraged some male audience members to wear green carnations to the opening performance of *Lady Windermere's Fan* in 1891, giving Hichens the inspiration for the title of *The Green Carnation*.

suddenly it began to rain, at first slowly with great heavy drops, and then faster and faster in a pitiless, hissing shower; the gutters flooded over, and the furious drops danced up from the stones. The two Johnnies walked on as fast as they could, whistling and calling "Hansom!" in vain; they were really getting very wet.

"Where the dickens are we?" said Phillipps. "Confound it all, I don't know. We ought to be in Oxford Street."[12]

They walked on a little farther, when suddenly, to their great joy, they found a dry archway, leading into a dark passage or courtyard. They took shelter silently, too thankful and too wet to say anything. Austin looked at his hat, it was a wreck; and Phillipps shook himself feebly, like a tired terrier.

"What a beastly nuisance this is," he muttered: "I only wish I could see a hansom."

Austin looked into the street, the rain was still falling in torrents; he looked up the passage, and noticed for the first time that it led to a great house, which towered grimly against the sky. It seemed all dark and gloomy, except that from some chink in a shutter a light shone out. He pointed it out to Phillipps, who stared vacantly about him, then exclaimed:

"Hang it! I know where we are now. At least, I don't exactly know, you know, but I once came by here with Wylliams, and he told me there was some club or somethin' down this passage; I don't recollect exactly what he said. Hullo! why there goes Wylliams. I say, Wylliams, tell us where we are?"

A gentleman had brushed past them in the darkness, and was walking fast down the passage. He heard his name and turned round, looking rather annoyed.

"Well, Phillipps, what do you want? Good evening, Austin; you seem rather wet, both of you."

"I should think we were wet; got caught in the rain. Didn't you tell me once there was some club down here? I wish you'd take us in, if you're a member."

Mr. Wylliams looked steadfastly at the two forlorn young men for a moment, hesitated, and said:

"Well, gentlemen, you may come with me if you like. But I must impose a condition; that you both give me your word of honour never to mention the club, or anything that you see while you are in it, to any individual whatsoever."

"Certainly not," replied Austin; "of course we shouldn't dream of doing so, should we, Phillipps?"

"No, no; go ahead, Wylliams, we'll keep it dark enough."

The party moved slowly down the passage till they came to the house. It was very large and very old; it looked as though it might have been an embassy of the last century. Wylliams whistled, knocked twice at the door, and whistled again, and it was opened by a man in black.

---

[12] Oxford Street is a major London thoroughfare in the West End containing mostly shops and restaurants. Oxford Circus is about a 15-minute walk from Piccadilly Circus.

"Friends of yours, Mr. Wylliams?"

Wylliams nodded, and they passed on.

"Now mind," he whispered, as they paused at a door, "you are not to recognise anybody, and nobody will recognise you."

The two friends nodded, and the door was opened, and they entered a vast room, brilliantly lighted with electric lamps.[13] Men were standing in knots, walking up and down, and smoking at little tables; it was just like any club smoking-room. Conversation was going on, but in a low murmur, and every now and then someone would stop talking, and look anxiously at a door at the other end of the room, and then turn round again. It was evident that they were waiting for something or somebody. Austin and Phillipps were sitting on a sofa, lost in amazement; nearly every face was familiar to them. The flower of the Row was in that strange club-room;[14] several young noblemen, a young fellow who had just come into an enormous fortune, three or four fashionable artists and literary men, an eminent actor, and a well-known canon. What could it mean? They were all supposed to be scattered far and wide over the habitable globe, and yet here they were. Suddenly there came a loud knock at the door; every man started, and those who were sitting got up. A servant appeared.

"The President is awaiting you, gentlemen," he said, and vanished.

One by one the members filed out, and Wylliams and the two guests brought up the rear. They found themselves in a room still larger than the first, but almost quite dark. The president sat at a long table, and before him burned two candles, which barely lighted up his face. It was the famous Duke of Dartington, the largest landowner in England.[15] As soon as the members had entered, he said in a cold hard voice, "Gentlemen, you know our rules, the book is prepared. Whoever opens it at the black page is at the disposal of the committee and myself. We had better begin." Someone began to read out the names in a low distinct voice, pausing between each name, and the member called came up to the table and opened at random the pages of a big folio volume that lay between the two candles.[16] The gloomy light made it difficult to distinguish features, but Phillipps heard a groan beside him, and recognised an old friend. His face was working fearfully, the man was evidently in an agony of terror. One by one the members opened the book; as each man did so he passed out by another door.

---

[13] Thomas Edison (1837–1941) patented the incandescent electric lamp in 1880. The fact that this club is lit with them (rather than gas lamps, which were still widely used) means it is at the cutting edge of modern technology and aesthetics.

[14] 'The flower of the Row' refers to the most fashionable young men of Rotten Row.

[15] Machen has invented this title. Dartington is a village in Devon, so some readers might have heard an echo of the Duke of Devonshire, the head of one of England's oldest and wealthiest aristocratic families.

[16] A folio is a large book (usually about 15 inches in height) made of sheets of paper that have been folded once in order to make two leaves (four pages).

At last there was only one left; it was Phillipps's friend. There was foam upon his lips as he passed up to the table, and his hand shook as he opened the leaves. Wylliams had passed out after whispering to the president, and had returned to his friend's side. He could hardly hold them back as the unfortunate man groaned in agony and leant against the table: he had opened the book at the black page. "Kindly come with me, Mr. D'Aubigny," said the president, and they passed out together.[17]

"We can go now," said Wylliams, "I think the rain has gone off. Remember your promise, gentlemen. You have been at a meeting of the Lost Club. You will never see that young man again. Good night."

"It isn't *murder*, is it?" gasped Austin.

"Oh no, not at all. Mr. D'Aubigny will, I hope, live for many years; he has disappeared, merely disappeared. Good night; there's a hansom that will do for you."

The two friends went to their homes in dead silence. They did not meet again for three weeks, and each thought the other looked ill and shaken. They walked drearily, with grave averted faces, down Piccadilly, each afraid to begin the recollection of the terrible club. Of a sudden Phillipps stopped as if he had been shot. "Look there, Austin," he muttered, "look at that." The posters of the evening papers were spread out beside the pavement, and on one of them Austin saw in large blue letters, "Mysterious disappearance of a Gentleman." Austin bought a copy and turned over the leaves with shaking fingers till he found the brief paragraph — "Mr. St. John D'Aubigny, of Stoke D'Aubigny, in Sussex, has disappeared under mysterious circumstances. Mr. D'Aubigny was staying at Strathdoon, in Scotland, and came up to London, as is stated, on business, on August 16th.[18] It has been ascertained that he arrived safely at King's Cross, and drove to Piccadilly Circus, where he got out. It is said that he was last seen at the corner of Glass House Street, leading from Regent Street into Soho.[19] Since the above date the unfortunate gentleman, who was much liked in London society, has not been heard of. Mr. D'Aubigny was to have been married in September. The police are extremely reticent."

"Good God! Austin, this is dreadful. You remember the date. Poor fellow, poor fellow."

---

[17] The surname D'Aubigny belonged to several Anglo-Norman noblemen during the Middle Ages. The titular heroine of Gautier's novel *Mademoiselle de Maupin* (1835), a major early influence on the Decadent movement, is the bisexual, cross-dressing Julie d'Aubigny (1670/73–1707).

[18] Strathdon (also Strathdown) is the name of a village and the general surrounding area in the highlands of Aberdeenshire, Scotland. It was known for its witches, as recorded in *The Folk-lore Journal*, James Grant's (1822–1887) *The Mysteries of All Nations* (1880), and elsewhere.

[19] Glasshouse Street is a short street linking Piccadilly Circus to Regent Street, just south of the disreputable district of Soho.

"Phillipps, I think I shall go home, I feel sick."

D'Aubigny was never heard of again. But the strangest part of a strange story remains to be told. The two friends called upon Wylliams, and charged him with being a member of the Lost Club, and an accomplice in the fate of D'Aubigny. The placid Mr. Wylliams at first stared at the two pale, earnest faces, and finally roared with laughter.

"My dear fellows, what on earth are you talking about? I never heard such a cock-and-bull in my life. As you say, Phillipps, I once pointed out to you a house said to be a club, as we were walking through Soho; but that was a low gambling club, frequented by German waiters. I am afraid the fact is that Azario's Chianti was rather too strong for you. However, I will try and convince you of your mistake."

Wylliams forthwith summoned his man, who swore that he and his master were in Cairo during the whole of August, and offered to produce the hotel bills.[20] Phillipps shook his head, and they went away. Their next step was to try and find out the archway where they had taken shelter, and after a good deal of trouble they succeeded. They knocked at the door of the gloomy house, whistling as Wylliams had done. They were admitted by a respectable mechanic in a white apron, who was evidently astonished at the whistle; in fact he was inclined to suspect the influence of a "drop too much." However, he willingly showed them over the premises. The place was a billiard table factory, and had been so (as they learnt in the neighbourhood) for many years. The rooms must once have been large and magnificent, but most of them had been divided into three or four separate workshops by wooden partitions.

Phillipps sighed; he could do no more for his lost friend; but both he and Austin remained unconvinced. In justice to Mr. Wylliams, it must be stated that Lord Henry Harcourt assured Phillipps that he had seen Wylliams in Cairo about the middle of August; he thought, but could not be sure, on the 16th; and, also, that the recent disappearances of some well known men about town are patient of explanations which would exclude the agency of the Lost Club.[21]

'The Lost Club', *The Whirlwind* (20 December 1890), pp. 182–84.

---

[20] 'His man' refers to his valet, the male servant who takes care of his master's personal needs.

[21] The uncommon phrase 'patient of explanations' also appears in Thomas De Quincey's (1785–1859) *Confessions of an Opium Eater* (1821), where it describes a person who is open to accept the explanations given. According to Fred J. Hando, Machen had purchased De Quincey's book while still a youth living in Wales (Hando, *The Pleasant Land of Gwent*, p. 57).

2

The Great God Pan (1894)[1]

THE EXPERIMENT

'I am glad you came, Clarke; very glad indeed. I was not sure you could spare the time.'

'I was able to make arrangements for a few days; things are not very lively just now. But have you no misgivings, Raymond? Is it absolutely safe?'

The two men were slowly pacing the terrace in front of Dr. Raymond's house. The sun still hung above the western mountain-line, but it shone with a dull red glow that cast no shadows, and all the air was quiet; a sweet breath came from the great wood on the hillside above, and with it, at intervals, the soft murmuring call of the wild doves. Below, in the long lovely valley, the river wound in and out between the lonely hills, and, as the sun hovered and vanished into the west, a faint mist, pure white, began to rise from the hills. Dr. Raymond turned sharply to his friend.

'Safe? Of course it is. In itself the operation is a perfectly simple one; any surgeon could do it.'

'And there is no danger at any other stage?'

'None; absolutely no physical danger whatsoever, I give you my word. You are always timid, Clarke, always; but you know my history. I have devoted myself to transcendental medicine for the last twenty years.[2] I have heard myself called quack and charlatan and impostor, but all the while I knew I was on the right

---

[1]   In Greek mythology, Pan is a demi-god associated with Arcadia, nature, the wild, and the pastoral, and is affiliated primarily with shepherds, satyrs, and nymphs. Like satyrs, he has the hindquarters, legs, tail, and horns of a goat. In accordance with Machen's depiction of Pan in this work, the demi-god is understood as not necessarily a single entity but as multiple or all-pervasive, and thus he is often not seen even though his presence is sensed. In *The Great God Pan*, Machen has the reader sense Pan's presence on more than one occasion, but the demi-god and his offspring remain allusive.

[2]   A spiritual philosophy of healing, transcendental medicine has roots in traditional medicine from India and seventeenth-century biomedicine from England. In the later nineteenth century, it was recognized as a non-normative practice that overlapped with mesmerism, hypnotism, spiritualism, and mysticism. Elements of transcendental medicine are now considered part of neuroscience. In Stevenson's *Strange Case of Dr Jekyll and Mr Hyde*, Hyde refers to the 'virtue of transcendental medicine' immediately before revealing himself as Jekyll to Dr Lanyon.

path. Five years ago I reached the goal, and since then every day has been a preparation for what we shall do to-night.'

'I should like to believe it is all true.' Clarke knit his brows, and looked doubtfully at Dr. Raymond. 'Are you perfectly sure, Raymond, that your theory is not a phantasmagoria — a splendid vision, certainly, but a mere vision after all?'[3]

Dr. Raymond stopped in his walk and turned sharply. He was a middle-aged man, gaunt and thin, of a pale yellow complexion, but as he answered Clarke and faced him, there was a flush on his cheek.

'Look about you, Clarke. You see the mountain, and hill following after hill, as wave on wave, you see the woods and orchards, the fields of ripe corn, and the meadows reaching to the reed-beds by the river. You see me standing here beside you, and hear my voice; but I tell you that all these things — yes, from that star that has just shone out in the sky to the solid ground beneath our feet — I say that all these are but dreams and shadows: the shadows that hide the real world from our eyes. There *is* a real world, but it is beyond this glamour and this vision, beyond these "chases in Arras, dreams in a career,"[4] beyond them all as beyond a veil. I do not know whether any human being has ever lifted that veil; but I do know, Clarke, that you and I shall see it lifted this very night from before another's eyes. You may think this all strange nonsense; it may be strange, but it is true, and the ancients knew what lifting the veil means. They called it seeing the god Pan.'[5]

Clarke shivered; the white mist gathering over the river was chilly.

'It is wonderful indeed,' he said. 'We are standing on the brink of a strange world, Raymond, if what you say is true. I suppose the knife is absolutely necessary?'

---

[3]   A phantasmagoria is a type of optical entertainment usually using magic lantern projections to display a series of images. It was popular in Europe during the eighteenth and nineteenth centuries. Over time, the term became increasingly used to refer to dreamlike visions. Machen had considered giving his novella *The Hill of Dreams* the name *Phantasmagoria*.
[4]   These lines refer to hunting scenes on an arras (hanging tapestry), and are taken from George Herbert's (1593–1633) poem 'Dotage' (1633), a meditation on fleeting and illusory pleasures.
[5]   Raymond's turn to science to extend visible reality to the spiritual, what Clarke calls the 'real world', is Neoplatonist in formulation. It also echoes English Aestheticist author Walter Pater's description in *Studies in the History of the Renaissance* (1873) of the fluidity between the external landscape and internal elements of the body, which reads in part: 'the passage of the blood, the wasting and repairing of the lenses of the eye, the modification of the tissues of the brain by every ray of light and sound [are] processes which science reduces to simpler and more elementary forces. Like the elements of which we are composed, the action of these forces extends beyond us; it rusts iron and ripens corn. Far out on every side of us these elements are broadcast, driven by many forces' (Walter Pater, *The Renaissance* (London: Macmillan, 1873), pp. 207–08).

'Yes; a slight lesion in the grey matter, that is all; a trifling rearrangement of certain cells, a microscopical alteration that would escape the attention of ninety-nine brain specialists out of a hundred. I don't want to bother you with "shop," Clarke; I might give you a mass of technical detail which would sound very imposing, and would leave you as enlightened as you are now. But I suppose you have read, casually, in out-of-the-way corners of your paper, that immense strides have been made recently in the physiology of the brain. I saw a paragraph the other day about Digby's theory, and Browne Faber's discoveries.[6] Theories and discoveries! Where they are standing now, I stood fifteen years ago, and I need not tell you that I have not been standing still for the last fifteen years. It will be enough if I say that five years ago I made the discovery that I alluded to when I said that ten years ago I reached the goal. After years of labour, after years of toiling and groping in the dark, after days and nights of disappointment and sometimes of despair, in which I used now and then to tremble and grow cold with the thought that perhaps there were others seeking for what I sought, at last, after so long, a pang of sudden joy thrilled my soul, and I knew the long journey was at an end. By what seemed then and still seems a chance, the suggestion of a moment's idle thought followed up upon familiar lines and paths that I had tracked a hundred times already, the great truth burst upon me, and I saw, mapped out in lines of light, a whole world, a sphere unknown; continents and islands, and great oceans in which no ship has sailed (to my belief) since a Man first lifted up his eyes and beheld the sun, and the stars of heaven, and the quiet earth beneath. You will think this all high-flown language, Clarke, but it is hard to be literal. And yet; I do not know whether what I am hinting at cannot be set forth in plain and lonely terms. For instance, this world of ours is pretty well girded now with the telegraph wires and cables; thought, with something less than the speed of thought, flashes from sunrise to sunset, from north to south, across the floods and the desert places.[7] Suppose that an electrician of to-day were suddenly to perceive that he and his friends have merely been playing with pebbles and mistaking them for the foundations of the world; suppose that such a man saw uttermost space lie open before the current, and words of men flash forth to the sun and beyond the sun into the systems beyond, and the voice of articulate-speaking men echo in the waste void that bounds our thought. As analogies go, that is a pretty good analogy of

---

[6] Sir Kenelm Digby (1603–1665) was a natural philosopher who theorized the brain's construction in atomist terms, and whose investigations included alchemy and sympathetic magic. No historical reference to Browne Faber has been found. Roger Luckhurst suggests the name echoes that of Charles Brown-Sequard (1817–1894), a brain neurologist (Roger Luckhurst, ed., *Late Victorian Gothic Tales* (Oxford: Oxford University Press, 2005), p. 279).
[7] Francis Ronalds (1788–1873) built the first working telegraph in 1816, but its commercial value was not recognized for decades afterward. The first transatlantic cable was successfully lain in 1866.

what I have done; you can understand now a little of what I felt as I stood here one evening; it was a summer evening, and the valley looked much as it does now; I stood here, and saw before me the unutterable, the unthinkable gulf that yawns profound between two worlds, the world of matter and the world of spirit; I saw the great empty deep stretch dim before me, and in that instant a bridge of light leapt from the earth to the unknown shore, and the abyss was spanned.[8] You may look in Browne Faber's book, if you like, and you will find that to the present day men of science are unable to account for the presence, or to specify the functions of a certain group of nerve-cells in the brain. That group is, as it were, land to let, a mere waste place for fanciful theories. I am not in the position of Browne Faber and the specialists, I am perfectly instructed as to the possible functions of those nerve-centres in the scheme of things. With a touch I can bring them into play, with a touch, I say, I can set free the current, with a touch I can complete the communication between this world of sense and — we shall be able to finish the sentence later on. Yes, the knife is necessary; but think what that knife will effect. It will level utterly the solid wall of sense, and probably, for the first time since man was made, a spirit will gaze on a spirit-world. Clarke, Mary will see the god Pan!'

'But you remember what you wrote to me? I thought it would be requisite that she — '

He whispered the rest into the doctor's ear.

'Not at all, not at all. That is nonsense. I assure you. Indeed, it is better as it is; I am quite certain of that.'

'Consider the matter well, Raymond. It's a great responsibility. Something might go wrong; you would be a miserable man for the rest of your days.'

'No, I think not, even if the worst happened. As you know, I rescued Mary from the gutter, and from almost certain starvation, when she was a child; I think her life is mine, to use as I see fit.[9] Come, it is getting late; we had better go in.'

Dr. Raymond led the way into the house, through the hall, and down a long dark passage. He took a key from his pocket and opened a heavy door, and

---

[8] Raymond's description brings to mind Marie Corelli's (1855–1924) highly successful first novel, *A Romance of Two Worlds* (1886), which — inspired in part by new scientific research in psychical studies, spiritualism, and electricity — uses the metaphor of the transatlantic cable to describe the electric communication between this world and the spiritual. Like Machen, Corelli resisted being represented as part of the British Decadent movement.

[9] Systems for assisting orphans were far from ideal in the Victorian era and adoption was often informal, with parental treatment not being monitored by any external body. A common trope in Decadent works, including Pater's *Marius the Epicurean* (1885) and Wilde's *Picture of Dorian Gray* (1890, 1891), *The Great God Pan* includes more than one parentless child, although Machen is unique in focussing on the female orphan. Dickens (one of Machen's favourite writers) features a virtuous female orphan in *The Old Curiosity Shop* (1840–1841).

motioned Clarke into his laboratory. It had once been a billiard-room, and was lighted by a glass dome in the centre of the ceiling, whence there still shone a sad grey light on the figure of the doctor as he lit a lamp with a heavy shade and placed it on a table in the middle of the room.

Clarke looked about him. Scarcely a foot of wall remained bare; there were shelves all around laden with bottles and phials of all shapes and colours, and at one end stood a little Chippendale book-case. Raymond pointed to this.

'You see that parchment Oswald Crollius? He was one of the first to show me the way, though I don't think he ever found it himself. That is a strange saying of his: "In every grain of wheat there lies hidden the soul of a star." '[10]

There was not much furniture in the laboratory. The table in the centre, a stone slab with a drain in one corner, the two armchairs on which Raymond and Clarke were sitting; that was all, except an odd-looking chair at the furthest end of the room. Clarke looked at it, and raised his eyebrows.

'Yes, that is the chair,' said Raymond. 'We may as well place it in position.' He got up and wheeled the chair to the light, and began raising and lowering it, letting down the seat, setting the back at various angles, and adjusting the foot-rest. It looked comfortable enough, and Clarke passed his hand over the soft green velvet, as the doctor manipulated the levers.

'Now, Clarke, make yourself quite comfortable. I have a couple hours' work before me; I was obliged to leave certain matters to the last.'

Raymond went to the stone slab, and Clarke watched him drearily as he bent over a row of phials and lit the flame under the crucible. The doctor had a small hand-lamp, shaded as the larger one, on a ledge above his apparatus, and Clarke, who sat in the shadows, looked down at the great dreary room, wondering at the bizarre effects of brilliant light and undefined darkness contrasting with one another. Soon he became conscious of an odd odour, at first the merest suggestion of odour, in the room; and as it grew more decided he felt surprised that he was not reminded of the chemist's shop or the surgery. Clarke found himself idly endeavouring to analyse the sensation, and half conscious, he began to think of a day, fifteen years ago, that he had spent

---

[10] Oswald Crollius (c. 1560–1609) was a German alchemist, Neoplatonist, and physician. In 'Discovering the Great and Deep Mysteries of Nature', he argues that, while 'all living things, but also all growing things, even stones and metalls, and whatever are in the Universall Nature of things, are indued [sic] with a syderiall spirit, which is called Heaven or the Astrum', 'when we say that all the form of things proceedeth from the astra's, it is not meant of the visible coales of Heaven, nor of the invisible body of the Astra's in the Firmament, but of every things [sic] own proper Astrum'. 'False Philosophers thinke that the stars of the Firmanent do infuse virtue into herbs and trees', when in fact 'the externall stars do neither incline nor necessitate Man, but Man rather inclines the Stars' (Oswald Crollius, 'Discovering the Great and Deep Mysteries of Nature', in *Philosophy Reformed and Improved in Four Profound Tractates* (London: M.S., 1657), pp. 29–30); see also his *Basilica chymica* (1608).

roaming through the woods and meadows near his old home. It was a burning day at the beginning of August, the heat had dimmed the outlines of all things and all distances with a faint mist, and people who observed the thermometer spoke of an abnormal register, of a temperature that was almost tropical. Strangely that wonderful hot day of 185- rose up again in Clarke's imagination; the sense of dazzling all-pervading sunlight seemed to blot out the shadows and the lights of the laboratory, and he felt again the heated air beating in gusts about his face, saw the shimmer rising from the turf, and heard the myriad murmur of the summer.[11]

'I hope the smell doesn't annoy you, Clarke; there's nothing unwholesome about it. It may make you a bit sleepy, that's all.'

Clarke heard the words quite distinctly, and knew that Raymond was speaking to him, but for the life of him he could not rouse himself from his lethargy. He could only think of the lonely walk he had taken fifteen years ago; it was his last look at the fields and woods he had known since he was a child, and now it all stood out in brilliant light, as a picture, before him. Above all there came to his nostrils the scent of summer, the smell of flowers mingled, and the odour of the woods, of cool shaded places, deep in the green depths, drawn forth by the sun's heat; and the scent of the good earth, lying as it were with arms stretched forth, and smiling lips, overpowered all. His fancies made him wander, as he had wandered long ago, from the fields into the wood, tracking a little path between the shining undergrowth of beech-trees; and the trickle of water dropping from the limestone rock sounded as a clear melody in the dream. Thoughts began to go astray and to mingle with other recollections; the beech-alley was transformed to a path between ilex-trees, and here and there a vine climbed from bough to bough, and sent up waving tendrils and drooped with purple grapes, and the sparse grey green leaves of a wild olive-tree stood out against the dark shadows of the ilex.[12] Clarke, in the deep folds of dream, was conscious that the path from his father's house had led him into an undiscovered country, and he was wondering at the strangeness of it all, when suddenly, in place of the hum and murmur of the summer, an infinite silence seemed to fall on all things, and the wood was hushed, and for a moment in time he stood face to face there with a presence, that was neither man nor beast, neither the living nor the dead, but all things mingled, the form of all things but

---

[11] Ron Weighell has proposed that the influence of the scent in this scene echoes 'a magical technique based on the theory of cabalistic correspondence' where perfumes are used 'to create an atmosphere conducive to visions of the relevant deity' (Ron Weighell, 'Sorcery and Sanctity: the Spagyric Quest of Arthur Machen', quoted in Valentine, *Arthur Machen*, p. 26).
[12] The ilex tree belongs to the genus *Ilex* (e.g. a holly or a holm oak) and is associated by some pagans with longevity, health, and fertility. The tree also appears in Machen's dreamlike descriptions in *The Hill of Dreams*.

devoid of all form.[13] And in that moment, the sacrament of body and soul was dissolved, and a voice seemed to cry 'let us go hence,' and then the darkness of darkness beyond the stars, the darkness of everlasting.

When Clarke woke up with a start he saw Raymond pouring a few drops of some oily fluid into a green phial, which he stoppered tightly.

'You have been dozing,' he said; 'the journey must have tired you out. It is done now. I am going to fetch Mary; I shall be back in ten minutes.'

Clarke lay back in his chair and wondered. It seemed as if he had but passed from one dream into another. He half expected to see the walls of the laboratory melt and disappear, and to awake in London, shuddering at his own sleeping fancies. But at last the door opened, and the doctor returned, and behind him came a girl of about seventeen, dressed all in white. She was so beautiful that Clarke did not wonder at what the doctor had written to him. She was blushing now over face and neck and arms, but Raymond seemed unmoved.

'Mary,' he said, 'the time has come. You are quite free. Are you willing to trust yourself to me entirely?'

'Yes, dear.'

'Do you hear that, Clarke? You are my witness. Here is the chair, Mary. It is quite easy. Just sit in it and lean back. Are you ready?'

'Yes, dear, quite ready. Give me a kiss before you begin.'

The doctor stooped and kissed her mouth, kindly enough. 'Now shut your eyes,' he said. The girl closed her eyelids, as if she were tired, and longed for sleep, and Raymond held the green phial to her nostrils. Her face grew white, whiter than her dress; she struggled faintly, and then with the feeling of submission strong within her, crossed her arms upon her breast as a little child about to say her prayers. The bright light of the lamp beat full upon her, and Clarke watched changes fleeting over that face as the changes of the hills when the summer clouds float across the sun. And then she lay all white and still, and the doctor turned up one of her eyelids. She was quite unconscious. Raymond pressed hard on one of the levers and the chair instantly sank back. Clarke saw him cutting away a circle, like a tonsure, from her hair, and the lamp was moved nearer.[14] Raymond took a small glittering instrument from a little case, and Clarke turned away shuddering. When he looked again the doctor was binding up the wound he had made.

'She will awake in five minutes.' Raymond was still perfectly cool. 'There is nothing more to be done; we can only wait.'

---

[13] The phrase 'undiscovered country' is suggestive of William Shakespeare's (1564–1616) character Hamlet's 'To be, or not to be' soliloquy, wherein he reasons that the main obstacle to suicide is 'the dread of something after death / The undiscovered country from whose bourn / No traveller returns' (*Hamlet*, 3.1.80–82).

[14] A tonsure is the part of a cleric's or monk's head left bare by shaving his hair. Common in mediaeval Christianity, a tonsure signified devotion and humility.

The minutes passed slowly; they could hear a slow, heavy ticking. There was an old clock in the passage. Clarke felt sick and faint; his knees shook beneath him, he could hardly stand.

Suddenly, as they watched, they heard a long-drawn sigh, and suddenly did the colour that had vanished return to the girl's cheeks, and suddenly her eyes opened. Clarke quailed before them. They shone with an awful light, looking far away, and a great wonder fell upon her face, and her hands stretched out as if to touch what was invisible; but in an instant the wonder faded, and gave place to the most awful terror. The muscles of her face were hideously convulsed, she shook from head to foot; the soul seemed struggling and shuddering within the house of flesh. It was a horrible sight, and Clarke rushed forward, as she fell shrieking to the floor.

Three days later Raymond took Clarke to Mary's bedside. She was lying wide-awake, rolling her head from side to side, and grinning vacantly.

'Yes,' said the doctor, still quite cool, 'it is a great pity; she is a hopeless idiot. However, it could not be helped; and, after all, she has seen the Great God Pan.'

MR. CLARKE'S MEMOIRS

Mr. Clarke, the gentleman chosen by Dr. Raymond to witness the strange experiment of the god Pan, was a person in whose character caution and curiosity were oddly mingled; in his sober moments he thought of the unusual and eccentric with undisguised aversion, and yet, deep in his heart, there was a wide-eyed inquisitiveness with respect to all the more recondite and esoteric elements in the nature of men. The latter tendency had prevailed when he accepted Raymond's invitation, for though his considered judgment had always repudiated the doctor's theories as the wildest nonsense, yet he secretly hugged a belief in fantasy, and would have rejoiced to see that belief confirmed. The horrors that he witnessed in the dreary laboratory were to a certain extent salutary; he was conscious of being involved in an affair not altogether reputable, and for many years afterwards he clung bravely to the commonplace, and rejected all occasions of occult investigation. Indeed, on some homœopathic principle, he for some time attended the séances of distinguished mediums, hoping that the clumsy tricks of these gentlemen would make him altogether disgusted with mysticism of every kind, but the remedy, though caustic, was not efficacious.[15] Clarke knew that he still pined for the unseen, and little by

---

[15] German physician Samuel Hahnemann (1755–1843) invented homeopathy, a method of treating diseases by using tiny doses of drugs to produce symptoms that are similar to the diseases themselves. As this passage suggests, Machen was highly sceptical of more fashionable forms of occulture such as séances, where a spiritualist medium took on the role of messenger between the living and the dead. In 1898, Machen declared that 'there are few steps between the laboratory and the séance' (Arthur Machen, 'Science and the Ghost

little, the old passion began to reassert itself, as the face of Mary, shuddering and convulsed with an unknowable terror, faded slowly from his memory. Occupied all day in pursuits both serious and lucrative, the temptation to relax in the evening was too great, especially in the winter months, when the fire cast a warm glow over his snug bachelor apartment, and a bottle of some choice claret stood ready by his elbow. His dinner digested, he would make a brief pretence of reading the evening paper, but the mere catalogue of news soon palled upon him, and Clarke would find himself casting glances of warm desire in the direction of an old Japanese bureau, which stood at a pleasant distance from the hearth. Like a boy before a jam-closet, for a few minutes he would hover indecisive, but lust always prevailed, and Clarke ended by drawing up his chair, lighting a candle, and sitting down before the bureau. Its pigeon-holes and drawers teemed with documents on the most morbid subjects, and in the well reposed a large manuscript volume, in which he had painfully entered the gems of his collection. Clarke had a fine contempt for published literature; the most ghostly story ceased to interest him if it happened to be printed; his sole pleasure was in the reading, compiling, arranging, and rearranging what he called his 'Memoirs to prove the Existence of the Devil,' and engaged in this pursuit the evening seemed to fly and the night appeared too short.[16]

On one particular evening, an ugly December night, black with fog, and raw with frost, Clarke hurried over his dinner, and scarcely deigned to observe his customary ritual of taking up the paper and laying it down again. He paced two or three times up and down the room, and opened the bureau, stood still a moment, and sat down. He leant back, absorbed in one of those dreams to which he was subject, and at length drew out his book, and opened it at the last entry. There were three or four pages densely covered with Clarke's round, set penmanship, and at the beginning he had written in a somewhat larger hand:

> Singular Narrative told me by my Friend, Dr. Phillips. He assures me that all the Facts related therein are strictly and wholly True, but refuses to give either the Surnames of the Persons concerned, or the Place where these Extraordinary Events occurred.

Mr. Clarke began to read over the account for the tenth time, glancing now and then at the pencil notes he had made when it was told him by his friend. It was one of his humours to pride himself on a certain literary ability; he thought

---

Story', *Literature* (17 September 1898), 251). Within spiritual discourse, the term 'occult' generally refers to secret practices, studies, and training in natural magic, while 'mysticism' involves engagements with an otherworldly realm that rely less on the acquirement of special knowledge. Further discussion of Machen's experience of the occult appears in the introduction to this edition.

[16] Similar renderings of collecting as 'lust' or an obsession appear in other Decadent works such as Huysmans's *A Rebours* and Wilde's *Picture of Dorian Gray*, both of which describe the collection of gems (to which Machen alludes here).

well of his style, and took pains in arranging the circumstances in dramatic
order. He read the following story:

The persons concerned in this statement are Helen V., who, if she is still alive,
must now be a woman of twenty-three, Rachel M., since deceased, who was a
year younger than the above, and Trevor W., an imbecile, aged eighteen. These
persons were at the period of the story inhabitants of a village on the borders
of Wales, a place of some importance in the time of the Roman occupation,
but now a scattered hamlet, of not more than five hundred souls. It is situated
on rising ground, about six miles from the sea, and is sheltered by a large and
picturesque forest.[17]

Some eleven years ago, Helen V. came to the village under rather peculiar
circumstances. It is understood that she, being an orphan, was adopted in her
infancy by a distant relative, who brought her up in his own house till she was
twelve years old. Thinking, however, that it would be better for the child to
have playmates of her own age, he advertised in several local papers for a good
home in a comfortable farm-house for a girl of twelve, and this advertisement
was answered by Mr. R., a well-to-do farmer in the above-mentioned village.
His references proving satisfactory, the gentleman sent his adopted daughter
to Mr. R., with a letter, in which he stipulated that the girl should have a room
to herself, and stated that her guardians need be at no trouble in the matter of
education, as she was already sufficiently educated for the position in life which
she would occupy. In fact, Mr. R. was given to understand that the girl was to
be allowed to find her own occupations, and to spend her time almost as she
liked. Mr. R. duly met her at the nearest station, a town some seven miles away
from his house, and seems to have remarked nothing extraordinary about the
child, except that she was reticent as to her former life and her adopted father.
She was, however, of a very different type from the inhabitants of the village;
her skin was a pale, clear olive, and her features were strongly marked, and of
a somewhat foreign character. She appears to have settled down, easily enough,
into farm-house life, and became a favourite with the children, who sometimes
went with her on her rambles in the forest, for this was her amusement. Mr.
R. states that he has known her to go out by herself directly after their early
breakfast, and not return till after dusk, and that, feeling uneasy at a young girl
being out alone for so many hours, he communicated with her adopted father,
who replied in a brief note that Helen must do as she chose. In the winter, when
the forest paths are impassable, she spent most of her time in her bed-room,
where she slept alone, according to the instructions of her relative. It was on
one of these expeditions to the forest that the first of the singular incidents
with which this girl is connected occurred, the date being about a year after

---

[17] The description fits Machen's hometown of Caerleon, known as Isca Silurum when it was
occupied by the Romans. It had a Roman road, as mentioned shortly in the text.

her arrival at the village. The preceding winter had been remarkably severe, the snow drifting to a great depth, and the frost continuing for an unexampled period, and the summer following was as noteworthy for its extreme heat. On one of the very hottest days in this summer, Helen V. left the farm-house for one of her long rambles in the forest, taking with her, as usual, some bread and meat for lunch. She was seen by some men in the fields making for the old Roman Road, a green causeway which traverses the highest part of the wood, and they were astonished to observe that the girl had taken off her hat, though the heat of the sun was already tropical. As it happened, a labourer, Joseph W. by name, was working in the forest near the Roman Road, and at twelve o'clock, his little son, Trevor, brought the man his dinner of bread and cheese. After the meal, the boy, who was about seven years old at the time, left his father at work, and, as he said, went to look for flowers in the wood, and the man, who could hear him shouting with delight over his discoveries, felt no uneasiness. Suddenly, however, he was horrified at hearing the most dreadful screams, evidently the result of great terror, proceeding from the direction in which his son had gone, and he hastily threw down his tools and ran to see what had happened. Tracing his path by the sound, he met the little boy, who was running headlong, and was evidently terribly frightened, and on questioning him the man elicited that after picking a posy of flowers he felt tired, and lay down on the grass and fell asleep. He was suddenly awakened, as he stated, by a peculiar noise, a sort of singing he called it, and on peeping through the branches he saw Helen V. playing on the grass with a 'strange naked man,' who he seemed unable to describe further. He said he felt dreadfully frightened, and ran away crying for his father. Joseph W. proceeded in the direction indicated by his son, and found Helen V. sitting on the grass in the middle of a glade or open space left by charcoal burners.[18] He angrily charged her with frightening his little boy, but she entirely denied the accusation and laughed at the child's story of a 'strange man,' to which he himself did not attach much credence. Joseph W. came to the conclusion that the boy had woke up with a sudden fright, as children sometimes do, but Trevor persisted in his story, and continued in such evident distress that at last his father took him home, hoping that his mother would be able to soothe him. For many weeks, however, the boy gave his parents much anxiety; he became nervous and strange in his manner, refusing to leave the cottage by himself, and constantly alarming the household by waking in the night with cries of 'the man in the wood! father! father!' In course of time, however, the impression seemed to have worn off, and about three months later he accompanied his father to the house of a gentleman in the neighbourhood, for whom Joseph W. occasionally did work. The man was shown into the study, and the little boy was

---

[18] Charcoal burning is an ancient practice whereby wood is heated in a large, earthen kiln in order to carbonize it (i.e. to transform it into charcoal).

left sitting in the hall, and a few minutes later, while the gentleman was giving
W. his instructions, they were both horrified by a piercing shriek and the sound
of a fall, and rushing out they found the child lying senseless on the floor, his
face contorted with terror. The doctor was immediately summoned, and after
some examination he pronounced the child to be suffering from a kind of fit,
apparently produced by a sudden shock. The boy was taken to one of the bedrooms, and after some time recovered consciousness, but only to pass into a
condition described by the medical man as one of violent hysteria.[19] The doctor
exhibited a strong sedative, and in the course of two hours pronounced him fit
to walk home, but in passing through the hall the paroxysms of fright returned
and with additional violence. The father perceived that the child was pointing
at some object, and heard the old cry, 'the man in the wood,' and looking in the
direction indicated saw a stone head of grotesque appearance, which had been
built into the wall above one of the doors. It seems that the owner of the house
had recently made alterations in his premises, and on digging the foundations
for some offices, the men had found a curious head, evidently of the Roman
period, which had been placed in the hall in the manner described. The head
is pronounced by the most experienced archæologists of the district to be that
of a faun or satyr.[†20]

From whatever cause arising, this second shock seemed too severe for the
boy Trevor, and at the present date he suffers from a weakness of intellect,
which gives but little promise of amending. The matter caused a good deal of
sensation at the time, and the girl Helen was closely questioned by Mr. R., but
to no purpose, she steadfastly denying that she had frightened or in any way
molested Trevor.

The second event with which this girl's name is connected took place about
six years ago, and is of a still more extraordinary character.

At the beginning of the summer of 188–, Helen contracted a friendship of
a peculiarly intimate character with Rachel M., the daughter of a prosperous

---

[19]   When Machen was writing this text, hysteria (from the Greek *hystera*, meaning 'uterus')
was recognized almost exclusively as a psychological condition experienced by women,
with one of the symptoms being strong sexual desire. Masturbation was one medically
recognized cure. In the late nineteenth century, the French neurologist Jean-Martin
Charcot (1825–1893) and Sigmund Freud (1856–1939) both contributed to arguments for
hysteria as a psychological, rather than physical or supernatural, disorder, with Freud
eventually declaring it as a condition found in both women and men.
[†] [This note is Machen's own.] Dr. Phillips tells me that he has seen the head in question, and
assures me that he has never received such a vivid presentment of intense evil.
[20]   In classical mythology, fauns were males who were goats from the waist down and
had goat horns. Satyrs were most often depicted with the ears and tail of a goat, although
originally they were portrayed with horses' ears and tails. A satyr is figured as an attendant
on the god Dionysus and noted for his wanton and lustful behaviour, often depicted with an
erection. The Roman deity Faunus is associated with Pan.

farmer in the neighbourhood. This girl, who was a year younger than Helen, was considered by most people to be the prettier of the two, though Helen's features had to a great extent softened as she became older. The two girls, who were together on every available opportunity, presented a singular contrast, the one with her clear, olive skin and almost Italian appearance, and the other of the proverbial red and white of our rural districts. It must be stated that the payments made to Mr. R. for the maintenance of Helen were known in the village for their excessive liberality, and the impression was general that she would one day inherit a large sum of money from her relative. The parents of Rachel were therefore not averse to their daughter's friendship with the girl, and even encouraged the intimacy, though they now bitterly regret having done so. Helen still retained her extraordinary fondness for the forest, and on several occasions Rachel accompanied her, the two friends setting out early in the morning, and remaining in the wood until dusk. Once or twice after these excursions Mrs. M. thought her daughter's manner rather peculiar; she seemed languid and dreamy, and as it has been expressed, 'different from herself,' but these peculiarities seem to have been thought too trifling for remark. One evening, however, after Rachel had come home, her mother heard a noise which sounded like suppressed weeping in the girl's room, and on going in found her lying, half undressed, upon the bed, evidently in the greatest distress. As soon as she saw her mother, she exclaimed, 'Ah, mother, mother, why did you let me go to the forest with Helen?' Mrs. M. was astonished at so strange a question, and proceeded to make inquiries. Rachel told her a wild story. She said— —

Clarke closed the book with a snap, and turned his chair towards the fire. When his friend sat one evening in that very chair, and told his story, Clarke had interrupted him at a point a little subsequent to this, had cut short his words in a paroxysm of horror. 'My God!' he had exclaimed, 'think, think what you are saying. It is too incredible, too monstrous; such things can never be in this quiet world, where men and women live and die, and struggle, and conquer, or maybe fail, and fall down under sorrow, and grieve and suffer strange fortunes for many a year; but not this, Phillips, not such things as this. There must be some explanation, some way out of the terror. Why, man, if such a case were possible, our earth would be a nightmare.'

But Phillips had told his story to the end, concluding:

'Her flight remains a mystery to this day; she vanished in broad sunlight; they saw her walking in a meadow, and a few moments later she was not there.'

Clarke tried to conceive the thing again, as he sat by the fire, and again his mind shuddered and shrank back, appalled before the sight of such awful, unspeakable elements enthroned as it were, and triumphant in human flesh. Before him stretched the long dim vista of the green causeway in the forest, as his friend had described it; he saw the swaying leaves and the quivering shadows on the grass, he saw the sunlight and the flowers, and far away, far in the long distance, the two figures moved towards him. One was Rachel, but the other?

Clarke had tried his best to disbelieve it all, but at the end of the account, as he had written it in his book, he had placed the inscription:

ET DIABOLUS INCARNATUS EST. ET HOMO
FACTUS EST.[21]

THE CITY OF RESURRECTIONS

'Herbert! Good God! Is it possible?'

'Yes, my name's Herbert. I think I know your face too, but I don't remember your name. My memory is very queer.'

'Don't you recollect Villiers of Wadham?'[22]

'So it is, so it is. I beg your pardon, Villiers, I didn't think I was begging of an old college friend. Goodnight.'

'My dear fellow, this haste is unnecessary. My rooms are close by, but we won't go there just yet. Suppose we walk up Shaftesbury Avenue a little way?[23] But how in heaven's name have you come to this pass, Herbert?'

'It's a long story, Villiers, and a strange one too, but you can hear it if you like.'

'Come on, then. Take my arm, you don't seem very strong.'

The ill-assorted pair moved slowly up Rupert Street; the one in dirty, evil-looking rags, and the other attired in the regulation uniform of a man about town, trim, glossy, and eminently well-to-do. Villiers had emerged from his restaurant after an excellent dinner of many courses, assisted by an ingratiating little flask of Chianti, and, in that frame of mind which was with him almost chronic, had delayed a moment by the door, peering round in the dimly-lighted street in search of those mysterious incidents and persons with which the streets of London teem in every quarter and every hour. Villiers prided himself as a practised explorer of such obscure mazes and byways of London life, and in this unprofitable pursuit he displayed an assiduity which was worthy of more serious employment. Thus he stood by the lamp-post surveying the passers-by with undisguised curiosity, and with that gravity known only to the systematic diner, had just enunciated in his mind the formula: 'London has been called the city of encounters; it is more than that, it is the city of Resurrections,' when these reflections were suddenly interrupted by a piteous whine at his

---

[21] 'And the devil was incarnate. And was made man'. The second part of this Latin passage is a reiteration of part of the Nicene Creed, a fourth-century CE profession of Christian faith that includes reference to Christ becoming a man in the words 'et homo factus est'.

[22] A college at the University of Oxford.

[23] A major thoroughfare in the West End of London.

elbow, and a deplorable appeal for alms. He looked around in some irritation, and with a sudden shock found himself confronted with the embodied proof of his somewhat stilted fancies. There, close beside him, his face altered and disfigured by poverty and disgrace, his body barely covered by greasy ill-fitting rags, stood his old friend Charles Herbert, who had matriculated on the same day as himself, with whom he had been merry and wise for twelve revolving terms.[24] Different occupations and varying interests had interrupted the friendship, and it was six years since Villiers had seen Herbert; and now he looked upon this wreck of a man with grief and dismay, mingled with a certain inquisitiveness as to what dreary chain of circumstances had dragged him down to such a doleful pass. Villiers felt together with compassion all the relish of the amateur in mysteries, and congratulated himself on his leisurely speculations outside the restaurant.

They walked on in silence for some time, and more than one passer-by stared in astonishment at the unaccustomed spectacle of a well-dressed man with an unmistakable beggar hanging on to his arm, and, observing this, Villiers led the way to an obscure street in Soho.[25] Here he repeated his question.

'How on earth has it happened, Herbert? I always understood you would succeed to an excellent position in Dorsetshire. Did your father disinherit you? Surely not?'

'No, Villiers; I came into all the property at my poor father's death; he died a year after I left Oxford. He was a very good father to me, and I mourned his death sincerely enough. But you know what young men are; a few months later I came up to town and went a good deal into society. Of course I had excellent introductions, and I managed to enjoy myself very much in a harmless sort of way. I played a little, certainly, but never for heavy stakes, and the few bets I made on races brought me in money — only a few pounds, you know, but enough to pay for cigars and such petty pleasures. It was in my second season that the tide turned. Of course you have heard of my marriage?'

'No, I never heard anything about it.'

'Yes, I married, Villiers. I met a girl, a girl of the most wonderful and most strange beauty, at the house of some people whom I knew. I cannot tell you her age; I never knew it, but, so far as I can guess, I should think she must have been about nineteen when I made her acquaintance. My friends had come to know her at Florence; she told them she was an orphan, the child of an English father and an Italian mother, and she charmed them as she charmed me. The first time I saw her was at an evening party; I was standing by the door talking to a friend, when suddenly above the hum and babble of conversation I heard a voice which seemed to thrill to my heart. She was singing an Italian song.

---

[24] To matriculate is to enrol in a college or university.
[25] On Soho, see note 9 of 'The Lost Club'.

I was introduced to her that evening, and in three months I married Helen.
Villiers, that woman, if I can call her woman, corrupted my soul. The night of
the wedding I found myself sitting in her bedroom in the hotel, listening to her
talk. She was sitting up in bed, and I listened to her as she spoke in her beautiful
voice, spoke of things which even now I would not dare whisper in the blackest
night, though I stood in the midst of a wilderness. You, Villiers, you may think
you know life, and London, and what goes on, day and night, in this dreadful
city;[26] for all I can say you may have heard the talk of the vilest, but I tell you
you can have no conception of what I know, no, not in your most fantastic,
hideous dreams can you have imaged forth the faintest shadow of what I have
heard — and seen. Yes, seen; I have seen the incredible, such horrors that even I
myself sometimes stop in the middle of the street, and ask whether it is possible
for a man to behold such things and live. In a year, Villiers, I was a ruined man,
in body and soul, — in body and soul.'

'But your property, Herbert? You had land in Dorset.'

'I sold it all; the fields and woods, the dear old house — everything.'

'And the money?'

'She took it all from me.'

'And then left you?'

'Yes; she disappeared one night. I don't know where she went, but I am sure
if I saw her again it would kill me. The rest of my story is of no interest; sordid
misery, that is all. You may think, Villiers, that I have exaggerated and talked
for effect; but I have not told you half. I could tell you certain things which
would convince you, but you would never know a happy day again. You would
pass the rest of your life, as I pass mine, a haunted man, a man who has seen
hell.'

Villiers took the unfortunate man to his rooms, and gave him a meal.
Herbert could eat little, and scarcely touched the glass of wine set before him.
He sat moody and silent by the fire, and seemed relieved when Villiers sent him
away with a small present of money.

'By the way, Herbert,' said Villiers, as they parted at the door, 'what was your
wife's name? You said Helen, I think? Helen what?'

'The name she passed under when I met her was Helen Vaughan, but what
her real name was I can't say.[27] I don't think she had a name. No, no, not in that
sense. Only human beings have names, Villiers; I can't say anymore. Goodbye;
yes, I will not fail to call if I see any way in which you can help me. Good-night.'

The man went out into the bitter night, and Villiers returned to his fireside.

---

[26] Machen appears to be thinking of James Thomson's (1834–1882) long poem *The City of
Dreadful Night* (1874), a despairing depiction of modern London.

[27] The name suggests Thomas Vaughan, the Welsh alchemist and physician. The surname
also appears in *The Hill of Dreams*, in which there is also reference to a historical Vaughan,
likely Thomas or his brother Henry (1621–1695).

There was something about Herbert which shocked him inexpressibly; not his poor rags or the marks which poverty had set upon his face, but rather an indefinite terror which hung about him like a mist. He had acknowledged that he himself was not devoid of blame; the woman, he had avowed, had corrupted him body and soul, and Villiers felt that this man, once his friend, had been an actor in scenes evil beyond the power of words. His story needed no confirmation; he himself was the embodied proof of it. Villiers mused curiously over the story he had heard, and wondered whether he had heard both the first and the last of it. 'No,' he thought, 'certainly not the last, probably only the beginning. A case like this is like a nest of Chinese boxes; you open one after another and find a quainter workmanship in every box. Most likely poor Herbert is merely one of the outside boxes; there are stranger ones to follow.'

Villiers could not take his mind away from Herbert and his story, which seemed to grow wilder as the night wore on. The fire began to burn low, and the chilly air of the morning crept into the room; Villiers got up with a glance over his shoulder, and, shivering slightly, went to bed.

A few days later he saw at his club a gentleman of his acquaintance, named Austin, who was famous for his intimate knowledge of London life, both in its tenebrous and luminous phases. Villiers, still full of his encounter in Soho and its consequences, thought Austin might possibly be able to shed some light on Herbert's history, and so after some casual talk he suddenly put the question:

'Do you happen to know anything of a man named Herbert — Charles Herbert?'

Austin turned round sharply and stared at Villiers with some astonishment.

'Charles Herbert? Weren't you in town three years ago? No; then you have not heard of the Paul Street case? It caused a good deal of sensation at the time.'

'What was the case?'

'Well, a gentleman, a man of very good position, was found dead, stark dead, in the area of a certain house in Paul Street, off Tottenham Court Road. Of course the police did not make the discovery; if you happen to be sitting up all night and have a light in your window, the constable will ring the bell, but if you happen to be lying dead in somebody's area, you will be left alone.[28] In this instance as in many others the alarm was raised by some kind of vagabond; I don't mean a common tramp, or a public-house loafer, but a gentleman, whose business or pleasure, or both, made him a spectator of the London streets at five o'clock in the morning. This individual was, as he said, "going home," it did not appear whence or whither, and had occasion to pass through Paul Street between four and five A.M. Something or other caught his eye at Number 20; he said, absurdly enough, that the house had the most unpleasant physiognomy he had ever observed, but, at any rate, he glanced down the area, and was a

---

[28] An area is an open, sunken space next to a building.

good deal astonished to see a man lying on the stones, his limbs all huddled together, and his face turned up. Our gentleman thought his face looked peculiarly ghastly, and so set off at a run in search of the nearest policeman. The constable was at first inclined to treat the matter lightly, suspecting a mere drunken freak; however, he came, and after looking at the man's face changed his tone, quickly enough. The early bird, who had picked up this fine worm, was sent off for a doctor, and the policeman rang and knocked at the door till a slatternly servant girl came down looking more than half asleep. The constable pointed out the contents of the area to the maid, who screamed loudly enough to wake up the street, but she knew nothing of the man; had never seen him at the house, and so forth. Meanwhile the original discoverer had come back with a medical man, and the next thing was to get into the area. The gate was open, so the whole quartet stumped down the steps. The doctor hardly needed a moment's examination; he said the poor fellow had been dead for several hours, and he was moved away to the police-station for the time being. It was then the case began to get interesting. The dead man had not been robbed, and in one of his pockets were papers identifying him as — well, as a man of good family and means, a favourite in society, and nobody's enemy, as far as could be known. I don't give his name, Villiers, because it has nothing to do with the story, and because it's no good raking up these affairs about the dead, when there are relations living. The next curious point was that the medical men couldn't agree as to how he met his death. There were some slight bruises on his shoulders, but they were so slight that it looked as if he had been pushed roughly out of the kitchen door, and not thrown over the railings from the street, or even dragged down the steps. But there were positively no other marks of violence about him, certainly none that would account for his death; and when they came to the autopsy there wasn't a trace of poison of any kind. Of course the police wanted to know all about the people at Number 20, and here again, so I have heard from private sources, one or two other very curious points came out. It appears that the occupants of the house were a Mr. and Mrs. Charles Herbert; he was said to be a landed proprietor, though it struck most people that Paul Street was not exactly the place to look for county gentry. As for Mrs. Herbert, nobody seemed to know who or what she was, and, between ourselves, I fancy the divers after her history found themselves in rather strange waters. Of course they both denied knowing anything about the deceased, and in default of any evidence against them they were discharged. But some very odd things came out about them. Though it was between five and six in the morning when the dead man was removed, a large crowd had collected, and several of the neighbours ran to see what was going on. They were pretty free with their comments, by all accounts, and from these it appeared that Number 20 was in very bad odour in Paul Street. The detectives tried to trace down these rumours to some solid foundation of fact, but could not get hold of anything. People shook their heads and raised their eyebrows and thought the Herberts rather "queer," "would rather not be seen going into their house," and so on, but there was nothing tangible. The authorities were morally certain that the man met his death in some way or another in the house and was thrown out by the kitchen door, but they couldn't prove it, and the absence of any indications of violence or poisoning left them helpless. An odd case, wasn't it? But curiously enough, there's something more that I haven't told you. I happened to know one of the doctors who was consulted as to the cause of death, and some time after the inquest I met him, and asked him about it. "Do you really mean to tell me," I said, "that you were baffled by the case, that you actually don't know what the man died of?" "Pardon me," he replied, "I know perfectly well what caused death. Blank died of fright, of sheer, awful terror; I never saw features so hideously contorted in the entire course of my practice, and I have seen the faces of a whole host of dead." The doctor was usually a cool customer enough, and a certain vehemence in his manner struck me, but I couldn't get anything more out of him. I suppose the Treasury didn't see their way to prosecuting the Herberts for frightening a man to death; at any rate, nothing was done, and the case dropped out of men's minds. Do you happen to know anything of Herbert?'

'Well,' replied Villiers, 'he was an old college friend of mine.'

'You don't say so? Have you ever seen his wife?'

'No, I haven't. I have lost sight of Herbert for many years.'

'It's queer, isn't it, parting with a man at the college gate or at Paddington, seeing nothing of him for years, and then finding him pop up his head in such an odd place. But I should like to have seen Mrs. Herbert; people said extraordinary things about her.'

'What sort of things?'

'Well, I hardly know how to tell you. Every one who saw her at the police court said she was at once the most beautiful woman and the most repulsive they had ever set eyes on. I have spoken to a man who saw her, and I assure you he positively shuddered as he tried to describe the woman, but he couldn't tell why. She seems to have been a sort of enigma; and I expect if that one dead man could have told tales, he would have told some uncommonly queer ones. And there you are again in another puzzle; what could a respectable country gentleman like Mr. Blank (we'll call him that if you don't mind) want in such a very queer house as Number 20? It's altogether a very odd case, isn't it?'

'It is indeed, Austin; an extraordinary case. I didn't think, when I asked you about my old friend, I should strike on such strange metal. Well, I must be off; good-day.'

Villiers went away, thinking of his own conceit of the Chinese boxes; here was quaint workmanship indeed.

THE DISCOVERY IN PAUL STREET

A few months after Villiers's meeting with Herbert, Mr. Clarke was sitting, as usual, by his after-dinner hearth, resolutely guarding his fancies from wandering in the direction of the bureau. For more than a week he had succeeded in keeping away from the 'Memoirs,' and he cherished hopes of a complete self-reformation; but, in spite of his endeavours, he could not hush the wonder and the strange curiosity that the last case he had written down had excited within him. He had put the case, or rather the outline of it, conjecturally to a scientific friend, who shook his head, and thought Clarke getting queer, and on this particular evening Clarke was making an effort to rationalise the story, when a sudden knock at his door roused him from his meditations.

'Mr. Villiers to see you sir.'

'Dear me, Villiers, it is very kind of you to look me up; I have not seen you for many months; I should think nearly a year. Come in, come in. And how are you, Villiers? Want any advice about investments?'

'No, thanks, I fancy everything I have in that way is pretty safe. No, Clarke, I have really come to consult you about a rather curious matter that has been brought under my notice of late. I am afraid you will think it all rather absurd when I tell my tale, I sometimes think so myself, and that's just what I made up my mind to come to you, as I know you're a practical man.'

Mr. Villiers was ignorant of the 'Memoirs to prove the Existence of the Devil.'

'Well, Villiers, I shall be happy to give you my advice, to the best of my ability. What is the nature of the case?'

'It's an extraordinary thing altogether. You know my ways; I always keep my eyes open in the streets, and in my time I have chanced upon some queer customers, and queer cases too, but this, I think, beats all. I was coming out of a restaurant one nasty winter night about three months ago; I had had a capital dinner and a good bottle of Chianti, and I stood for a moment on the pavement, thinking what a mystery there is about London streets and the companies that pass along them. A bottle of red wine encourages these fancies, Clarke, and I dare say I should have thought a page of small type, but I was cut short by a beggar who had come behind me, and was making the usual appeals. Of course I looked round, and this beggar turned out to be what was left of an old friend of mine, a man named Herbert. I asked him how he had come to such a wretched pass, and he told me. We walked up and down one of those long dark Soho streets, and there I listened to his story. He said he had married a beautiful girl, some years younger than himself, and, as he put it, she had corrupted him body and soul. He wouldn't go into details; he said he dare not, that what he had seen and heard haunted him by night and day, and when I looked in his face I knew he was speaking the truth. There was something about the man that made me shiver. I don't know why, but it was there. I gave him a little money and sent him away, and I assure you that when he was gone I gasped for breath. His presence seemed to chill one's blood.'

'Isn't all this just a little fanciful, Villiers? I suppose the poor fellow had made an imprudent marriage, and, in plain English, gone to the bad.'

'Well, listen to this.' Villiers told Clarke the story he had heard from Austin.

'You see,' he concluded, 'there can be but little doubt that this Mr. Blank, whoever he was, died of sheer terror; he saw something so awful, so terrible, that it cut short his life. And what he saw, he most certainly saw in that house, which, somehow or other, had got a bad name in the neighbourhood. I had the curiosity to go and look at the place for myself. It's a saddening kind of street; the houses are old enough to be mean and dreary, but not old enough to be quaint. As far as I could see most of them are let in lodgings, furnished and unfurnished, and almost every door has three bells to it. Here and there the ground floors have been made into shops of the commonest kind; it's a dismal street in every way. I found Number 20 was to let, and I went to the agent's and got the key. Of course I should have heard nothing of the Herberts in that quarter, but I asked the man, fair and square, how long they had left the house, and whether there had been other tenants in the meanwhile. He looked at me queerly for a minute, and told me the Herberts had left immediately after the unpleasantness, as he called it, and since then the house had been empty.'

Mr. Villiers paused for a moment.

'I have always been rather fond of going over empty houses; there's a sort of fascination about the desolate empty rooms, with the nails sticking in the walls, and the dust thick upon the window-sills. But I didn't enjoy going over Number 20 Paul Street. I had hardly put my foot inside the passage before I noticed a queer, heavy feeling about the air of the house. Of course all empty houses are stuffy, and so forth, but this was something quite different; I can't describe it to you, but it seemed to stop the breath. I went into the front room and the back room, and the kitchens downstairs; they were all dirty and dusty enough, as you would expect, but there was something strange about them all. I couldn't define it to you, I only know I felt queer. It was one of the rooms on the first floor, though, that was the worst. It was a largish room, and once on a time the paper must have been cheerful enough, but when I saw it, paint, paper, and everything were most doleful. But the room was full of horror; I felt my teeth grinding as I put my hand on the door, and when I went in, I thought I should have fallen fainting to the floor. However I pulled myself together, and stood against the end wall, wondering what on earth there could be about the room to make my limbs tremble, and my heart beat as if I were at the hour of death. In one corner there was a pile of newspapers littered about on the floor and I began looking at them; they were papers of three or four years ago, some of them half torn, and some crumpled as if they had been used for packing. I turned the whole pile over, and amongst them I found a curious drawing; I will show it to you presently. But I couldn't stay in the room; I felt it was overpowering me. I was thankful to come out, safe and sound, into the open air. People stared at me as I walked along the street, and one man said I was drunk. I was staggering about from one side of the pavement to the other, and it was as much as I could do to take the key back to the agent and get home. I was in bed for a week, suffering from what my doctor called nervous shock and exhaustion. One of those days I was reading the evening paper, and happened to notice a paragraph headed: "Starved to Death." It was the usual style of thing; a model lodging-house in Marylebone, a door locked for several days, and a dead man in his chair when they broke in. "The deceased," said the paragraph, "was known as Charles Herbert, and is believed to have been once a prosperous country gentleman. His name was familiar to the public three years ago in connection with the mysterious death in Paul Street, Tottenham Court Road, the deceased being the tenant of the house Number 20, in the area of which a gentleman of good position was found dead under circumstances not devoid of suspicion." A tragic ending, wasn't it? But after all, if what he told me were true, which I am sure it was, the man's life was all a tragedy, and a tragedy of a stranger sort than they put on the boards.'

'And that is the story, is it?' said Clarke musingly.

'Yes, that is the story.'

'Well, really, Villiers, I scarcely know what to say about it. There are no doubt circumstances in the case which seem peculiar, the finding of the dead man in the area of Herbert's house, for instance, and the extraordinary opinion of the physician as to the cause of death, but, after all, it is conceivable that the facts may be explained in a straightforward manner. As to your own sensations, when you went to see the house, I would suggest that they were due to a vivid imagination; you must have been brooding, in a semi-conscious way, over what you had heard. I don't exactly see what more can be said or done in the matter; you evidently think there is a mystery of some kind, but Herbert is dead; where then do you propose to look?'

'I propose to look for the woman; the woman whom he married. *She* is the mystery.'

The two men sat silent by the fireside; Clarke secretly congratulating himself on having successfully kept up the character of advocate of the commonplace, and Villiers wrapt in his gloomy fancies.

'I think I will have a cigarette,' he said at last, and put his hand in his pocket to feel for the cigarette-case.

'Ah!' he said, starting slightly, 'I forgot I had something to show you. You remember my saying that I had found a rather curious sketch amongst the pile of old newspapers at the house in Paul Street? — here it is.'

Villiers drew out a small thin parcel from his pocket. It was covered with brown paper, and secured with string, and the knots were troublesome. In spite of himself Clarke felt inquisitive; he bent forward on his chair as Villiers painfully undid the string, and unfolded the outer covering. Inside was a second wrapping of tissue, and Villiers took it off and handed the small piece of paper to Clarke without a word.

There was dead silence in the room for five minutes or more; the two men sat so still that they could hear the ticking of the tall old-fashioned clock that stood outside in the hall, and in the mind of one of them the slow monotony of sound woke up a far, far memory. He was looking intently at the small pen-and-ink sketch of a woman's head; it had evidently been drawn with great care, and by a true artist, for the woman's soul looked out of the eyes, and the lips were parted with a strange smile. Clarke gazed still at the face; it brought to his memory one summer evening long ago; he saw again the long lovely valley, the river winding between the hills, the meadows and the cornfields, the dull red sun, and the cold white mist rising from the water. He heard a voice speaking to him across the waves of many years, and saying, 'Clarke, Mary will see the God Pan!' and then he was standing in the grim room beside the doctor, listening to the heavy ticking of the clock, waiting and watching, watching the figure lying on the green chair beneath the lamp-light. Mary rose up, and he looked into her eyes, and his heart grew cold within him.

'Who is this woman?' he said at last. His voice was dry and hoarse.

'That is the woman whom Herbert married.'

Clarke looked again at the sketch; it was not Mary after all. There certainly was Mary's face, but there was something else, something he had not seen on Mary's features when the white-clad girl entered the laboratory with the doctor, nor at her terrible awakening, nor when she lay grinning on the bed. Whatever it was, the glance that came from those eyes, the smile on the full lips, or the expression of the whole face, Clarke shuddered before it in his inmost soul, and thought, unconsciously, of Dr. Phillip's words, 'the most vivid presentment of evil I have ever seen.'[29] He turned the paper over mechanically in his hand and glanced at the back.

'Good God! Clarke, what is the matter? You are as white as death.'

Villiers had started wildly from his chair, as Clarke fell back with a groan, and let the paper drop from his hands.

'I don't feel very well, Villiers, I am subject to these attacks. Pour me out a little wine; thanks, that will do. I shall be better in a few minutes.'

---

[29] The visceral impact of Helen's portrait on its viewers echoes the psychological and emotional impact of Dorian's likeness in Wilde's *Picture of Dorian Gray*, which Machen claimed to have read when it was first published in 1890 (Valentine, *Arthur Machen*, p. 29). *The Great God Pan* differs in having the narrative itself address the notion of a portrait as a potent medium of unexplainable psychic force.

Villiers picked up the fallen sketch and turned it over as Clarke had done.

'You saw that?' he said. 'That's how I identified it as being a portrait of Herbert's wife, or I should say his widow. How do you feel now?'

'Better, thanks, it was only a passing faintness. I don't think I quite catch your meaning. What did you say enabled you to identify the picture?'

'This word — Helen — written on the back. Didn't I tell you her name was Helen? Yes; Helen Vaughan.'

Clarke groaned; there could be no shadow of doubt.

'Now, don't you agree with me,' said Villiers, 'that in the story I have told you to-night, and in the part this woman plays in it, there are some very strange points?'

'Yes, Villiers,' Clarke muttered, 'it is a strange story indeed; a strange story indeed. You must give me time to think it over; I may be able to help you or I may not. Must you be going now? Well, good-night, Villiers, good-night. Come and see me in the course of a week.'

THE LETTER OF ADVICE

'Do you know, Austin,' said Villiers, as the two friends were pacing sedately along Piccadilly one pleasant morning in May, 'do you know I am convinced that what you told me about Paul Street and the Herberts is a mere episode in an extraordinary history. I may as well confess to you that when I asked you about Herbert a few months ago I had just seen him.'

'You had seen him? Where?'

'He begged of me in the street one night. He was in the most pitiable plight, but I recognized the man, and I got him to tell me his history, or at least the outline of it. In brief, it amounted to this — he had been ruined by his wife.'

'In what manner?'

'He would not tell me; he would only say that she had destroyed him body and soul. The man is dead now.'

'And what has become of his wife?'

'Ah, that's what I should like to know, and I mean to find her sooner or later. I know a man named Clarke, a dry fellow, in fact a man of business, but shrewd enough. You understand my meaning; not shrewd in the mere business sense of the word, but a man who really knows something about men and life. Well, I laid the case before him, and he was evidently impressed. He said it needed consideration, and asked me to come again in the course of a week. A few days later I received this extraordinary letter.'

Austin took the envelope, drew out the letter, and read it curiously. It ran as follows: —

'MY DEAR VILLIERS, — I have thought over the matter on which you consulted me the other night, and my advice to you is this. Throw the portrait into the fire, blot out the story from your mind. Never give it another thought, Villiers, or you will be sorry. You will think, no doubt, that I am in possession of some secret information, and to a certain extent that is the case. But I only know a little; I am like a traveller who has peered over an abyss, and has drawn back in terror. What I know is strange enough and horrible enough, but beyond my knowledge there are depths and horrors more frightful still, more incredible than any tale told of winter nights about the fire. I have resolved, and nothing shall shake that resolve, to explore no whit further, and if you value your happiness you will make the same determination.

'Come and see me by all means; but we will talk on more cheerful topics than this.'

Austin folded the letter methodically, and returned it to Villiers.

'It is certainly an extraordinary letter,' he said, 'what does he mean by the portrait?'

'Ah! I forgot to tell you I have been to Paul Street and have made a discovery.'

Villiers told his story as he had told it to Clarke, and Austin listened in silence. He seemed puzzled.

'How very curious that you should experience such an unpleasant sensation in that room!' he said at length. 'I hardly gather that it was a mere matter of the imagination; a feeling of repulsion, in short.'

'No, it was more physical than mental. It was as if I were inhaling at every breath some deadly fume, which seemed to penetrate to every nerve and bone and sinew of my body. I felt racked from head to foot, my eyes began to grow dim; it was like the entrance of death.'

'Yes, yes, very strange certainly. You see, your friend confesses that there is some very black story connected with this woman. Did you notice any particular emotion in him when you were telling your tale?'

'Yes, I did. He became very faint, but he assured me that it was a mere passing attack to which he was subject.'

'Did you believe him?'

'I did at the time, but I don't now. He heard what I had to say with a good deal of indifference, till I showed him the portrait. It was then he was seized with the attack of which I spoke. He looked ghastly, I assure you.'

'Then he must have seen the woman before. But there might be another explanation; it might have been the name, and not the face, which was familiar to him. What do you think?'

'I couldn't say. To the best of my belief it was after turning the portrait in his hands that he nearly dropped from his chair. The name, you know, was written on the back.'

'Quite so. After all, it is impossible to come to any resolution in a case like this. I hate melodrama, and nothing strikes me as more commonplace and tedious than the ordinary ghost story of commerce; but really, Villiers, it looks as if there were something very queer at the bottom of all this.'

The two men had, without noticing it, turned up Ashley Street, leading northward from Piccadilly. It was a long street, and rather a gloomy one, but here and there a brighter taste had illuminated the dark houses with flowers, and gay curtains, and a cheerful paint on the doors. Villiers glanced up as Austin stopped speaking, and looked at one of these houses; geraniums, red and white, drooped from every sill, and daffodil-coloured curtains were draped back from each window.

'It looks cheerful, doesn't it?' he said.

'Yes, and the inside is still more cheery. One of the pleasantest houses of the season, so I have heard. I haven't been there myself, but I've met several men who have, and they tell me it's uncommonly jovial.'

'Whose house is it?'

'A Mrs. Beaumont's.'

'And who is she?'

'I couldn't tell you. I have heard she comes from South America, but, after all, who she is is of little consequence. She is a very wealthy woman, there's no doubt of that, and some of the best people have taken her up. I hear she has some wonderful claret, really marvellous wine, which must have cost a fabulous sum. Lord Argentine was telling me about it; he was there last Sunday evening. He assures me he has never tasted such a wine, and Argentine, as you know, is an expert. By the way, that reminds me, she must be an oddish sort of woman, this Mrs. Beaumont. Argentine asked her how old the wine was, and what do you think she said? "About a thousand years, I believe." Lord Argentine thought she was chaffing him, you know, but when he laughed she said she was speaking quite seriously, and offered to show him the jar. Of course, he couldn't say anything more after that; but it seems rather antiquated for a beverage, doesn't it? Why, here we are at my rooms. Come in, won't you?'

'Thanks, I think I will. I haven't seen the curiosity-shop for some time.'

It was a room furnished richly, yet oddly, where every chair and bookcase and table, and every rug and jar and ornament seemed to be a thing apart, preserving each its own individuality.

'Anything fresh lately?' said Villiers after a while.

'No; I think not; you saw those queer jugs, didn't you? I thought so. I don't think I have come across anything for the last few weeks.'

Austin glanced around the room from cupboard to cupboard, from shelf to shelf, in search of some new oddity. His eyes fell at last on an old chest, pleasantly and quaintly carved, which stood in a dark corner of the room.

'Ah,' he said, 'I was forgetting, I have got something to show you.' Austin unlocked the chest, drew out a thick quarto volume, laid it on the table, and resumed the cigar he had put down.[30]

---

[30] A quarto is a medium-sized volume whose pages are made by folding a sheet twice to create four leaves with two pages each.

'Did you know Arthur Meyrick the painter, Villiers?'[31]

'A little; I met him two or three times at the house of a friend of mine. What has become of him? I haven't heard his name mentioned for some time.'

'He's dead.'

'You don't say so! Quite young, wasn't he?'

'Yes; only thirty when he died.'

'What did he die of?'

'I don't know. He was an intimate friend of mine, and a thoroughly good fellow. He used to come here and talk to me for hours, and he was one of the best talkers I have met. He could even talk about painting, and that's more than can be said of most painters. About eighteen months ago he was feeling rather overworked, and partly at my suggestion he went off on a sort of roving expedition, with no very definite end or aim about it. I believe New York was to be his first port, but I never heard from him. Three months ago I got this book, with a very civil letter from an English doctor practising at Buenos Ayres, stating that he had attended the late Mr. Meyrick during his illness, and that the deceased had expressed an earnest wish that the enclosed packet should be sent to me after his death. That was all.'

'And haven't you written for further particulars?'

'I have been thinking of doing so. You would advise me to write to the doctor?'

'Certainly. And what about the book?'

'It was sealed up when I got it. I don't think the doctor had seen it.'

'It is something very rare? Meyrick was a collector, perhaps?'

'No, I think not, hardly a collector. Now, what do you think of those Ainu jugs?'[32]

'They are peculiar, but I like them. But aren't you going to show me poor Meyrick's legacy?'

'Yes, yes, to be sure. The fact is, it's rather a peculiar sort of thing, and I haven't shown it to any one. I wouldn't say anything about it if I were you. There it is.'

Villiers took the book, and opened it at haphazard. 'It isn't a printed volume, then?' he said.

'No. It is a collection of drawings in black and white by my poor friend Meyrick.'

Villiers turned to the first page, it was blank; the second bore a brief inscription, which he read:

---

[31] In Eliot's novel *Daniel Deronda* (1876), the artist Van Meyrick tends to view women through portraiture.

[32] The Ainu are the original indigenous inhabitants of the islands now known as Japan, whose animistic religion was based on the cult of a bear.

Silet per diem universus, nec sine horrore secretus est; lucet nocturnis ignibus, chorus Ægipanum undique personatur: audiuntur et cantus tibiarum, et tinnitus cymbalorum per oram maritimam.[33]

On the third page was a design which made Villiers start and look up at Austin; he was gazing abstractedly out of the window. Villiers turned page after page, absorbed, in spite of himself, in the frightful Walpurgis Night of evil, strange monstrous evil, that the dead artist had set forth in hard black and white.[34] The figures of Fauns and Satyrs and Ægipans danced before his eyes, the darkness of the thicket, the dance on the mountain-top, the scenes by lonely shores, in green vineyards, by rocks and desert places, passed before him: a world before which the human soul seemed to shrink back and shudder. Villiers whirled over the remaining pages; he had seen enough, but the picture on the last leaf caught his eye, as he almost closed the book.

'Austin!'

'Well, what is it?'

'Do you know who that is?'

It was a woman's face, alone on the white page.

'Know who it is? No, of course not.'

'I do.'

'Who is it?'

'It is Mrs. Herbert.'

'Are you sure?'

'I am perfectly sure of it. Poor Meyrick! He is one more chapter in her history.'

'But what do you think of the designs?'

'They are frightful. Lock the book up again, Austin. If I were you I would burn it; it must be a terrible companion, even though it be in a chest.'

'Yes, they are singular drawings. But I wonder what connection there could be between Meyrick and Mrs. Herbert, or what link between her and these designs?'

'Ah, who can say? It is possible that the matter may end here, and we shall never know, but in my own opinion this Helen Vaughan, or Mrs. Herbert, is only the beginning. She will come back to London, Austin; depend on it, she will come back, and we shall hear more about her then. I doubt it will be very pleasant news.'

---

[33] 'The universe is silent all day, but not without secret horrors; by night it glows with fires, and from every direction the chorus of the Aegipans sounds: the blast of pipes and the ringing of cymbals are heard along the ocean shore'. This quotation is from *De Mirabilibus Mundi* (*The Wonders of the World*) by the Roman writer Gaius Julius Solinus (fl. third century CE). Similar to satyrs, Aegipans are goat-legged deities associated with Pan.

[34] Walpurgis Night (in German, Walpurgisnacht) is celebrated on the eve of 30 April — before the feast day of the eighth-century Saint Walpurga, which takes place on 1 May (May Day, one of the main holidays for many in pagan Europe). In parts of Europe, Walpurgis Night is associated with witches and sorcery.

THE SUICIDES

Lord Argentine was a great favourite in London society.[35] At twenty he had been a poor man, decked with the surname of an illustrious family, but forced to earn a livelihood as best he could, and the most speculative of money-lenders would not have entrusted him with fifty pounds on the chance of his ever changing his name for a title, and his poverty for a great fortune. His father had been near enough to the fountain of good things to secure one of the family livings, but the son, even if he had taken orders, would scarcely have obtained so much as this, and moreover felt no vocation for the ecclesiastical estate.[36] Thus he fronted the world with no better armour than the bachelor's gown and the wits of a younger son's grandson, with which equipment he contrived in some way to make a very tolerable fight of it. At twenty-five Mr. Charles Aubernoun saw himself still a man of struggles and of warfare with the world, but out of the seven who stood before him and the high places of his family three only remained. These three, however, were 'good lives,' but yet not proof against the Zulu assegais and typhoid fever, and so one morning Aubernoun woke up and found himself Lord Argentine, a man of thirty who had faced the difficulties of existence, and had conquered.[37] The situation amused him immensely, and he resolved that riches should be as pleasant to him as poverty had always been. Argentine, after some little consideration, came to the conclusion that dining, regarded as a fine art, was perhaps the most amusing pursuit open to fallen humanity, and thus his dinners became famous in London, and an invitation to his table a thing covetously desired. After ten years of lordship and dinners Argentine still declined to be jaded, still persisted in enjoying life, and by a kind of infection had become recognised as the cause of joy in others, in short as the best of company. His sudden and tragical death therefore caused a wide and deep sensation. People could scarce believe it, even though the newspaper was before their eyes, and the cry of 'Mysterious Death of a Nobleman' came ringing up from the street. But there stood the brief paragraph: 'Lord Argentine was found dead this morning by his valet under distressing circumstances. It is stated that there can be no doubt that his lordship committed suicide, though no motive can be assigned for the act. The deceased nobleman was widely known in society, and much liked for his genial manner and sumptuous hospitality. He is succeeded by, etc., etc.'

By slow degrees the details came to light, but the case still remained a

---

[35] 'Society' refers to the unofficial community of wealthy, prominent, and fashionable people.

[36] To take orders is to enter the Christian ministry.

[37] An assegai is a pole weapon (typically a pointed spear or javelin), used across Africa but closely associated with Zulu and Nguni people. This reference suggests that at least one of the three in line ahead of Charles Aubernoun to inherit the family wealth died in the Anglo–Zulu war of 1879.

mystery. The chief witness at the inquest was the dead nobleman's valet, who said that the night before his death Lord Argentine had dined with a lady of good position, whose name was suppressed in the newspaper reports. At about eleven o'clock Lord Argentine had returned, and informed his man that he should not require his services till the next morning. A little later the valet had occasion to cross the hall and was somewhat astonished to see his master quietly letting himself out at the front door. He had taken off his evening clothes, and was dressed in a Norfolk coat and knickerbockers, and wore a low brown hat.[38] The valet had no reason to suppose that Lord Argentine had seen him, and though his master rarely kept late hours, thought little of the occurrence till the next morning, when he knocked at the bedroom door at a quarter to nine as usual. He received no answer, and, after knocking two or three times, entered the room, and saw Lord Argentine's body leaning forward at an angle from the bottom of the bed. He found that his master had tied a cord securely to one of the short bed-posts, and, after making a running noose and slipping it round his neck, the unfortunate man must have resolutely fallen forward, to die by slow strangulation. He was dressed in the light suit in which the valet had seen him go out, and the doctor who was summoned pronounced that life had been extinct for more than four hours. All papers, letters, and so forth seemed in perfect order, and nothing was discovered which pointed in the most remote way to any scandal either great or small. Here the evidence ended; nothing more could be discovered. Several persons had been present at the dinner-party at which Lord Argentine had assisted, and to all these he seemed in his usual genial spirits. The valet, indeed, said he thought his master appeared a little excited when he came home, but he confessed that the alteration in his manner was very slight, hardly noticeable, indeed. It seemed hopeless to seek for any clue, and the suggestion that Lord Argentine had been suddenly attacked by acute suicidal mania was generally accepted.[39]

It was otherwise, however, when within three weeks, three more gentlemen, one of them a nobleman, and the two others men of good position and ample means, perished miserably in almost precisely the same manner. Lord Swanleigh was found one morning in his dressing-room, hanging from a peg affixed to the wall, and Mr. Collier-Stuart and Mr. Herries had chosen to die

---

[38] Common sports attire at the time, a Norfolk coat is a single-breasted jacket with a belt, designed to be loose for sport shooting, and knickerbockers are loose-legged pants usually synching below the knee.

[39] Acute suicidal mania was a recognized diagnosis at this time. In an extensively read 1881 article, William Knighton (dates unknown) observes that suicidal mania is the result of a range of influences but, in the West, is greater among men than women due to men's careers and greater burden of social and financial responsibility. He also proposes that 'the excited forms that religion and "spiritualism" take' have increased suicides in the United States (William Knighton, 'Suicidal Mania', *Contemporary Review*, 39 (1881), pp. 81–90 (p. 89)).

as Lord Argentine. There was no explanation in either case; a few bald facts; a living man in the evening, and a dead body with a black swollen face in the morning. The police had been forced to confess themselves powerless to arrest or to explain the sordid murders of Whitechapel; but before the horrible suicides of Piccadilly and Mayfair they were dumfoundered, for not even the mere ferocity which did duty as an explanation of the crimes of the East End, could be of service in the West.[40] Each of these men who had resolved to die a tortured shameful death was rich, prosperous, and to all appearances in love with the world, and not the acutest research could ferret out any shadow of a lurking motive in either case. There was a horror in the air, and men looked at one another's faces when they met, each wondering whether the other was to be the victim of a fifth nameless tragedy. Journalists sought in vain in their scrap-books for materials whereof to concoct reminiscent articles; and the morning paper was unfolded in many a house with a feeling of awe; no man knew when or where the blow would next light.

A short while after the last of these terrible events, Austin came to see Mr. Villiers. He was curious to know whether Villiers had succeeded in discovering any fresh traces of Mrs. Herbert, either through Clarke or by other sources, and he asked the question soon after he had sat down.

'No,' said Villiers, 'I wrote to Clarke, but he remains obdurate, and I have tried other channels, but without any result. I can't find out what became of Helen Vaughan after she left Paul Street, but I think she must have gone abroad. But to tell the truth, Austin, I haven't paid much attention to the matter for the last few weeks; I knew poor Herries intimately, and his terrible death has been a great shock to me, a great shock.'

'I can well believe it,' answered Austin gravely, 'you know Argentine was a friend of mine. If I remember rightly, we were speaking of him that day you came to my rooms.'

'Yes; it was in connection with that house in Ashley Street, Mrs. Beaumont's house. You said something about Argentine's dining there.'

'Quite so. Of course you know it was there Argentine dined the night before — before his death.'

'No, I haven't heard that.'

'Oh, yes; the name was kept out of the papers to spare Mrs. Beaumont. Argentine was a great favourite of hers, and it is said she was in a terrible state for some time after.'

A curious look came over Villiers' face; he seemed undecided whether to speak or not. Austin began again.

---

[40] In Machen's time, Piccadilly and Mayfair were comfortable neighbourhoods located in West London. Whitechapel, in the city's East End, was crowded, populated by poor immigrant families, and known to be ridden with crime and disease. The Whitechapel murders of 1888 were perpetuated by the notorious serial killer Jack the Ripper, credited with murdering at least five women in the district.

'I never experienced such a feeling of horror as when I read the account of Argentine's death. I didn't understand it at the time, and I don't now. I knew him well, and it completely passes my understanding for what possible cause he — or any of the others for the matter of that — could have resolved in cold blood to die in such an awful manner. You know how men babble away each other's characters in London, you may be sure any buried scandal or hidden skeleton would have been brought to light in such a case as this; but nothing of the sort has taken place. As for the theory of mania, that is very well, of course, for the coroner's jury, but everybody knows that it's all nonsense. Suicidal mania is not smallpox.'

Austin relapsed into gloomy silence. Villiers sat silent also, watching his friend. The expression of indecision still fleeted across his face; he seemed as if weighing his thoughts in the balance, and the considerations he was revolving left him still silent. Austin tried to shake off the remembrance of tragedies as hopeless and perplexed as the labyrinth of Dædalus, and began to talk in an indifferent voice of the more pleasant incidents and adventures of the season.[41]

'That Mrs. Beaumont,' he said, 'of whom we were speaking, is a great success; she has taken London almost by storm. I met her the other night at Fulham's; she is really a remarkable woman.'

'You have met Mrs. Beaumont?'

'Yes; she had quite a court around her. She would be called very handsome, I suppose, and yet there is something about her face which I didn't like. The features are exquisite, but the expression is strange. And all the time I was looking at her, and afterwards, when I was going home, I had a curious feeling that that very expression was in some way or another familiar to me.'

'You must have seen her in the Row.'[42]

'No, I am sure I never set eyes on the woman before; it is that which makes it puzzling. And to the best of my belief I have never seen anybody like her; what I felt was a kind of dim far-off memory, vague but persistent. The only sensation I can compare it to, is that odd feeling one sometimes has in a dream, when fantastic cities and wondrous lands and phantom personages appear familiar and accustomed.'

Villiers nodded and glanced aimlessly round the room, possibly in search of something on which to turn the conversation. His eyes fell on an old chest somewhat like that in which the artist's strange legacy lay hid beneath a Gothic scutcheon.[43]

'Have you written to the doctor about poor Meyrick?' he asked.

---

[41] According to Greek myth, the Athenian architect Daedalus built a labyrinth in Crete to confine the Minotaur (a monster with the body of a man and the head of a bull).

[42] Rotten Row (originally *Route de Roi*), a fashionable thoroughfare in London.

[43] Usually spelt 'escutcheon', a shield on which a coat of arms is painted.

'Yes; I wrote asking for full particulars as to his illness and death. I don't expect to have an answer for another three weeks or a month. I thought I might as well inquire whether Meyrick knew an Englishwoman named Herbert, and if so, whether the doctor could give me any information about her. But it's very possible that Meyrick fell in with her at New York, or Mexico, or San Francisco; I have no idea as to the extent or direction of his travels.'

'Yes, and it's very possible that the woman may have more than one name.'

'Exactly. I wish I had thought of asking you to lend me the portrait of her which you possess. I might have enclosed it in my letter to Dr. Matthews.'

'So you might; that never occurred to me. We might even now do so. Hark! what are those boys calling?'

While the two men had been talking together a confused noise of shouting had been gradually growing louder. The noise rose from the eastward and swelled down Piccadilly, drawing nearer and nearer, a very torrent of sound; surging up streets usually quiet, and making every window a frame for a face, curious or excited. The cries and voices came echoing up the silent street where Villiers lived, growing more distinct as they advanced, and, as Villiers spoke, an answer rang up from the pavement:

'The West End Horrors; Another Awful Suicide; Full Details!'

Austin rushed down the stairs and bought a paper and read out the paragraph to Villiers as the uproar in the street rose and fell. The window was open and the air seemed full of noise and terror.

'Another gentleman has fallen a victim to the terrible epidemic of suicide which for the last month has prevailed in the West End. Mr. Sidney Crashaw of Stoke House, Fulham, and King's Pomeroy, Devon, was found, after a prolonged search, hanging dead from the branch of a tree in his garden at one o'clock to-day. The deceased gentleman dined last night at the Carlton Club and seemed in his usual health and spirits. He left the Club at about ten o'clock, and was seen walking leisurely up St. James's Street a little later.[44] Subsequent to this his movements cannot be traced. On the discovery of the body medical aid was at once summoned, but life had evidently been long extinct. So far as is known Mr. Crashaw had no trouble or anxiety of any kind. This painful suicide, it will be remembered, is the fifth of the kind in the last month. The authorities at Scotland Yard are unable to suggest any explanation of these terrible occurrences.'

Austin put down the paper in mute horror.

'I shall leave London to-morrow,' he said, 'it is a city of nightmares. How awful this is, Villiers!'

Mr. Villiers was sitting by the window quietly looking out into the street. He

---

[44] The Carlton Club is a Conservative gentleman's club in the West End of London, established in 1832.

had listened to the newspaper report attentively, and the hint of indecision was no longer on his face.

'Wait a moment, Austin,' he replied, 'I have made up my mind to mention a little matter that occurred last night. It is stated, I think, that Crashaw was last seen alive in St. James's Street shortly after ten?'

'Yes, I think so. I will look again. Yes, you are quite right.'

'Quite so. Well, I am in a position to contradict that statement at all events. Crashaw was seen after that; considerably later indeed.'

'How do you know?'

'Because I happened to see Crashaw myself at about two o'clock this morning.'

'You saw Crashaw? You, Villiers?'

'Yes, I saw him quite distinctly; indeed, there were but a few feet between us.'

'Where, in heaven's name, did you see him?'

'Not far from here. I saw him in Ashley Street. He was just leaving a house.'

'Did you notice what house it was?'

'Yes. It was Mrs. Beaumont's.'

'Villiers! Think what you are saying; there must be some mistake. How could Crashaw be in Mrs. Beaumont's house at two o'clock in the morning? Surely, surely, you must have been dreaming, Villiers; you were always rather fanciful.'

'No; I was wide awake enough. Even if I had been dreaming as you say, what I saw would have roused me effectually.'

'What you saw? What did you see? Was there anything strange about Crashaw? But I can't believe it; it is impossible.'

'Well, if you like I will tell you what I saw, or if you please, what I think I saw, and you can judge for yourself.'

'Very good, Villiers.'

The noise and clamour of the street had died away, though now and then the sound of shouting still came from the distance, and the dull, leaden silence seemed like the quiet after an earthquake or a storm. Villiers turned from the window and began speaking.

'I was at a house near Regent's Park last night, and when I came away the fancy took me to walk home instead of taking a hansom. It was a clear pleasant night enough, and after a few minutes I had the streets pretty much to myself. It's a curious thing, Austin, to be alone in London at night, the gas-lamps stretching away in perspective, and the dead silence, and then perhaps the rush and clatter of a hansom on the stones, and the fire starting up under the horse's hoofs. I walked along pretty briskly, for I was feeling a little tired of being out in the night, and as the clocks were striking two I turned down Ashley Street, which, you know, is on my way. It was quieter than ever there, and the lamps were fewer; altogether, it looked as dark and gloomy as a forest in winter. I had done about half the length of the street when I heard a door closed very softly, and naturally I looked up to see who was abroad like myself at such an hour. As it happens, there is a street lamp close to the house in question, and I saw a man standing on the step. He had just shut the door and his face was towards me, and I recognized Crashaw directly. I never knew him to speak to, but I had often seen him, and I am positive that I was not mistaken in my man. I looked into his face for a moment, and then — I will confess the truth — I set off at a good run, and kept it up till I was within my own door.'

'Why?'

'Why? Because it made my blood run cold to see that man's face. I could never have supposed that such an infernal medley of passions could have glared out of any human eyes; I almost fainted as I looked. I knew I had looked into the eyes of a lost soul, Austin, the man's outward form remained, but all hell was within it. Furious lust, and hate that was like fire, and the loss of all hope and horror that seemed to shriek aloud to the night, though his teeth were shut; and the utter blackness of despair. I am sure that he did not see me; he saw nothing that you or I can see, but he saw what I hope we never shall. I do not know when he died; I suppose in an hour, or perhaps two, but when I passed down Ashley Street and heard the closing door, that man no longer belonged to this world; it was a devil's face I looked upon.'

There was an interval of silence in the room when Villiers ceased speaking. The light was failing, and all the tumult of an hour ago was quite hushed. Austin had bent his head at the close of the story, and his hand covered his eyes.

'What can it mean?' he said at length.

'Who knows, Austin, who knows? It's a black business, but I think we had better keep it to ourselves, for the present at any rate. I will see if I cannot learn anything about that house through private channels of information, and if I do light upon anything I will let you know.'

THE ENCOUNTER IN SOHO

Three weeks later Austin received a note from Villiers, asking him to call either that afternoon or the next. He chose the nearer date and found Villiers sitting as usual by the window, apparently lost in meditation on the drowsy traffic of the street. There was a bamboo table by his side, a fantastic thing, enriched with gilding and queer painted scenes, and on it lay a little pile of papers arranged and docketed as neatly as anything in Mr. Clarke's office.

'Well, Villiers, have you made any discoveries in the last three weeks?'

'I think so; I have here one or two memoranda which struck me as singular, and there is a statement to which I shall call your attention.'

'And these documents relate to Mrs. Beaumont? It was really Crashaw whom you saw that night standing on the doorstep of the house in Ashley Street?'

'As to that matter my belief remains unchanged, but neither my inquiries nor their results have any special relation to Crashaw. But my investigations have had a strange issue; I have found out who Mrs. Beaumont is!'

'Who is she? In what way do you mean?'

'I mean that you and I know her better under another name.'

'What name is that?'

'Herbert.'

'Herbert!' Austin repeated the word, dazed with astonishment.

'Yes, Mrs. Herbert of Paul Street, Helen Vaughan of earlier adventures unknown to me. You had reason to recognise the expression of her face; when you go home look at the face in Meyrick's book of horrors, and you will know the sources of your recollection.'

'And you have proof of this?'

'Yes, the best of proof; I have seen Mrs. Beaumont, or shall we say Mrs. Herbert?'

'Where did you see her?'

'Hardly in a place where you would expect to see a lady who lives in Ashley Street, Piccadilly. I saw her entering a house in one of the meanest and most disreputable streets in Soho. In fact, I had made an appointment, though not with her, and she was precise both to time and place.'

'All this seems very wonderful, but I cannot call it incredible. You must remember, Villiers, that I have seen this woman, in the ordinary adventure of London society, talking and laughing, and sipping her chocolate in a commonplace drawing-room with commonplace people. But you know what you are saying.'

'I do; I have not allowed myself to be led by surmises or fancies. It was with no thought of finding Helen Vaughan that I searched for Mrs. Beaumont in the dark waters of the life of London, but such has been the issue.'

'You must have been in strange places, Villiers.'

'Yes, I have been in very strange places. It would have been useless, you know, to go to Ashley Street, and ask Mrs. Beaumont to give me a short sketch of her previous history. No; assuming, as I had to assume, that her record was not of the cleanest, it would be pretty certain that at some previous time she must have moved in circles not quite so refined as her present ones. If you see mud on the top of a stream, you may be sure that it was once at the bottom. I went to the bottom. I have always been fond of diving into Queer Street for my amusement,[45] and I found my knowledge of that locality and its inhabitants

---

[45] To be on Queer Street is to be in financial difficulties, with the phrase often being associated with an area of London that had a number of bankruptcy courts. The phrase is used in this way in Dickens's *Our Mutual Friend* (1864) and Stevenson's *Strange Case of Dr Jekyll and Mr Hyde* (1886), texts with which Machen was familiar when writing *The Great God Pan*. In this work, Machen more frequently uses the word 'queer' and variants to refer to feeling strange, uncomfortable, or anxious.

very useful. It is, perhaps, needless to say that my friends had never heard the name of Beaumont, and as I had never seen the lady, and was quite unable to describe her, I had to set to work in an indirect way. The people there know me; I have been able to do some of them a service now and again, so they made no difficulty about giving their information; they were aware I had no communication direct or indirect with Scotland Yard. I had to cast out a good many lines though, before I got what I wanted, and when I landed the fish I did not for a moment suppose it was my fish. But I listened to what I was told out of a constitutional liking for useless information, and I found myself in possession of a very curious story, though, as I imagined, not the story I was looking for. It was to this effect. Some five or six years ago a woman named Raymond suddenly made her appearance in the neighbourhood to which I am referring. She was described to me as being quite young, probably not more than seventeen or eighteen, very handsome, and looking as if she came from the country. I should be wrong in saying that she found her level in going to this particular quarter, or associating with these people, for from what I was told, I should think the worst den in London far too good for her. The person from whom I got my information, as you may suppose, no great Puritan, shuddered and grew sick in telling me of the nameless infamies which were laid to her charge. After living there for a year, or perhaps a little more, she disappeared as suddenly as she came, and they saw nothing of her till about the time of the Paul Street case. At first she came to her old haunts only occasionally, then more frequently, and finally took up her abode there as before, and remained for six or eight months. It's of no use my going into details as to the life that woman led; if you want particulars you can look at Meyrick's legacy. Those designs were not drawn from his imagination. She again disappeared, and the people of the place saw nothing of her till a few months ago. My informant told me that she had taken some rooms in a house which he pointed out, and these rooms she was in the habit of visiting two or three times a week and always at ten in the morning. I was led to expect that one of these visits would be paid on a certain day about a week ago, and I accordingly managed to be on the look-out in company with my cicerone at a quarter to ten, and the hour and the lady came with equal punctuality.[46] My friend and I were standing under an archway, a little way back from the street, but she saw us, and gave me a glance that I shall be long in forgetting. That look was quite enough for me; I knew Miss Raymond to be Mrs. Herbert; as for Mrs. Beaumont she had quite gone out of my head. She went into the house, and I watched it till four o'clock, when she came out, and then I followed her. It was a long chase, and I had to be very careful to keep a long way in the background, and yet not lose sight of the woman. She

---

[46] A cicerone is a guide, typically at museums, archaeological sites, and other historic places.

took me down to the Strand, and then to Westminster, and then up St. James's Street, and along Piccadilly. I felt queerish when I saw her turn up Ashley Street; the thought that Mrs. Herbert was Mrs. Beaumont came into my mind, but it seemed too impossible to be true. I waited at the corner, keeping my eye on her all the time, and I took particular care to note the house at which she stopped. It was the house with the gay curtains, the home of flowers, the house out of which Crashaw came the night he hanged himself in his garden. I was just going away with my discovery, when I saw an empty carriage come round and draw up in front of the house, and I came to the conclusion that Mrs. Herbert was going out for a drive, and I was right. There, as it happened, I met a man I know, and we stood talking together a little distance from the carriage-way, to which I had my back. We had not been there for ten minutes when my friend took off his hat, and I glanced round and saw the lady I had been following all day. "Who is that?" I said, and his answer was, "Mrs. Beaumont; lives in Ashley Street." Of course there could be no doubt after that. I don't know whether she saw me, but I don't think she did. I went home at once, and, on consideration, I thought that I had a sufficiently good case with which to go to Clarke.'

'Why to Clarke?'

'Because I am sure that Clarke is in possession of facts about this woman, facts of which I know nothing.'

'Well, what then?'

Mr. Villiers leaned back in his chair and looked reflectively at Austin for a moment before he answered:

'My idea was that Clarke and I should call on Mrs. Beaumont.'

'You would never go into such a house as that? No, no, Villiers, you cannot do it. Besides, consider; what result...'

'I will tell you soon. But I was going to say that my information does not end here; it has been completed in an extraordinary manner.

'Look at this neat little packet of manuscript; it is paginated, you see, and I have indulged in the civil coquetry of a ribbon of red tape. It has almost a legal air, hasn't it? Run your eye over it, Austin. It is an account of the entertainment Mrs. Beaumont provided for her choicer guests. The man who wrote this escaped with his life, but I do not think he will live many years. The doctors tell him he must have sustained some severe shock to the nerves.'

Austin took the manuscript, but never read it. Opening the neat pages at haphazard his eye was caught by a word and a phrase that followed it; and, sick at heart, with white lips and a cold sweat pouring like water from his temples, he flung the paper down.

'Take it away, Villiers, never speak of this again. Are you made of stone, man? Why, the dread and horror of death itself, the thoughts of the man who stands in the keen morning air on the black platform, bound, the bell tolling in his ears, and waits for the harsh rattle of the bolt, are as nothing compared to this. I will not read it; I should never sleep again.'

'Very good. I can fancy what you saw. Yes; it is horrible enough; but after all, it is an old story, an old mystery played in our day, and in dim London streets instead of amidst the vineyards and the olive gardens. We know what happened to those who chanced to meet the Great God Pan, and those who are wise know that all symbols are symbols of something, not of nothing. It was, indeed, an exquisite symbol beneath which men long ago veiled their knowledge of the most awful, most secret forces which lie at the heart of all things; forces before which the souls of men must wither and die and blacken, as their bodies blacken under the electric current. Such forces cannot be named, cannot be spoken, cannot be imagined except under a veil and a symbol, a symbol to the most of us appearing a quaint, poetic fancy, to some a foolish tale. But you and I, at all events, have known something of the terror that may dwell in the secret place of life, manifested under human flesh; that which is without form taking to itself a form.[47] Oh, Austin, how can it be? How is it that the very sunlight does not turn to blackness before this thing, the hard earth melt and boil beneath such a burden?'

Villiers was pacing up and down the room, and the beads of sweat stood out on his forehead. Austin sat silent for a while, but Villiers saw him make a sign upon his breast.

'I say again, Villiers, you will surely never enter such a house as that? You would never pass out alive.'

'Yes, Austin, I shall go out alive — I, and Clarke with me.'

'What do you mean? You cannot, you would not dare...'

'Wait a moment. The air was very pleasant and fresh this morning; there was a breeze blowing, even through this dull street, and I thought I would take a walk. Piccadilly stretched before me a clear, bright vista, and the sun flashed on the carriages and on the quivering leaves in the park. It was a joyous morning, and men and women looked at the sky and smiled as they went about their work or their pleasure, and the wind blew as blithely as upon the meadows and the scented gorse. But somehow or other I got out of the bustle and the gaiety, and found myself walking slowly along a quiet, dull street, where there seemed to be no sunshine and no air, and where the few foot-passengers loitered as they walked, and hung indecisively about corners and archways. I walked along,

---

[47] Machen here suggests a correlation between Symbolist poetry and systems of otherworldly communication. The dangerous potency of such communicative practices demands that training in its use remain occult. In his highly influential Symbolist manifesto published in *Figaro* in 1886, the poet Jean Moréas (1856–1910) — Greek, but writing primarily in French — argues that Symbolist works of literature and art offer not representations of the otherworldly but, through symbols, allusions to and linkages with a primordial realm of being. Machen likewise avoids any explicit rendering of the source of horror.

hardly knowing where I was going or what I did there, but feeling impelled, as one sometimes is, to explore still further, with a vague idea of reaching some unknown goal. Thus I forged up the street, noting the small traffic of the milk-shop, and wondering at the incongruous medley of penny pipes, black tobacco, sweets, newspapers, and comic songs which here and there jostled one another in the short compass of a single window. I think it was a cold shudder that suddenly passed through me that first told me I had found what I wanted. I looked up from the pavement and stopped before a dusty shop, above which the lettering had faded, where the red bricks of two hundred years ago had grimed to black; where the windows had gathered to themselves the fog and the dirt of winters innumerable. I saw what I required; but I think it was five minutes before I had steadied myself and could walk in and ask for it in a cool voice and with a calm face. I think there must even then have been a tremor in my words, for the old man who came out from his back parlour, and fumbled slowly amongst his goods, looked oddly at me as he tied the parcel. I paid what he asked, and stood leaning by the counter, with a strange reluctance to take up my goods and go. I asked about the business, and learnt that trade was bad and the profits cut down sadly; but then the street was not what it was before traffic had been diverted, but that was done forty years ago, "just before my father died," he said. I got away at last, and walked along sharply; it was a dismal street indeed, and I was glad to return to the bustle and the noise. Would you like to see my purchase?'

Austin said nothing, but nodded his head slightly; he still looked white and sick. Villiers pulled out a drawer in the bamboo table, and showed Austin a long coil of cord, hard and new; and at one end was a running noose.

'It is the best hempen cord,' said Villiers, 'just as it used to be made for the old trade, the man told me. Not an inch of jute from end to end.'

Austin set his teeth hard, and stared at Villiers, growing whiter as he looked.

'You would not do it,' he murmured at last. 'You would not have blood on your hands. My God!' he exclaimed, with sudden vehemence, 'you cannot mean this, Villiers, that you will make yourself a hangman?'

'No. I shall offer a choice, and leave the thing alone with this cord in a locked room for fifteen minutes. If when we go in it is not done, I shall call the nearest policeman. That is all.'

'I must go now. I cannot stay here any longer; I cannot bear this. Good-night.'

'Good-night, Austin.'

The door shut, but in a moment it was open again, and Austin stood, white and ghastly, in the entrance.

'I was forgetting,' he said, 'that I too have something to tell. I have received a letter from Dr. Harding of Buenos Ayres. He says that he attended Meyrick for three weeks before his death.'

'And does he say what carried him off in the prime of life? It was not fever?'

'No, it was not fever. According to the doctor, it was an utter collapse of the whole system, probably caused by some severe shock. But he states that the patient would tell him nothing, and that he was consequently at some disadvantage in treating the case.'

'Is there anything more?'

'Yes. Dr. Harding ends his letter by saying: "I think this is all the information I can give you about your poor friend. He had not been long in Buenos Ayres, and knew scarcely any one, with the exception of a person who did not bear the best of characters, and has since left — a Mrs. Vaughan."'

THE FRAGMENTS

[Amongst the papers of the well-known physician, Dr. Robert Matheson, of Ashley Street, Piccadilly, who died suddenly, of apoplectic seizure, at the beginning of 1892, a leaf of manuscript paper was found, covered with pencil jottings. These notes were in Latin, much abbreviated, and had evidently been made in great haste. The MS. was only deciphered with great difficulty, and some words have up to the present time evaded all the efforts of the expert employed. The date, 'xxv Jul. 1888,' is written on the right-hand corner of the MS. The following is a translation of Dr. Matheson's manuscript.]

'Whether science would benefit by these brief notes if they could be published, I do not know, but rather doubt. But certainly I shall never take the responsibility of publishing or divulging one word of what is here written, not only on account of my oath freely given to those two persons who were present, but also because the details are too abominable. It is probably that, upon mature consideration, and after weighting the good and evil, I shall one day destroy this paper, or at least leave it under seal to my friend D., trusting in his discretion, to use it or to burn it, as he may think fit.

'As was befitting, I did all that my knowledge suggested to make sure that I was suffering under no delusion. At first astounded, I could hardly think, but in a minute's time I was sure that my pulse was steady and regular, and that I was in my real and true senses. I ran over the anatomy of the foot and arm and repeated the formulæ of some of the carbon compounds, and then fixed my eyes quietly on what was before me.

'Though horror and revolting nausea rose up within me, and an odour of corruption choked my breath, I remained firm. I was then privileged or accursed, I dare not say which, to see that which was on the bed, lying there black like ink, transformed before my eyes. The skin, and the flesh, and the muscles, and the bones, and the firm structure of the human body that I had thought to be unchangeable, and permanent as adamant, began to melt and dissolve.

'I knew that the body may be separated into its elements by external agencies, but I should have refused to believe what I saw. For here there was some internal force, of which I knew nothing, that caused dissolution and change.

'Here too was all the work by which man had been made repeated before my eyes. I saw the form waver from sex to sex, dividing itself from itself, and then again reunited. Then I saw the body descend to the beasts whence it ascended, and that which was on the heights go down to the depths, even to the abyss of all being. The principle of life, which makes organism, always remained, while the outward form changed.

'The light within the room had turned to blackness, not the darkness of night, in which objects are seen dimly, for I could see clearly and without difficulty. But it was the negation of light; objects were presented to my eyes, if I may say so, without any medium, in such a manner that if there had been a prism in the room I should have seen no colours represented in it.

'I watched, and at last I saw nothing but a substance as jelly. Then the ladder was ascended again ... [*Here the MS. is illegible*] ... for one instance I saw a Form, shaped in dimness before me, which I will not further describe. But the symbol of this form may be seen in ancient sculptures, and in paintings which survived beneath the lava, too foul to be spoken of ... as a horrible and unspeakable shape, neither man nor beast, was changed into human form, there came finally death.

'I who saw all this, not without great horror and loathing of soul, here write my name, declaring all that I have set on this paper to be true.

'ROBERT MATHESON, Med. Dr.'

*   *   *   *   *

... Such, Raymond, is the story of what I know, and what I have seen. The burden of it was too heavy for me to bear alone, and yet I could tell it to none but you. Villiers, who was with me at the last, knows nothing of that awful secret of the wood, of how what we both saw die, lay upon the smooth sweet turf amidst the summer flowers, half in sun and half in shadow, and holding the girl Rachel's hand, called and summoned those companions, and shaped in solid form, upon the earth we tread on, the horror which we can but hint at, which we can only name under a figure. I would not tell Villiers of this, nor of that resemblance, which struck me as with a blow upon my heart, when I saw the portrait, which filled the cup of terror at the end. What this can mean I dare not guess. I know that what I saw perish was not Mary, and yet in the last agony Mary's eyes looked into mine. Whether there can be any one who can show the last link in this chain of awful mystery, I do not know, but if there be any one who can do this, you, Raymond, are the man. And if you know the secret, it rests with you to tell it or not, as you please.

I am writing this letter to you immediately on my getting back to town. I have been in the country for the last few days; perhaps you may be able to guess in what part. While the horror and wonder of London was at its height, — for 'Mrs. Beaumont,' as I have told you, was well known in society, — I wrote to my friend Dr. Phillips, giving some brief outline, or rather hint, of what had happened, and asking him to tell me the name of the village where the events he had related to me occurred. He gave me the name, as he said with the less hesitation, because Rachel's father and mother were dead, and the rest of the family had gone to a relative in the State of Washington six months before. The parents, he said, had undoubtedly died of grief and horror caused by the terrible death of their daughter, and by what had gone before that death. On the evening of the day which I received Phillips's letter I was at Caermaen,[48] and standing beneath the mouldering Roman walls, white with the winters of seventeen hundred years, I looked over the meadow where once had stood the older temple of the 'God of the Deeps,' and saw a house gleaming in the sunlight. It was the house where Helen had lived. I stayed at Caermaen for several days. The people of the place, I found, knew little and had guessed less. Those whom I spoke to on the matter seemed surprised that an antiquarian (as I professed myself to be) should trouble about a village tragedy, of which they gave a very commonplace version, and, as you may imagine, I told nothing of what I knew. Most of my time was spent in the great wood that rises just above the village and climbs the hillside, and goes down to the river in the valley; such another long lovely valley, Raymond, as that on which we looked one summer night, walking to and fro before your house. For many an hour I strayed through the maze of the forest, turning now to right and now to left, pacing slowly down long alleys of undergrowth, shadowy and chill, even under the midday sun, and halting beneath great oaks; lying on the short turf of a clearing where the faint sweet scent of wild roses came to me on the wind and mixed with the heavy perfume of the elder whose mingled odour is like the odour of the room of the dead, a vapour of incense and corruption.[49] I stood by rough banks at the edges of the wood, gazing at all the pomp and procession of the foxgloves towering amidst the bracken and shining red in the broad sunshine, and beyond them into deep thickets of close undergrowth where springs boil up from the rock and nourish the water-weeds, dank and evil.[50] But in all my wanderings I avoided one part of

---

[48] Caermaen is a fictitious place in Wales based on Machen's childhood village of Caerleon and used as a main setting in his *The Hill of Dreams*.

[49] In Celtic myth, the elder is a symbol of both death and regeneration, and is believed to ward off evil.

[50] Poisonous plants, foxgloves have been associated with fairies.

the wood; it was not till yesterday that I climbed to the summit of the hill, and stood upon the ancient Roman road that threads the highest ridge of the wood. Here they had walked, Helen and Rachel, along this quiet causeway, upon the pavement of green turf, shut in on either side by high banks of red earth, and tall hedges of shining beech, and here I followed in their steps, looking out, now and again, through partings in the boughs, and seeing on one side the sweep of the wood stretching far to right and left, and sinking into the broad level, and beyond, the yellow sea, and the land over the sea. On the other side was the valley and the river, and hill following hill as wave on wave, and wood and meadow, and cornfield, and white houses gleaming, and a great wall of mountain, and far blue peaks in the north. And so at least, I came to the place. The track went up a gentle slope, and widened out into an open space with a wall of thick undergrowth around it, and then, narrowing again, passed on into the distance and the faint blue mist of summer heat. And into this pleasant summer glade Rachel passed a girl, and left it, who shall say what? I did not stay long there.

*   *   *   *   *

In a small town near Caermaen there is a museum, containing for the most part Roman remains which have been found in the neighbourhood at various times. On the day after my arrival at Caermaen I walked over to the town in question, and took the opportunity of inspecting this museum. After I had seen most of the sculptured stones, the coffins, rings, coins, and fragments of tessellated pavement which the place contains, I was shown a small square pillar of white stone, which had been recently discovered in the wood of which I have been speaking, and, as I found on inquiry, in that open space where the Roman road broadens out. On one side of the pillar was an inscription, of which I took a note. Some of the letters have been defaced, but I do not think there can be any doubt as to those which I supply. The inscription is as follows:

> DEVOMNODENT*i*
> FLA*v*IVSSENILISPOSSV*it*
> PROPTERNVP*tias*
> *qua*SVIDITSVBVMB*ra*

'To the great god Nodens (the god of the Great Deep or Abyss), Flavius Senilis has erected this pillar on account of the marriage which he saw beneath the shade.'[51]

---

[51] Nodens is a Celtic deity who, in ancient Britain, was associated with the sea, rivers, hunting, and dogs. In 1805, a Roman temple complex devoted to him was excavated in Lydney Park, Gloucestershire; there is record of the complex being in communication with a Roman camp in Machen's hometown of Caerleon (Harry Mengden Scarth, 'Roman Remains in Lydney Park, Gloucestershire', *Transactions of the Bristol and Gloucestershire*

The custodian of the museum informed me that local antiquaries were much puzzled, not by the inscription, or by any difficulty in translating it, but as to the circumstance or rite to which allusion is made.

$*$ $*$ $*$ $*$ $*$

... And now, my dear Clarke, as to what you tell me about Helen Vaughan, whom you say you saw die under circumstances of the utmost and almost incredible horror. I was interested in your account, but a good deal, nay, all of what you told me, I knew already. I can understand the strange likeness you remarked both in the portrait and in the actual face; you have seen Helen's mother. You remember that still summer night so many years ago, when I talked to you of the world beyond the shadows, and of the god Pan. You remember Mary. She was the mother of Helen Vaughan, who was born nine months after that night.

Mary never recovered her reason. She lay, as you saw her, all the while upon her bed, and a few days after the child was born, she died. I fancy that just at the last she knew me; I was standing by the bed, and the old look came into her eyes for a second, and then she shuddered and groaned and died. It was an ill work I did that night, when you were present; I broke open the door of the house of life, without knowing or caring what might pass forth or enter in. I recollect your telling me at the time, sharply enough, and rightly enough too, in one sense, that I had ruined the reason of a human being by a foolish experiment, based on an absurd theory. You did well to blame me, but my theory was not all absurdity. What I said Mary would see, she saw, but I forgot that no human eyes could look on such a vision with impunity. And I forgot, as I have just said, that when the house of life is thus thrown open, there may enter in that for which we have no name, and human flesh may become the veil of a horror one dare not express. I played with energies which I did not understand and you have seen the ending of it. Helen Vaughan did well to bind the cord about her neck and die, though the death was horrible. The blackened face, the hideous form upon the bed, changing and melting before your eyes from woman to man, from man to beast, and from beast to worse than beast, all the strange horror that you witnessed, surprises me but little. What you say the doctor whom you sent for saw and shuddered at I noticed long ago; I knew what I had done the moment the child was born, and when it was scarcely five years old I surprised it, not once or twice but several times with a playmate, you may guess of what

Archaeological Society (London: Longmans, Green and Co, 1879), pp. 210–21 (p. 215)). Machen's Latin inscription closely echoes those on an existing marker at Lydney Park. The latter has missing characters, so translations vary, but Harry Mengden Scarth (1814–1890) translates it as follows: 'To the greatest God | for the second time | Flavius Senilis, | Head of the Religion, | has erected this | from voluntary contributions' (p. 215).

kind. It was for me a constant, an incarnate horror, and after a few years I felt I could bear it no longer, and I sent Helen Vaughan away. You know now what frightened the boy in the wood. The rest of the strange story, and all else that you tell me, as discovered by your friend, I have contrived to learn from time to time, almost to the last chapter. And now Helen is with her companions. ...

THE END

NOTE. — *Helen Vaughan was born on August 5th, 1865, at the Red House, Breconshire, and died on July 25th, 1888, in her house in a street off Piccadilly, called Ashley Street in the story.*[52]

from *The Great God Pan and The Inmost Light*
(London: John Lane, 1894), pp. 1–109

---

[52] Breconshire, now part of Powys, was a county in Wales located just north of Caerleon, where Machen grew up as a boy.

3

The Recluse of Bayswater (1895)[1]

Amongst the many friends who were favoured with the occasional pleasure of Mr. Dyson's society was Mr. Edgar Russell, realist and obscure struggler, who occupied a small back room on the second floor of a house in Abingdon Grove, Notting Hill.[2] Turning off from the main street, and walking a few paces onward, one was conscious of a certain calm, a drowsy peace, which made the feet inclined to loiter, and this was ever the atmosphere of Abingdon Grove. The houses stood a little back, with gardens where the lilac, and laburnum, and blood-red may blossomed gaily in their seasons,[3] and there was a corner where an older house in another street had managed to keep a back garden of real extent, a walled-in garden, whence there came a pleasant scent of greenness after the rains of early summer, where old elms held memories of the open fields, where there was yet sweet grass to walk on.[4] The houses in Abingdon Grove belonged chiefly to the nondescript stucco period of thirty-five years ago, tolerably built, with passable accommodation for moderate incomes; they had largely passed into the state of lodgings, and cards bearing the inscription

---

[1] *The Three Impostors* is an episodic novel made up of shorter pieces, including 'The Recluse of Bayswater'. An episodic novel consists of generally self-contained stories joined together by an often thin, overarching narrative, a recurring character or characters, and/ or a repeated motif or theme. Machen's well-known story 'The Novel of the White Powder' is embedded within 'The Recluse of Bayswater', with this larger frame allowing Machen to maintain the narrative flow of the book's main character, Dyson. The frame of this episode also offers a counter-reading of 'White Powder' by giving additional information on the narrator of that story. H. P. Lovecraft comments that 'White Powder' and 'The Novel of the Black Seal' (also from *The Three Impostors*) 'perhaps represent the highwater mark of Machen's skill as a terror-weaver' (H. P. Lovecraft, 'Supernatural Horror in Literature', Project Gutenberg Australia, <http://gutenberg.net.au/ebooks06/0601181h.html> [accessed 3 March 2016]).
[2] Machen himself rented a flat in Notting Hill when he first moved to London.
[3] 'Blood-red may' is a traditional name for the hawthorn, the berries of which are bright red. In pre-Christian Britain and Ireland, the hawthorn carried spiritual and mystical significance, associated, for example, with the festival of Beltane (also known as May Day).
[4] An area of London, Bayswater is north of Kensington Gardens and west of Paddington. By Machen's time, it was well established and populated by wealthy people who owned grand homes, as well as others somewhat further down the socio-economic scale, who lived in flats that had been carved out of older houses.

'Furnished apartments' were not infrequent over the doors. Here, then, in a house of sufficiently good appearance, Mr. Russell had established himself; for he looked upon the traditional dirt and squalor of Grub Street as a false and obsolete convention, and preferred, as he said, to live within sight of green leaves.[5] Indeed, from his room one had a magnificent view of a long line of gardens, and a screen of poplars shut out the melancholy back premises of Wilton Street during the summer months. Mr. Russell lived chiefly on bread and tea, for his means were of the smallest; but when Dyson came to see him, he would send out the slavey for six ale, and Dyson was always at liberty to smoke as much of his own tobacco as he pleased.[6] The landlady had been so unfortunate as to have her drawing-room floor vacant for many months; a card had long proclaimed the void within; and Dyson, when he walked up the steps one evening in early autumn, had a sense that something was missing, and, looking at the fanlight, saw the appealing card had disappeared.

'You have let your first floor, have you?' he said, as he greeted Mr. Russell.

'Yes; it was taken about a fortnight ago by a lady.'

'Indeed,' said Dyson, always curious; 'a young lady?'

'Yes; I believe so. She is a widow, and wears a thick crape veil. I have met her once or twice on the stairs and in the street; but I should not know her face.'

'Well,' said Dyson, when the beer had arrived, and the pipes were in full blast, 'and what have you been doing? Do you find the work getting any easier?'

'Alas!' said the young man, with an expression of great gloom, 'the life is a purgatory, and all but a hell. I write, picking out my words, weighing and balancing the force of every syllable, calculating the minutest effects that language can produce, erasing and rewriting, and spending a whole evening over a page of manuscript. And then, in the morning, when I read what I have written— Well, there is nothing to be done but to throw it in the wastepaper basket, if the verso has been already written on, or to put it in the drawer if the other side happens to be clean.[7] When I have written a phrase which undoubtedly embodies a happy turn of thought, I find it dressed up in feeble commonplace; and when the style is good, it serves only to conceal the baldness of superannuated fancies. I sweat over my work, Dyson — every finished line means so much agony. I envy the lot of the carpenter in the side street who has a craft which he understands. When he gets an order for a table he does not

---

[5]   Called Milton Street since 1830, relatively impoverished Grub Street — located in central London — had a high population of booksellers and struggling writers who often worked as 'hack' writers for the many low-end publishing firms in the area. The term 'Grub Street' became shorthand for low-brow literature and writers, as well as seedy living.

[6]   A slavey is a female servant who does a range of tasks within a household or boarding house.

[7]   The verso is the back side of a page or piece of paper (the front side is known as the recto).

writhe with anguish; but if I were so unlucky as to get an order for a book, I think I should go mad.'

'My dear fellow, you take it all too seriously. You should let the ink flow more readily. Above all, firmly believe, when you sit down to write, that you are an artist, and that whatever you are about is a masterpiece. Suppose ideas fail you, say, as I heard one of our most exquisite artists say, "It's of no consequence; the ideas are all there, at the bottom of that box of cigarettes!" You, indeed, smoke tobacco, but the application is the same.[8] Besides, you must have some happy moments; and these should be ample consolation.'

'Perhaps you are right. But such moments are so few; and then there is the torture of a glorious conception matched with execution beneath the standard of the Family Story Paper.[9] For instance, I was happy for two hours a night or two ago; I lay awake and saw visions. But then the morning!'

'What was your idea?'

'It seemed to me a splendid one: I thought of Balzac and the *Comédie Humaine,* of Zola and the Rougon-Macquart family.[10] It dawned upon me that I would write the history of a street. Every house should form a volume. I fixed upon the street, I saw each house, and read as clearly as in letters the physiology and psychology of each; the little byway stretched before me in its actual shape — a street that I know and have passed down a hundred times, with some twenty houses, prosperous and mean, and lilac bushes in purple blossom. And yet it was, at the same time, a symbol, a *via dolorosa* of hopes cherished and disappointed,[11] of years of monotonous existence without content or discontent, of tragedies and obscure sorrows; and on the door of one of those houses I saw the red stain of blood, and behind a window two shadows, blackened and faded, on the blind, as they swayed on tightened cords — the shadows of a man and a woman hanging in a vulgar gaslit parlour. These were my fancies; but when pen touched paper they shrivelled and vanished away.'

---

[8]   The reference to tobacco here is to loose tobacco, as in a pipe.

[9]   Various periodicals contained the phrase 'Family Story Paper' in their name. Russell is here looking down his nose not at a particular publication, but at the type of literature that was being published in inexpensive family story papers — such as the *Family Herald* and *Cassell's Illustrated Family Paper* — which printed undemanding, populist fiction and poetry. They were miles away from the high-brow literary periodicals in which Russell would like to publish his work.

[10]   Honoré de Balzac (1799–1850) was a French author. *La Comédie humaine* is the title of the collection of 20 years of his realist novels, short stories, and essays (which also contain some fantastic and mystical elements). French author Émile Zola (1840–1902) was inspired by *La Comédie humaine* to compose his own series of 20 novels called *Les Rougon-Macquart* (1871–1893). Zola's works depart from Balzac's in their strict adherence to literary naturalism.

[11]   The expression *'via dolorosa'* is Latin for 'road of sorrow', referring to the route Christ took on his way to be crucified at Golgotha, but is also used as a general term for a painful, difficult journey or experience.

'Yes,' said Dyson, 'there is a lot in that. I envy you the pains of transmuting vision into reality, and, still more, I envy you the day when you will look at your bookshelf and see twenty goodly books upon the shelves — the series complete and done for ever. Let me entreat you to have them bound in solid parchment, with gold lettering. It is the only real cover for a valiant book. When I look in at the windows of some choice shop, and see the bindings of Levant morocco, with pretty tools and panellings, and your sweet contrasts of red and green, I say to myself, "These are not books, but *bibelots*."[12] A book bound so — a true book, mind you — is like a Gothic statue draped in brocade of Lyons.'[13]

'Alas!' said Russell, 'we need not discuss the binding — the books are not begun.'

The talk went on as usual till eleven o'clock, when Dyson bade his friend good night. He knew the way downstairs, and walked down by himself; but, greatly to his surprise, as he crossed the first-floor landing the door opened slightly, and a hand was stretched out, beckoning.

Dyson was not the man to hesitate under such circumstances. In a moment he saw himself involved in adventure; and, as he told himself, the Dysons had never disobeyed a lady's summons. Softly, then, with due regard for the lady's honour, he would have entered the room, when a low but clear voice spoke to him —

'Go downstairs and open the door and shut it again rather loudly. Then come up to me; and for Heaven's sake, walk softly.'

Dyson obeyed her commands, not without some hesitation, for he was afraid of meeting the landlady or the maid on his return journey. But, walking like a cat, and making each step he trod on crack loudly, he flattered himself that he had escaped observation; and as he gained the top of the stairs the door opened wide before him, and he found himself in the lady's drawing-room, bowing awkwardly.

'Pray be seated, sir. Perhaps this chair will be the best; it was the favoured chair of my landlady's deceased husband. I would ask you to smoke, but the odour would betray me. I know my proceedings must seem to you unconventional; but I saw you arrive this evening, and I do not think you would refuse to help a woman who is so unfortunate as I am.'

Mr. Dyson looked shyly at the young lady before him. She was dressed in deep mourning, but the piquant smiling face and charming hazel eyes ill accorded with the heavy garments and the mouldering surface of the crape.

'Madam,' he said gallantly, 'your instinct has served you well. We will not trouble, if you please, about the question of social conventions; the chivalrous

---

[12] Levant morocco is a high-quality leather made in the Levant region bordering the eastern Mediterranean, which, in the present day, includes Syria, Lebanon, Israel, and Palestine. A bibelot is a small, curious, and usually rare object.

[13] The French city of Lyon was famous for its brocade, a woven silk fabric adorned with elaborate designs stitched with gold, silver, and other colourful threads.

gentleman knows nothing of such matters. I hope I may be privileged to serve you.'

'You are very kind to me, but I knew it would be so. Alas! sir, I have had experience of life, and I am rarely mistaken. Yet man is too often so vile and so misjudging that I trembled even as I resolved to take this step, which, for all I knew, might prove to be both desperate and ruinous.'

'With me you have nothing to fear,' said Dyson. 'I was nurtured in the faith of chivalry, and I have always endeavoured to remember the proud traditions of my race. Confide in me, then, and count upon my secrecy, and if it prove possible, you may rely on my help.'

'Sir, I will not waste your time, which I am sure is valuable, by idle parleyings. Learn, then, that I am a fugitive, and in hiding here; I place myself in your power; you have but to describe my features, and I fall into the hands of my relentless enemy.'

Mr. Dyson wondered for a passing instant how this could be, but he only renewed his promise of silence, repeating that he would be the embodied spirit of dark concealment.

'Good,' said the lady, 'the Oriental fervour of your style is delightful. In the first place, I must disabuse your mind of the conviction that I am a widow. These gloomy vestments have been forced on me by strange circumstance; in plain language, I have deemed it expedient to go disguised. You have a friend, I think, in the house, Mr. Russell? He seems of a coy and retiring nature.'

'Excuse me, madam,' said Dyson, 'he is not coy, but he is a realist; and perhaps you are aware that no Carthusian monk can emulate the cloistral seclusion in which a realistic novelist loves to shroud himself.[14] It is his way of observing human nature.'

'Well, well,' said the lady; 'all this, though deeply interesting, is not germane to our affair. I must tell you my history.'

With these words the young lady proceeded to relate the

NOVEL OF THE WHITE POWDER.

My name is Leicester; my father, Major-General Wyn Leicester, a distinguished officer of artillery, succumbed five years ago to a complicated liver complaint acquired in the deadly climate of India. A year later my only brother, Francis, came home after an exceptionally brilliant career at the University, and settled down with the resolution of a hermit to master what has been well called the great legend of the law. He was a man who seemed to live in utter indifference to everything that is called pleasure; and though he was handsomer than most men, and could talk as merrily and wittily as if he were a mere vagabond, he

---

[14] The Carthusians are a particularly austere monastic order founded in France by St Bruno (d.1101) in 1086.

avoided society, and shut himself up in a large room at the top of the house to make himself a lawyer. Ten hours a day of hard reading was at first his allotted portion; from the first light in the east to the late afternoon he remained shut up with his books, taking a hasty half-hour's lunch with me as if he grudged the wasting of the moments, and going out for a short walk when it began to grow dusk. I thought that such relentless application must be injurious, and tried to cajole him from the crabbed text-books, but his ardour seemed to grow rather than diminish, and his daily tale of hours increased. I spoke to him seriously, suggesting some occasional relaxation, if it were but an idle afternoon with a harmless novel; but he laughed, and said that he read about feudal tenures when he felt in need of amusement, and scoffed at the notion of theatres, or a month's fresh air.[15] I confessed that he looked well, and seemed not to suffer from his labours, but I knew that such unnatural toil would take revenge at last, and I was not mistaken. A look of anxiety began to lurk about his eyes, and he seemed languid, and at last he avowed that he was no longer in perfect health; he was troubled, he said, with a sensation of dizziness, and awoke now and then of nights from fearful dreams, terrified and cold with icy sweats. 'I am taking care of myself,' he said, 'so you must not trouble; I passed the whole of yesterday afternoon in idleness, leaning back in that comfortable chair you gave me, and scribbling nonsense on a sheet of paper. No, no; I will not overdo my work; I shall be well enough in a week or two, depend upon it.'

Yet in spite of his assurances I could see that he grew no better, but rather worse; he would enter the drawing-room with a face all miserably wrinkled and despondent, and endeavour to look gaily when my eyes fell on him, and I thought such symptoms of evil omen, and was frightened sometimes at the nervous irritation of his movements, and at glances which I could not decipher. Much against his will, I prevailed on him to have medical advice, and with an ill grace he called in our old doctor.

Dr. Haberden cheered me after his examination of his patient.

'There is nothing really much amiss,' he said to me. 'No doubt he reads too hard, and eats hastily, and then goes back again to his books in too great a hurry, and the natural consequence is some digestive trouble and a little mischief in the nervous system. But I think — I do, indeed, Miss Leicester — that we shall be able to set this all right. I have written him a prescription which ought to do great things. So you have no cause for anxiety.'

My brother insisted on having the prescription made up by a chemist in the neighbourhood; it was an odd, old-fashioned shop, devoid of the studied

---

[15] Feudal tenures were a system of land-holding in Western Europe during the Middle Ages, whereby a person had possession and use, but not ownership, of a parcel of land in exchange for certain payments and/or other obligations (e.g. military service) to its owner, who was usually a member of the nobility.

coquetry and calculated glitter that make so gay a show on the counters and shelves of the modern apothecary; but Francis liked the old chemist, and believed in the scrupulous purity of his drugs. The medicine was sent in due course, and I saw that my brother took it regularly after lunch and dinner. It was an innocent-looking white powder, of which a little was dissolved in a glass of cold water; I stirred it in, and it seemed to disappear, leaving the water clear and colourless. At first Francis seemed to benefit greatly; the weariness vanished from his face, and he became more cheerful than he had ever been since the time when he left school; he talked gaily of reforming himself, and avowed to me that he had wasted his time.

'I have given too many hours to law,' he said, laughing; 'I think you have saved me in the nick of time. Come, I shall be Lord Chancellor yet, but I must not forget life.[16] You and I will have a holiday together before long; we will go to Paris and enjoy ourselves, and keep away from the Bibliothèque Nationale.'[17]

I confessed myself delighted with the prospect.

'When shall we go?' I said. 'I can start the day after to-morrow if you like.'

'Ah! that is perhaps a little too soon; after all, I do not know London yet, and I suppose a man ought to give the pleasures of his own country the first choice. But we will go off together in a week or two, so try and furbish up your French. I only know law French myself, and I am afraid that wouldn't do.'[18]

We were just finishing dinner, and he quaffed off his medicine with a parade of carousal as if it had been wine from some choicest bin.[19]

'Has it any particular taste?' I said.

'No; I should not know I was not drinking water,' and he got up from his chair and began to pace up and down the room as if he were undecided as to what he should do next.

'Shall we have coffee in the drawing-room?' I said; 'or would you like to smoke?'

'No; I think I will take a turn; it seems a pleasant evening. Look at the afterglow; why, it is as if a great city were burning in flames, and down there between the dark houses it is raining blood fast, fast.[20] Yes, I will go out; I may be in soon, but I shall take my key; so good night, dear, if I don't see you again.'

---

[16] The Lord Chancellor, typically a lawyer, is a senior Cabinet member and functionary in the United Kingdom's government, with a range of legislative and executive functions.

[17] The national library of France, which, in the 1890s, was the largest repository of books in the world.

[18] Law French was the language of English law courts from the Norman Conquest (1066 CE) until the seventeenth century. Its legacy remains in the many French-derived words in modern English legal terminology.

[19] The phrase 'parade of carousal' means ostentatiously, as though he were at a drunken feast.

[20] Bloody rain is an ancient sign foreshadowing calamity and destruction. This bad omen appears in Homer's (before 700 BCE) *Iliad* (Book XI) and in a number of other classical, mediaeval, and early modern works.

The door slammed behind him, and I saw him walk lightly down the street, swinging his malacca cane, and I felt grateful to Dr. Haberden for such an improvement.[21]

I believe my brother came home very late that night, but he was in a merry mood the next morning.

'I walked on without thinking where I was going,' he said, 'enjoying the freshness of the air, and livened by the crowds as I reached more frequented quarters. And then I met an old college friend, Orford, in the press of the pavement, and then — well, we enjoyed ourselves. I have felt what it is to be young and a man; I find I have blood in my veins, as other men have. I made an appointment with Orford for to-night; there will be a little party of us at the restaurant. Yes; I shall enjoy myself for a week or two, and hear the chimes at midnight, and then we will go for our little trip together.'[22]

Such was the transmutation of my brother's character that in a few days he became a lover of pleasure, a careless and merry idler of western pavements, a hunter out of snug restaurants, and a fine critic of fantastic dancing; he grew fat before my eyes, and said no more of Paris, for he had clearly found his paradise in London. I rejoiced, and yet wondered a little; for there was, I thought, something in his gaiety that indefinitely displeased me, though I could not have defined my feeling. But by degrees there came a change; he returned still in the cold hours of the morning, but I heard no more about his pleasures, and one morning as we sat at breakfast together I looked suddenly into his eyes and saw a stranger before me.

'O Francis!' I cried. 'O Francis, Francis, what have you done?' and rending sobs cut the words short. I went weeping out of the room; for though I knew nothing, yet I knew all, and by some odd play of thought I remembered the evening when he first went abroad to prove his manhood, and the picture of the sunset sky glowed before me; the clouds like a city in burning flames, and the rain of blood. Yet I did battle with such thoughts, resolving that perhaps, after all, no great harm had been done, and in the evening at dinner I resolved to press him to fix a day for our holiday in Paris. We had talked easily enough, and my brother had just taken his medicine, which he had continued all the while. I was about to begin my topic, when the words forming in my mind vanished, and I wondered for a second what icy and intolerable weight oppressed my heart and suffocated me as with the unutterable horror of the coffin-lid nailed down on the living.[23]

---

[21] Often capitalized, a Malacca cane is a brown-coloured walking stick of *Calamus rotang*, an East Indian rattan palm.

[22] In Shakespeare's play *Henry IV, Part 2* (III.ii.196), Sir John Falstaff says to Justice Shallow, 'We have heard the chimes at midnight', meaning that, when they were young, they often stayed up late carousing.

[23] Premature burial — formally known as vivisepulture — is a common phobia. 'The

We had dined without candles; the room had slowly grown from twilight to gloom, and the walls and corners were indistinct in the shadow. But from where I sat I looked out into the street; and as I thought of what I would say to Francis, the sky began to flush and shine, as it had done on a well-remembered evening, and in the gap between two dark masses that were houses an awful pageantry of flame appeared — lurid whorls of writhed cloud, and utter depths burning, grey masses like the fume blown from a smoking city, and an evil glory blazing far above shot with tongues of more ardent fire, and below as if there were a deep pool of blood. I looked down to where my brother sat facing me, and the words were shaped on my lips, when I saw his hand resting on the table. Between the thumb and forefinger of the closed hand there was a mark, a small patch about the size of a sixpence, and somewhat of the colour of a bad bruise.[24] Yet, by some sense I cannot define, I knew that what I saw was no bruise at all; oh! if human flesh could burn with flame, and if flame could be black as pitch, such was that before me. Without thought or fashioning of words grey horror shaped within me at the sight, and in an inner cell it was known to be a brand.[25] For a moment the stained sky became dark as midnight, and when the light returned to me I was alone in the silent room, and soon after I heard my brother go out.

Late as it was, I put on my bonnet and went to Dr. Haberden, and in his great consulting room, ill lighted by a candle which the doctor brought in with him, with stammering lips, and a voice that would break in spite of my resolve, I told him all, from the day on which my brother began to take the medicine down to the dreadful thing I had seen scarcely half an hour before.

When I had done, the doctor looked at me for a minute with an expression of great pity on his face.

'My dear Miss Leicester,' he said, 'you have evidently been anxious about your brother; you have been worrying over him, I am sure. Come, now, is it not so?'

'I have certainly been anxious,' I said. 'For the last week or two I have not felt at ease.'

'Quite so; you know, of course, what a queer thing the brain is?'

'I understand what you mean; but I was not deceived. I saw what I have told you with my own eyes.'

'Yes, yes, of course. But your eyes had been staring at that very curious sunset we had to-night. That is the only explanation. You will see it in the proper light to-morrow, I am sure. But, remember, I am always ready to give any help that

---

Premature Burial' (1844) and 'Fall of the House of Usher' (1839), by Edgar Allan Poe — whom both Machen and the Decadents admired — are among the best-known stories involving the subject.

[24] The diameter of a sixpence coin was three-quarters of an inch or 1.9 cm.

[25] A mark made by burning, often to indicate ownership or criminal history.

is in my power; do not scruple to come to me, or to send for me if you are in any distress.'

I went away but little comforted, all confusion and terror and sorrow, not knowing where to turn. When my brother and I met the next day, I looked quickly at him, and noticed, with a sickening at heart, that the right hand, the hand on which I had clearly seen the patch as of a black fire, was wrapped up with a handkerchief.

'What is the matter with your hand, Francis?' I said in a steady voice.

'Nothing of consequence. I cut a finger last night, and it bled rather awkwardly. So I did it up roughly to the best of my ability.'

'I will do it neatly for you, if you like.'

'No, thank you, dear; this will answer very well. Suppose we have breakfast; I am quite hungry.'

We sat down, and I watched him. He scarcely ate or drank at all, but tossed his meat to the dog when he thought my eyes were turned away; there was a look in his eyes that I had never yet seen, and the thought flashed across my mind that it was a look that was scarcely human. I was firmly convinced that awful and incredible as was the thing I had seen the night before, yet it was no illusion, no glamour of bewildered sense, and in the course of the morning I went again to the doctor's house.

He shook his head with an air puzzled and incredulous, and seemed to reflect for a few minutes.

'And you say he still keeps up the medicine? But why? As I understand, all the symptoms he complained of have disappeared long ago; why should he go on taking the stuff when he is quite well. And, by the bye, where did he get it made up? At Sayce's? I never send any one there; the old man is getting careless. Suppose you come with me to the chemist's; I should like to have some talk with him.'

We walked together to the shop; old Sayce knew Dr. Haberden, and was quite ready to give any information.

'You have been sending that in to Mr. Leicester for some weeks I think on my prescription,' said the doctor, giving the old man a pencilled scrap of paper.

The chemist put on his great spectacles with trembling uncertainty, and held up the paper with a shaking hand.

'Oh yes,' he said, 'I have very little of it left; it is rather an uncommon drug, and I have had it in stock some time. I must get in some more, if Mr. Leicester goes on with it.'

'Kindly let me have a look at the stuff,' said Haberden; and the chemist gave him a glass bottle. He took out the stopper and smelt the contents, and looked strangely at the old man.

'Where did you get this?' he said, 'and what is it? For one thing, Mr. Sayce, it is not what I prescribed. Yes, yes, I see the label is right enough, but I tell you this is not the drug.'

'I have had it a long time,' said the old man in feeble terror; 'I got it from Burbage's in the usual way. It is not prescribed often, and I have had it on the shelf for some years. You see there is very little left.'

'You had better give it to me,' said Haberden. 'I am afraid something wrong has happened.'[26]

We went out of the shop in silence, the doctor carrying the bottle neatly wrapped in paper under his arm.

'Dr. Haberden,' I said when we had walked a little way — 'Dr. Haberden.'

'Yes,' he said, looking at me gloomily enough.

'I should like you to tell me what my brother has been taking twice a day for the last month or so.'

'Frankly, Miss Leicester, I don't know. We will speak of this when we get to my house.'

We walked on quickly without another word till we reached Dr. Haberden's. He asked me to sit down, and began pacing up and down the room, his face clouded over, as I could see, with no common fears.

'Well,' he said at length, 'this is all very strange; it is only natural that you should feel alarmed, and I must confess that my mind is far from easy. We will put aside, if you please, what you told me last night and this morning, but the fact remains that for the last few weeks Mr. Leicester has been impregnating his system with a drug which is completely unknown to me. I tell you, it is not what I ordered; and what that stuff in the bottle really is remains to be seen.'

He undid the wrapper, and cautiously tilted a few grains of the white powder on to a piece of paper, and peered curiously at it.

'Yes,' he said, 'it is like the sulphate of quinine, as you say; it is flaky.[27] But smell it.'

He held the bottle to me, and I bent over it. It was a strange, sickly smell, vaporous and overpowering, like some strong anæsthetic.

'I shall have it analysed,' said Haberden; 'I have a friend who has devoted his

---

[26] The Victorian period saw regular efforts to standardize requirements for the dispensation of lethal or potentially lethal medications. The 1851 Arsenic Act required clear labelling of danger but did not limit who was permitted to sell arsenic, as the category of pharmacist was not yet legally defined. This changed with the 1868 Pharmacy Act, which states that, in the UK, only doctors and pharmacists who passed examination and were then registered as members of the Pharmaceutical Society were allowed to dispense dangerous drugs or poisons. The 1885 Poisons Bill absorbed the Arsenic Act, while enhancing regulations on labelling and who was allowed to dispense poisons. Haberden equates the white powder with sulphate of quinine, which was not recognized as requiring such labelling. The label on Sayce's bottle does not appear to state 'poison', which the 1885 bill requires of poisons.

[27] Quinine sulphate was typically prescribed as a powder, and has been used since the seventeenth century as a treatment for malaria.

whole life to chemistry as a science.[28] Then we shall have something to go upon. No, no; say no more about that other matter; I cannot listen to that; and take my advice and think no more about it yourself.'

That evening my brother did not go out as usual after dinner.

'I have had my fling,' he said with a queer laugh, 'and I must go back to my old ways. A little law will be quite a relaxation after so sharp a dose of pleasure,' and he grinned to himself, and soon after went up to his room. His hand was still all bandaged.

Dr. Haberden called a few days later.

'I have no special news to give you,' he said. 'Chambers is out of town, so I know no more about that stuff than you do. But I should like to see Mr. Leicester if he is in.'

'He is in his room,' I said; 'I will tell him you are here.'

'No, no, I will go up to him; we will have a little quiet talk together. I dare say that we have made a good deal of fuss about very little; for, after all, whatever the white powder may be, it seems to have done him good.'

The doctor went upstairs, and standing in the hall I heard his knock, and the opening and shutting of the door; and then I waited in the silent house for an hour, and the stillness grew more and more intense as the hands of the clock crept round. Then there sounded from above the noise of a door shut sharply, and the doctor was coming down the stairs. His footsteps crossed the hall, and there was a pause at the door; I drew a long, sick breath with difficulty, and saw my face white in a little mirror, and he came in and stood at the door. There was an unutterable horror shining in his eyes; he steadied himself by holding the back of a chair with one hand, his lower lip trembled like a horse's, and he gulped and stammered unintelligible sounds before he spoke.

'I have seen that man,' he began in a dry whisper. 'I have been sitting in his presence for the last hour. My God! And I am alive and in my senses! I, who have dealt with death all my life, and have dabbled with the melting ruins of the earthly tabernacle.[29] But not this, oh! not this,' and he covered his face with his hands as if to shut out the sight of something before him.

'Do not send for me again, Miss Leicester,' he said with more composure. 'I can do nothing in this house. Good-bye.'

As I watched him totter down the steps, and along the pavement towards his house, it seemed to me that he had aged by ten years since the morning.

My brother remained in his room. He called out to me in a voice I hardly recognised that he was very busy, and would like his meals brought to his door

---

[28] Chemistry developed as a science from alchemy, the practice of transmuting base substances into more valuable ones.

[29] Haberden is alluding to the biblical passage 'For we know that if our earthly house of this tabernacle were dissolved, we have a building of God, an house not made with hands, eternal in the heavens' (II Corinthians 5. 1).

and left there, and I gave the order to the servants. From that day it seemed as if the arbitrary conception we call time had been annihilated for me; I lived in an ever-present sense of horror, going through the routine of the house mechanically, and only speaking a few necessary words to the servants. Now and then I went out and paced the streets for an hour or two and came home again; but whether I were without or within, my spirit delayed before the closed door of the upper room, and, shuddering, waited for it to open. I have said that I scarcely reckoned time; but I suppose it must have been a fortnight after Dr. Haberden's visit that I came home from my stroll a little refreshed and lightened. The air was sweet and pleasant, and the hazy form of green leaves, floating cloudlike in the square, and the smell of blossoms, had charmed my senses, and I felt happier and walked more briskly. As I delayed a moment at the verge of the pavement, waiting for a van to pass by before crossing over to the house, I happened to look up at the windows, and instantly there was the rush and swirl of deep cold waters in my ears, my heart leapt up, and fell down, down as into a deep hollow, and I was amazed with a dread and terror without form or shape. I stretched out a hand blindly through folds of thick darkness, from the black and shadowy valley, and held myself from falling, while the stones beneath my feet rocked and swayed and tilted, and the sense of solid things seemed to sink away from under me.[30] I had glanced up at the window of my brother's study, and at that moment the blind was drawn aside, and something that had life stared out into the world. Nay, I cannot say I saw a face or any human likeness; a living thing, two eyes of burning flame glared at me, and they were in the midst of something as formless as my fear, the symbol and presence of all evil and all hideous corruption. I stood shuddering and quaking as with the grip of ague, sick with unspeakable agonies of fear and loathing, and for five minutes I could not summon force or motion to my limbs. When I was within the door, I ran up the stairs to my brother's room, and knocked.

'Francis, Francis,' I cried, 'for Heaven's sake, answer me. What is the horrible thing in your room? Cast it out, Francis; cast it from you.'

I heard a noise as of feet shuffling slowly and awkwardly, and a choking, gurgling sound, as if some one was struggling to find utterance, and then the noise of a voice, broken and stifled, and words that I could scarcely understand.

'There is nothing here,' the voice said. 'Pray do not disturb me. I am not very well to-day.'

I turned away, horrified, and yet helpless. I could do nothing, and I wondered why Francis had lied to me, for I had seen the appearance beyond the glass too plainly to be deceived, though it was but the sight of a moment. And I sat still, conscious that there had been something else, something I had seen in the first flash of terror, before those burning eyes had looked at me. Suddenly

---

[30] Likely an allusion to the biblical 'valley of the shadow of death' (Psalm 23. 4).

I remembered; as I lifted my face the blind was being drawn back, and I had had an instant's glance of the thing that was moving it, and in my recollection I knew that a hideous image was engraved for ever on my brain. It was not a hand; there were no fingers that held the blind, but a black stump pushed it aside, the mouldering outline and the clumsy movement as of a beast's paw had glowed into my senses before the darkling waves of terror had overwhelmed me as I went down quick into the pit. My mind was aghast at the thought of this, and of the awful presence that dwelt with my brother in his room; I went to his door and cried to him again, but no answer came. That night one of the servants came up to me and told me in a whisper that for three days food had been regularly placed at the door and left untouched; the maid had knocked, but had received no answer; she had heard the noise of shuffling feet that I had noticed. Day after day went by, and still my brother's meals were brought to his door and left untouched; and though I knocked and called again and again, I could get no answer. The servants began to talk to me; it appeared they were as alarmed as I; the cook said that when my brother first shut himself up in his room she used to hear him come out at night and go about the house; and once, she said, the hall door had opened and closed again, but for several nights she had heard no sound. The climax came at last; it was in the dusk of the evening, and I was sitting in the darkening dreary room when a terrible shriek jarred and rang harshly out of the silence, and I heard a frightened scurry of feet dashing down the stairs. I waited, and the servant-maid staggered into the room and faced me, white and trembling.

'O Miss Helen!' she whispered; 'oh! for the Lord's sake, Miss Helen, what has happened? Look at my hand, miss; look at that hand!'

I drew her to the window, and saw there was a black wet stain upon her hand.

'I do not understand you,' I said. 'Will you explain to me?'

'I was doing your room just now,' she began. 'I was turning down the bed-clothes, and all of a sudden there was something fell upon my hand, wet, and I looked up, and the ceiling was black and dripping on me.'

I looked hard at her and bit my lip.

'Come with me,' I said. 'Bring your candle with you.'

The room I slept in was beneath my brother's, and as I went in I felt I was trembling. I looked up at the ceiling, and saw a patch, all black and wet, and a dew of black drops upon it, and a pool of horrible liquor soaking into the white bed-clothes.

I ran upstairs, and knocked loudly.

'O Francis, Francis, my dear brother,' I cried, 'what has happened to you?'

And I listened. There was a sound of choking, and a noise like water bubbling and regurgitating, but nothing else, and I called louder, but no answer came.

In spite of what Dr. Haberden had said, I went to him; with tears streaming down my cheeks I told him of all that had happened, and he listened to me with a face set hard and grim.

'For your father's sake,' he said at last, 'I will go with you, though I can do nothing.'

We went out together; the streets were dark and silent, and heavy with heat and a drought of many weeks. I saw the doctor's face white under the gas-lamps, and when we reached the house his hand was shaking.

We did not hesitate, but went upstairs directly. I held the lamp, and he called out in a loud, determined voice —

'Mr. Leicester, do you hear me? I insist on seeing you. Answer me at once.'

There was no answer, but we both heard that choking noise I have mentioned.

'Mr. Leicester, I am waiting for you. Open the door this instant, or I shall break it down.' And he called a third time in a voice that rang and echoed from the walls —

'Mr. Leicester! For the last time I order you to open the door.'

'Ah!' he said, after a pause of heavy silence, 'we are wasting time here. Will you be so kind as to get me a poker, or something of the kind.'

I ran into a little room at the back where odd articles were kept, and found a heavy adze-like tool that I thought might serve the doctor's purpose.[31]

'Very good,' he said, 'that will do, I dare say. I give you notice, Mr. Leicester,' he cried loudly at the keyhole, 'that I am now about to break into your room.'

Then I heard the wrench of the adze, and the woodwork split and cracked under it; with a loud crash the door suddenly burst open, and for a moment we started back aghast at a fearful screaming cry, no human voice, but as the roar of a monster, that burst forth inarticulate and struck at us out of the darkness.

'Hold the lamp,' said the doctor, and we went in and glanced quickly round the room.

'There it is,' said Dr. Haberden, drawing a quick breath; 'look, in that corner.'

I looked, and a pang of horror seized my heart as with a white-hot iron. There upon the floor was a dark and putrid mass, seething with corruption and hideous rottenness, neither liquid nor solid, but melting and changing before our eyes, and bubbling with unctuous oily bubbles like boiling pitch. And out of the midst of it shone two burning points like eyes, and I saw a writhing and stirring as of limbs, and something moved and lifted up that might have been an arm. The doctor took a step forward, raised the iron bar and struck at the burning points; he drove in the weapon, and struck again and again in a fury of loathing. At last the thing was quiet.

·   ·   ·   ·   ·   ·

A week or two later, when I had to some extent recovered from the terrible shock, Dr. Haberden came to see me.

---

[31] First appearing in the Stone Age, an adze is a tool similar to an axe, used for roughly carving wood.

'I have sold my practice,' he began, 'and to-morrow I am sailing on a long voyage. I do not know whether I shall ever return to England; in all probability I shall buy a little land in California, and settle there for the remainder of my life. I have brought you this packet, which you may open and read when you feel able to do so. It contains the report of Dr. Chambers on what I submitted to him. Good-bye, Miss Leicester, good-bye.'

When he was gone I opened the envelope; I could not wait, and proceeded to read the papers within. Here is the manuscript, and if you will allow me, I will read you the astounding story it contains.

'My dear Haberden,' the letter began, 'I have delayed inexcusably in answering your questions as to the white substance you sent me. To tell you the truth, I have hesitated for some time as to what course I should adopt, for there is a bigotry and an orthodox standard in physical science as in theology, and I knew that if I told you the truth I should offend rooted prejudices which I once held dear myself. However, I have determined to be plain with you, and first I must enter into a short personal explanation.

'You have known me, Haberden, for many years as a scientific man; you and I have often talked of our profession together, and discussed the hopeless gulf that opens before the feet of those who think to attain to truth by any means whatsoever except the beaten way of experiment and observation in the sphere of material things. I remember the scorn with which you have spoken to me of men of science who have dabbled a little in the unseen, and have timidly hinted that perhaps the senses are not, after all, the eternal, impenetrable bounds of all knowledge, the everlasting walls beyond which no human being has ever passed. We have laughed together heartily, and I think justly, at the "occult" follies of the day, disguised under various names — the mesmerisms, spiritualisms, materialisations, theosophies, all the rabble rant of imposture, with their machinery of poor tricks and feeble conjuring, the true back-parlour magic of shabby London streets.[32] Yet, in spite of what I have said, I must confess to you that I am no materialist, taking the word of course in its usual signification.[33] It is now many years since I have convinced myself,

---

[32] In Machen's time, 'mesmerism' could mean simply a type of hypnosis, or refer specifically to the variety developed by the Austrian physician F. A. Mesmer (1733–1815). Spiritualism is the belief that the spirits of the dead can communicate with the living, especially through a medium. This belief developed into a major movement during the Victorian period, and was often conflated with Theosophy, the occult, and mysticism. On spiritualism, see the excerpt of Florence Marryat's work in this edition. Materialization is the process of the spirits of the dead — and other entities, such as angels and demons — taking material form. Theosophy is a religious or philosophical body of thought, influenced by eastern spiritualities, that claims mystical knowledge of the divine. The introduction to this edition offers further discussion of Machen's recurring contrasts of science, spirituality, superstition, and hoaxes.

[33] By materialist, Chambers means one who believes that nature, including consciousness and thought, are all fundamentally made up of or the products of physical matter.

convinced myself a sceptic remember, that the old iron-bound theory is utterly and entirely false. Perhaps this confession will not wound you so sharply as it would have done twenty years ago; for I think you cannot have failed to notice that for some time hypotheses have been advanced by men of pure science which are nothing less than transcendental, and I suspect that most modern chemists and biologists of repute would not hesitate to subscribe the *dictum* of the old Schoolman, *Omnia exeunt in mysterium*, which means, I take it, that every branch of human knowledge if traced up to its source and final principles vanishes into mystery.[34] I need not trouble you now with a detailed account of the painful steps which led me to my conclusions; a few simple experiments suggested a doubt as to my then standpoint, and a train of thought that rose from circumstances comparatively trifling brought me far; my old conception of the universe has been swept away, and I stand in a world that seems as strange and awful to me as the endless waves of the ocean seen for the first time, shining, from a peak in Darien.[35] Now I know that the walls of sense that seemed so impenetrable, that seemed to loom up above the heavens and to be founded below the depths, and to shut us in for evermore, are no such everlasting impassable barriers as we fancied, but thinnest and most airy veils that melt away before the seeker, and dissolve as the early mist of the morning about the brooks. I know that you never adopted the extreme materialistic position; you did not go about trying to prove a universal negative, for your logical sense withheld you from that crowning absurdity;[36] but I am sure that you will find all that I am saying strange and repellent to your habits of thought. Yet, Haberden, what I tell you is the truth, nay, to adopt our common language, the sole and scientific truth, verified by experience; and the universe is verily more splendid and more awful than we used to dream. The whole universe, my friend, is a tremendous sacrament; a mystic, ineffable force and energy, veiled by an outward form of matter; and man, and the sun and the other stars, and the flower of the grass, and the crystal in the test-tube, are each and every one as spiritual, as material, and subject to an inner working.[37]

'You will perhaps wonder, Haberden, whence all this tends; but I think a little thought will make it clear. You will understand that from such a standpoint the whole view of things is changed, and what we thought incredible and absurd

---

[34] In the Middle Ages, a Schoolman was somebody who studied scholasticism, such as Thomas Aquinas (1225–1274). On scholasticism, see note 17 of *The Hill of Dreams*. The Latin phrase 'all things pass into mystery' is recognized as a dictum of Aquinus and other scholastic theologians.

[35] Machen evokes the final lines of Romantic poet John Keats's (1795–1821) sonnet 'On First Looking into Chapman's Homer' (1816), but with a sense of horror rather than the imaginative epiphany of Keats's speaker.

[36] In logic, a universal negative is the categorical proposition that every β is not an α.

[37] This passage brings to mind 'Discovering the Great and Deep Mysteries of Nature' (1657) by Oswald Crollius, mentioned in *The Great God Pan*; see note 10 of that work.

may be possible enough. In short, we must look at legend and belief with other eyes, and be prepared to accept tales that had become mere fables. Indeed, this is no such great demand. After all, modern science will concede as much, in a hypocritical manner; you must not, it is true, believe in witchcraft, but you may credit hypnotism; ghosts are out of date, but there is a good deal to be said for the theory of telepathy. Give a superstition a Greek name, and believe in it, should almost be a proverb.

'So much for my personal explanation. You sent me, Haberden, a phial, stoppered and sealed, containing a small quantity of a flaky white powder, obtained from a chemist who has been dispensing it to one of your patients. I am not surprised to hear that this powder refused to yield any results to your analysis. It is a substance which was known to a few many hundred years ago, but which I never expected to have submitted to me from the shop of a modern apothecary. There seems no reason to doubt the truth of the man's tale; he no doubt got, as he says, the rather uncommon salt you prescribed from the wholesale chemist's; and it has probably remained on his shelf for twenty years, or perhaps longer. Here what we call chance and coincidence begins to work; during all these years the salt in the bottle was exposed to certain recurring variations of temperature, variations probably ranging from 40° to 80°. And, as it happens, such changes, recurring year after year at irregular intervals, and with varying degrees of intensity and duration, have constituted a process, and a process so complicated and so delicate, that I question whether modern scientific apparatus directed with the utmost precision could produce the same result. The white powder you sent me is something very different from the drug you prescribed; it is the powder from which the wine of the Sabbath, the *Vinum Sabbati*, was prepared. No doubt you have read of the Witches' Sabbath, and have laughed at the tales which terrified our ancestors; the black cats, and the broomsticks, and dooms pronounced against some old woman's cow.[38] Since I have known the truth I have often reflected that it is on the whole a happy thing that such burlesque as this is believed, for it serves to conceal much that it is better should not be known generally. However, if you care to read the appendix to Payne Knight's monograph, you will find that the true Sabbath was something very different, though the writer has very nicely refrained from printing all he knew.[39] The secrets of the true Sabbath were the secrets of remote times surviving into the Middle Ages, secrets of an evil science which existed long before Aryan man entered Europe.[40] Men and women, seduced from their homes on specious pretenses, were met by beings well qualified to

---

[38] A Witches' Sabbath is a nocturnal gathering of witches, often on one of the eight festivals of the ancient pagan calendar (such as the eve of May Day or the autumnal equinox).

[39] Richard Payne Knight (1750–1824) was a British classicist and archaeologist. He discusses the Witches' Sabbath in *A Discourse on the Worship of Priapus* (1786).

[40] The Aryans are a prehistoric people who spoke an early Indo-European language.

assume, as they did assume, the part of devils, and taken by their guides to some desolate and lonely place, known to the initiate by long tradition, and unknown to all else. Perhaps it was a cave in some bare and wind-swept hill, perhaps some inmost recess of a great forest, and there the Sabbath was held. There, in the blackest hour of night, the *Vinum Sabbati* was prepared, and this evil graal was poured forth and offered to the neophytes, and they partook of an infernal sacrament; *sumentes calicem principis inferorum*, as an old author well expresses it.[41] And suddenly, each one that had drunk found himself attended by a companion, a shape of glamour and unearthly allurement, beckoning him apart, to share in joys more exquisite, more piercing than the thrill of any dream, to the consummation of the marriage of the Sabbath. It is hard to write of such things as these, and chiefly because that shape that allured with loveliness was no hallucination, but, awful as it is to express, the man himself. By the power of that Sabbath wine, a few grains of white powder thrown into a glass of water, the house of life was riven asunder and the human trinity dissolved, and the worm which never dies, that which lies sleeping within us all, was made tangible and an external thing, and clothed with a garment of flesh. And then, in the hour of midnight, the primal fall was repeated and re-presented, and the awful thing veiled in the mythos of the Tree in the Garden was done anew. Such was the *nuptiæ Sabbati*.[42]

'I prefer to say no more; you, Haberden, know as well as I do that the most trivial laws of life are not to be broken with impunity; and for so terrible an act as this, in which the very inmost place of the temple was broken open and defiled, a terrible vengeance followed. What began with corruption ended also with corruption.'

Underneath is the following in Dr. Haberden's writing: —

'The whole of the above is unfortunately strictly and entirely true. Your brother confessed all to me on that morning when I saw him in his room. My attention was first attracted to the bandaged hand, and I forced him to show it me. What I saw made me, a medical man of many years standing, grow sick with loathing, and the story I was forced to listen to was infinitely more frightful than I could have believed possible. It has tempted me to doubt the Eternal Goodness which can permit nature to offer such hideous possibilities; and if you had not with your own eyes seen the end, I should have said to you —

---

[41] In Old French, graal is the word for grail, or chalice; Machen appears to be using the term as a metonym for the wine. Neophytes are novices or recent converts. The Latin phrase translates as 'taking the cup of the Prince of Hell'.
[42] 'The Tree in the Garden' is an allusion to the biblical tree of the knowledge of good and evil (Genesis 2. 17). The phrase '*nuptiæ Sabbati*' is Latin for 'wedding Sabbath'.

disbelieve it all. I have not, I think, many more weeks to live, but you are young, and may forget all this.'

'JOSEPH HABERDEN, M.D.'

In the course of two or three months I heard that Dr. Haberden had died at sea shortly after the ship left England.

Miss Leicester ceased speaking, and looked pathetically at Dyson, who could not refrain from exhibiting some symptoms of uneasiness.

He stuttered out some broken phrases expressive of his deep interest in her extraordinary history, and then said with a better grace —

'But, pardon me, Miss Leicester, I understood you were in some difficulty. You were kind enough to ask me to assist you in some way.'

'Ah,' she said, 'I had forgotten that; my own present trouble seems of such little consequence in comparison with what I have told you. But as you are so good to me, I will go on. You will scarcely believe it, but I found that certain persons suspected, or rather pretended to suspect, that I had murdered my brother. These persons were relatives of mine, and their motives were extremely sordid ones; but I actually found myself subject to the shameful indignity of being watched. Yes, sir, my steps were dogged when I went abroad, and at home I found myself exposed to constant if artful observation. With my high spirit this was more than I could brook, and I resolved to set my wits to work and elude the persons who were shadowing me. I was so fortunate as to succeed; I assumed this disguise, and for some time have lain snug and unsuspected. But of late I have reason to believe that the pursuer is on my track; unless I am greatly deceived, I saw yesterday the detective who is charged with the odious duty of observing my movements. You, sir, are watchful and keen-sighted; tell me, did you see any one lurking about this evening?'

'I hardly think so,' said Dyson, 'but perhaps you would give me some description of the detective in question.'

'Certainly; he is a youngish man, dark, with dark whiskers. He has adopted spectacles of large size in the hope of disguising himself effectually, but he cannot disguise his uneasy manner, and the quick, nervous glances he casts to right and left.'

This piece of description was the last straw for the unhappy Dyson, who was foaming with impatience to get out of the house, and would gladly have sworn eighteenth-century oaths, if propriety had not frowned on such a course.

'Excuse me, Miss Leicester,' he said with cold politeness, 'I cannot assist you.'

'Ah!' she said sadly, 'I have offended you in some way. Tell me what I have done, and I will ask you to forgive me.'

'You are mistaken,' said Dyson, grabbing his hat, but speaking with some difficulty; 'you have done nothing. But, as I say, I cannot help you. Perhaps,' he added, with some tinge of sarcasm, 'my friend Russell might be of service.'

'Thank you,' she replied; 'I will try him,' and the lady went off into a shriek of laughter, which filled up Mr. Dyson's cup of scandal and confusion.

He left the house shortly afterwards, and had the peculiar delight of a five-mile walk, through streets which slowly changed from black to grey, and from grey to shining passages of glory for the sun to brighten. Here and there he met or overtook strayed revellers, but he reflected that no one could have spent the night in a more futile fashion than himself; and when he reached his home he had made resolves for reformation. He decided that he would abjure all Milesian and Arabian methods of entertainment, and subscribe to Mudie's for a regular supply of mild and innocuous romance.[43]

'The Recluse of Bayswater', *The Three Impostors*
(London: John Lane, 1895), pp. 197–243.

---

[43] In *Lebor Gabála Érenn*, a mediaeval Christian history of Ireland (the earliest version being of the eleventh century), the Milesians are the Gaels. In this context, 'Milesian and Arabian methods of entertainment' likely refers to mythic tales. Mudie's was a popular lending library known for its support of bland, middle-class values. On Mudie's, see note 72 of *The Hill of Dreams*.

4

The Hill of Dreams (1907)

I

There was a glow in the sky as if great furnace doors were opened.

But all the afternoon his eyes had looked on glamour; he had strayed in fairyland. The holidays were nearly done, and Lucian Taylor had gone out resolved to lose himself, to discover strange hills and prospects that he had never seen before.[1] The air was still, breathless, exhausted after heavy rain, and the clouds looked as if they had been moulded of lead. No breeze blew upon the hill, and down in the well of the valley not a dry leaf stirred, not a bough shook in all the dark January woods.

About a mile from the rectory he had diverged from the main road by an opening that promised mystery and adventure.[2] It was an old neglected lane, little more than a ditch, worn ten feet deep by its winter waters, and shadowed by great untrimmed hedges, densely woven together. On each side were turbid streams, and here and there a torrent of water gushed down the banks, flooding the lane. It was so deep and dark that he could not get a glimpse of the country through which he was passing, but the way went down and down to some unconjectured hollow.

Perhaps he walked two miles between the high walls of the lane before its descent ceased, but he thrilled with the sense of having journeyed very far, all the long way from the known to the unknown. He had come as it were into the bottom of a bowl amongst the hills, and black woods shut out the world. From the road behind him, from the road before him, from the unseen wells

---

[1]   The first name of Machen's protagonist harks back to that of the highly regarded late-classical prose writer Lucian (117–c. 180 CE), known in particular for his social satires. In Walter Pater's novel *Marius the Epicurean* (1885), the aesthete Flavian introduces the hero to the works of Lucian, 'writings seeming to overflow with that intellectual light turned upon dim places, which, at least in seasons of mental fair weather, can make people laugh where they have been wont, perhaps, to pray' (Water Pater, *Marius the Epicurean* (London: Macmillan, 1907), p. 51). Machen implied that he had read Pater's novel only after having written *The Hill of Dreams*, and that he was disappointed by it. The name Lucian also carries aural hints of Lucifer, a proud angel who, according to Christian mythology, rebelled against God and was punished, a narrative that accords with Lucian's sense of his choice to pursue an artistic literary career rather than a more familiar path.

[2]   A rectory is the home of the Anglican clergyman (the rector) in charge of a parish.

beneath the trees, rivulets of waters swelled and streamed down towards the centre to the brook that crossed the lane. Amid the dead and wearied silence of the air, beneath leaden and motionless clouds, it was strange to hear such a tumult of gurgling and rushing water, and he stood for a while on the quivering footbridge and watched the rush of dead wood and torn branches and wisps of straw all hurrying madly past him, to plunge into the heaped spume, the barmy froth that had gathered against a fallen tree.

Then he climbed again, and went up between limestone rocks, higher and higher, till the noise of waters became indistinct, a faint humming like swarming hives in summer. He walked some distance on level ground, till there was a break in the banks and a stile on which he could lean and look out. He found himself, as he had hoped, afar and forlorn; he had strayed into outland and occult territory.[3] From the eminence of the lane, skirting the brow of a hill, he looked down into deep valleys and dingles, and beyond, across the trees, to remoter country, wild bare hills and dark wooded lands meeting the grey still sky.[4] Immediately beneath his feet the ground sloped steep down to the valley, a hillside of close grass patched with dead bracken, and dotted here and there with stunted thorns, and below there were deep oakwoods, all still and silent, and lonely as if no one ever passed that way.[5] The grass and bracken and thorns and woods, all were brown and grey beneath the leaden sky, and as Lucian looked he was amazed, as though he were reading a wonderful story, the meaning of which was a little greater than his understanding. Then, like the hero of a fairy-book, he went on and on, catching now and again glimpses of the amazing country into which he had penetrated, and perceiving rather than seeing that as the day waned everything grew more grey and somber. As he advanced he heard the evening sounds of the farms, the low of the cattle, and the barking of the sheepdogs; a faint thin noise from far away. It was growing late, and as the shadows blackened he walked faster, till once more the lane began to descend, there was a sharp turn, and he found himself, with a good deal of relief, and a little disappointment, on familiar ground. He had nearly described a circle, and knew this end of the lane very well; it was not much more than a mile from home. He walked smartly down the hill; the air

---

[3] The term 'occult' here means simply something hidden or unfamiliar. The term also connotes things that require special training or have a supernatural aspect, and this passage supports a reading of Lucian's experience at the ancient mound as more than simply mysterious. On Machen's interest in occult history and beliefs, see the introduction to this edition, as well as his essay 'Literature of Occultism' and the excerpt from *Hieroglyphics*, both included in this edition.

[4] A dingle is a deep chasm between two hills or mountains.

[5] The oak is one of the most sacred trees in pagan Europe, figuring in Classical, Norse, and Celtic mythology. In pagan Gaul and the British Isles, the oak (and mistletoe that grows on oaks) held particular significance for Druids, highly educated teachers and priests amongst the ancient Celtic peoples.

was all glimmering and indistinct, transmuting trees and hedges into ghostly shapes, and the walls of the White House Farm flickered on the hillside, as if they were moving towards him. Then a change came. First, a little breath of wind brushed with a dry whispering sound through the hedges, the few leaves left on the boughs began to stir, and one or two danced madly, and as the wind freshened and came up from a new quarter, the sapless branches above rattled against one another like bones. The growing breeze seemed to clear the air and lighten it. He was passing the stile where a path led to old Mrs. Gibbon's desolate little cottage, in the middle of the fields, at some distance even from the lane, and he saw the light blue smoke of her chimney rise distinct above the gaunt greengage trees, against a pale band that was broadening along the horizon.[6] As he passed the stile with his head bent, and his eyes on the ground, something white started out from the black shadow of the hedge, and in the strange twilight, now tinged with a flush from the west, a figure seemed to swim past him and disappear. For a moment he wondered who it could be, the light was so flickering and unsteady, so unlike the real atmosphere of the day, when he recollected it was only Annie Morgan, old Morgan's daughter at the White House.[7] She was three years older than he, and it annoyed him to find that though she was only fifteen, there had been a dreadful increase in her height since the summer holidays. He had got to the bottom of the hill, and, lifting up his eyes, saw the strange changes of the sky. The pale band had broadened into a clear vast space of light, and above, the heavy leaden clouds were breaking apart and driving across the heaven before the wind. He stopped to watch, and looked up at the great mound that jutted out from the hills into mid-valley. It was a natural formation, and always it must have had something of the form of a fort, but its steepness had been increased by Roman art, and there were high banks on the summit which Lucian's father had told him were the *vallum* of the camp, and a deep ditch had been dug to the north to sever it from the hillside.[8] On this summit oaks had grown, queer stunted-looking

---

[6]   Greengages are light-green plums introduced to Britain by Sir William Gage (1695–1744) in the eighteenth century. The colour green features strongly not only in a number of Machen's works, but also within the decadent movement (see note 11 of 'The Lost Club').

[7]   While 'Morgan' is not an uncommon name in Wales, the nature of Machen's novella hints at an allusion to Morgan le Fay, King Arthur's fairy sister.

[8]   A vallum is the defensive earthworks of a Roman fort or settlement. Such barriers are usually built out of earth and rocks, and topped by wooden stakes or tree trunks. The Roman fort described here owes much to Machen's birthplace of Caerleon (Welsh for 'fortress of the legion', a legion being a unit of a Roman army). Caerleon has extensive remains of the legionary fortress of Isca, one of the three most important military bases during the Roman occupation of Britain. Isca was founded in 74 or 75 CE, and there is evidence of Roman occupation as late as 380 CE. Adding to the site's ancient and legendary status is its association with Arthurian adventures and, by some, even with Camelot (King Arthur's seat).

trees with twisted and contorted trunks, and writhing branches; and these now stood out black against the lighted sky. And then the air changed once more; the flush increased, and a spot like blood appeared in the pond by the gate, and all the clouds were touched with fiery spots and dapples of flame; here and there it looked as if awful furnace doors were being opened.

The wind blew wildly, and it came up through the woods with a noise like a scream, and a great oak by the roadside ground its boughs together with a dismal grating jar. As the red gained in the sky, the earth and all upon it glowed, even the grey winter fields and the bare hillsides crimsoned, the water pools were cisterns of molten brass, and the very road glittered. He was wonder-struck, almost aghast, before the scarlet magic of the afterglow. The old Roman fort was invested with fire; flames from heaven were smitten about its walls, and above there was a dark floating cloud, like a fume of smoke, and every haggard writhing tree showed as black as midnight against the blast of the furnace.

When he got home he heard his mother's voice calling: 'Here's Lucian at last. Mary, Master Lucian has come, you can get the tea ready.' He told a long tale of his adventures, and felt somewhat mortified when his father seemed perfectly acquainted with the whole course of the lane, and knew the names of the wild woods through which he had passed in awe.

'You must have gone by the Darren, I suppose' — that was all he said.[9] 'Yes, I noticed the sunset; we shall have some stormy weather. I don't expect to see many in church to-morrow.'

There was buttered toast for tea 'because it was holidays.' The red curtains were drawn, and a bright fire was burning, and there was the old familiar furniture, a little shabby, but charming from association. It was much pleasanter than the cold and squalid schoolroom; and much better to be reading *Chambers's Journal* than learning Euclid;[10] and better to talk to his father and mother than to be answering such remarks as: 'I say, Taylor, I've torn my trousers; how much do you charge for mending?' 'Lucy, dear, come quick and sew this button on my shirt.'[11]

That night the storm woke him, and he groped with his hands amongst the bedclothes, and sat up, shuddering, not knowing where he was. He had seen himself, in a dream, within the Roman fort, working some dark horror, and

---

[9]   The Darran Valley (spelt with an 'a') in south-east Wales is not far from Caerleon.

[10]   Founded by William (1800–1883) and Robert Chambers (1802–1871), *Chambers's Journal* (1854–1910) was a popular and respected weekly magazine that published fiction as well as articles on history, science, religion, and other topics. It had been preceded by *Chambers's Edinburgh Journal*, before the publication moved to London. Euclid (born *c.* 300 BCE) was the most important mathematician of the classical world, especially influential in the development of geometry.

[11]   In addition to feminizing him, these schoolmates are punning on Lucian's surname, Taylor.

the furnace doors were opened and a blast of flame from heaven was smitten upon him.

Lucian went slowly, but not discreditably, up the school, gaining prizes now and again, and falling in love more and more with useless reading and unlikely knowledge. He did his elegiacs and iambics well enough, but he preferred exercising himself in the rhymed Latin of the middle ages.[12] He liked history, but he loved to meditate on a land laid waste, Britain deserted by the legions, the rare pavements riven by frost, Celtic magic still brooding on the wild hills and in the black depths of the forest, the rosy marbles stained with rain, and the walls growing grey. The masters did not encourage these researches; a pure enthusiasm, they felt, should be for cricket and football, the *dilettanti* might even play fives and read Shakespeare without blame, but healthy English boys should have nothing to do with decadent periods.[13] He was once found guilty of recommending Villon to a school-fellow named Barnes.[14] Barnes tried to extract unpleasantness from the text during preparation, and rioted in his place, owing to his incapacity for the language. The matter was a serious one; the headmaster had never heard of Villon, and the culprit gave up the name of his literary admirer without remorse. Hence, sorrow for Lucian, and complete immunity for the miserable illiterate Barnes, who resolved to confine his researches to the Old Testament, a book which the headmaster knew well. As for Lucian, he plodded on, learning his work decently, and sometimes doing very creditable Latin and Greek prose. His school-fellows thought him quite mad, and tolerated him, and indeed were very kind to him in their barbarous manner. He often remembered in after life acts of generosity and good nature

---

[12] An elegiac is a classical verse form comprising two lines, each written in a specific, complex metre; they are often found in poems about mourning. Iambics are verses or poems written in iambs, a type of two-syllable unit of verse. During the classical period, Latin poetry rarely rhymed; however, many mediaeval poets writing in Latin deployed rhyme in their works, much as other authors were doing in vernacular languages.

[13] Dilettanti are people who pursue a subject, art, language, or other topic in a superficial way, primarily for their own amusement. Played in a three-sided court, fives is an English variant of handball, in which players strike a ball with their gloved hands. Decadent periods are those that some people regard as socially and aesthetically in a state of decline and decay. Artistic and literary works from such times are often characterized by hyper-refinement, artificiality, and non-normative morality. While the masters mentioned here are critical of an historical era of Celtic spirituality and the declining period of Roman influence in what became Britain, Machen is also alluding to the Decadent movement of his own time, itself characterized by a Celtic revival and a strong interest in Greek and Roman paganism.

[14] François Villon (1431–1463?) was a mediaeval French poet who frequently lived as a vagabond, outlaw, and prisoner, and who wrote about his tumultuous experiences in various verse forms. Several nineteenth-century British poets emulated and translated Villon, including Dante Gabriel Rossetti (1828–1882) and Algernon Charles Swinburne, both part of the broader community of the Decadent movement.

done by wretches like Barnes, who had no care for old French nor for curious metres, and such recollections always moved him to emotion. Travelers tell such tales; cast upon cruel shores amongst savage races, they have found no little kindness and warmth of hospitality.

He looked forward to the holidays as joyfully as the rest of them. Barnes and his friend Duscot used to tell him their plans and anticipation; they were going home to brothers and sisters, and to cricket, more cricket, or to football, more football, and in the winter there were parties and jollities of all sorts. In return he would announce his intention of studying the Hebrew language, or perhaps Provençal, with a walk up a bare and desolate mountain by way of open-air amusement, and on a rainy day for choice.[15] Whereupon Barnes would impart to Duscot his confident belief that old Taylor was quite cracked. It was a queer, funny life that of school, so very unlike anything in *Tom Brown*.[16] He once saw the headmaster patting the head of the bishop's little boy, while he called him 'my little man,' and smiled hideously. He told the tale grotesquely in the lower fifth room the same day, and earned much applause, but forfeited all liking directly by proposing a voluntary course of scholastic logic.[17] One barbarian threw him to the ground and another jumped on him, but it was done very pleasantly.[18] There were, indeed, some few of a worse class in the school, solemn sycophants, prigs perfected from tender years, who thought life already 'serious,' and yet, as the headmaster said, were 'joyous, manly young fellows.'[19] Some of these dressed for dinner at home, and talked of dances when

---

[15] Provençal is a Romance language once widely spoken in south-eastern France. The mediaeval lyric poets known as the troubadours wrote in Provençal from the twelfth through the fourteenth centuries.

[16] Thomas Hughes's (1822–1896) popular novel *Tom Brown's School Days* (1853) recounts the story of Tom's life as a student at Rugby School, where he initially faces bullying but eventually triumphs both academically and athletically.

[17] In English public schools, the lower fifth is year 10 of a student's journey through the educational system. Such students are usually 14 to 15 years old. Scholastic logic is the mode of reasoning at the heart of scholasticism, which was the dominant form of philosophical and theological teaching during the Middle Ages in Western Europe, and which emphasized the ability of reason to illuminate and support Christian faith. Leading scholastics included Peter Abelard (1079–1142) and Thomas Aquinas (1225–1274).

[18] Machen's term 'barbarian' is notable, coming from the original Greek for foreigner. As the Roman empire rapidly declined politically and militarily during the late fourth and fifth centuries CE, barbarians were the people who ravaged the Italian peninsula and sacked Rome. This decline of the Roman empire was recognized, in Machen's time, as a key Decadent era, having been discussed as such in Montesquieu's (1689–1755) *Considérations sur les causes de la grandeur des Romains et de leur décadence* (1734), Voltaire's (1694–1778) *Essai sur l'histoire générale et sur les mœurs et l'esprit des nations* (1756), and Edward Gibbon's (1737–1794) *The History of the Decline and Fall of the Roman Empire* (1776–1788). Machen thus suggests that Lucian would be seen as one of the Decadents.

[19] The headmaster is deploying language associated with 'muscular Christianity', a largely nineteenth-century movement within the Church of England which aimed to instil in

they came back in January. But this virulent sort was comparatively infrequent, and achieved great success in after life. Taking his school days on the whole, he always spoke up for the system, and years afterwards he described with enthusiasm the strong beer at a roadside tavern, some way out of the town. But he always maintained that the taste for tobacco, acquired in early life, was the great note of the English Public School.[20]

Three years after Lucian's discovery of the narrow lane and the vision of the flaming fort, the August holidays brought him home at a time of great heat. It was one of those memorable years of English weather, when some Provençal spell seems wreathed round the island in the northern sea, and the grasshoppers chirp loudly as the cicadas, the hills smell of rosemary, and white walls of the old farmhouses blaze in the sunlight as if they stood in Arles or Avignon or famed Tarascon by Rhone.[21] Lucian's father was late at the station, and consequently Lucian bought the *Confessions of an English Opium Eater* which he saw on the bookstall.[22] When his father did drive up, Lucian noticed that the old trap had had a new coat of dark paint, and that the pony looked advanced in years.[23]

'I was afraid that I should be late, Lucian,' said his father, 'though I made old Polly go like anything. I was just going to tell George to put her into the trap when young Philip Harris came to me in a terrible state. He said his father fell down "all of a sudden like" in the middle of the field, and they couldn't make him speak, and would I please to come and see him. So I had to go, though I couldn't do anything for the poor fellow. They had sent for Dr. Burrows, and I am afraid he will find it a bad case of sunstroke. The old people say they never remember such a heat before.'

The pony jogged steadily along the burning turnpike road, taking revenge for the hurrying on the way to the station. The hedges were white with the limestone dust, and the vapour of heat palpitated over the fields. Lucian showed his *Confessions* to his father, and began to talk of the beautiful bits

---

young men a sense that manly exertion and physical strength are essential components of an upright Christian life. The eponymous hero of *Tom Brown's School Days* is a prime example of a muscular Christian hero.

[20] In England, a public school is an independent secondary-level school. Unlike state-supported institutions, students must pay (often quite high fees) to attend public schools; famous examples include Rugby and Eton.

[21] Three cities in the south-east of France, located on the Rhône River. In the first volume of his autobiography, Machen describes Gwent, the region in which he grew up, with 'white farms, that shine radiant in the sunlight' (*Far Off Things*, p. 12).

[22] Thomas De Quincey's *Confessions* (1821) recounts his life as a student, his adventures in the London underworld, his education at the University of Oxford, and the effects of his addiction to opium. He and his book were inspiring for many later Decadent writers in Britain and elsewhere.

[23] A trap is a light carriage, usually with two wheels.

he had already found. Mr. Taylor knew the book well — had read it many years before. Indeed he was almost as difficult to surprise as that character in Daudet, who had one formula for all the chances of life, and when he saw the drowned Academician dragged out of the river, merely observed *'J'ai vu tout ça.'*[24] Mr. Taylor the parson, as his parishioners called him, had read the fine books and loved the hills and woods, and now knew no more of pleasant or sensational surprises. Indeed the living was much depreciated in value,[25] and his own private means were reduced almost to vanishing point, and under such circumstances the great style loses many of its finer savours. He was very fond of Lucian, and cheered by his return, but in the evening he would be a sad man again, with his head resting on one hand, and eyes reproaching sorry fortune.

Nobody called out 'Here's your master with Master Lucian; you can get tea ready,' when the pony jogged up to the front door. His mother had been dead a year, and a cousin kept house. She was a respectable person called Deacon, of middle age, and ordinary standards; and, consequently, there was cold mutton on the table. There was a cake, but nothing of flour, baked in ovens, would rise at Miss Deacon's evocation. Still, the meal was laid in the beloved 'parlour,' with the view of hills and valleys and climbing woods from the open window, and the old furniture was still pleasant to see, and the old books in the shelves had many memories. One of the most respected of the armchairs had become weak in the castors and had to be artfully propped up, but Lucian found it very comfortable after the hard forms. When tea was over he went out and strolled in the garden and orchards, and looked over the stile down into the brake, where foxgloves and bracken and broom mingled with the hazel undergrowth, where he knew of secret glades and untracked recesses, deep in the woven green, the cabinets for many years of his lonely meditations. Every path about his home, every field and hedgerow had dear and friendly memories for him; and the odour of the meadowsweet was better than the incense steaming in the sunshine.[26] He loitered, and hung over the stile till the far-off woods began to

---

[24] This reference is to French author Alphonse Daudet's (1840–1897) novel *L'Immortel* (1888), a satire on the Académie Française, an organization whose main purpose is to maintain the purity of the French language and set the rules for its correct usage. Academicians — the members of the Académie — are known as 'les immortels'. Daudet paints a bleak picture of the members' hypocrisy, scheming, and vanity. In his novel, the character Réhu often cynically and wearily notes that he has seen various things happen before; Lucian's quotation 'J'ai vu tout ca' ('I have seen all that') is a mis-remembering of Réhu's more common expression 'J'ai vu ca, moi' ('I have seen that, myself').

[25] Also known as a benefice, a living is a clergyman's position that provides income through a return on fixed assets, such as property. The term can also be used to refer to the income itself.

[26] In prehistoric Britain, some people left meadowsweet at burial sites, possibly as tributes or offerings. In folk medicine, the plant has been used to treat cancer, tumours, and rheumatism.

turn purple, till the white mists were wreathing in the valley.

Day after day, through all that August, morning and evening were wrapped in haze; day after day the earth shimmered in the heat, and the air was strange, unfamiliar. As he wandered in the lanes and sauntered by the cool sweet verge of the woods, he saw and felt that nothing was common or accustomed, for the sunlight transfigured the meadows and changed all the form of the earth. Under the violent Provençal sun, the elms and beeches looked exotic trees, and in the early morning when the mists were thick the hills had put on an unearthly shape.

The one adventure of the holidays was the visit to the Roman fort, to that fantastic hill about whose steep bastions and haggard oaks he had seen the flames of sunset writhing nearly three years before. Ever since that Saturday evening in January, the lonely valley had been a desirable place to him; he had watched the green battlements in summer and winter weather, had seen the heaped mounds rising dimly amidst the drifting rain, had marked the violent height swim up from the ice-white mists of summer evenings, had watched the fairy bulwarks glimmer and vanish in hovering April twilight. In the hedge of the lane there was a gate on which he used to lean and look down south to where the hill surged up so suddenly, its summit defined on summer evenings not only by the rounded ramparts but by the ring of dense green foliage that marked the circle of oak trees.[27] Higher up the lane, on the way he had come that Saturday afternoon, one could see the white walls of Morgan's farm on the hillside to the north, and on the south there was the stile with the view of old Mrs. Gibbon's cottage smoke; but down in the hollow, looking over the gate, there was no hint of human work, except those green and antique battlements, on which the oaks stood in circle, guarding the inner wood.

The ring of the fort drew him with stronger fascination during that hot August weather. Standing, or as his headmaster would have said, 'mooning' by the gate, and looking into that enclosed and secret valley, it seemed to his fancy as if there were a halo about the hill, an aureole that played like flame around it. One afternoon as he gazed from his station by the gate the sheer sides and the swelling bulwarks were more than ever things of enchantment; the green oak ring stood out against the sky as still and bright as in a picture, and Lucian, in spite of his respect for the law of trespass, slid over the gate. The farmers and their men were busy on the uplands with the harvest, and the adventure was irresistible. At first he stole along by the brook in the shadow of the alders, where the grass and the flowers of wet meadows grew richly; but as he drew nearer to the fort, and its height now rose sheer above him, he left all shelter, and began desperately to mount. There was not a breath of wind; the sunlight shone down on the bare hillside; the loud chirp of the grasshoppers was the

---

[27] Prehistoric Druids are believed to have conducted their rites in circles of oak trees.

only sound. It was a steep ascent and grew steeper as the valley sank away. He turned for a moment, and looked down towards the stream which now seemed to wind remote between the alders; above the valley there were small dark figures moving in the cornfield, and now and again there came the faint echo of a high-pitched voice singing through the air as on a wire.[28] He was wet with heat; the sweat streamed off his face, and he could feel it trickling all over his body. But above him the green bastions rose defiant, and the dark ring of oaks promised coolness. He pressed on, and higher, and at last began to crawl up the *vallum*, on hands and knees, grasping the turf and here and there the roots that had burst through the red earth. And then he lay, panting with deep breaths, on the summit.

Within the fort it was all dusky and cool and hollow; it was as if one stood at the bottom of a great cup. Within, the wall seemed higher than without, and the ring of oaks curved up like a dark green vault. There were nettles growing thick and rank in the foss;[29] they looked different from the common nettles in the lanes, and Lucian, letting his hand touch a leaf by accident, felt the sting burn like fire. Beyond the ditch there was an undergrowth, a dense thicket of trees, stunted and old, crooked and withered by the winds into awkward and ugly forms; beech and oak and hazel and ash and yew twisted and so shortened and deformed that each seemed, like the nettle, of no common kind. He began to fight his way through the ugly growth, stumbling and getting hard knocks from the rebound of the twisted boughs. His foot struck once or twice against something harder than wood, and looking down he saw stones white with the leprosy of age, but still showing the work of the axe. And farther, the roots of the stunted trees gripped the foot-high relics of a wall; and a round heap of fallen stones nourished rank, unknown herbs, that smelt poisonous. The earth was black and unctuous, and bubbling under the feet, left no track behind. From it, in the darkest places where the shadow was thickest, swelled the growth of an abominable fungus, making the still air sick with its corrupt odour, and he shuddered as he felt the horrible thing pulped beneath his feet. Then there was a gleam of sunlight, and as he thrust the last boughs apart, he stumbled into the open space in the heart of the camp. It was a lawn of sweet close turf in the centre of the matted brake, of clean firm earth from which no shameful growth sprouted, and near the middle of the glade was a stump of a felled yew-tree, left untrimmed by the woodman.[30] Lucian thought it must have been made for a

---

[28] The expression 'as on a wire' is likely an analogy to voices faintly heard through late nineteenth-century telephonic technology.

[29] A foss (or fosse) is a moat or similar type of defensive ditch dug around a fortification and often filled with water.

[30] Yew trees were sacred for many peoples in pagan Britain and Ireland, symbolizing death, reincarnation, and everlasting life. They were often planted — and are still today found — in churchyards.

seat; a crooked bough through which a little sap still ran was a support for the back, and he sat down and rested after his toil. It was not really so comfortable a seat as one of the school forms, but the satisfaction was to find anything at all that would serve for a chair. He sat there, still panting after the climb and his struggle through the dank and jungle-like thicket, and he felt as if he were growing hotter and hotter; the sting of the nettle was burning his hand, and the tingling fire seemed to spread all over his body.

Suddenly, he knew that he was alone. Not merely solitary; that he had often been amongst the woods and deep in the lanes; but now it was a wholly different and a very strange sensation. He thought of the valley winding far below him, all its fields by the brook green and peaceful and still, without path or track. Then he had climbed the abrupt surge of the hill, and passing the green and swelling battlements, the ring of oaks, and the matted thicket, had come to the central space. And behind there were, he knew, many desolate fields, wild as common, untrodden, unvisited. He was utterly alone. He still grew hotter as he sat on the stump, and at last lay down at full length on the soft grass, and more at his ease felt the waves of heat pass over his body.

And then he began to dream, to let his fancies stray over half-imagined, delicious things, indulging a virgin mind in its wanderings. The hot air seemed to beat upon him in palpable waves, and the nettle sting tingled and itched intolerably; and he was alone upon the fairy hill, within the great mounds, within the ring of oaks, deep in the heart of the matted thicket.[31] Slowly and timidly he began to untie his boots, fumbling with the laces, and glancing all the while on every side at the ugly misshapen trees that hedged the lawn. Not a branch was straight, not one was free, but all were interlaced and grew one about another; and just above ground, where the cankered stems joined the protuberant roots, there were forms that imitated the human shape, and faces and twining limbs that amazed him. Green mosses were hair, and tresses were stark in grey lichen; a twisted root swelled into a limb; in the hollows of the rotted bark he saw the masks of men. His eyes were fixed and fascinated by the simulacra of the wood, and could not see his hands, and so at last, and suddenly, it seemed, he lay in the sunlight, beautiful with his olive skin, dark haired, dark eyed, the gleaming bodily vision of a strayed faun.[32]

---

[31] In pagan Celtic mythology, fairies were often said to live in an otherworld located beneath hills, some of which were prehistoric burial mounds. In 1880, antiquarian W. N. Johns (dates unknown) argued that, because the remains of a Roman villa had been discovered beneath the base of the Caerleon mound, the mound itself was post-Roman, and built by locals in accord with pre-Roman traditions (W. N. Johns, *Historical Traditions and Facts Relating to Newport and Caerleon* (Newport: self-published, 1880), p. 81).

[32] A simulacrum (plural: simulacra) is an image or representation of something, often connoting an ideal or unreal resemblance. On fauns, see note 20 of *The Great God Pan*. The faun depicted here is distinctly more embodied and erotic then the phenomenon referenced in Machen's *Great God Pan*. At this moment in the narrative, Lucian appears to

Quick flames now quivered in the substance of his nerves, hints of mysteries, secrets of life passed trembling through his brain, unknown desires stung him. As he gazed across the turf and into the thicket, the sunshine seemed really to become green, and the contrast between the bright glow poured on the lawn and the black shadow of the brake made an odd flickering light, in which all the grotesque postures of stem and root began to stir; the wood was alive. The turf beneath him heaved and sank as with the deep swell of the sea. He fell asleep, and lay still on the grass, in the midst of the thicket.

He found out afterwards that he must have slept for nearly an hour. The shadows had changed when he awoke; his senses came to him with a sudden shock, and he sat up and stared at his bare limbs in stupid amazement. He huddled on his clothes and laced his boots, wondering what folly had beset him. Then, while he stood indecisive, hesitating, his brain a whirl of puzzled thought, his body trembling, his hands shaking; as with electric heat, sudden remembrance possessed him. A flaming blush shone red on his cheeks, and glowed and thrilled through his limbs. As he awoke, a brief and slight breeze had stirred in a nook of the matted boughs, and there was a glinting that might have been the flash of sudden sunlight across shadow, and the branches rustled and murmured for a moment, perhaps at the wind's passage.

He stretched out his hands, and cried to his visitant to return; he entreated the dark eyes that had shone over him, and the scarlet lips that had kissed him.[33] And then panic fear rushed into his heart, and he ran blindly, dashing through the wood. He climbed the *vallum*, and looked out, crouching, lest anybody should see him. Only the shadows were changed, and a breath of cooler air mounted from the brook; the fields were still and peaceful, the black figures moved, far away, amidst the corn, and the faint echo of the high-pitched voices sang thin and distant on the evening wind. Across the stream, in the cleft on the hill, opposite to the fort, the blue wood smoke stole up a spiral pillar from the chimney of old Mrs. Gibbon's cottage. He began to run full tilt down the steep surge of the hill, and never stopped till he was over the gate and in the lane again. As he looked back, down the valley to the south, and saw the violent ascent, the green swelling bulwarks, and the dark ring of oaks; the sunlight seemed to play about the fort with an aureole of flame.

---

envision himself, within the simulacra, as a faun. Three paragraphs later, however, Machen's reference to a dark-eyed 'visitant' constructs the faun as an entity separate from the hero. In classical manifestations, fauns, satyrs, and Pan all have the ability to seem nowhere and everywhere simultaneously — an ambiguous, often eerie presence in the natural landscape. Machen here appropriately has Lucian sense that 'the wood was alive'.

[33] The description brings to mind Laurence Housman's (1865–1959) drawing 'The Reflected Faun' (1894), in which a faun in a grove smells a flower while his simulacrum in a pond kisses an androgynous figure. The image appeared in the first volume of the *Yellow Book*, a Decadent periodical published by John Lane, who also published Machen's *The Great God Pan* and *The Inmost Light* as one book (1894) and *The Three Imposters* (1895).

'Where on earth have you been all this time, Lucian?' said his cousin when he got home. 'Why, you look quite ill. It is really madness of you to go walking in such weather as this. I wonder you haven't got a sunstroke. And the tea must be nearly cold. I couldn't keep your father waiting, you know.'

He muttered something about being rather tired, and sat down to his tea. It was not cold, for the 'cosy' had been put over the pot, but it was black and bitter strong, as his cousin expressed it. The draught was unpalatable, but it did him good, and the thought came with great consolation that he had only been asleep and dreaming queer, nightmarish dreams. He shook off all his fancies with resolution, and thought the loneliness of the camp, and the burning sunlight, and possibly the nettle sting, which still tingled most abominably, must have been the only factors in his farrago of impossible recollections. He remembered that when he had felt the sting, he had seized a nettle with thick folds of his handkerchief, and having twisted off a good length, had put it in his pocket to show his father. Mr. Taylor was almost interested when he came in from his evening stroll about the garden and saw the specimen.

'Where did you manage to come across that, Lucian?' he said. 'You haven't been to Caermaen, have you?'[34]

'No. I got it in the Roman fort by the common.'

'Oh, the twyn.[35] You must have been trespassing then. Do you know what it is?'

'No. I thought it looked different from the common nettles.'

'Yes; it's a Roman nettle — *urtica pilulifera*. It's a rare plant. Burrows says it's to be found at Caermaen, but I was never able to come across it. I must add it to the *flora* of the parish.'

Mr. Taylor had begun to compile a *flora* accompanied by a *hortus siccus*, but both stayed on high shelves dusty and fragmentary.[36] He put the specimen on his desk, intending to fasten it in the book, but the maid swept it away, dry and withered, in a day or two.

Lucian tossed and cried out in his sleep that night, and the awakening in the morning was, in a measure, a renewal of the awakening in the fort. But the impression was not so strong, and in a plain room it seemed all delirium, a phantasmagoria.[37] He had to go down to Caermaen in the afternoon, for

---

[34] Caermaen is not an actual place, but the name and some of the descriptions evoke Machen's birthplace, Caerleon. Caermaen also appears in *The Great God Pan*.

[35] Lucian's father uses the Welsh word for 'hill' or 'knoll'.

[36] A *flora* is a collection that systematically describes plants found in a particular area, while a *hortus siccus* is a collection of dried plants. Mr Taylor is, evidently, one of the many amateur botanists that proliferated across Britain during the Victorian period.

[37] On 'phantasmagoria', see note 3 of *The Great God Pan*. Machen uses the motif of the phantasmagoria throughout *The Hill of Dreams* to address both the false façade of London society and Lucian's psychological state.

Mrs. Dixon, the vicar's wife, had 'commanded' his presence at tea. Mr. Dixon, though fat and short and clean shaven, ruddy of face, was a safe man, with no extreme views on anything. He 'deplored' all extreme party convictions, and thought the great needs of our beloved Church were conciliation, moderation, and above all 'amolgamation' — so he pronounced the word.[38] Mrs. Dixon was tall, imposing, splendid, well fitted for the episcopal order, with gifts that would have shone at the palace. There were daughters, who studied German Literature, and thought Miss Frances Ridley Havergal wrote poetry, but Lucian had no fear of them; he dreaded the boys.[39] Everybody said they were such fine, manly fellows, such gentlemanly boys, with such a good manner, sure to get on in the world. Lucian had said 'Bother!' in a very violent manner when the gracious invitation was conveyed to him, but there was no getting out of it. Miss Deacon did her best to make him look smart; his ties were all so disgraceful that she had to supply the want with a narrow ribbon of a sky-blue tint; and she brushed him so long and so violently that he quite understood why a horse sometimes bites and sometimes kicks the groom. He set out between two and three in a gloomy frame of mind; he knew too well what spending the afternoon with honest manly boys meant. He found the reality more lurid than his anticipation. The boys were in the field, and the first remark he heard when he got in sight of the group was:

'Hullo, Lucian, how much for the tie?' 'Fine tie,' another, a stranger, observed. 'You bagged it from the kitten, didn't you?'

Then they made up a game of cricket, and he was put in first. He was l.b.w. in his second over, so they all said, and had to field for the rest of the afternoon.[40] Arthur Dixon, who was about his own age, forgetting all the laws of hospitality, told him he was a beastly muff when he missed a catch, rather a difficult catch. He missed several catches, and it seemed as if he were always panting after balls, which, as Edward Dixon said, any fool, even a baby, could have stopped. At last the game broke up, solely from Lucian's lack of skill, as everybody declared. Edward Dixon, who was thirteen, and had a swollen red face and a

---

[38] The 'beloved Church' refers to the Church of England (also called the Anglican Church), a Protestant Christian denomination governed according to an episcopal model (i.e. by bishops). In the eighteenth and nineteenth centuries, the Church of England splintered into various theological directions (e.g. High Church, Low Church). Like Mr Dixon, however, many people sought to restore unity amongst the various factions and members.

[39] Frances Ridley Havergal (1836–1879) did write religious poetry, but was best known for her hymns. Machen, through the narrator, is being sarcastic, implying that the daughters have so little feeling for real poetry that they put Ridley's work in this category.

[40] In cricket, a batsman is disqualified if the person is 'leg before wicket' — that is, if an umpire decides that a batsman's body or padding have gotten in the way of a ball that would otherwise have hit the wicket. An over is a set number of balls bowled to a batsman. A cricket match is divided into two innings; during each innings, one team bats and one team fields.

projecting eye, wanted to fight him for spoiling the game, and the others agreed that he funked the fight in a rather dirty manner. The strange boy, who was called De Carti, and was understood to be distantly related to Lord De Carti of M'Carthytown, said openly that the fellows at his place wouldn't stand such a sneak for five minutes. So the afternoon passed off very pleasantly indeed, till it was time to go into the vicarage for weak tea, home-made cake, and unripe plums. He got away at last. As he went out at the gate he heard De Carti's final observation:

'We like to dress well at our place. His governor must be beastly poor to let him go about like that. D'y' see his trousers are all ragged at heel? Is old Taylor a gentleman?'

It had been a very gentlemanly afternoon, but there was a certain relief when the vicarage was far behind, and the evening smoke of the little town, once the glorious capital of Siluria, hung haze-like over the ragged roofs and mingled with the river mist.[41] He looked down from the height of the road on the huddled houses, saw the points of light start out suddenly from the cottages on the hillside beyond, and gazed at the long lovely valley fading in the twilight, till the darkness came and all that remained was the somber ridge of the forest. The way was pleasant through the solemn scented lane, with glimpses of dim country, the vague mystery of night overshadowing the woods and meadows. A warm wind blew gusts of odour from the meadowsweet by the brook, now and then bee and beetle span homeward through the air, booming a deep note as from a great organ far away, and from the verge of the wood came the 'who-oo, who-oo, who-oo' of the owls, a wild strange sound that mingled with the whirr and rattle of the night-jar, deep in the bracken. The moon swam up through the films of misty cloud, and hung, a golden glorious lantern, in mid-air; and, set in the dusky hedge, the little green fires of the glowworms appeared. He sauntered slowly up the lane, drinking in the religion of the scene, and thinking the country by night as mystic and wonderful as a dimly-lit cathedral. He had quite forgotten the 'manly young fellows' and their sports, and only wished as the land began to shimmer and gleam in the moonlight that he knew by some medium of words or colour how to represent the loveliness about his way.

'Had a pleasant evening, Lucian?' said his father when he came in.

'Yes, I had a nice walk home. Oh, in the afternoon we played cricket. I didn't care for it much. There was a boy named De Carti there; he is staying with the Dixons. Mrs. Dixon whispered to me when we were going into tea, "He's a second cousin of Lord De Carti's," and she looked quite grave as if she were in church.'

---

[41] Silurum is the country of the Silures, the ancient Britons who lived in south-east Wales at the time of the Roman conquest. Isca, or Isca Silurum, was the Roman name for Caerleon, Machen's hometown (on Isca, see note 8 to *The Hill of Dreams*).

The parson grinned grimly and lit his old pipe.

'Baron De Carti's great-grandfather was a Dublin attorney,' he remarked. 'Which his name was Jeremiah M'Carthy.[42] His prejudiced fellow-citizens called him the Unjust Steward, also the Bloody Attorney, and I believe that "to hell with M'Carthy" was quite a popular cry about the time of the Union.'[43]

Mr. Taylor was a man of very wide and irregular reading and a tenacious memory; he often used to wonder why he had not risen in the Church. He had once told Mr. Dixon a singular and *drolatique* anecdote concerning the bishop's college days,[44] and he never discovered why the prelate did not bow according to his custom when the name of Taylor was called at the next visitation. Some people said the reason was lighted candles, but that was impossible, as the Reverend and Honourable Smallwood Stafford, Lord Beamys's son, who had a cure of souls in the cathedral city, was well known to burn no end of candles, and with him the bishop was on the best of terms.[45] Indeed the bishop often stayed at Coplesey (pronounced 'Copsey') Hall, Lord Beamys's place in the west.

Lucian had mentioned the name of De Carti with intention, and had perhaps exaggerated a little Mrs. Dixon's respectful manner. He knew such incidents cheered his father, who could never look at these subjects from a proper point of view, and, as people said, sometimes made the strangest remarks for a clergyman. This irreverent way of treating serious things was one of the great bonds between father and son, but it tended to increase their isolation. People said they would often have liked to ask Mr. Taylor to garden-parties, and tea-parties, and other cheap entertainments, if only he had not been such an *extreme* man and so *queer*. Indeed, a year before, Mr. Taylor had gone to a garden-party at the Castle, Caermaen, and had made such fun of the bishop's recent address on missions to the Portuguese, that the Gervases and Dixons and all who heard him were quite shocked and annoyed. And, as Mrs. Meyrick of Lanyravon observed, his black coat was perfectly *green* with age; so on the whole the Gervases did not like to invite Mr. Taylor again.[46] As for the son,

---

[42] Machen is here likely mocking the pretensions of newly elevated Irish peers. 'De Carti' is a spurious Normanization of the common Irish surname 'M'Carthy' (or 'McCarthy'), meant to sound ancient and noble.

[43] An 'unjust steward' appears in the Bible (Luke 16. 1–13). The Act of Union came into effect on 1 January 1801. It brought Ireland into union with Great Britain, thus creating the United Kingdom of Great Britain and Ireland.

[44] *drolatique* (French): humorous.

[45] For some Anglicans who leaned towards Low Church views, lighting candles during religious services and for private prayer seemed unpleasantly akin to what they regarded as superstitious Roman Catholic practices. To have a 'cure of souls' is to have spiritual oversight over the people of a certain district or parish. 'Cure' is from the Latin 'cura', meaning 'care'.

[46] Lanyravon (the old anglicized spelling for Llanyrafon) is a community in south-east Wales.

nobody cared to have him; Mrs. Dixon, as she said to her husband, really asked him out of charity.

'I am afraid he seldom gets a real meal at home,' she remarked, 'so I thought he would enjoy a good wholesome tea for once in a way. But he is such an *unsatisfactory* boy, he would only have one slice of that nice plain cake, and I couldn't get him to take more than two plums. They were really quite ripe too, and boys are usually so fond of fruit.'

Thus Lucian was forced to spend his holidays chiefly in his own company, and make the best he could of the ripe peaches on the south wall of the rectory garden. There was a certain corner where the heat of that hot August seemed concentrated, reverberated from one wall to the other, and here he liked to linger of mornings, when the mists were still thick in the valleys, 'mooning,' meditating, extending his walk from the quince to the medlar and back again, beside the mouldering walls of mellowed brick.[47] He was full of a certain wonder and awe, not unmixed with a swell of strange exultation, and wished more and more to be alone, to think over that wonderful afternoon within the fort. In spite of himself the impression was fading; he could not understand that feeling of mad panic terror that drove him through the thicket and down the steep hillside; yet, he had experienced so clearly the physical shame and reluctance of the flesh; he recollected that for a few seconds after his awakening the sight of his own body had made him shudder and writhe as if it had suffered some profoundest degradation. He saw before him a vision of two forms; a faun with tingling and pricking flesh lay expectant in the sunlight, and there was also the likeness of a miserable shamed boy, standing with trembling body and shaking, unsteady hands. It was all confused, a procession of blurred images, now of rapture and ecstasy, and now of terror and shame, floating in a light that was altogether phantasmal and unreal. He dared not approach the fort again; he lingered in the road to Caermaen that passed behind it, but a mile away, and separated by the wild land and a strip of wood from the towering battlements. Here he was looking over a gate one day, doubtful and wondering, when he heard a heavy step behind him, and glancing round quickly saw it was old Morgan of the White House.

'Good afternoon, Master Lucian,' he began. 'Mr. Taylor pretty well, I suppose? I be goin' to the house a minute; the men in the fields are wantin' some more cider. Would you come and taste a drop of cider, Master Lucian? It's very good, sir, indeed.'

Lucian did not want any cider, but he thought it would please old Morgan if he took some, so he said he should like to taste the cider very much indeed. Morgan was a sturdy, thick-set old man of the ancient stock; a stiff churchman,

---

[47] Both quince and medlar are small trees that belong to the *malaceous* (apple) family. Medlar fruit is edible only once it has begun to decay.

who breakfasted regularly on fat broth and Caerphilly cheese in the fashion of
his ancestors; hot, spiced elder wine was for winter nights, and gin for festal
seasons.[48] The farm had always been the freehold of the family, and when
Lucian, in the wake of the yeoman, passed through the deep porch by the
oaken door, down into the long dark kitchen, he felt as though the seventeenth
century still lingered on.[49] One mullioned window, set deep in the sloping wall,
gave all the light there was through quarries of thick glass in which there were
whorls and circles, so that the lapping rose-branch and the garden and the fields
beyond were distorted to the sight. Two heavy beams, oaken but whitewashed,
ran across the ceiling; a little glow of fire sparkled in the great fireplace, and
a curl of blue smoke fled up the cavern of the chimney. Here was the genuine
chimney-corner of our fathers; there were seats on each side of the fireplace
where one could sit snug and sheltered on December nights, warm and merry
in the blazing light, and listen to the battle of the storm, and hear the flame spit
and hiss at the falling snowflakes. At the back of the fire were great blackened
tiles with raised initials and a date — I. M., 1684.[50]

'Sit down, Master Lucian, sit down, sir,' said Morgan.

'Annie,' he called through one of the numerous doors, 'here's Master Lucian,
the parson, would like a drop of cider. Fetch a jug, will you, directly?'

'Very well, father,' came the voice from the dairy, and presently the girl
entered, wiping the jug she held. In his boyish way Lucian had been a good
deal disturbed by Annie Morgan; he could see her on Sundays from his seat in
church, and her skin, curiously pale, her lips that seemed as though they were
stained with some brilliant pigment, her black hair, and the quivering black
eyes, gave him odd fancies which he had hardly shaped to himself. Annie had
grown into a woman in three years, and he was still a boy. She came into the
kitchen, curtsying and smiling.

'Good-day, Master Lucian, and how is Mr. Taylor, sir?'

'Pretty well, thank you. I hope you are well.'

'Nicely, sir, thank you. How nice your voice do sound in church, Master
Lucian, to be sure. I was telling father about it last Sunday.'

Lucian grinned and felt uncomfortable, and the girl set down the jug on the
round table and brought a glass from the dresser. She bent close over him as
she poured out the green oily cider, fragrant of the orchard; her hand touched

---

[48] As a 'stiff churchman', old Morgan is a conservative-leaning supporter of the Church of
England. Caerphilly is a hard, white cheese made in the Welsh town of the same name.

[49] As a freehold property, Morgan's farm had been owned by his family and passed down
through inheritance for several generations. A yeoman is a farmer who works his own land
by raising crops and/or livestock on it.

[50] Likely the initials of Morgan's ancestor who constructed the dwelling in 1684, which
accords with Lucian's sense that he was stepping back into the seventeenth century. The
upper-case 'I' is perhaps a Latinization of the letter 'J'.

his shoulder for a moment, and she said, 'I beg your pardon, sir,' very prettily. He looked up eagerly at her face; the black eyes, a little oval in shape, were shining, and the lips smiled. Annie wore a plain dress of some black stuff, open at the throat; her skin was beautiful. For a moment the ghost of a fancy hovered unsubstantial in his mind; and then Annie curtsied as she handed him the cider, and replied to his thanks with, 'And welcome kindly, sir.'

The drink was really good; not thin, nor sweet, but round and full and generous, with a fine yellow flame twinkling through the green when one held it up to the light. It was like a stray sunbeam hovering on the grass in a deep orchard, and he swallowed the glassful with relish, and had some more, warmly commending it. Mr. Morgan was touched.

'I see you do know a good thing, sir,' he said. 'Iss, indeed, now, it's good stuff, though it's my own makin'. My old grandfather he planted the trees in the time of the wars, and he was a very good judge of an apple in his day and generation.[51] And a famous grafter he was, to be sure.[52] You will never see no swelling in the trees he grafted at all whatever. Now there's James Morris, Penyrhaul, he's a famous grafter, too, and yet them Redstreaks he grafted for me five year ago, they be all swollen-like below the graft already.[53] Would you like to taste a Blemmin pippin, now, Master Lucian?[54] there be a few left in the loft, I believe.'

Lucian said he should like an apple very much, and the farmer went out by another door, and Annie stayed in the kitchen talking. She said Mrs. Trevor, her married sister, was coming to them soon to spend a few days.

'She's got such a beautiful baby,' said Annie, 'and he's quite sensible-like already, though he's only nine months old. Mary would like to see you, sir, if you would be so kind as to step in; that is, if it's not troubling you at all, Master Lucian. I suppose you must be getting a fine scholar now, sir?'

'I am doing pretty well, thank you,' said the boy. 'I was first in my form last term.'

'Fancy! To think of that! D'you hear, father, what a scholar Master Lucian be getting?'

'He be a rare grammarian, I'm sure,' said the farmer. 'You do take after your father, sir; I always do say that nobody have got such a good deliverance in the pilpit.'

---

[51] Morgan's grandfather would most likely have served in the British Army during the Napoleonic Wars (1796–1815).

[52] A grafter is one who splices a piece of one plant (the scion) into another (the stock), such that the two plants continue to grow. Grafting is usually done to reproduce an original cultivar, to ward off diseases, or to generate a new hybrid variety.

[53] Penyrhaul, today known as Penyrheol, is a suburb of Swansea in south-west Wales.

[54] Redstreaks and Blenheim Orange pippins (Morgan's accent leads him to say 'Blemmin') are old varieties of British apples.

Lucian did not find the Blenheim Orange as good as the cider, but he ate it with all the appearance of relish, and put another, with thanks, into his pocket. He thanked the farmer again when he got up to go; and Annie curtsied and smiled, and wished him good-day, and welcome, kindly.

Lucian heard her saying to her father as he went out what a nice-mannered young gentleman he was getting, to be sure; and he went on his way, thinking that Annie was really very pretty, and speculating as to whether he would have the courage to kiss her, if they met in a dark lane. He was quite sure she would only laugh, and say, 'Oh, Master Lucian!'

For many months he had occasional fits of recollection, both cold and hot; but the bridge of time, gradually lengthening, made those dreadful and delicious images grow more and more indistinct, till at last they all passed into that wonderland which a youth looks back upon in amazement, not knowing why this used to be a symbol of terror or that of joy. At the end of each term he would come home and find his father a little more despondent, and harder to cheer even for a moment; and the wall paper and the furniture grew more and more dingy and shabby. The two cats, loved and ancient beasts, that he remembered when he was quite a little boy, before he went to school, died miserably, one after the other. Old Polly, the pony, at last fell down in the stable from the weakness of old age, and had to be killed there; the battered old trap ran no longer along the well-remembered lanes. There was long meadow grass on the lawn, and the trained fruit trees on the wall had got quite out of hand. At last, when Lucian was seventeen, his father was obliged to take him from school; he could no longer afford the fees.[55] This was the sorry ending of many hopes, and dreams of a double-first, a fellowship, distinction and glory that the poor parson had long entertained for his son, and the two moped together, in the shabby room, one on each side of the sulky fire, thinking of dead days and finished plans, and seeing a grey future in the years that advanced towards them. At one time there seemed some chance of a distant relative coming forward to Lucian's assistance; and indeed it was quite settled that he should go up to London with certain definite aims. Mr. Taylor told the good news to his acquaintances — his coat was too green now for any pretence of friendship; and Lucian himself spoke of his plans to Burrows the doctor and Mr. Dixon, and one or two others.[56] Then the whole scheme fell through, and the parson and his son suffered much sympathy. People, of course, had to say they were sorry, but in reality the news was received with high spirits, with the joy with which one sees a stone, as it rolls down a steep place, give yet another bounding

---

[55] Machen's own family could not afford to send him to university, and he failed the examination for the Royal College of Surgeons, which would have allowed him to go into medicine.

[56] The greenness of his coat suggests excess wear or a patina of age, such as the verdigris that forms on copper or brass through long exposure to the elements.

leap towards the pool beneath. Mrs. Dixon heard the pleasant tidings from Mrs. Colley, who came in to talk about the Mothers' Meeting and the Band of Hope.[57] Mrs. Dixon was nursing little Æthelwig, or some such name, at the time, and made many affecting observations on the general righteousness with which the world was governed.[58] Indeed, poor Lucian's disappointment seemed distinctly to increase her faith in the Divine Order, as if it had been some example in Butler's *Analogy*.[59]

'Aren't Mr. Taylor's views very *extreme*?' she said to her husband the same evening.

'I am afraid they are,' he replied. 'I was quite *grieved* at the last Diocesan Conference at the way in which he spoke.[60] The dear old bishop had given an address on Auricular Confession; he was *forced* to do so, you know, after what had happened, and I must say that I never felt prouder of our beloved Church.'[61]

Mr. Dixon told all the Homeric story of the conference, reciting the achievements of the champions, 'deploring' this and applauding that.[62] It seemed that Mr. Taylor had had the audacity to quote authorities which the bishop could not very well repudiate, though they were directly opposed to the 'safe' episcopal pronouncement.[63]

Mrs. Dixon of course was grieved; it was 'sad' to think of a clergyman behaving so shamefully.

'But you know, dear,' she proceeded, 'I have been thinking about that

---

[57] In the nineteenth century, women who belonged to a parish or a specific congregation would sometimes get together in a Mothers' Meeting for fellowship and to share advice. The Band of Hope was a temperance organization that sought to steer children away from the perceived dangers of alcohol.

[58] The best-known Athelwig in English history was the Abbot of Evesham (*c.* 1013/16–1077/78 CE). Machen is poking fun at the Dixons' pretensions of bestowing an ancient Anglo-Saxon name on their baby.

[59] Joseph Butler (1692–1752) was a theologian and Anglican clergyman (eventually becoming the Bishop of Durham), author of the *Analogy of Religion Natural and Revealed to the Constitution and Course of Nature* (1736). This highly influential book shaped the discussion of Christian morality well into the nineteenth century; however, as Mrs Dixon's response to Lucian reveals, its arguments were certainly not accepted by all members of the Church of England.

[60] A diocesan conference is a gathering of the Anglican clergy and lay representatives of a particular diocese (an area under a bishop's jurisdiction) to plan, debate, and conduct diocese-related business.

[61] As opposed to an internal confession to one's self or God, an auricular confession is a confession of one's sins made privately to a priest. Auricular confessions were regarded by some in the Church of England as suspiciously Roman Catholic.

[62] In a humorous send-up of Mr Dixon's inflated pretensions, Machen is likening the conference to an epic such as the ancient Greek poet Homer's (before 700 BCE) *Iliad* and *Odyssey*.

[63] Mr Dixon is referring to the views espoused by the 'dear old bishop' mentioned earlier — the man who oversaw the conference. Mr Taylor, a clergyman in the diocese, is at odds with the bishop on some matter of church doctrine (possibly having to do with confession).

unfortunate Taylor boy and his disappointments, and after what you've just told me, I am sure it's some kind of judgment on them both. Has Mr. Taylor forgotten the vows he took at his ordination? But don't you think, dear, I am right, and that he has been punished: "the sins of the fathers"?'[64]

Somehow or other Lucian divined this atmosphere of threatenings and judgments, and shrank more and more from the small society of the countryside. For his part, when he was not 'mooning' in the beloved fields and woods of happy memory, he shut himself up with books, reading whatever could be found on the shelves, and amassing a store of incongruous and obsolete knowledge. Long did he linger with the men of the seventeenth century; delaying the gay sunlit streets with Pepys, and listening to the charmed sound of the Restoration Revel; roaming by peaceful streams with Izaak Walton, and the great Catholic divines; enchanted with the portrait of Herbert the loving ascetic; awed by the mystic breath of Crashaw. Then the cavalier poets sang their gallant songs; and Herrick made Dean Prior magic ground by the holy incantation of a verse.[65] And in the old proverbs and homely sayings of the time he found the good and beautiful English life, a time full of grace and dignity and rich merriment. He dived deeper and deeper into his books; he had taken all obsolescence to be his province; in his disgust at the stupid usual questions, 'Will it pay?' 'What good is it?' and so forth, he would only read what was uncouth and useless. The strange pomp and symbolism of the Cabala, with its hint of more terrible things; the Rosicrucian mysteries of Fludd, the enigmas of Vaughan, dreams of

---

[64] The Bible cautions several times that God will punish the children (to the third and fourth generation) of fathers who have sinned (e.g. Exodus 20. 5; Numbers 14. 18; Deuteronomy 5. 9). While Mrs Dixon's use of the word 'sins' is quite common, the King James Bible — the standard version of the Bible for nineteenth-century Anglicans — uses, instead, the noun 'iniquity'.

[65] Giving a sense of Lucian's intellectual and spiritual distance from his own time, Machen has clustered together here a number of seventeenth-century literary and religious references: Samuel Pepys (1633–1703), an English diarist and public official, whose diary (deciphered and published in the nineteenth century) presents an intimate portrait of daily life in mid-seventeenth-century London; the Restoration, which marked the return — in the person of King Charles II — of monarchical government to England in 1660, and was a period of great social and aesthetic 'revel'; Izaak Walton (1593–1683), whose book *The Compleat Angler* portrays peaceful countryside life; who exactly Machen means by 'the great Catholic divines' is unclear, but likely includes men who wrote about nature as a reflection of God, such as St Bernard of Clairvaux (1090–1153), St Bonaventure (1221–1274), and St Francis of Assisi (1182?–1226); George Herbert (1593–1633), an Anglican priest and religious poet, and a member of a noble Welsh family (Walton wrote a biography of him); Richard Crashaw (1612?–1649), an English poet noted for his fusion of sensuality and Roman Catholic mysticism; and Robert Herrick (1591–1694), an English poet noted for his lyrical poems praising simple country delights, who was also an Anglican priest in the parish of Dean Prior, Devonshire.

alchemists — all these were his delight.[66] Such were his companions, with the hills and hanging woods, the brooks and lonely waterpools; books, the thoughts of books, the stirrings of imagination, all fused into one phantasy by the magic of the outland country.[67] He held himself aloof from the walls of the fort; he was content to see the heaped mounds, the violent height with faery bulwarks, from the gate in the lane, and to leave all within the ring of oaks in the mystery of his boyhood's vision.[68] He professed to laugh at himself and at his fancies of that hot August afternoon, when sleep came to him within the thicket, but in his heart of hearts there was something that never faded — something that glowed like the red glint of a gypsy's fire seen from afar across the hills and mists of the night, and known to be burning in a wild land. Sometimes, when he was sunken in his books, the flame of delight shot up, and showed him a whole province and continent of his nature, all shining and aglow; and in the midst of the exultation and triumph he would draw back, a little afraid. He had become ascetic in his studious and melancholy isolation, and the vision of such ecstasies frightened him. He began to write a little; at first very tentatively and feebly, and then with more confidence. He showed some of his verses to his father, who told him with a sigh that he had once hoped to write — in the old days at Oxford, he added.

'They are very nicely done,' said the parson; 'but I'm afraid you won't find anybody to print them, my boy.'

So he pottered on; reading everything, imitating what struck his fancy, attempting the effect of the classic metres in English verse, trying his hand at a masque, a Restoration comedy, forming impossible plans for books which rarely got beyond half a dozen lines on a sheet of paper; beset with splendid fancies

---

[66] In this sentence, Machen is clustering together various non-Christian mystical elements. The Kabbalah (less commonly spelt Cabala) is an esoteric Jewish system of thought that, proponents claimed, enabled them to foretell the future and know the truth of holy scriptures. Rosicrucian mysteries are forms of occult knowledge held by members of the secret Rosicrucian society. Robert Fludd (1574–1637) was a well-known early modern English Rosicrucian who espoused a mystical pantheism. Vaughan is either Thomas Vaughan, a Welsh physician and alchemist, or, less likely, his twin brother Henry, a Welsh physician and poet, many of whose religious verses contain a mystical dimension. Alchemists engaged in the ancient and secretive practice — most common during the Middle Ages and early modern period — of using magic and chemistry either to transmute base elements into other matter (such as lead into gold) and/or to discover the elixir or meaning of life. Machen discusses alchemy in 'The Literature of Occultism' (1899), included in this edition.

[67] Machen's association of magic and wild nature ('the outland country') is notable because teaching in natural magic was a standard element of Victorian occult societies, such as the highly influential Hermetic Order of the Golden Dawn, founded in 1888.

[68] In the nineteenth century, spelling 'fairy' as 'faerie' (a common early modern form of the word) gave to the concept an extra patina of age and mystery. Bulwarks are the defensive earthen ramparts Machen earlier refers to as the fort's *vallum*.

which refused to abide before the pen.[69] But the vain joy of conception was not altogether vain, for it gave him some armour about his heart.

The months went by, monotonous, and sometimes blotted with despair. He wrote and planned and filled the waste-paper basket with hopeless efforts. Now and then he sent verses or prose articles to magazines, in pathetic ignorance of the trade. He felt the immense difficulty of the career of literature without clearly understanding it; the battle was happily in a mist, so that the host of the enemy, terribly arrayed, was to some extent hidden. Yet there was enough of difficulty to appal; from following the intricate course of little nameless brooks, from hushed twilight woods, from the vision of the mountains, and the breath of the great wind, passing from deep to deep, he would come home filled with thoughts and emotions, mystic fancies which he yearned to translate into the written word. And the result of the effort seemed always to be bathos![70] Wooden sentences, a portentous stilted style, obscurity, and awkwardness clogged the pen; it seemed impossible to win the great secret of language; the stars glittered only in the darkness, and vanished away in clearer light. The periods of despair were often long and heavy, the victories very few and trifling; night after night he sat writing after his father had knocked out his last pipe, filling a page with difficulty in an hour, and usually forced to thrust the stuff away in despair, and go unhappily to bed, conscious that after all his labour he had done nothing. And these were moments when the accustomed vision of the land alarmed him, and the wild domed hills and darkling woods seemed symbols of some terrible secret in the inner life of that stranger — himself. Sometimes when he was deep in his books and papers, sometimes on a lonely walk, sometimes amidst the tiresome chatter of Caermaen 'society,' he would thrill with a sudden sense of awful hidden things, and there ran that quivering flame through his nerves that brought back the recollection of the matted thicket, and that earlier appearance of the bare black boughs enwrapped with flames. Indeed, though he avoided the solitary lane, and the sight of the sheer height, with its ring of oaks and moulded mounds, the image of it grew more intense as the symbol of certain hints and suggestions. The exultant and insurgent flesh seemed to have its

---

[69] Classic (or classical) metres are the complex metrical patterns developed by the Greeks and adapted by the Romans, based on the number of syllables in a line. A masque is a type of drama popular in England — especially amongst the aristocracy — during the early seventeenth century. Masques featured music, dance, ornate poetry, and mythological and pastoral characters. A Restoration comedy is a comic play written in England from 1660 (when the English monarchy was restored after the republican Commonwealth) to about 1710. In reaction to the dour, anti-theatrical ethos of the Commonwealth, Restoration authors such as Sir George Etherege (1634?–1691) and William Congreve (1670–1729) wrote plays characterized by verbal wit and socio-erotic licentiousness, generally referred to as comedies of manners.

[70] An anticlimactic, often ludicrous plunge from lofty ideals and pretensions into mere triteness.

temple and castle within those olden walls, and he longed with all his heart to escape, to set himself free in the wilderness of London, and to be secure amidst the murmur of modern streets.

II

Lucian was growing really anxious about his manuscript. He had gained enough experience at twenty-three to know that editors and publishers must not be hurried; but his book had been lying at Messrs. Beit's office for more than three months. For six weeks he had not dared to expect an answer, but afterwards life had become agonising. Every morning, at post-time, the poor wretch nearly choked with anxiety to know whether his sentence had arrived, and the rest of the day was racked with alternate pangs of hope and despair. Now and then he was almost assured of success; conning over these painful and eager pages in memory, he found parts that were admirable, while again, his inexperience reproached him, and he feared he had written a raw and awkward book, wholly unfit for print.[71] Then he would compare what he remembered of it with notable magazine articles and books praised by reviewers, and fancy that after all there might be good points in the thing; he could not help liking the first chapter for instance. Perhaps the letter might come tomorrow. So it went on; week after week of sick torture made more exquisite by such gleams of hope; it was as if he were stretched in anguish on the rack, and the pain relaxed and kind words spoken now and again by the tormentors, and then once more the grinding pang and burning agony. At last he could bear suspense no longer, and he wrote to Messrs. Beit, inquiring in a humble manner whether the manuscript had arrived in safety. The firm replied in a very polite letter, expressing regret that their reader had been suffering from a cold in the head, and had therefore been unable to send in his report. A final decision was promised in a week's time, and the letter ended with apologies for the delay and a hope that he had suffered no inconvenience. Of course the 'final decision' did not come at the end of the week, but the book was returned at the end of three weeks, with a circular thanking the author for his kindness in submitting the manuscript, and regretting that the firm did not see their way to producing it. He felt relieved; the operation that he had dreaded and deprecated for so long was at last over, and he would no longer grow sick of mornings when the letters were brought in. He took his parcel to the sunny corner of the garden, where the old wooden seat stood sheltered from the biting March winds. Messrs. Beit had put in with the circular one of their short lists, a neat booklet, headed: *Messrs. Beit & Co.'s Recent Publications.*

He settled himself comfortably on the seat, lit his pipe, and began to read:

---

[71] To 'con over' is to carefully examine.

'*A Bad Un to Beat*: a Novel of Sporting Life, by the Honourable Mrs. Scudamore Runnymede, author of *Yoicks, With the Mudshire Pack, The Sportleigh Stables*, etc., etc., 3 vols. At all Libraries.' The *Press*, it seemed, pronounced this to be 'a charming book'. Mrs. Runnymede has wit and humour enough to furnish forth half-a-dozen ordinary sporting novels.' 'Told with the sparkle and vivacity of a past-mistress in the art of novel writing,' said the *Review*; while Miranda, of *Smart Society*, positively bubbled with enthusiasm. 'You must forgive me, Aminta,' wrote this young person, 'if I have not sent the description I promised of Madame Lulu's new creations and others of that ilk. I must a tale unfold; Tom came in yesterday and began to rave about the Honourable Mrs. Scudamore Runnymede's last novel, *A Bad Un to Beat*. He says all the Smart Set are talking of it, and it seems the police have to regulate the crowd at Mudie's.[72] You know I read everything Mrs. Runnymede writes, so I set out Miggs directly to beg, borrow or steal a copy, and I confess I burnt the midnight oil before I laid it down. Now, mind you get it, you will find it so awfully *chic*.' Nearly all the novelists on Messrs. Beit's list were ladies, their works all ran to three volumes, and all of them pleased the *Press*, the *Review*, and Miranda of *Smart Society*. One of these books, *Millicent's Marriage*, by Sarah Pocklington Sanders, was pronounced fit to lie on the schoolroom table, on the drawing-room bookshelf, or beneath the pillow of the most gently nurtured of our daughters. 'This,' the reviewer went on, 'is high praise, especially in these days when we are deafened by the loud-voiced clamour of self-styled "artists." We would warn the young men who prate so persistently of style and literature, construction and prose harmonies, that we believe the English reading public will have none of them. Harmless amusement, a gentle flow of domestic interest, a faithful reproduction of the open and manly life of the hunting field, pictures of innocent and healthy English girlhood such as Miss Sanders here affords us; these are the topics that will always find a welcome in our homes, which remain bolted and barred against the abandoned artist and the scrofulous stylist.'

He turned over the pages of the little book and chuckled in high relish; he discovered an honest enthusiasm, a determination to strike a blow for the good and true that refreshed and exhilarated. A beaming face, spectacled and whiskered probably, an expansive waistcoat, and a tender heart, seemed to shine through the words which Messrs. Beit had quoted; and the alliteration of the final sentence; that was good too; there was style for you if you wanted

---

[72] Started in London in 1842 by Charles Edward Mudie (1818–1890), Mudie's was a popular lending library that charged a small amount for the loan of books. Because of its market share, Mudie's had a deep effect on the morality and structure of the popular novel. He and other lenders favoured novels that appealed to middle-class propriety, especially when offered as three-volume publications (or triple-deckers), with each volume being loaned separately. The popularity of this format — which Machen disparages in the next paragraph — had waned considerably by the mid-1890s.

it. The champion of the blushing cheek and the gushing eye showed that he too could handle the weapons of the enemy if he cared to trouble himself with such things. Lucian leant back and roared with indecent laughter till the tabby tom-cat who had succeeded to the poor dead beasts looked up reproachfully from his sunny corner, with a face like the reviewer's, innocent and round and whiskered. At last he turned to his parcel and drew out some half-dozen sheets of manuscript, and began to read in a rather desponding spirit; it was pretty obvious, he thought, that the stuff was poor and beneath the standard of publication. The book had taken a year and a half in the making; it was a pious attempt to translate into English prose the form and mystery of the domed hills, the magic of occult valleys, the sound of the red swollen brook swirling through leafless woods. Day-dreams and toil at nights had gone into the eager pages, he had laboured hard to do his very best, writing and rewriting, weighing his cadences, beginning over and over again, grudging no patience, no trouble if only it might be pretty good; good enough to print and sell to a reading public which had become critical. He glanced through the manuscript in his hand, and to his astonishment, he could not help thinking that in its measure it was decent work. After three months his prose seemed fresh and strange as if it had been wrought by another man, and in spite of himself he found charming things, and impressions that were not commonplace. He knew how weak it all was compared with his own conceptions; he had seen an enchanted city, awful, glorious, with flame smitten about its battlements, like the cities of the Sangraal, and he had moulded his copy in such poor clay as came to his hand;[73] yet, in spite of the gulf that yawned between the idea and the work, he knew as he read that the thing accomplished was very far from a failure. He put back the leaves carefully, and glanced again at Messrs. Beit's list. It had escaped his notice that *A Bad Un to Beat* was in its third three-volume edition. It was a great thing, at all events, to know in what direction to aim, if he wished to succeed. If he worked hard, he thought, he might some day win the approval of the coy and retiring Miranda of *Smart Society*; that modest maiden might in his praise interrupt her task of disinterested advertisement, her philanthropic counsels to 'go to Jumper's, and mind you ask for Mr. C. Jumper, who will show you the lovely blue paper with the yellow spots at ten shillings the piece.' He put down

---

[73]　The Sangraal refers to the chalice or other type of vessel used by Christ and his disciples at the Last Supper. Often called the Holy Grail and imbued with miraculous powers, it was reputedly given to Joseph of Arimathea (a follower of Jesus), who brought it to England. Legends of the Sangraal combine elements of Christian and pagan Celtic lore, and there are a number of mediaeval tales — especially in the Arthurian canon — about knights setting out on quests to find it. The 'cities of the Sangraal' are likely those locales that feature in such quest tales, including Jerusalem, Turin, and Glastonbury. Machen wrote at length about the Sangraal history, generally concluding that its origin is Celtic, albeit heavily mingled with later Christian mythology.

the pamphlet, and laughed again at the books and the reviewers: so that he might not weep. This then was English fiction, this was English criticism, and farce, after all, was but an ill-played tragedy.

The rejected manuscript was hidden away, and his father quoted Horace's maxim as to the benefit of keeping literary works for some time 'in the wood.'[74] There was nothing to grumble at, though Lucian was inclined to think the duration of the reader's catarrh a little exaggerated.[75] But this was a trifle; he did not arrogate to himself the position of a small commercial traveller, who expects prompt civility as a matter of course, and not at all as a favour. He simply forgot his old book, and resolved that he would make a better one if he could. With the hot fit of resolution, the determination not to be snuffed out by one refusal upon him, he began to beat about in his mind for some new scheme. At first it seemed that he had hit upon a promising subject; he began to plot out chapters and scribble hints for the curious story that had entered his mind, arranging his circumstances and noting the effects to be produced with all the enthusiasm of the artist. But after the first breath the aspect of the work changed; page after page was tossed aside as hopeless, the beautiful sentences he had dreamed of refused to be written, and his puppets remained stiff and wooden, devoid of life or motion. Then all the old despairs came back, the agonies of the artificer who strives and perseveres in vain; the scheme that seemed of amorous fire turned to cold hard ice in his hands. He let the pen drop from his fingers, and wondered how he could have ever dreamed of writing books. Again, the thought occurred that he might do something if he could only get away, and join the sad procession in the murmuring London streets, far from the shadow of those awful hills. But it was quite impossible; the relative who had once promised assistance was appealed to, and wrote expressing his regret that Lucian had turned out a 'loafer,' wasting his time in scribbling, instead of trying to earn his living. Lucian felt rather hurt at this letter, but the parson only grinned grimly as usual. He was thinking of how he signed a cheque many years before, in the days of his prosperity, and the cheque was payable to this didactic relative, then in but a poor way, and of a thankful turn of mind.

The old rejected manuscript had almost passed out of his recollection. It was recalled oddly enough. He was looking over the *Reader*, and enjoying the admirable literary criticisms, some three months after the return of his book, when his eye was attracted by a quoted passage in one of the notices. The thought and style both wakened memory, the cadences were familiar

---

[74] Either Machen is misremembering an observation by the Roman poet Horace (65–8 BCE) or deliberately misconstruing it. In *Ars Poetica* (*Art of Poetry*), Horace comments on the preservation of worthy verses by rubbing them with oil of cedar and placing them in cases made of cypress.

[75] Catarrh is an inflammation, usually of the respiratory tract, accompanied by a phlegmy cough.

and beloved. He read through the review from the beginning; it was a very favourable one, and pronounced the volume an immense advance on Mr. Ritson's previous work. 'Here, undoubtedly, the author has discovered a vein of pure metal,' the reviewer added, 'and we predict that he will go far.' Lucian had not yet reached his father's stage, he was unable to grin in the manner of that irreverent parson. The passage selected for high praise was taken almost word for word from the manuscript now resting in his room, the work that had not reached the high standard of Messrs. Beit & Co., who, curiously enough, were the publishers of the book reviewed in the *Reader*. He had a few shillings in his possession, and wrote at once to a bookseller in London for a copy of *The Chorus in Green*, as the author had oddly named the book. He wrote on June 21st, and thought he might fairly expect to receive the interesting volume by the 24th; but the postman, true to his tradition, brought nothing for him, and in the afternoon he resolved to walk down to Caermaen, in case it might have come by a second post; or it might have been mislaid at the office; they forgot parcels sometimes, especially when the bag was heavy and the weather hot. This 24th was a sultry and oppressive day; a grey veil of cloud obscured the sky, and a vaporous mist hung heavily over the land, and fumed up from the valleys. But at five o'clock, when he started, the clouds began to break, and the sunlight suddenly streamed down through the misty air, making ways and channels of rich glory, and bright islands in the gloom. It was a pleasant and shining evening when, passing by devious back streets to avoid the barbarians (as he very rudely called the respectable inhabitants of the town), he reached the post-office; which was also the general shop.

'Yes, Mr. Taylor, there is something for you, sir,' said the man. 'Williams the postman forgot to take it up this morning,' and he handed over the packet. Lucian took it under his arm and went slowly through the ragged winding lanes till he came into the country. He got over the first stile on the road, and sitting down in the shelter of a hedge, cut the strings and opened the parcel. *The Chorus in Green* was got up in what reviewers call a dainty manner: a bronze-green cloth, well-cut gold lettering, wide margins and black 'old-face' type, all witnessed to the good taste of Messrs. Beit & Co. He cut the pages hastily and began to read. He soon found that he had wronged Mr. Ritson — that old literary hand had by no means stolen his book wholesale, as he had expected. There were about two hundred pages in the pretty little volume, and of these about ninety were Lucian's, dovetailed into a rather different scheme with skill that was nothing short of exquisite. And Mr. Ritson's own work was often very good; spoilt here and there for some tastes by the 'cataloguing' method, a somewhat materialistic way of taking an inventory of the holy country things; but, for that very reason, contrasting to great advantage with Lucian's hints and dreams and note of haunting. And here and there Mr. Ritson had made little alterations in the style of the passages he had conveyed, and most of these alterations were amendments, as Lucian was obliged to confess, though he would have liked to argue one or two points with his collaborator and corrector. He lit his pipe and leant back comfortably in the hedge, thinking things over, weighing very coolly his experience of humanity, his contact with the 'society' of the countryside, the affair of *The Chorus in Green*, and even some little incidents that had struck him as he was walking through the streets of Caermaen that evening. At the post-office, when he was inquiring for his parcel, he had heard two old women grumbling in the street; it seemed, so far as he could make out, that both had been disappointed in much the same way. Each had applied for an alms at the vicarage; they were probably shiftless old wretches who had liked beer for supper all their lives, and had forgotten the duties of economy and 'laying up treasure on earth'. One was a Roman Catholic, hardened, and beyond the reach of conversion; she had been advised to ask alms of the priests, 'who are always creeping and crawling about.' The other old sinner was a dissenter, and, 'Mr. Dixon has quite enough to do to relieve good Church people.'[76] Mrs. Dixon, assisted by Henrietta, was, it seemed, the lady high almoner, who dispensed these charities.[77] As she said to Mrs. Colley, they would end by keeping all the beggars in the county, and they really couldn't afford it. A large family was an expensive thing, and the girls *must* have new frocks. 'Mr. Dixon is always telling me and the girls that we must not *demoralise* the people by indiscriminate charity.' Lucian had heard of these sage counsels, and thought of them as he listened to the bitter complaints of the gaunt, hungry old women. In the back street by which he passed out of the town he saw a large 'healthy' boy kicking a sick cat; the poor creature had just strength enough to crawl under an outhouse door; probably to die in torments. He did not find much satisfaction in thrashing the boy, but he did it with hearty good will. Further on, at the corner where the turnpike used to be, was a big notice, announcing a meeting at the schoolroom in aid of the missions to the Portuguese. 'Under the Patronage of the Lord Bishop of the Diocese,' was the imposing headline; the Reverend Merivale Dixon, vicar of Caermaen, was to be in the chair, supported by Stanley Gervase, Esq., J. P., and by many of the clergy and gentry of the neighbourhood. Senhor Diabo, 'formerly a Romanist priest, now an evangelist in Lisbon,' would address the meeting.[78] 'Funds are urgently

---

[76] A dissenter is a British Protestant who does not conform to the rules and theology of the Church of England.

[77] An almoner is a person who, on behalf of an organization such as a church, dispenses charity to needy people. By labelling Mrs Dixon 'the lady high almoner', Machen is gently satirizing the character's elevated, sanctimonious sense of her self and her social position.

[78] Evidently, Senhor Diabo is a former Roman Catholic Portuguese priest who has converted to Protestantism. While an evangelist can simply be someone who preaches the stories and doctrines of Christ, in the nineteenth century the term often designated a

needed to carry on this good work,' concluded the notice. So he lay well back in the shade of the hedge, and thought whether some sort of an article could not be made by vindicating the terrible Yahoos; one might point out that they were in many respects a simple and unsophisticated race, whose faults were the result of their enslaved position, while such virtues as they had were all their own. They might be compared, he thought, much to their advantage, with more complex civilisations. There was no hint of anything like the Beit system of publishing in existence amongst them; the great Yahoo nation would surely never feed and encourage a scabby Houyhnhnm, expelled for his foulness from the horse-community, and the witty dean, in all his minuteness, had said nothing of 'safe' Yahoos.[79] On reflection, however, he did not feel quite secure of this part of his defence; he remembered that the leading brutes had favourites, who were employed in certain simple domestic offices about their masters, and it seemed doubtful whether the contemplated vindication would not break down on this point. He smiled queerly to himself as he thought of these comparisons, but his heart burnt with a dull fury. Throwing back his unhappy memory, he recalled all the contempt and scorn he had suffered; as a boy he had heard the masters murmuring their disdain of him and of his desire to learn other than ordinary school work. As a young man he had suffered the insolence of these wretched people about him; their cackling laughter at his poverty jarred and grated in his ears; he saw the acrid grin of some miserable idiot woman, some creature beneath the swine in intelligence and manners, merciless, as he went by with his eyes on the dust, in his ragged clothes. He and his father seemed to pass down an avenue of jeers and contempt, and contempt from such animals as these! This putrid filth, moulded into human shape, made only to fawn on the rich and beslaver them, thinking no foulness too foul if it were done in honour of those in power and authority; and no refined cruelty of contempt too cruel if it were contempt of the poor and humble and oppressed; it was to this obscene and ghastly throng that he was something to be pointed at. And these men and women spoke of sacred things, and knelt before the awful altar of God, before the altar of tremendous fire, surrounded as they professed by Angels and Archangels and all the Company of Heaven; and in their very church they had one aisle for the rich and another for the poor. And the species was not peculiar to Caermaen; the rich business men in London and the successful brother author were probably amusing themselves at the expense of the poor struggling

---

Protestant who enthusiastically encouraged people to experience guilt for their sins and to become reconciled to God through a personal relationship with Christ.

[79] In *Gulliver's Travels* (1726), the Anglo-Irish satirist Jonathan Swift (1667–1745) wrote about the Yahoos — a race of vile-mannered, uncouth beings that have the shape of humans — who are ruled over by the Houyhnhnms, a race of highly intelligent, rational horses. Machen refers to Swift as 'the witty dean' because the satirist had served from 1713 to 1745 as the dean of St Patrick's Cathedral, Dublin.

creature they had injured and wounded; just as the 'healthy' boy had burst into a great laugh when the miserable sick cat cried out in bitter agony, and trailed its limbs slowly, as it crept away to die. Lucian looked into his own life and his own will; he saw that in spite of his follies, and his want of success, he had not been consciously malignant, he had never deliberately aided in oppression, or looked on it with enjoyment and approval, and he felt that when he lay dead beneath the earth, eaten by swarming worms, he would be in a purer company than now, when he lived amongst human creatures. And he was to call this loathsome beast, all sting and filth, brother! 'I had rather call the devils my brothers,' he said in his heart, 'I would fare better in hell.' Blood was in his eyes, and as he looked up the sky seemed of blood, and the earth burnt with fire.[80]

The sun was sinking low on the mountain when he set out on the way again. Burrows, the doctor, coming home in his trap, met him a little lower on the road, and gave him a friendly good-night.

'A long way round on this road, isn't it?' said the doctor. 'As you have come so far, why don't you try the short cut across the fields? You will find it easily enough; second stile on the left hand, and then go straight ahead.'

He thanked Dr. Burrows and said he would try the short cut, and Burrows span on homeward. He was a gruff and honest bachelor, and often felt very sorry for the lad, and wished he could help him. As he drove on, it suddenly occurred to him that Lucian had an awful look on his face, and he was sorry he had not asked him to jump in, and come to supper. A hearty slice of beef, with strong ale, whisky and soda afterwards, a good pipe, and certain Rabelaisian tales which the doctor had treasured for many years, would have done the poor fellow a lot of good, he was certain.[81] He half turned round on his seat, and looked to see if Lucian were still in sight, but he had passed the corner, and the doctor drove on, shivering a little; the mists were beginning to rise from the wet banks of the river.

Lucian trailed slowly along the road, keeping a look out for the stile the doctor had mentioned. It would be a little of an adventure, he thought, to find his way by an unknown track; he knew the direction in which his home lay, and he imagined he would not have much difficulty in crossing from one stile to another. The path led him up a steep bare field, and when he was at the top, the town and the valley winding up to the north stretched before him. The river was stilled at the flood, and the yellow water, reflecting the sunset, glowed in its deep pools like dull brass. These burning pools, the level meadows fringed with

---

[80] Lucian's hallucinations echo some of the apocalyptic imagery of blood and fire found in the Book of Revelation in the Bible.

[81] Stories by the French writer and physician François Rabelais (c. 1490–1553) are noted for their combination of energetic humour and penetrating considerations of philosophy and politics. He was best known for his scatological satire *The Life of Gargantua and of Pantagruel.*

shuddering reeds, the long dark sweep of the forest on the hill, were all clear and distinct, yet the light seemed to have clothed them with a new garment, even as voices from the streets of Caermaen sounded strangely, mounting up thin with the smoke. There beneath him lay the huddled cluster of Caermaen, the ragged and uneven roofs that marked the winding and sordid streets, here and there a pointed gable rising above its meaner fellows; beyond he recognised the piled mounds that marked the circle of the amphitheatre, and the dark edge of trees that grew where the Roman wall whitened and waxed old beneath the frosts and rains of eighteen hundred years.[82] Thin and strange, mingled together, the voices came up to him on the hill; it was as if an outland race inhabited the ruined city and talked in a strange language of strange and terrible things. The sun had slid down the sky, and hung quivering over the huge dark dome of the mountain like a burnt sacrifice, and then suddenly vanished. In the afterglow the clouds began to writhe and turn scarlet, and shone so strangely reflected in the pools of the snake-like river, that one would have said the still waters stirred, the fleeting and changing of the clouds seeming to quicken the stream, as if it bubbled and sent up gouts of blood. But already about the town the darkness was forming; fast, fast the shadows crept upon it from the forest, and from all sides banks and wreaths of curling mist were gathering, as if a ghostly leaguer were being built up against the city, and the strange race who lived in its streets.[83] Suddenly there burst out from the stillness the clear and piercing music of the *réveillé*, calling, recalling, iterated, reiterated, and ending with one long high fierce shrill note with which the steep hills rang.[84] Perhaps a boy in the school band was practising on his bugle, but for Lucian it was magic. For him it was the note of the Roman trumpet, *tuba mirum spargens sonum*, filling all the hollow valley with its command, reverberated in dark places in the far forest, and resonant in the old graveyards without the walls.[85] In his imagination he saw the earthen gates of the tombs broken open, and the serried legion swarming to the eagles.[86] Century by century they passed up; they rose, dripping, from the river bed, they rose from the level, their armour shone in

---

[82] Roman soldiers first occupied Isca (Caerleon) in 75 CE, and the last of them withdrew in the late third century CE.

[83] 'Leaguer' is an archaic term for a siege.

[84] A *reveille* is an early morning bugle or drum signal alerting soldiers to gather.

[85] The Latin phrase is from the mediaeval hymn 'Dies Irae' ('Day of Wrath'), meaning 'The trumpet scatters a wondrous sound'. The 'Dies Irae' paints a poetic picture of the Last Judgement. In Machen's time, the 'Dies Irae' was frequently recited or sung at Roman Catholic funerals and sometimes at Anglican services, although more commonly in English.

[86] A legion was a main unit of the Roman army, comprising 3000 to 6000 soldiers. Legions' common emblems were eagles, which usually surmounted the standards that soldiers followed into battle. The Legio II Augustus (Augustus's Second Legion) was stationed at Isca (Caerleon).

the quiet orchard, they gathered in ranks and companies from the cemetery, and as the trumpet sounded, the hill fort above the town gave up its dead. By hundreds and thousands the ghostly battle surged about the standard, behind the quaking mist, ready to march against the mouldering walls they had built so many years before.

He turned sharply; it was growing very dark, and he was afraid of missing his way. At first the path led him by the verge of a wood; there was a noise of rustling and murmuring from the trees as if they were taking evil counsel together. A high hedge shut out the sight of the darkening valley, and he stumbled on mechanically, without taking much note of the turnings of the track, and when he came out from the wood shadow to the open country, he stood for a moment quite bewildered and uncertain. A dark wild twilight country lay before him, confused dim shapes of trees near at hand, and a hollow below his feet, and the further hills and woods were dimmer, and all the air was very still. He gazed about him, scanning the dusky earth, and trying to make out some familiar shape, some well-known form of hill or wood. Suddenly the darkness about him glowed; a furnace fire had shot up on the mountain, and for a moment the little world of the woodside and the steep hill shone in a pale light, and he thought he saw his path beaten out in the turf before him. The great flame sank down to a red glint of fire, and it led him on down the ragged slope, his feet striking against ridges of ground, and falling from beneath him at a sudden dip. The bramble bushes shot out long prickly vines, amongst which he was entangled, and lower, he was held back by wet bubbling earth. He had descended into a dark and shady valley, beset and tapestried with gloomy thickets; the weird wood noises were the only sounds, strange, unutterable mutterings, dismal, inarticulate. He pushed on in what he hoped was the right direction, stumbling from stile to gate, peering through mist and shadow, and still vainly seeking for any known landmark. Presently another sound broke upon the grim air, the murmur of water poured over stones, gurgling against the old misshapen roots of trees, and running clear in a deep channel. He passed into the chill breath of the brook, and almost fancied he heard two voices speaking in its murmur; there seemed a ceaseless utterance of words, an endless argument. With a mood of horror pressing on him, he listened to the noise of waters, and the wild fancy seized him that he was not deceived, that two unknown beings stood together there in the darkness and tried the balances of his life, and spoke his doom.[87] The hour in the matted thicket rushed over the great bridge of years to his thought; he had sinned against the earth, and the earth trembled and shook for vengeance. He stayed still for a moment, quivering with fear, and at last

---

[87] Another likely echo of biblical passages in which a person's character is represented through the metaphor of balances (scales); for example, 'Thou art weighed in the balances, and art found wanting' (Daniel 5. 27).

went on blindly, no longer caring for the path, if only he might escape from
the toils of that dismal shuddering hollow. As he plunged through the hedges
the bristling thorns tore his face and hands; he fell amongst stinging-nettles
and was pricked as he beat out his way amidst the gorse. He raced headlong,
his head over his shoulder, through a windy wood, bare of undergrowth; there
lay about the ground mouldering stumps, the relics of trees that had thundered
to their fall, crashing and tearing to earth, long ago; and from these remains
there flowed out a pale thin radiance, filling the spaces of the sounding wood
with a dream of light. He had lost all count of the track; he felt he had fled for
hours, climbing and descending, and yet not advancing; it was as if he stood
still and the shadows of the land went by, in a vision. But at last a hedge, high
and straggling, rose before him, and as he broke through it, his feet slipped, and
he fell headlong down a steep bank into a lane. He lay still, half-stunned, for
a moment, and then rising unsteadily, he looked desperately into the darkness
before him, uncertain and bewildered. In front it was black as a midnight
cellar, and he turned about, and saw a glint in the distance, as if a candle were
flickering in a farm-house window. He began to walk with trembling feet
towards the light, when suddenly something pale started out from the shadows
before him, and seemed to swim and float down the air. He was going down
hill, and he hastened onwards, and he could see the bars of a stile framed dimly
against the sky, and the figure still advanced with that gliding motion. Then, as
the road declined to the valley, the landmark he had been seeking appeared. To
his right there surged up in the darkness the darker summit of the Roman fort,
and the streaming fire of the great full moon glowed through the bars of the
wizard oaks, and made a halo shine about the hill. He was now quite close to the
white appearance, and saw that it was only a woman walking swiftly down the
lane; the floating movement was an effect due to the somber air and the moon's
glamour. At the gate, where he had spent so many hours gazing at the fort, they
walked foot to foot, and he saw it was Annie Morgan.

'Good evening, Master Lucian,' said the girl, 'it's very dark, sir, indeed.'

'Good evening, Annie,' he answered, calling her by her name for the first
time, and he saw that she smiled with pleasure. 'You are out late, aren't you?'

'Yes, sir; but I've been taking a bit of supper to old Mrs. Gibbon. She's been
very poorly the last few days, and there's nobody to do anything for her.'

Then there were really people who helped one another; kindness and pity
were not mere myths, fictions of 'society,' as useful as Doe and Roe, and as non-
existent.[88] The thought struck Lucian with a shock; the evening's passion and

---

[88] Doe and Roe refer to John Doe and Richard Roe, two fictitious names used for centuries
in English legal cases in which certain individuals (e.g. witnesses) require their identities
to be protected. Outside of strictly legal circumstances, Doe and Roe came to stand as
convenient placeholders for ordinary people, not tied to any specific, actual individuals.

delirium, the wild walk and physical fatigue had almost shattered him in body and mind. He was 'degenerate,' *decadent*,[89] and the rough rains and blustering winds of life, which a stronger man would have laughed at and enjoyed, were to him 'hail-storms and fire-showers.'[90] After all, Messrs. Beit, the publishers, were only sharp men of business, and these terrible Dixons and Gervases and Colleys merely the ordinary limited clergy and gentry of a quiet country town; sturdier sense would have dismissed Dixon as an old humbug, Stanley Gervase, Esquire, J. P., as a 'bit of a bounder,' and the ladies as 'rather a shoddy lot.' But he was walking slowly now in painful silence, his heavy, lagging feet striking against the loose stones. He was not thinking of the girl beside him; only something seemed to swell and grow and swell within his heart; it was all the torture of his days, weary hopes and weary disappointment, scorn rankling and throbbing, and the thought 'I had rather call the devils my brothers and live with them in hell.'[91] He choked and gasped for breath, and felt involuntary muscles working in his face, and the impulses of a madman stirring him; he himself was in truth the realisation of the vision of Caermaen that night, a city with mouldering walls beset by the ghostly legion. Life and the world and the laws of the sunlight had passed away, and the resurrection and kingdom of the dead began.[92] The Celt assailed him, beckoning from the weird wood he

---

[89] Machen uses the terms 'degenerate' and 'decadent' here to refer to a state of unhealthy hyper-sensitivity, both physically and mentally. This was a common rendering of the Decadent individual in literature and art, but it was particularly familiar at this historical moment because of the popularity of Britain's most famous Decadent artist, Aubrey Beardsley, who died of tuberculosis at the age of 25. Machen's adjective 'degenerate' owes something to Max Nordau's (1849–1923) *Degeneration* (1892–1893; English translation 1895), which mounted a powerful case that Western civilization was being plagued and eroded by Decadent, anti-social art and morality. Amongst its many scathing criticisms, Nordau's book vigorously attacks the homosexual Irish writer Wilde, a man who at the time was regarded by many as the exemplar of the Decadent artist. Nordau's study preceded Wilde's 1895 trail for 'gross indecency', which itself preceded Machen's writing of *The Hill of Dreams*. As Machen knew Wilde and was part of the literary community that included members of the Decadent movement, he would have been familiar with the case and the potent connotations of the term 'decadent' when he wrote this passage. Wilde's lover Douglas wrote a notably positive review of *The Hill of Dreams* upon its publication.

[90] This is a quotation from Thomas Carlyle (1795–1881), who wrote of the death of the Scottish poet Robert Burns (1759–1796) that 'he passed, not softly yet speedily, into that still country, where the hail-storms and fire-showers do not reach, and the heaviest-laden wayfarer at length lays down his load' ('Burns', *Edinburgh Review*, 48 (December, 1828), pp. 267–312; reprinted in Thomas Carlyle, *Critical and Miscellaneous Essays* (London: James Fraser, 1893), pp. 287–350, p. 339).

[91] Lucian's thoughts echo words spoken by Satan in John Milton's (1608–1674) epic *Paradise Lost* (1667). In Book I, for example, the rebel angel famously declares it is 'Better to reign in Hell, than serve in Heaven' (line 263).

[92] Machen is drawing on the idea of a kingdom of the dead present in many Celtic traditions, both pagan and hybridized pagan-Christian. The passage also glances at the Christian belief in the eventual resurrection of the dead, both of good and wicked people (e.g. John 5. 28–29; Acts 25. 15).

called the world, and his far-off ancestors, the 'little people,' crept out of their caves, muttering charms and incantations in hissing inhuman speech; he was beleaguered by desires that had slept in his race for ages.[93]

'I am afraid you are very tired, Master Lucian. Would you like me to give you my hand over this rough bit?'

He had stumbled against a great round stone and had nearly fallen. The woman's hand sought his in the darkness; as he felt the touch of the soft warm flesh, he moaned, and a pang shot through his arm to his heart. He looked up and found he had only walked a few paces since Annie had spoken; he had thought they had wandered for hours together. The moon was just mounting above the oaks, and the halo round the dark hill brightened. He stopped short, and keeping his hold of Annie's hand, looked into her face. A hazy glory of moonlight shone around them and lit up their eyes. He had not greatly altered since his boyhood; his face was pale olive in colour, thin and oval; marks of pain had gathered about the eyes, and his black hair was already stricken with grey. But the eager, curious gaze still remained, and what he saw before him lit up his sadness with a new fire. She stopped too, and did not offer to draw away, but looked back with all her heart. They were alike in many ways; her skin was also of that olive colour, but her face was sweet as a beautiful summer night, and her black eyes showed no dimness, and the smile on the scarlet lips was like a flame when it brightens a dark and lonely land.

'You are sorely tired, Master Lucian, let us sit down here by the gate.'

It was Lucian who spoke next: 'My dear, my dear.' And their lips were together again, and their arms locked together, each holding the other fast. And then the poor lad let his head sink down on his sweetheart's breast, and burst into a passion of weeping. The tears streamed down his face, and he shook with sobbing, in the happiest moment that he had ever lived. The woman bent over him and tried to comfort him, but his tears were his consolation and his triumph. Annie was whispering to him, her hand laid on his heart; she was whispering beautiful, wonderful words, that soothed him as a song. He did not know what they meant.

'Annie, dear, dear Annie, what are you saying to me? I have never heard such beautiful words. Tell me, Annie, what do they mean?'

She laughed, and said it was only nonsense that the nurses sang to the children.

'No, no, you are not to call me Master Lucian any more,' he said, when they parted, 'you must call me Lucian; and I, I worship you, my dear Annie.'

---

[93] As a Welshman, Lucian is experiencing an interior awakening of his pagan Celtic ancestry. The 'little people' are akin to the fairies Machen refers to earlier, a mysterious, supernatural race that many Celtic traditions said lived in earthen mounds of the kind Lucian had previously discovered. On this race, see also Machen's 'The Ceremony', included in this collection.

He fell down before her, embracing her knees, and adored, and she allowed him, and confirmed his worship. He followed slowly after her, passing the path which led to her home with a longing glance. Nobody saw any difference in Lucian when he reached the rectory. He came in with his usual dreamy indifference, and told how he had lost his way by trying the short cut. He said he had met Dr. Burrows on the road, and that he had recommended the path by the fields. Then, as dully as if he had been reading some story out of a newspaper, he gave his father the outlines of the Beit case, producing the pretty little book called *The Chorus in Green*. The parson listened in amazement.

'You mean to tell me that *you* wrote this book?' he said. He was quite roused.

'No; not all of it. Look; that bit is mine, and that; and the beginning of this chapter. Nearly the whole of the third chapter is by me.'

He closed the book without interest, and indeed he felt astonished at his father's excitement. The incident seemed to him unimportant.

'And you say that eighty or ninety pages of this book are yours, and these scoundrels have stolen your work?'

'Well, I suppose they have. I'll fetch the manuscript, if you would like to look at it.'

The manuscript was duly produced, wrapped in brown paper, with Messrs. Beit's address label on it, and the post-office dated stamps.

'And the other book has been out a month.'

The parson, forgetting the sacerdotal office, and his good habit of grinning, swore at Messrs. Beit and Mr. Ritson, calling them damned thieves, and then began to read the manuscript, and to compare it with the printed book.[94]

'Why, it's splendid work. My poor fellow,' he said after a while, 'I had no notion you could write so well. I used to think of such things in the old days at Oxford; "old Bill," the tutor, used to praise my essays, but I never wrote anything like this. And this infernal ruffian of a Ritson has taken all your best things and mixed them up with his own rot to make it go down. Of course you'll expose the gang?'

Lucian was mildly amused; he couldn't enter into his father's feelings at all. He sat smoking in one of the old easy chairs, taking the rare relish of a hot grog with his pipe, and gazing out of his dreamy eyes at the violent old parson. He was pleased that his father liked his book, because he knew him to be a deep and sober scholar and a cool judge of good letters; but he laughed to himself when he saw the magic of print. The parson had expressed no wish to read the manuscript when it came back in disgrace; he had merely grinned, said something about boomerangs, and quoted Horace with relish. Whereas now, before the book in its neat case, lettered with another man's name, his approbation of the writing and his disapproval of the 'scoundrels,' as he called

---

[94] 'Sacerdotal' means priestly.

them, were loudly expressed, and, though a good smoker, he blew and puffed vehemently at his pipe.

'You'll expose the rascals, of course, won't you?' he said again.

'Oh no, I think not. It really doesn't matter much, does it? After all, there are some very weak things in the book; doesn't it strike you as "young"' I have been thinking of another plan, but I haven't done much with it lately. But I believe I've got hold of a really good idea this time, and if I can manage to see the heart of it I hope to turn out a manuscript worth stealing. But it's so hard to get at the core of an idea — the heart, as I call it,' he went on after a pause. 'It's like having a box you can't open, though you know there's something wonderful inside. But I do believe I've a fine thing in my hands, and I mean to try my best to work it.'

Lucian talked with enthusiasm now, but his father, on his side, could not share these ardours. It was his part to be astonished at excitement over a book that was not even begun, the mere ghost of a book flitting elusive in the world of unborn masterpieces and failures. He had loved good letters, but he shared unconsciously in the general belief that literary attempt is always pitiful, though he did not subscribe to the other half of the popular faith — that literary success is a matter of very little importance. He thought well of books, but only of printed books; in manuscripts he put no faith, and the *paulo-post-futurum* tense he could not in any manner conjugate.[95] He returned once more to the topic of palpable interest.

'But about this dirty trick these fellows have played on you. You won't sit quietly and bear it, surely? It's only a question of writing to the papers.'

'They wouldn't put the letter in. And if they did, I should only get laughed at. Some time ago a man wrote to the *Reader*, complaining of his play being stolen. He said that he had sent a little one-act comedy to Burleigh, the great dramatist, asking for his advice. Burleigh gave his advice and took the idea for his own very successful play. So the man said, and I daresay it was true enough. But the victim got nothing by his complaint. "A pretty state of things," everybody said. "Here's a Mr. Tomson, that no one has ever heard of, bothers Burleigh with his rubbish, and then accuses him of petty larceny. Is it likely that a man of Burleigh's position, a playwright who can make his five thousand a year easily, would borrow from an unknown Tomson?" I should think it very likely, indeed,' Lucian went on, chuckling, 'but that was their verdict. No; I don't think I'll write to the papers.'

'Well, well, my boy, I suppose you know your own business best. I think you are mistaken, but you must do as you like.'

---

[95] In ancient Greek, the *paolo post futurum* is a future passive tense. As an adverb, the expression came to mean that which might happen in the distant future, or perhaps never; it connotes things fanciful and unrealistic. Machen here signals that Lucian's father is sceptical of his son fulfilling his vision for a new literary work, but also that the hero's mind is straying from real-world concerns and that he cannot foresee what will eventually become of him.

'It's all so unimportant,' said Lucian, and he really thought so. He had sweeter things to dream of, and desired no communion of feeling with that madman who had left Caermaen some few hours before. He felt he had made a fool of himself, he was ashamed to think of the fatuity of which he had been guilty; such boiling hatred was not only wicked, but absurd. A man could do no good who put himself into a position of such violent antagonism against his fellow-creatures; so Lucian rebuked his heart, saying that he was old enough to know better. But he remembered that he had sweeter things to dream of; there was a secret ecstasy that he treasured and locked tight away, as a joy too exquisite even for thought till he was quite alone; and then there was that scheme for a new book that he had laid down hopelessly some time ago; it seemed to have arisen into life again within the last hour; he understood that he had started on a false tack, he had taken the wrong aspect of his idea. Of course the thing couldn't be written in that way; it was like trying to read a page turned upside down; and he saw those characters he had vainly sought suddenly disambushed, and a splendid inevitable sequence of events unrolled before him.[96]

It was a true resurrection; the dry plot he had constructed revealed itself as a living thing, stirring and mysterious, and warm as life itself. The parson was smoking stolidly to all appearance, but in reality he was full of amazement at his own son, and now and again he slipped sly furtive glances towards the tranquil young man in the arm-chair by the empty hearth. In the first place, Mr. Taylor was genuinely impressed by what he had read of Lucian's work; he had so long been accustomed to look upon all effort as futile, that success amazed him. In the abstract, of course, he was prepared to admit that some people did write well and got published and made money, just as other persons successfully backed an outsider at heavy odds; but it had seemed as improbable that Lucian should show even the beginnings of achievement in one direction as in the other. Then the boy evidently cared so little about it; he did not appear to be proud of being worth robbing, nor was he angry with the robbers.

He sat back luxuriously in the disreputable old chair, drawing long slow wreaths of smoke, tasting his whisky from time to time, and evidently well at ease with himself. The father saw him smile, and it suddenly dawned upon him that his son was very handsome; he had such kind gentle eyes and a kind mouth, and his pale cheeks were flushed like a girl's. Mr. Taylor felt moved. What a harmless young fellow Lucian had been; no doubt a little queer and different from others, but wholly inoffensive, and patient under disappointment. And Miss Deacon, her contribution to the evening's discussion had been characteristic; she had remarked, firstly, that writing was a very unsettling occupation, and secondly, that it was extremely foolish to entrust one's property to people of whom one knew nothing. Father and son had smiled together at these observations, which

---

[96] Rather than 'disambushed', Machen may have intended 'disabused'.

were probably true enough. Mr. Taylor at last left Lucian alone; he shook hands with a good deal of respect, and said, almost deferentially:

'You mustn't work too hard, old fellow. I wouldn't stay up too late, if I were you, after that long walk. You must have gone miles out of your way.'

'I'm not tired now, though. I feel as if I could write my new book on the spot'; and the young man laughed a gay sweet laugh that struck the father as a new note in his son's life.

He sat still a moment after his father had left the room. He cherished his chief treasure of thought in its secret place; he would not enjoy it yet. He drew up a chair to the table at which he wrote, or tried to write, and began taking pens and paper from the drawer. There was a great pile of ruled paper there; all of it used, on one side, and signifying many hours of desperate scribbling, of heart-searching and rack of his brain; an array of poor, eager lines written by a waning fire with waning hope; all useless and abandoned. He took up the sheets cheerfully, and began in delicious idleness to look over these fruitless efforts. A page caught his attention; he remembered how he wrote it while a November storm was dashing against the panes; and there was another, with a queer blot in one corner; he had got up from his chair and looked out, and all the earth was white fairyland, and the snowflakes whirled round and round in the wind. Then he saw the chapter begun of a night in March: a great gale blew that night and rooted up one of the ancient yews in the churchyard. He had heard the trees shrieking in the woods, and the long wail of the wind, and across the heaven a white moon fled awfully before the streaming clouds. And all these poor abandoned pages now seemed sweet, and past unhappiness was transmuted into happiness, and the nights of toil were holy. He turned over half a dozen leaves and began to sketch out the outlines of the new book on the unused pages; running out a skeleton plan on one page, and dotting fancies, suggestions, hints on others. He wrote rapidly, overjoyed to find that loving phrases grew under his pen; a particular scene he had imagined filled him with desire; he gave his hand free course, and saw the written work glowing; and action and all the heat of existence quickened and beat on the wet page. Happy fancies took shape in happier words, and when at last he leant back in his chair he felt the stir and rush of the story as if it had been some portion of his own life. He read over what he had done with a renewed pleasure in the nimble and flowing workmanship, and as he put the little pile of manuscript tenderly in the drawer he paused to enjoy the anticipation of to-morrow's labour.

And then——but the rest of the night was given to tender and delicious things, and when he went up to bed a scarlet dawn was streaming from the east.

III

For days Lucian lay in a swoon of pleasure, smiling when he was addressed, sauntering happily in the sunlight, hugging recollection warm to his heart. Annie had told him that she was going on a visit to her married sister, and said, with a caress, that he must be patient. He protested against her absence, but she fondled him, whispering her charms in his ear till he gave in, and then they said good-bye, Lucian adoring on his knees. The parting was as strange as the meeting, and that night when he laid his work aside, and let himself sink deep into the joys of memory, all the encounter seemed as wonderful and impossible as magic.

'And you really don't mean to do anything about those rascals?' said his father.

'Rascals? Which rascals? Oh, you mean Beit. I had forgotten all about it. No; I don't think I shall trouble. They're not worth powder and shot.'

And he returned to his dream, pacing slowly from the medlar to the quince and back again. It seemed trivial to be interrupted by such questions; he had not even time to think of the book he had recommenced so eagerly, much less of this labour of long ago. He recollected without interest that it cost him many pains, that it was pretty good here and there, and that it had been stolen, and it seemed that there was nothing more to be said on the matter. He wished to think of the darkness in the lane, of the kind voice that spoke to him, of the kind hand that sought his own, as he stumbled on the rough way. So far, it was wonderful. Since he had left school and lost the company of the worthy barbarians who had befriended him there, he had almost lost the sense of kinship with humanity; he had come to dread the human form as men dread the hood of the cobra. To Lucian a man or a woman meant something that stung, that spoke words that rankled, and poisoned his life with scorn. At first such malignity shocked him: he would ponder over words and glances and wonder if he were not mistaken, and he still sought now and then for sympathy. The poor boy had romantic ideas about women; he believed they were merciful and pitiful, very kind to the unlucky and helpless. Men perhaps had to be different; after all, the duty of a man was to get on in the world, or, in plain language, to make money, to be successful; to cheat rather than to be cheated, but always to be successful; and he could understand that one who fell below this high standard must expect to be severely judged by his fellows. For example, there was young Bennett, Miss Spurry's nephew. Lucian had met him once or twice when he was spending his holidays with Miss Spurry, and the two young fellows had compared literary notes together. Bennett showed some beautiful things he had written, over which Lucian had grown both sad and enthusiastic. It was such exquisite magic verse, and so much better than anything he ever hoped to write, that there was a touch of anguish in his congratulations. But when Bennett, after many vain prayers to his aunt, threw up a safe position in the bank, and betook himself to a London garret, Lucian was not surprised at the general verdict.

Mr. Dixon, as a clergyman, viewed the question from a high standpoint and found it all deplorable, but the general opinion was that Bennett was a hopeless young lunatic. Old Mr. Gervase went purple when his name was mentioned, and the young Dixons sneered very merrily over the adventure.

'I always thought he was a beastly young ass,' said Edward Dixon, 'but I didn't think he'd chuck away his chances like that. Said he couldn't stand a bank! I hope he'll be able to stand bread and water. That's all those littery fellows get, I believe, except Tennyson and Mark Twain and those sort of people.'[97]

Lucian of course sympathised with the unfortunate Bennett, but such judgments were after all only natural. The young man might have stayed in the bank and succeeded to his aunt's thousand a year, and everybody would have called him a very nice young fellow — 'clever, too.' But he had deliberately chosen, as Edward Dixon had said, to chuck his chances away for the sake of literature; piety and a sense of the main chance had alike pointed the way to a delicate course of wheedling, to a little harmless practising on Miss Spurry's infirmities, to frequent compliances of a soothing nature, and the 'young ass' had been blind to the direction of one and the other. It seemed almost right that the vicar should moralise, that Edward Dixon should sneer, and that Mr. Gervase should grow purple with contempt. Men, Lucian thought, were like judges, who may pity the criminal in their hearts, but are forced to vindicate the outraged majesty of the law by a severe sentence. He felt the same considerations applied to his own case; he knew that his father should have had more money, that his clothes should be newer and of a better cut, that he should have gone to the university and made good friends. If such had been his fortune he could have looked his fellow-men proudly in the face, upright and unashamed. Having put on the whole armour of a first-rate West End tailor, with money in his purse, having taken anxious thought for the morrow, and having some useful friends and good prospects; in such a case he might have held his head high in a gentlemanly and Christian community.[98] As it was he had usually avoided the reproachful glance of his fellows, feeling that he deserved their condemnation. But he had cherished for a long time his romantic

---

[97] The English poet Alfred Tennyson (1809–1892) was appointed poet laureate in 1850. He became famous for poems such as 'The Lady of Shalott' (1832), *In Memoriam* (1850), and *Idylls of the King*, an Arthurian epic Lucian would surely have admired, as Machen himself did. Machen first read Tennyson in his father's library. Mark Twain (pseud. Samuel Langhorne Clemens (1835–1910)) was an American novelist, essayist, and humourist, the author of *The Adventures of Tom Sawyer* (1876) and *The Adventures of Huckleberry Finn* (1883), among other works.

[98] London's West End was primarily a fashionable part of the city with many theatres. It was also noted as a fashion district, and a tailor located there would have served a wealthy clientele.

sentimentalities about women; literary conventions borrowed from the minor poets and pseudo-medievalists, or so he thought afterwards.[99] But, fresh from school, wearied a little with the perpetual society of barbarian though worthy boys, he had in his soul a charming image of womanhood, before which he worshipped with mingled passion and devotion. It was a nude figure, perhaps, but the shining arms were to be wound about the neck of a vanquished knight; there was rest for the head of a wounded lover; the hands were stretched forth to do works of pity, and the smiling lips were to murmur not love alone, but consolation in defeat. Here was the refuge for a broken heart; here the scorn of men would but make tenderness increase; here was all pity and all charity with loving-kindness. It was a delightful picture, conceived in the 'come rest on this bosom,' and 'a ministering angel thou' manner, with touches of allurement that made devotion all the sweeter.[100] He soon found that he had idealised a little; in the affair of young Bennett, while the men were contemptuous the women were virulent. He had been rather fond of Agatha Gervase, and she, so other ladies said, had 'set her cap' at him.[101] Now, when he rebelled, and lost the goodwill of his aunt, dear Miss Spurry, Agatha insulted him with all conceivable rapidity. 'After all, Mr. Bennett,' she said, 'you will be nothing better than a beggar; now, will you? You mustn't think me cruel, but I can't help speaking the truth. *Write books!*' Her expression filled up the incomplete sentence; she waggled with indignant emotion. These passages came to Lucian's ears, and indeed the Gervases boasted of 'how well poor Agatha had behaved.'

'Never mind, Gathy,' old Gervase had observed. 'If the impudent young puppy comes here again, we'll see what Thomas can do with the horse-whip.'

'Poor dear child,' Mrs. Gervase added in telling the tale, 'and she was so fond of him too. But of course it couldn't go on after his shameful behaviour.'

But Lucian was troubled; he sought vainly for the ideal womanly, the tender note of 'come rest on this bosom.' Ministering angels, he felt convinced, do not rub red pepper and sulfuric acid into the wounds of suffering mortals.

Then there was the case of Mr. Vaughan, a squire in the neighbourhood, at whose board all the aristocracy of Caermaen had feasted for years. Mr. Vaughan had a first-rate cook, and his cellar was rare, and he was never so happy as when he shared his good things with his friends. His mother kept his house, and they delighted all the girls with frequent dances, while the men sighed over the amazing champagne. Investments proved disastrous, and Mr. Vaughan had to

---

[99] This could be a glance at such poets as Tennyson and the Pre-Raphaelites, who turned to the Middle Ages for inspiration, subject matter, and style.

[100] Machen slightly misquotes the first line of Irish poet Thomas Moore's (1779–1852) lyric 'Come, rest on this bosom, my own stricken deer', a popular tune in the nineteenth century. The line 'A ministering angel thou' appears in Sir Walter Scott's epic poem *Marmion* (1808).

[101] An idiomatic expression (already old-fashioned by Machen's day) describing a woman who deliberately sets out to attract a man's romantic attention.

sell the grey manor-house by the river. He and his mother took a little modern stucco villa in Caermaen, wishing to be near their dear friends. But the men were 'very sorry; rough on you, Vaughan. Always thought those Patagonians were risky, but you wouldn't hear of it.[102] Hope we shall see you before very long; you and Mrs. Vaughan must come to tea some day after Christmas.'

'Of course we are all very sorry for them,' said Henrietta Dixon. 'No, we haven't called on Mrs. Vaughan yet. They have no regular servant, you know; only a woman in the morning. I hear old mother Vaughan, as Edward will call her, does nearly everything. And their house is absurdly small; it's little more than a cottage. One really can't call it a gentleman's house.'

Then Mr. Vaughan, his heart in the dust, went to the Gervases and tried to borrow five pounds of Mr. Gervase. He had to be ordered out of the house, and, as Edith Gervase said, it was all very painful; 'he went out in such a funny way,' she added, 'just like the dog when he's had a whipping. Of course it's sad, even if it is all his own fault, as everybody says, but he looked so ridiculous as he was going down the steps that I couldn't help laughing.' Mr. Vaughan had heard the ringing, youthful laughter as he crossed the lawn.

Young girls like Henrietta Dixon and Edith Gervase naturally viewed the Vaughans' comical position with all the high spirits of their age, but the elder ladies could not look at matters in this frivolous light.

'Hush, dear, hush,' said Mrs. Gervase, 'it's all too shocking to be a laughing matter. Don't you agree with me, Mrs. Dixon? The sinful extravagance that went on at Pentre always *frightened* me.[103] You remember that ball they gave last year? Mr. Gervase assured me that the champagne must have cost *at least* a hundred and fifty shillings the dozen.'

'It's dreadful, isn't it,' said Mrs. Dixon, 'when one thinks of how many poor people there are who would be thankful for a crust of bread?'

'Yes, Mrs. Dixon,' Agatha joined in, 'and you know how absurdly the Vaughans spoilt the cottagers. Oh, it was really wicked; one would think Mr. Vaughan wished to make them above their station. Edith and I went for a walk one day nearly as far as Pentre, and we begged a glass of water of old Mrs. Jones who lives in that pretty cottage near the brook. She began praising the Vaughans in the most fulsome manner, and showed us some flannel things they had given her at Christmas. I assure you, my dear Mrs. Dixon, the flannel was the very best quality; no lady could wish for better. It couldn't have cost less than half-a-crown a yard.'[104]

---

[102] Evidently, Mr Vaughan has invested in a scheme in Patagonia, in southern Argentina.

[103] Pentre is a village in south-east Wales.

[104] It is difficult to establish the relative expense of an item at one historical moment in time due to constant changes in currency value, the impact of import/export developments for different items, vacillations in the income standard for various careers, and other factors. In this instance, Machen makes the relative value of the item to the characters clear, although this is not always the case.

'I know, my dear, I know. Mr. Dixon always said it couldn't last. How often I have heard him say that the Vaughans were pauperising all the common people about Pentre, and putting every one else in a most unpleasant position. Even from a worldly point of view it was very poor taste on their part. So different from the *true* charity that Paul speaks of.'[105]

'I only wish they had given away nothing worse than flannel,' said Miss Colley, a young lady of very strict views. 'But I assure you there was a perfect orgy, I can call it nothing else, every Christmas. Great joints of prime beef, and barrels of strong beer, and snuff and tobacco distributed wholesale; as if the poor wanted to be encouraged in their disgusting habits. It was really impossible to go through the village for weeks after; the whole place was poisoned with the fumes of horrid tobacco pipes.'

'Well, we see how that sort of thing ends,' said Mrs. Dixon, summing up judicially. 'We had intended to call, but I really think it would be impossible after what Mrs. Gervase has told us. The idea of Mr. Vaughan trying to sponge on poor Mr. Gervase in that shabby way! I think meanness of that kind is so hateful.'

It was the practical side of all this that astonished Lucian. He saw that in reality there was no high-flown quixotism in a woman's nature:[106] the smooth arms, made he had thought for caressing, seemed muscular; the hands meant for the doing of works of pity in his system, appeared dexterous in the giving of 'stingers,' as Barnes might say, and the smiling lips could sneer with great ease. Nor was he more fortunate in his personal experiences. As has been told, Mrs. Dixon spoke of him in connection with 'judgments,' and the younger ladies did not exactly cultivate his acquaintance. Theoretically they 'adored' books and thought poetry 'too sweet,' but in practice they preferred talking about mares and fox-terriers and their neighbours.

They were nice girls enough, very like other young ladies in other country towns, content with the teaching of their parents, reading the Bible every morning in their bedrooms, and sitting every Sunday in church amongst the well-dressed 'sheep' on the right hand.[107] It was not their fault if they failed to

---

[105] In the Bible (1 Corinthians 13. 2–8, 13), St Paul offers a lengthy discussion of 'charity' (today often translated as 'love').

[106] The term 'quixotism' means extravagance or impracticality, based on the hero of *The History of the Valorous and Wittie Knight-Errant Don-Quixote of the Mancha* (two volumes published in 1605 and 1615), a romance in prose by Spanish author Miguel de Cervantes (1547–1616). Machen first encountered the work as a youth in his father's library.

[107] Christians are sometimes referred to as 'sheep' in the Bible (e.g. John 21. 15–17), but here Machen also seems to use the metaphor to describe people who uncritically follow rules and conventions. In Christian theology, to be 'on the right hand' indicates a place of honour and holiness. Machen is also echoing St Matthew's apocalyptic vision of Christ's second coming, in which Christ will separate all nations 'one from another, as a shepherd divideth his sheep from the goats: / And he shall set the sheep on his right hand, but the goats on the left' (Matthew 25. 32–33).

satisfy the ideal of an enthusiastic dreamy boy, and indeed, they would have thought his feigned woman immodest, absurdly sentimental, a fright ('never wears stays, my dear') and *horrid*.

At first he was a good deal grieved at the loss of that charming tender woman, the work of his brain. When the Miss Dixons went haughtily by with a scornful waggle, when the Miss Gervases passed in the wagonette, laughing as the mud splashed him, the poor fellow would look up with a face of grief that must have been very comic; 'like a dying duck,' as Edith Gervase said. Edith was really very pretty, and he would have liked to talk to her, even about fox-terriers, if she would have listened. One afternoon at the Dixons' he really forced himself upon her, and with all the obtuseness of an enthusiastic boy tried to discuss the *Lotus Eaters* of Tennyson.[108] It was too absurd. Captain Kempton was making signals to Edith all the time, and Lieutenant Gatwick had gone off in disgust, and he had promised to bring her a puppy 'by Vick out of Wasp.' At last the poor girl could bear it no longer:

'Yes, it's very sweet,' she said at last. 'When did you say you were going to London, Mr. Taylor?'

It was about the time that his disappointment became known to everybody, and the shot told. He gave her a piteous look and slunk off, 'just like the dog when he's had a whipping,' to use Edith's own expression. Two or three lessons of this description produced their due effect; and when he saw a male Dixon or Gervase approaching him he bit his lip and summoned up his courage. But when he descried a 'ministering angel' he made haste and hid behind a hedge or took to the woods. In course of time the desire to escape became an instinct, to be followed as a matter of course; in the same way he avoided the adders on the mountain. His old ideals were almost if not quite forgotten; he knew that the female of the *bête humaine*, like the adder, would in all probability sting, and he therefore shrank from its trail, but without any feeling of special resentment.[109] The one had a poisoned tongue as the other had a poisoned fang, and it was well to leave them both alone. Then had come that sudden fury of rage against all humanity, as he went out of Caermaen carrying the book that had been stolen from him by the enterprising Beit. He shuddered as he thought of how nearly he had approached the verge of madness, when his eyes filled with blood and

---

[108] Tennyson's poem 'The Lotos-Eaters' (1832) is an imaginative reworking of Odysseus's encounter with a people called the Lotus Eaters in Book 9 of Homer's epic *The Odyssey*. The Lotus Eaters lured some of Odysseus's men to eat a mysterious, narcotic plant that induced forgetfulness, causing them to abandon their voyage. The figure of the Lotus Eater became recognized as a precursor for nineteenth-century Decadents envisioned to be lounging about, taking drugs for imaginative stimulation, and indulging in sensual pleasures.

[109] The phrase '*bête humaine*' is an allusion to Émile Zola's novel *La Bête humaine* (*The Human Beast*, sometimes rendered as *The Beast Within*) (1890), which features psychological mania, adultery, jealousy, rage, and murder.

the earth seemed to burn with fire. He remembered how he had looked up to the horizon and the sky was blotched with scarlet; and the earth was deep red, with red woods and red fields. There was something of horror in the memory, and in the vision of that wild night walk through dim country, when every shadow seemed a symbol of some terrible impending doom. The murmur of the brook, the wind shrilling through the wood, the pale light flowing from the mouldered trunks, and the picture of his own figure fleeing and fleeting through the shades; all these seemed unhappy things that told a story in fatal hieroglyphics. And then the life and laws of the sunlight had passed away, and the resurrection and kingdom of the dead began. Though his limbs were weary, he had felt his muscles grow strong as steel; a woman, one of the hated race, was beside him in the darkness, and the wild beast woke within him, ravening for blood and brutal lust; all the raging desires of the dim race from which he came assailed his heart. The ghosts issued out from the weird wood and from the caves in the hills, besieging him, as he had imagined the spiritual legion besieging Caermaen, beckoning him to a hideous battle and a victory that he had never imagined in his wildest dreams. And then out of the darkness the kind voice spoke again, and the kind hand was stretched out to draw him up from the pit. It was sweet to think of that which he had found at last; the boy's picture incarnate, all the passion and compassion of his longing, all the pity and love and consolation. She, that beautiful passionate woman offering up her beauty in sacrifice to him, she was worthy indeed of his worship. He remembered how his tears had fallen upon her breast, and how tenderly she had soothed him, whispering those wonderful unknown words that sang to his heart. And she had made herself defenceless before him, caressing and fondling the body that had been so despised. He exulted in the happy thought that he had knelt down on the ground before her, and had embraced her knees and worshipped. The woman's body had become his religion; he lay awake at night looking into the darkness with hungry eyes, wishing for a miracle, that the appearance of the so-desired form might be shaped before him. And when he was alone in quiet places in the wood, he fell down again on his knees, and even on his face, stretching out vain hands in the air, as if they would feel her flesh. His father noticed in those days that the inner pocket of his coat was stuffed with papers; he would see Lucian walking up and down in a secret shady place at the bottom of the orchard, reading from his sheaf of manuscript, replacing the leaves, and again drawing them out. He would walk a few quick steps, and pause as if enraptured, gazing in the air as if he looked through the shadows of the world into some sphere of glory, feigned by his thought. Mr. Taylor was almost alarmed at the sight; he concluded of course that Lucian was writing a book. In the first place, there seemed something immodest in seeing the operation performed under one's eyes; it was as if the 'make-up' of a beautiful

actress were done on the stage, in full audience; as if one saw the rounded
calves fixed in position, the fleshings drawn on, the voluptuous outlines of
the figure produced by means purely mechanical, blushes mantling from the
paint-pot, and the golden tresses well secured by the wigmaker. Books, Mr.
Taylor thought, should swim into one's ken mysteriously; they should appear
all printed and bound, without apparent genesis; just as children are suddenly
told that they have a little sister, found by mamma in the garden. But Lucian
was not only engaged in composition; he was plainly rapturous, enthusiastic;
Mr. Taylor saw him throw up his hands, and bow his head with strange gesture.
The parson began to fear that his son was like some of those mad Frenchmen
of whom he had read, young fellows who had a sort of fury of literature, and
gave their whole lives to it, spending days over a page, and years over a book,
pursuing art as Englishmen pursue money, building up a romance as if it were a
business. Now Mr. Taylor held firmly by the 'walking-stick' theory; he believed
that a man of letters should have a real profession, some solid employment in
life.[110] 'Get something to do,' he would have liked to say, 'and then you can write
as much as you please. Look at Scott, look at Dickens and Trollope.'[111] And then
there was the social point of view; it might be right, or it might be wrong, but
there could be no doubt that the literary man, as such, was not thought much
of in English society. Mr. Taylor knew his Thackeray, and he remembered that
old Major Pendennis, society personified, did not exactly boast of his nephew's
occupation. Even Warrington was rather ashamed to own his connection with
journalism, and Pendennis himself laughed openly at his novel-writing as an
agreeable way of making money, a useful appendage to the cultivation of dukes,
his true business in life.[112] This was the plain English view, and Mr. Taylor was
no doubt right enough in thinking it good, practical common sense. Therefore
when he saw Lucian loitering and sauntering, musing amorously over his
manuscript, exhibiting manifest signs of that fine fury which Britons have ever
found absurd, he felt grieved at heart, and more than ever sorry that he had not
been able to send the boy to Oxford.

'B. N. C. would have knocked all this nonsense out of him,' he thought.[113] 'He

---

[110] French philosopher René Descartes (1596–1650) proposed that light was material and that
humans' perception of light was akin to a blind man sensing objects by aid of his walking-
stick. Machen uses the analogy to suggest that Mr Taylor would have preferred it if his son
had actual employment, as opposed to more amorphous prospects.

[111] It was in his father's library that Machen first encountered Scott's and Dickens's writing,
the latter becoming one of his favourite authors. Anthony Trollope (1815–1882) was also an
English novelist.

[112] English novelist William Makepeace Thackeray (1811–1863) was noted in particular
for his social satire. In The History of Pendennis (1848–1850), Arthur Pendennis moves to
London to seek his fortune, sharing rooms with his friend George Warrington, a journalist
who helps the protagonist with his writing career. Major Pendennis, Arthur's uncle and a
snob, does not think highly of journalists.

[113] B. N. C. stands for Brasenose College (founded 1509), a constituent college of the
University of Oxford.

would have taken a double First like my poor father and made something of a figure in the world.[114] However, it can't be helped.' The poor man sighed, and lit his pipe, and walked in another part of the garden.

But he was mistaken in his diagnosis of the symptoms. The book that Lucian had begun lay unheeded in the drawer; it was a secret work that he was engaged on, and the manuscripts that he took out of that inner pocket never left him day or night. He slept with them next to his heart, and he would kiss them when he was quite alone, and pay them such devotion as he would have paid to her whom they symbolized. He wrote on these leaves a wonderful ritual of praise and devotion; it was the liturgy of his religion. Again and again he copied and recopied this madness of a lover; dallying all days over the choice of a word, searching for more exquisite phrases. No common words, no such phrases as he might use in a tale would suffice; the sentences of worship must stir and be quickened, they must glow and burn, and be decked out as with rare work of jewellery.[115] Every part of that holy and beautiful body must be adored; he sought for terms of extravagant praise, he bent his soul and mind low before her, licking the dust under her feet, abased and yet rejoicing as a Templar before the image of Baphomet.[116] He exulted more especially in the knowledge that there was nothing of the conventional or common in his ecstasy; he was not the fervent, adoring lover of Tennyson's poems, who loves with passion and yet with a proud respect, with the love always of a gentleman for a lady. Annie was not a lady; the Morgans had farmed their land for hundreds of years; they were what Mrs. Gervase and Miss Colley and the rest of them called common people. Tennyson's noble gentleman thought of their ladies with something of reticence; they imagined them dressed in flowing and courtly robes, walking with slow dignity; they dreamed of them as always stately, the future mistresses of their houses, mothers of their heirs. Such lovers bowed, but not too low, remembering their own honour, before those who were to be equal companions and friends as well as wives. It was not such conceptions as these that he embodied in the

---

[114] 'Taking a double First' may refer to obtaining first-class honours in two subjects studied at university, but more likely refers to receiving first-class results in both parts of an undergraduate degree.

[115] Machen's language would have reminded many of the popular phrase 'to burn always with this hard, gem-like flame', from Walter Pater's *The Renaissance* (1873), arguably the most influential work of Aestheticist writing ever. Against Pater's intent, the image here became shorthand for leading a Decadent life of sensuous pleasure in the moment.

[116] The Templars (also known as the Knights Templar and the Knights of the Temple of Solomon) were a religio-military order founded in Jerusalem around 1118 CE. They caused controversy amongst officials in the Roman Catholic Church because of their rapidly expanding wealth and power, and their enemies began to accuse them of sacrilegious practices (e.g. the worship of Baphomet, a mysterious idol or deity associated with demonic practices). Pope Clement V dissolved the Templars in 1312, and their leaders were burned at the stake as heretics.

amazing emblems of his ritual; he was not, he told himself, a young officer, 'something in the city,' or a rising barrister engaged to a Miss Dixon or a Miss Gervase. He had not thought of looking out for a nice little house in a good residential suburb where they would have pleasant society; there were to be no consultations about wall-papers, or jocose whispers from friends as to the necessity of having a room that would do for a nursery. No glad young thing had leant on his arm while they chose the suite in white enamel, and the china for 'our bedroom,' the modest salesman doing his best to spare their blushes. When Edith Gervase married she would get mamma to look out for two really good servants, 'as we must begin quietly,' and mamma would make sure that the drains and everything were right. Then her 'girl friends' would come on a certain solemn day to see all her 'lovely things.' 'Two dozen of everything!' 'Look, Ethel, did you ever see such ducky frills?' 'And that insertion, isn't it quite too sweet?' 'My dear Edith, you *are* a lucky girl.' 'All the underlinen specially made by Madame Lulu!' 'What delicious things!' 'I hope he knows what a prize he is winning.' 'Oh! do look at those lovely ribbon-bows!' 'You darling, how happy you must be.' 'Real Valenciennes!'[117] Then a whisper in the lady's ear, and her reply, 'Oh, *don't*, Nelly!' So they would chirp over their treasures, as in Rabelais they chirped over their cups;[118] and everything would be done in due order till the wedding-day, when mamma, who had strained her sinews and the commandments to bring the match about, would weep and look indignantly at the unhappy bridegroom. 'I *hope* you'll be kind to her, Robert.' Then in a rapid whisper to the bride: 'Mind, you *insist* on Wyman's flushing the drains when you come back; servants are so careless and dirty too. Don't let him go about by himself in Paris. Men are so *queer*; one never knows. You *have* got the pills?' And aloud, after these *secreta*, 'God bless you, my dear; good-bye! *cluck, cluck*, good-bye!'[119]

There were stranger things written in the manuscript pages that Lucian cherished, sentences that burnt and glowed like 'coals of fire which hath a most vehement flame.'[120] There were phrases that stung and tingled as he wrote them, and sonorous words poured out in ecstasy and rapture, as in some of the

---

[117] A type of fine lace first made in the fifteenth century in the French city of Valenciennes.
[118] In Rabelais's sixteenth-century *The Life of Gargantua and of Pantagruel*, the phrase 'chirped over their cups' depicts people festively chatting while indulging in food and drink.
[119] The Latin *secreta* (plural of *secretum*) refers to that which is secreted. The Latin for 'secrets' is *arcana* or *occulta*, concepts that Machen would not have wanted to associate with the shallow character of Mrs Dixon.
[120] From the Bible's Song of Solomon 8. 6. The nineteenth-century Decadents admired the Song for its forthright sexuality and strong female voice. In contrast to Mrs Dixon's concerns about the cleanliness of the plumbing, Machen here again brings to mind (as he had in the previous paragraph) Pater's advice that the individual 'burn always with this hard, gem-like flame'.

old litanies.[121] He hugged the thought that a great part of what he had invented was in the true sense of the word occult: page after page might have been read aloud to the uninitiated without betraying the inner meaning.[122] He dreamed night and day over these symbols, he copied and re-copied the manuscript nine times before he wrote it out fairly in a little book which he made himself of a skin of creamy vellum.[123] In his mania for acquirements that should be entirely useless he had gained some skill in illumination, or limning as he preferred to call it, always choosing the obscurer word as the obscurer arts.[124] First he set himself to the severe practice of the text; he spent many hours and days of toil in struggling to fashion the serried columns of black letter, writing and re-writing till he could shape the massive character with firm true hand. He cut his quills with the patience of a monk in the scriptorium, shaving and altering the nib, lightening and increasing the pressure and flexibility of the points, till the pen satisfied him, and gave a stroke both broad and even.[125] Then he made experiments in inks, searching for some medium that would rival the glossy black letter of the old manuscripts; and not till he could produce a fair page of text did he turn to the more entrancing labour of the capitals and borders and ornaments.[126] He mused long over the Lombardic letters, as glorious in their way as a cathedral, and trained his hand to execute the bold and flowing lines; and then there was the art of the border, blossoming in fretted splendour all about the page. His cousin, Miss Deacon, called it all a great waste of time, and his father thought he would have done much better in trying to improve his ordinary handwriting, which was both ugly and illegible. Indeed, there seemed but a poor demand for the limner's art. He sent some specimens of his skill to an 'artistic firm' in London; a verse of the 'Maud,' curiously emblazoned,

---

[121] A litany is a form of prayer comprising invocations (or supplications) and responses. By characterizing them as old, Lucian is likely harking back to familiar litanies he would have heard as a boy at his father's church.

[122] Machen is exploring the relationship between beautiful writing and occult spirituality, and the possibility of the former allowing access to the latter.

[123] Vellum is an animal skin (such as that of calf or lamb) specially prepared for use as a writing surface. Mediaeval monks and others wrote on and made books out of pieces of vellum; however, the practice largely died out in Europe with the invention of the printing press. Lucian's careful attention to the fabric of the book and to book arts in general is reminiscent of other Decadent literary characters, such as the protagonists of Huysmans's *A Rebours* and Wilde's *Picture of Dorian Gray*.

[124] An illumination is a painted design that decorates the pages of a mediaeval book or manuscript.

[125] A scriptorium is a room in a monastery for writing and copying manuscripts.

[126] These 'capitals, borders and ornaments' are types of illuminations often used to decorate mediaeval manuscripts, gaining renewed popularity from the Pre-Raphaelite movement's interest in the book arts. 'Lombardic letters', referred to in the next sentence, are a type of calligraphy from Lombardy, Italy, characterized by particularly broad letters with ornate designs, usually reserved for an initial letter (first letter) in a paragraph or section.

and a Latin hymn with the notes pricked on a red stave.[127] The firm wrote civilly, telling him that his work, though good, was not what they wanted, and enclosing an illuminated text. 'We have great demand for this sort of thing,' they concluded, 'and if you care to attempt something in this style we should be pleased to look at it.' The said text was 'Thou, God, seest me.'[128] The letter was of a degraded form, bearing much the same relation to the true character as a 'churchwarden gothic' building does to Canterbury Cathedral; the colours were varied.[129] The initial was pale gold, the *h* pink, the *o* black, the *u* blue, and the first letter was somehow connected with a bird's nest containing the young of the pigeon, who were waited on by the female bird.

'What a pretty text,' said Miss Deacon. 'I should like to nail it up in my room. Why don't you try to do something like that, Lucian? You might make something by it.'

'I sent them these,' said Lucian, 'but they don't like them much.'

'My dear boy! I should think not! Like them! What were you thinking of to draw those queer stiff flowers all round the border? Roses? They don't look like roses at all events. Where do you get such ideas from?'

'But the design is appropriate; look at the words.'

'My dear Lucian, I can't read the words; it's such a queer old-fashioned writing. Look how plain that text is; one can see what it's about. And this other one; I can't make it out at all.'

'It's a Latin hymn.'

'A Latin hymn? Is it a Protestant hymn? I may be old-fashioned, but *Hymns Ancient and Modern* is quite good enough for me.[130] This is the music, I suppose? But, my dear boy, there are only four lines, and who ever heard of notes shaped like that: you have made some square and some diamond-shape? Why didn't you look in your poor mother's old music? It's in the ottoman in the drawing-room. I could have shown you how to make the notes; there are crotchets, you know, and quavers.'[131]

---

[127] 'Maud' likely refers to Tennyson's poem of that name (1855). A 'stave' (more commonly 'staff' in North America) is the set of five parallel lines used for musical notation.

[128] In the Bible (Genesis 16. 13), Hagar speaks these words when she is alone in the wilderness and pregnant with Abraham's son, Ishmael.

[129] Machen's simile indicates that the sample sent to Lucian is a degraded form of its mediaeval predecessor. Canterbury Cathedral — the seat of the Archbishop of Canterbury — is renowned for the quality of its gothic architecture (e.g. the soaring fifteenth-century tower), whereas 'churchwarden gothic' can be taken to refer to later examples of the gothic architectural style as they appear in diluted and adulterated form in churches across England. In the Anglican Church, a 'churchwarden' is the lay person who looks after a church's secular affairs.

[130] In the second half of the nineteenth century, the main source of hymns sung in Anglican churches was *Hymns Ancient and Modern* (1861, followed by revised and expanded editions), a collection of relatively recent English hymns as well as ancient hymns translated into English.

[131] Crotchets (printed thus: ♩) and quavers (printed thus: ♪) are two types of musical notes,

Miss Deacon laid down the illuminated *Urbs Beata* in despair; she felt convinced that her cousin was 'next door to an idiot.'[132]

And he went out into the garden and raged behind a hedge. He broke two flower-pots and hit an apple-tree very hard with his stick, and then, feeling more calm, wondered what was the use of trying to do anything. He would not have put the thought into words, but in his heart he was aggrieved that his cousin liked the pigeons and the text, and did not like his emblematical roses and the Latin hymn. He knew he had taken great pains over the work, and that it was well done, and being still a young man he expected praise. He found that in this hard world there was a lack of appreciation; a critical spirit seemed abroad. If he could have been scientifically observed as he writhed and smarted under the strictures of 'the old fool,' as he rudely called his cousin, the spectacle would have been extremely diverting. Little boys sometimes enjoy a very similar entertainment; either with their tiny fingers or with mamma's nail scissors they gradually deprive a fly of its wings and legs. The odd gyrations and queer thin buzzings of the creature as it spins comically round and round never fail to provide a fund of harmless amusement. Lucian, indeed, fancied himself a very ill-used individual; but he should have tried to imitate the nervous organisation of the flies, which, as mamma says, 'can't really feel.'[133]

But now, as he prepared the vellum leaves, he remembered his art with joy; he had not laboured to do beautiful work in vain. He read over his manuscript once more, and thought of the designing of the pages. He made sketches on furtive sheets of paper, and hunted up books in his father's library for suggestions. There were books about architecture, and mediæval iron work, and brasses which contributed hints for adornment; and not content with mere pictures he sought in the woods and hedges, scanning the strange forms of trees, and the poisonous growth of great water-plants, and the parasite twining of honeysuckle and briony.[134] In one of these rambles he discovered a red earth which he made into a pigment, and he found in the unctuous juice of a certain fern an ingredient which he thought made his black ink still more glossy. His book was written all in symbols, and in the same spirit of symbolism he decorated it, causing wonderful foliage to creep about the text, and showing the

---

each indicating the length of time each note should be held (a quaver is held for half the duration of a crotchet). In North America, crotchets and quavers are today usually referred to as quarter and eighth notes, respectively.

[132] *Urbs Beata* is Latin for 'Blessed city of Jerusalem, called vision of peace', the name of a mediaeval hymn.

[133] The idea that flies and other non-human animals cannot feel was given a great deal of currency by Descartes, whose mechanistic theory of non-human animals' physiology — essentially, that they are a type of machine and, therefore, cannot feel pain — was especially influential and debated in the nineteenth century.

[134] Honeysuckle and briony (or bryony) are types of climbing vines. The berries of both plants are poisonous to humans.

blossom of certain mystical flowers, with emblems of strange creatures, caught and bound in rose thickets. All was dedicated to love and a lover's madness, and there were songs in it which haunted him with their lilt and refrain. When the book was finished it replaced the loose leaves as his constant companion by day and night. Three times a day he repeated his ritual to himself, seeking out the loneliest places in the woods, or going up to his room; and from the fixed intentness and rapture of his gaze, the father thought him still severely employed in the questionable process of composition. At night he contrived to wake for his strange worship; and he had a peculiar ceremony when he got up in the dark and lit his candle. From a steep and wild hillside, not far from the house, he had cut from time to time five large boughs of spiked and prickly gorse. He had brought them into the house, one by one, and had hidden them in the big box that stood beside his bed. Often he woke up weeping and murmuring to himself the words of one of his songs, and then when he had lit the candle, he would draw out the gorse-boughs, and place them on the floor, and taking off his nightgown, gently lay himself down on the bed of thorns and spines. Lying on his face, with the candle and the book before him, he would softly and tenderly repeat the praises of his dear, dear Annie, and as he turned over page after page, and saw the raised gold of the majuscules glow and flame in the candle-light, he pressed the thorns into his flesh.[135] At such moments he tasted in all its acute savour the joy of physical pain; and after two or three experiences of such delights he altered his book, making a curious sign in vermilion on the margin of the passages where he was to inflict on himself this sweet torture. Never did he fail to wake at the appointed hour, a strong effort of will broke through all the heaviness of sleep, and he would rise up, joyful though weeping, and reverently set his thorny bed upon the floor, offering his pain with his praise. When he had whispered the last word, and had risen from the ground, his body would be all freckled with drops of blood; he used to view the marks with pride. Here and there a spine would be left deep in the flesh, and he would pull these out roughly, tearing through the skin. On some nights when he had pressed with more fervour on the thorns his thighs would stream with blood, red beads standing out on the flesh, and trickling down to his feet. He had some difficulty in washing away the bloodstains so as not to leave any traces to attract the attention of the servant; and after a time he returned no more to his bed when his duty had been accomplished. For a coverlet he had a dark rug, a good deal worn, and in this he would wrap his naked bleeding body, and lie down on the hard floor, well content to add an aching rest to the account of his pleasures. He was covered with scars, and those that healed during the day were torn open afresh at night; the pale olive skin was red with the angry marks of blood, and the graceful form of the young man appeared like the body

---

[135] Majuscules are capital letters.

of a tortured martyr.[136] He grew thinner and thinner every day, for he ate but little; the skin was stretched on the bones of his face, and the black eyes burnt in dark purple hollows. His relations noticed that he was not looking well.

'Now, Lucian, it's perfect madness of you to go on like this,' said Miss Deacon, one morning at breakfast. 'Look how your hand shakes; some people would say that you have been taking brandy. And all that you want is a little medicine, and yet you won't be advised. You know it's not my fault; I have asked you to try Dr. Jelly's Cooling Powders again and again.'

He remembered the forcible exhibition of the powders when he was a boy, and felt thankful that those days were over. He only grinned at his cousin and swallowed a great cup of strong tea to steady his nerves, which were shaky enough. Mrs. Dixon saw him one day in Caermaen; it was very hot, and he had been walking rather fast. The scars on his body burnt and tingled, and he tottered as he raised his hat to the vicar's wife. She decided without further investigation that he must have been drinking in public-houses.[137]

'It seems a mercy that poor Mrs. Taylor was taken,' she said to her husband. 'She has certainly been spared a great deal. That wretched young man passed me this afternoon; he was quite intoxicated.'

'How very sad,' said Mr. Dixon. 'A little port, my dear?'

'Thank you, Merivale, I will have another glass of sherry. Dr. Burrows is always scolding me and saying I *must* take something to keep up my energy, and this sherry is so weak.'

The Dixons were not teetotallers. They regretted it deeply, and blamed the doctor, who 'insisted on some stimulant.' However, there was some consolation in trying to convert the parish to total abstinence, or, as they curiously called it, temperance. Old women were warned of the sin of taking a glass of beer for supper; aged labourers were urged to try Cork-ho, the new temperance drink; an uncouth beverage, styled coffee, was dispensed at the reading-room. Mr. Dixon preached an eloquent 'temperance' sermon, soon after the above conversation, taking as his text: *Beware of the leaven of the Pharisees.*[138] In his

---

[136] The early centuries of the Christian church are especially known for the scores of martyrs who suffered and died for their religious beliefs. Lucian's suffering recalls mediaeval and early modern illustrations of young, attractive male martyrs such as St Sebastian, a Roman officer who, in the third century, converted to Christianity and was executed by being shot full of arrows.

[137] Pubs, which Machen also refers to as publics.

[138] A line spoken by Jesus (Matthew 16. 6), warning his disciples to avoid not the literal leaven used by the Pharisees and the Sadducees when they make bread but, metaphorically, their doctrines. By focusing on his parishioners' consumption of alcoholic beverages, Mr Dixon is misconstruing the meaning of the biblical passage much as Jesus's disciples did — taking the literal rather than the metaphorical sense. The Pharisees and the Sadducees were ancient Jewish sects that held radically differing philosophical and theological views;

discourse he showed that fermented liquor and leaven had much in common, that beer was at the present day 'put away' during Passover by the strict Jews; and in a moving peroration he urged his dear brethren, 'and more especially those amongst us who are poor in this world's goods,' to beware indeed of that evil leaven which was sapping the manhood of our nation.[139] Mrs. Dixon cried after church:

'Oh, Merivale, what a beautiful sermon! How earnest you were. I hope it will do good.'

Mr. Dixon swallowed his port with great decorum, but his wife fuddled herself every evening with cheap sherry. She was quite unaware of the fact, and sometimes wondered in a dim way why she always had to scold the children after dinner. And so strange things sometimes happened in the nursery, and now and then the children looked queerly at one another after a red-faced woman had gone out, panting.

Lucian knew nothing of his accuser's trials, but he was not long in hearing of his own intoxication. The next time he went down to Caermaen he was hailed by the doctor.

'Been drinking again today?' 'No,' said Lucian in a puzzled voice. 'What do you mean?'

'Oh, well, if you haven't, that's all right, as you'll be able to take a drop with me. Come along in?'

Over the whisky and pipes Lucian heard of the evil rumours affecting his character.

'Mrs. Dixon assured me you were staggering from one side of the street to the other. You quite frightened her, she said. Then she asked me if I recommended her to take one or two ounces of spirit at bedtime for the palpitation; and of course I told her two would be better. I have my living to make here, you know. And upon my word, I think she wants it; she's always gurgling inside like waterworks. I wonder how old Dixon can stand it.'

'I like "ounces of spirit,"' said Lucian. 'That's taking it medicinally, I suppose. I've often heard of ladies who have to "take it medicinally"; and that's how it's done?'

'That's it. "Dr Burrows won't *listen* to me": "I tell him how I dislike the taste of spirits, but he says they are absolutely *necessary* for my constitution": "my medical man *insists* on something at bedtime"; that's the style.'

Lucian laughed gently; all these people had become indifferent to him;

---

by the nineteenth century, the name Pharisees had come to stand for people who were sanctimonious and self-righteous.

[139] Mr Dixon is especially patronizing towards the less-well-off members of his congregation, implying that alcoholic beverages are particularly harmful for them. In his language, there are echoes of biblical injunctions for the rich to help the poor (e.g. 1 Timothy 6. 17–18; 1 John 4. 17), but he seems not to heed them.

he could no longer feel savage indignation at their little hypocrisies and malignancies. Their voices uttering calumny, and morality, and futility had become like the thin shrill angry note of a gnat on a summer evening; he had his own thoughts and his own life, and he passed on without heeding.

'You come down to Caermaen pretty often, don't you?' said the doctor. 'I've seen you two or three times in the last fortnight.'

'Yes, I enjoy the walk.'

'Well, look me up whenever you like, you know. I am often in just at this time, and a chat with a human being isn't bad, now and then. It's a change for me; I'm often afraid I shall lose my patients.'

The doctor had the weakness of these terrible puns, dragged headlong into the conversation. He sometimes exhibited them before Mrs. Gervase, who would smile in a faint and dignified manner, and say:

'Ah, I see. Very amusing indeed. We had an old coachman once who was very clever, I believe, at that sort of thing, but Mr. Gervase was obliged to send him away, the laughter of the other domestics was so very boisterous.'

Lucian laughed, not boisterously, but good-humouredly, at the doctor's joke. He liked Burrows, feeling that he was a man and not an automatic gabbling machine.

'You look a little pulled down,' said the doctor, when Lucian rose to go. 'No, you don't want my medicine. Plenty of beef and beer will do you more good than drugs. I daresay it's the hot weather that has thinned you a bit. Oh, you'll be all right again in a month.'

As Lucian strolled out of the town on his way home, he passed a small crowd of urchins assembled at the corner of an orchard. They were enjoying themselves immensely. The 'healthy' boy, the same whom he had seen some weeks ago operating on a cat, seemed to have recognised his selfishness in keeping his amusements to himself. He had found a poor lost puppy, a little creature with bright pitiful eyes, almost human in their fond, friendly gaze. It was not a well-bred little dog; it was certainly not that famous puppy 'by Vick out of Wasp'; it had rough hair and a foolish long tail which it wagged beseechingly, at once deprecating severity and asking kindness. The poor animal had evidently been used to gentle treatment; it would look up in a boy's face, and give a leap, fawning on him, and then bark in a small doubtful voice, and cower a moment on the ground, astonished perhaps at the strangeness, the bustle and animation. The boys were beside themselves with eagerness; there was quite a babble of voices, arguing, discussing, suggesting. Each one had a plan of his own which he brought before the leader, a stout and sturdy youth.

'Drown him! What be you thinkin' of, mun?' he was saying. ''tain't no sport at all. You shut your mouth, gwaes. Be you goin' to ask your mother for the boiling water? Iss, Bob Williams, I do know all that: but where be you a-going to get the fire from? Be quiet, mun, can't you? Thomas Trevor, be this dog yourn or mine? Now, look you, if you don't all of you shut your bloody mouths, I'll take the dog 'ome and keep him. There now!'

He was a born leader of men. A singular depression and lowness of spirit showed itself on the boys' faces. They recognised that the threat might very possibly be executed, and their countenances were at once composed to humble attention. The puppy was still cowering on the ground in the midst of them: one or two tried to relieve the tension of their feelings by kicking him in the belly with their hobnail boots. It cried out with the pain and writhed a little, but the poor little beast did not attempt to bite or even snarl. It looked up with those beseeching friendly eyes at its persecutors, and fawned on them again, and tried to wag its tail and be merry, pretending to play with a straw on the road, hoping perhaps to win a little favour in that way.

The leader saw the moment for his master-stroke. He slowly drew a piece of rope from his pocket.

'What do you say to that, mun? Now, Thomas Trevor! We'll hang him over that there bough. Will that suit you, Bobby Williams?'

There was a great shriek of approval and delight. All was again bustle and animation. 'I'll tie it round his neck?' 'Get out, mun, you don't know how it be done.' 'Iss, I do, Charley.' 'Now, let me, gwaes, now do let me.' 'You be sure he won't bite?' 'He bain't mad, be he?' 'Suppose we were to tie up his mouth first?'

The puppy still fawned and curried favour, and wagged that sorry tail, and lay down crouching on one side on the ground, sad and sorry in his heart, but still with a little gleam of hope; for now and again he tried to play, and put up his face, praying with those fond, friendly eyes. And then at last his gambols and poor efforts for mercy ceased, and he lifted up his wretched voice in one long dismal whine of despair. But he licked the hand of the boy that tied the noose.[140]

He was slowly and gently swung into the air as Lucian went by unheeded; he struggled, and his legs twisted and writhed. The 'healthy' boy pulled the rope, and his friends danced and shouted with glee. As Lucian turned the corner, the poor dangling body was swinging to and fro, the puppy was dying, but he still kicked a little.

Lucian went on his way hastily, and shuddering with disgust. The young of the human creature were really too horrible; they defiled the earth, and made

---

[140] Animal rights received extensive advocacy during the Victorian period, with dogs — recognized as intimate and loyal pets and companions — gaining particular attention. Machen's description here echoes Dr George Hoggan's immensely influential letter in the *Morning Post* (2 February 1875), in which Hoggan describes the cruelty of animal experimentation and depicts a dog licking the vivisector's hands as if begging for mercy. Attitudes during the 1890s were also shaped by the findings of the 1887 Select Committee, set up to investigate responses to rabies, which led to a broader consideration of the regulation of pets.

existence unpleasant, as the pulpy growth of a noxious and obscene fungus spoils an agreeable walk. The sight of those malignant little animals with mouths that uttered cruelty and filth, with hands dexterous in torture, and feet swift to run all evil errands, had given him a shock and broken up the world of strange thoughts in which he had been dwelling. Yet it was no good being angry with them: it was their nature to be very loathsome. Only he wished they would go about their hideous amusements in their own back gardens where nobody could see them at work; it was too bad that he should be interrupted and offended in a quiet country road. He tried to put the incident out of his mind, as if the whole thing had been a disagreeable story, and the visions amongst which he wished to move were beginning to return, when he was again rudely disturbed. A little girl, a pretty child of eight or nine, was coming along the lane to meet him. She was crying bitterly and looking to left and right, and calling out some word all the time.

'Jack, Jack, Jack! Little Jackie! Jack!'

Then she burst into tears afresh, and peered into the hedge, and tried to peep through a gate into a field.

'Jackie, Jackie, Jackie!'

She came up to Lucian, sobbing as if her heart would break, and dropped him an old-fashioned curtsy.

'Oh, please sir, have you seen my little Jackie?'

'What do you mean?' said Lucian. 'What is it you've lost?'

'A little dog, please sir. A little terrier dog with white hair. Father gave me him a month ago, and said I might keep him. Someone did leave the garden gate open this afternoon, and he must 'a got away, sir, and I was so fond of him, sir, he was so playful and loving, and I be afraid he be lost.'

She began to call again, without waiting for an answer.

'Jack, Jack, Jack!'

'I'm afraid some boys have got your little dog,' said Lucian. 'They've killed him. You'd better go back home.'

He went on, walking as fast as he could in his endeavour to get beyond the noise of the child's crying. It distressed him, and he wished to think of other things. He stamped his foot angrily on the ground as he recalled the annoyances of the afternoon, and longed for some hermitage on the mountains, far above the stench and the sound of humanity.

A little farther, and he came to Croeswen, where the road branched off to right and left.[141] There was a triangular plot of grass between the two roads; there the cross had once stood, 'the goodly and famous roode' of the old local chronicle.[142] The words echoed in Lucian's ears as he went by on the right

---

[141] Croeswen is a community in south-east Wales.

[142] The phrase 'the goodly and famous roode' is from *Rites of Durham*, and Machen uses

hand. 'There were five steps that did go up to the first pace, and seven steps to
the second pace, all of clene hewn ashler. And all above it was most curiously
and gloriously wrought with thorowgh carved work; in the highest place was
the Holy Roode with Christ upon the Cross having Marie on the one syde and
John on the other. And below were six splendent and glisteringe archaungels
that bore up the roode, and beneath them in their stories were the most fair and
noble ymages of the xii Apostles and of divers other Saints and Martirs. And
in the lowest storie there was a marvelous ymagerie of divers Beasts, such as
oxen and horses and swine, and little dogs and peacocks, all done in the finest
and most curious wise, so that they all seemed as they were caught in a Wood
of Thorns, the which is their torment of this life.[143] And here once in the year
was a marvelous solemn service, when the parson of Caermaen came out with
the singers and all the people, singing the psalm *Benedicite omnia opera* as they
passed along the road in their procession.[144] And when they stood at the roode
the priest did there his service, making certain prayers for the beasts, and then
he went up to the first pace and preached a sermon to the people, shewing them
that as our lord Jhu dyed upon the Tree of his deare mercy for us, so we too owe
mercy to the beasts his Creatures, for that they are all his poor lieges and silly
servants. And that like as the Holy Aungells do their suit to him on high, and
the Blessed xii Apostles and the Martirs, and all the Blissful Saints served him
aforetime on earth and now praise him in heaven, so also do the beasts serve
him, though they be in torment of life and below men. For their spirit goeth
downward, as Holy Writ teacheth us.'[145]

It was a quaint old record, a curious relic of what the modern inhabitants of
Caermaen called the Dark Ages.[146] A few of the stones that had formed the base

---

fragments of the same text to construct some of the rest of the paragraph. This important
anonymous manuscript from the mid-sixteenth century describes the monuments and rites
of Durham Cathedral in the north of England, prior to the Reformation. The phrase 'clene
hewn ashler' — a slight variant of which appears in Robert Willis's (1800–1875) *Architectural
Nomenclature of the Middle Ages* (1844) — suggests Machen also used an architectural
document as a source. 'Roode' (or 'rood') is the word for an often large crucifix commonly
located inside a mediaeval church, at the entry to the choir or chancel.

[143] 'Mary Walked through a Wood of Thorns' is a mid-nineteenth-century German song of
pilgrimage. It became a popular Christmas song in various European languages, including
English.

[144] Not a psalm but a canticle, the 'Benedicite, omnia opera Domini' is a joyful prayer of
thanksgiving for God's works of creation. In the English version from the 1662 *Book of
Common Prayer*, the canticle begins 'O all ye works of the Lord, bless ye the Lord'.

[145] Whether the spirits/souls of non-human animals go to heaven has been a longstanding
and vexed question for theologians, philosophers, and animal rights activists. Machen's
language here seems to echo the biblical passage, enigmatically phrased as a question:
'Who knoweth the spirit of man that goeth upward, and the spirit of the beast that goeth
downward to the earth?' (Ecclesiastes 3. 22).

[146] The term 'the Dark Ages' has generally been used to refer to the centuries following the
fall of the Western Roman Empire in the fourth and fifth centuries CE to approximately

of the cross still remained in position, grey with age, blotched with black lichen and green moss. The remainder of the famous rood had been used to mend the roads, to build pigsties and domestic offices; it had turned Protestant, in fact.[147] Indeed, if it had remained, the parson of Caermaen would have had no time for the service; the coffee-stall, the Portuguese Missions, the Society for the Conversion of the Jews, and important social duties took up all his leisure. Besides, he thought the whole ceremony unscriptural.

Lucian passed on his way, wondering at the strange contrasts of the Middle Ages. How was it that people who could devise so beautiful a service believed in witchcraft, demoniacal possession and obsession, in the incubus and succubus, and in the Sabbath and in many other horrible absurdities?[148] It seemed astonishing that anybody could even pretend to credit such monstrous tales, but there could be no doubt that the dread of old women who rode on broomsticks and liked black cats was once a very genuine terror.

A cold wind blew up from the river at sunset, and the scars on his body began to burn and tingle. The pain recalled his ritual to him, and he began to recite it as he walked along. He had cut a branch of thorn from the hedge and placed it next to his skin, pressing the spikes into the flesh with his hand till the warm blood ran down. He felt it was an exquisite and sweet observance for her sake; and then he thought of the secret golden palace he was building for her, the rare and wonderful city rising in his imagination. As the solemn night began to close about the earth, and the last glimmer of the sun faded from the hills, he gave himself anew to the woman, his body and his mind, all that he was, and all that he had.

IV

In the course of the week Lucian again visited Caermaen. He wished to view the amphitheatre more precisely, to note the exact position of the ancient walls, to gaze up the valley from certain points within the town, to imprint minutely and clearly on his mind the surge of the hills about the city, and the dark tapestry of the hanging woods. And he lingered in the museum where the relics of the Roman occupation had been stored; he was interested in the fragments of

---

1000 CE. The term implies a collapse of civic institutions and learning, which Machen questions in his phrasing here.

[147] During the sixteenth-century Protestant Reformation in Britain, many objects associated with Roman Catholicism's perceived idolatry and superstition were either destroyed or repurposed for secular uses.

[148] An 'incubus' is an evil spirit or demon in male form said to descend upon and have sexual relations with women when they are sleeping. A 'succubus' is the female counterpart, said to have sexual relations with sleeping men. On the nocturnal Sabbath, or Witches' Sabbath, see note 38 to 'The Recluse of Bayswater'.

tessellated floors,[149] in the glowing gold of drinking cups, the curious beads of fused and coloured glass, the carved amber-work, the scent-flagons that still retained the memory of unctuous odours, the necklaces, brooches, hairpins of gold and silver, and other intimate objects which had once belonged to Roman ladies. One of the glass flagons, buried in damp earth for many hundred years, had gathered in its dark grave all the splendours of the light, and now shone like an opal with a moonlight glamour and gleams of gold and pale sunset green, and imperial purple. Then there were the wine jars of red earthenware, the memorial stones from graves, and the heads of broken gods, with fragments of occult things used in the secret rites of Mithras.[150] Lucian read on the labels where all these objects were found: in the churchyard, beneath the turf of the meadow, and in the old cemetery near the forest; and whenever it was possible he would make his way to the spot of discovery, and imagine the long darkness that had hidden gold and stone and amber. All these investigations were necessary for the scheme he had in view, so he became for some time quite a familiar figure in the dusty deserted streets and in the meadows by the river. His continual visits to Caermaen were a tortuous puzzle to the inhabitants, who flew to their windows at the sound of a step on the uneven pavements. They were at a loss in their conjectures; his motive for coming down three times a week must of course be bad, but it seemed undiscoverable. And Lucian on his side was at first a good deal put out by occasional encounters with members of the Gervase or Dixon or Colley tribes; he had often to stop and exchange a few conventional expressions, and such meetings, casual as they were, annoyed and distracted him. He was no longer infuriated or wounded by sneers or contempt or by the cackling laughter of the young people when they passed him on the road (his hat was a shocking one and his untidiness terrible), but such incidents were unpleasant just as the smell of a drain was unpleasant, and threw the strange mechanism of his thoughts out of gear for the time. Then he had been disgusted by the affair of the boys and the little dog; the loathsomeness of it had quite broken up his fancies. He had read books of modern occultism, and remembered some of the experiments described. The adept, it was alleged, could transfer the sense of consciousness from the brain to the foot or hand, he could annihilate the world around him and pass into another sphere.[151] Lucian wondered whether he could not perform some such operation for his own benefit. Human beings were constantly annoying him and getting in his way; was it not possible to annihilate the race, or at all events to reduce them to wholly insignificant forms? A certain process suggested itself

---

[149] Tessellated floors are made of mosaics.

[150] The cult of Mithras, an ancient Persian god, spread throughout the Roman Empire during the first two centuries CE and was especially popular amongst the legions. Worship involved secret, male-only rites.

[151] An adept is a person who is highly skilled and knowledgeable in a certain art or science.

to his mind, a work partly mental and partly physical, and after two or three experiments he found to his astonishment and delight that it was successful. Here, he thought, he had discovered one of the secrets of true magic; this was the key to the symbolic transmutations of the eastern tales.[152] The adept could, in truth, change those who were obnoxious to him into harmless and unimportant shapes, not as in the letter of the old stories, by transforming the enemy, but by transforming himself. The magician puts men below him by going up higher, as one looks down on a mountain city from a loftier crag. The stones on the road and such petty obstacles do not trouble the wise man on the great journey, and so Lucian, when obliged to stop and converse with his fellow-creatures, to listen to their poor pretences and inanities, was no more inconvenienced than when he had to climb an awkward stile in the course of a walk. As for the more unpleasant manifestations of humanity, after all they no longer concerned him. Men intent on the great purpose did not suffer the current of their thoughts to be broken by the buzzing of a fly caught in a spider's web, so why should he be perturbed by the misery of a puppy in the hands of village boys? The fly, no doubt, endured its tortures; lying helpless and bound in those slimy bands, it cried out in its thin voice when the claws of the horrible monster fastened on it; but its dying agonies had never vexed the reverie of a lover. Lucian saw no reason why the boys should offend him more than the spider, or why he should pity the dog more than he pitied the fly. The talk of the men and women might be wearisome and inept and often malignant; but he could not imagine an alchemist at the moment of success, a general in the hour of victory, or a financier with a gigantic scheme of swindling well on the market being annoyed by the buzz of insects. The spider is, no doubt, a very terrible brute with a hideous mouth and hairy tiger-like claws when seen through the microscope; but Lucian had taken away the microscope from his eyes. He could now walk the streets of Caermaen confident and secure, without any dread of interruption, for at a moment's notice the transformation could be effected. Once Dr. Burrows caught him and made him promise to attend a bazaar that was to be held in aid of the Hungarian Protestants; Lucian assented the more willingly as he wished to pay a visit to certain curious mounds on a hill a little way out of the town, and he calculated on slinking off from the bazaar early in the afternoon. Lord Beamys was visiting Sir Vivian Ponsonby, a local magnate, and had kindly promised to drive over and declare the bazaar open. It was a solemn moment when the carriage drew up and the great man alighted. He was rather an evil-looking old nobleman, but the clergy and gentry, their wives and sons and daughters welcomed him with great and unctuous joy. Conversations

---

[152] Machen employs the term 'magic' here as used within occult spirituality, where it refers to the use of secret, learned practices to cause changes in consciousness that would enhance the individual's spiritual maturity and engagement with the universal will.

were broken off in mid-sentence, slow people gaped, not realising why their
friends had so suddenly left them, the Meyricks came up hot and perspiring in
fear lest they should be too late, Miss Colley, a yellow virgin of austere regard,
smiled largely, Mrs. Dixon beckoned wildly with her parasol to the 'girls' who
were idly strolling in a distant part of the field, and the archdeacon ran at full
speed. The air grew dark with bows, and resonant with the genial laugh of the
archdeacon, the cackle of the younger ladies, and the shrill parrot-like voices of
the matrons; those smiled who had never smiled before, and on some maiden
faces there hovered that look of adoring ecstasy with which the old masters
graced their angels. Then, when all the due rites had been performed, the
company turned and began to walk towards the booths of their small Vanity
Fair.[153] Lord Beamys led the way with Mrs. Gervase, Mrs. Dixon followed with
Sir Vivian Ponsonby, and the multitudes that followed cried, saying, 'What a
dear old man!' — 'Isn't it *kind* of him to come all this way?' — 'What a sweet
expression, isn't it?' — 'I think he's an old love' — 'One of the good old sort'
— 'Real English nobleman' — 'Oh most correct, I assure you; if a girl gets into
trouble, notice to quit at once' — 'Always stands by the Church' — 'Twenty
livings in his gift' — 'Voted for the Public Worship Regulation Act' — 'Ten
thousand acres strictly preserved.'[154] The old lord was leering pleasantly and
muttering to himself: 'Some fine gals here. Like the looks of that filly with the
pink hat. Ought to see more of her. She'd give Lotty points.'

The pomp swept slowly across the grass: the archdeacon had got hold of Mr.
Dixon, and they were discussing the misdeeds of some clergyman in the rural
deanery.

'I can scarce credit it,' said Mr. Dixon.

'Oh, I assure you, there can be no doubt. We have witnesses. There can be
no question that there was a procession at Llanfihangel on the Sunday before
Easter; the choir and minister went round the church, carrying palm branches
in their hands.'[155]

'Very shocking.'

'It has distressed the bishop. Martin is a hard-working man enough, and all

---

[153] In John Bunyan's (1628–1688) Christian allegory *The Pilgrim's Progress* (Part 1: 1678; Part
2: 1684), the town of Vanity has a perpetual fair characterized by frivolity and flamboyance.
The term 'Vanity Fair' thereafter came to indicate any group or place that was preoccupied
with such concerns. Thackeray's novel *Vanity Fair* (1847–1848) in part satirized social
pretension and shallowness.
[154] The 1874 Public Worship Regulation Act of Parliament was intended to suppress
what some believed was a growing Roman Catholic-style character within the rites and
ceremonies of the Church of England.
[155] The Sunday before Easter, commonly known as Palm Sunday, commemorates Jesus's
entry intro Jerusalem riding an ass, before which people strewed palm branches. In
Anglican and many other Western churches, palm leaves are distributed to parishioners on
Palm Sunday.

that, but those sort of things can't be tolerated. The bishop told me that he had set his face against processions.'

'Quite right: the bishop is perfectly right. Processions are unscriptural.'

'It's the thin end of the wedge, you know, Dixon.'

'Exactly. I have always resisted anything of the kind here.'

'Right. *Principiis obsta*, you know.[156] Martin is so *imprudent*. There's a *way* of doing things.'

The 'scriptural' procession led by Lord Beamys broke up when the stalls were reached, and gathered round the nobleman as he declared the bazaar open.

Lucian was sitting on a garden-seat, a little distance off, looking dreamily before him. And all that he saw was a swarm of flies clustering and buzzing about a lump of tainted meat that lay on the grass. The spectacle in no way interrupted the harmony of his thoughts, and soon after the opening of the bazaar he went quietly away, walking across the fields in the direction of the ancient mounds he desired to inspect.

All these journeys of his to Caermaen and its neighbourhood had a peculiar object; he was gradually levelling to the dust the squalid kraals of modern times, and rebuilding the splendid and golden city of Siluria.[157] All this mystic town was for the delight of his sweetheart and himself; for her the wonderful villas, the shady courts, the magic of tessellated pavements, and the hangings of rich stuffs with their intricate and glowing patterns. Lucian wandered all day through the shining streets, taking shelter sometimes in the gardens beneath the dense and gloomy ilex trees,[158] and listening to the plash and trickle of the fountains. Sometimes he would look out of a window and watch the crowd and colour of the market-place, and now and again a ship came up the river bringing exquisite silks and the merchandise of unknown lands in the Far East. He had made a curious and accurate map of the town he proposed to inhabit, in which every villa was set down and named. He drew his lines to scale with the gravity of a surveyor, and studied the plan till he was able to find his way from house to house on the darkest summer night. On the southern slopes about the town there were vineyards, always under a glowing sun, and sometimes he ventured to the furthest ridge of the forest, where the wild people still lingered, that he might catch the golden gleam of the city far away, as the light quivered and scintillated on the glittering tiles. And there were gardens outside the city gates where strange and brilliant flowers grew, filling the hot air with their odour, and scenting the breeze that blew along the streets. The dull modern life was

---

[156] Latin for 'resist the beginnings' (usually of something deemed to be negative); the expression is commonly translated by the idiomatic 'nip it in the bud'.

[157] In Afrikaans, a kraal is a rural village of huts, often enclosed by a fence; it can also mean an enclosure for livestock.

[158] The ilex tree (e.g. a holly or a holm oak) is associated by some pagans with longevity, health, and fertility. It also appears in *The Great God Pan*.

far away, and people who saw him at this period wondered what was amiss; the abstraction of his glance was obvious, even to eyes not over-sharp. But men and women had lost all their power of annoyance and vexation; they could no longer even interrupt his thought for a moment. He could listen to Mr. Dixon with apparent attention, while he was in reality enraptured by the entreating music of the double flute, played by a girl in the garden of Avallaunius, for that was the name he had taken.[159] Mr. Dixon was innocently discoursing archæology, giving a brief *résumé* of the view expressed by Mr. Wyndham at the last meeting of the antiquarian society.

'There can be no doubt that the temple of Diana stood there in pagan times,' he concluded, and Lucian assented to the opinion, and asked a few questions which seemed pertinent enough.[160] But all the time the flute notes were sounding in his ears, and the ilex threw a purple shadow on the white pavement before his villa. A boy came forward from the garden; he had been walking amongst the vines and plucking the ripe grapes, and the juice had trickled down over his breast. Standing beside the girl, unashamed in the sunlight, he began to sing one of Sappho's love songs.[161] His voice was as full and rich as a woman's, but purged of all emotion; he was an instrument of music in the flesh.[162] Lucian looked at him steadily; the white perfect body shone against the roses and the blue of the sky, clear and gleaming as marble in the glare of the sun. The words he sang burned and flamed with passion, and he was as unconscious of their meaning as the twin pipes of the flute. And the girl was smiling. The vicar shook hands and went on, well pleased with his remarks on the temple of Diana and also with Lucian's polite interest.

'He is by no means wanting in intelligence,' he said to his family. 'A little curious in manner, perhaps, but not stupid.'

---

[159] A double flute is a wind instrument (usually with a single or double reed). One of the most famous classical references to the double flute is in the musical competition between Apollo, who plays a lyre, and the satyr Marsyas, often depicted playing a double flute. Machen's original title for *The Hill of Dreams* was *The Garden of Avallaunius*, the name being his fusion of the Latin name Vallaunius with that of the island of Avalon from Arthurian legend. In Machen's hometown of Caerleon, there was found a Roman memorial marker to Tadia Vallaunius and her son. It is noted and illustrated in John Edward Lee's *Isca Silurum: or, An Illustrated Catalogue of the Museum of Antiquities at Caerleon* (London: Longman, Green, Longman and Roberts, 1862). In 1899, when Machen became a member of the Golden Dawn, he took the name Frater Avallaunius (*frater* (Latin): brother).

[160] Diana is the ancient Roman goddess of the moon, most often figured as chaste.

[161] Sappho (*c.* 630–*c.* 570 BCE) was a Greek poet from the isle of Lesbos. While only fragments of her work survive, her love lyrics — in which she often represents intense erotic desire and emotional suffering — have been deeply respected by and influential for many subsequent poets, including the English Romantics and members of the Aesthetic and Decadent movements.

[162] In George Du Maurier's (1834–1896) immensely popular, anti-aesthete novel *Trilby* (1894), the evil Svengali hypnotizes the eponymous heroine and converts her into 'a singing machine [...] a flexible flageolet of flesh and blood' (George Du Maurier, *Trilby* (Oxford: Oxford University Press, 1995), p. 299). A flageolet is a simple type of wind instrument.

'Oh, papa,' said Henrietta, 'don't you think he is rather silly? He can't talk about anything — anything interesting, I mean. And he pretends to know a lot about books, but I heard him say the other day he had never read *The Prince of the House of David* or *Ben-Hur*.[163] Fancy!'

The vicar had not interrupted Lucian. The sun still beat upon the roses, and a little breeze bore the scent of them to his nostrils together with the smell of grapes and vine-leaves. He had become curious in sensation, and as he leant back upon the cushions covered with glistening yellow silk, he was trying to analyse a strange ingredient in the perfume of the air. He had penetrated far beyond the crude distinctions of modern times, beyond the rough: 'there's a smell of roses,' 'there must be sweetbriar somewhere.' Modern perceptions of odour were, he knew, far below those of the savage in delicacy. The degraded black fellow of Australia could distinguish odours in a way that made the consumer of 'damper' stare in amazement, but the savage's sensations were all strictly utilitarian.[164] To Lucian as he sat in the cool porch, his feet on the marble, the air came laden with scents as subtly and wonderfully interwoven and contrasted as the harmonica of a great master.[165] The stained marble of the pavement gave a cool reminiscence of the Italian mountain, the blood-red roses palpitating in the sunlight sent out an odour mystical as passion itself, and there was the hint of inebriation in the perfume of the trellised vines. Besides these, the girl's desire and the unripe innocence of the boy were as distinct as benzoin and myrrh, both delicious and exquisite, and exhaled as freely as the scent of the roses.[166] But there was another element that puzzled him, an aromatic suggestion of the forest. He understood it at last; it was the vapour of the great red pines that grew beyond the garden; their spicy needles were burning in the sun, and the smell was as fragrant as the fume of incense blown from far. The soft entreaty of the flute and the swelling rapture of the boy's voice beat on the air together, and Lucian wondered whether there were in the nature of things any true distinction between the impressions of sound and scent and colour. The violent blue of the sky, the song, and the odours seemed rather varied symbols of one mystery than distinct entities. He could almost imagine that the boy's innocence was indeed a perfume, and that the palpitating roses had become a sonorous chant.

In the curious silence which followed the last notes, when the boy and girl

---

[163] Popular American novels. Joseph Holt Ingraham (1809–1860) wrote *The Prince of the House of David; or Three Years in the Holy City* (1855) and Lewis Wallace (1827–1905) wrote *Ben-Hur: A Tale of the Christ* (1880).

[164] Historically, damper was a staple among Australians working away from domestic conveniences. This basic wheat bread is traditionally cooked in the ashes of an outdoor fire.

[165] Machen is likely referring not to the simple mouth organ, but to the eighteenth-century musical instrument consisting of a series of glasses or glass bowls over which one runs one fingers to produce sound. A late version of the instrument added a keyboard.

[166] Benzoin and myrrh are exotic plant-derived aromatic resins used in the production of perfume, cosmetics, and incense.

had passed under the purple ilex shadow, he fell into a reverie. The fancy that sensations are symbols and not realities hovered in his mind, and led him to speculate as to whether they could not actually be transmuted one into another.[167] It was possible, he thought, that a whole continent of knowledge had been undiscovered; the energies of men having been expended in unimportant and foolish directions. Modern ingenuity had been employed on such trifles as locomotive engines, electric cables, and cantilever bridges; on elaborate devices for bringing uninteresting people nearer together; the ancients had been almost as foolish, because they had mistaken the symbol for the thing signified. It was not the material banquet which really mattered, but the thought of it; it was almost as futile to eat and take emetics and eat again as to invent telephones and high-pressure boilers.[168] As for some other ancient methods of enjoying life, one might as well set oneself to improve calico printing at once.[169]

'Only in the garden of Avallaunius,' said Lucian to himself, 'is the true and exquisite science to be found.'

He could imagine a man who was able to live in one sense while he pleased; to whom, for example, every impression of touch, taste, hearing, or seeing should be translated into odour; who at the desired kiss should be ravished with the scent of dark violets, to whom music should be the perfume of a rose-garden at dawn.

When, now and again, he voluntarily resumed the experience of common life, it was that he might return with greater delight to the garden in the city of refuge. In the actual world the talk was of Nonconformists, the lodger franchise, and the Stock Exchange;[170] people were constantly reading newspapers, drinking Australian Burgundy, and doing other things equally absurd. They either looked shocked when the fine art of pleasure was mentioned, or confused it with going to musical comedies, drinking bad whisky, and keeping late hours in disreputable and vulgar company. He found to his amusement that the profligate were by many degrees duller than the pious, but that the most tedious

---

[167] For the next three paragraphs, Machen explores synaesthesia — when the stimulation of one sense fosters a correlative experience in another. The concept was central to the works of the Decadents and Symbolists, who created literature and art intended to induce not only other sensory experiences but the experiences of supernatural and spiritual realms of being. A subject of medical and scientific interest since it was recognized in 1812, synaesthesia only became a popular phenomenon with Arthur Rimbaud's (1854–1891) poem 'Voyelles' (1883). Occultists and Theosophists, such as Annie Besant (1847–1933), Charles Webster Leadbeater (1854–1934), and Pamela Colman Smith (1871–1958), explored and experimented with synaesthesia.

[168] Emetics are substances taken in order to induce vomiting.

[169] Calico printing is the printing of a figured pattern on plain-woven cotton cloth.

[170] Nonconformists are English Protestants who do not belong to the Church of England. During the nineteenth century, there was extensive debate in the United Kingdom on whether to allow lodgers (i.e. renters) the right to vote.

of all were the persons who preached promiscuity, and called their system of 'pigging' the 'New Morality.'[171]

He went back to the city lovingly, because it was built and adorned for his love. As the metaphysicians insist on the consciousness of the ego as the implied basis of all thought, so he knew that it was she in whom he had found himself, and through whom and for whom all the true life existed.[172] He felt that Annie had taught him the rare magic which had created the garden of Avallaunius. It was for her that he sought strange secrets and tried to penetrate the mysteries of sensation, for he could only give her wonderful thoughts and a wonderful life, and a poor body stained with the scars of his worship.

It was with this object, that of making the offering of himself a worthy one, that he continually searched for new and exquisite experiences.[173] He made lovers come before him and confess their secrets; he pried into the inmost mysteries of innocence and shame, noting how passion and reluctance strive together for the mastery. In the amphitheatre he sometimes witnessed strange entertainments in which such tales as *Daphnis and Chloe* and *The Golden Ass* were performed before him.[174] These shows were always given at night-time; a circle of torch-bearers surrounded the stage in the centre, and above, all the tiers of seats were dark. He would look up at the soft blue of the summer sky, and at the vast dim mountain hovering like a cloud in the west, and then at the scene illumined by a flaring light, and contrasted with violent shadows. The subdued mutter of conversation in a strange language rising from bench after bench, swift hissing whispers of explanation, now and then a shout or a cry as the interest deepened, the restless tossing of the people as the end drew near, an arm lifted, a cloak thrown back, the sudden blaze of a torch lighting up purple or white or the gleam of gold in the black serried ranks; these were impressions

---

[171] 'Pigging' is slang for living a makeshift life without any sort of plan. 'New Morality' is a fairly common term applied to various attitudes or ways of life that were at one time condemned but that have acquired respectability, and even popularity, amongst certain segments of a population.

[172] Metaphysicians are those engaged in understanding and explaining metaphysics, one of the more recondite branches of philosophy, addressing topics such as ontology, cosmology, and epistemology.

[173] This passage of *The Hill of Dreams* is particularly suggestive of Pater's 'Conclusion' to *The Renaissance*, where he famously encourages his readers to 'catch at any exquisite passion, or any contribution to knowledge that seems, by a lifted horizon, to set the spirit free for a moment, or any stirring of the senses' (Walter Pater, *Studies in the History of the Renaissance* (London: Macmillan, 1873), p. 211).

[174] *Daphnis and Chloe* is a second-century CE Greek pastoral romance by Longus (fl. second century CE), featuring mistaken identities, young love, and adventure; the god Pan at one point intervenes to save Chloe. *The Golden Ass* (also known as *Metamorphoses*) is another second-century CE romance. Written in Latin by Apuleius (*c.* 124–170 CE), it recounts the character Lucius's involvement with magic (he is turned into a donkey) and his subsequent adventures; ultimately, he is saved by the Egyptian goddess Isis and joins her cult.

that seemed always amazing. And above, the dusky light of the stars, around, the sweet-scented meadows, and the twinkle of lamps from the still city, the cry of the sentries about the walls, the wash of the tide filling the river, and the salt savour of the sea. With such a scenic ornament he saw the tale of Apuleius represented, heard the names of Fotis and Byrrhaena and Lucius proclaimed, and the deep intonation of such sentences as *Ecce Veneris hortator et armiger Liber advenit ultro.*[175] The tale went on through all its marvellous adventures, and Lucian left the amphitheatre and walked beside the river where he could hear indistinctly the noise of voices and the singing Latin, and note how the rumour of the stage mingled with the murmur of the shuddering reeds and the cool lapping of the tide. Then came the farewell of the cantor, the thunder of applause, the crash of cymbals, the calling of the flutes, and the surge of the wind in the great dark wood.[176]

At other times it was his chief pleasure to spend a whole day in a vineyard planted on the steep slope beyond the bridge. A grey stone seat had been placed beneath a shady laurel, and here he often sat without motion or gesture for many hours. Below him the tawny river swept round the town in a half circle; he could see the swirl of the yellow water, its eddies and miniature whirlpools, as the tide poured up from the south. And beyond the river the strong circuit of the walls, and within, the city glittered like a charming piece of mosaic. He freed himself from the obtuse modern view of towns as places where human beings live and make money and rejoice or suffer, for from the standpoint of the moment such facts were wholly impertinent. He knew perfectly well that for his present purpose the tawny sheen and shimmer of the tide was the only fact of importance about the river, and so he regarded the city as a curious work in jewellery. Its radiant marble porticoes, the white walls of the villas, a dome of burning copper, the flash and scintillation of tiled roofs, the quiet red of brickwork, dark groves of ilex, and cypress, and laurel, glowing rose-gardens, and here and there the silver of a fountain, seemed arranged and contrasted with a wonderful art, and the town appeared a delicious ornament, every cube of colour owing its place to the thought and inspiration of the artificer. Lucian, as he gazed from his arbour amongst the trellised vines, lost none of the subtle pleasures of the sight; noting every *nuance* of colour, he let his eyes dwell for a moment on the scarlet flash of poppies, and then on a glazed roof which in the glance of the sun seemed to spout white fire. A square of vines was like some

---

[175] Fotis, Byrrhaenna, and Lucius are characters in Apuleius's *The Golden Ass*. 'Look, Venus' prompter and arms-bearer, Bacchus, has come too' — the translation given in Apuleius, *Metamorphoses*, vol. 1, ed. and trans. by J. Arthur Hanson (Cambridge, MA: Harvard University Press — The Loeb Classical Library, 1989), bk. 2, chap. 11, p. 81.

[176] In a cathedral or other church, the cantor is the person who sings text to which the congregation responds; in a synagogue, the cantor is the person who leads prayers and sings liturgical texts.

rare green stone; the grapes were massed so richly amongst the vivid leaves, that even from far off there was a sense of irregular flecks and stains of purple running through the green. The laurel garths were like cool jade; the gardens, where red, yellow, blue and white gleamed together in a mist of heat, had the radiance of opal; the river was a band of dull gold.[177] On every side, as if to enhance the preciousness of the city, the woods hung dark on the hills; above, the sky was violet, specked with minute feathery clouds, white as snowflakes. It reminded him of a beautiful bowl in his villa; the ground was of that same brilliant blue, and the artist had fused into the work, when it was hot, particles of pure white glass.

For Lucian this was a spectacle that enchanted many hours; leaning on one hand, he would gaze at the city glowing in the sunlight till the purple shadows grew down the slopes and the long melodious trumpet sounded for the evening watch. Then, as he strolled beneath the trellises, he would see all the radiant facets glimmering out, and the city faded into haze, a white wall shining here and there, and the gardens veiled in a dim glow of colour. On such an evening he would go home with the sense that he had truly lived a day, having received for many hours the most acute impressions of beautiful colour.

Often he spent the night in the cool court of his villa, lying amidst soft cushions heaped upon the marble bench. A lamp stood on the table at his elbow, its light making the water in the cistern twinkle. There was no sound in the court except the soft continual plashing of the fountain. Throughout these still hours he would meditate, and he became more than ever convinced that man could, if he pleased, become lord of his own sensations. This, surely, was the true meaning concealed under the beautiful symbolism of alchemy. Some years before he had read many of the wonderful alchemical books of the later Middle Ages, and had suspected that something other than the turning of lead into gold was intended. This impression was deepened when he looked into *Lumen de Lumine* by Vaughan, the brother of the Silurist, and he had long puzzled himself in the endeavour to find a reasonable interpretation of the hermetic mystery, and of the red powder, 'glistering and glorious as the sun.'[178] And the solution shone out at last, bright and amazing, as he lay quiet in the court of Avallaunius.

---

[177] A garth is a courtyard surrounded by a cloister. The laurel is a small evergreen tree, the foliage of which has been used since ancient times as a symbol of victory or high distinction, both political and artistic.

[178] In *Lumen de Lumine: or a New Magicall Light Discovered, and Communicated to the World* (London: H. Blunden, 1651), Thomas Vaughan recounts a dream wherein Thalia, the Temple of Nature's guardian, reveals to him the composition of all creation. A hermetic mystery is one that is associated with Hermes Trismegistus (the name that Neoplatonists and others gave to the Egyptian god Thoth) and, not uncommonly, the Greek god Hermes, the messenger of the gods. In general, such mysteries pertain to alchemical, magical, and other mystical doctrines. In *Lumen de Lumine*, Vaughan refers to the philosophers mixing ingredients to make a 'bloudie [i.e. bloody] powder', 'shining like the Sun' (pp. 95, 94).

He knew that he himself had solved the riddle, that he held in his hand the powder of projection, the philosopher's stone transmuting all it touched to fine gold; the gold of exquisite impressions.[179] He understood now something of the alchemical symbolism; the crucible and the furnace, the 'Green Dragon,' and the 'Son Blessed of the Fire' had, he saw, a peculiar meaning.[180] He understood too why the uninitiated were warned of the terror and danger through which they must pass; and the vehemence with which the adepts disclaimed all desire for material riches no longer struck him as singular. The wise man does not endure the torture of the furnace in order that he may be able to compete with operators in pork and company promoters; neither a steam yacht, nor a grouse-moor, nor three liveried footmen would add at all to his gratifications. Again Lucian said to himself:

'Only in the court of Avallaunius is the true science of the exquisite to be found.'

He saw the true gold into which the beggarly matter of existence may be transmuted by spagyric art; a succession of delicious moments, all the rare flavours of life concentrated, purged of their lees, and preserved in a beautiful vessel.[181] The moonlight fell green on the fountain and on the curious pavements, and in the long sweet silence of the night he lay still and felt that thought itself was an acute pleasure, to be expressed perhaps in terms of odour or colour by the true artist.

And he gave himself other and even stranger gratifications. Outside the city walls, between the baths and the amphitheatre, was a tavern, a place where wonderful people met to drink wonderful wine. There he saw priests of Mithras and Isis and of more occult rites from the East, men who wore robes of bright colours, and grotesque ornaments, symbolising secret things.[182] They spoke

---

[179] The philosopher's stone is the alchemical stone or substance believed to have the power to transmute base metals into precious ones such as gold, as well as to extend life.

[180] Machen refers to consuming 'the juices of the Green Dragon' as the act of attaining alchemical knowledge in 'The Spagyric Quest of Beroaldus Cosmopolita', in his *Thesaurus Incantatus* (London: Thomas Marvell, 1888), pp. 3–16. The phrase 'Son Blessed of the Fire' can be found in various alchemical works as early as those of the sixteenth-century French alchemist Denis Zachaire (pseud., 1510–1556). The phrase appears in 'The Spagyric Quest' (p. 13), and also in 'More Alchemy' (*Household Words*, 33 (1856), pp. 43–49 (p. 46)), which Machen claimed to have read as a boy in his father's library; the latter article describes 'Son Blessed of the Fire' as the philosopher's stone.

[181] The word 'spagyric' — from the Greek for 'collect' and 'extract' — means alchemical. The lees are the residue or dregs.

[182] On Mithras, see note 150 of *The Hill of Dreams*. Isis is the Egyptian goddess of fertility who came to be worshipped as well by many Greeks and Romans. Isis also became a central figure in the new occultism, with the first temple of the Hermetic Order of the Golden Dawn being named the Isis-Urania Temple. In the 1890s, the last founding leader of the Order, MacGregor Mathers, and his wife, Moina, offered public performances of the 'Ceremony of Isis' in Paris.

amongst themselves in a rich jargon of coloured words, full of hidden meanings and the sense of matters unintelligible to the uninitiated, alluding to what was concealed beneath roses, and calling each other by strange names. And there were actors who gave the shows in the amphitheatre, officers of the legion who had served in wild places, singers, and dancing girls, and heroes of strange adventure.

The walls of the tavern were covered with pictures painted in violent hues; blues and reds and greens jarring against one another and lighting up the gloom of the place. The stone benches were always crowded, the sunlight came in through the door in a long bright beam, casting a dancing shadow of vine leaves on the further wall. There a painter had made a joyous figure of the young Bacchus driving the leopards before him with his ivy-staff, and the quivering shadow seemed a part of the picture.[183] The room was cool and dark and cavernous, but the scent and heat of the summer gushed in through the open door. There was ever a full sound, with noise and vehemence, there, and the rolling music of the Latin tongue never ceased.

'The wine of the siege, the wine that we saved,' cried one.

'Look for the jar marked *Faunus*, you will be glad.'

'Bring me the wine of the Owl's Face.'

'Let us have the wine of Saturn's Bridge.'[184]

The boys who served brought the wine in dull red jars that struck a charming note against their white robes. They poured out the violet and purple and golden wine with calm sweet faces as if they were assisting in the mysteries, without any sign that they heard the strange words that flashed from side to side. The cups were all of glass; some were of deep green, of the colour of the sea near the land, flawed and specked with the bubbles of the furnace. Others were of brilliant scarlet, streaked with irregular bands of white, and having the appearance of white globules in the moulded stem. There were cups of dark glowing blue, deeper and more shining than the blue of the sky, and running through the substance of the glass were veins of rich gamboge yellow, twining from the brim to the foot. Some cups were of a troubled and clotted red, with alternating blotches of dark and light, some were variegated with white and yellow stains, some wore a film of rainbow colours, some glittered, shot

---

[183] Bacchus is the Roman god of wine and drunken revelry, known as Dionysus by the Greeks. In the 1860s, the homosexual Pre-Raphaelite artist Simeon Solomon (1840–1905) — appreciated by Decadents such as Pater and Swinburne — painted three works of Bacchus with his staff and/or a leopard-skin robe.

[184] Faunus is a Roman woodland deity, regarded as the counterpart to the Greek Pan. Owls, seen to have solemn faces, were sometimes associated in Roman mythology with bloodshed and death. Saturn is the Roman god of agriculture, who ruled during a period of prosperity and peaceful labour. He is also known as the god of liberation, generation, and dissolution. The raucous festival of Saturnalia occurred as a lead up to the winter solstice when the nights begin to shorten, beginning the move toward spring.

with gold threads through the clear crystal, some were as if sapphires hung suspended in running water, some sparkled with the glint of stars, some were black and golden like tortoiseshell.

A strange feature was the constant and fluttering motion of hands and arms. Gesture made a constant commentary on speech; white fingers, whiter arms, and sleeves of all colours, hovered restlessly, appeared and disappeared with an effect of threads crossing and recrossing on the loom. And the odour of the place was both curious and memorable; something of the damp cold breath of the cave meeting the hot blast of summer, the strangely mingled aromas of rare wines as they fell plashing and ringing into the cups, the drugged vapour of the East that the priests of Mithras and Isis bore from their steaming temples; these were always strong and dominant. And the women were scented, sometimes with unctuous and overpowering perfumes, and to the artist the experiences of those present were hinted in subtle and delicate *nuances* of odour.

They drank their wine and caressed all day in the tavern. The women threw their round white arms about their lover's necks, they intoxicated them with the scent of their hair, the priests muttered their fantastic jargon of Theurgy.[185] And through the sonorous clash of voices there always seemed the ring of the cry:

'Look for the jar marked *Faunus*; you will be glad.'

Outside, the vine tendrils shook on the white walls glaring in the sunshine; the breeze swept up from the yellow river, pungent with the salt sea savour.

These tavern scenes were often the subject of Lucian's meditation as he sat amongst the cushions on the marble seat. The rich sound of the voices impressed him above all things, and he saw that words have a far higher reason than the utilitarian office of imparting a man's thought. The common notion that language and linked words are important only as a means of expression he found a little ridiculous; as if electricity were to be studied solely with the view of 'wiring' to people, and all its other properties left unexplored, neglected. Language, he understood, was chiefly important for the beauty of its sounds, by its possession of words resonant, glorious to the ear, by its capacity, when exquisitely arranged, of suggesting wonderful and indefinable impressions, perhaps more ravishing and farther removed from the domain of strict thought than the impressions excited by music itself. Here lay hidden the secret of the sensuous art of literature; it was the secret of suggestion, the art of causing delicious sensation by the use of words. In a way, therefore, literature was independent of thought; the mere English listener, if he had an ear attuned, could recognise the beauty of a splendid Latin phrase.

Here was the explanation of the magic of *Lycidas*.[186] From the standpoint of the

---

[185] Magic involving communication with and aid by supernatural forces.

[186] *Lycidas* (1638) is a pastoral elegy by John Milton (1608–1674) mourning the death of his friend Edward King.

formal understanding it was an affected lament over some wholly uninteresting and unimportant Mr. King; it was full of nonsense about 'shepherds' and 'flocks' and 'muses' and such stale stock of poetry; the introduction of St. Peter on a stage thronged with nymphs and river gods was blasphemous, absurd, and, in the worst taste;[187] there were touches of greasy Puritanism, the twang of the conventicle was only too apparent.[188] And *Lycidas* was probably the most perfect piece of pure literature in existence; because every word and phrase and line were sonorous, ringing and echoing with music.[189]

'Literature,' he re-enunciated in his mind, 'is the sensuous art of causing exquisite impressions by means of words.'

And yet there was something more; besides the logical thought, which was often a hindrance, a troublesome though inseparable accident, besides the sensation, always a pleasure and a delight, besides these there were the indefinable inexpressible images which all fine literature summons to the mind. As the chemist in his experiments is sometimes astonished to find unknown, unexpected elements in the crucible or the receiver, as the world of material things is considered by some a thin veil of the immaterial universe, so he who reads wonderful prose or verse is conscious of suggestions that cannot be put into words, which do not rise from the logical sense, which are rather parallel to than connected with the sensuous delight.[190] The world so disclosed is rather the world of dreams, rather the world in which children sometimes live, instantly appearing, and instantly vanishing away, a world beyond all expression or analysis, neither of the intellect nor of the senses. He called these

---

[187] St Peter was one of Christ's disciples and a leader of the early Christian church. He was martyred at Rome during the time of the emperor Nero (37–68 CE). Nymphs, in Greek and Roman mythology, are a class of minor female deities inhabiting natural places, such as mountains, streams, and forests.

[188] Puritanism is a set of Protestant beliefs that arose in England in the sixteenth century and flourished in the seventeenth (until the Restoration of the monarchy in 1660). Puritanism departed from mainstream Anglicanism by closely following Calvinist theology, emphasizing such tenets as predestination, humanity's sinfulness, antipathy towards church hierarchy, and the individual Christian's ability to discern religious truth. Milton was a major Puritan apologist. A conventicle is a secret, illegal meeting, often for prayer and worship, of Protestants who dissented from the Church of England during the sixteenth and seventeenth centuries.

[189] Machen is interested in the ways in which words mean beyond their literal meaning. The conclusion here that the best literature is that which is closest to being music echoes Pater's well-known argument, in the essay 'The School of Giorgione' (included in the third edition of *The Renaissance* (1888)), that all types of art aspire to the condition of music, in which form and content are inseparable. In a 1944 piece, Machen notes with agreement, 'Pater held that music is the art of arts; that the rest excel as they aspire towards it' (Arthur Machen, Introduction to Fred J. Hando, *The Pleasant Land of Gwent*, p. 12).

[190] Machen was fascinated by the veil as not only concealing other realms of being from the visible world, but also revealing them, especially to the initiated. See *The Great God Pan* and his pamphlet *Beneath the Barley: A Note on the Origins of Eleusinia* (1931).

fancies of his 'Meditations of a Tavern,' and was amused to think that a theory of letters should have risen from the eloquent noise that rang all day about the violet and golden wine.

'Let us seek for more exquisite things,' said Lucian to himself. He could almost imagine the magic transmutation of the senses accomplished, the strong sunlight was an odour in his nostrils; it poured down on the white marble and the palpitating roses like a flood. The sky was a glorious blue, making the heart joyous, and the eyes could rest in the dark green leaves and purple shadow of the ilex. The earth seemed to burn and leap beneath the sun, he fancied he could see the vine tendrils stir and quiver in the heat, and the faint fume of the scorching pine needles was blown across the gleaming garden to the seat beneath the porch. Wine was before him in a cup of carved amber; a wine of the colour of a dark rose, with a glint as of a star or of a jet of flame deep beneath the brim; and the cup was twined about with a delicate wreath of ivy. He was often loath to turn away from the still contemplation of such things, from the mere joy of the violent sun, and the responsive earth. He loved his garden and the view of the tessellated city from the vineyard on the hill, the strange clamour of the tavern, and white Fotis appearing on the torch-lit stage. And there were shops in the town in which he delighted, the shops of the perfume makers, and jewellers, and dealers in curious ware. He loved to see all things made for ladies' use, to touch the gossamer silks that were to touch their bodies, to finger the beads of amber and the gold chains which would stir above their hearts, to handle the carved hairpins and brooches, to smell odours which were already dedicated to love.

But though these were sweet and delicious gratifications, he knew that there were more exquisite things of which he might be a spectator. He had seen the folly of regarding fine literature from the standpoint of the logical intellect, and he now began to question the wisdom of looking at life as if it were a moral representation. Literature, he knew, could not exist without some meaning, and considerations of right and wrong were to a certain extent inseparable from the conception of life, but to insist on ethics as the chief interest of the human pageant was surely absurd. One might as well read *Lycidas* for the sake of its denunciation of 'our corrupted Clergy,' or Homer for 'manners and customs.'[191] An artist entranced by a beautiful landscape did not greatly concern himself with the geological formation of the hills, nor did the lover of a wild sea inquire as to the chemical analysis of the water. Lucian saw a coloured and complex life displayed before him, and he sat enraptured at the spectacle, not concerned to know whether actions were good or bad, but content if they were curious.

In this spirit he made a singular study of corruption. Beneath his feet, as he

---

[191] The headnote to Milton's *Lycidas* explains that, in the poem, the author 'foretells the ruin of our corrupted Clergy'.

sat in the garden porch, was a block of marble through which there ran a scarlet stain. It began with a faint line, thin as a hair, and grew as it advanced, sending out offshoots to right and left, and broadening to a pool of brilliant red. There were strange lives into which he looked that were like the block of marble; women with grave sweet faces told him the astounding tale of their adventures, and how, as they said, they had met the faun when they were little children. They told him how they had played and watched by the vines and the fountains, and dallied with the nymphs, and gazed at images reflected in the water pools, till the authentic face appeared from the wood. He heard others tell how they had loved the satyrs for many years before they knew their race; and there were strange stories of those who had longed to speak but knew not the word of the enigma, and searched in all strange paths and ways before they found it.[192]

He heard the history of the woman who fell in love with her slave-boy, and tempted him for three years in vain. He heard the tale from the woman's full red lips, and watched her face, full of the ineffable sadness of lust, as she described her curious stratagems in mellow phrases. She was drinking a sweet yellow wine from a gold cup as she spoke, and the odour in her hair and the aroma of the precious wine seemed to mingle with the soft strange words that flowed like an unguent from a carven jar. She told how she bought the boy in the market of an Asian city, and had him carried to her house in the grove of fig-trees. 'Then,' she went on, 'he was led into my presence as I sat between the columns of my court. A blue veil was spread above to shut out the heat of the sun, and rather twilight than light shone on the painted walls, and the wonderful colours of the pavement, and the images of Love and the Mother of Love.[193] The men who brought the boy gave him over to my girls, who undressed him before me, one drawing gently away his robe, another stroking his brown and flowing hair, another praising the whiteness of his limbs, and another caressing him, and speaking loving words in his ear. But the boy looked sullenly at them all, striking away their hands, and pouting with his lovely and splendid lips, and I saw a blush, like the rosy veil of dawn, reddening his body and his cheeks. Then I made them bathe him, and anoint him with scented oils from head to foot, till his limbs shone and glistened with the gentle and mellow glow of an ivory statue. Then I said: "You are bashful, because you shine alone amongst us all; see, we too will be your fellows." The girls began first of all, fondling and kissing one another, and doing for each other the offices of waiting-maids. They drew out the pins and loosened the bands of their hair, and I never knew before that they were so lovely. The soft and shining tresses flowed down, rippling like sea-waves; some had hair golden and radiant as this wine in my cup, the faces of

---

[192] On satyrs, see *The Great God Pan*, note 20.
[193] The Roman god Cupid (in Greek mythology, Eros) and his mother, Venus (in Greek mythology, Aphrodite).

others appeared amidst the blackness of ebony; there were locks that seemed of burnished and scintillating copper, some glowed with hair of tawny splendour, and others were crowned with the brightness of the sardonyx. Then, laughing, and without the appearance of shame, they unfastened the brooches and the bands which sustained their robes, and so allowed silk and linen to flow swiftly to the stained floor, so that one would have said there was a sudden apparition of the fairest nymphs. With many festive and jocose words they began to incite each other to mirth, praising the beauties that shone on every side, and calling the boy by a girl's name, they invited him to be their playmate. But he refused, shaking his head, and still standing dumbfounded and abashed, as if he saw a forbidden and terrible spectacle. Then I ordered the women to undo my hair and my clothes, making them caress me with the tenderness of the fondest lover, but without avail, for the foolish boy still scowled and pouted out his lips, stained with an imperial and glorious scarlet.'

She poured out more of the topaz-coloured wine in her cup, and Lucian saw it glitter as it rose to the brim and mirrored the gleam of the lamps. The tale went on, recounting a hundred strange devices. The woman told how she had tempted the boy by idleness and ease, giving him long hours of sleep, and allowing him to recline all day on soft cushions, that swelled about him, enclosing his body. She tried the experiment of curious odours: causing him to smell always about him the oil of roses, and burning in his presence rare gums from the East. He was allured by soft dresses, being clothed in silks that caressed the skin with the sense of a fondling touch. Three times a day they spread before him a delicious banquet, full of savour and odour and colour; three times a day they endeavoured to intoxicate him with delicate wine.

'And so,' the lady continued, 'I spared nothing to catch him in the glistening nets of love; taking only sour and contemptuous glances in return. And at last in an incredible shape I won the victory, and then, having gained a green crown fighting in agony against his green and crude immaturity, I devoted him to the theatre, where he amused the people by the splendour of his death.'

On another evening he heard the history of the man who dwelt alone, refusing all allurements, and was at last discovered to be the lover of a black statue.[194] And there were tales of strange cruelties, of men taken by mountain robbers, and curiously maimed and disfigured, so that when they escaped and

---

[194] Machen glances here at the tale in Ovid's (43 BCE–17/18 CE) *Metamorphoses* of Pygmalion, a sculptor who fell in love with a statue he had created. Aphrodite (Greek goddess of love, beauty, and pleasure) brought the statue to life for him. In the myth, however, the statue is fashioned of white ivory; its blackness in Machen's rendering is a notable departure, perhaps connoting illicit desires and sexuality. French artist and sculptor Jean-Léon Gérôme's (1824–1904) experiments with tinted sculptures include the work *Pygmalion and Galatea* (c. 1891). His oil painting *Pygmalion and Galatea* (1890), which includes Eros hovering in the corner, had been a huge success. Gérôme was known for his orientalist works, and was especially admired by the author Théophile Gautier, an inspiration for the Decadent movement.

returned to the town, they were thought to be monsters and killed at their own doors. Lucian left no dark or secret nook of life unvisited; he sat down, as he said, at the banquet, resolved to taste all the savours, and to leave no flagon unvisited.

His relations grew seriously alarmed about him at this period. While he heard with some inner ear the suave and eloquent phrases of singular tales, and watched the lamp-light in amber and purple wine, his father saw a lean pale boy, with black eyes that burnt in hollows, and sad and sunken cheeks.

'You ought to try and eat more, Lucian,' said the parson; 'and why don't you have some beer?'

He was pecking feebly at the roast mutton and sipping a little water; but he would not have eaten or drunk with more relish if the choicest meat and drink had been before him.

His bones seemed, as Miss Deacon said, to be growing through his skin; he had all the appearance of an ascetic whose body has been reduced to misery by long and grievous penance. People who chanced to see him could not help saying to one another: 'How ill and wretched that Lucian Taylor looks!' They were of course quite unaware of the joy and luxury in which his real life was spent, and some of them began to pity him, and to speak to him kindly.

It was too late for that. The friendly words had as much lost their meaning as the words of contempt. Edward Dixon hailed him cheerfully in the street one day:

'Come in to my den, won't you, old fellow?' he said. 'You won't see the pater.[195] I've managed to bag a bottle of his old port. I know you smoke like a furnace, and I've got some ripping cigars. You will come, won't you! I can tell you the pater's booze is first rate.'

He gently declined and went on. Kindness and unkindness, pity and contempt had become for him mere phrases; he could not have distinguished one from the other. Hebrew and Chinese, Hungarian and Pushtu would be pretty much alike to an agricultural labourer; if he cared to listen he might detect some general differences in sound, but all four tongues would be equally devoid of significance.

To Lucian, entranced in the garden of Avallaunius, it seemed very strange that he had once been so ignorant of all the exquisite meanings of life. Now, beneath the violet sky, looking through the brilliant trellis of the vines, he saw the picture; before, he had gazed in sad astonishment at the squalid rag which was wrapped about it.

V

And he was at last in the city of the unending murmuring streets, a part of the stirring shadow, of the amber-lighted gloom.

---

[195] Latin for 'father', a not uncommon word in nineteenth-century England.

It seemed a long time since he had knelt before his sweetheart in the lane, the moon-fire streaming upon them from the dark circle of the fort, the air and the light and his soul full of haunting, the touch of the unimaginable thrilling his heart; and now he sat in a terrible 'bed-sitting-room' in a western suburb, confronted by a heap and litter of papers on the desk of a battered old bureau.

He had put his breakfast-tray out on the landing, and was thinking of the morning's work, and of some very dubious pages that he had blackened the night before. But when he had lit his disreputable briar,[196] he remembered there was an unopened letter waiting for him on the table; he had recognised the vague, staggering script of Miss Deacon, his cousin. There was not much news; his father was 'just the same as usual,' there had been a good deal of rain, the farmers expected to make a lot of cider, and so forth. But at the close of the letter Miss Deacon became useful for reproof and admonition.

'I was at Caermaen on Tuesday,' she said, 'and called on the Gervases and the Dixons. Mr. Gervase smiled when I told him you were a literary man, living in London, and said he was afraid you wouldn't find it a very practical career. Mrs. Gervase was very proud of Henry's success; he passed fifth for some examination, and will begin with nearly four hundred a year. I don't wonder the Gervases are delighted. Then I went to the Dixons, and had tea. Mrs. Dixon wanted to know if you had published anything yet, and I said I thought not. She showed me a book everybody is talking about, called the *Dog and the Doctor*.[197] She says it's selling by thousands, and that one can't take up a paper without seeing the author's name. She told me to tell you that you ought to try to write something like it. Then Mr. Dixon came in from the study, and your name was mentioned again. He said he was afraid you had made rather a mistake in trying to take up literature as if it were a profession, and seemed to think that a place in a house of business would be more *suitable* and more practical. He pointed out that you had not had the advantages of a university training, and said that you would find men who had made good friends, and had the *tone* of the university, would be before you at every step. He said Edward was doing very well at Oxford. He writes to them that he knows several noblemen, and that young Philip Bullingham (son of Sir John Bullingham) is his most intimate friend; of course this is *very* satisfactory for the Dixons. I am afraid, my dear

---

[196] A tobacco pipe made from the branch of a briar bush.

[197] No work by this name is found, although sentimental depictions of dogs were common in Victorian literature and art. The painter Edwin Henry Landseer (1802–1873) was famous for his paintings of canines displaying various human character traits, and the popular author Ouida published articles defending the rights of dogs. In her novel *Puck* (1881), the eponymous canine narrates the narrative of his difficult life as a pet. Machen's own painful portrayal of dog abuse in *The Hill of Dreams* would have encouraged Victorian readers to consider the correlation between animal abuse and the degradation of other humans, an issue explored by Henry Salt (1851–1939) and other animal rights activists of the period.

Lucian, you have rather overrated your powers. Wouldn't it be better, even now, to look out for some *real work* to do, instead of wasting your time over those silly old books? I know quite well how the Gervases and the Dixons feel; they think idleness so injurious for a young man, and likely to lead to *bad habits.* You know, my dear Lucian, I am only writing like this because of my affection for you, so I am sure, my dear boy, you won't be offended.'

Lucian pigeon-holed the letter solemnly in the receptacle lettered 'Barbarians.' He felt that he ought to ask himself some serious questions: 'Why haven't I passed fifth? why isn't Philip (son of Sir John) my most intimate friend? why am I an idler, liable to fall into bad habits?' but he was eager to get to his work, a curious and intricate piece of analysis. So the battered bureau, the litter of papers, and the thick fume of his pipe, engulfed him and absorbed him for the rest of the morning. Outside were the dim October mists, the dreary and languid life of a side street, and beyond, on the main road, the hum and jangle of the gliding trains. But he heard none of the uneasy noises of the quarter, not even the shriek of the garden gates nor the yelp of the butcher on his rounds, for delight in his great task made him unconscious of the world outside.

He had come by curious paths to this calm hermitage between Shepherd's Bush and Acton Vale.[198] The golden weeks of the summer passed on in their enchanted procession, and Annie had not returned, neither had she written. Lucian, on his side, sat apart, wondering why his longing for her were not sharper. As he thought of his raptures he would smile faintly to himself, and wonder whether he had not lost the world and Annie with it. In the garden of Avallaunius his sense of external things had grown dim and indistinct; the actual, material life seemed every day to become a show, a fleeting of shadows across a great white light. At last the news came that Annie Morgan had been married from her sister's house to a young farmer, to whom it appeared, she had been long engaged, and Lucian was ashamed to find himself only conscious of amusement, mingled with gratitude. She had been the key that opened the shut palace, and he was now secure on the throne of ivory and gold. A few days after he had heard the news he repeated the adventure of his boyhood; for the second time he scaled the steep hillside, and penetrated the matted brake. He expected violent disillusion, but his feeling was rather astonishment at the activity of boyish imagination. There was no terror nor amazement now in the green bulwarks, and the stunted undergrowth did not seem in any way extraordinary. Yet he did not laugh at the memory of his sensations, he was not angry at the cheat. Certainly it had been all illusion, all the heats and chills of boyhood,

---

[198] At the end of the nineteenth century, Shepherd's Bush and Acton Vale were suburbs west of London. In *Far Off Things* (1922), Machen describes living at Clarendon Road, Notting Hill Gate, in the area of Holland Park, which is just east of Shepherd's Bush. Acton Vale was just west of Shepherd's Bush. For the most part, Machen describes both Shepherd's Bush and Acton Vale as dreary, raw, ugly suburbs.

its thoughts of terror were without significance. But he recognised that the illusions of the child only differed from those of the man in that they were more picturesque; belief in fairies and belief in the Stock Exchange as bestowers of happiness were equally vain, but the latter form of faith was ugly as well as inept. It was better, he knew, and wiser, to wish for a fairy coach than to cherish longings for a well-appointed brougham and liveried servants.

He turned his back on the green walls and the dark oaks without any feeling of regret or resentment. After a little while he began to think of his adventures with pleasure; the ladder by which he had mounted had disappeared, but he was safe on the height. By the chance fancy of a beautiful girl he had been redeemed from a world of misery and torture, the world of external things into which he had come a stranger, by which he had been tormented. He looked back at a kind of vision of himself seen as he was a year before, a pitiable creature burning and twisting on the hot coals of the pit, crying lamentably to the laughing bystanders for but one drop of cold water wherewith to cool his tongue. He confessed to himself, with some contempt, that he had been a social being, depending for his happiness on the goodwill of others; he had tried hard to write, chiefly, it was true, from love of the art, but a little from a social motive. He had imagined that a written book and the praise of responsible journals would ensure him the respect of the county people. It was a quaint idea, and he saw the lamentable fallacies naked; in the first place, a painstaking artist in words was not respected by the respectable; secondly, books should not be written with the object of gaining the goodwill of the landed and commercial interests; thirdly and chiefly, no man should in any way depend on another.

From this utter darkness, from danger of madness, the ever dear and sweet Annie had rescued him. Very beautifully and fitly, as Lucian thought, she had done her work without any desire to benefit him, she had simply willed to gratify her own passion, and in doing this had handed to him the priceless secret. And he, on his side, had reversed the process; merely to make himself a splendid offering for the acceptance of his sweetheart, he had cast aside the vain world, and had found the truth, which now remained with him, precious and enduring.

And since the news of the marriage he found that his worship of her had by no means vanished; rather in his heart was the eternal treasure of a happy love, untarnished and spotless; it would be like a mirror of gold without alloy, bright and lustrous for ever. For Lucian, it was no defect in the woman that she was desirous and faithless; he had not conceived an affection for certain moral or intellectual accidents, but for the very woman. Guided by the self-evident axiom that humanity is to be judged by literature, and not literature by humanity, he detected the analogy between *Lycidas* and Annie.[199] Only the

---

[199] This was a popular axiom among the Decadents, challenging the Aristotelian claim

dullard would object to the nauseous cant of the one, or to the indiscretions of the other. A sober critic might say that the man who could generalise Herbert and Laud, Donne and Herrick, Sanderson and Juxon, Hammond and Lancelot Andrewes into 'our corrupted Clergy' must be either an imbecile or a scoundrel, or probably both.[200] The judgment would be perfectly true, but as a criticism of *Lycidas* it would be a piece of folly. In the case of the woman one could imagine the attitude of the conventional lover; of the chevalier who, with his tongue in his cheek, 'reverences and respects' all women, and coming home early in the morning writes a leading article on St. English Girl.[201] Lucian, on the other hand, felt profoundly grateful to the delicious Annie, because she had at precisely the right moment voluntarily removed her image from his way. He confessed to himself that, latterly, he had a little dreaded her return as an interruption; he had shivered at the thought that their relations would become what was so terribly called an 'intrigue' or 'affair.' There would be all the threadbare and common stratagems, the vulgarity of secret assignations, and an atmosphere suggesting the period of Mr. Thomas Moore and Lord Byron and 'segars.'[202] Lucian had been afraid of all this; he had feared lest love itself should destroy love.

He considered that now, freed from the torment of the body, leaving untasted the green water that makes thirst more burning, he was perfectly initiated in the true knowledge of the splendid and glorious love. There seemed to him a monstrous paradox in the assertion that there could be no true love without a corporal presence of the beloved; even the popular sayings of 'absence makes

---

that art is the product of the human compulsion to imitate the real world. In his essay 'The Decay of Lying' (1889), Wilde has a character counter Aristotle explicitly, declaring that 'Life imitates Art far more than Art imitates Life' (Oscar Wilde, 'The Decay of Lying', *Intentions* (London: A. R. Keller & Co., 1907), pp. 7–63 (p. 46)).

[200] On Herbert and Herrick, see note 65 of *The Hill of Dreams*; William Laud (1573-1645): academic and Archbishop of Canterbury; John Donne (1573-1631), poet and member of the Anglican clergy; Robert Sanderson (1587-1663), theologian; William Juxon (1582-1663), Archbishop of Canterbury; Henry Hammond (1605-1660), Anglican theologian; and Lancelot Andrewes (1555-1626), scholar and Anglican bishop.

[201] Used ironically here, the cited phrase appears in Plato's (*c.*428–*c.*348 BCE) *Dialogues*: 'reverences and respects temperance and courage and magnanimity and wisdom, and wishes to live chastely with the chaste object of his affection'. The Aestheticist poet and Renaissance scholar John Addington Symonds (1840–1893) cites the passage in his *A Problem in Greek Ethics: Being an Inquiry into the Phenomenon of Sexual Inversion* (1873) to note Plato's valorisation of ideal friendship over physical desire (London, private printing, 1901, p. 50). The term 'St. English Girl' appears to be Machen's, suggesting that he is mocking the false idealization of English women as saintly and virtuous.

[202] Machen is alluding to an era that over-idealized women. He offers a similar critique in an earlier quotation of Moore's poetry. The Romantic poet Lord George Gordon Byron (1788–1824) is known both for his idealization of women in poems such as 'She Walks in Beauty' (1813) and for his various sexual relationships. 'Segars' appears to be a playful pronunciation of 'cigars'.

the heart grow fonder,' and 'familiarity breeds contempt,' witnessed to the contrary. He thought, sighing, and with compassion, of the manner in which men are continually led astray by the cheat of the senses. In order that the unborn might still be added to the born, nature had inspired men with the wild delusion that the bodily companionship of the lover and the beloved was desirable above all things, and so, by the false show of pleasure, the human race was chained to vanity, and doomed to an eternal thirst for the non-existent.

Again and again he gave thanks for his own escape; he had been set free from a life of vice and sin and folly, from all the dangers and illusions that are most dreaded by the wise. He laughed as he remembered what would be the common view of the situation. An ordinary lover would suffer all the sting of sorrow and contempt; there would be grief for a lost mistress, and rage at her faithlessness, and hate in the heart; one foolish passion driving on another, and driving the man to ruin. For what would be commonly called the real woman he now cared nothing; if he had heard that she had died in her farm in Utter Gwent, he would have experienced only a passing sorrow, such as he might feel at the death of any one he had once known.[203] But he did not think of the young farmer's wife as the real Annie; he did not think of the frost-bitten leaves in winter as the real rose. Indeed, the life of many reminded him of the flowers; perhaps more especially of those flowers which to all appearance are for many years but dull and dusty clumps of green, and suddenly, in one night, burst into the flame of blossom, and fill all the misty lawns with odour; till the morning. It was in that night that the flower lived, not through the long unprofitable years; and, in like manner, many human lives, he thought, were born in the evening and dead before the coming of day. But he had preserved the precious flower in all its glory, not suffering it to wither in the hard light, but keeping it in a secret place, where it could never be destroyed. Truly now, and for the first time, he possessed Annie, as a man possesses gold which he has dug from the rock and purged of its baseness.

He was musing over these things when a piece of news, very strange and unexpected, arrived at the rectory. A distant, almost a mythical relative, known from childhood as 'Cousin Edward in the Isle of Wight,' had died, and by some strange freak had left Lucian two thousand pounds. It was a pleasure to give his father five hundred pounds, and the rector on his side forgot for a couple of days to lean his head on his hand. From the rest of the capital, which was well invested, Lucian found he would derive something between sixty and seventy pounds a year, and his old desires for literature and a refuge in the murmuring streets returned to him. He longed to be free from the incantations

---

[203] Machen grew up in the county of Monmouthshire, which Machen called by its older Celtic name of Gwent. 'Utter Gwent' refers to what was recognized as the utmost, or in some way greatest, part of Gwent.

that surrounded him in the country, to work and live in a new atmosphere; and so, with many good wishes from his father, he came to the retreat in the waste places of London.

He was in high spirits when he found the square, clean room, horribly furnished, in the by-street that branched from the main road, and advanced in an unlovely sweep to the mud pits and the desolation that was neither town nor country. On every side monotonous grey streets, each house the replica of its neighbour, to the east an unexplored wilderness, north and west and south the brickfields and market-gardens, everywhere the ruins of the country, the tracks where sweet lanes had been, gangrened stumps of trees, the relics of hedges, here and there an oak stripped of its bark, white and haggard and leprous, like a corpse. And the air seemed always grey, and the smoke from the brickfields was grey.

At first he scarcely realised the quarter into which chance had led him. His only thought was of the great adventure of letters in which he proposed to engage, and his first glance round his 'bed-sitting-room' showed him that there was no piece of furniture suitable for his purpose. The table, like the rest of the suite, was of bird's-eye maple; but the maker seemed to have penetrated the druidic secret of the rocking-stone, the thing was in a state of unstable equilibrium perpetually.[204] For some days he wandered through the streets, inspecting the second-hand furniture shops, and at last, in a forlorn byway, found an old Japanese bureau, dishonoured and forlorn, standing amongst rusty bedsteads, sorry china, and all the refuse of homes dead and desolate. The bureau pleased him in spite of its grime and grease and dirt. Inlaid mother-of-pearl, the gleam of lacquer dragons in red gold, and hints of curious design shone through the film of neglect and ill-usage, and when the woman of the shop showed him the drawers and well and pigeon-holes, he saw that it would be an apt instrument for his studies.

The bureau was carried to his room and replaced the 'bird's-eye' table under the gas-jet. As Lucian arranged what papers he had accumulated: the sketches of hopeless experiments, shreds and tatters of stories begun but never completed, outlines of plots, two or three notebooks scribbled through and through with impressions of the abandoned hills, he felt a thrill of exaltation at the prospect of work to be accomplished, of a new world all open before him.

He set out on the adventure with a fury of enthusiasm; his last thought at night when all the maze of streets was empty and silent was of the problem, and his dreams ran on phrases, and when he awoke in the morning he was eager to

---

[204] Stones that can be made to rock but that seem impossible to push over have been found throughout the world. Some are the product of erosion while others may have been constructed through human influence. A number of rocking stones in Britain and Ireland are thought to have been associated with Druids, witches, or other spiritual groups.

get back to his desk. He immersed himself in a minute, almost a microscopic analysis of fine literature. It was no longer enough, as in the old days, to feel the charm and incantation of a line or a word; he wished to penetrate the secret, to understand something of the wonderful suggestion, all apart from the sense, that seemed to him the *differentia* of literature, as distinguished from the long follies of 'character-drawing,' 'psychological analysis,' and all the stuff that went to make the three-volume novel of commerce.[205]

He found himself curiously strengthened by the change from the hills to the streets. There could be no doubt, he thought, that living a lonely life, interested only in himself and his own thoughts, he had become in a measure inhuman. The form of external things, black depths in woods, pools in lonely places, those still valleys curtained by hills on every side, sounding always with the ripple of their brooks, had become to him an influence like that of a drug, giving a certain peculiar colour and outline to his thoughts. And from early boyhood there had been another strange flavour in his life, the dream of the old Roman world, those curious impressions that he had gathered from the white walls of Caermaen, and from the looming bastions of the fort. It was in reality the subconscious fancies of many years that had rebuilt the golden city, and had shown him the vine-trellis and the marbles and the sunlight in the garden of Avallaunius. And the rapture of love had made it all so vivid and warm with life, that even now, when he let his pen drop, the rich noise of the tavern and the chant of the theatre sounded above the murmur of the streets. Looking back, it was as much a part of his life as his schooldays, and the tessellated pavements were as real as the square of faded carpet beneath his feet.

But he felt that he had escaped. He could now survey those splendid and lovely visions from without, as if he read of opium dreams, and he no longer dreaded a weird suggestion that had once beset him, that his very soul was being moulded into the hills, and passing into the black mirror of still waterpools. He had taken refuge in the streets, in the harbour of a modern suburb, from the vague, dreaded magic that had charmed his life. Whenever he felt inclined to listen to the old wood-whisper or to the singing of the fauns he bent more earnestly over his work, turning a deaf ear to the incantation.

In the curious labour of the bureau he found refreshment that was continually renewed. He experienced again, and with a far more violent impulse, the enthusiasm that had attended the writing of his book a year or two before, and so, perhaps, passed from one drug to another. It was, indeed, with something of rapture that he imagined the great procession of years all to be devoted to the intimate analysis of words, to the construction of the sentence, as if it were a piece of jewellery or mosaic.

---

[205] The *differentia* is that trait, element, or factor that distinguishes one thing from another, or one type of thing from another.

Sometimes, in the pauses of the work, he would pace up and down his cell, looking out of the window now and again and gazing for an instant into the melancholy street. As the year advanced the days grew more and more misty, and he found himself the inhabitant of a little island wreathed about with the waves of a white and solemn sea. In the afternoon the fog would grow denser, shutting out not only sight but sound; the shriek of the garden gates, the jangling of the tram-bell echoed as if from a far way. Then there were days of heavy incessant rain; he could see a grey drifting sky and the drops plashing in the street, and the houses all dripping and saddened with wet.

He cured himself of one great aversion. He was no longer nauseated at the sight of a story begun and left unfinished. Formerly, even when an idea rose in his mind bright and wonderful, he had always approached the paper with a feeling of sickness and dislike, remembering all the hopeless beginnings he had made. But now he understood that to begin a romance was almost a separate and special art, a thing apart from the story, to be practiced with sedulous care. Whenever an opening scene occurred to him he noted it roughly in a book, and he devoted many long winter evenings to the elaboration of these beginnings. Sometimes the first impression would yield only a paragraph or a sentence, and once or twice but a splendid and sonorous word, which seemed to Lucian all dim and rich with unsurmised adventure. But often he was able to write three or four vivid pages, studying above all things the hint and significance of the words and actions, striving to work into the lines the atmosphere of expectation and promise, and the murmur of wonderful events to come.

In this one department of his task the labour seemed almost endless. He would finish a few pages and then rewrite them, using the same incident and nearly the same words, but altering that indefinite something which is scarcely so much style as manner, or atmosphere. He was astonished at the enormous change that was thus effected, and often, though he himself had done the work, he could scarcely describe in words how it was done. But it was clear that in this art of manner, or suggestion, lay all the chief secrets of literature, that by it all the great miracles were performed. Clearly it was not style, for style in itself was untranslatable, but it was that high theurgic magic that made the English *Don Quixote*, roughly traduced by some Jarvis, perhaps the best of all English books.[206] And it was the same element that made the journey of Roderick Random to London, ostensibly a narrative of coarse jokes and common experiences and burlesque manners, told in no very choice diction, essentially

---

[206] On *Don Quixote*, see note 106 of *The Hill of Dreams*. Machen is referring here to Tobias Smollett's (1721–1771) *The Adventures of Roderick Random* (1748). In the preface, Smollett notes the influence of Cervantes's work, which he translated into English in 1755. An English translation of *Don Quixote* was produced by Charles Jarvis (also recorded as Jervis) in 1742. According to Thomas Hart, this edition was more popular than Smollett's during Machen's time (Thomas R. Hart, review, *Cervantes: Bulletin of the Cervantes Society of America*, 8:1 (1988), pp. 118–22 (p. 118)).

a wonderful vision of the eighteenth century, carrying to one's very nostrils the aroma of the Great North Road iron-bound under black frost, darkened beneath shuddering woods, haunted by highwaymen, with an adventure waiting beyond every turn, and great old echoing inns in the midst of lonely winter lands.

It was this magic that Lucian sought for his opening chapters; he tried to find that quality that gives to words something beyond their sound and beyond their meaning, that in the first lines of a book should whisper things unintelligible but all significant. Often he worked for many hours without success, and the grim wet dawn once found him still searching for hieroglyphic sentences, for words mystical, symbolic. On the shelves, in the upper part of his bureau, he had placed the books which, however various as to matter, seemed to have a part in this curious quality of suggestion, and in that sphere which might almost be called supernatural. To these books he often had recourse, when further effort appeared altogether hopeless, and certain pages in Coleridge and Edgar Allan Poe had the power of holding him in a trance of delight, subject to emotions and impressions which he knew to transcend altogether the realm of the formal understanding.[207] Such lines as:

> Bottomless vales and boundless floods,
> And chasms, and caves, and Titan woods,
> With forms that no man can discover
> For the dews that drip all over;

had for Lucian more than the potency of a drug, lulling him into a splendid waking-sleep, every word being a supreme incantation. And it was not only his mind that was charmed by such passages, for he felt at the same time a strange and delicious bodily languor that held him motionless, without the desire or power to stir from his seat.[208] And there were certain phrases in *Kubla Khan* that had such a magic that he would sometimes wake up, as it were, to the consciousness that he had been lying on the bed or sitting in the chair by the bureau, repeating a single line over and over again for two or three hours. Yet he knew perfectly well that he had not been really asleep; a little effort recalled a constant impression of the wall-paper, with its pink flowers on a buff ground, and of the muslin-curtained window, letting in the grey winter light. He had been some seven months in London when this odd experience first occurred to him. The day opened dreary and cold and clear, with a gusty and restless wind whirling round the corner of the street, and lifting the dead leaves and scraps

---

[207] Romantic poet Samuel Taylor Coleridge (1772–1834) claimed to have written *Kubla Khan; or, A Vision in a Dream: A Fragment* (completed 1797; pub. 1816) after an opium-induced dream. American author Poe was admired by French and British Decadents for his gothic and macabre tales. The quotation immediately after this reference is from Poe's poem 'Dream-Land' (1844).

[208] The description is suggestive of Tennyson's poem 'The Lotos-Eaters'. See note 108 in *The Hill of Dreams*.

of paper that littered the roadway into eddying mounting circles, as if a storm of black rain were to come. Lucian had sat late the night before, and rose in the morning feeling weary and listless and heavy-headed. While he dressed, his legs dragged him as with weights, and he staggered and nearly fell in bending down to the mat outside for his tea-tray. He lit the spirit lamp on the hearth with shaking, unsteady hands, and could scarcely pour out the tea when it was ready.[209] A delicate cup of tea was one of his few luxuries; he was fond of the strange flavour of the green leaf, and this morning he drank the straw-coloured liquid eagerly, hoping it would disperse the cloud of languor.[210] He tried his best to coerce himself into the sense of vigour and enjoyment with which he usually began the day, walking briskly up and down and arranging his papers in order. But he could not free himself from depression; even as he opened the dear bureau a wave of melancholy came upon him, and he began to ask himself whether he were not pursuing a vain dream, searching for treasures that had no existence. He drew out his cousin's letter and read it again, sadly enough. After all, there was a good deal of truth in what she said; he had 'overrated' his powers, he had no friends, no real education. He began to count up the months since he had come to London; he had received his two thousand pounds in March, and in May he had said good-bye to the woods and to the dear and friendly paths. May, June, July, August, September, October, November, and half of December had gone by, and what had he to show? Nothing but the experiment, the attempt, futile scribblings which had no end nor shining purpose. There was nothing in his desk that he could produce as evidence of his capacity, no fragment even of accomplishment. It was a thought of intense bitterness, but it seemed as if the barbarians were in the right — a place in a house of business would have been more suitable. He leaned his head on his desk overwhelmed with the severity of his own judgment. He tried to comfort himself again by the thought of all the hours of happy enthusiasm he had spent amongst his papers, working for a great idea with infinite patience. He recalled to mind something that he had always tried to keep in the background of his hopes, the foundation stone of his life, which he had hidden out of sight. Deep in his heart was the hope that he might one day write a valiant book; he scarcely dared to entertain the aspiration, he felt his incapacity too deeply, but yet this longing was the foundation of all his painful and patient effort. This he had proposed in secret to himself, that if he laboured without ceasing, without tiring, he might produce something which would at all events be art, which would stand wholly apart from the objects shaped like books, printed with printers' ink, and called by the name of books that he had read. Giotto, he knew, was a painter, and the man who imitated

---

[209] A spirit lamp is one fuelled by alcohol (i.e. spirits).

[210] In Irish writer Sheridan Le Fanu's (1814–1873) short story 'Green Tea' (1872), a clergyman interested in the work of mystic and theologian Emanuel Swedenborg (1688–1772) suffers hallucinations after drinking too much green tea.

walnut-wood on the deal doors opposite was a painter, and he had wished to be a very humble pupil in the class of the former.[211] It was better, he thought, to fail in attempting exquisite things than to succeed in the department of the utterly contemptible; he had vowed he would be the dunce of Cervantes's school rather than top-boy in the academy of *A Bad Un to Beat* and *Millicent's Marriage*.[212] And with this purpose he had devoted himself to laborious and joyous years, so that however mean his capacity, the pains should not be wanting. He tried now to rouse himself from a growing misery by the recollection of this high aim, but it all seemed hopeless vanity. He looked out into the grey street, and it stood a symbol of his life, chill and dreary and grey and vexed with a horrible wind. There were the dull inhabitants of the quarter going about their common business; a man was crying 'mackerel' in a doleful voice, slowly passing up the street, and staring into the white-curtained 'parlours,' searching for the face of a purchaser behind the India-rubber plants, stuffed birds, and piles of gaudy gilt books that adorned the windows.[213] One of the blistered doors over the way banged, and a woman came scurrying out on some errand, and the garden gate shrieked two melancholy notes as she opened it and let it swing back after her. The little patches called gardens were mostly untilled, uncared for, squares of slimy moss, dotted with clumps of coarse ugly grass, but here and there were the blackened and rotting remains of sunflowers and marigolds. And beyond, he knew, stretched the labyrinth of streets more or less squalid, but all grey and dull, and behind were the mud pits and the steaming heaps of yellowish bricks, and to the north was a great wide cold waste, treeless, desolate, swept by bitter wind. It was all like his own life, he said again to himself, a maze of unprofitable dreariness and desolation, and his mind grew as black and hopeless as the winter sky. The morning went thus dismally till twelve o'clock, and he put on his hat and great-coat. He always went out for an hour every day between twelve and one; the exercise was a necessity, and the landlady made his bed in the interval. The wind blew the smoke from the chimneys into his face as he shut the door, and with the acrid smoke came the prevailing odour of the

---

[211] Giotto de Bondone (1266/7–1337), a Florentine painter and architect.

[212] The two novels are among those Lucian had seen in Bait's catalogue earlier in *The Hill of Dreams*. Notably, George John Whyte-Melville (1821–1878) actually published a poem 'A Rum 'Un To Follow — A Bad 'Un To Beat' in *Baily's Monthly Magazine: Or Sports and Pastimes* in 1869, and it is much like what Machen challenges here. The common phrase 'bad 'un to beat' describes a sportsperson or animal that is difficult to defeat in competition.

[213] Machen's critique of popular novels, the suburbs, and, here, the Victorian domestic interior is an indirect attack on middle-class conservatism and habitual complacency, something that Robert Louis Stevenson, a favourite author of Machen's, railed against in works such as *An Inland Voyage* (1878). Here, Machen appears to criticize the rise of the concept of the House Beautiful, on which Wilde lectured in North America in 1882. A key element of the concept is the new sense, among the middle classes, of the home as not only a private sanctuary but also a display of taste intended for consumption by visitors.

street, a blend of cabbage-water and burnt bones and the faint sickly vapour from the brickfields. Lucian walked mechanically for the hour, going eastward, along the main road. The wind pierced him, and the dust was blinding, and the dreariness of the street increased his misery. The row of common shops, full of common things, the blatant public-houses, the Independent chapel, a horrible stucco parody of a Greek temple with a façade of hideous columns that was a nightmare, villas like smug Pharisees, shops again, a church in cheap Gothic, an old garden blasted and riven by the builder, these were the pictures of the way.[214] When he got home again he flung himself on the bed, and lay there stupidly till sheer hunger roused him. He ate a hunch of bread and drank some water, and began to pace up and down the room, wondering whether there were no escape from despair. Writing seemed quite impossible, and hardly knowing what he did he opened his bureau and took out a book from the shelves. As his eyes fell on the page the air grew dark and heavy as night, and the wind wailed suddenly, loudly, terribly.

'By woman wailing for her Demon lover.'[215] The words were on his lips when he raised his eyes again. A broad band of pale clear light was shining into the room, and when he looked out of the window he saw the road all brightened by glittering pools of water, and as the last drops of the rain-storm starred these mirrors the sun sank into the wrack. Lucian gazed about him, perplexed, till his eyes fell on the clock above his empty hearth. He had been sitting, motionless, for nearly two hours without any sense of the passage of time, and without ceasing he had murmured those words as he dreamed an endless wonderful story. He experienced somewhat the sensations of Coleridge himself; strange, amazing, ineffable things seemed to have been presented to him, not in the form of the idea, but actually and materially, but he was less fortunate than Coleridge in that he could not, even vaguely, image to himself what he had seen. Yet when he searched his mind he knew that the consciousness of the room in which he sat had never left him; he had seen the thick darkness gather, and had heard the whirl of rain hissing through the air. Windows had been shut down with a crash, he had noted the pattering footsteps of people running to shelter, the landlady's voice crying to some one to look at the rain coming in under the door. It was like peering into some old bituminous picture, one could see at last that the mere blackness resolved itself into the likeness of trees and rocks and travellers.[216] And against this background of his room, and the storm, and the noises of the street, his vision stood out illuminated, he felt he had descended to the very depths, into the caverns that are hollowed beneath the soul. He tried

---

[214] Independents are English Protestants who are not members of the Church of England. On Pharisees, see note 138 of *The Hill of Dreams*.

[215] A line from Coleridge's *Kubla Khan*.

[216] Bitumen is a flammable mixture of hydrocarbons and other substances, often used by Victorians for outdoor lighting.

vainly to record the history of his impressions; the symbols remained in his memory, but the meaning was all conjecture.

The next morning, when he awoke, he could scarcely understand or realise the bitter depression of the preceding day. He found it had all vanished away and had been succeeded by an intense exaltation. Afterwards, when at rare intervals he experienced the same strange possession of the consciousness, he found this to be the invariable result, the hour of vision was always succeeded by a feeling of delight, by sensations of heightened and intensified powers. On that bright December day after the storm he rose joyously, and set about the labour of the bureau with the assurance of success, almost with the hope of formidable difficulties to be overcome. He had long busied himself with those curious researches which Poe had indicated in the *Philosophy of Composition*, and many hours had been spent in analysing the singular effects which may be produced by the sound and resonance of words.[217] But he had been struck by the thought that in the finest literature there were more subtle tones than the loud and insistent music of 'never more,' and he endeavoured to find the secret of those pages and sentences which spoke, less directly, and less obviously, to the soul rather than to the ear, being filled with a certain grave melody and the sensation of singing voices. It was admirable, no doubt, to write phrases that showed at a glance their designed rhythm, and rang with sonorous words, but he dreamed of a prose in which the music should be less explicit, of names rather than notes. He was astonished that morning at his own fortune and facility; he succeeded in covering a page of ruled paper wholly to his satisfaction, and the sentences, when he read them out, appeared to suggest a weird elusive chanting, exquisite but almost imperceptible, like the echo of the plainsong reverberated from the vault of a monastic church.[218]

He thought that such happy mornings well repaid him for the anguish of depression which he sometimes had to suffer, and for the strange experience of 'possession' recurring at rare intervals, and usually after many weeks of severe diet. His income, he found, amounted to about sixty-five pounds a year, and he lived for weeks at a time on fifteen shillings a week. During these austere periods his only food was bread, at the rate of a loaf a day; but he drank huge draughts of green tea, and smoked a black tobacco, which seemed to him a more potent mother of thought than any drug from the scented East. 'I hope you go to some nice place for dinner,' wrote his cousin; 'there used to be some excellent eating-houses in London where one could get a good cut from the joint, *with plenty of gravy*, and a boiled potato, for a shilling. Aunt Mary writes that you

---

[217] In 'Philosophy of Composition' (1846), Poe discusses his technique of writing by choosing an effect first and building from there, using his gothic poem 'The Raven' (1845) as an example.

[218] Plainsong is a body of songs or chants characterized by a single melodic line. It is commonly used in Christian liturgy.

should try Mr. Jones's in Water Street, Islington, whose father came from near Caermaen, and was always most comfortable in her day. I daresay the walk there would do you good. It is such a pity you smoke that horrid tobacco. I had a letter from Mrs. Dolly (Jane Diggs, who married your cousin John Dolly) the other day, and she said they would have been delighted to take you for only twenty-five shillings a week for the sake of the family if you had not been a smoker. She told me to ask you if you had ever seen a horse or a dog smoking tobacco. They are such nice, comfortable people, and the children would have been company for you. Johnnie, who used to be such a dear little fellow, has just gone into an office in the City, and seems to have excellent prospects. How I wish, my dear Lucian, that you could do something in the same way. Don't forget Mr. Jones's in Water Street, and you might mention your name to him.'

Lucian never troubled Mr. Jones; but these letters of his cousin's always refreshed him by the force of contrast. He tried to imagine himself a part of the Dolly family, going dutifully every morning to the City on the bus, and returning in the evening for high tea.[219] He could conceive the fine odour of hot roast beef hanging about the decorous house on Sunday afternoons, papa asleep in the dining-room, mamma lying down, and the children quite good and happy with their 'Sundays books.' In the evening, after supper, one read the *Quiver* till bedtime.[220] Such pictures as these were to Lucian a comfort and a help, a remedy against despair. Often when he felt overwhelmed by the difficulty of the work he had undertaken, he thought of the alternative career, and was strengthened.

He returned again and again to that desire of a prose which should sound faintly, not so much with an audible music, but with the memory and echo of it. In the night, when the last tram had gone jangling by, and he had looked out and seen the street all wrapped about in heavy folds of the mist, he conducted some of his most delicate experiments. In that white and solitary midnight of the suburban street he experienced the curious sense of being on a tower, remote and apart and high above all the troubles of the earth. The gas lamp, which was nearly opposite, shone in a pale halo of light, and the houses themselves were merely indistinct marks and shadows amidst that palpable whiteness, shutting out the world and its noises. The knowledge of the swarming life that was so still, though it surrounded him, made the silence seem deeper than that of the mountains before the dawn; it was as if he alone stirred and looked out amidst a host sleeping at his feet. The fog came in by the open window in freezing puffs, and as Lucian watched he noticed that it shook and wavered like the sea, tossing

---

[219] In nineteenth-century Britain, high tea was the standard late-afternoon or early evening meal.

[220] John Cassell (1817–1865) established *The Quiver* (1861–1926) as an illustrated magazine reflecting his evangelical and temperance interests. It was aimed at a middle-class readership.

up wreaths and drifts across the pale halo of the lamp, and, these vanishing, others succeeded. It was as if the mist passed by from the river to the north, as if it still passed by in the silence.

He would shut his window gently, and sit down in his lighted room with all the consciousness of the white advancing shroud upon him. It was then that he found himself in the mood for curious labours, and able to handle with some touch of confidence the more exquisite instruments of the craft.[221] He sought for that magic by which all the glory and glamour of mystic chivalry were made to shine through the burlesque and gross adventures of Don Quixote, by which Hawthorne had lit his infernal Sabbath fires, and fashioned a burning aureole about the village tragedy of the *Scarlet Letter*.[222] In Hawthorne the story and the suggestion, though quite distinct and of different worlds, were rather parallel than opposed to one another; but Cervantes had done a stranger thing. One read of Don Quixote, beaten, dirty, and ridiculous, mistaking windmills for giants, sheep for an army; but the impression was of the enchanted forest, of Avalon, of the San Graal, 'far in the spiritual city.'[223] And Rabelais showed him, beneath the letter, the Tourainian sun shining on the hot rock above Chinon, on the maze of narrow, climbing streets, on the high-pitched, gabled roofs, on the grey-blue *tourelles*, pricking upward from the fantastic labyrinth of walls.[224] He heard the sound of sonorous plainsong from the monastic choir, of gross exuberant gaiety from the rich vineyards; he listened to the eternal mystic mirth of those that halted in the purple shadow of the *sorbier* by the white, steep road.[225] The gracious and ornate *châteaux* on the Loire and the Vienne rose fair and shining to confront the incredible secrets of vast, dim, far-lifted Gothic naves, that seemed ready to take the great deep, and float away from the mist and dust of earthly streets to anchor in the haven of the clear city that hath foundations.[226] The rank tale of the *garde-robe*, of the

---

[221] Machen's use of the term 'craft' signals Lucian's vision of writing as a form of natural magic. It also accords with the theory of literary aesthetics he articulates in *Hieroglyphics* (1902), excerpted in this edition.

[222] Cervantes's eponymous hero, Don Quixote, attempts to live the valorous life of knights from a past golden age, often with comic effect; Machen recognizes a parallel to his own veneration of Arthurian legend. *The Scarlet Letter: A Romance* (1850), by American author Nathaniel Hawthorne (1804–1864), addresses issues of sin, guilt, and gender politics.

[223] Part of Welsh history, Avalon is first referenced in Geoffrey of Monmouth's (*c*. 1100–1155) semi-historical *Historia Regum Britanniae* (*The History of the Kings of Britain*) (1136) as the location where King Arthur's sword was forged and where he went to recover from his wounds. On the San Graal (Sangraal), or Holy Grail, see note 73 of *The Hill of Dreams*. The quotation is taken from Tennyson's 'The Holy Grail' in his *Idylls of the King*, which he wrote while staying in Machen's home town of Caerleon.

[224] Rabelais was likely born in Chinon, a town in the region of Touraine, which takes its name from the Celtic tribe of the Turones. *tourelles* (French): turrets.

[225] *sorbier* (French): mountain ash.

[226] The Loire and the Vienne are major French rivers.

farm-kitchen, mingled with the reasoned, endless legend of the schools, with luminous Platonic argument; the old pomp of the Middle Ages put on the robe of a fresh life.[227] There was a smell of wine and of incense, of June meadows and of ancient books, and through it all he hearkened, intent, to the exultation of chiming bells ringing for a new feast in a new land. He would cover pages with the analysis of these marvels, tracking the suggestion concealed beneath the words, and yet glowing like the golden threads in a robe of samite, or like that device of the old binders by which a vivid picture appeared on the shut edges of a book. He tried to imitate this art, to summon even the faint shadow of the great effect, rewriting a page of Hawthorne, experimenting and changing an epithet here and there, noting how sometimes the alteration of a trifling word would plunge a whole scene into darkness, as if one of those blood-red fires had instantly been extinguished. Sometimes, for severe practice, he attempted to construct short tales in the manner of this or that master. He sighed over these desperate attempts, over the clattering pieces of mechanism which would not even simulate life; but he urged himself to an infinite perseverance. Through the white hours he worked on amidst the heap and litter of papers; books and manuscripts overflowed from the bureau to the floor; and if he looked out he saw the mist still pass by, still passing from the river to the north.

It was not till the winter was well advanced that he began at all to explore the region in which he lived. Soon after his arrival in the grey street he had taken one or two vague walks, hardly noticing where he went or what he saw; but for all the summer he had shut himself in his room, beholding nothing but the form and colour of words. For his morning walk he almost invariably chose the one direction, going along the Uxbridge Road towards Notting Hill, and returning by the same monotonous thoroughfare.[228] Now, however, when the new year was beginning its dull days, he began to diverge occasionally to right and left, sometimes eating his luncheon in odd corners, in the bulging parlours of eighteenth-century taverns, that still fronted the surging sea of modern streets, or perhaps in brand new 'publics' on the broken borders of the brickfields, smelling of the clay from which they had swollen. He found

---

[227] *garderobe* (French): a small private room, usually in a medieval building. The term became most often used to refer to a toilet, as Machen implies with his use of the word 'rank', as in 'foul smelling'. Machen may be alluding to a tale in Italian author Giovanni Boccaccio's (1313–1375) collection the *Decameron* (c. 1353), in which the character Andreuccio goes to the toilet, steps on a weak board, and falls through the floor onto faeces below. In his writings, Greek philosopher Plato used the structure of a dialogue or debate to record differing philosophical positions without necessarily concluding with a clear preference. Another common Platonic pattern of argument involves extrapolating on a plausible claim to the point of absurdity.

[228] In *Far Off Things*, Machen notes that he often felt isolated and lonely when, upon first arriving in London, he had lived at 23 Clarendon Road, Notting Hill. He found pleasure, however, in taking rambling walks in search of countryside.

waste by-places behind railway embankments where he could smoke his pipe sheltered from the wind; sometimes there was a wooden fence by an old pear-orchard where he sat and gazed at the wet desolation of the market-gardens, munching a few currant biscuits by way of dinner. As he went farther afield a sense of immensity slowly grew upon him; it was as if, from the little island of his room, that one friendly place, he pushed out into the grey unknown, into a city that for him was uninhabited as the desert.

He came back to his cell after these purposeless wanderings always with a sense of relief, with the thought of taking refuge from grey. As he lit the gas and opened the desk of his bureau and saw the pile of papers awaiting him, it was as if he had passed from the black skies and the stinging wind and the dull maze of the suburb into all the warmth and sunlight and violent colour of the south.

VI

It was in this winter after his coming to the grey street that Lucian first experienced the pains of desolation. He had all his life known the delights of solitude, and had acquired that habit of mind which makes a man find rich company on the bare hillside and leads him into the heart of the wood to meditate by the dark waterpools. But now in the blank interval when he was forced to shut up his desk, the sense of loneliness overwhelmed him and filled him with unutterable melancholy. On such days he carried about with him an unceasing gnawing torment in his breast; the anguish of the empty page awaiting him in his bureau, and the knowledge that it was worse than useless to attempt the work. He had fallen into the habit of always using this phrase 'the work' to denote the adventure of literature; it had grown in his mind to all the austere and grave significance of 'the great work' on the lips of the alchemists; it included every trifling and laborious page and the vague magnificent fancies that sometimes hovered before him. All else had become mere by-play, unimportant, trivial; the work was the end, and the means and the food of his life — it raised him up in the morning to renew the struggle, it was the symbol which charmed him as he lay down at night. All through the hours of toil at the bureau he was enchanted, and when he went out and explored the unknown coasts, the one thought allured him, and was the coloured glass between his eyes and the world. Then as he drew nearer home his steps would quicken, and the more weary and grey the walk, the more he rejoiced as he thought of his hermitage and of the curious difficulties that awaited him there. But when, suddenly and without warning, the faculty disappeared, when his mind seemed a hopeless waste from which nothing could arise, then he became subject to a misery so piteous that the barbarians themselves would have been sorry for him. He had known some foretaste of these bitter and inexpressible griefs in the old country days, but then he had immediately taken refuge in the hills, he had rushed to the dark woods as to an anodyne, letting his heart drink in all the wonder and magic of the wild land. Now in these days of January, in the suburban street, there was no such refuge.

He had been working steadily for some weeks, well enough satisfied on the whole with the daily progress, glad to awake in the morning, and to read over what he had written on the night before. The new year opened with faint and heavy weather and a breathless silence in the air, but in a few days the great frost set in. Soon the streets began to suggest the appearance of a beleaguered city, the silence that had preceded the frost deepened, and the mist hung over the earth like a dense white smoke. Night after night the cold increased, and people seemed unwilling to go abroad, till even the main thoroughfares were empty and deserted, as if the inhabitants were lying close in hiding. It was at this dismal time that Lucian found himself reduced to impotence. There was a sudden break in his thought, and when he wrote on valiantly, hoping against hope, he only grew more aghast on the discovery of the imbecilities he had committed to paper. He ground his teeth together and persevered, sick at heart, feeling as if all the world were fallen from under his feet, driving his pen on mechanically, till he was overwhelmed. He saw the stuff he had done without veil or possible concealment, a lamentable and wretched sheaf of verbiage, worse, it seemed, than the efforts of his boyhood. He was no longer tautological, he avoided tautology with the infernal art of a leader-writer, filling his wind bags and mincing his words as if he had been a trained journalist on the staff of the *Daily Post*.[229] There seemed all the matter of an insufferable tragedy in these thoughts; that his patient and enduring toil was in vain, that practice went for nothing, and that he had wasted the labour of Milton to accomplish the tenth-rate. Unhappily he could not 'give in'; the longing, the fury for the work burnt within him like a burning fire; he lifted up his eyes in despair.

It was then, while he knew that no one could help him, that he languished for help, and then, though he was aware that no comfort was possible, he fervently wished to be comforted. The only friend he had was his father, and he knew that his father would not even understand his distress. For him, always, the printed book was the beginning and end of literature; the agony of the maker, his despair and sickness, were as accursed as the pains of labour. He was ready to read and admire the work of the great Smith, but he did not wish to hear of the period when the great Smith had writhed and twisted like a scotched worm, only hoping to be put out of his misery, to go mad or die, to escape somehow from the bitter pains.[230] And Lucian knew no one else. Now and then he read

---

[229] At the time Machen was writing, a number of British cities had their own *Daily Post* publication.

[230] The term 'Smith' is generic for author, as in 'wordsmith'. The term 'scotched' means crushed.

in the paper the fame of the great *littérateurs*; the Gypsies were entertaining the Prince of Wales, the Jolly Beggars were dining with the Lord Mayor, the Old Mumpers were mingling amicably and gorgeously with the leading members of the Stock Exchange.[231] He was so unfortunate as to know none of these gentlemen, but it hardly seemed likely that they could have done much for him in any case. Indeed, in his heart, he was certain that help and comfort from without were in the nature of things utterly impossible, his ruin and grief were within, and only his own assistance could avail. He tried to reassure himself, to believe that his torments were a proof of his vocation, that the facility of the novelist who stood six years deep in contracts to produce romances was a thing wholly undesirable, but all the while he longed for but a drop of that inexhaustible fluency which he professed to despise.

He drove himself out from that dreary contemplation of the white paper and the idle pen. He went into the frozen and deserted streets, hoping that he might pluck the burning coal from his heart, but the fire was not quenched. As he walked furiously along the grim iron roads he fancied that those persons who passed him cheerfully on their way to friends and friendly hearths shrank from him into the mists as they went by. Lucian imagined that the fire of his torment and anguish must in some way glow visibly about him; he moved, perhaps, in a nimbus that proclaimed the blackness and the flames within. He knew, of course, that in misery he had grown delirious, that the well-coated, smooth-hatted personages who loomed out of the fog upon him were in reality shuddering only with cold, but in spite of common sense he still conceived that he saw on their faces an evident horror and disgust, and something of the repugnance that one feels at the sight of a venomous snake, half-killed, trailing its bleeding vileness out of sight. By design Lucian tried to make for remote and desolate places, and yet when he had succeeded in touching on the open country, and knew that the icy shadow hovering through the mist was a field, he longed for some sound and murmur of life, and turned again to roads where pale lamps were glimmering, and the dancing flame of firelight shone across the frozen shrubs. And the sight of these homely fires, the thought of affection and consolation waiting by them, stung him the more sharply perhaps because of the contrast with his own chills and weariness and helpless sickness, and chiefly because he knew that he had long closed an everlasting door between his heart and such felicities. If those within had come out and had called him by his name to enter and be comforted, it would have been quite unavailing, since between them and him there was a great gulf fixed. Perhaps for the first time he realised that he had lost the art of humanity for ever. He had thought when he closed his ears to the wood whisper and changed the fauns' singing

---

[231] Mumpers are beggars or those who sponge off wealthier people. No known historical referent was found for Machen's titles of Gypsies, Jolly Beggars, and Old Mumpers.

for the murmur of the streets, the black pools for the shadows and amber light of London, that he had put off the old life, and had turned his soul to healthy activities, but the truth was that he had merely exchanged one drug for another. He could not be human, and he wondered whether there were some drop of the fairy blood in his body that made him foreign and a stranger in the world.[232]

He did not surrender to desolation without repeated struggles. He strove to allure himself to his desk by the promise of some easy task; he would not attempt invention, but he had memoranda and rough jottings of ideas in his note-books, and he would merely amplify the suggestions ready to his hand. But it was hopeless, again and again it was hopeless. As he read over his notes, trusting that he would find some hint that might light up the dead fires, and kindle again that pure flame of enthusiasm, he found how desperately his fortune had fallen. He could see no light, no colour in the lines he had scribbled with eager trembling fingers; he remembered how splendid all these things had been when he wrote them down, but now they were meaningless, faded into grey. The few words he had dashed on to the paper, enraptured at the thought of the happy hours they promised, had become mere jargon, and when he understood the idea it seemed foolish, dull, unoriginal. He discovered something at last that appeared to have a grain of promise, and determined to do his best to put it into shape, but the first paragraph appalled him; it might have been written by an unintelligent schoolboy. He tore the paper in pieces, and shut and locked his desk, heavy despair sinking like lead into his heart. For the rest of that day he lay motionless on the bed, smoking pipe after pipe in the hope of stupefying himself with tobacco fumes. The air in the room became blue and thick with smoke; it was bitterly cold, and he wrapped himself up in his great-coat and drew the counterpane over him. The night came on and the window darkened, and at last he fell asleep.

He renewed the effort at intervals, only to plunge deeper into misery. He felt the approaches of madness, and knew that his only hope was to walk till he was physically exhausted, so that he might come home almost fainting with fatigue, but ready to fall asleep the moment he got into bed. He passed the mornings in a kind of torpor, endeavouring to avoid thought, to occupy his mind with the pattern of the paper, with the advertisements at the end of a book, with the curious greyness of the light that glimmered through the mist into his room, with the muffled voices that rumbled now and then from the street. He tried to make out the design that had once coloured the faded carpet on the floor, and wondered about the dead artist in Japan, the adorner of his bureau. He speculated as to what his thoughts had been as he inserted the rainbow mother-of-pearl and made that great flight of shining birds, dipping their wings as they

---

[232] In Shakespeare's play *Romeo and Juliet* (*c.* 1591–1595), Capulet says of his 14-year-old daughter, Juliet, 'My child is yet a stranger in the world' (I.2.8).

rose from the reeds, or how he had conceived the lacquer dragons in red gold, and the fantastic houses in the garden of peach-trees. But sooner or later the oppression of his grief returned, the loud shriek and clang of the garden-gate, the warning bell of some passing bicyclist steering through the fog, the noise of his pipe falling to the floor, would suddenly awaken him to the sense of misery. He knew that it was time to go out; he could not bear to sit still and suffer. Sometimes he cut a slice of bread and put it in his pocket, sometimes he trusted to the chance of finding a public-house, where he could have a sandwich and a glass of beer. He turned always from the main streets and lost himself in the intricate suburban byways, willing to be engulfed in the infinite whiteness of the mist.

The roads had stiffened into iron ridges, the fences and trees were glittering with frost crystals, everything was of strange and altered aspect. Lucian walked on and on through the maze, now in a circle of shadowy villas, awful as the buried streets of Herculaneum, now in lanes dipping into the open country, that led him past great elm-trees whose white boughs were all still, and past the bitter lonely fields where the mist seemed to fade away into grey darkness.[233] As he wandered along these unfamiliar and ghastly paths he became the more convinced of his utter remoteness from all humanity, he allowed that grotesque suggestion of there being something visibly amiss in his outward appearance to grow upon him, and often he looked with a horrible expectation into the faces of those who passed by, afraid lest his own senses gave him false intelligence, and that he had really assumed some frightful and revolting shape. It was curious that, partly by his own fault, and largely, no doubt, through the operation of mere coincidence, he was once or twice strongly confirmed in this fantastic delusion. He came one day into a lonely and unfrequented byway, a country lane falling into ruin, but still fringed with elms that had formed an avenue leading to the old manor-house. It was now the road of communication between two far outlying suburbs, and on these winter nights lay as black, dreary, and desolate as a mountain track. Soon after the frost began, a gentleman had been set upon in this lane as he picked his way between the corner where the bus had set him down, and his home where the fire was blazing, and his wife watched the clock. He was stumbling uncertainly through the gloom, growing a little nervous because the walk seemed so long, and peering anxiously for the lamp at the end of his street, when the two footpads rushed at him out of the fog.[234] One caught him from behind, the other struck him with a heavy bludgeon, and as he lay senseless they robbed him of his watch and money, and vanished across

---

[233] In 79 CE, the Roman town of Herculaneum was buried by volcanic eruptions from Mount Vesuvius. As a result, many of the buildings, mosaics, paintings, and furnishings were preserved.
[234] Footpads are highway robbers travelling on foot.

the fields. The next morning all the suburb rang with the story; the unfortunate merchant had been grievously hurt, and wives watched their husbands go out in the morning with sickening apprehension, not knowing what might happen at night. Lucian of course was ignorant of all these rumours, and struck into the gloomy by-road without caring where he was or whither the way would lead him.

He had been driven out that day as with whips, another hopeless attempt to return to the work had agonised him, and existence seemed an intolerable pain. As he entered the deeper gloom, where the fog hung heavily, he began, half consciously, to gesticulate; he felt convulsed with torment and shame, and it was a sorry relief to clench his nails into his palm and strike the air as he stumbled heavily along, bruising his feet against the frozen ruts and ridges. His impotence was hideous, he said to himself, and he cursed himself and his life, breaking out into a loud oath, and stamping on the ground. Suddenly he was shocked at a scream of terror, it seemed in his very ear, and looking up he saw for a moment a woman gazing at him out of the mist, her features distorted and stiff with fear. A momentary convulsion twitched her arms into the ugly mimicry of a beckoning gesture, and she turned and ran for dear life, howling like a beast.

Lucian stood still in the road while the woman's cries grew faint and died away. His heart was chilled within him as the significance of this strange incident became clear. He remembered nothing of his violent gestures; he had not known at the time that he had sworn out loud, or that he was grinding his teeth with impotent rage. He only thought of that ringing scream, of the horrible fear on the white face that had looked upon him, of the woman's headlong flight from his presence. He stood trembling and shuddering, and in a little while he was feeling his face, searching for some loathsome mark, for the stigmata of evil branding his forehead. He staggered homewards like a drunken man, and when he came into the Uxbridge Road some children saw him and called after him as he swayed and caught at the lamp-post. When he got to his room he sat down at first in the dark. He did not dare to light the gas. Everything in the room was indistinct, but he shut his eyes as he passed the dressing-table, and sat in a corner, his face turned to the wall. And when at last he gathered courage and the flame leapt hissing from the jet, he crept piteously towards the glass, and ducked his head, crouching miserably, and struggling with his terrors before he could look at his own image.

To the best of his power he tried to deliver himself from these more grotesque fantasies; he assured himself that there was nothing terrific in his countenance but sadness, that his face was like the face of other men.[235] Yet he could not

---

[235] The attention to the face as exposing one's sins is central to a number of neo-gothic novels of this period, including Stevenson's *Strange Case of Dr Jekyll and Mr Hyde* and Wilde's *Picture of Dorian Gray*.

forget that reflection he had seen in the woman's eyes, how the surest mirrors had shown him a horrible dread, her soul itself quailing and shuddering at an awful sight. Her scream rang and rang in his ears; she had fled away from him as if he offered some fate darker than death.

He looked again and again into the glass, tortured by a hideous uncertainty. His senses told him there was nothing amiss, yet he had had a proof, and yet, as he peered more earnestly, there was, it seemed, something strange and not altogether usual in the expression of the eyes. Perhaps it might be the unsteady flare of the gas, or perhaps a flaw in the cheap looking-glass, that gave some slight distortion to the image. He walked briskly up and down the room and tried to gaze steadily, indifferently, into his own face. He would not allow himself to be misguided by a word. When he had pronounced himself incapable of humanity, he had only meant that he could not enjoy the simple things of common life. A man was not necessarily monstrous, surrounded by a red halo of malediction, merely because he did not appreciate high tea, a quiet chat about the neighbours, and a happy noisy evening with the children. But with what message, then, did he appear charged that the woman's mouth grew so stark? Her hands had jerked up as if they had been pulled with frantic wires; she seemed for the instant like a horrible puppet. Her scream was a thing from the nocturnal Sabbath.[236]

He lit a candle and held it close up to the glass so that his own face glared white at him, and the reflection of the room became an indistinct darkness. He saw nothing but the candle flame and his own shining eyes, and surely they were not as the eyes of common men. As he put down the light, a sudden suggestion entered his mind, and he drew a quick breath, amazed at the thought. He hardly knew whether to rejoice or to shudder. For the thought he conceived was this: that he had mistaken all the circumstances of the adventure, and had perhaps repulsed a sister who would have welcomed him to the Sabbath.

He lay awake all night, turning from one dreary and frightful thought to the other, scarcely dozing for a few hours when the dawn came. He tried for a moment to argue with himself when he got up; knowing that his true life was locked up in the bureau, he made a desperate attempt to drive the phantoms and hideous shapes from his mind. He was assured that his salvation was in the work, and he drew the key from his pocket, and made as if he would have opened the desk. But the nausea, the remembrances of repeated and utter failure, were too powerful. For many days he hung about the Manor Lane, half dreading, half desiring another meeting, and he swore he would not again mistake the cry of rapture, nor repulse the arms extended in a frenzy of delight. In those days he dreamed of some dark place where they might celebrate and make the marriage of the Sabbath, with such rites as he had dared to imagine.

---

[236] On the nocturnal Sabbath, see note 38 of 'The Recluse of Bayswater'.

It was perhaps only the shock of a letter from his father that rescued him from these evident approaches to madness. Mr. Taylor wrote how they had missed him at Christmas, how the farmers had inquired after him, of the homely familiar things that recalled his boyhood, his mother's voice, the friendly fireside, and the good old fashions that had nurtured him. He remembered that he had once been a boy, loving the cake and puddings and the radiant holly, and all the seventeenth-century mirth that lingered on in the ancient farm-houses. And there came to him the more holy memory of Mass on Christmas morning. How sweet the dark and frosty earth had smelt as he walked beside his mother down the winding lane, and from the stile near the church they had seen the world glimmering to the dawn, and the wandering lanthorns advancing across the fields.[237] Then he had come into the church and seen it shining with candles and holly, and his father in pure vestments of white linen sang the longing music of the liturgy at the altar, and the people answered him, till the sun rose with the grave notes of the Paternoster, and a red beam stole through the chancel window.[238]

The worst horror left him as he recalled the memory of these dear and holy things. He cast away the frightful fancy that the scream he had heard was a shriek of joy, that the arms, rigidly jerked out, invited him to an embrace. Indeed, the thought that he had longed for such an obscene illusion, that he had gloated over the recollection of that stark mouth, filled him with disgust. He resolved that his senses were deceived, that he had neither seen nor heard, but had for a moment externalized his own slumbering and morbid dreams. It was perhaps necessary that he should be wretched, that his efforts should be discouraged, but he would not yield utterly to madness.

Yet when he went abroad with such good resolutions, it was hard to resist an influence that seemed to come from without and within. He did not know it, but people were everywhere talking of the great frost, of the fog that lay heavy on London, making the streets dark and terrible, of strange birds that came fluttering about the windows in the silent squares. The Thames rolled out duskily, bearing down the jarring ice-blocks, and as one looked on the black water from the bridges it was like a river in a northern tale. To Lucian it all seemed mythical, of the same substance as his own fantastic thoughts. He rarely saw a newspaper, and did not follow from day to day the systematic readings of the thermometer, the reports of ice-fairs, of coaches driven across the river at Hampton, of the skating on the fens; and hence the iron roads, the beleaguered silence and the heavy folds of mist appeared as amazing as a picture, significant, appalling. He could not look out and see a common suburban street foggy and

---

[237] lanthorns: lanterns (archaic).
[238] 'Paternoster' is Latin for the Lord's Prayer, from the Latin for 'Our Father'. A vestment is a ceremonial robe and a liturgy is the standard procedure of religious worship.

dull, nor think of the inhabitants as at work or sitting cheerfully eating nuts about their fires; he saw a vision of a grey road vanishing, of dim houses all empty and deserted, and the silence seemed eternal. And when he went out and passed through street after street, all void, by the vague shapes of houses that appeared for a moment and were then instantly swallowed up, it seemed to him as if he had strayed into a city that had suffered some inconceivable doom, that he alone wandered where myriads had once dwelt. It was a town great as Babylon, terrible as Rome, marvellous as Lost Atlantis, set in the midst of a white wilderness surrounded by waste places.[239] It was impossible to escape from it; if he skulked between hedges, and crept away beyond the frozen pools, presently the serried stony lines confronted him like an army, and far and far they swept away into the night, as some fabled wall that guards an empire in the vast dim East. Or in that distorting medium of the mist, changing all things, he imagined that he trod an infinite desolate plain, abandoned from ages, but circled and encircled with dolmen and menhir that loomed out at him, gigantic, terrible.[240] All London was one grey temple of an awful rite, ring within ring of wizard stones circled about some central place, every circle was an initiation, every initiation eternal loss.[241] Or perhaps he was astray for ever in a land of grey rocks. He had seen the light of home, the flicker of the fire on the walls; close at hand, it seemed, was the open door, and he had heard dear voices calling to him across the gloom, but he had just missed the path. The lamps vanished, the voices sounded thin and died away, and yet he knew that those within were waiting, that they could not bear to close the door, but waited, calling his name, while he had missed the way, and wandered in the pathless desert of the grey rocks. Fantastic, hideous, they beset him wherever he turned, piled up into

---

[239] W. T. Stead, whom Machen disliked for his populist approach to psychism and communicating with the dead, popularized the vision of London as Babylon in a highly influential article on child prostitution (W. T. Stead, 'The Maiden Tribute of Modern Babylon', *Pall Mall Gazette* (6, 7, 8, and 10 July 1885)).

[240] A dolmen is a group of vertical megaliths topped with a capstone and typically covered in rocks and dirt to create a human burial mound, or tumulus. They were primarily constructed during the neolithic period. Menhirs are standing stones, which were erected singly or often in a circle during various pre-historic periods.

[241] The description brings to mind the nine concentric rings of the inferno in Dante Alighieri's (c. 1265–1321) *Divine Comedy* (1308–1320). In *The Drama of Kings* (1871), author Robert William Buchanan (1841–1901) uses the phrase 'ring within ring' as a set refrain. Buchanan is best known now for his attack on Aestheticism, 'The Fleshly School of Poetry', (1871; expanded version 1872). Famous critiques of the piece include Rossetti's 'The Stealthy School of Criticism' (1871) and Swinburne's *Under the Microscope* (1872). Buchanan later distanced himself from the article as well, focussing his literary career instead on spirituality and mysticism. *The Drama of Kings* includes the essay 'On Mystic Realism', which carries a sceptical attitude much like Lucian's in this scene. Buchanan also states in the essay that, with his writing, he attempts 'to combine two qualities which the modern mind is accustomed to regard apart — reality and mystery, earthliness and spirituality' (Robert Buchanan, *The Drama of Kings* (London: Strathan, 1871), p. 465).

strange shapes, pricked with sharp peaks, assuming the appearance of goblin towers, swelling into a vague dome like a fairy rath, huge and terrible.[242] And as one dream faded into another, so these last fancies were perhaps the most tormenting and persistent; the rocky avenues became the camp and fortalice of some half-human, malignant race who swarmed in hiding, ready to bear him away into the heart of their horrible hills. It was awful to think that all his goings were surrounded, that in the darkness he was watched and surveyed, that every step but led him deeper and deeper into the labyrinth.

When, of an evening, he was secure in his room, the blind drawn down and the gas flaring, he made vigorous efforts toward sanity. It was not of his free will that he allowed terror to overmaster him, and he desired nothing better than a placid and harmless life, full of work and clear thinking. He knew that he deluded himself with imagination, that he had been walking through London suburbs and not through Pandemonium, and that if he could but unlock his bureau all those ugly forms would be resolved into the mist.[243] But it was hard to say if he consoled himself effectually with such reflections, for the return to common sense meant also the return to the sharp pangs of defeat. It recalled him to the bitter theme of his own inefficiency, to the thought that he only desired one thing of life, and that this was denied him. He was willing to endure the austerities of a monk in a severe cloister, to suffer cold, to be hungry, to be lonely and friendless, to forbear all the consolation of friendly speech, and to be glad of all these things, if only he might be allowed to illuminate the manuscript in quietness. It seemed a hideous insufferable cruelty, that he should so fervently desire that which he could never gain.

He was led back to the old conclusion; he had lost the sense of humanity, he was wretched because he was an alien and a stranger amongst citizens. It seemed probable that the enthusiasm of literature, as he understood it, the fervent desire for the fine art, had in it something of the inhuman, and dissevered the enthusiast from his fellow-creatures. It was possible that the barbarian suspected as much, that by some slow process of rumination he had arrived at his fixed and inveterate hatred of all artists. It was no doubt a dim unconscious impression, by no means a clear reasoned conviction; the average Philistine, if pressed for the reasons of his dislike, would either become inarticulate, ejaculating 'faugh' and 'pah' like an old-fashioned Scots Magazine, or else he would give some imaginary and absurd reason, alleging that all 'littery men' were poor, that composers never cut their hair, that painters were rarely public-school men, that sculptors couldn't ride straight to hounds to save their lives,

---

[242] Relatively common in Ireland, a rath is a circular earthen wall creating a space used as a dwelling, stronghold, or fortalice (small fort). Some recognize them as inhabited by the little people or fairies.
[243] In Milton's *Paradise Lost*, Pandemonium is the capital of Hell.

but clearly these imbecilities were mere afterthoughts;[244] the average man hated the artist from a deep instinctive dread of all that was strange, uncanny, alien to his nature; he gibbered, uttered his harsh, semi-bestial 'faugh,' and dismissed Keats to his gallipots from much the same motives as usually impelled the black savage to dismiss the white man on an even longer journey.[245]

Lucian was not especially interested in this hatred of the barbarian for the maker, except from this point, that it confirmed him in his belief that the love of art dissociated the man from the race. One touch of art made the whole world alien, but surely miseries of the civilised man cast amongst savages were not so much caused by dread of their ferocity as by the terror of his own loneliness. He feared their spears less than his own thoughts; he would perhaps in his last despair leave his retreat and go forth to perish at their hands, so that he might at least die in company, and hear the sound of speech before death. And Lucian felt most keenly that in his case there was a double curse; he was as isolated as Keats, and as inarticulate as his reviewers. The consolation of the work had failed him, and he was suspended in the void between two worlds.

It was no doubt the composite effect of his failures, his loneliness of soul, and solitude of life, that had made him invest those common streets with such grim and persistent terrors. He had perhaps yielded to a temptation without knowing that he had been tempted, and, in the manner of De Quincey, had chosen the subtle in exchange for the more tangible pains.[246] Unconsciously, but still of free will, he had preferred the splendour and the gloom of a malignant vision before his corporal pains, before the hard reality of his own impotence. It was better to dwell in vague melancholy, to stray in the forsaken streets of a city doomed from ages, to wander amidst forlorn and desperate rocks than to awake to a gnawing and ignoble torment, to confess that a house of business would have been more suitable and more practical, that he had promised what he could never perform. Even as he struggled to beat back the phantasmagoria of the mist, and resolved that he would no longer make all the streets a stage of apparitions, he hardly realised what he had done, or that the ghosts he had called might depart and return again.

He continued his long walks, always with the object of producing a physical weariness and exhaustion that would enable him to sleep of nights. But even when he saw the foggy and deserted avenues in their proper shape, and allowed his eyes to catch the pale glimmer of the lamps, and the dancing flame of the

---

[244] Machen appears simply to be mocking conventional middle-class periodicals. *Scots Magazine* itself has been in publication, on and off, since 1739, but not when Machen was writing *The Hill of Dreams*.

[245] Romantic poet John Keats had first studied for a career in medicine. Despite having published for only four years before dying from tuberculosis at the age of 25, Keats had become a highly revered author by Machen's time. Gallipots are small containers that apothecaries used to hold medicines and ointments.

[246] The reference is to De Quincey's opium addiction.

firelight, he could not rid himself of the impression that he stood afar off, that between those hearths and himself there was a great gulf fixed. As he paced down the footpath he could often see plainly across the frozen shrubs into the homely and cheerful rooms. Sometimes, late in the evening, he caught a passing glimpse of the family at tea, father, mother, and children laughing and talking together, well pleased with each other's company. Sometimes a wife or a child was standing by the garden gate peering anxiously through the fog, and the sight of it all, all the little details, the hideous but comfortable armchairs turned ready to the fire, maroon-red curtains being drawn close to shut out the ugly night, the sudden blaze and illumination as the fire was poked up so that it might be cheerful for father; these trivial and common things were acutely significant. They brought back to him the image of a dead boy — himself. They recalled the shabby old 'parlour' in the country, with its shabby old furniture and fading carpet, and renewed a whole atmosphere of affection and homely comfort. His mother would walk to the end of the drive and look out for him when he was late (wandering then about the dark woodlands); on winter evenings she would make the fire blaze, and have his slippers warming by the hearth, and there was probably buttered toast 'as a treat.' He dwelt on all these insignificant petty circumstances, on the genial glow and light after the muddy winter lanes, on the relish of the buttered toast and the smell of the hot tea, on the two old cats curled fast asleep before the fender, and made them instruments of exquisite pain and regret. Each of these strange houses that he passed was identified in his mind with his own vanished home; all was prepared and ready as in the old days, but he was shut out, judged and condemned to wander in the frozen mist, with weary feet, anguished and forlorn, and they that would pass from within to help him could not, neither could he pass to them. Again, for the hundredth time, he came back to the sentence: he could not gain the art of letters and he had lost the art of humanity. He saw the vanity of all his thoughts; he was an ascetic caring nothing for warmth and cheerfulness and the small comforts of life, and yet he allowed his mind to dwell on such things. If one of those passers-by, who walked briskly, eager for home, should have pitied him by some miracle and asked him to come in, it would have been worse than useless, yet he longed for pleasures that he could not have enjoyed. It was as if he were come to a place of torment, where they who could not drink longed for water, where they who could feel no warmth shuddered in the eternal cold. He was oppressed by the grim conceit that he himself still slept within the matted thicket, imprisoned by the green bastions of the Roman fort. He had never come out, but a changeling had gone down the hill, and now stirred about the earth.[247]

Beset by such ingenious terrors, it was not wonderful that outward events and common incidents should abet his fancies. He had succeeded one day in escaping from the mesh of the streets, and fell on a rough and narrow lane that stole into a little valley. For the moment he was in a somewhat happier mood;

---

[247] In Celtic and other folklore, a changeling is an infant (often a fairy child or an unattractive child) secretly substituted by the fairies for another human child.

the afternoon sun glowed through the rolling mist, and the air grew clearer. He saw quiet and peaceful fields, and a wood descending in a gentle slope from an old farmstead of warm red brick. The farmer was driving the slow cattle home from the hill, and his loud halloo to his dog came across the land a cheerful mellow note. From another side a cart was approaching the clustered barns, hesitating, pausing while the great horses rested, and then starting again into lazy motion. In the well of the valley a wandering line of bushes showed where a brook crept in and out amongst the meadows, and, as Lucian stood, lingering, on the bridge, a soft and idle breath ruffled through the boughs of a great elm. He felt soothed, as by calm music, and wondered whether it would not be better for him to live in some such quiet place, within reach of the streets and yet remote from them. It seemed a refuge for still thoughts; he could imagine himself sitting at rest beneath the black yew tree in the farm garden, at the close of a summer day. He had almost determined that he would knock at the door and ask if they would take him as a lodger, when he saw a child running towards him down the lane. It was a little girl, with bright curls tossing about her head, and, as she came on, the sunlight glowed upon her, illuminating her brick-red frock and the yellow king-cups in her hat.[248] She had run with her eyes on the ground, chirping and laughing to herself, and did not see Lucian till she was quite near him. She started and glanced into his eyes for a moment, and began to cry; he stretched out his hand, and she ran from him screaming, frightened no doubt by what was to her a sudden and strange apparition. He turned back towards London, and the mist folded him in its thick darkness, for on that evening it was tinged with black.

It was only by the intensest strain of resolution that he did not yield utterly to the poisonous anodyne which was always at his hand. It had been a difficult struggle to escape from the mesh of the hills, from the music of the fauns, and even now he was drawn by the memory of these old allurements. But he felt that here, in his loneliness, he was in greater danger, and beset by a blacker magic. Horrible fancies rushed wantonly into his mind; he was not only ready to believe that something in his soul sent a shudder through all that was simple and innocent, but he came trembling home one Saturday night, believing, or half-believing, that he was in communion with evil. He had passed through the clamorous and blatant crowd of the 'high street,' where, as one climbed the hill, the shops seemed all aflame, and the black night air glowed with the flaring gas-jets and the naphtha-lamps, hissing and wavering before the February wind.[249] Voices, raucous, clamant, abominable, were belched out of the blazing public-houses as the doors swung to and fro, and above these doors were hideous

---

[248] A king-cup is a small, golden, cup-shaped plant common to marshlands.
[249] Naphtha-lamps burn liquid hydrocarbon. They were common at markets and outdoor performances.

brassy lamps, very slowly swinging in a violent blast of air, so that they might have been infernal thuribles, censing the people.[250] Some man was calling his wares in one long continuous shriek that never stopped or paused, and, as a respond, a deeper, louder voice roared to him from across the road. An Italian whirled the handle of his piano-organ in a fury, and a ring of imps danced mad figures around him, danced and flung up their legs till the rags dropped from some of them, and they still danced on. A flare of naphtha, burning with a rushing noise, threw a light on one point of the circle, and Lucian watched a lank girl of fifteen as she came round and round to the flash. She was quite drunk, and had kicked her petticoats away, and the crowd howled laughter and applause at her. Her black hair poured down and leapt on her scarlet bodice; she sprang and leapt round the ring, laughing in Bacchic frenzy, and led the orgy to triumph. People were crossing to and fro, jostling against each other, swarming about certain shops and stalls in a dense dark mass that quivered and sent out feelers as if it were one writhing organism. A little farther a group of young men, arm in arm, were marching down the roadway chanting some music-hall verse in full chorus, so that it sounded like plainsong. An impossible hubbub, a hum of voices angry as swarming bees, the squeals of five or six girls who ran in and out, and dived up dark passages and darted back into the crowd; all these mingled together till his ears quivered. A young fellow was playing the concertina, and he touched the keys with such slow fingers that the tune wailed solemn into a dirge; but there was nothing so strange as the burst of sound that swelled out when the public-house doors were opened.[251]

He walked amongst these people, looked at their faces, and looked at the children amongst them. He had come out thinking that he would see the English working class, 'the best-behaved and the best-tempered crowd in the world,' enjoying the simple pleasure of the Saturday night's shopping.[252] Mother bought the joint for Sunday's dinner, and perhaps a pair of boots for father; father had an honest glass of beer, and the children were given bags of sweets, and then all these worthy people went decently home to their well-earned rest. De Quincey had enjoyed the sight in his day, and had studied the rise and fall of onions and potatoes.[253] Lucian, indeed, had desired to take these simple

---

[250] Thuribles are metal censers suspended by chains used for burning incense during religious services.

[251] A concertina is a reed-based instrument akin to an accordion, using bellows and buttons for playing. Developed in the nineteenth century, it was often used for traditional folk music.

[252] In a warning against placing confidence in democracy and the masses, Arthur Winnington-Ingram (1858–1946) wrote in 1896 that 'the best-tempered crowd in the world is an English crowd', but that its constituents are also ignorant and easily led (Arthur Winnington-Ingram, *The Men Who Crucified Christ* (London: Wells Gardner, Darton & Co., 1896), p. 51).

[253] In *Confessions*, De Quincey describes his experiences of the poor and working classes,

emotions as an opiate, to forget the fine fret and fantastic trouble of his own existence in plain things and the palpable joy of rest after labour. He was only afraid lest he should be too sharply reproached by the sight of these men who fought bravely year after year against starvation, who knew nothing of intricate and imagined grief, but only the weariness of relentless labour, of the long battle for their wives and children. It would be pathetic, he thought, to see them content with so little, brightened by the expectation of a day's rest and a good dinner, forced, even then, to reckon every penny, and to make their children laugh with halfpence. Either he would be ashamed before so much content, or else he would be again touched by the sense of his inhumanity which could take no interest in the common things of life. But still he went to be at least taken out of himself, to be forced to look at another side of the world, so that he might perhaps forget a little while his own sorrows.

He was fascinated by what he saw and heard. He wondered whether De Quincey also had seen the same spectacle, and had concealed his impressions out of reverence for the average reader. Here there were no simple joys of honest toilers, but wonderful orgies, that drew out his heart to horrible music. At first the violence of sound and sight had overwhelmed him; the lights flaring in the night wind, the array of naphtha lamps, the black shadows, the roar of voices. The dance about the piano-organ had been the first sign of an inner meaning, and the face of the dark girl as she came round and round to the flame had been amazing in its utter furious abandon. And what songs they were singing all around him, and what terrible words rang out, only to excite peals of laughter. In the public-houses the workmen's wives, the wives of small tradesmen, decently dressed in black, were drinking their faces to a flaming red, and urging their husbands to drink more. Beautiful young women, flushed and laughing, put their arms round the men's necks and kissed them, and then held up the glass to their lips. In the dark corners, at the openings of side streets, the children were talking together, instructing each other, whispering what they had seen; a boy of fifteen was plying a girl of twelve with whisky, and presently they crept away. Lucian passed them as they turned to go, and both looked at him. The boy laughed, and the girl smiled quietly. It was above all in the faces around him that he saw the most astounding things, the Bacchic fury unveiled and unashamed. To his eyes it seemed as if these revellers recognised him as a fellow, and smiled up in his face, aware that he was in the secret. Every instinct of religion, of civilisation even, was swept away; they gazed at one another and at him, absolved of all scruples, children of the earth and nothing more. Now and then a couple detached themselves from the swarm, and went away into the darkness, answering the jeers and laughter of their friends as they vanished.

---

noting his pleasurable entry into their discussions of wages and the price of household goods.

On the edge of the pavement, not far from where he was standing, Lucian noticed a tall and lovely young woman who seemed to be alone. She was in the full light of a naphtha flame, and her bronze hair and flushed cheeks shone illuminate as she viewed the orgy. She had dark brown eyes, and a strange look as of an old picture in her face; and her eyes brightened with an argent gleam. He saw the revellers nudging each other and glancing at her, and two or three young men went up and asked her to come for a walk. She shook her head and said 'No thank you' again and again, and seemed as if she were looking for somebody in the crowd.

'I'm expecting a friend,' she said at last to a man who proposed a drink and a walk afterwards; and Lucian wondered what kind of friend would ultimately appear. Suddenly she turned to him as he was about to pass on, and said in a low voice:

'I'll go for a walk with you if you like; you just go on, and I'll follow in a minute.'

For a moment he looked steadily at her. He saw that the first glance had misled him; her face was not flushed with drink as he had supposed, but it was radiant with the most exquisite colour, a red flame glowed and died on her cheek, and seemed to palpitate as she spoke. The head was set on the neck nobly, as in a statue, and about the ears the bronze hair strayed into little curls. She was smiling and waiting for his answer.

He muttered something about being very sorry, and fled down the hill out of the orgy, from the noise of roaring voices and the glitter of the great lamps very slowly swinging in the blast of wind. He knew that he had touched the brink of utter destruction; there was death in the woman's face, and she had indeed summoned him to the Sabbath. Somehow he had been able to refuse on the instant, but if he had delayed he knew he would have abandoned himself to her, body and soul. He locked himself in his room and lay trembling on the bed, wondering if some subtle sympathy had shown the woman her perfect companion. He looked in the glass, not expecting now to see certain visible and outward signs, but searching for the meaning of that strange glance that lit up his eyes. He had grown even thinner than before in the last few months, and his cheeks were wasted with hunger and sorrow, but there were still about his features the suggestion of a curious classic grace, and the look as of a faun who has strayed from the vineyards and olive gardens. He had broken away, but now he felt the mesh of her net about him, a desire for her that was a madness, as if she held every nerve in his body and drew him to her, to her mystic world, to the rosebush where every flower was a flame.

He dreamed all night of the perilous things he had refused, and it was loss to awake in the morning, pain to return to the world. The frost had broken and the fog had rolled away, and the grey street was filled with a clear grey light.

Again he looked out on the long dull sweep of the monotonous houses, hidden
for the past weeks by a curtain of mist. Heavy rain had fallen in the night,
and the garden rails were still dripping, the roofs still dark with wet, all down
the line the dingy white blinds were drawn in the upper windows. Not a soul
walked the street; every one was asleep after the exertions of the night before;
even on the main road it was only at intervals that some straggler paddled by.
Presently a woman in a brown ulster shuffled off on some errand, then a man
in shirt-sleeves poked out his head, holding the door half-open, and stared up at
a window opposite.[254] After a few minutes he slunk in again, and three loafers
came slouching down the street, eager for mischief or beastliness of some sort.
They chose a house that seemed rather smarter than the rest, and, irritated by
the neat curtains, the little grass plot with its dwarf shrub, one of the ruffians
drew out a piece of chalk and wrote some words on the front door. His friends
kept watch for him, and the adventure achieved, all three bolted, bellowing
yahoo laughter. Then a bell began, tang, tang, tang, and here and there children
appeared on their way to Sunday-school, and the chapel 'teachers' went by
with verjuice eyes and lips, scowling at the little boy who cried 'Piper, piper!'[255]
On the main road many respectable people, the men shining and ill-fitted,
the women hideously bedizened, passed in the direction of the Independent
nightmare, the stuccoed thing with Doric columns, but on the whole life was
stagnant.[256] Presently Lucian smelt the horrid fumes of roast beef and cabbage;
the early risers were preparing the one-o'clock meal, but many lay in bed and
put off dinner till three, with the effect of prolonging the cabbage atmosphere
into the late afternoon. A drizzly rain began as the people were coming out of
church, and the mothers of little boys in velvet and little girls in foolishness
of every kind were impelled to slap their offspring, and to threaten them with
father. Then the torpor of beef and beer and cabbage settled down on the street;
in some houses they snorted and read the Parish Magazine, in some they snored
and read the murders and collected filth of the week;[257] but the only movement

---

[254] An ulster is a basic worker's overcoat. In the Victorian period, to appear in public with
the sleeves of one's shirt uncovered was considered by the middle class to be highly casual,
or even base.
[255] Verjuice is a sour liquid, akin to vinegar, made of various fruits such as crab apples,
lemons, and, in particular, unripe grapes.
[256] In ancient Greek architecture, Doric columns are wider and simpler than the designs of
the other two principal types, the Ionic and Corinthian.
[257] The Parish Magazine is the periodical commonly published by an Anglican parish,
combining religious articles and local news and notices. The other magazines Machen
describes are the penny dreadfuls and other inexpensive publications popular for their
sensationalist stories of crime and violence. Many argued that the materials themselves
encouraged crime. See, for example, Wilkie Collins, 'The Unknown Public', *Household
Words*, 18 (August 1858), pp. 217–22; the anonymous 'Boyish Freaks', *Chambers's Journal of
Popular Literature, Science and Arts*, 5 (April 1888), pp. 252–55; and Hugh Chisholm, 'How
to Counteract the "Penny Dreadful"', *Fortnightly Review*, 64 (November 1895), pp. 765–75.

of the afternoon was a second procession of children, now bloated and distended with food, again answering the summons of tang, tang, tang. On the main road the trams, laden with impossible people, went humming to and fro, and young men who wore bright blue ties cheerfully haw-hawed and smoked penny cigars. They annoyed the shiny and respectable and verjuice-lipped, not by the frightful stench of the cigars, but because they were cheerful on Sunday. By and by the children, having heard about Moses in the Bulrushes and Daniel in the Lion's Den, came straggling home in an evil humour.[258] And all the day it was as if on a grey sheet grey shadows flickered, passing by.

And in the rose-garden every flower was a flame! He thought in symbols, using the Persian imagery of a dusky court, surrounded by white cloisters, gilded by gates of bronze. The stars came out, the sky glowed a darker violet, but the cloistered wall, the fantastic trellises in stone, shone whiter. It was like a hedge of may-blossom, like a lily within a cup of lapis-lazuli, like sea-foam tossed on the heaving sea at dawn.[259] Always those white cloisters trembled with the lute music, always the garden sang with the clear fountain, rising and falling in the mysterious dusk. And there was a singing voice stealing through the white lattices and the bronze gates, a soft voice chanting of the Lover and the Beloved, of the Vineyard, of the Gate and the Way. Oh! the language was unknown; but the music of the refrain returned again and again, swelling and trembling through the white nets of the latticed cloisters. And every rose in the dusky air was a flame.

The shadowy air was full of the perfume of eastern things. The attar of roses must have been sprinkled in the fountain; the odour seemed to palpitate in the nostrils, as the music and singing on the ears.[260] A thin spire of incense rose from a rich brass censer, and floated in filmy whorls across the oleander blossoms. And there were hints of strange drugs, the scent of opium and *asrar*, breathing deep reverie and the joy of long meditation.[261] The white walls, the

---

[258] Machen references Bible stories, commonly told to children, regarding the discovery of baby Moses in 'an ark of bulrushes' (Exodus 2. 1–6) and Daniel being imprisoned among lions as punishment for violating King Darius's decree (Daniel 6. 1–28).

[259] Lapis lazuli is a deep blue, semi-precious stone first mined in what is now Afghanistan and introduced to Europe in the late Middle Ages. The stone is mentioned in Huysmans's *A Rebours* and Wilde's *Picture of Dorian Gray*. In his discussion of Decadent artist Gustave Moreau's (1826–1898) *Galatée*, Huysmans describes the sky as lapis lazuli (Joris-Karl Huysmans, 'Le Salon officiel de 1880', *La Reformé*, 1880; repr. *L'Art moderne* (Paris: Charpentier, 1883), pp. 127–66).

[260] Originally from Persia, attar of roses is a fragrance derived from the essential oil of the flower.

[261] From the Arabic term for 'secret', asrar is an ancient scent made of saffron and ouhd, and associated with the semi-fantastic state experienced in a Middle Eastern or oriental garden. The two main alchemical texts by the renowned Persian physician, alchemist, and philosopher Ar-Rasi (854–925 CE) are *al-Asrar* and *Sirr al-Asrar* (*The Secrets* and *The Secret of Secrets*).

latticed cloisters of the court, seemed to advance and retreat, to flush and pale as the stars brightened and grew larger into silver worlds; all the faery-work of the chancelled stone hovered and glimmered beneath the sky, dark as the violet, dark as wine. The singing voice swelled to rapture and passion as the song chanted the triumph of the Lover and the Beloved, how their souls were melted together as the juice of the grape is mingled in the vintage, how they found the Gate and the Way. And all the blossoms in the dusky air, all the flowers in the garden, all the roses upon the tree, were aflame.

He had seen the life which he expressed by these symbols offered to him, and he had refused it; and he was alone in the grey street, with its lamps just twinkling through the dreary twilight, the blast of a ribald chorus sounding from the main road, a doggerel hymn whining from some parlour, to the accompaniment of the harmonium.[262] He wondered why he had turned away from that woman who knew all secrets, in whose eyes were all the mysteries. He opened the desk of his bureau, and was confronted by the heap and litter of papers, lying in confusion as he had left them. He knew that there was the motive of his refusal; he had been unwilling to abandon all hope of the work. The glory and the torment of his ambition glowed upon him as he looked at the manuscript; it seemed so pitiful that such a single desire should be thwarted. He was aware that if he chose to sit down now before the desk he could, in a manner, write easily enough — he could produce a tale which would be formally well constructed and certain of favourable reception. And it would not be the utterly commonplace, entirely hopeless favourite of the circulating library; it would stand in those ranks where the real thing is skilfully counterfeited, amongst the books which give the reader his orgy of emotions, and yet contrive to be superior, and 'art,' in his opinion. Lucian had often observed this species of triumph, and had noted the acclamation that never failed the clever sham, the literary lie. *Romola*, for example, had made the great host of the serious, the portentous, shout for joy, while the real book, *The Cloister and the Hearth*, was a comparative failure.[263]

He knew that he could write a *Romola*; but he thought the art of counterfeiting half-crowns less detestable than this shabby trick of imitating literature. He had refused definitely to enter the atelier of the gentleman who pleased his clients by ingeniously simulating the grain of walnut; and though he had seen the old oaken aumbry kicked out contemptuously into the farmyard, serving perhaps the necessities of hens or pigs, he would not apprentice himself to the masters

---

[262] A harmonium is a keyboard instrument akin to an organ. It is also known as a reed organ because sound is made by pumping air through metal reeds.

[263] In Eliot's novel *Romola* (1862–1863), the heroine struggles with issues of family, religion, morality, and politics during the Italian Renaissance. Set in the fifteenth century, Reade's novel *The Cloister and the Hearth* (1861) explores the conflicts between religious devotion and family commitment, in part through the portrayal of a young man's travels and strife.

of veneer.[264] He paced up and down the room, glancing now and again at his papers, and wondering if there were no hope for him. A great thing he could never do, but he had longed to do a true thing, to imagine sincere and genuine pages.

He was stirred again to this fury for the work by the event of the evening before, by all that had passed through his mind since the melancholy dawn. The lurid picture of that fiery street, the flaming shops and flaming glances, all its wonders and horrors, lit by the naphtha flares and by the burning souls, had possessed him; and the noises, the shriek and the whisper, the jangling rattle of the piano-organ, the long-continued scream of the butcher as he dabbled in the blood, the lewd litany of the singers, these seemed to be resolved into an infernal overture, loud with the expectation of lust and death. And how the spectacle was set in the cloud of dark night, a phantom play acted on that fiery stage, beneath those hideous brassy lamps, very slowly swinging in a violent blast. As all the medley of outrageous sights and sounds now fused themselves within his brain into one clear impression, it seemed that he had indeed witnessed and acted in a drama, that all the scene had been prepared and vested for him, and that the choric songs he had heard were but preludes to a greater act. For in that woman was the consummation and catastrophe of it all, and the whole stage waited for their meeting. He fancied that after this the voices and the lights died away, that the crowd sank swiftly into the darkness, and that the street was at once denuded of the great lamps and of all its awful scenic apparatus.

Again, he thought, the same mystery would be represented before him; suddenly on some dark and gloomy night, as he wandered lonely on a deserted road, the wind hurrying before him, suddenly a turn would bring him again upon the fiery stage, and the antique drama would be re-enacted. He would be drawn to the same place, to find that woman still standing there; again he would watch the rose radiant and palpitating upon her cheek, the argent gleam in her brown eyes, the bronze curls gilding the white splendour of her neck. And for the second time she would freely offer herself. He could hear the wail of the singers swelling to a shriek, and see the dusky dancers whirling round in a faster frenzy, and the naphtha flares tinged with red, as the woman and he went away into the dark, into the cloistered court where every flower was a flame, whence he would never come out.

His only escape was in the desk; he might find salvation if he could again hide his heart in the heap and litter of papers, and again be rapt by the cadence of a phrase. He threw open his window and looked out on the dim world and the glimmering amber lights. He resolved that he would rise early in the morning, and seek once more for his true life in the work.

But there was a strange thing. There was a little bottle on the mantelpiece, a

---

[264] An atelier is an artist's studio. An aumbry is a small cupboard inset into the wall of a church.

bottle of dark blue glass, and he trembled and shuddered before it, as if it were a fetish.

VII

It was very dark in the room. He seemed by slow degrees to awake from a long and heavy torpor, from an utter forgetfulness, and as he raised his eyes he could scarcely discern the pale whiteness of the paper on the desk before him. He remembered something of a gloomy winter afternoon, of driving rain, of gusty wind: he had fallen asleep over his work, no doubt, and the night had come down.

He lay back in his chair, wondering whether it were late; his eyes were half closed, and he did not make the effort and rouse himself. He could hear the stormy noise of the wind, and the sound reminded him of the half-forgotten days. He thought of his boyhood, and the old rectory, and the great elms that surrounded it. There was something pleasant in the consciousness that he was still half dreaming; he knew he could wake up whenever he pleased, but for the moment he amused himself by the pretence that he was a little boy again, tired with his rambles and the keen air of the hills. He remembered how he would sometimes wake up in the dark at midnight, and listen sleepily for a moment to the rush of the wind straining and crying amongst the elms, and hear it beat upon the walls, and then he would fall to dreams again, happy in his warm, snug bed.

The wind grew louder, and the windows rattled. He half opened his eyes and shut them again, determined to cherish that sensation of long ago. He felt tired and heavy with sleep; he imagined that he was exhausted by some effort; he had, perhaps, been writing furiously, without rest. He could not recollect at the instant what the work had been; it would be delightful to read the pages when he had made up his mind to bestir himself.

Surely that was the noise of boughs, swaying and grinding in the wind. He remembered one night at home when such a sound had roused him suddenly from a deep sweet sleep. There was a rushing and beating as of wings upon the air, and a heavy dreary noise, like thunder far away upon the mountain. He had got out of bed and looked from behind the blind to see what was abroad. He remembered the strange sight he had seen, and he pretended it would be just the same if he cared to look out now. There were clouds flying awfully from before the moon, and a pale light that made the familiar land look strange and terrible. The blast of wind came with a great shriek, and the trees tossed and bowed and quivered; the wood was scourged and horrible, and the night air was ghastly with a confused tumult, and voices as of a host. A huge black cloud rolled across the heaven from the west and covered up the moon, and there came a torrent of bitter hissing rain.

It was all a vivid picture to him as he sat in his chair, unwilling to wake. Even as he let his mind stray back to that night of the past years, the rain beat sharply on the window-panes, and though there were no trees in the grey suburban street, he heard distinctly the crash of boughs. He wandered vaguely from thought to thought, groping indistinctly amongst memories, like a man trying to cross from door to door in a darkened unfamiliar room. But, no doubt, if he were to look out, by some magic the whole scene would be displayed before him. He would not see the curve of monotonous two-storied houses, with here and there a white blind, a patch of light, and shadows appearing and vanishing, not the rain plashing in the muddy road, not the amber of the gas-lamp opposite, but the wild moonlight poured on the dearly loved country; far away the dim circle of the hills and woods, and beneath him the tossing trees about the lawn, and the wood heaving under the fury of the wind.

He smiled to himself, amidst his lazy meditations, to think how real it seemed, and yet it was all far away, the scenery of an old play long ended and forgotten. It was strange that after all these years of trouble and work and change he should be in any sense the same person as that little boy peeping out, half frightened, from the rectory window. It was as if on looking in the glass one should see a stranger, and yet know that the image was a true reflection.

The memory of the old home recalled his father and mother to him, and he wondered whether his mother would come if he were to cry out suddenly. One night, on just such a night as this, when a great storm blew from the mountain, a tree had fallen with a crash and a bough had struck the roof, and he awoke in a fright, calling for his mother. She had come and had comforted him, soothing him to sleep, and now he shut his eyes, seeing her face shining in the uncertain flickering candle light, as she bent over his bed. He could not think she had died; the memory was but a part of the evil dreams that had come afterwards.

He said to himself that he had fallen asleep and dreamed sorrow and agony, and he wished to forget all the things of trouble. He would return to happy days, to the beloved land, to the dear and friendly paths across the fields. There was the paper, white before him, and when he chose to stir, he would have the pleasure of reading his work. He could not quite recollect what he had been about, but he was somehow conscious that he had been successful and had brought some long labour to a worthy ending. Presently he would light the gas, and enjoy the satisfaction that only the work could give him, but for the time he preferred to linger in the darkness, and to think of himself as straying from stile to stile through the scented meadows, and listening to the bright brook that sang to the alders.

It was winter now, for he heard the rain and the wind, and the swaying of the trees, but in those old days how sweet the summer had been. The great hawthorn bush in blossom, like a white cloud upon the earth, had appeared to him in twilight, he had lingered in the enclosed valley to hear the nightingale, a voice swelling out from the rich gloom, from the trees that grew around the well. The scent of the meadowsweet was blown to him across the bridge of years, and with it came the dream and the hope and the longing, and the afterglow red in the sky, and the marvel of the earth. There was a quiet walk that he knew so well; one went up from a little green by-road, following an unnamed brooklet scarce a foot wide, but yet wandering like a river, gurgling over its pebbles, with its dwarf bushes shading the pouring water. One went through the meadow grass, and came to the larch wood that grew from hill to hill across the stream, and shone a brilliant tender green, and sent vague sweet spires to the flushing sky. Through the wood the path wound, turning and dipping, and beneath, the brown fallen needles of last year were soft and thick, and the resinous cones gave out their odour as the warm night advanced, and the shadows darkened. It was quite still; but he stayed, and the faint song of the brooklet sounded like the echo of a river beyond the mountains. How strange it was to look into the wood, to see the tall straight stems rising, pillar-like, and then the dusk, uncertain, and then the blackness. So he came out from the larch wood, from the green cloud and the vague shadow, into the dearest of all hollows, shut in on one side by the larches and before him by high violent walls of turf, like the slopes of a fort, with a clear line dark against the twilight sky, and a weird thorn bush that grew large, mysterious, on the summit, beneath the gleam of the evening star.

And he retraced his wanderings in those deep old lanes that began from the common road and went away towards the unknown, climbing steep hills, and piercing the woods of shadows, and dipping down into valleys that seemed virgin, unexplored, secret for the foot of man. He entered such a lane not knowing where it might bring him, hoping he had found the way to fairyland, to the woods beyond the world, to that vague territory that haunts all the dreams of a boy. He could not tell where he might be, for the high banks rose steep, and the great hedges made a green vault above. Marvellous ferns grew rich and thick in the dark red earth, fastening their roots about the roots of hazel and beech and maple, clustering like the carven capitals of a cathedral pillar. Down, like a dark shaft, the lane dipped to the well of the hills, and came amongst the limestone rocks. He climbed the bank at last, and looked out into a country that seemed for a moment the land he sought, a mysterious realm with unfamiliar hills and valleys and fair plains all golden, and white houses radiant in the sunset light.

And he thought of the steep hillsides where the bracken was like a wood, and of bare places where the west wind sang over the golden gorse, of still circles in mid-lake, of the poisonous yew-tree in the middle of the wood, shedding its crimson cups on the dank earth. How he lingered by certain black waterpools hedged in on every side by drooping wych-elms and black-stemmed alders, watching the faint waves widening to the banks as a leaf or a twig dropped from the trees.[265]

And the whole air and wonder of the ancient forest came back to him. He had found his way to the river valley, to the long lovely hollow between the hills, and went up and up beneath the leaves in the warm hush of midsummer, glancing back now and again through the green alleys, to the river winding in mystic esses beneath, passing hidden glens receiving the streams that rushed down the hillside, ice-cold from the rock, passing the immemorial tumulus, the graves where the legionaries waited for the trumpet, the grey farmhouses sending the blue wreaths of wood smoke into the still air.[266] He went higher and higher, till at last he entered the long passage of the Roman road, and from this, the ridge and summit of the wood, he saw the waves of green swell and dip and sink towards the marshy level and the gleaming yellow sea. He looked on the surging forest, and thought of the strange deserted city mouldering into a petty village on its verge, of its encircling walls melting into the turf, of vestiges of an older temple which the earth had buried utterly.

It was winter now, for he heard the wail of the wind, and a sudden gust drove the rain against the panes, but he thought of the bee's song in the clover, of the foxgloves in full blossom, of the wild roses, delicate, enchanting, swaying on a long stem above the hedge. He had been in strange places, he had known sorrow and desolation, and had grown grey and weary in the work of letters, but he lived again in the sweetness, in the clear bright air of early morning, when the sky was blue in June, and the mist rolled like a white sea in the valley. He laughed when he recollected that he had sometimes fancied himself unhappy in those days; in those days when he could be glad because the sun shone, because the wind blew fresh on the mountain. On those bright days he had been glad, looking at the fleeting and passing of the clouds upon the hills, and had gone up higher to the broad dome of the mountain, feeling that joy went up before him.

He remembered how, a boy, he had dreamed of love, of an adorable and ineffable mystery which transcended all longing and desire. The time had come when all the wonder of the earth seemed to prefigure this alone, when he found the symbol of the Beloved in hill and wood and stream, and every flower and every dark pool discoursed a pure ecstasy. It was the longing for longing, the love of love, that had come to him when he awoke one morning just before the dawn, and for the first time felt the sharp thrill of passion.

He tried in vain to express to himself the exquisite joys of innocent desire. Even now, after troubled years, in spite of some dark cloud that overshadowed the background of his thought, the sweetness of the boy's imagined pleasure

---

[265] The wych or Scots elm is the most common form of elm. The Old English word 'wych' means pliable or supple.
[266] A legionary (or legionnaire) is a Roman soldier.

came like a perfume into his reverie. It was no love of a woman but the desire of womanhood, the Eros of the Unknown, that made the heart tremble. He hardly dreamed that such a love could ever be satisfied, that the thirst of beauty could be slaked. He shrank from all contact of actuality, not venturing so much as to imagine the inner place and sanctuary of the mysteries. It was enough for him to adore in the outer court, to know that within, in the sweet gloom, were the vision and the rapture, the altar and the sacrifice.

He remembered, dimly, the passage of many heavy years since that time of hope and passion, but, perhaps, the vague shadow would pass away, and he could renew the boy's thoughts, the unformed fancies that were part of the bright day, of the wild roses in the hedgerow. All other things should be laid aside, he would let them trouble him no more after this winter night. He saw now that from the first he had allowed his imagination to bewilder him, to create a fantastic world in which he suffered, moulding innocent forms into terror and dismay. Vividly, he saw again the black circle of oaks, growing in a haggard ring upon the bastions of the Roman fort. The noise of the storm without grew louder, and he thought how the wind had come up the valley with the sound of a scream, how a great tree had ground its boughs together, shuddering before the violent blast. Clear and distinct, as if he were standing now in the lane, he saw the steep slopes surging from the valley, and the black crown of the oaks set against the flaming sky, against a blaze and glow of light as if great furnace doors were opened. He saw the fire, as it were, smitten about the bastions, about the heaped mounds that guarded the fort, and the crooked evil boughs seemed to writhe in the blast of flame that beat from heaven. Strangely with the sight of the burning fort mingled the impression of a dim white shape floating up the dusk of the lane towards him, and he saw across the valley of years a girl's face, a momentary apparition that shone and vanished away.

Then there was a memory of another day, of violent summer, of white farmhouse walls blazing in the sun, and a far call from the reapers in the cornfields. He had climbed the steep slope and penetrated the matted thicket and lay in the heat alone on the soft short grass that grew within the fort. There was a cloud of madness, and confusion of broken dreams that had no meaning or clue but only an indefinable horror and defilement. He had fallen asleep as he gazed at the knotted fantastic boughs of the stunted brake about him, and when he woke he was ashamed, and fled away fearing that 'they' would pursue him. He did not know who 'they' were, but it seemed as if a woman's face watched him from between the matted boughs, and that she summoned to her side awful companions who had never grown old through all the ages.

He looked up, it seemed, at a smiling face that bent over him, as he sat in the cool dark kitchen of the old farmhouse, and wondered why the sweetness of those red lips and the kindness of the eyes mingled with the nightmare in the fort, with the horrible Sabbath he had imagined as he lay sleeping on the hot soft turf. He had allowed these disturbed fancies, all this mad wreck of terror and shame that he had gathered to his mind, to trouble him for too long a time; presently he would light up the room, and leave all the old darkness of his life behind him, and from henceforth he would walk in the day.

He could still distinguish, though very vaguely, the pile of papers before him, and he remembered, now, that he had finished a long task that afternoon, before he fell asleep. He could not trouble himself to recollect the exact nature of the work, but he was sure that he had done well; in a few minutes, perhaps, he would strike a match, and read the title, and amuse himself with his own forgetfulness. But the sight of the papers lying there in order made him think of his beginnings, of those first unhappy efforts which were so impossible and so hopeless. He saw himself bending over the table in the old familiar room, desperately scribbling, and then laying down his pen dismayed at the sad results on the page. It was late at night, his father had been long in bed, and the house was still. The fire was almost out, with only a dim glow here and there amongst the cinders, and the room was growing chilly. He rose at last from his work and looked out on a dim earth and a dark and cloudy sky.

Night after night he had laboured on, persevering in his effort, even through the cold sickness of despair, when every line was doomed as it was made. Now, with the consciousness that he knew at least the conditions of literature, and that many years of thought and practice had given him some sense of language, he found these early struggles both pathetic and astonishing. He could not understand how he had persevered so stubbornly, how he had had the heart to begin a fresh page when so many folios of blotted, painful effort lay torn, derided, impossible in their utter failure. It seemed to him that it must have been a miracle or an infernal possession, a species of madness, that had driven him on, every day disappointed, and every day hopeful.

And yet there was a joyous side to the illusion. In these dry days that he lived in, when he had bought, by a long experience and by countless hours of misery, a knowledge of his limitations, of the vast gulf that yawned between the conception and the work, it was pleasant to think of a time when all things were possible, when the most splendid design seemed an affair of a few weeks. Now he had come to a frank acknowledgment; so far as he was concerned, he judged every book wholly impossible till the last line of it was written, and he had learnt patience, the art of sighing and putting the fine scheme away in the pigeon-hole of what could never be. But to think of those days! Then one could plot out a book that should be more curious than Rabelais, and jot down the outlines of a romance to surpass Cervantes, and design renaissance tragedies and volumes of *contes*, and comedies of the Restoration;[267] everything was to

---

[267] *contes* (French): tales.

be done, and the masterpiece was always the rainbow cup, a little way before him.[268]

He touched the manuscript on the desk, and the feeling of the pages seemed to restore all the papers that had been torn so long ago. It was the atmosphere of the silent room that returned, the light of the shaded candle falling on the abandoned leaves. This had been painfully excogitated while the snowstorm whirled about the lawn and filled the lanes, this was of the summer night, this of the harvest moon rising like a fire from the tithebarn on the hill.[269] How well he remembered those half-dozen pages of which he had once been so proud; he had thought out the sentences one evening, while he leaned on the foot-bridge and watched the brook swim across the road. Every word smelt of the meadowsweet that grew thick upon the banks; now, as he recalled the cadence and the phrase that had seemed so charming, he saw again the ferns beneath the vaulted roots of the beech, and the green light of the glowworm in the hedge.

And in the west the mountains swelled to a great dome, and on the dome was a mound, the memorial of some forgotten race, that grew dark and large against the red sky, when the sun set. He had lingered below it in the solitude, amongst the winds, at evening, far away from home; and oh, the labour and the vain efforts to make the form of it and the awe of it in prose, to write the hush of the vast hill, and the sadness of the world below sinking into the night, and the mystery, the suggestion of the rounded hillock, huge against the magic sky.

He had tried to sing in words the music that the brook sang, and the sound of the October wind rustling through the brown bracken on the hill. How many pages he had covered in the effort to show a white winter world, a sun without warmth in a grey-blue sky, all the fields, all the land white and shining, and one high summit where the dark pines towered, still in the still afternoon, in the pale violet air.

To win the secret of words, to make a phrase that would murmur of summer and the bee, to summon the wind into a sentence, to conjure the odour of the night into the surge and fall and harmony of a line; this was the tale of the long evenings, of the candle flame white upon the paper and the eager pen.

He remembered that in some fantastic book he had seen a bar or two of music, and, beneath, the inscription that here was the musical expression of Westminster Abbey.[270] His boyish effort seemed hardly less ambitious, and he

---

[268] Rainbow-cup coins, from the German *Regenbogenschüsselchen*, are actual Celtic gold coins, which myth claimed to be located at the end of rainbows.

[269] A tithebarn is a barn in which the local church stored farmers' payments in produce of an annual tax, equal to a tithe — one tenth of their produce or earnings.

[270] Used for all but two coronations beginning with William the Conqueror (c. 1028–1087) in 1066, Westminster Abbey was re-founded by Queen Elizabeth I (1533–1603) in 1560 as a Church of England 'Royal Peculiar', making it directly responsible to the sovereign. Machen here refers to music capturing the spiritual character of the institution. In

no longer believed that language could present the melody and the awe and the loveliness of the earth. He had long known that he, at all events, would have to be content with a far approach, with a few broken notes that might suggest, perhaps, the magistral everlasting song of the hill and the streams.

But in those far days the impossible was but a part of wonderland that lay before him, of the world beyond the wood and the mountain. All was to be conquered, all was to be achieved; he had but to make the journey and he would find the golden world and the golden word, and hear those songs that the sirens sang. He touched the manuscript; whatever it was, it was the result of painful labour and disappointment, not of the old flush of hope, but it came of weary days, of correction and re-correction. It might be good in its measure; but afterwards he would write no more for a time. He would go back again to the happy world of masterpieces, to the dreams of great and perfect books, written in an ecstasy.

Like a dark cloud from the sea came the memory of the attempt he had made, of the poor piteous history that had once embittered his life. He sighed and said alas, thinking of his folly, of the hours when he was shaken with futile, miserable rage. Some silly person in London had made his manuscript more saleable and had sold it without rendering an account of the profits, and for that he had been ready to curse humanity. Black, horrible, as the memory of a stormy day, the rage of his heart returned to his mind, and he covered his eyes, endeavouring to darken the picture of terror and hate that shone before him. He tried to drive it all out of his thought, it vexed him to remember these foolish trifles; the trick of a publisher, the small pomposities and malignancies of the country folk, the cruelty of a village boy, had inflamed him almost to the pitch of madness. His heart had burnt with fury, and when he looked up the sky was blotched, and scarlet as if it rained blood.

Indeed he had almost believed that blood had rained upon him, and cold blood from a sacrifice in heaven; his face was wet and chill and dripping, and he had passed his hand across his forehead and looked at it. A red cloud had seemed to swell over the hill, and grow great, and come near to him; he was but an ace removed from raging madness.

It had almost come to that; the drift and the breath of the scarlet cloud had well-nigh touched him. It was strange that he had been so deeply troubled by such little things, and strange how after all the years he could still recall the anguish and rage and hate that shook his soul as with a spiritual tempest.

The memory of all that evening was wild and troubled; he resolved that it should vex him no more, that now, for the last time, he would let himself be tormented by the past. In a few minutes he would rise to a new life, and forget all the storms that had gone over him.

'Shakespeare's English Kings', Pater refers to King Henry III (1207–1272) as having the 'deep religious expression of Westminster Abbey' (Walter Pater, 'Shakespeare's English Kings', *Appreciations* (London: Macmillan, 1890), pp. 192–313 (p. 196)).

Curiously, every detail was distinct and clear in his brain. The figure of the doctor driving home, and the sound of the few words he had spoken came to him in the darkness, through the noise of the storm and the pattering of the rain. Then he stood upon the ridge of the hill and saw the smoke drifting up from the ragged roofs of Caermaen, in the evening calm; he listened to the voices mounting thin and clear, in a weird tone, as if some outland folk were speaking in an unknown tongue of awful things.

He saw the gathering darkness, the mystery of twilight changing the huddled squalid village into an unearthly city, into some dreadful Atlantis, inhabited by a ruined race.[271] The mist falling fast, the gloom that seemed to issue from the black depths of the forest, to advance palpably towards the walls, were shaped before him; and beneath, the river wound, snake-like, about the town, swimming to the flood and glowing in its still pools like molten brass. And as the water mirrored the afterglow and sent ripples and gouts of blood against the shuddering reeds, there came suddenly the piercing trumpet-call, the loud reiterated summons that rose and fell, that called and recalled, echoing through all the valley, crying to the dead as the last note rang.[272] It summoned the legion from the river and the graves and the battlefield, the host floated up from the sea, the centuries swarmed about the eagles, the array was set for the last great battle, behind the leaguer of the mist.

He could imagine himself still wandering through the dim, unknown, terrible country, gazing affrighted at hills and woods that seemed to have put on an unearthly shape, stumbling amongst the briars that caught his feet. He lost his way in a wild country, and the red light that blazed up from the furnace on the mountains only showed him a mysterious land, in which he strayed aghast, with the sense of doom weighing upon him. The dry mutter of the trees, the sound of an unseen brook, made him afraid as if the earth spoke of his sin, and presently he was fleeing through a desolate shadowy wood, where a pale light flowed from the mouldering stumps, a dream of light that shed a ghostly radiance.

And then again the dark summit of the Roman fort, the black sheer height rising above the valley, and the moonfire streaming around the ring of oaks, glowing about the green bastions that guarded the thicket and the inner place.

The room in which he sat appeared the vision, the trouble of the wind and rain without was but illusion, the noise of the waves in the seashell. Passion and tears and adoration and the glories of the summer night returned, and the calm sweet face of the woman appeared, and he thrilled at the soft touch of her hand on his flesh.

---

[271] Machen's language in this paragraph, as well as many of his descriptions during Lucian's increasingly hallucinatory experiences, bring to mind James Thomson's poem *The City of Dreadful Night*.

[272] Machen is alluding to the Day of Judgement in the Bible.

She shone as if she had floated down into the lane from the moon that swam between films of cloud above the black circle of the oaks. She led him away from all terror and despair and hate, and gave herself to him with rapture, showing him love, kissing his tears away, pillowing his cheek upon her breast.

His lips dwelt upon her lips, his mouth upon the breath of her mouth, her arms were strained about him, and oh! she charmed him with her voice, with sweet kind words, as she offered her sacrifice. How her scented hair fell down, and floated over his eyes, and there was a marvellous fire called the moon, and her lips were aflame, and her eyes shone like a light on the hills.

All beautiful womanhood had come to him in the lane. Love had touched him in the dusk and had flown away, but he had seen the splendour and the glory, and his eyes had seen the enchanted light.

AVE ATQUE VALE[273]

The old words sounded in his ears like the ending of a chant, and he heard the music's close. Once only in his weary hapless life, once the world had passed away, and he had known her, the dear, dear Annie, the symbol of all mystic womanhood.

The heaviness of languor still oppressed him, holding him back amongst these old memories, so that he could not stir from his place. Oddly, there seemed something unaccustomed about the darkness of the room, as if the shadows he had summoned had changed the aspect of the walls. He was conscious that on this night he was not altogether himself; fatigue, and the weariness of sleep, and the waking vision had perplexed him. He remembered how once or twice when he was a little boy he had opened his eyes on the midnight darkness startled by an uneasy dream, and had stared with a frightened gaze into nothingness, not knowing where he was, all trembling, and breathing quick, till he touched the rail of his bed, and the familiar outlines of the looking-glass and the chiffonier began to glimmer out of the gloom. So now he touched the pile of manuscript and the desk at which he had worked so many hours, and felt reassured, though he smiled at himself, and he felt the old childish dread, the longing to cry out for some one to bring a candle, and show him that he really was in his own room. He glanced up for an instant, expecting to see perhaps the glitter of the brass gas jet that was fixed in the wall, just beside his bureau, but it was too dark, and he could not rouse himself and make the effort that would drive the cloud and the muttering thoughts away.

He leant back again, picturing the wet street without, the rain driving like fountain spray about the gas lamp, the shrilling of the wind on those waste places to the north. It was strange how in the brick and stucco desert where no

---

[273] Latin for 'Hail and Farewell', famously used by the Roman poet Catullus (c. 84–54 BCE) in an elegy on the ashes of his dead brother (Catullus 101). 'Ave atque Vale' is also the title of Swinburne's elegy on Baudelaire.

trees were, he all the time imagined the noise of tossing boughs, the grinding of the boughs together. There was a great storm and tumult in this wilderness of London, and for the sound of the rain and the wind he could not hear the hum and jangle of the trams, and the jar and shriek of the garden gates as they opened and shut. But he could imagine his street, the rain-swept desolate curve of it, as it turned northward, and beyond the empty suburban roads, the twinkling villa windows, the ruined field, the broken lane, and then yet another suburb rising, a solitary gas-lamp glimmering at a corner, and the plane tree lashing its boughs, and driving great showers against the glass.

It was wonderful to think of. For when these remote roads were ended one dipped down the hill into the open country, into the dim world beyond the glint of friendly fires. To-night, how waste they were, these wet roads, edged with the red-brick houses, with shrubs whipped by the wind against one another, against the paling and the wall. There the wind swayed the great elms scattered on the sidewalk, the remnants of the old stately fields, and beneath each tree was a pool of wet, and a torment of raindrops fell with every gust. And one passed through the red avenues, perhaps by a little settlement of flickering shops, and passed the last sentinel wavering lamp, and the road became a ragged lane, and the storm screamed from hedge to hedge across the open fields. And then, beyond, one touched again upon a still remoter avant-guard of London, an island amidst the darkness, surrounded by its pale of twinkling, starry lights.

He remembered his wanderings amongst these outposts of the town, and thought how desolate all their ways must be to-night. They were solitary in wet and wind, and only at long intervals some one pattered and hurried along them, bending his eyes down to escape the drift of rain. Within the villas, behind the close-drawn curtains, they drew about the fire, and wondered at the violence of the storm, listening for each great gust as it gathered far away, and rocked the trees, and at last rushed with a huge shock against their walls as if it were the coming of the sea. He thought of himself walking, as he had often walked, from lamp to lamp on such a night, treasuring his lonely thoughts, and weighing the hard task awaiting him in his room. Often in the evening, after a long day's labour, he had thrown down his pen in utter listlessness, feeling that he could struggle no more with ideas and words, and he had gone out into driving rain and darkness, seeking the word of the enigma as he tramped on and on beneath these outer battlements of London.

Or on some grey afternoon in March or November he had sickened of the dull monotony and the stagnant life that he saw from his window, and had taken his design with him to the lonely places, halting now and again by a gate, and pausing in the shelter of a hedge through which the austere wind shivered, while, perhaps, he dreamed of Sicily, or of sunlight on the Provençal olives. Often as he strayed solitary from street to field, and passed the Syrian fig tree imprisoned in Britain, nailed to an ungenial wall, the solution of the puzzle became evident, and he laughed and hurried home eager to make the page speak, to note the song he had heard on his way.

Sometimes he had spent many hours treading this edge and brim of London, now lost amidst the dun fields, watching the bushes shaken by the wind, and now looking down from a height whence he could see the dim waves of the town, and a barbaric water tower rising from a hill, and the snuff-coloured cloud of smoke that seemed blown up from the streets into the sky.

There were certain ways and places that he had cherished; he loved a great old common that stood on high ground, curtained about with ancient spacious houses of red brick, and their cedarn gardens.[274] And there was on the road that led to this common a space of ragged uneven ground with a pool and a twisted oak, and here he had often stayed in autumn and looked across the mist and the valley at the great theatre of the sunset, where a red cloud like a charging knight shone and conquered a purple dragon shape, and golden lances glittered in a field of faery green.

Or sometimes, when the unending prospect of trim, monotonous, modern streets had wearied him, he had found an immense refreshment in the discovery of a forgotten hamlet, left in a hollow, while all new London pressed and surged on every side, threatening the rest of the red roofs with its vulgar growth. These little peaceful houses, huddled together beneath the shelter of trees, with their bulging leaded windows and uneven roofs, somehow brought back to him the sense of the country, and soothed him with the thought of the old farm-houses, white or grey, the homes of quiet lives, harbours where, perhaps, no tormenting thoughts ever broke in.

For he had instinctively determined that there was neither rest nor health in all the arid waste of streets about him. It seemed as if in those dull rows of dwellings, in the prim new villas red and white and staring, there must be a leaven working which transformed all to base vulgarity.[275] Beneath the dull sad slates, behind the blistered doors, love turned to squalid intrigue, mirth to drunken clamour, and the mystery of life became a common thing; religion was sought for in the greasy piety and flatulent oratory of the Independent chapel, the stuccoed nightmare of the Doric columns. Nothing fine, nothing rare, nothing exquisite, it seemed, could exist in the weltering suburban sea, in the habitations which had risen from the stench and slime of the brickfields. It was as if the sickening fumes that steamed from the burning bricks had been sublimed into the shape of houses, and those who lived in these grey places could also claim kinship with the putrid mud.

---

[274] cedarn: cedar.

[275] With this paragraph, Machen offers an extended metaphor of inverted alchemy as a type of cultural or sociological transformation into something base. Alchemy is recognized as the transmutation of 'base' or 'common' metals into gold, but also as an attempt to reveal the 'mystery of life', to use Machen's wording here.

Hence he had delighted in the few remains of the past that he could find still surviving on the suburb's edge, in the grave old houses that stood apart from the road, in the mouldering taverns of the eighteenth century, in the huddled hamlets that had preserved only the glow and the sunlight of all the years that had passed over them. It appeared to him that vulgarity and greasiness and squalor had come with a flood, that not only the good but also the evil in man's heart had been made common and ugly, that a sordid scum was mingled with all the springs, of death as of life. It would be alike futile to search amongst these mean two-storied houses for a splendid sinner as for a splendid saint; the very vices of these people smelt of cabbage water and a pothouse vomit.[276]

And so he had often fled away from the serried maze that encircled him, seeking for the old and worn and significant as an antiquary looks for the fragments of the Roman temple amidst the modern shops. In some way the gusts of wind and the beating rain of the night reminded him of an old house that had often attracted him with a strange indefinable curiosity. He had found it on a grim grey day in March, when he had gone out under a leaden-moulded sky, cowering from a dry freezing wind that brought with it the gloom and the doom of far unhappy Siberian plains. More than ever that day the suburb had oppressed him; insignificant, detestable, repulsive to body and mind, it was the only hell that a vulgar age could conceive or make, an inferno created not by Dante but by the jerry-builder.[277] He had gone out to the north, and when he lifted up his eyes again he found that he had chanced to turn up by one of the little lanes that still strayed across the broken fields. He had never chosen this path before because the lane at its outlet was so wholly degraded and offensive, littered with rusty tins and broken crockery, and hedged in with a paling fashioned out of scraps of wire, rotting timber, and bending worn-out rails. But on this day, by happy chance, he had fled from the high road by the first opening that offered, and he no longer groped his way amongst obscene refuse, sickened by the bloated bodies of dead dogs, and fetid odours from unclean decay, but the malpassage had become a peaceful winding lane, with warm shelter beneath its banks from the dismal wind.[278] For a mile he had walked on quietly, and then a turn in the road showed him a little glen or hollow, watered by such a tiny rushing brooklet as his own woods knew, and beyond, alas, the glaring foreguard of a 'new neighbourhood'; raw red villas, semi-detached, and then a row of lamentable shops.

But as he was about to turn back, in the hope of finding some other outlet, his

---

[276] A pothouse is a low-end pub.

[277] A jerry-builder is a person who constructs buildings poorly and of cheap material, generally to maximize profit.

[278] Machen echoes Baudelaire's Decadent work *Les Fleurs du mal* (1857), suggesting that his neologism 'malpassage' refers to the sickly or evil passage that he has just described in notably Decadent terms.

attention was charmed by a small house that stood back a little from the road on his right hand. There had been a white gate, but the paint had long faded to grey and black, and the wood crumbled under the touch, and only moss marked out the lines of the drive. The iron railing round the lawn had fallen, and the poor flower-beds were choked with grass and a faded growth of weeds. But here and there a rosebush lingered amidst suckers that had sprung grossly from the root, and on each side of the hall door were box trees, untrimmed, ragged, but still green. The slate roof was all stained and livid, blotched with the drippings of a great elm that stood at one corner of the neglected lawn, and marks of damp and decay were thick on the uneven walls, which had been washed yellow many years before. There was a porch of trellis work before the door, and Lucian had seen it rock in the wind, swaying as if every gust must drive it down. There were two windows on the ground floor, one on each side of the door, and two above, with a blind space where a central window had been blocked up.

This poor and desolate house had fascinated him. Ancient and poor and fallen, disfigured by the slate roof and the yellow wash that had replaced the old mellow dipping tiles and the warm red walls, and disfigured again by spots and patches of decay; it seemed as if its happy days were for ever ended. To Lucian it appealed with a sense of doom and horror; the black streaks that crept upon the walls, and the green drift upon the roof, appeared not so much the work of foul weather and dripping boughs, as the outward signs of evil working and creeping in the lives of those within.

The stage seemed to him decked for doom, painted with the symbols of tragedy; and he wondered as he looked whether any one were so unhappy as to live there still. There were torn blinds in the windows, but he had asked himself who could be so brave as to sit in that room, darkened by the dreary box, and listen of winter nights to the rain upon the window, and the moaning of wind amongst the tossing boughs that beat against the roof.

He could not imagine that any chamber in such a house was habitable. Here the dead had lain, through the white blind the thin light had filtered on the rigid mouth, and still the floor must be wet with tears and still that great rocking elm echoed the groaning and the sobs of those who watched. No doubt, the damp was rising, and the odour of the earth filled the house, and made such as entered draw back, foreseeing the hour of death.

Often the thought of this strange old house had haunted him; he had imagined the empty rooms where a heavy paper peeled from the walls and hung in dark strips; and he could not believe that a light ever shone from those windows that stared black and glittering on the neglected lawn. But to-night the wet and the storm seemed curiously to bring the image of the place before him, and as the wind sounded he thought how unhappy those must be, if any there were, who sat in the musty chambers by a flickering light, and listened to the elm-tree moaning and beating and weeping on the walls.

And to-night was Saturday night; and there was about that phrase something that muttered of the condemned cell, of the agony of a doomed man. Ghastly to his eyes was the conception of any one sitting in that room to the right of the door behind the larger box tree, where the wall was cracked above the window and smeared with a black stain in an ugly shape.

He knew how foolish it had been in the first place to trouble his mind with such conceits of a dreary cottage on the outskirts of London. And it was more foolish now to meditate these things, fantasies, feigned forms, the issue of a sad mood and a bleak day of spring. For soon, in a few moments, he was to rise to a new life. He was but reckoning up the account of his past, and when the light came he was to think no more of sorrow and heaviness, of real or imagined terrors. He had stayed too long in London, and he would once more taste the breath of the hills, and see the river winding in the long lovely valley; ah! he would go home.

Something like a thrill, the thrill of fear, passed over him as he remembered that there was no home. It was in the winter, a year and a half after his arrival in town, that he had suffered the loss of his father. He lay for many days prostrate, overwhelmed with sorrow and with the thought that now indeed he was utterly alone in the world. Miss Deacon was to live with another cousin in Yorkshire; the old home was at last ended and done. He felt sorry that he had not written more frequently to his father: there were things in his cousin's letters that had made his heart sore. 'Your poor father was always looking for your letters,' she wrote, 'they used to cheer him so much. He nearly broke down when you sent him that money last Christmas; he got it into his head that you were starving yourself to send it him. He was hoping so much that you would have come down this Christmas, and kept asking me about the plum-puddings months ago.'

It was not only his father that had died, but with him the last strong link was broken, and the past life, the days of his boyhood, grew faint as a dream. With his father his mother died again, and the long years died, the time of his innocence, the memory of affection. He was sorry that his letters had gone home so rarely; it hurt him to imagine his father looking out when the post came in the morning, and forced to be sad because there was nothing. But he had never thought that his father valued the few lines that he wrote, and indeed it was often difficult to know what to say. It would have been useless to write of those agonising nights when the pen seemed an awkward and outlandish instrument, when every effort ended in shameful defeat, or of the happier hours when at last wonder appeared and the line glowed, crowned and exalted. To poor Mr. Taylor such tales would have seemed but trivial histories of some Oriental game, like an odd story from a land where men have time for the infinitely little, and can seriously make a science of arranging blossoms in a jar, and discuss perfumes instead of politics. It would have been useless to write to the rectory of his only interest, and so he wrote seldom.

And then he had been sorry because he could never write again and never see his home. He had wondered whether he would have gone down to the old place at Christmas, if his father had lived. It was curious how common things evoked the bitterest griefs, but his father's anxiety that the plum-pudding should be good, and ready for him, had brought the tears into his eyes. He could hear him saying in a nervous voice that attempted to be cheerful: 'I suppose you will be thinking of the Christmas puddings soon, Jane; you remember how fond Lucian used to be of plum-pudding. I hope we shall see him this December.' No doubt poor Miss Deacon paled with rage at the suggestion that she should make Christmas pudding in July; and returned a sharp answer; but it was pathetic. The wind wailed, and the rain dashed and beat again and again upon the window. He imagined that all his thoughts of home, of the old rectory amongst the elms, had conjured into his mind the sound of the storm upon the trees, for, to-night, very clearly he heard the creaking of the boughs, the noise of boughs moaning and beating and weeping on the walls, and even a pattering of wet, on wet earth, as if there were a shrub near the window that shook off the raindrops, before the gust.

That thrill, as it were a shudder of fear, passed over him again, and he knew not what had made him afraid. There was some dark shadow on his mind that saddened him; it seemed as if a vague memory of terrible days hung like a cloud over his thought, but it was all indefinite, perhaps the last grim and ragged edge of the melancholy wrack that had swelled over his life and the bygone years. He shivered and tried to rouse himself and drive away the sense of dread and shame that seemed so real and so awful, and yet he could not grasp it. But the torpor of sleep, the burden of the work that he had ended a few hours before, still weighed down his limb and bound his thoughts. He could scarcely believe that he had been busy at his desk a little while ago, and that just before the winter day closed in and the rain began to fall he had laid down the pen with a sigh of relief, and had slept in his chair. It was rather as if he had slumbered deeply through a long and weary night, as if an awful vision of flame and darkness and the worm that dieth not had come to him sleeping. But he would dwell no more on the darkness; he went back to the early days in London when he had said farewell to the hills and to the waterpools, and had set to work in this little room in the dingy street.

How he had toiled and laboured at the desk before him! He had put away the old wild hopes of the masterpiece conceived and executed in a fury of inspiration, wrought out in one white heat of creative joy; it was enough if by dint of long perseverance and singleness of desire he could at last, in pain and agony and despair, after failure and disappointment and effort constantly renewed, fashion something of which he need not be ashamed. He had put himself to school again, and had, with what patience he could command, ground his teeth into the rudiments, resolved that at last he would tear out the heart of the mystery. They were good nights to remember, these; he was glad to think of the little ugly room, with its silly wall-paper and its 'bird's-eye' furniture, lighted up, while he sat at the bureau and wrote on into the cold stillness of the London morning, when the flickering lamplight and the daystar shone together. It was an interminable labour, and he had always known it to be as hopeless as alchemy. The gold, the great and glowing masterpiece, would never shine amongst the dead ashes and smoking efforts of the crucible, but in the course of the life, in the interval between the failures, he might possibly discover curious things.

These were the good nights that he could look back on without any fear or shame, when he had been happy and content on a diet of bread and tea and tobacco, and could hear of some imbecility passing into its hundredth thousand, and laugh cheerfully — if only that last page had been imagined aright, if the phrases noted in the still hours rang out their music when he read them in the morning. He remembered the drolleries and fantasies that the worthy Miss Deacon used to write to him, and how he had grinned at her words of reproof, admonition, and advice. She had once instigated Dolly *fils* to pay him a visit, and that young prop of respectability had talked about the extraordinary running of Bolter at the Scurragh meeting in Ireland;[279] and then, glancing at Lucian's books, had inquired whether any of them had 'warm bits.' He had been kind though patronising, and seemed to have moved freely in the most brilliant society of Stoke Newington. He had not been able to give any information as to the present condition of Edgar Allan Poe's old school. It appeared eventually that his report at home had not been a very favourable one, for no invitation to high tea had followed, as Miss Deacon had hoped. The Dollys knew many nice people, who were well off, and Lucian's cousin, as she afterwards said, had done *her* best to introduce him to the *beau monde* of those northern suburbs.[280]

But after the visit of the young Dolly, with what joy he had returned to the treasures which he had concealed from profane eyes. He had looked out and seen his visitor on board the tram at the street corner, and he laughed out loud, and locked his door. There had been moments when he was lonely, and wished to hear again the sound of friendly speech; but after such an irruption of suburban futility, it was a keen delight to feel that he was secure on his tower, that he could absorb himself in his wonderful task as safe and silent as if he were in mid-desert.

But there was one period that he dared not revive; he could not bear to think of those weeks of desolation and terror in the winter after his coming to London. His mind was sluggish, and he could not quite remember how many years had passed since that dismal experience; it sounded all an old story, but yet it was

---

[279] *fils* (French): son.
[280] *beau monde* (French): fashionable society (literally, 'beautiful world').

still vivid, a flaming scroll of terror from which he turned his eyes away. One awful scene glowed into his memory, and he could not shut out the sight of an orgy, of dusky figures whirling in a ring, of lurid naphtha flares blazing in the darkness, of great glittering lamps, like infernal thuribles, very slowly swaying in a violent blast of air. And there was something else, something which he could not remember, but it filled him with terror, but it slunk in the dark places of his soul, as a wild beast crouches in the depths of a cave.

Again, and without reason, he began to image to himself that old mouldering house in the field. With what a loud incessant noise the wind must be clamouring about on this fearful night, how the great elm swayed and cried in the storm, and the rain dashed and pattered on the windows, and dripped on the sodden earth from the shaking shrubs beside the door. He moved uneasily on his chair, and struggled to put the picture out of his thoughts; but in spite of himself he saw the stained uneven walls, that ugly blot of mildew above the window, and perhaps a feeble gleam of light filtered through the blind, and some one, unhappy above all and forever lost, sat within the dismal room. Or rather, every window was black, without a glimmer of hope, and he who was shut in thick darkness heard the wind and the rain, and the noise of the elm-tree moaning and beating and weeping on the walls.

For all his effort the impression would not leave him, and as he sat before his desk looking into the vague darkness he could almost see that chamber which he had so often imagined; the low whitewashed ceiling held up by a heavy beam, the smears of smoke and long usage, the cracks and fissures of the plaster. Old furniture, shabby, deplorable, battered, stood about the room; there was a horsehair sofa worn and tottering, and a dismal paper, patterned in livid red, blackened and mouldered near the floor, and peeled off and hung in strips from the dank walls. And there was that odour of decay, of the rank soil steaming, of rotting wood, a vapour that choked the breath and made the heart full of fear and heaviness.

Lucian again shivered with a thrill of dread; he was afraid that he had overworked himself and that he was suffering from the first symptoms of grave illness. His mind dwelt on confused and terrible recollections, and with a mad ingenuity gave form and substance to phantoms; and even now he drew a long breath, almost imagining that the air in his room was heavy and noisome, that it entered his nostrils with some taint of the crypt. And his body was still languid, and though he made a half motion to rise he could not find enough energy for the effort, and he sank again into the chair. At all events, he would think no more of that sad house in the field; he would return to those long struggles with letters, to the happy nights when he had gained victories.

He remembered something of his escape from the desolation and the worse than desolation that had obsessed him during that first winter in London. He had gone free one bleak morning in February, and after those dreary terrible weeks the desk and the heap and litter of papers had once more engulfed and absorbed him. And in the succeeding summer, of a night when he lay awake and listened to the birds, shining images came wantonly to him. For an hour, while the dawn brightened, he had felt the presence of an age, the resurrection of the life that the green fields had hidden, and his heart stirred for joy when he knew that he held and possessed all the loveliness that had so long mouldered. He could scarcely fall asleep for eager and leaping thoughts, and as soon as his breakfast was over he went out and bought paper and pens of a certain celestial stationer in Notting Hill.[281] The street was not changed as he passed to and fro on his errand. The rattling wagons jostled by at intervals, a rare hansom came spinning down from London, there sounded the same hum and jangle of the gliding trams.[282] The languid life of the pavement was unaltered; a few people, unclassed, without salience or possible description, lounged and walked from east to west, and from west to east, or slowly dropped into the byways to wander in the black waste to the north, or perhaps to go astray in the systems that stretched towards the river. He glanced down these by-roads as he passed, and was astonished, as always, at their mysterious and desert aspect. Some were utterly empty; lines of neat, appalling residences, trim and garnished as if for occupation, edging the white glaring road; and not a soul was abroad, and not a sound broke their stillness. It was a picture of the desolation of midnight lighted up, but empty and waste as the most profound and solemn hours before the day. Other of these by-roads, of older settlement, were furnished with more important houses, standing far back from the pavement, each in a little wood of greenery, and thus one might look down as through a forest vista, and see a way smooth and guarded with low walls and yet untrodden, and all a leafy silence. Here and there in some of these echoing roads a figure seemed lazily advancing in the distance, hesitating and delaying, as if lost in the labyrinth. It was difficult to say which were the more dismal, these deserted streets that wandered away to right and left, or the great main thoroughfare with its narcotic and shadowy life. For the latter appeared vast, interminable, grey, and those who travelled by it were scarcely real, the bodies of the living, but rather the uncertain and misty shapes that come and go across the desert in an Eastern tale, when men look up from the sand and see a caravan pass them, all in silence, without a cry or a greeting. So they passed and repassed each other on those pavements, appearing and vanishing, each intent on his own secret, and wrapped in obscurity. One might have sworn that not a man saw his neighbour who met him or jostled him, that here every one was a phantom for the other, though the lines of their paths crossed and recrossed, and their eyes stared like the eyes

---

[281] In this context, 'celestial' is used as a synonym for 'excellent'.
[282] A hansom is a two-wheeled horse-drawn cab.

of live men. When two went by together, they mumbled and cast distrustful glances behind them as though afraid all the world was an enemy, and the pattering of feet was like the noise of a shower of rain. Curious appearances and simulations of life gathered at points in the road, for at intervals the villas ended and shops began in a dismal row, and looked so hopeless that one wondered who could buy. There were women fluttering uneasily about the greengrocers, and shabby things in rusty black touched and retouched the red lumps that an unshaven butcher offered, and already in the corner public there was a confused noise, with a tossing of voices that rose and fell like a Jewish chant, with the senseless stir of marionettes jerked into an imitation of gaiety. Then, in crossing a side street that seemed like grey mid-winter in stone, he trespassed from one world to another, for an old decayed house amidst its garden held the opposite corner. The laurels had grown into black skeletons, patched with green drift, the ilex gloomed over the porch, the deodar had blighted the flower-beds.[283] Dark ivies swarmed over an elm-tree, and a brown clustering fungus sprang in gross masses on the lawn, showing where the roots of dead trees mouldered. The blue verandah, the blue balcony over the door, had faded to grey, and the stucco was blotched with ugly marks of weather, and a dank smell of decay, that vapour of black rotten earth in old town gardens, hung heavy about the gates. And then a row of musty villas had pushed out in shops to the pavement, and the things in faded black buzzed and stirred about the limp cabbages, and the red lumps of meat.

It was the same terrible street, whose pavements he had trodden so often, where sunshine seemed but a gaudy light, where the fume of burning bricks always drifted. On black winter nights he had seen the sparse lights glimmering through the rain and drawing close together, as the dreary road vanished in long perspective. Perhaps this was its most appropriate moment, when nothing of its smug villas and skeleton shops remained but the bright patches of their windows, when the old house amongst its mouldering shrubs was but a dark cloud, and the streets to the north and south seemed like starry wastes, beyond them the blackness of infinity. Always in the daylight it had been to him abhorred and abominable, and its grey houses and purlieus had been fungus-like sproutings, an efflorescence of horrible decay.

But on that bright morning neither the dreadful street nor those who moved about it appalled him. He returned joyously to his den, and reverently laid out the paper on his desk. The world about him was but a grey shadow hovering on a shining wall; its noises were faint as the rustling of trees in a distant wood. The lovely and exquisite forms of those who served the Amber Venus were his distinct, clear, and manifest visions, and for one amongst them who came to

---

[283] Deodar (Hindu: wood of the gods) is a type of cedar indigenous to the Himalayas, cedar also having spiritual connotations in Celtic tradition.

him in a fire of bronze hair his heart stirred with the adoration of love. She it was who stood forth from all the rest and fell down prostrate before the radiant form in amber, drawing out her pins in curious gold, her glowing brooches of enamel, and pouring from a silver box all her treasures of jewels and precious stones, chrysoberyl and sardonyx, opal and diamond, topaz and pearl. And then she stripped from her body her precious robes and stood before the goddess in the glowing mist of her hair, praying that to her who had given all and came naked to the shrine, love might be given, and the grace of Venus. And when at last, after strange adventures, her prayer was granted, then when the sweet light came from the sea, and her lover turned at dawn to that bronze glory, he saw beside him a little statuette of amber. And in the shrine, far in Britain where the black rains stained the marble, they found the splendid and sumptuous statue of the Golden Venus, the last fine robe of silk that the lady had dedicated falling from her fingers, and the jewels lying at her feet. And her face was like the lady's face when the sun had brightened it on that day of her devotion.

The bronze mist glimmered before Lucian's eyes; he felt as though the soft floating hair touched his forehead and his lips and his hands. The fume of burning bricks, the reek of cabbage water, never reached his nostrils that were filled with the perfume of rare unguents, with the breath of the violet sea in Italy. His pleasure was an inebriation, an ecstasy of joy that destroyed all the vile Hottentot kraals and mud avenues as with one white lightning flash, and through the hours of that day he sat enthralled, not contriving a story with patient art, but rapt into another time, and entranced by the urgent gleam in the lady's eyes.[284]

The little tale of *The Amber Statuette* had at last issued from a humble office in the spring after his father's death. The author was utterly unknown; the author's Murray was a wholesale stationer and printer in process of development, so that Lucian was astonished when the book became a moderate success.[285] The reviewers had been sadly irritated, and even now he recollected with cheerfulness an article in an influential daily paper, an article pleasantly headed: 'Where are the disinfectants?'[286]

And then— but all the months afterwards seemed doubtful, there were only broken revelations of the laborious hours renewed, and the white nights when he had seen the moonlight fade and the gaslight grow wan at the approach of dawn.

---

[284] Hottentot (Dutch or Afrikaans): the Khoi people of southwestern Africa.

[285] The phrase 'the author's Murray' is probably a reference to John Murray, an English publishing house founded in 1768 and, during Machen's period, publisher to Queen Victoria (1819–1901). Authors published by Murray include Jane Austen (1775–1817), Charles Darwin (1809–1882), Sir Arthur Conan Doyle (1859–1930), and Herman Melville (1819–1891).

[286] Machen similarly appears to have found pleasure in the particularly virulent negative reviews of his own works.

He listened. Surely that was the sound of rain falling on sodden ground, the heavy sound of great swollen drops driven down from wet leaves by the gust of wind, and then again the strain of boughs sang above the tumult of the air; there was a doleful noise as if the storm shook the masts of a ship. He had only to get up and look out of the window and he would see the treeless empty street, and the rain starring the puddles under the gas-lamp, but he would wait a little while.

He tried to think why, in spite of all his resolutions, a dark horror seemed to brood more and more over all his mind. How often he had sat and worked on just such nights as this, contented if the words were in accord though the wind might wail, though the air were black with rain. Even about the little book that he had made there seemed some taint, some shuddering memory, that came to him across the gulf of forgetfulness. Somehow the remembrance of the offering to Venus, of the phrases that he had so lovingly invented, brought back again the dusky figures that danced in the orgy, beneath the brassy glittering lamps; and again the naphtha flares showed the way to the sad house in the fields, and the red glare lit up the mildewed walls and the black hopeless windows. He gasped for breath, he seemed to inhale a heavy air that reeked of decay and rottenness, and the odour of the clay was in his nostrils.

That unknown cloud that had darkened his thoughts grew blacker and engulfed him, despair was heavy upon him, his heart fainted with a horrible dread. In a moment, it seemed, a veil would be drawn away and certain awful things would appear.

He strove to rise from his chair, to cry out, but he could not. Deep, deep the darkness closed upon him, and the storm sounded far away. The Roman fort surged up, terrific, and he saw the writhing boughs in a ring, and behind them a glow and heat of fire. There were hideous shapes that swarmed in the thicket of the oaks; they called and beckoned to him, and rose into the air, into the flame that was smitten from heaven about the walls. And amongst them was the form of the beloved, but jets of flame issued from her breasts, and beside her was a horrible old woman, naked; and they, too, summoned him to mount the hill.

He heard Dr. Burrows whispering of the strange things that had been found in old Mrs. Gibbon's cottage, obscene figures, and unknown contrivances. She was a witch, he said, and the mistress of the witches.

He fought against the nightmare, against the illusion that bewildered him. All his life, he thought, had been an evil dream, and for the common world he had fashioned an unreal red garment, that burned in his eyes. Truth and the dream were so mingled that now he could not divide one from the other. He had let Annie drink his soul beneath the hill, on the night when the moonfire shone, but he had not surely seen her exalted in the flame, the Queen of the Sabbath. Dimly he remembered Dr. Burrows coming to see him in London, but had he not imagined all the rest?

Again he found himself in the dusky lane, and Annie floated down to him from the moon above the hill. His head sank upon her breast again, but, alas, it was aflame. And he looked down, and he saw that his own flesh was aflame, and he knew that the fire could never be quenched.

There was a heavy weight upon his head, his feet were nailed to the floor, and his arms bound tight beside him. He seemed to himself to rage and struggle with the strength of a madman; but his hand only stirred and quivered a little as it lay upon the desk.

Again he was astray in the mist; wandering through the waste avenues of a city that had been ruined from ages. It had been splendid as Rome, terrible as Babylon, and for ever the darkness had covered it, and it lay desolate for ever in the accursed plain. And far and far the grey passages stretched into the night, into the icy fields, into the place of eternal gloom.

Ring within ring the awful temple closed around him; unending circles of vast stones, circle within circle, and every circle less throughout all ages. In the centre was the sanctuary of the infernal rite, and he was borne thither as in the eddies of a whirlpool, to consummate his ruin, to celebrate the wedding of the Sabbath. He flung up his arms and beat the air, resisting with all his strength, with muscles that could throw down mountains; and this time his little finger stirred for an instant, and his foot twitched upon the floor.

Then suddenly a flaring street shone before him. There was darkness round about him, but it flamed with hissing jets of light and naphtha fires, and great glittering lamps swayed very slowly in a violent blast of air. A horrible music, and the exultation of discordant voices, swelled in his ears, and he saw an uncertain tossing crowd of dusky figures that circled and leapt before him. There was a noise like the chant of the lost, and then there appeared in the midst of the orgy, beneath a red flame, the figure of a woman. Her bronze hair and flushed cheeks were illuminate, and an argent light shone from her eyes, and with a smile that froze his heart her lips opened to speak to him. The tossing crowd faded away, falling into a gulf of darkness, and then she drew out from her hair pins of curious gold, and glowing brooches in enamel, and poured out jewels before him from a silver box, and then she stripped from her body her precious robes, and stood in the glowing mist of her hair, and held out her arms to him. But he raised his eyes and saw the mould and decay gaining on the walls of a dismal room, and a gloomy paper was dropping to the rotting floor. A vapour of the grave entered his nostrils, and he cried out with a loud scream; but there was only an indistinct guttural murmur in his throat.

And presently the woman fled away from him, and he pursued her. She fled away before him through midnight country, and he followed after her, chasing her from thicket to thicket, from valley to valley. And at last he captured her and won her with horrible caresses, and they went up to celebrate and make the marriage of the Sabbath. They were within the matted thicket, and they writhed in the flames, insatiable, for ever. They were tortured, and tortured one another, in the sight of thousands who gathered thick about them; and their desire rose up like a black smoke.

Without, the storm swelled to the roaring of an awful sea, the wind grew to a shrill long scream, the elm-tree was riven and split with the crash of a thunderclap. To Lucian the tumult and the shock came as a gentle murmur, as if a brake stirred before a sudden breeze in summer. And then a vast silence overwhelmed him.

A few minutes later there was a shuffling of feet in the passage, and the door was softly opened. A woman came in, holding a light, and she peered curiously at the figure sitting quite still in the chair before the desk. The woman was half dressed, and she had let her splendid bronze hair flow down, her cheeks were flushed, and as she advanced into the shabby room, the lamp she carried cast quaking shadows on the mouldering paper, patched with marks of rising damp, and hanging in strips from the wet, dripping wall. The blind had not been drawn, but no light nor glimmer of light filtered through the window, for a great straggling box tree that beat the rain upon the panes shut out even the night. The woman came softly, and as she bent down over Lucian an argent gleam shone from her brown eyes, and the little curls upon her neck were like golden work upon marble. She put her hand to his heart, and looked up, and beckoned to some one who was waiting by the door.

'Come in, Joe,' she said. 'It's just as I thought it would be: "Death by misadventure";' and she held up a little empty bottle of dark blue glass that was standing on the desk. 'He would take it, and I always knew he would take a drop too much one of these days.'

'What's all those papers that he's got there?'

'Didn't I tell you? It was crool to see him. He'd got it into 'is 'ead he could write a book; he's been at it for the last six months. Look 'ere.'

She spread the neat pile of manuscript broadcast over the desk, and took a sheet at haphazard. It was all covered with illegible hopeless scribblings; only here and there it was possible to recognise a word.

'Why, nobody could read it, if they wanted to.'

'It's all like that. He thought it was beautiful. I used to 'ear him jabbering to himself about it, dreadful nonsense it was he used to talk. I did my best to tongue him out of it, but it wasn't any good.'

'He must have been a bit dotty. He's left you everything?'

'Yes.'

'You'll have to see about the funeral.'

'There'll be the inquest and all that first.'

'You've got evidence to show he took the stuff.'

'Yes, to be sure I have. The doctor told him he would be certain to do for himself, and he was found two or three times quite silly in the streets. They had to drag him away from a house in Halden Road. He was carrying on dreadful, shaking at the gaite, and calling out it was 'is 'ome and they wouldn't let him in. I heard Dr. Manning myself tell 'im in this very room that he'd kill 'imself one of these days. Joe! Aren't you ashamed of yourself. I declare you're quite rude, and it's almost Sunday too. Bring the light over here, can't you?'

The man took up the blazing paraffin lamp, and set it on the desk, beside the scattered heap of that terrible manuscript. The flaring light shone through the dead eyes into the dying brain, and there was a glow within, as if great furnace doors were opened.

The Hill of Dreams (London: Grant Richards, 1907). Machen worked on this novella, considered by many to be his greatest work, from 1895 to 1897.

5

The Bowmen (1914)

It was during the Retreat of the Eighty Thousand, and the authority of the censorship is sufficient excuse for not being more explicit.[1] But it was on the most awful day of that awful time, on the day when ruin and disaster came so near that their shadow fell over London far away; and, without any certain news, the hearts of men failed within them and grew faint; as if the agony of their brothers in the battlefield had entered into their souls.

On this dreadful day, then, when three hundred thousand men in arms with all their artillery swelled like a flood against the little English army, there was one point above all other points in our battle line that was for a time in awful danger, not merely of defeat, but of utter annihilation. With the permission of the censorship and the military experts, this corner may, perhaps, be described as salient, and if this angle were crushed and broken, then the English force as a whole would be shattered, the Allied left would be turned, and Sedan would inevitably follow.[2]

All the morning the German guns had thundered and shrieked against this corner and against the thousand or so of men who held it. The men joked at the shells and found funny names for them, and had bets about them and greeted them with scraps of music-hall songs. But the shells came on and burst and tore good Englishmen limb from limb, and tore brother from brother, and as the heat of the day increased, so did the fury of that terrific cannonade. There was no help, it seemed. The English artillery was good, but there was not nearly enough of it; it was being steadily battered into scrap iron.

There comes a moment in a storm at sea when people say to one another, "It is at its worst; it can blow no harder," and then there is a blast ten times more fierce than any before it. So it was in these British trenches.

---

[1]   The 'Retreat' refers to the withdrawal of 80,000 Allied troops from Mons, Belgium, in August and September 1914. That year, the British government passed legislation giving the War Office powers to censor press coverage of the war. Machen implies that the narrator of this story is a journalist for the *Evening News*, which did in fact first publish 'The Bowmen' in 1914. As Machen himself was a writer for the paper, he was intentionally encouraging readers to read the work, at least initially, as factual.

[2]   Sedan is an area in the Ardennes in northern France, the location of a definitive Prussian victory against the French in the Franco–Prussian war (1870–1871).

There were no stouter hearts in the whole world than the hearts of those men; but even they were appalled as this seven times heated hell of the German cannonade fell upon them and overwhelmed them and rent them and destroyed them. And at this very moment they saw from their trenches that a tremendous host was moving against their lines. Five hundred of the thousand remained; and as far as they could see the German infantry was pressing on against them, column upon column, a grey world of men, ten thousand of them as it appeared afterwards.

There was no hope at all. They shook hands, some of them. One man improvised a new version of the battle-song: "Goodbye, goodbye to Tipperary," ending with "And we shan't get there!"[3] And they all went on firing steadily. The officers pointed out that such an opportunity for fancy shooting might never occur again, the Germans dropped line after line, the Tipperary humorist asked, "What price Sidney-street?" and the few machine guns did their best.[4] But everybody knew it was of no use. The dead grey bodies lay in companies and battalions; but others came on and on and on, and they swarmed and stirred and advanced from beyond and beyond.

"World without end. Amen," said one of the British soldiers, with some irrelevance as he took aim and fired.[5] And then he remembered a queer vegetarian restaurant in London where he had once or twice eaten queer dishes of cutlets made of lentils and nuts that pretended to be 'steaks.[6] On all the plates in this restaurant there was printed a figure of St. George in blue, with the motto, *Adsit Anglis Sanctus Georgius* — may Saint George be a present help to the English. This soldier happened to know Latin and other useless things, and now as he fired at his man in the grey advancing mass — 300 yards away — he uttered the pious vegetarian motto. He went on firing to the end, and at last Bill on his right had to clout him cheerfully over the head to make him stop,

---

[3] The chorus of the popular wartime song 'It's a Long Way to Tipperary' (1912) typically ends with the line 'It's a long, long way to Tipperary, but my heart's right there'. The song does not normally include the words 'Goodbye, goodbye to Tipperary' in the title or elsewhere.

[4] An allusion to the Siege of Sidney Street (also known as the Battle of Stepney), a 1911 gunfight between two burglars and a combination of London's Metropolitan Police and City Police that even entailed the presence of Winston Churchill who, at the time, was home secretary. The siege ended with one burglar shot dead and the other dying of smoke inhalation when the building in which the two were hidden burst into flame. Churchill would not allow the fire to be suppressed, resulting in a wall collapsing and killing another person.

[5] The cited phrase is the last words of the familiar Christian doxology (a short hymn of praise) often known as the 'Gloria Patri', the final sentence of which is 'As it was in the beginning, is now and ever shall be, world without end. Amen.'

[6] Possibly a reference to St George's Cafe in St Martin's Lane, a contemporary vegetarian restaurant known amongst authors and journalists. As Machen's mockery implies, the author himself was never a vegetarian. St George is the patron saint of England.

pointing out as he did so that the King's ammunition cost money, and was not lightly to be wasted in drilling funny patterns into dead Germans.

For, as the Latin scholar uttered his invocation he felt something between a shudder and an electric shock pass through his body. The roar of the battle died down in his ears to a gentle murmur; instead of it, he says, he heard a great voice and a shout louder than a thunder-peal, crying, "Array, array, array!"[7]

His heart grew hot as a burning coal, it grew cold as ice within him, as it seemed to him that a tumult of voices answered to this summons. He heard, or seemed to hear thousands shouting: "St. George! St. George!"

"Ha! messire; ha! sweet saint, grant us good deliverance!"[8]

"St. George for merry England!"[9]

"Harow! Harow!"[10] Monseigneur St. George, succour us."[11]

"Ha! St. George! Ha! St. George; a long bow and a strong bow."

"Knight of Heaven, aid us!"[12]

And as the soldier heard these voices he saw before him, beyond the trench, a long line of shapes, with a shining about them. They were like men who drew the bow, and with another shout, their cloud of arrows flew singing and tingling through the air towards the German host.

*   *   *   *   *

The other men in the trench were firing all the while. They had no hope; but they aimed just as if they had been shooting at Bisley.[13]

---

[7] A call to marshal the British ranks into a proper line of battle.

[8] 'Messire' is French for 'master' or 'my lord'.

[9] In the nineteenth and early twentieth centuries, 'merry [or merrie] England' was a not uncommon term that characterized a supposedly healthier, happier, and more authentic society, largely rustic, that existed prior to the Industrial Revolution. William Hazlitt (1778–1830) helped to popularize the term in his essay 'Merry England' (1825), the headnote for which is 'St. George for merry England!' It opens with words that would have appealed to Machen: 'This old-fashioned epithet might be supposed to have been bestowed ironically, or on the old principle — *Ut lucus a non lucendo* [light though it does not shine]. Yet there is something in the sound that hits the fancy, and a sort of truth beyond appearances' (William Hazlitt, 'Essay XV: Merry England', in *The Complete Works of William Hazlitt*, ed. by P. P. Howe, vol. 17 (New York: AMS Press, 1967), pp. 152–62 (p. 152)).

[10] To 'harow' something means to harvest or despoil it. The 1915 book version uses the modern spelling 'harrow'; however, the original Middle English form of the word intensifies the supernatural, transhistorical nature of the story's events by suggesting that temporal and ontological boundaries are collapsing and the English soldiers of 1914 are themselves being possessed by their mediaeval forebears. There might also be an echo here of the mediaeval tale of Christ's 'harrowing' of Hell, his descent into the underworld to free the souls of righteous people held captive.

[11] 'Monseigneur' is a French title given to nobles and other high-ranking people.

[12] St George is called Heaven's knight here because of his reputation for martial combat on behalf of God's truth and power (e.g. in Book 1 of Edmund Spenser's (c. 1552–1599) epic poem *The Faerie Queene* (1596)).

[13] Bisley, a village in Surrey in the south of England, is the home of the United Kingdom's National Rifle Association and National Shooting Centre. It hosted shooting events at the 1908 Olympic Games.

Suddenly one of them lifted up his voice in plain English.

"Gawd help us!" he bellowed to the man next to him, "but we're blooming marvels! Look at those grey ... gentlemen, look at them! D'ye see them? They're not going down in dozens, nor in 'undreds; it's thousands, it is. Look! look! there's a regiment gone while I'm talking to ye."

"Shut it!" the other soldier bellowed, taking aim, "what are ye gassing about?"

But he gulped with astonishment even as he spoke: for, indeed, the grey men were falling by the thousand. The English could hear the guttural scream of the German officers, the crackle of their revolvers as they shot the reluctant: and still line after line crashed to the earth.[14]

*   *   *   *   *

All the while the Latin-bred soldier heard the cry,

"Harow! harow! monseigneur, dear saint, quick to our aid! St. George help us!"

The singing arrows darkened the air; the heathen horde melted from before them.

*   *   *   *   *

"More machine guns!" Bill yelled to Tom.

"Don't hear them," Tom yelled back; "but, thank God, anyway; they've got it in the neck."

In fact, there were ten thousand dead German soldiers left before that salient of the English army, and consequently there was no Sedan. In Germany, a country ruled by scientific principles, the Great General Staff decided that the contemptible English must have employed turpinite shells, as no wounds were discernible on the bodies of the dead German soldiers.[15] But the man who knew

---

[14] The German officers are executing their own soldiers who are refusing to fight. During the First World War, such men were accused of cowardice.

[15] The phrase 'contemptible English' alludes to an order from Kaiser Wilhelm II in August 1914, which supposedly referred to British forces as a 'contemptible little Army'. The British Expeditionary Forces adopted the term, calling itself the Old Contemptibles. As no original copy of the order has been found, its authenticity has been called into question. Turpinite (or Turpenite) is a fictitious poisonous gas supposedly invented by Eugène Turpin and used by the French army against the Germans in the first months of the First World War. The legitimacy of using poison gas during war had been debated and worried about since the mid-nineteenth century, and poison gas projectiles had been prohibited by the two Hague Conventions (1899, 1907). Nevertheless, the Germans launched the First World War's first full-scale use of poison gas — 150 tons of chlorine — when they attacked French, British, and Canadian troops at Ypres on 22 April 1915. Machen may initially have been one of those who believed the myth of Turpinite's existence; as Richard Bleiler observes, one of Machen's only notable revisions to this story, when it was republished in the 1915 *The Angels of Mons: The Bowmen and Other Legends of the War*, was to replace the word 'Turpinite' with 'an

what nuts tasted like when they called themselves steak, knew also that St. George had brought his Agincourt Bowmen to help the English.[16]

'The Bowmen', *Evening News* (29 September 1914), p. 3.

---

unknown gas of a poisonous nature' (Richard J. Bleiler, *The Strange Case of "The Angels of Mons"* (Jefferson, NC: McFarland, 2015), p. 19).

[16] On 25 October 1415, King Henry V (1386–1422) defeated a much larger French army at the village of Agincourt in northern France. The English victory was due in large part to the prowess of archers wielding longbows.

6

The Rose Garden (1924)

And afterwards she went very softly, and opened the window and looked out. Behind her, the room was in a mystical semi-darkness; chairs and tables were hovering, ill-defined shapes; there was but the faintest illusory glitter from the talc moons in the rich Indian curtain which she had drawn across the door. The yellow silk draperies of the bed were but suggestions of colour, and the pillow and the white sheets glimmered as a white cloud in a far sky at twilight.

She turned from the dusky room, and with dewy tender eyes gazed out across the garden towards the lake. She could not rest nor lay herself down to sleep; though it was late, and half the night had passed, she could not rest. A sickle moon was slowly drawing upwards through certain filmy clouds that stretched in a long band from east to west, and a pallid light began to flow from the dark water, as if there also some vague planet were rising. She looked with eyes insatiable for wonder; and she found a strange eastern effect in the bordering of reeds, in their spearlike shapes, in the liquid ebony that they shadowed, in the fine inlay of pearl and silver as the moon shone free; a bright symbol in the steadfast calm of the sky.

There were faint stirring sounds heard from the fringe of reeds, and now and then the drowsy, broken cry of the waterfowl, for they knew that the dawn was not far off. In the centre of the lake was a carved white pedestal, and on it shone a white boy, holding the double flute to his lips.[1]

Beyond the lake the park began, and sloped gently to the verge of the wood, now but a dark cloud beneath the sickle moon. And then beyond, and farther still, undiscovered hills, grey bands of cloud, and the steep pale height of the heaven. She gazed on with her tender eyes, bathing herself, as it were, in the deep rest of the night, veiling her soul with the half-light and the half-shadow, stretching out her delicate hands into the coolness of the misty silvered air, wondering at her hands.

And then she turned from the window, and made herself a divan of cushions on the Persian carpet, and half sat, half lay there, as motionless, as ecstatic as a poet dreaming under roses, far in Ispahan.[2] She had gazed out, after all, to

---

[1] A double flute is a wind instrument often depicted as played by the satyr Marsyas.

[2] Ispahan (also known as Isfahan) is an ancient city in central Iran. It is famous for its

assure herself that sight and the eyes showed nothing but a glimmering veil, a gauze of curious lights and figures: that in it there was no reality nor substance. He had always told her that there was only one existence, one science, one religion, that the external world was but a variegated shadow which might either conceal or reveal the truth; and now she believed.

He had shewn her that bodily rapture might be the ritual and expression of the ineffable mysteries, of the world beyond sense, that must be entered by the way of sense; and now she believed.[3] She had never much doubted any of his words, from the moment of their meeting a month before. She had looked up as she sat in the arbour, and her father was walking down through the avenue of roses, bringing to her the stranger, thin and dark, with a pointed beard and melancholy eyes. He murmured something to himself as they shook hands; she could hear the rich, unknown words that sounded as the echo of far music. Afterwards he had told her what those words signified:

> "How say ye that I was lost? I wandered among roses.
> Can he go astray that enters the rose garden?
> The Lover in the house of the Beloved is not forlorn.
> I wandered among roses. How say ye that I was lost?"[4]

His voice, murmuring the strange words, had persuaded her, and now she had the rapture of the perfect knowledge. She had looked out into the silvery uncertain night in order that she might experience the sense that for her these things no longer existed. She was not any more a part of the garden, or of the lake, or of the wood, or of the life that she had led hitherto. Another line that he had quoted came to her:

"The kingdom of I and We forsake and your home in annihilation make."[5]

---

mixing of cultures and religions, and for ornate Persian and Islamic architecture. The trope of the roses of Ispahan appeared in various European works of the nineteenth century, including English diplomat James Morier's (1782–1849) *Adventures of Hajji Baba of Ispahan* (1824); French poet Leconte de Lisle's (1818–1894) 'Les roses d'Ispahan' (date unknown), and Pierre Loti's (1850–1923) collection *Vers Ispahan* (1904).

[3] In the section of *Hieroglyphics* (1902) excerpted in this collection, Machen describes an otherworldly 'Shadowy Companion [...] who whispers to us his ineffable secrets, which we clumsily endeavour to set down in mortal language'. Decades later, in the privately published pamphlet *Beneath the Barley*, he proposes that literature is 'the art of exhibiting symbols which may hint at the ineffable mysteries behind them; the art of the veil, which reveals what it conceals' (unpaginated).

[4] No source for this passage has been established, although the language echoes aspects of Edward Granville Browne's (1862–1926) translations of poetry by the Babis of Persia. See the following note.

[5] Machen attributes this line to the Babis of Persia, defining his source of the translated passage as Edward Granville Browne ('Ars Artium', *The Academy* (25 July 1908), pp. 84–85 (p. 85)). Browne offers the translation in his article 'The Bábís of Persia: II. Their Literature and Doctrines', *Journal of the Royal Asiatic Society of Great Britain and Ireland*, 21:4 (October 1889), pp. 881–1009. Machen's description also suggests lines from Andrew

It had seemed at first almost nonsense — if it had been possible for him to talk nonsense; but now she was filled and thrilled with the meaning of it. Herself was annihilated; at his bidding she had destroyed all her old feelings and emotions, her likes and dislikes, all the inherited loves and hates that her father and mother had given her; the old life had been thrown utterly away.

It grew light, and when the dawn burned she fell asleep, murmuring:

"How say ye that I was lost?"

'The Rose Garden', *Ornaments in Jade* (New York:Alfred A. Knopf, 1924), pp. 3–5. Machen wrote this story in 1897, although it was not published until 1924.

Marvell's (1621–1678) poem 'The Garden', which Machen would have known: 'Annihilating all that's made / To a green thought in a green shade'.

7

The Turanians (1924)[1]

The smoke of the tinkers' camp rose a thin pale blue from the heart of the wood.[2]

Mary had left her mother at work on "things," and had gone out with a pale and languid face into the hot afternoon. She had talked of walking across the fields to the Green, and of having a chat with the doctor's daughter, but she had taken the other path that crept down towards the hollow and the dark thickets of the wood.[3]

After all, she had felt too lazy to rouse herself, to make the effort of conversation, and the sunlight scorched the path that was ruled straight from stile to stile across the brown August fields, and she could see, even from far away, how the white dust-clouds were smoking on the road by the Green. She hesitated, and at last went down under the far-spreading oak-trees, by a winding way of grass that cooled her feet.

Her mother, who was very kind and good, used to talk to her sometimes on the evils of "exaggeration," on the necessity of avoiding phrases violently expressed, words of too fierce an energy.[4] She remembered how she had run into the house a few days before and had called her mother to look at a rose in the garden that "burnt like a flame." Her mother had said the rose was very pretty, and a little later had hinted her doubts as to the wisdom of "such very strong expressions."

"I know, my dear Mary," she had said, "that in your case it isn't affectation. You really *feel* what you say, don't you? Yes; but is it nice to feel like that? Do you think that it's quite *right*, even?"

---

[1] The Persian term 'Turanians' refers to an ancient, largely nomadic people from a sparsely populated region of central Asia to the south and east of the Aral Sea.

[2] Tinkers mend pots, kettles, pans, and other household metal items. They are often itinerant and, in the nineteenth century, the word was used by some as a synonym for gypsy.

[3] Common in British towns and villages, a green is a grassy, park-like area jointly owned and used by a community's members.

[4] Machen appears here to be lightly mocking those reviewers who had critiqued his own Decadent style for its exaggeration and excess. The phrase 'burnt like a flame' that Mary's mother questions, for example, echoes not only Pater's famous dictum in *The Renaissance* (1873) that the aim of life is 'to burn always with this hard, gem-like flame', but also the phrase 'burst into the flame of blossom' and the many other flaming objects in *The Hill of Dreams*.

The mother had looked at the girl with a curious wistfulness, almost as if she would say something more, and sought for the fit words, but could not find them. And then she merely remarked:

"You haven't seen Alfred Moorhouse since the tennis party, have you? I must ask him to come next Tuesday; you like him?"

The daughter could not quite see the link between her fault of "exaggeration" and the charming young barrister, but her mother's warning recurred to her as she strayed down the shadowed path, and felt the long dark grass cool and refreshing about her feet. She would not have put this sensation into words, but she thought it was as though her ankles were gently, sweetly kissed as the rich grass touched them, and her mother would have said it was not right to think such things.

And what a delight there was in the colours all about her! It was as though she walked in a green cloud; the strong sunlight was filtered through the leaves, reflected from the grass, and made all visible things, the tree-stems, the flowers, and her own hands seem new, transformed into another likeness. She had walked by the wood-path over and over again, but to-day it had become full of mystery and hinting, and every turn brought a surprise.

To-day the mere sense of being alone under the trees was an acute secret joy, and as she went down deeper and the wood grew dark about her, she loosened her brown hair, and when the sun shone over the fallen tree she saw her hair was not brown but bronze and golden, glowing on her pure white dress.

She stayed by the well in the rock, and dared to make the dark water her mirror, looking to right and left with shy glances and listening for the rustle of parted boughs, before she would match her gold with luminous ivory.[5] She saw wonders in a glass as she leaned over the shadowed mysterious pool, and smiled at the smiling nymph, whose lips parted as if to whisper secrets.[6]

As she went on her way, the thin blue smoke rose from a gap in the trees, and she remembered her childish dread of "the gipsies." She walked a little farther, and laid herself to rest on a smooth patch of turf, and listened to the strange intonations that sounded from the camp. "Those horrible people" she had heard the yellow folk called, but she found now a pleasure in voices that sang and, indistinctly heard, were almost chanting, with a rise and fall of notes and a wild wail, and the solemnity of unknown speech. It seemed a fit music for the

---

[5]   Machen is evoking the image of Narcissus, the youth in Greek mythology who fell in love with his own reflection in a pool of water. After wasting away and dying from unfulfilled desire, Narcissus was transformed into the narcissus flower. The figure is popular in the art and literature of the Decadent movement, with particular attention to the beauty of male youth; Machen's rendering of a female version is unique in this regard.
[6]   In Greek and Roman mythology, nymphs — female deities — were companions of fauns and the demi-god Pan, to which Machen alludes below in his reference to the grace of the younger 'faun-like' Turanian men, introducing the sexuality of Pan's relationship to the nymphs.

unknown woodland, in harmony with the drip of the well, and the birds' sharp notes, and the rustle and hurry of the wood creatures.

She rose again and went on till she could see the red fire between the boughs; and the voices thrilled into an incantation. She longed to summon up courage, and talk to these strange wood-folk, but she was afraid to burst into the camp. So she sat down under a tree and waited, hoping that one of them might happen to come her way.

There were six or seven men, as many women, and a swarm of fantastic children, lolling and squatting about the fire, gabbling to one another in their singsong speech. They were people of curious aspect, short and squat, high-cheekboned, with dingy yellow skin and long almond eyes; only in one or two of the younger men there was a suggestion of a wild, almost faunlike grace, as of creatures who always moved between the red fire and the green leaf. Though everybody called them gipsies, they were in reality Turanian metal-workers, degenerated into wandering tinkers; their ancestors had fashioned the bronze battle-axes, and they mended pots and kettles. Mary waited under the tree, sure that she had nothing to fear, and resolved not to run away if one of them appeared.

The sun sank into a mass of clouds and the air grew close and heavy; a mist steamed up about the trees, a blue mist like the smoke of a wood-fire. A strange smiling face peered out from between the leaves, and the girl knew that her heart leapt as the young man walked towards her.

The Turanians moved their camp that night. There was a red glint, like fire, in the vast shadowy west, and then a burning paten floated up from a wild hill.[7] A procession of weird bowed figures passed across the crimson disk, one stumbling after another in long single file, each bending down beneath his huge shapeless pack, and the children crawled last, goblinlike, fantastic.

The girl was lying in her white room, caressing a small green stone, a curious thing cut with strange devices, awful with age. She held it close to the luminous ivory, and the gold poured upon it.[8]

She laughed for joy, and murmured and whispered to herself, asking herself questions in the bewilderment of her delight. She was afraid to say anything to her mother.

'The Turanians', *Ornaments in Jade* (New York: Alfred A. Knopf, 1924), pp. 6–9.
    Machen wrote this story in 1897, although it was not published until 1924.

---

[7] During the Christian Eucharist celebration, the bread is placed on a metal plate called a paten.

[8] This description of a green stone etched with strange markings is a witty allusion to the collection *Ornaments in Jade* in which this story appeared. The title suggests that the reader is to understand the collection itself, symbolically, as a green stone and the stories as ornamental markings, strange and not wholly decipherable.

8

The Idealist (1924)

"Did you notice Symonds while Beever was telling that story just now?" said one clerk to another.[1]

"No. Why? Didn't he like it?"

The second clerk had been putting away his papers and closing his desk in a grave and business-like manner, but when Beever's story was recalled to him he began to bubble anew, tasting the relish of the tale for a second time.

"He's a fair scorcher, old Beever," he remarked between little gasps of mirth. "But didn't Symonds like it?"

"Like it? He looked disgusted, I can tell you. Made a face, something in this style:" and the man drew his features into a design of sour disapproval, as he gave his hat the last polish with his coatsleeve.

"Well, I'm off now," he said. "I want to get home early, as there's tart for tea," and he fashioned another grimace, an imitation of his favourite actor's favourite contortion.

"Well, good-bye," said his friend. "You are a hot 'un, you are. You're worse than Beever. See you on Monday. What will Symonds say?" and he shouted after him as the door swung to and fro.

Charles Symonds, who had failed to see the humour of Mr. Beever's tale, had left the office a few minutes earlier and was now pacing slowly westward, mounting Fleet Street.[2] His fellow clerk had not been much amiss in his observation. Symonds had heard the last phrases of Beever's story, and unconsciously had looked half round towards the group, angry and disgusted at their gross and stupid merriment. Beever and his friends seemed to him guilty of sacrilege; he likened them to plough-boys pawing and deriding an exquisite painted panel, blaring out their contempt and brutal ignorance. He could not control his features; in spite of himself he looked loathing at the three yahoos.

---

[1]   Although not similar in character, the hero's name brings to mind John Addington Symonds (1840–1893), an Aestheticist poet, highly respected literary critic, and advocate for same-sex male love.

[2]   The story follows its hero's rather direct walk westward roughly 6 miles across London along Fleet Street (known for its publishing industry), the Strand, and Piccadilly to Fulham, on the north bank of the Thames. At the end of the nineteenth century, Fulham had seen a major growth in suburban housing.

He would have given anything if he could have found words and told them what he thought, but even to look displeasure was difficult. His shyness was a perpetual amusement to the other clerks, who often did little things to annoy him, and enjoyed the spectacle of Symonds inwardly raging and burning like Etna, but too hopelessly diffident to say a word. He would turn dead man's white, and grind his teeth at an insult, and pretend to join in the laugh, and pass it off as a joke. When he was a boy his mother was puzzled by him, not knowing whether he were sullen or insensible, or perhaps very good-tempered.

He climbed Fleet Street, still raw with irritation, partly from a real disgust at the profane coarseness of the clerks, and partly from a feeling that they talked so because they knew he hated such gross farces and novels. It was hideous to live and work with such foul creatures, and he glanced back fury at the City, the place of the stupid, the blatant, the intolerable.

He passed into the rush and flood of the Strand, into the full tide of a Saturday afternoon, still meditating the outrage, and constructing a cutting sentence for future use, heaping up words which should make Beever tremble. He was quite aware that he would never utter one of those biting phrases, but the pretence soothed him, and he began to remember other things. It was in late November and the clouds were already gathering for the bright solemnity of the sunset, flying to their places before the wind. They curled into fantastic shapes, high up there in the wind's whirlpool, and Symonds, looking towards the sky, was attracted by two grey writhing clouds that drew together in the west, in the far perspective of the Strand. He saw them as if they had been living creatures, noting every change and movement and transformation, till the shaking winds made them one and drove a vague form away to the south.

The curious interest he had taken in the cloud shapes had driven away the thought of the office, of the fetid talk which he so often heard. Beever and his friends ceased to exist, and Symonds escaped to his occult and private world which no one had ever divined. He lived far away down in Fulham, but he let the buses rock past him, and walked slowly, endeavouring to prolong the joys of anticipation. Almost with a visible gesture he drew himself apart, and went solitary, his eyes downcast, and gazing not on the pavement but on certain clear imagined pictures.

He quickened his steps as he passed along the northern pavement of Leicester Square, hurrying to escape the sight of the enamelled strange spectra who were already beginning to walk and stir abroad, issuing from their caves and waiting for the gas-light.[3] He scowled as he looked up and chanced to see on a hoarding an icon with raddled cheeks and grinning teeth, at which some young men were leering; and one was recalling this creature's great song:

"And that's the way they do it.
How d'ye fink it's done?

---

[3]   Machen's allusion in this sentence is to prostitutes waiting for night.

Oh, *that's* the way they do it.

Doesn't it taike the bun?"

Symonds scowled at the picture of her, remembering how Beever had voted her "good goods," how the boys bellowed the chorus under his windows of Saturday nights. Once he had opened the window as they passed by, and had sworn at them and cursed them, in a whisper, lest he should be overheard.

He peered curiously at the books in a Piccadilly shop; now and then when he could save a few pounds he had made purchases there, but the wares which the bookseller dealt in were expensive, and he was obliged to be rather neatly dressed at the office, and he had other esoteric expenses. He had made up his mind to learn Persian and he hesitated as to whether he should turn back now, and see if he could pick up a grammar in Great Russell Street at a reasonable price. But it was growing dark, and the mists and shadows that he loved were gathering and inviting him onwards to those silent streets near the river.

When he at last diverged from the main road he made his way by a devious and eccentric track, threading an intricate maze of streets which to most people would have been dull and gloomy and devoid of interest. But to Symonds these backwaters of London were as bizarre and glowing as a cabinet of Japanese curios; he found here his delicately chased bronzes, work in jade, the flush and flame of extraordinary colours. He delayed at a corner, watching a shadow on a lighted blind, watching it fade and blacken and fade, conjecturing its secrets, inventing dialogue for this drama in *Ombres Chinoises*.[4] He glanced up at another window, and saw a room vivid, in a hard yellow light of flaming gas, and lurked in the shelter of an old elm till he was perceived and the curtains were drawn hastily. On the way he had chosen, it was his fortune to pass many well-ordered decent streets, by villas detached and semi-detached, half hidden behind flowering-shrubs and evergreens. At this hour, on a Saturday in November, few were abroad, and Symonds was often able, crouching down by the fence, to peer into a lighted room, to watch persons who thought themselves utterly unobserved. As he came near to his home he went through meaner streets, and he stopped at a corner, observing two children at play, regarding them with the minute scrutiny of an entomologist at the microscope. A woman who had been out shopping crossed the road and drove the children home, and Symonds moved on, hastily, but with a long sigh of enjoyment.

---

[4] *Ombres Chinoises* (French: Chinese shadows), also called magic lantern shows, are plays enacted by the use of moving shadow silhouettes. Similar to Machen's story, Wilde's poem 'The Harlot's House' (1882) depicts as a drama the view of silhouettes moving behind the curtains of a brothel. Wilde suggests that those inside the house are immoral, while Machen's story demonstrates the hypocrisy and even deviancy of those on the street who accuse others of sins the viewers assume are taking place. In this sense, the story echoes Gautier's argument in the preface to *Mademoiselle de Maupin* (1835) that critics insisting on finding immorality in literature are themselves obsessed with deviancy.

His breath came quick, in gusts, as he drew out his latch-key. He lived in an old Georgian house, and he raced up the stairs, and locked the door of the great lofty room in which he lived. The evening was damp and chilly, but the sweat streamed down his face. He stuck a match, and there was a strange momentary vision of the vast room, almost empty of furniture, a hollow space bordered by grave walls and the white glimmer of the corniced ceiling.

He lit a candle, opened a large box that stood in a corner, and set to work. He seemed to be fitting together some sort of lay figure;[5] a vague hint of the human shape increased under his hands. The candle sparkled at the other end of the room, and Symonds was sweating over his task in a cavern of dark shadow. His nervous shaking fingers fumbled over that uncertain figure, and then he began to draw out incongruous monstrous things. In the dusk, white silk shimmered, laces and delicate frills hovered for a moment, as he bungled over the tying of knots, the fastening of bands. The old room grew rich, heavy, vaporous with subtle scents; the garments that were passing through his hands had been drenched with fragrance. Passion had contorted his face; he grinned stark in the candlelight.[6]

When he had finished the work he drew it with him to the window, and lighted three more candles. In his excitement, that night he forgot the effect of *Ombres Chinoises*, and those who passed and happened to look up at the white staring blind found singular matter for speculation.

'The Idealist', *Ornaments in Jade* (New York: Alfred A. Knopf, 1924), pp. 10–15. Machen wrote this story in 1897, although it was not published until 1924.

---

[5]   A lay figure is a mannequin with bendable joints, used by artists instead of a living model to arrange clothing and material in natural poses.

[6]   Machen contributes here to a tradition made popular by E. T. A. Hoffmann's (1776–1822) short story 'Der Sandmann' (1816), in which the German author depicts an attractive female automaton named Olympia. The trope also appears in such Decadent works as Rachilde's (1860–1953) *Monsieur Vénus* (1884) and Villiers de L'Isle-Adam's (1838–1889) *L'Eve future* (1886).

The Ceremony (1924)

From her childhood, from those early and misty days which began to seem unreal, she recollected the grey stone in the wood.

It was something between the pillar and the pyramid in shape, and its grey solemnity amidst the leaves and the grass shone and shone from those early years, always with some hint of wonder.[1] She remembered how, when she was quite a little girl, she had strayed one day, on a hot afternoon, from her nurse's side, and only a little way in the wood the grey stone rose from the grass, and she cried out and ran back in panic terror.

"What a silly little girl," the nurse had said. "It's only the … stone." She had quite forgotten the name that the servant had given, and she was always ashamed to ask as she grew older.

But always that hot day, that burning afternoon of her childhood when she had first looked consciously on the grey image in the wood, remained not a memory but a sensation. The wide wood swelling like the sea, the tossing of the bright boughs in the sunshine, the sweet smell of the grass and flowers, the beating of the summer wind upon her cheek, the gloom of the underglade rich, indistinct, gorgeous, significant as old tapestry; she could feel it and see it all, and the scent of it was in her nostrils. And in the midst of the picture, where strange plants grew gross in shadow, was the old grey shape of the stone.

But there were in her mind broken remnants of another and far earlier impression.[2] It was all uncertain, the shadow of a shadow, so vague that it might well have been a dream that had mingled with the confused waking thoughts of a little child. She did not know that she remembered, she rather remembered the memory. But again it was a summer day, and a woman, perhaps the same nurse, held her in her arms, and went through the wood. The woman carried bright flowers in one hand; the dream had in it a glow of bright red, and the

---

[1] This pillar is likely a prehistoric standing stone (also known as a cromlech). Some standing stones are remnants of tombs, while others form part of stone circles, such as Stonehenge. In the nineteenth century, it was not uncommon for people to regard standing stones as sites of occult Druidic activity; for instance, in his poem *Milton* (c. 1810), William Blake (1757–1827) writes of 'stony Druid Temples'.

[2] On Machen's Wordsworthian conception of childhood imagination and its relation to pre-birth memory, see the introduction to this edition.

perfume of cottage roses. Then she saw herself put down for a moment on the grass, and the red colour stained the grim stone, and there was nothing else — except that one night she woke up and heard the nurse sobbing.

She often used to think of the strangeness of very early life; one came, it seemed, from a dark cloud, there was a glow of light, but for a moment, and afterwards the night. It was as if one gazed at a velvet curtain, heavy, mysterious, impenetrable blackness, and then, for the twinkling of an eye, one spied through a pinhole a storied town that flamed, with fire about its walls and pinnacles. And then again the folding darkness, so that sight became illusion, almost in the seeing. So to her was that earliest, doubtful vision of the grey stone, of the red colour spilled upon it, with the incongruous episode of the nursemaid, who wept at night.

But the later memory was clear; she could feel, even now, the inconsequent terror that sent her away shrieking, running to the nurse's skirts. Afterwards, through the days of girlhood, the stone had taken its place amongst the vast array of unintelligible things which haunt every child's imagination. It was part of life, to be accepted and not questioned; her elders spoke of many things which she could not understand, she opened books and was dimly amazed, and in the Bible there were many phrases which seemed strange. Indeed, she was often puzzled by her parents' conduct, by their looks at one another, by their half-words, and amongst all these problems which she hardly recognized as problems, was the grey ancient figure rising from dark grass.

Some semi-conscious impulse made her haunt the wood where shadow enshrined the stone. One thing was noticeable; that all through the summer months the passers-by dropped flowers there. Withered blossoms were always on the ground, amongst the grass, and on the stone fresh blooms constantly appeared. From the daffodil to the Michaelmas daisy there was marked the calendar of the cottage gardens, and in the winter she had seen sprays of juniper and box, mistletoe and holly.[3] Once she had been drawn through the bushes by a red glow, as if there had been a fire in the wood, and when she came to the place, all the stone shone and all the ground about it was bright with roses.

In her eighteenth year she went one day into the wood, carrying with her a book that she was reading. She hid herself in a nook of hazel, and her soul

---

[3] All four of these evergreens are recorded as having held varying degrees of sacred importance for pre-Christian Britons. Juniper has a history of being used in ritual incense, while box (or boxwood) was recognized as a symbol of longevity. The green leaves and red berries of the holly tree signified the durability of life even in the darkness of winter. For their part, Druids are said to have believed in mistletoe's powers of healing and fertility. Various nineteenth-century artists depicted scenes of Druids and mistletoe, most notably George Henry (1858–1943) and Edward Atkinson Hornel's (1864–1933) *The Druids: Bringing in the Mistletoe* (1890) and Henri Paul Motte's (1846–1922) *Druids Cutting the Mistletoe on the Sixth Day of the Moon* (c. 1900).

was full of poetry, when there was a rustling, the rapping of parted boughs returning to their place. Her concealment was but a little way from the stone, and she peered through the net of boughs, and saw a girl timidly approaching. She knew her quite well; it was Annie Dolben, the daughter of a labourer, lately a promising pupil at Sunday school. Annie was a nice-mannered girl, never failing in her curtsy, wonderful for her knowledge of the Jewish Kings.[4] Her face had taken an expression that whispered, that hinted strange things; there was a light and a glow behind the veil of flesh. And in her hand she bore lilies.

The lady hidden in hazels watched Annie come close to the grey image; for a moment her whole body palpitated with expectation, almost the sense of what was to happen dawned upon her. She watched Annie crown the stone with flowers, she watched the amazing ceremony that followed.[5]

And yet, in spite of all her blushing shame, she herself bore blossoms to the wood a few months later. She laid white hothouse lilies upon the stone, and orchids of dying purple, and crimson exotic flowers. Having kissed the grey image with devout passion, she performed there all the antique immemorial rite.

'The Ceremony', *Ornaments in Jade* (New York: Alfred A. Knopf, 1924), pp. 20–23. Machen wrote this story in 1897, although it was not published until 1924.

---

[4] These were the Hebrew rulers, such as David and Solomon, of ancient Judah and Israel, the main biblical records of whom appear in I and II Samuel and I and II Kings.

[5] Crowning the standing stone with flowers is reminiscent of pagan celebrations at Beltane (held on the first of May in the Northern hemisphere), which mark the earth's re-awakening to abundant life and fertility after winter's dormancy and death.

Ritual (1937)

Once upon a time, as we say in English, or *olim*, as the Latins said in their more austere and briefer way, I was sent forth on a May Monday to watch London being happy on their Whitsun holiday.[1] This is the sort of appointment that used to be known in newspaper offices as an annual; and the difficulty for the men engaged in this business is to avoid seeing the same sights as those witnessed a year before and saying much the same things about them as were said on Whit-Monday twelvemonth. Queuing up for Madame Tussaud's waxworks, giving buns to diverse creatures in the Zoo, gazing at those Easter Island gods in the portico of the British Museum, waiting for all sorts of early doors to open; all these are spectacles of the day. And the patient man who boards the buses from suburbs may chance to hear a lady from Hornsey expounding to her neighbour on the seat, an inhabitant of Enfield Wash, the terrible gaieties that Piccadilly Circus witnesses when the electric signs are fairly lit.[2]

On the Whit-Monday in question, I saw and recorded some of these matters; and then strolled westward along Piccadilly, by the palings of the Green Park.[3] The conventional business of the day had been more or less attended to: now for the systematic prowl: one never knows where one may find one's goods. And then and there, I came across some boys, half-a-dozen or so of them, playing what struck me as a very queer game on the fresh turf of the Park, under the tender and piercing green of the young leaves. I have forgotten the preliminary elaborations of the sport; but there seemed to be some sort of dramatic action, perhaps with dialogue, but this I could not hear. Then one boy stood alone, with the five or six others about him. They pretended to hit the solitary boy, and he fell to the ground and lay motionless, as if dead. Then the others covered him up with their coats, and ran away. And then, if I remember, the boy who had been ritually smitten, slaughtered, and buried, rose to his feet, and the very odd game began all over again.[4]

---

[1] In Machen's time, 'Whit Monday' was a public holiday. It was the Monday immediately after Whit Sunday, which is the name Anglicans (especially in England) give to Pentecost, the seventh Sunday after Easter.

[2] Hornsey and Enfield Wash are suburbs in North London. Piccadilly Circus is a traffic circle and open square in London's bustling West End.

[3] Green Park is located in central London, just north of Buckingham Palace.

[4] A number of children's games in Great Britain involve pretended death and resurrection;

Here, I thought, was something a little out of the way of the accustomed doings and pleasures of the holiday crowds, and I returned to my office and embodied an account of this Green Park sport in my tale of Whit-Monday in London; with some allusion to the curious analogy between the boys' game and certain matters of a more serious nature. But it would not do. A spectacled Reader came down out of his glass cage, and held up a strip of proof.[5]

"Hiram Abiff?" he queried in a low voice, as he placed the galley-slip on my desk, and pointed to the words with his pen.[6] "It's not usual to mention these things in print."

I assured the Reader that I was not one of the Widow's offspring, but he still shook his head gravely, and I let him have his way, willing to avoid all *admiratio*.[7] It was, I thought, a curious little incident, and to this day I have never heard an explanation of the coincidence — mere chance, very likely — between the pastime in the Park and those matters which it is not usual to mention in print.

But a good many years later, this business of the Green Park was recalled to me by a stranger experience in a very different part of London. A friend of mine, an American, who had travelled in many outland territories of the earth, asked me to show him some of the less known quarters of London.

"Do not misunderstand me, sir," he said, in his measured, almost Johnsonian manner, "I do not wish to see your great city in its alleged sensational aspects.[8] I am not yearning to probe the London underworld, nor do I wish to view any opium joints or blind-pigs for cocaine addicts.[9] In such matters, I have already accumulated more than sufficient experience in other quarters of the world. But if you would just shew me those aspects which are so ordinary that nobody ever sees them, I shall be greatly indebted to you."

I remembered how I had once awed two fellow-citizens of his by taking

---

in 'Dead Man Arise' (also known as 'Green Man Arise'), for example, the 'dead' child lies on the ground and is covered up by coats, a blanket, hay, or some other material (Iona and Peter Opie, *Children's Games in Street and Playground* (Oxford: Oxford University Press, 1969), pp. 106–08).

[5]   In the newspaper business, a Reader is the person who evaluates manuscripts prior to publication. In Machen's day, such a person often worked in an office that was situated above the main newsroom floor and had interior windows overlooking the newsroom.

[6]   According to the tenets of the Freemasons (a secret fraternal order), Hiram Abiff was the architect of King Solomon's temple who was attacked and killed by men seeking the secrets of a master mason. As with many things in Freemasonry, members keep his legend and the rites associated with him hidden from the general public. A galley-slip (or galley proof) is a strip of paper with printed text that needs to be proofread before publication.

[7]   Machen's narrator is saying that he is not a Freemason. In the Bible, Solomon's architect, Hiram, is said to be 'a widow's son of the tribe Naphtali' (1 Kings 7. 14). *Admiratio* (Latin): wonder or admiration.

[8]   The word 'Johnsonian' refers to the serious style of Dr Samuel Johnson (1709–1784), an English critic, poet, and lexicographer.

[9]   'Blind-pigs' is a slang term for saloons in which liquor is illegally sold and consumed.

them to a street not very far from King's Cross Station, and shewing them how each house was guarded by twin plaster sphinxes of a deadly chocolate-red, which crouched on either side of the flights of steps leading to the doorways.[10] I remembered how the late Arnold Bennett had come exploring in this region, and seen the sphinxes and had noted them in his diary with a kind of dumb surmise, venturing no comment.[11] So I said that I thought I understood. We set out, and soon we were deep in that unknown London which is at our very doors.

"Dickens had been here," I said in my part as Guide and Interpreter. "You know 'Little Dorrit'? Then this might be Mr. Casby's very street, which set out meaning to run down into the valley and up again to the top of the hill, but got out of breath and stopped still after twenty yards."[12]

The American gentleman relished the reference and his surroundings. He pointed out to me curious work in some of the iron balconies before the first floor windows in the grey houses, making a rough sketch of the design of one of them in his note-book. We wandered here and there, and up and down at haphazard, by strange wastes and devious ways, till I, in spite of my fancied knowledge, found myself in a part that I did not remember to have seen before. There were timber yards with high walls about them. There were cottages that seemed to have strayed from the outskirts of some quiet provincial town, off the main road. One of these lay deep in the shadow of an old mulberry, and ripening grapes hung from a vine on a neighbouring wall. The hollyhocks in the neat little front gardens were almost over; there were still brave displays of snapdragons and marigolds. But round the corner, barrows piled with pale bananas and flaming oranges filled the roadway, and the street market resounded with raucous voices, praise of fruit and fish, and loud bargainings, and gossip at its highest pitch. We pushed our way through the crowd, and left the street of the market, and presently came into the ghostly quiet of a square: high, severe houses, built of whitish bricks, complete in 1840 Gothic, all neat and well-kept, and for all sign of life or movement, uninhabited.

---

[10] A sphinx is a mythic ancient Egyptian creature with the head of a human (or other animal) and the body of a lion. They are usually portrayed as mysterious and dangerous, as in Sophocles's (495?–406 BCE) drama *Oedipus Rex*. Increasingly associated with the mystery of the female and with the *femme fatale*, sphinxes appear frequently in Decadent and Symbolist art and literature, Gustave Moreau's painting *Oedipus and the Sphinx* (1867) being perhaps best known. Other works include Franz von Stuck's (1863–1928) paintings *The Kiss of the Sphinx* (1895) and *Sphinx* (1904); Fernand Khnopff's (1858–1921) painting *Caresses* (also known as *The Caress*, 1896); illustrations by Beardsley and Charles Ricketts (1866–1931); and Wilde's story 'A Sphinx without a Secret' (1887) and poem 'Sphinx' (1894). Wilde nicknamed his friend Ada Leverson (1862–1933), Sphinx.

[11] Enoch Arnold Bennett (1867–1931) was an English author and critic. In his fiction, he largely adhered to literary realism.

[12] In Dickens's novel *Little Dorrit* (serial publication, 1855–1857), the minor character Mr Casby is a heartless man who appears the soul of generosity but, in fact, is intent on squeezing every penny out of the residents of Bleeding Heart Yard.

And then, when we had barely rested our ears from the market jangle, there came what I suppose was an overflow from that region. A gang of small boys surged into the square and broke its peace. There were about a dozen of them, more or less, and I took it that they were playing soldiers. They marched, two and two, in their dirty and shabby order, apparently under the command of a young ruffian somewhat bigger and taller than the rest. Two of them banged incessantly with bits of broken wood on an old meat tin and a battered iron tea tray, and all of them howled as barbarously as any crooner, but much louder. They went about and about, and then diverged into an empty road that looked as if it led nowhere in particular, and there drew up, and formed themselves into a sort of hollow square, their captain in the middle. The tin pan music went on steadily, but less noisily; it had become a succession of slow beats, and the howls had turned into a sort of whining chant.

But it remained a very horrible row, and I was moving on to get away from the noise, when my American interposed.

"If you wouldn't mind our tarrying here for a few moments," he said apologetically. "This pastime of your London boys interests me very much. You may think it strange, but I find it more essentially exciting than the Eton and Harrow Cricket Match of which I witnessed some part a few weeks ago."[13]

So we looked on from an unobtrusive corner. The boys, evidently, agreed with my friend, and found their game absorbing. I don't think that they had noticed us or knew that we were there.

They went through their queer performance. The bangs or beats on the tin and the tray grew softer and slower, and the yells had died into a monotonous drone. The leader went inside the square, from boy to boy, and seemed to whisper into the ear of each one. Then he passed round a second time, standing before each, and making a sort of summoning or beckoning gesture with his hand. Nothing happened. I did not find the sport essentially exciting; but looking at the American, I observed that he was watching it with an expression of the most acute interest and amazement. Again the big boy went about the square. He stopped dead before a little fellow in a torn jacket. He threw out his arms wide, with a gesture of embrace, and then drew them in. He did this three times, and at the third repetition of the ceremony, the little chap in the torn jacket cried out with a piercing scream and fell forward as if dead.

The banging of the tins and the howl of the voices went up to heaven with a hideous dissonance.

My American friend was gasping with astonishment as we passed on our way.

"This is an amazing city," he said. "Do you know, sir, that those boys were

---

[13]   Eton and Harrow are old, prestigious public (i.e. fee-paying) schools for boys in England.

acting all as if they'd been Asiki doing their Njoru ritual.[14] I've seen it in East Africa. But there the black man that falls down stays down. He's dead."

A week or two later, I was telling the tale to some friends. One of them pulled an evening paper out of his pocket.

"Look at that," said he, pointing with is finger. I read the headlines:

MYSTERY DEATH IN NORTH LONDON SQUARE
HOME OFFICE DOCTOR PUZZLED
HEART VESSELS RUPTURED
"PLAYING SOLDIERS"
BOY FALLS DEAD
CORONER DIRECTS OPEN VERDICT

'Ritual', in *Path and Pavement: Twenty New Tales of Britain*, ed. by John Rowland (London: Eric Grant, 1937), pp. 143–51.

---

[14] In the novel *The Yellow God: An Idol of Africa* (1908), H. Rider Haggard (1856–1925) invents the Asiki tribe. At one point, he describes an Asiki ceremony as follows: 'Louder and louder brayed the music and beat the drums, wilder and wilder grew the shrieks. [...] Then suddenly the Asika stood still and threw up her arms, whereon all the thousands present stood still also. Again she threw up her arms, and they fell upon their faces and lay as though they were dead' (H. Rider Haggard, *The Yellow God: An Idol of Africa* (Cassell: London, 1908), pp. 225–26).

PART II
Non-Fiction

The Literature of Occultism (1899)

There is a sense, of course, in which all fine literature, both in prose and in verse, belongs to the region of things mysterious and occult.[1] Formerly it might have been maintained that music was the purest of all the arts, that the shuddering and reverberant summons of the organ, the far, faint echo of a distant choir singing spoke clearly to the soul without the material impediment of a story, without that "body" which must clothe the spirit of pictures and sculptured forms, being as they are representations of the visible things around us.[2] But since Wagner came and conquered, music has become more and more an intellectual exercise, and to the modern musical critic every bar must be capable of interpretation, of an intelligible translation, if it is to be absolved in the judgment.[3]

Since then, music has frankly become a "mixed" art, a "criticism of life" in the medium of sound; we who try to understand literature may well insist that our fine prose and our fine poetry have a part in them, and that part the most precious, which is wholly super-intellectual, non-intelligible, occult. The lines of Keats, the "magic casements, opening on the foam of perilous seas, in faëry lands forlorn," will occur to every one as an instance of this mysterious element in poetry.[4] Poe's ode to Helen is another example, and there are passages in the old prose writers and sentences in Browne and Jeremy Taylor which thrill the heart with an inexplicable, ineffable charm.[5] This, perhaps, is the true literature

---

[1]   While working for the publisher George Redway, Machen produced a catalogue entitled *The Literature of Occultism and Archaeology* (1885). On occultism, see the introduction to this edition.

[2]   On Pater's argument regarding music as the ideal art form, see *The Hill of Dreams*, note 191.

[3]   Wilhelm Richard Wagner (1813–1883), German composer much admired by the Decadents. He is recognized for his revolutionary work on synthesizing various forms of art — music, visuals, poetry, and drama — into a single experience. Friedrich Nietzsche (1844–1900) would argue that Wagner's work marked a major cultural shift in the West from Apollonian rationalism, which Nietzsche called Decadent, to a Dionysian, life-affirming freedom.

[4]   The passage is from Keats's 'Ode to a Nightingale' (1819), in which — apropos to Machen's subject — the bird's voice leads the poet to contrast its eternal beauty to his own mortality.

[5]   Poe is the author of 'To Helen' (1831; revised 1845). By this time in his career, Machen had

of occultism. These are the runes which call up the unknown spirits from the mind.

But there is a literature which is occult in a more special sense, which either undertakes to explain and comment on the secrets of man's life, or is explicitly founded on mysterious beliefs of one kind or another. Books of this sort have, it is well known, existed from the earliest times; perhaps, indeed, when the last explorer leaves Babylon, bringing with him positively the most antique inscription in the world, he will find an incantation written on the brick or on the rock. It will be said, no doubt, that there would be nothing strange in such a discovery, that early man living in a world which he understood either dimly or not at all would naturally devise occult causes for occult effects, would imagine that he too by esoteric means could pass behind the veil, and attain to the knowledge of the secret workings of the universe. But we know that such beliefs were by no means peculiar to the Egyptian of prehistoric times, we are able to trace all through the ages the one conviction of an occult world lying a little beyond the world of sense, and probably at the present day there are as many students of and believers in magic, white and black, as there were in the awful hanging gardens of Babylon. But though belief is as fervent as ever, the expression of it has lamentably deteriorated, as may be seen in "Letters from Julia," written by the hand of Mr. W. T. Stead, which we mentioned a few weeks ago.[6] The modern disciples of Isis speak in a tongue that differs from that of the ancient initiates.[7] They who wish to learn the message of the new hierophant may read the review, or even the book in question, but here, where we discourse of literature and of literature only, we cannot enter into the squalid chapter of back-parlour magic, into the inanities, the follies, the impostures of modern theosophy and modern spiritualism.[8] And here we must not even speak of

---

used the name Helen for characters in *The Great God Pan* and *The Three Impostors*. Thomas Browne (1605–1682) was an English author and expert in religion, esotericism, and medicine. Jeremy Taylor (1613–1667) was an Anglican cleric renowned for the beauty of his prose.

[6] An influential publisher, journalist, and author, Stead was heavily engaged with spiritualism, editing *Borderland: A Psychical Quarterly* (1893–1897) as a magazine for the general reader. He claimed that *Letters from Julia or Light from the Borderland* (1897) was the product of automatic writing, with a dead person communicating through his unconscious. Machen had no patience for what he saw as the charlatanism of such popular occulture.

[7] On Isis, see note 182 of *The Hill of Dreams*. Her persona was a major influence on the occult during Machen's time.

[8] A hierophant is a chief priest. The Theosophical Society was founded in New York in 1875 by Helena Blavatsky (Elena Petrovna Blavatskaya, 1831–1891), William Quan Judge (1851–1896), and Henry Steel Olcott (1832–1907), with influences going back centuries. A popular middle-class movement, it was influenced by eastern religions. Having its heyday in the Victorian period, spiritualism is the belief that the dead can communicate with the living through such forms as dreams, spirit photography, table rapping, and automatic writing. Machen's attitude to Theosophy and spiritualism are discussed in the introduction to this edition.

"imposture," for we know nothing of these persons, save that they cannot write books.

But this literature of occultism was not always vulgar. Futile, perhaps, it was always, or perhaps, like the ritual of Freemasonry, it did once point the way to veritable enigmas;[9] if it could never tell the secret, it may have whispered that there was a secret, that we are the sons of God and it doth not yet appear what we shall be. But no one could look into the alchemical writings of the middle ages and deny them the name of literature. Alchemy, in spite of all confident pronouncements on the subject, remains still a mystery, the very nature and object of the quest are unknown.[10] The baser alchemists — there were quacks and impostors and dupes then as now — no doubt sought or pretended to seek some method of making gold artificially, but the sages, those who practised the true spagyric art, were engaged in some infinitely more mysterious adventure. The Life of Nicholas Flamel is decisive on this point, and Thomas Vaughan, the brother of the Silurist, was certainly not hinting at any chemical or material transmutation when he wrote his "Lumen de Lumine" and the "Magia Adamica."[11] The theory has been advanced that the true alchemists were, in fact, the successors of the hierophants of Eleusis,[12] that their transmutation was a transmutation of man, not of metal, that their "first matter" was "that hermaphrodite, the son of Adam, who, though in the form of a man, ever bears about him in his body the body of Eve, his wife,"[13] that their fine gold,

---

[9]   Freemasonry is an international, male-only secret order (Free and Accepted Masons). Rooted in the stonemason organizations of the Middle Ages, it maintains a moral order communicated by occult symbols and rituals. Membership involves a process of teachings and initiation.

[10]   Alchemy, also referred to as the spagyric art (from the Greek for 'collect' and 'extract'), is the secretive use of magic and chemistry to transmute base elements into other matter, such as lead into gold, and/or to discover the elixir or meaning of life. Machen's exposure to alchemical texts is outlined in the introduction.

[11]   Practitioners of alchemy are believed to include the French Nicholas Flamel (c. 1330–1418) and the Welsh Thomas Vaughan, whose brother, the poet Henry Vaughan, described himself as a descendent of the Celtic tribe of the Silures. Thomas Vaughan's works include *Lumen de Lumine* (1651) and the *Magia Adamica* (1650).

[12]   The Eleusinian Mysteries were initiation rituals of what is believed to have been an ancient Greek agrarian cult of Demeter (goddess of the harvest) and her daughter Persephone. Ministered by hierophants, the secret mysteries and rites addressed Persephone's transformation as she accompanied Hades to the underworld before returning to her mother.

[13]   The quotation Machen presents here has not been traced, but there is a tradition of interpreting Adam as possessing sex and/or gender fluidity. A key source for this argument is the biblical account of the creation of Eve from one of Adam's ribs (Genesis 3. 21–23). The term 'hermaphrodite' comes from Hermaphroditus, the child of the gods Hermes and Aphrodite. Ovid (43 BCE–17/18 CE), in the *Metamorphoses*, Book 4, tells how Hermaphroditus and the nymph Salmacis were physically united and transformed into a creature containing both sexes.

glistening and glorious as the sun, symbolised the soul, freed from the bonds of matter, in communion with the source of all things, initiated in the perfect mysteries. However that may be, there can be no question as to the beauty of the best alchemical treatises, of that strange symbolism which spoke of the Bird of Hermes, of the Red Dragon, of the Son Blessed of the Fire.[14] The curious in such matters may consult Ashmole's "Fasciculus Chemicus," and the extraordinary "Opusculum" of Denys Zachaire.[15]

In the space of an article it is, of course, impossible to sketch out even a brief scheme of old occult literature. We must pass over the Greeks, in spite of the songs of the Initiated that Aristophanes has given us, in spite of that Thessalian magic which Apuleius moulded to such exquisite literary ends.[16] We must decline the question of the origin of alchemy, which a distinguished French chemist has characteristically referred to some misunderstood trade receipts, relating to methods of gilding and bronzing the baser metals. Then there is the great question of the Sabbath.[17] Popular opinion says that in the Dark Ages people were mad about witchcraft, and that they tortured old women till they confessed to anything rather than suffer another turn of the rack. It is a harmless superstition, this theory of the poor old woman with her black cat, but it may be noted that Payne Knight's monograph on the "Worship of Priapus" throws a very different light on the matter, that Hawthorne understood something of the real Sabbath.[18] The terror and the flame of it glow behind all the chapters of the "Scarlet Letter," and those who can read between the lines see the same red glare in "Young Goodman Brown." We must leave, too, the problem of Rosicrucianism, concerning which Mr. A. E. Waite has said the last words in his "Real History of the Rosicrucians," a kind of historical counterblast to the fantastic and entertaining, but wholly unreliable work by the late Hargrave

---

[14] The Bird of Hermes appears in the alchemical Ripley Scroll, ascribed to the alchemist George Ripley (died *c.* 1490), with the symbol open to interpretation. In alchemy, the red dragon is both the oil of lead and, once perfected, the red powder. The red dragon is also the symbol of Wales and associated with King Arthur (as Machen notes in *Chronicles of Clemendy* (1888)). The phrase 'Son Blessed of the Fire' appears in works as early as those of sixteenth-century French alchemist Denis Zachaire, author of *Opusculum* (1600).

[15] In 1650, Elias Ashmole offered an English translation of alchemist Arthur Dee's (1579–1651) *Fasciculus Chemicus* (1629; revised *c.* 1631–1633).

[16] Aristophanes (444–*c.* 386 BCE) was a Greek playwright whose plays, most notably *The Frogs*, include songs sung by those initiated into the Eleusinian Mysteries. Thessalian magic was practised by witches in the region of Thessaly in Greece from the first to third centuries BCE; involving invocations to the goddess of the moon, the practices are referenced in various texts throughout Western history. Apuleius's novel *Metamorphoses*, also known as *The Golden Ass*, focuses on the adventures of a man eager to practise magic.

[17] On the Witches' Sabbath, see note 38 of 'The Recluse of Bayswater'.

[18] On Knight, see note 39 of 'The Recluse of Bayswater'. Hawthorne's novel *The Scarlet Letter* (1850) and story 'Young Goodman Brown' (1835) engage extensively with witchcraft and the supernatural.

Jennings.[19] The "Black Mass," which M. Huysmans exploited to such a purpose in "Là Bas" is a degenerate, *décadent* descendant of the medieval Sabbath, and is really only a revival of the blasphemous fooleries that went on in France about the time of the Revolution, when great persons assembled to adore a toad, which had received "All the Sacraments of the Church."[20] Indeed, there seems to be a constant Satanic tradition in France; in the middle ages one finds Gilles de Raiz,[21] and about ten years ago a clever writer described an appearance of Satan in Paris with extraordinary effectiveness, and this, be it remarked, was long before Léo Taxil had invented Diana Vaughan, and the diabolic rites of an inner Masonry.[22] Those who know anything of occultism will be aware that we have scarcely touched the fringes of the subject; we have said nothing of the Kabbala, nothing of the Evil Eye, perhaps the most widespread, ancient, and persistent of all beliefs, nothing of the malefic images, such as "Sister Helen" made in Rossetti's ballad, which are being made in our Somersetshire at the present time by village women who love and hate.[23] And all these beliefs and many others have left deep marks on our literature, and perhaps on our hearts also.

So far our subject has been chiefly the "expository" literature of the secret sciences, we have noted some few of the forms which occultism has assumed,

---

[19] Arising at the start of the seventeenth century in Germany, Rosicrucianism was a secret order claiming historical roots to ancient mysteries associated with hermeticism, Christianity, and the ancient Jewish belief system of the Kabbalah (also spelt Kabbala and Cabala). Waite's *Real History of the Rosicrucians* (1887) was published by George Redway while Machen was in the latter's employ. The 'problem' Machen refers to is the lack of proof of Rosicrucianism's ancient roots. Unlike Hargrave Jennings (1817–1890), a British Freemason and occult scholar who believed that Rosicrucianism arose from ancient mysteries, Waite and Machen were sceptical.

[20] Huysmans's *Là Bas* (1891, *The Damned*) depicts a man who explores contemporary Parisian Satanism, culminating in a Black Mass, commonly held during a Witches' Sabbath. The revolution referred to is the French Revolution (1789–1799). The seven sacraments of the Roman Catholic Church are baptism, confirmation, the Eucharist, penance, the anointment of the sick, Holy Orders, and matrimony.

[21] A baron and knight, Gilles de Raiz (*c.* 1404–1440; usually spelt Rais) is believed to have been interested in the occult, and spent much of his wealth on a self-authored theatrical spectacle. He was found guilty of the murder of multiple children (potentially hundreds) and hanged.

[22] Leo Taxil (1854–1907) was a French writer first known for anti-Catholic works such as *Les Pornographes sacrés* (1882) and *Les Maîtresses du Pape* (1884). He converted to Roman Catholicism in 1885 and, in the 1890s, falsely claimed that some writings he published had been written by a woman named Diana Vaughan who wished to confess her involvement in a Satanic cult associated with Freemasonry. Waite debunked Taxil's claims in *Devil Worship in France* (1896), and in 1897 Taxil admitted he had not actually converted.

[23] Various cultures recognize the concept of the Evil Eye, where a particularly malicious look can cast a curse upon its recipient. Dante Gabriel Rossetti's poem 'Sister Helen' (*c.* 1852; rev. 1861, 1880), set in Ireland, depicts the use of a witchcraft effigy to kill someone. A likely influence was the translation by Wilde's mother, Lady Jane Wilde (1821–1896), of Johannes Wilhelm Meinhold's (1797–1851) tale *Sidonia the Sorceress* (1848).

and have mentioned one or two of the leading books and leading cases. The imaginative literature inspired by or dealing with the mysteries is a far smaller field for criticism. Passing by the "Golden Ass" and all the mass of legends and songs that the middle ages have given us, doing reverence to King Arthur as we read that "here in this world he changed his life,"[24] leaving the strange Hermetic Poems of Sir George Ripley, and that mystical romance the "Chymical Marriage of Christian Rosycross," we may glance at the fiction of the present century and see how it has been influenced by the occult idea.[25] Sir Walter Scott dabbled slightly in the subject, as he dabbled in most antique and curious things, but occultism to him was merely a "property" with which he decked some of his pages, as he chose to deck his hall at Abbotsford with helmets and broadswords.[26] "Mervyn Clitheroe," by Harrison Ainsworth, and the "Lancashire Witches," by the same writer, are books to make boys quake of dark nights when they pass the black end of the lane, but Bulwer Lytton's "Strange Story" strikes a genuine and original note of terror, and few will forget the appearance of the *Scin Læca*, the Luminous Shadow of Icelandic belief.[27] And perhaps the "Haunters and the Haunted" comes still nearer to perfection, with its theory of the malignant dead, of the instruments by which they work. Hawthorne and Poe, so utterly unlike in most things, were at one in their love of haunting, but while Hawthorne suggested the presence of the infernal army camped all about us and around us, Poe found his terror and awe in the mortal human body, in his theory of a living death. He wrote the story of the corporeal frame that rots in death, and thinks while it decays. Those who have read Mrs. Oliphant's "Wizard's Son" have seen a splendid theme spoilt by weak and diffuse execution, but her "Beleaguered City" may stand with Mr. Kipling's very different "Mark of the Beast," that is among the little masterpieces of

---

[24] The quotation is from *Le Morte d'Arthur* (printed in 1485), written or compiled by Thomas Malory (c. 1416–1471) who, until the 1890s, was believed to be Welsh, like Machen. The work was popular among Pre-Raphaelites and Decadents. Beardsley's first published works, produced in 1893–1894, were illustrations for the text.

[25] The romance that Machen mentions is a Rosicrucian work, also known as (among other titles) the *Hermetick Romance, or the Chymical Wedding* (1616).

[26] Scott named the home and lands in which he lived from 1812 until his death Abbotsford. He published a series of essays entitled *Letters on Demonology and Witchcraft* (1830).

[27] William Harrison Ainsworth's (1805–1882) works include *The Life and Adventures of Mervyn Clitheroe* (1858) and his most successful novel, *The Lancashire Witches* (1848). Edward Bulwer Lytton's (1803–1873) occult-related works include *A Strange Story* (1861), *Zanoni* (1842), and *The Last Days of Pompeii* (1834), a study of the fall of a Decadent society, as well as the story 'The Haunted and the Haunters: or The House and the Brain' (1859). In *A Strange Story*, the Old English term *Scin-Læca* is translated as 'the shining corpse'. In witchcraft, it refers to a phantom, an astral body, or a glowing body (possibly associated with the dead) that can serve as a medium for supernatural engagement. Various Theosophists, Rosicrucians, and others claimed Bulwer Lytton as an influence. Upon its founding in 1867, the English Rosicrucian Society declared the author its Grand Patron, without his consent.

occult fiction.[28] In the one case spiritual awe, in the other panic terror, and the hint of awful possibilities are developed with the extremest skill, and after such successes as these it would be painful to contemplate the sorry imitation, the lath and plaster mysteries of "Mr. Isaacs," a book which recalls Madame Blavatsky and her sliding panels.[29] At the outset we barred all discussion of "Theosophy," so it will only be necessary to say that Mr. A. P. Sinnett once wrote two novels, which may be Theosophic, but are certainly not literature. "Jekyll and Hyde" remains to some of us Stevenson's most perfect work, and it may be that a too obvious undercurrent of allegory is its only flaw. But those who revel in the creations of a bizarre and powerful imagination will find no books in modern English literature to surpass Mr. M. P. Shiel's "Prince Zaleski" and "Shapes in the Fire," stories which tell of a wilder wonderland than Poe dreamed of in his most fantastic moments.[30] And "Pierrot," by Mr. De Vere Stacpoole, stands alone also, perfect in its pure and singular invention.[31] And we must say at the end as at the beginning that perhaps the true occultism is to be found in the books of those that never consciously designed to write of hidden things, that the "melodies unheard" are the mightiest incantations, that the "magic casements" open on the very vision of the world unseen.[32]

'The Literature of Occultism', *Literature: An International Gazette of Criticism*, New Series: 2 (17 January 1899), pp. 34–36.

---

[28] *The Wizard's Son* (1882) and *A Beleaguered City* (1880) are supernatural novels by the Scottish author Margaret Oliphant (1828–1897). English author Rudyard Kipling's (1865–1936) short story 'The Mark of the Beast' (1890) engages with issues of colonial abuse and disrespect of others' spiritualities.

[29] Francis Marion Crawford's (1854–1909) *Mr. Isaacs: A Tale of Modern India* (1882) addresses Theosophy and includes references to Helena Blavatsky, Henry Steel Olcott, and A. P. Sinnett (1840–1921).

[30] M. P. Shiel (1865–1947), a British author of West Indian descent, is best known for his horror and supernatural fiction. Shiel's *Prince Zaleski* (1895) and *Shapes in the Fire* (1896) were published by Machen's publisher John Lane. Both of Shiel's novels combine Decadence and horror, the former depicting a Decadent Russian detective living in exile in Wales.

[31] The Irish author Henry De Vere Stacpoole (1863–1951) was also a translator of poetry by Sappho and François Villon. *Pierrot* (1896) appeared in the short-lived Pierrot's Library series put out by John Lane. It combines an Aestheticist style with a story about a cross-dressing woman and a youth trapped in a haunted castle.

[32] In 'Ode on a Grecian Urn' (1820), Keats writes, 'Heard melodies are sweet, but those unheard / are sweeter'.

12

Excerpts from *Hieroglyphics: A Note upon Ecstasy in Literature* (1902)

*

If ecstasy be present, then I say there is fine literature, if it be absent, then, in spite of all the cleverness, all the talents, all the workmanship and observation and dexterity you may show me, then, I think, we have a product (possibly a very interesting one), which is not fine literature.

Of course you will allow me to contradict myself, or rather, to amplify myself before we begin to discuss the matter fully. I said my answer was the word, ecstasy; I still say so, but I may remark that I have chosen this word as the representative of many. Substitute, if you like, rapture, beauty, adoration, wonder, awe, mystery, sense of the unknown, desire for the unknown. All and each will convey what I mean; for some particular case one term may be more appropriate than another, but in every case there will be that withdrawal from the common life and the common consciousness which justifies my choice of "ecstasy" as the best symbol of my meaning. I claim, then, that here we have the touchstone which will infallibly separate the higher from the lower in literature, which will range the innumerable multitude of books in two great divisions, which can be applied with equal justice to a Greek drama, an eighteenth century novelist, and a modern poet, to an epic in twelve books, and to a lyric in twelve lines. I will convince you of my belief in my own nostrum by a bold experiment:[1] here is *Pickwick* and here is *Vanity Fair*; the one regarded as a popular "comic" book, the other as a serious masterpiece, showing vast insight into human character; and applying my test, I set *Pickwick* beside the Odyssey, and *Vanity Fair* on top of the political pamphlet.[2]

---

[1] A nostrum is a quirky plan or theory.
[2] *The Pickwick Papers* (1836–1837) and *Vanity Fair* (1847–1848) are novels by Dickens and Thackeray respectively.

*

What *is* a good style?[3] If you mean by a "good" style, one that delivers the author's meaning in the clearest possible manner, if its purpose and effect are obviously utilitarian, if it be designed solely with the view of imparting knowledge — the knowledge of what the author intends — then I must point out that "style" in this sense is or should be amongst the accomplishments of every commercial clerk — indeed, it will be merely a synonym for plain speaking and plain writing — and in this sense it is evidently not one of the marks of art, since the object of art is not information, but a peculiar kind of æsthetic delight. But if on the other hand style is to mean such a use and choice of words and phrases and cadences that the ear and the soul through the ear receive an impression of subtle but most beautiful music, if the sense and sound and colour of the words affect us with an almost inexplicable delight, then I say that while Idea is the soul, style is the glorified body of the very highest literary art. Style, in short, is the last perfection of the very best in literature, it is the outward sign of the burning grace within. But we must keep the systematic consideration of style for some other night; it's not a subject to be dealt with by the way, and I have only said so much because it was necessary to draw the line between language as a means of imparting facts (good style in the sense of our opponents) and language as an æsthetic instrument, which is a good, or rather a beautiful style in our sense. In the latter sense it is the form of fine literature, in the former sense it is the medium of all else that is expressed in words, from a bill of exchange upwards.

It seems to me, then, that we have considered one by one the alternative tests of fine literature which have been or may be proposed, and we have come to the conclusion that each and all are impossible. It is no longer permissible, I imagine, for you or for me to say: "This book is fine literature because it makes me cry, because it was so interesting that I couldn't put it down, because it is so natural and faithful to life, because it is so well (plainly and neatly) written." We have picked these reasons to pieces one by one, and the result is that we are driven back on my "word of the enigma" — Ecstasy; the infallible instrument, as I think, by which fine literature may be discerned from reading-matter, by which art may be known from artifice, and style from intelligent expression. At

---

[3]   This segment of *Hieroglyphics* brings to mind Pater's essay 'Style' (1888), in which he compares authors' works (including Thackeray's) in an effort to articulate what makes great as opposed to good literature. As Machen himself does here, Pater also addresses the ideal art of music: 'If music be the ideal of all art whatever, precisely because in music it is impossible to distinguish the form from the substance of matter, the subject from the expression, then, literature, by finding its specific excellence in the absolute correspondence of the term to its import, will be but fulfilling the condition of all artistic quality in things everywhere, of all good art. // Good art, but not necessarily great art' (*Appreciations* (London: Macmillan, 1889), p. 35).

any rate we have got our hypothesis, and you remember what stress Coleridge laid on the necessity of forming some hypothesis before entering on any investigation.

I believe we began to-night with the evening paper, and the strange glimpse it gives us, through a pinky-green veil, through a cloud of laborious nonsense about odds and winners and tips and all such foolery, into that ancient eternal desire of man for the unknown. And that, you remember, was one of the synonyms that I offered you for ecstasy; and so in a sense I expect that we shall have the evening paper close beside us all the way of our long voyage in quest of the lost Atlantis.

*

Well, I remember saying one night that you were here that ecstasy is at once the most exquisite of emotions and a whole philosophy of life. And it is to the philosophy of life that we are brought, in the last resort. You know that there are, speaking very generally, two solutions of existence; one is the materialistic or rationalistic, the other, the spiritual or mystic. If the former were true, then Keats would be a queer kind of madman, and the "Morte d'Arthur" would be an elaborate symptom of insanity;[4] if the latter is true, then "Pride and Prejudice" is not fine literature, and the works of George Eliot are the works of a superior insect — and nothing more.[5] You must make your choice: is the story of the Graal lunacy, or not?[6] You think it is not: then do not talk any more of turning glass into diamonds by careful polishing and cutting. Do not say: Mr A. spends five years over a book, and therefore what he writes is fine literature; Miss B. polishes off five novels in a year, and therefore she does not write fine literature. Do not say, Mr Shorthouse has got the name of a man who kept a private school in the time of Charles I quite right; therefore "John Inglesant" is fine literature, while the archæological details in "Ivanhoe" are all wrong, therefore it is not fine literature.[7] Good Lord! You might as well say: but my landlady's name is Mrs Stickings, and the girl (who left last month) was really called Mabel; *therefore* that story of mine was fine literature. What's that about sustained effort? Can you turn a deal ladder into a golden staircase by making it of a thousand rungs? What I say three times is right, eh? and if I tell the tale

---

[4]   Machen is referring to *Le Morte d'Arthur*, written or compiled by Malory.

[5]   *Pride and Prejudice* (1813) is a gently satirical novel of manners by Jane Austen. Eliot was and continues to be a highly respected novelist, and one of the few female authors with whose work Machen engages.

[6]   On the Graal, see *The Hill of Dreams*, note 73.

[7]   Joseph Henry Shorthouses's (1834–1903) historical romance *John Inglesant* (1881) is set during the English civil wars (1642–1646, 1648). Scott's historical romance *Ivanhoe* (1820) is set in England during the twelfth century.

of Mrs Stickings so that it extends to "our minimum length for three volume novels," it becomes fine literature.

Well, I really hope that we have at last settled the matter; that fine literature is simply the expression of the eternal things that are in man, that it is beauty clothed in words, that it is always ecstasy, that it always draws itself away, and goes apart into lonely places, far from the common course of life. Realise this, and you will never be misled into pronouncing mere reading-matter, however interesting, to be fine literature; and now that we clearly understand the difference between the two, I propose that we drop the "fine" and speak simply of literature.

But I assure you that, even after having established the grand distinction, it is by no means plain sailing. Everything terrestrial is so composite (except, perhaps, pure music) that one is confronted by an almost endless task of distinguishing matter from form, and body from spirit. Literature, we say, is ecstasy, but a book must be written about something and about somebody; it must be expressed in words, it must have arrangement and artifice, it must have accident as well as essence. Consider "Don Quixote" as an example; it is, I suppose, the finest prose romance in existence.[8] Essentially, it expresses the eternal quest of the unknown, that longing, peculiar to man, which makes him reach out towards infinity; and he lifts up his eyes, and he strains his eyes, looking across the ocean, for certain fabled, happy islands, for Avalon that is beyond the setting of the sun. And he comes into life from the unknown world, from glorious places, and all his days he journeys through the world, spying about him, going on and ever on, expecting beyond every hill to find the holy city, seeing signs, and omens, and tokens by the way, reminded every hour of his everlasting citizenship. "From the great deep to the great deep he goes".[9] it is true of King Arthur and of each one of us; and this, I take it, is the essence of "Don Quixote," and of all his forerunners and successors. Then, in the second place, you get the eternal moral of the book, and you will understand that I am not using "moral" in the vulgar sense. The eternal moral, then, of "Don Quixote" is the strife between temporal and eternal, between the soul and the body, between things spiritual and things corporal, between ecstasy and the common life. You read the book and you see that there is a perpetual jar, you are continually confronted by the great antinomy of life. It seems a mere comic incident when the knight dreaming of enchantment is knocked about, and made ridiculous; but I tell you it is the perpetual tragedy of life itself, symbolised. I say that it is, under a figure, the picture of humanity in the world, that you will find the truth it represents repeated again and again throughout all history. You

---

8   The reference is to Cervantes's *Don Quixote* (1605 and 1615).
9   From 'The Coming of Arthur' in Tennyson's *Idylls of the King*. The earliest literary mention of Arthur is in the Welsh poem *Gododdin* (c. 600 CE).

know that if one goes back resolutely to the first principles of things, one finds oneself, as it were, in a place where all lines that seemed parallel and eternally divided meet, and so it is with this tragedy symbolised by the Don Quixote. It is, you may say, the tragedy of the Unknown and the Known, of the Soul and Body, of the Idea and the Fact, of Ecstasy and Common Life; at last, I suppose, of Good and Evil. The source of it lies far beyond our understanding, but its symbol is shown again and again in Cervantes's page.

*

And then, there are other elements which must be accounted for if one is to judge a book as a whole, fairly and thoroughly. I may be so charmed with the writer's rapture, with the wonder and beauty of his idea, that I may forget the fact that the artist must also be the artificer; that while the soul conceives, the understanding must formulate the conception, that while ecstasy must suggest the conduct of the story, common-sense must help to range each circumstance in order, that while an inward, mysterious delight must dictate the burning phrases and sound in the music and melody of the words, cool judgment must go through every line, reminding the author that, if literature be the language of the Shadowy Companion it must yet be translated out of the unknown speech into the vulgar tongue.[10] Here then we have the elements of a book. Firstly the Idea or Conception, the thing of exquisite beauty which dwells in the author's soul, not yet clothed in words, nor even in thought, but a pure emotion. Secondly, when this emotion has taken definite form, is made incarnate as it were, in the shape of a story, which can be roughly jotted down on paper, we may speak of the Plot. Thirdly, the plot has to be systematised, to be drawn to scale, to be carried out to its legitimate conclusions, to be displayed by means of Incident; and here we have Construction. Fourthly, the story is to be written down, and Style is the invention of beautiful words which shall affect the reader by their meaning, by their sound, by their mysterious suggestion.

This, then, is the fourfold work of literature, and if you want to be perfect you must be perfect in each part. Art must inspire and shape each and all, but only the first, the Idea, is pure art; with Plot, and Construction, and Style there is an alloy of artifice. If then any given book can be shown to proceed from an Idea, it is to be placed in the class of literature, in the shelf of the "Odyssey" as I think I once expressed it. It may be placed very high in the class; the more it have of rapture in its every part, the higher it will be: or, it may be placed very low, because, for example, having once admired the Conception, the dream that came to the author from the other world, we are forced to admit that the

---

[10] Earlier in *Hieroglyphics*, Machen describes the 'Shadowy Companion' as an other-consciousness and a spiritual being.

Story or Plot was feebly imagined, that the Construction was clumsily carried out, that the Style is, æsthetically, non-existent. You will notice that I am never afraid of blaming my favourites, of finding fault with the books which I most adore. I can do so freely and without fear of consequences, since having once applied my test, and having found that "Pickwick," for example, is literature, I am not in the least afraid that I shall be compelled to eat my words if flaws in plot and style and construction are afterwards made apparent. The statue is gold; we have settled that much, and we need not fear that it will turn into lead, if we find that the graving and carving is poor enough. Once be sure that your temple *is* a temple, and I will warrant you against it being suddenly transmuted into a tub, through the discovery of scamped workmanship.

Well, suppose we begin to apply our analysis. Let us take the strange case of Mr R. L. Stevenson, and especially his "Jekyll and Hyde," which, in some ways, is his most characteristic and most effective book. Now I suppose that instructed opinion (granting its existence) was about equally divided as to the class in which this most skilful and striking story was to be placed. Many, I have no doubt, gave it a very high place in the ranks of imaginative literature, or (as we should now say) in the ranks of literature; while many other judges set it down as an extremely clever piece of sensationalism, and nothing more. Well, I think both these opinions are wrong; and I should be inclined to say that "Jekyll and Hyde" just scrapes by the skin of its teeth, as it were, into the shelves of literature, and no more. On the surface it would seem to be merely sensationalism; I expect that when you read it, you did so with breathless absorption, hurrying over the pages in your eagerness to find out the secret, and this secret once discovered, I imagine that "Jekyll and Hyde" retired to your shelf — and stays there, rather dusty. You have never opened it again? Exactly. I *have* read it for a second time, and I was astonished to find how it had, if I may say so, evaporated. At the first reading one was enthralled by mere curiosity, but when once this curiosity had been satisfied what remained? If I may speak from my own experience, simply a rather languid admiration of the ingenuity of the plot with its construction, combined with a slight feeling of impatience, such as one might experience if one were asked to solve a puzzle for the second time. You see that the secret once disclosed, all the steps which lead to the disclosure become, *ipso facto*, insignificant, or rather they become nothing at all, since their only significance and their only existence lay in the secret, and when the secret has ceased to be a secret, the signs and cyphers of it fall also into the world of nonentity. You may be amazed, and perplexed, and entranced by a cryptogram, while you are solving it, but the solution once attained, your cryptogram is either nothing or perilously near to nothingness.

Well, all this points, doesn't it, towards mere sensationalism, very cleverly done? But, as I said, I think "Jekyll and Hyde" just scrapes over the border-line and takes its place, very low down, among books that are literature. And

I base my verdict solely on the Idea, on the Conception that lies, buried rather deeply, beneath the Plot. The plot, in itself, strikes me as mechanical — this actual physical transformation, produced by a drug, linked certainly with a theory of ethical change, but not linked at all with the really mysterious, the really psychical — all this affects me, I say, as ingenious mechanism and nothing more; while I have shown how the construction is ingenious artifice, and the style is affected by the same plague of laboured ingenuity. Throughout it is a thoroughly conscious style, and in literature all the highest things are unconsciously, or at least, subconsciously produced. It has music, but it has no under-music, and there are no phrases in it that seem veils of dreams, echoes of the "inexpressive song." It is on the conception, then, alone, that I justify my inclusion of "Jekyll" amongst works of art; for it seems to me that, lurking behind the plot, we divine the presence of an Idea, of an inspiration. "Man is not truly one, but truly two," or, perhaps, a polity with many inhabitants, Dr Jekyll writes in his confession, and I think that I see here a trace that Mr Stevenson had received a vision of the mystery of human nature, compounded of the dust and of the stars, of a dim vast city, splendid and ruinous as drowned Atlantis deep beneath the waves, of a haunted quire where a flickering light burns before the Veil.[11] This, I believe, was the vision that came to the artist, but the admirable artificer seized hold of it at once and made it all his own, omitting what he did not understand, translating roughly from the unknown tongue, materialising, coarsening, hardening. Don't you see how thoroughly *physical* the actual plot is, and if one escapes for a moment from the atmosphere of the laboratory it is only to be confronted by the most obvious vein of moral allegory; and from this latter light, "Jekyll and Hyde" seems almost the vivid metaphor of a clever preacher. You mustn't imagine, you know, that I condemn the powder business as bad in itself, for (let us revert for a moment to philosophy) man is a sacrament, soul manifested under the form of body, and art has to deal with each and both and to show their interaction and interdependence. The most perfect form of literature is, no doubt, lyrical poetry which is, one might say, almost pure Idea, art with scarcely an alloy of artifice, expressed in magic words, in the voice of music. In a word, a perfect lyric, such as Keats's "Belle Dame Sans Mercy" is *almost* pure soul, a spirit with the luminous body of melody. But (in our age, at all events) a prose romance must put on a grosser and more material envelope than this, it must have incident, corporeity, relation to material things, and all these will occupy a considerable part of the whole. To a certain extent, then, the Idea must be materialised, but still it must always shine through the fleshly vestment; the body must never be mere body but always the body of the spirit, existing to conceal and yet to manifest the spirit; and here it seems to me that Mr Stevenson's story breaks down. The transformation of Jekyll into Hyde

---

[11] With the word 'quire' (also spelt 'choir'), Machen likely has in mind the area of a church in which priests perform religious services.

is solely material, as you read it, without artistic significance; it is simply an astounding incident, and not an outward sign of an inward mystery. As for the possible allegory I have too much respect for Mr Stevenson as an artificer to think that he would regard this element as anything but a very grave defect. Allegory, as Poe so well observed, is always a literary vice, and we are only able to enjoy the "Pilgrim's Progress" by forgetting that the allegory exists.[12] Yes, that seems to me the *vitium* of "Jekyll and Hyde":[13] the conception has been badly realised, and by badly I do not mean clumsily, because from the logical, literal standpoint, the plot and the construction are marvels of cleverness; but I mean inartistically: ecstasy, which as we have settled is the synonym of art, gave birth to the idea, but immediately abandoned it to artifice, and to artifice only, instead of presiding over and inspiring every further step in plot, in construction, and in style.

*

Do you remember the books that you read when you were a boy? I can think of stories that I read long ago (I have forgotten the very names of them) that filled me with emotions that I recognised, afterwards, as purely artistic. The sorriest pirate, the most wretchedly concealed treasure, poor Captain Mayne Reid at his boldest gave me then the sensations that I now search for in the "Odyssey" or in the thought of it;[14] and I looked into some of these shabby old tales years afterwards, and wondered how on earth I had managed to penetrate into "faëry lands forlorn" through such miserable stucco portals.[15] And you, you say, extracted somehow or other, from Harrison Ainsworth's "Lancashire Witches," that essence of the unknown that you now find in Poe, and I expect that everybody who loves literature could gather similar recollections.[16]

Well, it would be easy enough to solve the problem by saying that the emotions of children are of no consequence and don't count, but then I don't think that proposition is true. I think, on the contrary, that children, especially young children before they have been defiled by the horrors of "education," possess the artistic emotion in remarkable purity, that they reproduce, in a measure, the primitive man before he was defiled, artistically, by the horrors of civilisation. The ecstasy of the artist is but a recollection, a remnant from

---

[12] *The Pilgrim's Progress* (Part 1: 1678; Part 2: 1684) is a Christian allegory by John Bunyan.
[13] *vitium* (Latin): defect.
[14] Irish-American author Thomas Mayne Reid (1818–1883) wrote popular adventure novels, such as *The Rifle Rangers* (1850) and *The Scalp Hunters* (1860).
[15] The phrases 'faery lands forlorn' (with no umlaut) and 'magic casements' below appear in Keats's 'Ode to a Nightingale' (1820).
[16] Ainsworth's *The Lancashire Witches* (1848) recounts the story of the people convicted of and executed for witchcraft in Lancashire, England, in 1612.

the childish vision, and the child undoubtedly looks at the world through "magic casements." But you see all this is unconscious, or subconscious (to a less degree it is so in later life, and artists are rare simply because it is their almost impossible task to translate the emotion of the sub-consciousness into the speech of consciousness), and as you may sometimes see children uttering their conceptions in words that are nonsense, or next door to it, so nonsense or at any rate very poor stuff suffices with them to summon up the vision from the depths of the soul. Suppose we could catch a genius at the age of nine or ten and request him to utter what he felt; the boy would speak or write rubbish, and in the same way you would find that he read rubbish, and that it excited in him an ineffable joy and ecstasy. Coleridge was a Bluecoat boy when he read the "poems" of William Lisle Bowles, and admired them to enthusiasm, and I am quite sure that at some early period Poe had been enraptured by Mrs Radcliffe, and we know how Burns founded himself on Fergusson.[17] When men are young, the inward ecstasy, the "red powder of projection" is of such efficacy and virtue that the grossest and vilest matter is transmuted for them into pure gold, glistering and glorious as the sun.[18] The child (and with him you may link all primitive and childlike people) approaches books and pictures just as he approaches nature itself and life; and a wonderful vision appears where many of us can only see the common and insignificant.

Excerpts from *Hieroglyphics: A Note upon Ecstasy in Literature* (London: Grant Richards, 1902), pp. 11–12, 38–41, 71–75, 77–85, and 94–97.

---

[17] Some schools attired their pupils in long blue coats. William Lisle Bowles (1762–1850) was an English poet, priest, and literary critic; Coleridge admired his *Fourteen Sonnets* (1789), but the scare quotes around 'poems' imply Machen did not share the same regard. English writer Ann Radcliffe (1764–1832) wrote popular Gothic novels, such as *The Mysteries of Udolpho* (1794). Influential poet Robert Burns (1759–1796) acknowledged the inspiration of fellow Scottish poet Robert Fergusson's (1750–1774) *Poems* (1773).

[18] In alchemy, red powder refers to the gold transformed from lead, but also to the spiritual reality beyond our own everyday existence. Thomas Vaughan refers to the philosophers mixing ingredients to make a 'bloudie [i.e. bloody] powder', 'shining like the Sun' (*Lumen de Lumine* (London: H. Blunden, 1651), pp. 95, 94).

13

Introduction to
The Angels of Mons: The Bowmen
and Other Legends of the War (1915)

I have been asked to write an introduction to the story of "The Bowmen," on its publication in book form together with three other tales of similar fashion. And I hesitate. This affair of "The Bowmen" has been such an odd one from first to last, so many queer complications have entered into it, there have been so many and so divers currents and cross-currents of rumour and speculation concerning it, that I honestly do not know where to begin. I propose, then, to solve the difficulty by apologising for beginning at all.

For, usually and fitly, the presence of an introduction is held to imply that there is something of consequence and importance to be introduced. If, for example, a man has made an anthology of great poetry, he may well write an introduction justifying his principle of selection, pointing out here and there, as the spirit moves him, high beauties and supreme excellencies, discoursing of the magnates and lords and princes of literature, whom he is merely serving as groom of the chamber. Introductions, that is, belong to the masterpieces and classics of the world, to the great and ancient and accepted things; and I am here introducing a short, small story of my own which appeared in THE EVENING NEWS about ten months ago.[1]

I appreciate the absurdity, nay, the enormity of the position in all its grossness. And my excuse for these pages must be this: that though the story itself is nothing, it has yet had such odd and unforeseen consequences and adventures that the tale of them may possess some interest. And then, again, there are certain psychological morals to be drawn from the whole matter of the tale and its sequel of rumours and discussions that are not, I think, devoid of consequence; and so to begin at the beginning.

---

[1] From 1910 to 1921, Machen worked as a writer for the *Evening News*, a newspaper published from 1881 to 1980, with a brief reappearance in 1987.

This was in last August; to be more precise, on the last Sunday of last August. There were terrible things to be read on that hot Sunday morning between meat and mass. It was in *THE WEEKLY DISPATCH* that I saw the awful account of the retreat from Mons.[2] I no longer recollect the details; but I have not forgotten the impression that was then made on my mind. I seemed to see a furnace of torment and death and agony and terror seven times heated, and in the midst of the burning was the British Army. In the midst of the flame, consumed by it and yet aureoled in it, scattered like ashes and yet triumphant, martyred and for ever glorious. So I saw our men with a shining about them, so I took these thoughts with me to church, and, I am sorry to say, was making up a story in my head while the deacon was singing the Gospel.

This was not the tale of "The Bowmen." It was the first sketch, as it were, of "The Soldiers' Rest," which is reprinted in this volume.[3] I only wish I had been able to write it as I conceived it. The tale as it stands is, I think, a far better piece of craft than "The Bowmen," but the tale that came to me as the blue incense floated above the Gospel Book on the desk between the tapers: that indeed was a noble story — like all the stories that never get written.[4] I conceived the dead men coming up through the flames and in the flames, and being welcomed in the Eternal Tavern with songs and flowing cups and everlasting mirth. But every man is the child of his age, however much he may hate it; and our popular religion has long determined that jollity is wicked. As far as I can make out modern Protestantism believes that Heaven is something like Evensong in an English cathedral, the service by Stainer and the Dean preaching.[5] For those opposed to dogma of any kind — even the mildest — I suppose it is held that a Course of Ethical Lectures will be arranged.

Well, I have long maintained that on the whole the average church, considered as a house of preaching, is a much more poisonous place than the average tavern; still, as I say, one's age masters one, and clouds and bewilders the intelligence, and the real story of "The Soldiers' Rest," with its "sonus epulantium in æterno convivio," was ruined at the moment of its birth, and it was some time later that

---

[2]   The *Weekly Dispatch* was a Sunday newspaper published from 1801 to 1961, known as the *Sunday Dispatch* from 1928 onward. A city in Belgium, Mons was the site of the first major engagement — 23 August 1914 — of the British Expeditionary Force (BEF) against the German army during the First World War (1914–1918). Vastly outnumbered, the BEF undertook a two-week retreat to south of the river Marne, during which many lives were lost to the pursuing Germans.

[3]   A short story by Machen published in 1915.

[4]   The Gospel Book is a book containing the life and teachings of Jesus Christ as presented in the first four books of the New Testament.

[5]   Evensong is an Anglican form of evening worship, usually involving singing. Sir John Stainer (1840–1901) was an English organist and composer who wrote oratorios, cantatas, anthems, hymns, and services that became fixtures of Anglican worship. A dean is a senior leader in an Anglican cathedral.

the actual story, as here printed, got written.[6] And in the meantime the plot of
"The Bowmen" occurred to me. Now it has been murmured and hinted and
suggested and whispered in all sorts of quarters that before I wrote the tale I had
heard something. The most decorative of these legends is also the most precise:
"I know for a fact that the whole thing was given him in typescript by a lady-in-
waiting."[7] This was not the case; and all vaguer reports to the effect that I had
heard some rumours or hints of rumours are equally void of any trace of truth.

Again I apologise for entering so pompously into the minutiæ of my bit of
a story, as if it were the lost poems of Sappho; but it appears that the subject
interests the public, and I comply with my instructions. I take it, then, that the
origins of "The Bowmen" were composite. First of all, all ages and nations have
cherished the thought that spiritual hosts may come to the help of earthly arms,
that gods and heroes and saints have descended from their high immortal places
to fight for their worshippers and clients. Then Kipling's story of the ghostly
Indian regiment got in my head and got mixed with the mediævalism that is
always there; and so "The Bowmen" was written.[8] I was heartily disappointed
with it, I remember, and thought it — as I still think it — an indifferent piece
of work. However, I have tried to write for these thirty-five long years, and if I
have not become practised in letters, I am at least a past master in the Lodge of
Disappointment. Such as it was, "The Bowmen" appeared in THE EVENING NEWS
of September 29th, 1914.

Now the journalist does not, as a rule, dwell much on the prospect of fame;
and if he be an evening journalist, his anticipations of immortality are bounded
by twelve o'clock at night at the latest; and it may well be that those insects
which begin to live in the morning and are dead by sunset deem themselves
immortal. Having written my story, having groaned and growled over it and
printed it, I certainly never thought to hear another word of it. My colleague
"The Londoner" praised it warmly to my face, as his kindly fashion is;[9] entering,
very properly, a technical caveat as to the language of the battle-cries of the
bowmen. "Why should English archers use French terms?" he said. I replied
that the only reason was this — that a "Monseigneur" here and there struck me
as picturesque; and I reminded him that, as a matter of cold historical fact, most
of the archers of Agincourt were mercenaries from Gwent, my native country,

---

[6]   The Latin phrase translates as 'the sound of feasting at an eternal banquet'. Machen's
image of the afterlife as a place of eternal feasting is reminiscent of the pagan Norse belief
in Valhalla, a hall attended by the souls of warriors slain in battle.
[7]   A lady-in-waiting is a woman, usually aristocratic, who has been appointed to serve a
queen or princess.
[8]   Most likely this is a reference to Kipling's short story 'The Lost Legion' (1892). Set in
Afghanistan, the tale is notable for the spectral presence of an entire regiment of Indian
soldiers (now ghosts) that had rebelled against British rule in the Great Mutiny of 1857.
[9]   'The Londoner' is a person Machen uses here to differentiate the Anglocentrism of
mainstream English views regarding British history and his own Celtic foreignness.

who would appeal to Mihangel and to saints not known to the Saxon — Teilo, Iltyd, Dewi, Cadwaladyr Vendigeid.[10] And I thought that that was the first and last discussion of "The Bowmen." But in a few days from its publication the editor of *THE OCCULT REVIEW* wrote to me.[11] He wanted to know whether the story had any foundation in fact. I told him that it had no foundation in fact of any kind or sort; I forget whether I added that it had no foundation in rumour, but I should think not, since to the best of my belief there were no rumours of heavenly interposition in existence at that time. Certainly I had heard of none. Soon afterwards the editor of *LIGHT* wrote asking a like question, and I made him a like reply.[12] It seemed to me that I had stifled any "Bowmen" mythos in the hour of its birth.

A month or two later, I received several requests from editors of parish magazines to reprint the story. I — or, rather, my editor — readily gave permission; and then, after another month or two, the conductor of one of these magazines wrote to me, saying that the February issue containing the story had been sold out, while there was still a great demand for it. Would I allow them to reprint "The Bowmen" as a pamphlet, and would I write a short preface giving the exact authorities for the story? I replied that they might reprint in pamphlet form with all my heart, but that I could not give my authorities, since I had none, the tale being pure invention. The priest wrote again, suggesting — to my amazement — that I must be mistaken, that the main "facts" of "The Bowmen" must be true, that my share in the matter must surely have been confined to the elaboration and decoration of a veridical history. It seemed that my light fiction had been accepted by the congregation of this particular church as the solidest of facts; and it was then that it began to dawn on me that if I had failed in the art of letters, I had succeeded, unwittingly, in the art of deceit. This happened, I should think, some time in April, and the snowball of rumour that was then set rolling has been rolling ever since, growing bigger and bigger, till it is now swollen to a monstrous size.

It was at about this period that variants of my tale began to be told as

---

[10]   On 25 October 1415 at the village of Agincourt in northern France, King Henry V defeated a much larger French army, due in large part to his archers. Machen is listing important, semi-legendary, Welsh figures from the Dark Ages: Teilo, Iltyd (properly Illtud), and Dewi were saints. Cadwaladyr (more commonly spelled Cadwaladr) was the king of Gwent. In his article 'The Sangraal–II' (*The Academy* (24 August 1907), pp. 820–23 (p. 822)), Machen writes that 'Cadwallader', who 'loomed a more heroic figure than Arthur in the Welsh imagination', shares with the ancient Celtic hero Bràn the epithet 'Vendigeid', which he defines in English as 'Blessed' and in Latin as '*benedictus*'.

[11]   An illustrated monthly magazine (1905–1951), the *Occult Review* published articles by and about leading people involved in spiritualism and occulture during the first half of the twentieth century.

[12]   The periodical *Light* was first published by the London Spiritualist Alliance in 1881 and then, beginning in 1884, by the College of Psychic Studies. Still in operation today, *Light* focuses on the connections between the human and spirit realms.

authentic histories.[13] At first, these tales betrayed their relation to their original. In several of them the vegetarian restaurant appeared, and St. George was the chief character. In one case an officer — name and address missing — said that there was a portrait of St. George in a certain London restaurant, and that a figure, just like the portrait, appeared to him on the battlefield, and was invoked by him, with the happiest results. Another variant — this, I think, never got into print — told how dead Prussians had been found on the battlefield with arrow wounds in their bodies. This notion amused me, as I had imagined a scene, when I was thinking out the story, in which a German general was to appear before the Kaiser to explain his failure to annihilate the English.

"All-Highest," the general was to say, "it is true, it is impossible to deny it. The men were killed by arrows; the shafts were found in their bodies by the burying parties."

I rejected the idea as over-precipitous even for a mere fantasy. I was therefore entertained when I found that what I had refused as too fantastical for fantasy was accepted in certain occult circles as hard fact.

Other versions of the story appeared in which a cloud interposed between the attacking Germans and the defending British. In some examples the cloud served to conceal our men from the advancing enemy; in others, it disclosed shining shapes which frightened the horses of the pursuing German cavalry. St. George, it will he noted, has disappeared — he persisted some time longer in certain Roman Catholic variants — and there are no more bowmen, no more arrows. But so far angels are not mentioned; yet they are ready to appear, and I think that I have detected the machine which brought them into the story.

In "The Bowmen" my imagined soldier saw "a long line of shapes, with a shining about them." And Mr. A.P. Sinnett, writing in the May issue of THE OCCULT REVIEW, reporting what he had heard, states that "those who could see said they saw 'a row of shining beings' between the two armies." Now I conjecture that the word "shining" is the link between my tale and the derivative from it. In the popular view shining and benevolent supernatural beings are angels and nothing else, and must be angels, and so, I believe, the Bowmen of my story have become "the Angels of Mons." In this shape they have been received with respect and credence everywhere, or almost everywhere.

And here, I conjecture, we have the key to the large popularity of the delusion — as I think it. We have long ceased in England to take much interest in saints, and in the recent revival of the cultus of St. George, the saint is little more than a patriotic figurehead.[14] And the appeal to the saints to succour us is certainly not

---

[13]   Richard J. Bleiler reproduces a rich selection of various retellings of Machen's story in *The Strange Case of 'The Angels of Mons'* (Jefferson, NC: McFarland, 2015).

[14]   The cultus is a system of worship, sometimes used as an alternative rendering of the noun 'cult', as Machen does here.

a common English practice; it is held Popish by most of our countrymen.[15] But angels, with certain reservations, have retained their popularity, and so, when it was settled that the English army in its dire peril was delivered by angelic aid, the way was clear for general belief, and for the enthusiasms of the religion of the man in the street. And so soon as the legend got the title "The Angels of Mons" it became impossible to avoid it. It permeated the Press: it would not be neglected; it appeared in the most unlikely quarters — in *Truth and Town Topics*, *The New Church Weekly* (Swedenborgian) and *John Bull*.[16] The editor of *The Church Times* has exercised a wise reserve: he awaits that evidence which so far is lacking; but in one issue of the paper I noted that the story furnished a text for a sermon, the subject of a letter, and the matter for an article. People send me cuttings from provincial papers containing hot controversy as to the exact nature of the appearances; the "Office Window" of *The Daily Chronicle* suggests scientific explanations of the hallucination; the *Pall Mall* in a note about St. James says he is of the brotherhood of the Bowmen of Mons — this reversion to the bowmen from the angels being possibly due to the strong statements that I have made on the matter. The pulpits both of the Church and of Non-conformity have been busy: Bishop Welldon, Dean Hensley Henson (a disbeliever), Bishop Taylor Smith (the Chaplain-General), and many other clergy have occupied themselves with the matter.[17] Dr. Horton preached about the "angels" at Manchester;[18] Sir Joseph Compton Rickett (President of the National Federation of Free Church Councils) stated that the soldiers at the front had seen visions and dreamed dreams, and had given testimony of powers and principalities fighting for them or against them.[19] Letters come from all the ends of the earth to the Editor of *The Evening News* with theories, beliefs, explanations, suggestions. It is all somewhat wonderful; one can say that the

---

[15] Popish: according to the doctrines and traditions of the Roman Catholic Church.

[16] On Emanuel Swedenborg, see note 210 of *The Hill of Dreams*.

[17] James Edward Cowell Welldon (1854–1937) was the bishop of Calcutta from 1898 to 1902 and Dean of Manchester from 1906 to 1918, among other positions. Herbert Hensley Henson (1863–1947) was an Anglican priest who served as dean of Durham Cathedral from 1913 to 1918. By calling him a 'disbeliever', Machen is likely referring to a sermon Henson delivered on 25 July 1915 at Westminster Abbey, in which he referred sceptically to the growing myth of the Mons angels (see Rene Kollar, *Searching for Raymond: Anglicanism, Spiritualism, and Bereavement between the Two World Wars* (Lanham: Lexington, 2000), p. 7). John Taylor Smith (1860–1938) was an Anglican priest who served as the bishop of Sierra Leone from 1897 to 1901 and as the chaplain-general — the senior clergyman — of the British armed forces from 1901 to 1925.

[18] Robert Forman Horton (1855–1934) was a Nonconformist divine and the first non-Anglican fellow of a college at the University of Oxford (David W. Bebbington, *The Nonconformist Conscience: Chapel and Politics — 1870–1914* (London: Routledge, 2014), p. 1).

[19] Sir Joseph Compton-Rickett (1847–1919) was an English politician (Liberal), lay preacher, and author.

whole affair is a psychological phenomenon of considerable interest, fairly comparable with the great Russian delusion of last August and September.[20]

*   *   *   *

Now it is possible that some persons, judging by the tone of these remarks of mine, may gather the impression that I am a profound disbeliever in the possibility of any intervention of the super-physical order in the affairs of the physical order. They will be mistaken if they make this inference; they will be mistaken if they suppose that I think miracles in Judæa credible but miracles in France or Flanders incredible. I hold no such absurdities. But I confess, very frankly, that I credit none of the "Angels of Mons" legends, partly because I see, or think I see, their derivation from my own idle fiction, but chiefly because I have, so far, not received one jot or tittle of evidence that should dispose me to belief. It is idle, indeed, and foolish enough for a man to say: "I am sure that story is a lie, because the supernatural element enters into it"; here, indeed, we have the maggot writhing in the midst of corrupted offal denying the existence of the sun. But if this fellow be a fool — as he is — equally foolish is he who says, "If the tale has anything of the supernatural it is true, and the less evidence the better"; and I am afraid this tends to be the attitude of many who call themselves occultists. I hope that I shall never get to that frame of mind. So I say, not that super-normal interventions are impossible, not that they have not happened during this war — I know nothing as to that point, one way or the other — but that there is not one atom of evidence (so far) to support the current stories of the angels of Mons. For, be it remarked, these stories are specific stories. They rest on the second, third, fourth, fifth hand stories told by "a soldier," by "an officer," by "a Catholic correspondent," by "a nurse," by any number of anonymous people. Indeed, names have been mentioned. A lady's name has been drawn, most unwarrantably as it appears to me, into the discussion, and I have no doubt that this lady has been subject to a good deal of pestering and annoyance. She has written to the Editor of THE EVENING NEWS denying all knowledge of the supposed miracle. The Psychical Research Society's expert confesses that no real evidence has been proffered to her Society on the matter.[21] And then, to my amazement, she accepts as fact the proposition that some men on the battlefield have been "hallucinated," and proceeds to give the theory of sensory hallucination. She forgets that, by her own showing, there is no reason to suppose that anybody has been hallucinated at all. Someone (unknown) has met a nurse (unnamed) who has talked to a soldier (anonymous) who has seen

---

[20] Machen here likely refers to the disastrously unsuccessful Russian invasion of East Prussia in August and September 1914.
[21] The Society for Psychical Research was founded in London in 1882 to carry out research into paranormal phenomena, such as sightings of ghosts and communication with the dead.

angels. But THAT is not evidence; and not even Sam Weller at his gayest would have dared to offer it as such in the Court of Common Pleas.[22] So far, then, nothing remotely approaching proof has been offered as to any supernatural intervention during the Retreat from Mons. Proof may come; if so, it will be interesting and more than interesting.

But, taking the affair as it stands at present, how is it that a nation plunged in materialism of the grossest kind has accepted idle rumours and gossip of the supernatural as certain truth? The answer is contained in the question: it is precisely because our whole atmosphere is materialist that we are ready to credit anything — save the truth. Separate a man from good drink, he will swallow methylated spirit with joy. Man is created to be inebriated; to be "nobly wild, not mad."[23] Suffer the Cocoa Prophets and their company to seduce him in body and spirit, and he will get himself stuff that will make him ignobly wild and mad indeed.[24] It took hard, practical men of affairs, business men, advanced thinkers, Freethinkers, to believe in Madame Blavatsky and Mahatmas and the famous message from the Golden Shore: 'Judge's plan is right; follow him and STICK.'[25]

And the main responsibility for this dismal state of affairs undoubtedly lies on the shoulders of the majority of the clergy of the Church of England. Christianity, as Mr. W. L. Courtney has so admirably pointed out, is a great Mystery Religion; it is THE Mystery Religion.[26] Its priests are called to an awful and tremendous hierurgy;[27] its pontiffs are to be the pathfinders, the bridge-makers between the world of sense and the world of spirit. And, in fact, they pass their time in preaching, not the eternal mysteries, but a twopenny morality, in changing the Wine of Angels and the Bread of Heaven into gingerbeer and mixed biscuits: a sorry transubstantiation, a sad alchemy, as it seems to me.

Introduction to *The Angels of Mons: The Bowmen and Other Legends of the War* (London: Simpkin, Marshall, Hamilton, Kent, 1915), pp. 5–27.

---

[22] Sam Weller is a jovial character in Dickens's *Pickwick Papers*. The Court of Common Pleas is one of England's common-law courts from the early thirteenth century until the Judicature Act of 1873, when it was merged with other courts to form the High Court of Justice.

[23] A phrase from English poet Robert Herrick's 'An Ode to Ben Jonson'.

[24] Machen is arguing that if one allows (i.e. suffers) the Cocoa Prophets to influence one's spiritual engagement, the effect will be ignoble. The precise meaning of the term 'Cocoa Prophets' is unclear, but he is using it disparagingly against spiritualists, Theosophists, and others whom he depicts as charlatans in this piece and elsewhere.

[25] Freethinkers are people who form their own — sometimes unorthodox — opinions, especially about religion. Blavatsky claimed Mahatmas, or Masters, have profound mystical insights and are capable of supernatural acts. Upon her death, William Quan Judge (1851–1896) arranged for a piece of paper to be found with a message from Blavatsky from the afterlife (what Machen calls the Golden Shore) choosing Judge as the heir to her leadership.

[26] On Courtney, see his 'Novels and Nerves', included in this edition.

[27] A hierurgy is a holy act or a rite of worship.

14

Introduction to
The Great God Pan (1916)

"The Great God Pan" was first published in December, 1894. So the book is of full age, and I am glad to take the opportunity of a new edition to recall those early 'nineties when the tale was written and published — those 'nineties of which I was not even a small part, but no part at all. For those were the days of "The Yellow Book," of "Keynotes," and the "Keynotes Series," of Aubrey Beardsley and "The Woman Who Did," of many portentous things in writing and drawing and publishing.[1] "The Great God Pan" had the good fortune to issue from The Bodley Head, which was the centre of the whole movement, and no doubt the book profited by the noise that the movement was making.[2] But this was in a sense an illegitimate profit; since the story was conceived and written in solitude, and came from far off lonely days spent in a land remote from London, and from literary societies and sodalities.[3] So far as it stands for anything, it stands, not for the ferment of the 'nineties, but for the visions that a little boy saw in the late 'sixties and early 'seventies.

*   *   *   *   *

We all know the saying, *SI JEUNESSE SAVAIT.*[4] I have respected it for some years, and it is only lately that I have begun to have very grave doubts as to the truth of the implied statement. "If only youth understood" . . . but I have a very strong suspicion that if youth did understand it would be as unprofitable and unfruitful as the most barren years of old age. I believe that youth attains, so far

---

[1]   On the influential Decadent quarterly *The Yellow Book* (1894–1897), see the introduction to this edition. Beardsley, the periodical's art director until 1896, did much to codify the visual and, to a lesser extent, literary aesthetics of *fin-de-siècle* Decadence. The Bodley Head published both Machen's *The Great God Pan* and Grant Allen's novel *The Woman Who Did* (1895).

[2]   As suggested by the artefacts that Machen mentions, he is referring particularly to the British Decadent movement that attained a cultural sense of coherence in the 1890s, although British Decadent works were produced prior to this decade.

[3]   Sodalities are fellowships or associations.

[4]   French: 'If youth knew'.

as it does attain, just because it does not understand. The logical understanding is the prison-house of Wordsworth's supreme and magistral ode;[5] it is the house of prudent artifice, of the calculations of means to the end; it is the region where things can be done by recipe, where effects are all foreseen and intended. It is the house of matter and the house of mechanism. And when youth does anything well or pretty well, it is because youth has not wholly been overcast by the shadows of the prison-walls; it is because it does not understand. Nay; it is so even with age. Cervantes understood quite clearly that he was going to write a clever burlesque of the romances of chivalry, that he was going to make people laugh with a great deal of low comedy and broad farce and funny "business";[6] he understood, too, that he was to redeem his book from the charge of sheer vulgarity by inserting here and there some real literature, in the shape of certain elegant tales of sentiment and passion. He understood all this; but he did not in the least understand that he was to do something infinitely greater than all this; and so he did it and made "Don Quixote" a high, immortal masterpiece. This was the achievement of a youth recovered, of the happy state of ignorance restored; it is the clearest example that I know of the law that youth succeeds because it does not understand.

*   *   *   *   *

Here a horrible descent has to be made; so let it be made quickly. It is necessary to come down from the high and shining and remote peaks to the homely hillocks, in other words to explain how I came to write "The Great God Pan." I found out, long years afterwards, how it was done, how my effects were produced; but I am very certain that I understood nothing about the real origins and essences of the story while I was writing it. It all came from a lonely house standing on the slope of a hill, under a great wood, above a river in the country where I was born.

*   *   *   *   *

Llanddewi Rectory where I was bred looks out over a wonderful and enchanting country. The hill on which the house stands slopes down through apple orchards to a wild brake or thicket of undergrowth and bracken; in the heart of this little wood the well bubbles over and sends a brooklet to swell the

---

[5] William Wordsworth's 'Intimations of Immortality from Recollections of Early Childhood' (1807) describes birth as 'a sleep and a forgetting', where the child is born 'trailing clouds of glory' from God, which are gradually erased from the mind by 'the prison-house' of life. Machen's related conception of the imagination is discussed in the introduction to this edition.

[6] In Cervantes's *Don Quixote*, the hero chooses and comically fails to live the idealized life of a valorous knight.

Soar brook. Beyond the brake rising ground again, where Llanddewi Church stands amidst dark yews, age-old; hills rise higher to right and left of it, those to the right deeply wooded.[7] I have often spent an afternoon gazing at the woods in summer weather, watching the sheen of the sun and the stirring of the wind on those nearest, and thinking of what Ulysses said of his dear Zacynthus "wooded, quivering with leaves."[8] Then, beyond again, another height, Llanhenoc, and the distance was closed by the vast green wall of Wentwood, a remnant, still great, of the Wood of Gwent that once covered all the land of the lower Usk and the Wye. And just visible beneath this forest was the white of a house, which they told me was called Bertholly.[9]

And for some reason, or for no reason, this house which stood on the boundaries and green walls of my young world became an object of mysterious attraction to me. It became one of the many symbols of the world of wonder that were offered to me, it became, as it were, a great word in the secret language by which the mysteries were communicated. I thought of it always with something of awe, even of dread; its appearance was significant of ... I knew not what. Thus for many years; but I suppose I may have been twelve or thirteen when I saw Bertholly near at hand. My father had taken me to see a neighbouring clergyman who lived at a place called Tredonoc, and Tredonoc goes down to the banks of the Usk. On our way there we passed through a maze of hills and valleys, through woods, by deep lanes, by paths over sunken lands; we could see no distances. But after the call on the rector had been made, we went on a little and, cresting a slight hill saw suddenly before us a dream of mystic beauty — the valley of the Usk. Still, after many years have past, after many things have been broken for ever, I remember how it overwhelmed me and possessed me, as the soul is overwhelmed and subdued by the first kiss of the Beloved.

And there, under the great green of the forest, high above the mystic, silvery esses of the river was Bertholly, more inexplicable, more wonderful, more significant, the nearer it was seen.

*   *   *   *   *

---

[7] Machen's father was the Anglican priest for the parish of Llanddewi Fach, and Machen spent his youth living in his father's rectory about five miles from Caerleon. Soar Brook, a tributary of the Usk, runs not far from the rectory.

[8] Zacynthus is an Ionian island that, in Homer's epic *The Odyssey*, is part of Ulysses's dominion.

[9] Llanhenoc (today spelt as Llanhennock) is a village two miles from Caerleon. Wentwood is a hilly, forested area in south-east Wales, a remnant of the much larger Forest of Gwent, which extended between the rivers Usk and Wye. Bertholly house is mentioned as a beautiful place to visit — both for the building and its scenic location ('a most delicious view of the fertile valley and the distant mountains') — as early as 1801 (William Coxe, *An Historical Tour in Monmouthshire*, Part 1 (London: Cadell and Davies), p. 37).

Stevenson, I think, knew of the emotions which I am trying to express.[10] To his mind the matter presented itself thus: there are certain scenes, certain hills and valleys and groves of pines which demand that a story shall be written about them. I would refine; I would say that the emotions aroused by these external things reverberating in the heart, are indeed the story; or all that signifies in the story. But, our craft being that of letters, we must express what we feel through the medium of words. And once words are granted, we fall into the region of the logical understanding, we are forced to devise incidents and circumstances and plots, to "make up a story;" we translate a hill into a tale, conceive lovers to explain a brook, turn the perfect into the imperfect. The musician must be happier in his art, if he be not the sorry slave of those sorry follies which mimic the lowing of cattle by some big brazen horn. The true musician exercises a perfect art; there is no descent into the logic of plots for him.

For me; these thoughts of Bertholly in the awe of the forest and the breath of the winding river remained through many years, as something to be expressed. And to these were joined the dream I had made to myself of Cærleon-on-Usk, the town where I was born, a very ancient place, once the home of the legions, the centre of an exiled Roman culture in the heart of Celtdom.[11] I had seen a man looking at a bright gold coin that his gardener brought him from the making of a new fruit border. It shone in the sunlight: but there were eighteen hundred years upon it. I had seen the vase of glass, iridescent, wonderful as an opal, after these long centuries of sojourn in the earth, which, as they say, uttered sweet rich odours as it came up out of its deep æonian grave.[12] I had stood, dreaming under the mouldering remnants of the Roman city wall as the sun set red over Twyn Barlwm, I had noted the leering lineaments of Faunus built as an ornament into the wall of a modern house in Cærleon.[13] In fine, there was a dream ever with me of the ancient city and the former rites that it had witnessed; with the old hills and the old woods a deep green circle about it. Such, I believe, were the fountains of my story. Of course, I leave out the centre of it all, that is the heart of the author; but that is a secret hidden from him and revealed to the reviewers, certain of whom I propose presently to quote.

      *   *   *   *   *

---

[10] Works by Robert Louis Stevenson that address the spirit of place (or *genius loci*) include the travelogue *An Inland Voyage* (1878) and the essay 'Pan's Pipes' (1881).

[11] The Celtic and Roman influences on Machen's home town of Caerleon are discussed in the introduction to this edition.

[12] Eternal grave.

[13] Twyn Barlwm is today commonly known as Twmbarlwm; this hill in south-east Wales has the remains of an Iron Age — possibly Silurian — fort on the top. On Faunus, see note 184 of *The Hill of Dreams*. Machen also reimagines this moment in *The Great God Pan*, where he depicts a boy's panicked reaction on seeing the same face in a stone wall.

Well; I found myself in the year 1890 twenty-seven years old, and in some sort of way a man of letters. Let me hasten to explain that nobody of the slightest consequence knew anything about me or my doings; I had no literary connections of any kind or sort. But I had translated Margaret of Navarre's "Heptaméron," and Beroalde de Verville's "Moyen de Parvenir," and I had written a volume of tales in the manner of the Renaissance, a volume called "The Chronicle of Clemendy."[14] Altogether, I had acquired that ill habit of writing, that queer itch which so works that the patient if he be neither writing nor thinking of something to be written is bored and dull and unhappy. So I wrote.

I began like many a better man, on "turn-overs" for "The Globe." "The Globe" paid a guinea, but I found out that the "St. James's Gazette" paid two pounds for the same number of words, so I wrote as much as I could for the "St. James's Gazette."[15] These things were at first "essays" or articles upon things in general, on books, on country sights, on summer days or snowy lanes in winter, on old songs, old proverbs — or anything that got into my head. Then I chanced to meet Oscar Wilde, and dined with him, and at dinner he told me the plot of a story written by a friend of his, which he said was "wonderful."[16] It did not seem to me so sheerly wonderful; I did not see why I should not think of a plot as good or almost as good — always reserving, of course, my first principle, which has been so choice a comfort all my literary life: that nothing that I have written, am writing, or am to write can possibly be of the faintest use or profit to myself or to anybody else. But, anyhow, I tried my hand at a slight whimsical story (it was about a famous dinner-giving baronet who turned out to be his own cook) sent it to the "St. James's," and to my joy and surprise they printed it, and so I commenced story writer. My tales were strangely enough "society" tales; strangely enough, because I know about as much of "society" as of the habits of the Great Horned Owl.[17]

How it was that I did not send the tale of "The Great God Pan" to the "St. James's Gazette" I do not know. But in this summer of 1890 there was founded

---

[14] Margaret of Navarre (Marguerite de Navarre) (1492–1549) was the queen of Navarre and author of plays, poems, and the story collection *Heptaméron* (1558) in the manner of Boccaccio's *Decameron*. The most famous work by the polymath François Béroalde de Verville (1556–c. 1629) is *Le Moyen de parvenir* (c. 1610), a rollicking collection of often ribald stories and conversations. Machen's *The Chronicle of Clemendy* (1888) is a framed set of tales written in the language and style of seventeenth-century English prose.

[15] The *Globe* (1803–1921) and *St. James's Gazette* (1880–1905) were London newspapers.

[16] Wilde is the most famous contributor to the British Decadent movement, and one of the most influential by far. When Machen and he met, Wilde was already internationally recognized as the embodiment of the movement, while Machen was not yet known.

[17] Society tales are stories about people who are fashionable, wealthy, and prominent.

a new weekly paper called "The Whirlwind."[18] It advocated Jacobite principles, and it printed tales, and so when I thought of what is now the first chapter of "The Great God Pan" I sent it to "The Whirlwind," and there it appeared. I had no notion that there would be anything to follow this first chapter; and it was many months later, sometime in January, 1891, that I set out to write one of my short "society" tales, "The City of Resurrections," which is now the third chapter in the book. I finished the story and found it would never do, the occult horror suggested in it did not consort with the "social" framework: and suddenly it dawned on me that this short tale was a continuation of the "Whirlwind" story; that there were many other chapters to write: in brief, that I had somehow got hold of an idea. I was happy for a whole evening; while I thought of the curious and beautiful thing I was to invent. I thought of this curious and beautiful thing when I read through the proof sheets of the completed book for the first time, and then I groaned, realising what a great gulf was fixed (for me) between the idea and the fact.

But this is all too fast. I wrote, with horrid difficulty, with sick despairs, with a sinking heart, with hope ever failing, all but the last chapter of the book. Of course, I had got the whole thing plotted out carefully on paper, and as I went on story after story of my card-castle fell into ruins; this device, I found, would by no means serve; that incident would never convey the meaning intended. But somehow the thing was done; all but the last chapter; and that I could not do at all. There was no help for it, and I put the manuscript away, and had pretty well resigned myself to its remaining unfinished for ever. It was not until the following June that a possible way of ending the book occurred to me, and so in June, 1891, it was all finished. I sent the manuscript to Messrs. Blackwood of Edinburgh; and they very civilly declined it, praising its cleverness — it is not at all clever — but "shrinking" if I remember, "from the central idea."[19] I forget whether I tried other publishers vainly; but "The Great God Pan" was accepted by Mr. John Lane of the Bodley Head, and published by him in 1894.[20]

*   *   *   *   *

And then the reviews began to come in, and then the fun began; and I must confess that I enjoyed it all very much. For I would find this sort of thing waiting for me on the breakfast table.

---

[18] In addition to the first chapter of *The Great God Pan*, the *Whirlwind* also published Machen's story 'The Lost Club', included in this edition.

[19] William Blackwood & Sons published *Blackwood's Magazine*, as well as fiction by major authors, such as George Eliot, John Buchan (1875–1940), and E. M. Forster (1879–1970).

[20] Lane, discussed in the introduction to this edition, was the main publisher of *fin-de-siècle* literature contributing to the Decadent movement.

... It is not Mr. Machen's fault but his misfortune, that one shakes with laughter rather than with dread over the contemplation of his psychological bogey. — "Observer."

His horror, we regret to say, leaves us quite cold. Gallant gentlemen commit suicide at the mere sight of the accursed thing; here be murders, inquests, alarums, and excursions — and our flesh obstinately refuses to creep. Why? Possibly because we have had a surfeit of this morbid thaumaturgy of late, and "ken the biggin' o' t." — "Chronicle."[21]

In the hands of a student of occultism might be made very powerful. As it is, they just fail. — "Sunday Times."

If Mr. Arthur Machen's object were to make our flesh creep, we can only speak for ourselves and say that we have read the book without an emotion ... the story is, in fact, most elaborately absurd ... as meaningless as an allegory as it is absurd from any other point of view. — "Westminster."

Not the ghost of a creepy feeling will this story produce in the mind of anybody who reads it. — "Echo."

His bogles don't scare. In his next attempt, however, he may come out on the right side. — "Sketch."

"Really," laughed the Hostess, "is the Yellow Book a disease?" ... "Yes," continued the Philosopher, meditatively, ... "and as for "The House of Shame," and "The Great God Pan" — well there are some kinds of maladies which are not mentioned outside medical treatises!" — W. L. Courtney, in "The Daily Telegraph."[22]

We are afraid he only succeeds in being ridiculous. The book is, on the whole, the most acutely and intentionally disagreeable we have yet seen in English. We could say more, but refrain from doing so for fear of giving such a work advertisement. — "Manchester Guardian."

In all the glory of the binder's and printer's arts, we have two tales of no great distinction. — "National Observer."

---

[21] Thaumaturgy is the working of magic or miracles.
[22] H. B. Marriott Watson's (1863–1921) short story 'The House of Shame' appeared in volume 4 of *The Yellow Book* (1895). On Courtney, see his 'Novels and Nerves', included in this edition.

This book is gruesome, ghastly, and dull ... the majority of readers will turn from it in utter disgust. — "Lady's Pictorial."

These tricks have all their ludicrous side. — "Guardian."

It is an incoherent nightmare of sex and the supposed horrible mysteries behind it, such as might conceivably possess a man who was given to a morbid brooding over these matters, but which would soon lead to insanity if unrestrained .... innocuous from its absurdity. — "Westminster" (Second Notice).

       *   *   *   *   *

So well they kept the bridge in the brave days of old![23] I have turned the leaves of the scrap-book in which I have religiously preserved these cuttings with a tender melancholy, which, nevertheless, is not altogether sad. Indeed, I have felt more in the mood of the man who finds a crushed flower or a leaf in an old book that he seldom opens, that he has not looked into for years. He remembers the affair, whatever it was; he recognises that it was all over and done with very long ago, that it was a silly business at the best: and yet, the little faded flower brings back that night in spring, and makes him feel a boy again. He is wiser now; but then the white boughs of the May hung just over the walls of Paradise.[24] So I have read once more these little faded flowers of speech, and feel a boy again. Or rather, a sort of a boy, a boy of thirty who has been very nearly starved to death in a London lodging-house, who has toiled and despaired over the impossible alchemy of letters, finding nothing but ashes in his crucible, who has given many lonely years to the work. Such a boy I find once more in the leaves of my old scrap-book. I salute him across the great bridge of years and bid him farewell.

Introduction to *The Great God Pan* (London: Simpkin,
Marshall, Hamilton, Kent, 1916), pp. vii–xxiii.

---

[23] The phrase 'kept the bridge' is a military metaphor, here indicating defence of the conventions of mainstream literature.

[24] The blossoms of May — often known as hawthorn — are white flowers associated with the pagan festival of Beltane (held on the first of May), and are connected in British folklore with youth and passion.

PART III

Critical Contexts

Arthur Edward Waite:
Excerpts from *The Occult Sciences* (1891)

The claims of Hermetic philosophy to the consideration of serious thinkers in the nineteenth century are not to be confounded with those merely of an exalted intellectual system, or of a sublime and legitimate aspiration. These may, indeed, be urged in behalf of it with the force of unadulterated truthfulness, but not as the principal point. What the philosophy which is indiscriminately called transcendental, Hermetic, Rosicrucian, mystical, and esoteric or occult,[1] submits in its revived form to the scrutator[2] of life and her problems as a sufficing and rational cause for its resuscitation, and as an adequate ground for its recognition, is tersely this: — That it comprises an actual, positive, and realisable knowledge concerning the worlds which we denominate invisible, because they transcend the imperfect and rudimentary faculties of a partially developed humanity, and concerning the latent potentialities which constitute, by the fact of their latency, what is termed the interior man. In more strictly philosophical language, the Hermetic science is a method of transcending the phenomenal world, and attaining to the reality which is behind phenomena. At a time when many leaders of thought have substantially abandoned all belief in the existence of intelligence outside of the visible universe, it is almost superfluous to say that the mere claim of the mystics has an irresistible magnetic attraction for those who are conscious that deep down in the heart of every man there exists the hunger after the supernatural.

The mode of transcending the phenomenal world, as taught by the mystics, consists, and to some extent exclusively, of a form of intellectual ascension or development, which is equivalent to a conscious application of selective evolutionary laws by man himself to man. Those latent faculties which are

---

[1] Transcendental is used here as a synonym for mystical, referring to secret, supernatural beings and occurrences. On matters Hermetic, see note 178 of *The Hill of Dreams*, and on Rosicrucian mysteries, see note 19 of 'The Literature of Occultism'. 'Esoteric' and 'occult' are both, generally speaking, synonyms for secret. While esoteric knowledge and practices are those taught to only a select few, the term occult connotes those things that only people who have been properly educated and/or initiated can perceive or know.

[2] scrutator: one who investigates something or searches for meaning.

identified as Psychic Force pass, under this training, into objective life; they become the instruments of communication with the unseen world, and the modes of subsistence which are therein. In other words, the conscious evolution of the individual has germinated a new sense by which he is enabled to appreciate what is inappreciable by the grosser senses.

The powers of the interior man, and the possibility of communication with the unseen, are the subject of historical magic, which is filled with thaumaturgic accounts of experiments with these forces, and of the results of this communication.[3] Whether these alleged occurrences are to be accepted as substantiated facts is not the question on which the enlightened mystic desires to insist. The evidence which supports them may be, and is, important; it may be, and is, overwhelming; but it is not upon the wonders of the Past only that the Hermetic claim is sought to be established, or demands recognition, in the Present. Whatever be the evidential value for the success of the psychic experiments conducted by the investigators of old, they may at least be said to constitute a sufficient ground for a new series of scientific inquiries on the part of those persons who are devoting their intelligence and their energy to the solution of the grand mysteries of existence. Otherwise, the transcendental philosophy would be simply the revival of an archaic faith, and would be wholly unadapted to the necessities of today. It should be remembered, however, when speaking of scientific inquiry, that the reference is not confined to the professed scientists of the period, but to all who are capable of exact observation, and can appreciate the momentous character of the issues involved.

The standpoint indeed is this: the successful experiments of the past are capable of repetition in the present, and it is open to those who doubt it to be convinced by individual experience. In one of his most mystical utterances, Christ is recorded to have said that there are those who are eunuchs from their mother's womb, and that there are those who become eunuchs in the interests of the Kingdom of God; so also there are natural magicians and magicians who are the product of art, yet, generally speaking, the magician, unlike the poet, is not born but made, for the same potentialities abide in the whole of humanity, and they can be ultimately developed in all. What is wanted, therefore, is not merely persons possessed of the gifts of clairvoyance, or even of lucidity, of prophetic foresight, or of the qualities called mediumistic, but those who by the nature of their aspirations, and by the help of a favourable environment, are able to apply the arcane laws of evolution to their own interior selves. But there is another and an indispensable condition, namely the power to distinguish between Hermetic truth and the shameless frauds which have encompassed it from time immemorial. At present, the intellectual world is substantially divided into those who reject esoteric doctrine and practice as unmixedly

---

[3]   thaumaturgic: dealing with the working of magic or miracles.

fraudulent, and those whose credulity identifies its worst impostures and most puerile perversions with its highest forms of truth. Transcendentalism is concerned with the development and application of certain powerful forces resident in the interior man, and as these forces have been developed and applied in various directions, from many motives, and with a multiplicity of ends in view, historical mysticism is very diverse in its character, is often puerile, superstitious, dangerous, malevolent, and obscene, and from its nature has been always peculiarly liable to the counterfeits and charlatans.

Certain sections of modern mystics have expressed somewhat too freely their indignation against the Christian churches for the abuses and corruptions which they have generated during the undermining process of the ages. Now, the history of no doctrine and of no religion can compare in its abuses and corruptions with that of Magic; for every species of abomination of "unnatural love and more unnatural hate" have been fostered under the tenebrous wings of the goetic part of mysticism.[4] There, as in other matters, the height of aspiration finds its exact counterpoise in the abysses of spiritual degradation. It is the custom with many to shield occultism from the responsibility of these dishonourable histories by means of transliteral interpretations, just as it is the custom among the more credulous section of spiritualists to cloak every phase of fraud among "mediums" by accrediting the "spirit world" with the impostures of many of those who pose as the avenues of communication between the seen and the unseen. [...]

Every branch of the occult or secret sciences may be included under the word MAGIC, with the sole exception of astrology, which, important and interesting as it is, can hardly be termed a branch of arcane wisdom, as it depends solely on abstruse astronomical calculations, and on the appreciation of the value of those influences which are supposed to be diffused by the planets and the starry heavens over the lives of nations and individuals. But the doctrines concerning the nature and power of angels, ghosts, and spirits; the methods of evoking and controlling the shades of the dead, elementary spirits, and demons; the composition of talismans; the manufacture of gold by alchemy; all forms of divination, including clairvoyance in the crystal, and all the mysterious calculations which make up kabbalistic science, are all parts of magic.[5] It is necessary to make this statement at the outset to prevent misconception, because in an elementary hand-book it would be clearly a source of confusion to include subjects so apparently distinct under a single generic title; and we have therefore determined to make a few introductory remarks upon magic

---

[4] goetic: involving magic, usually black magic.
[5] On alchemy and the Kabbalah, see Machen's 'Literature of Occultism', included in this edition.

viewed as a whole, and then to treat each of its branches under special titles which will be readily intelligible to those who are seeking for the first time an acquaintance with the mysteries of the esoteric sciences.

The popular significance attached to the term magic diverges widely from the interpretations which are offered by its students. By the term magic, according to the common opinion, there is generally implied one of two things — either that it is the art of producing effects by the operation of causes which are apparently inadequate to their production, and are therefore in apparent defiance of the known order of nature; or that it is the art of evoking spirits,[†] and of forcing them to perform the bidding of the operator. The second alternative may be practically resolved into the first, for the invocation of invisible intelligences is inseparably connected in the minds of the vulgar with a certain hocus-pocus of preposterous rites and formulae, including the utterance of barbarous and, to them, meaningless words, which certainly appear to be inadequate to produce so stupendous an effect as a direct manifestation from a hidden side of Nature. Now, to establish communication with worlds which are normally beyond our reach is undoubtedly included in the great claims of the magus; and the art of evoking spirits, taken in its true and its highest sense, is the head and crown of Magic; but it is not in fact a violation of immutable natural laws, and the causes which are set in operation by its qualified initiates are really adequate to the effects which are produced, wonderful and incredible as they may appear. The popular conception of Magic, even when it is not identified with the trickeries of imposture and the pranks of the mountebank, is entirely absurd and gross.

"Magic, or, more accurately, Magism" says Christian in his *Histoire de la Magie*, "if anyone would condescend to return to its antique origin, could be no longer confounded with the superstitions which calumniate its memory.[6] Its name is derived to us from the Greek word Magos, a Magician, and Mageia, Magic, which are merely permutations of the terms Mog, Megh, Magh, which in Pehlvi and in Zend, both languages of the eldest East, signify 'priest,' 'wise,'

[†] [This note is Waite's own.] Four classes of the intelligences called 'spirits' are recognized by the science of the magi. There are the Angels who are the offspring of primeval creation, made and not begotten; there are the Devils, or Demons, the angelical hierarchies who fell from their first estate. There are the Elementary Spirits, who inhabit the four elements of ancient physical science, and are divided into Sylphs, Undines, Gnomes, and Salamanders — intelligences who reproduce their species after the manner of mankind. Finally, there are the Souls of departed men and women whose actual locality in the unseen world is variously described. Angels are involved in the higher branches of white magic, and Demons in the operation of the black art; Elementary Spirits are the classes most easily commanded, and they are the "familiars" of the middle ages. The Souls of the Dead were conjured commonly for the revelation of mundane secrets, occasionally for the disclosure of future events, but most frequently in the interests of bereaved affection.

[6] Pitois Christian's (1811–1877) *Histoire de la Magie* was published in 1870.

and 'excellent.'[7] It was thence also that, in a period anterior to historic Greece, there originated the Chaldæan name Maghdim, which is equivalent to 'supreme wisdom,' or sacred philosophy.[8] Thus, mere etymology indicates that Magic was the synthesis of those sciences once possessed by the Magi or philosophers of India, of Persia, of Chaldæa, and of Egypt, who were the priests of nature, the patriarchs of knowledge, and the founders of those vast civilisations whose ruins still maintain, without tottering, the burden of sixty centuries."

Ennemoser, in his "History of Magic" (as translated by Howitt), says: "Among the Parsees, the Medes, and the Egyptians, a higher knowledge of nature was understood by the term Magic, with which religion, and particularly astronomy, were associated.[9] The initiated and their disciples were called Magicians — that is, the Wise — which was also the case among the Greeks. ... Plato understood by Wisdom nothing less than a worship of the Divinity, and Apuleius says that Magus means, in the Persian language, a priest. ... India, Persia, Chaldea, and Egypt, were the cradles of the oldest Magic.[10] Zoroaster, Ostanes, the Brahmins, the Chaldean sages, and the Egyptian priests, were the primitive possessors of its secrets.[11] The priestly and sacrificial functions, the healing of the sick, and the preservation of the Secret Wisdom, were the objects of their life. They were either princes themselves, or surrounded princes as their counsellors. Justice, truth, and the power of self-sacrifice, were the great qualities with which each one of these must be endowed; and the neglect of any one of these virtues was punished in the most cruel manner."

A theosophical writer who is said to belong to the most advanced school, Dr Franz Hartmann, who is said to be a practical as well as theoretical student, who also lays claim to the successful performance of recondite alchemical experiments by the application of spiritual forces to material things, and who, therefore, should at any rate be competent to provide us with a tolerable definition of his art, has the following assertion at the beginning of one of his

---

[7] Pehlvi and Zend are ancient Indo-European languages spoken in the Persian Empire. Zend eventually ceased to be a language spoken by everyday people and, instead, became the language used to convey sacred mysteries.

[8] Chaldæan was the language spoken in Chaldæa (or Chaldea), part of ancient Mesopotamia.

[9] Joseph Ennemoser (1787–1854) wrote *Geschichte der Magie* (1844). William Howitt (1792–1879), a spiritualist, translated it from German into English in 1854. Parsees are Zoroastrians who live in India, and Medes are inhabitants of Media, an ancient territory roughly in the region of north-western Iran.

[10] Plato concerned himself with the relationship between impermanent physical Forms and the eternal, unchanging Ideas. On Plato and Apuleius, see notes 227 and 175 of *The Hill of Dreams*, respectively.

[11] Zoroaster (fl. sixth century BCE) was a religious teacher in ancient Persia and the reputed founder of Zoroastrianism. Ostanes is a shadowy figure about whom little precise and verifiable information is known; he is often regarded as the founder of alchemy in ancient Persia. In Hinduism, a Brahmin is a member of the highest, or priestly, caste.

books: — "whatever misinterpretation ancient or modern ignorance may have given to the word *Magic*, its only true significance is *The Highest Science, or Wisdom, based upon knowledge and practical experience*."[12] This definition reads an absolute value into a term which it does not historically possess, for though Magic be undoubtedly derived from a word which signifies Wisdom, it is Wisdom as conceived by the Magi to which it is alone equivalent, and so far as philosophy is concerned, magian Wisdom either may or may not be identical with the absolute and eternal Wisdom.

Magic, says Eliphas Lévi, is "the traditional science of the secrets of Nature which has come down to us from the Magi," a definition devoid of nonsense, and narrowly escaping perfection, the limitation of the source of esoteric knowledge to the Persian hierarchs being, we thing, its sole defect.[13]

By these definitions it is plain that Magic is not merely the art of invoking spirits, and that it is not merely concerned with establishing a communication with other forms of intelligent subsistence in the innumerable spheres of the transcendental. If such invocation be possible, if such communication can be truly established, it is evidently by the intervention of certain occult forces resident in the communicating individual, man. Now, it is reasonable to suppose that the same forces can be applied in other directions, and the synthesis of the methods and processes by which these forces are utilized in the several fields of experiment, combined with a further synthesis of methods and processes by which the latent potentialities of a variety of physical substances are developed into manifest activity, constitutes Magic in the full, perfect, and comprehensive sense of that much abused term.

Arthur Edward Waite, Excerpts from *The Occult Sciences: A Compendium of Transcendental Doctrine and Experiment* (London: Kegan Paul, 1891), pp. 1–4, 9–12. American-born Waite (1857–1947) spent most of his life in England. A friend of Machen, Waite was a respected writer on occult subjects, co-creator of the Rider–Waite Tarot deck, and a member at various times of the Order of the Golden Dawn, the Freemasons, and the Rosicrucians.

---

[12] Machen discusses Theosophy in 'The Literature of Occultism', included in this edition. Franz Hartmann (1838–1912) was a German physician and Theosophist, and a colleague of Blavatsky in India.

[13] Eliphas Lévi (aka Alphonse Louis Constant, 1810–1875) was an occult magician and friend of Théophile Gautier. He had a major influence on spiritualism and the Hermetic Order of the Golden Dawn. His work was published by Machen's employer, George Redway, and translated by Waite. The Magi are Zoroastrian priests said to wield supernatural power.

16

Florence Marryat:
Chapter XI, A Chance Séance with a
Stranger, from *The Spirit World* (1894)

I made a short tour through the provinces this spring, to deliver a lecture that proved, on the testimony of the Scriptures, that the practice of Spiritualism was both right and true.[1] In the course of my wanderings, I arrived at the city of Nottingham, where I was met by my host, Mr James Fraser Hewes.[2] It was on a Friday afternoon, and, as I was not to lecture until Saturday, Mr Hewes, with a view to filling up the time, asked me if I would like to attend a materialising séance that evening, with a Mrs Davidson, of South Shields.[3] I had never heard the name of this medium, though I am aware there are several good ones stowed away in the provincial towns, and I asked Mr Hewes what her mediumship was like; but he also had never had the pleasure of sitting with Mrs Davidson before, so could give me no information on the subject. She had been invited to Nottingham by a gentleman of the name of Bostock, who was sitting with her and his friends at his private residence. Mr and Mrs Hewes had been invited for that evening, but as for myself, I was supposed to be at Walsall, which was the last place I had lectured at. It was decided then that I should accompany my hosts to the meeting *incognita*, and after tea we set out for Mr Bostock's house. This gentleman, though doubtless possessing every virtue under the sun, does not understand the proper conditions for obtaining good materialisations. It was one of the few warm nights which we have enjoyed this spring, and his

---

[1] The practice of spiritualism refers to communicating with the spirits of the dead through a medium, séance, or other aid.

[2] James Fraser Hewes (*c.* 1865–1930) was an anti-vivisectionist and co-founder of the Spiritualist Society in Nottingham. The weekly *Two Worlds* interviewed him as a member of the 'young guard' of spiritualism (*Two Worlds: The People's Popular Penny Spiritual Paper*, 344:7 (15 June 1894), pp. 282–84 (p. 282)).

[3] In a materializing séance the spirits of the dead take on some kind of tangible, visible form (e.g. ghostly apparitions, impressions in moulds). Information on Mrs Davidson is limited. She gave a number of séances and, as is mentioned in the spiritualist periodical *Two Worlds*, they appear to have been as successful as that attended by Marryat.

séance-room was insufferably crowded by some thirty gentlemen and ladies, whilst, in order to darken the apartment, every breath of fresh air had been carefully excluded. I felt on entering it that I could not stay a minute there. It was like the atmosphere of a hothouse. By means of a very narrow gangway, we were enabled to get to the chairs reserved for our accommodation, which proved to be near the cabinet, mine being the sixth seat from it.[4] This cabinet — if it can be called so — was composed of a piece of green silesia nailed across one corner of the room, with just enough space behind it to admit a chair.[5] "Where is the medium?" I whispered to Mr Hewes. "In the next room," he replied. "She is so frightened of going into the cabinet that the spirits are obliged to bring her into the séance-room under control, or they would not be able to persuade her to enter it." And then he added: "How surprised they would be" — meaning the sitters — "if they knew *who* was sitting with them.[6] No one knows you will be in the town until to-morrow night." At this juncture Mrs Davidson entered the room. She is a miner's wife, and was dressed in accordance with her class. She has a pleasant face, but at this moment it looked worried and anxious. "Oh, this heat, this heat!" she exclaimed, looking in a bewildered way around her; "we shall never get anything in this heat." When I say *she* said so, I mean the spirit who was controlling her, and who was a man whose name I did not catch. Mr Bostock immediately asked what he should do — should he open the windows, etc. This proposal was seconded and acceded to, but still the medium looked uneasy. "So many — too many," she murmured; "we shall get nothing, I am afraid." Mr Bostock then asked if some of the sitters should be sent away, but the control did not think that would be fair. "We must not disappoint them like that," he replied; "and when they have come so far. We will do our best, friends, and no one can do more; but I am very much afraid that we shall get nothing." So it will be seen that no great things were expected from the evening's sitting; and as for myself, I simply prepared to remain in a warm bath till the séance concluded, and directed my attention to solely keeping as still and as cool as was possible under the circumstances. And here it would not be out of place, perhaps, to make a few remarks on the mistakes perpetrated in this particular by people who have organised many more séances perhaps than Mr Bostock. A séance-room should *never be crowded*, especially on a warm night. In order to procure materialisation, it is essential to have a moderate atmosphere, neither too hot nor too cold. The sitters, too, should be selected with discretion, being, if possible, equally divided between the sexes, and admitting none who are very feeble or diseased amongst them; and if half the claimants for admittance

---

[4]   A cabinet is a cornered-off area of a room from which a medium may conduct a séance.
[5]   Silesia is a lightly twilled fabric.
[6]   Sitters are those for whom the medium is operating and for whom messages from spirits may be intended.

have been used to sit at séances, and the other half have not, very few of the latter should be admitted at a time. They should be "sneaked in," as it were, by ones and twos, until their aura shall be thoroughly absorbed in that of the more experienced sitters. Such a system, if carefully carried out, would give the influences far less difficulties to contend against, and lead to a more successful issue.

But to return to Mrs Davidson's mediumship. We sat for some time in silence and "tears" (of perspiration) without anything occurring, then a voice issued from behind the curtain:[7] "Will the lady sitting in the sixth chair from the cabinet change seats with the lady who is sitting next to it?"

This move placed me close to the silesia curtain, so that I could hear the least movement inside of it. I had not sat there long, however, before the inside of the cabinet was illuminated by some mysterious spirit light, so that I could see the medium sitting in her chair with her black gown on, and the little shawl pinned across her shoulders, whilst her head was sunk forward on her breast. A lady who was sitting just behind me said she saw it too, *i.e.*, she perceived the strange illumination, which seemed to her as if she were facing an uncurtained window in the daylight, but she did not see the medium's figure as I did. Yet, though I perceived this quite plainly, I saw no spirits forming, as heretofore, nor anything except the medium. Presently a child's voice — one, I believe, of the medium's controls — asked the circle to sing something, and we joined in a well-known melody. The curtain was pulled on one side, and a little girl of about nine or ten years old in appearance peeped out and disappeared again. "Who is that?" demanded Mr Bostock; "can't you tell us?" "That's little Gertie," was the answer, "come for the lady sitting next the cabinet. Sing something livelier, please; she likes lively tunes." The sitters then struck up a hymn in quicker measure, and "Gertie" came out again. This time she held up her white skirts and swayed from one side to the other in a sort of slow dance, showing her little bare feet. I asked her to speak to me, or kiss me, but at each request she disappeared again, so I did not press the point. After she had shown herself four or five times she retreated, making way for my daughter "Florence," whose appearance I can never mistake, she is so slender and young and virginal looking — with such a saintly air about her, as if she came fresh from Heaven. Knowing her to be such a strong spirit — strong, I mean, in being able to show herself to mortal sight — I thought her presence might save the séance and turn it into a success, so I exclaimed: "Oh Florence, I am so glad you have come! Do show yourself more plainly if possible, for we are afraid we shall not have much of a séance this evening." But Florence did not appear inclined to come out into the room. On the contrary, as I addressed her, she drew backward, and laid her finger on her lip. I reiterated my request, and then she bent her head forward till

---

[7]   The phrase 'silence and tears' appears twice in Byron's poem 'When We Two Parted'.

I could hear her whisper: "Not to-night, mother; some one is coming." But I had not the least idea to whom she alluded. I begged her to tell me. "*Who* is it that is coming, Florence?" I said. She bent her head forward again, and whispered in a very low tone: "Eva." My heart literally stood still. This is the name of my beloved eldest daughter, whom I had the misfortune to lose in childbirth nearly seven years ago, and whom I have been longing and praying to see ever since, but without effect. I began to tremble so violently I could hardly keep still on my seat, and I felt as if I should suffocate, the announcement was so unexpected to me. Here was I, who had been entreating the Almighty for the last seven years to afford me a little glimpse of this most cherished possession of my life, doomed to meet her for the first time since she had been torn from my arms, in company with strangers, who knew nothing of my loss, nor could sympathise with it. I thought I must run out of the room to avoid making a fool of myself, though why one *should* be thought a fool for giving way to a natural emotion puzzles me. In a few more minutes the curtain was lifted, and my darling girl, with her little baby in her arms, stood before me, but well within the shelter of the cabinet. She held out her infant to me as though she would secure recognition by that means; but I could not look at either of them. The agony of my spirit quite overcame me, and I lost all control of myself. I sunk down on my knees as if God Himself had been before me, and sobbed as I had not done for years past. I did not expect that she would come again. I thought my uncontrollable grief would upset her, and perhaps spoil conditions, but I could not help it. Judge of my surprise, therefore, when my darling girl, having got rid of her baby, came right out of the cabinet again, and reaching my side where I knelt weeping, stooped over me, took my head, and laid it on her dear breast, and wiped away my tears with her veil, as she kept on kissing me, and repeating: "Don't cry, mother; don't cry." At the moment I could only press my head against her, and thank God that He had answered my constant prayer, and let me see my darling again; but looking back upon the interview, I can distinctly remember and describe the features which struck me most in it. Her veil, as it wiped my wet face, felt like silk net, but very fine and soft, and it effectually dried my tears, which net would not have done. It was also scented with some perfume like incense. I could feel the softness of her lips as she kissed me, and her warm breath coming through them, and her whole body seemed to be pervaded with the same subtle perfume, as if she had been a *sachet*. Her face was warm and very soft, like the flesh of a new-born baby, and those who regarded her more mechanically than I had the power to do, told me afterwards that she was very pale, and her head and face were much enveloped by her voluminous veil. After Eva had left, Florence informed us that she intended to, and would have, walked out into the circle with me, had not my emotion upset her so, that she lost the power of doing it. This, with the exception of a few remarks from inside the cabinet from Mrs Davidson's controls, concluded the séance. Only three spirits had appeared, and they had been my three daughters. I was very sorry for the other sitters, but it was not my fault. Nevertheless, I felt terribly guilty, and as if I, the one stranger amongst them, had monopolised the whole of their evening. The only consolation I had was in being told that, if I had not been there, they would have got nothing at all.

Florence Marryat, 'Chapter XI. A Chance Séance with a Stranger', *The Spirit World* (London: F. V. White, 1894), pp. 253–61. Marryat (1833–1899) was an English spiritualist, as well as an actress and prolific novelist. *The Spirit World* is a sequel to *There is No Death* (1891), her immensely popular account of séances.

17

William Leonard Courtney:
Novels and Nerves (1895)

It was, perhaps, rather a serious conversation to take place after dinner, but, at all events, it formed a more or less agreeable substitute for round games and a little music. The Hostess had a distinctly "literary" turn — in the most approved modern sense of that much-debated and demoralised adjective. In other words, she was supposed to have read Tolstoi in French, and had certainly made herself acquainted with the works of Zola and Maupassant.[1] Of other forms of writing — even of the English novelists of some thirty or forty years ago — she was profoundly and unblushingly ignorant, although she was quite prepared to agree with a recent lecturer at the Royal Institution that Dickens was a democratic vulgarian.[2] On the other hand, she could have stood a *viva voce* examination on the social dramas of Ibsen, on Maeterlinck's "Princess Maleine" and "The Intruder," and on the contents of all the four Yellow Books.[3] Indeed, the last Yellow Book lay on the table, with the pages turned down at Victoria Cross's "Theodora" and Mr. H.B. Marriott Watson's "The House of Shame."[4] The recent life of Mr. J.A. Symonds was near her elbow, and also

---

[1] The Russian novelist and philosopher Leo Tolstoy (1828–1910) was noted for his epic sweep and detailed characterizations; among his many works are *War and Peace* (1865–1869) and *Anna Karenina* (1875–1877). Émile Zola was famous for his work in naturalism. Guy de Maupassant (1850–1893) was a French novelist and short story writer noted for his psychological realism; for example in *Une Vie* (1883) and *Bel-Ami* (1885).

[2] The Royal Institution of Great Britain is a society dedicated to scientific exploration. Although popular, some readers criticized as vulgar Dickens's close descriptions of poverty and social decay amongst London's lower classes.

[3] A *viva voce* (Latin) is an oral examination. Henrik Ibsen (1828–1906) was a Norwegian playwright and poet noted for his social realism and his complex depictions of women's lives, as in the play *Hedda Gabler* (1890). Maurice Maeterlinck (1862–1949) was a Belgian author who wrote stories, plays, and poems informed by Symbolism and a sense of personal and social doom. His first and second plays were *La Princesse Maleine* (1889) and *L'Intruse* (1890). On the Decadent periodical *The Yellow Book* (1894–1897), see the introduction to this edition.

[4] Volume 4 of *The Yellow Book* (published in January 1895) includes 'Theodora' and 'The House of Shame'. The author Victoria Cross (pseud. for Annie Sophie Cory; 1868–1952) was known for her often exotic stories and novels; her first novel, *The Woman Who Didn't* (1895),

Mr. Garnet Smith's "The Melancholy of Stephen Allard," although I could not help noticing that the latter presented for the most part a virgin array of uncut pages.[5] She had her friends round her, on one side the Philosopher, on the other the Physician. Our Hostess always had an amiable weakness for noted men — a feeling which they, being after all human, repaid with interest.

"I see you have 'The Melancholy of Stephen Allard,'" said the Philosopher. "Have you finished it yet?"

"Well — no, not quite," answered our Hostess, with much frankness. "I am not sure that I care for cultured mournfulness. It is apt to grow to inordinate length, and to consist, like the play of 'Hamlet,' largely of quotations."

The Physician laughed. "What do you prefer," he asked. "Brutal cynicism?" His fingers were playing with the Yellow Book as he spoke.

"I understand you," she said. "'Theodora' and 'The House of Shame' are both a little strong — too highly peppered, perhaps — — "

"Except for the virginal palate of the modern female reader, of course," responded the Physician cheerfully, "which, as it has never attempted to assimilate simple food, solaces itself on Worcestershire sauce and piccalilli."

"Have you ever considered," said the Philosopher gravely, "that Pessimism is the note of a dying century? Each age has its characteristic extravagance. Classical antiquity had a naïve joy in life. The Middle Ages were inspired with a devotional spirit. Our own time is weary alike of religion and of existence; it has imbibed the Mephistophelian temper 'to deny,' it has preternatural acuteness and no faith, it is weary of its old ideals, and breaks its dolls because they are only full of sawdust."

"And is this the way you explain 'The Melancholy of Stephen Allard'?" asked the Hostess. "Surely all civilization is misery — to know is to suffer, as Leopardi says."[6]

"Yes," said the Philosopher, raising his eyebrows at the Italian pessimist's

---

was published in John Lane's Keynote series. Australian-born Henry Brereton Marriott Watson (1863–1921) was best known for his many romantic novels, although he has also been recognized as contributing to the Decadent, gothic writing popular during the *fin de siècle*.

[5]   On English author and historian John Addington Symonds, see note 1 of 'The Idealist'. Courtney here alludes to Symonds's defiance of Victorian social and moral norms by advocating for male–male homosexual history and desire. Symonds's friend Horatio Brown (1854–1926) published a biography of him in 1895. Garnet Smith (dates unknown) was an English author and essayist; his essays demonstrate extensive knowledge of both contemporary art and literature, as well as the aims and limitations of Decadence. *The Melancholy of Stephen Allard* (1894), which he probably authored although claiming only the role of editor, offers extensive considerations of melancholy, Decadence, and paganism. 'To be a man is to be self-conscious', the text reads, 'and to be self-conscious is to be diseased' (*The Melancholy of Stephen Allard: A Private Diary* (London: MacMillan, 1894), p. 97).

[6]   Giacomo Leopardi (1798–1837) was an Italian poet and essayist whose work is infused with a profound sense that humans are doomed to misery and suffering.

name, "culture no doubt induces the melancholy spirit, but only when a man either has nothing to do or has given up the idea of doing anything. Activity of any sort — even sweeping a crossing — is a tonic. Moral philosophy presupposes that life is worth living — that is why Pessimism is so unethical."

"At all events, Pessimism is interesting — which is more than can be said for your Théodicées and your rampant beliefs that this is the best of possible worlds.[7] Optimism is so commonplace and vulgar!"

The Philosopher smiled. He liked being scoffed at by the Hostess, because she was both ignorant and pretty. If she had been ugly and wise, he would have argued with her till the crack of doom.

"My dear Madam," burst in the Physician — he had been chafing for some time at being forced to keep silence — "philosophy cannot explain our present symptoms. What a barbarous idea this 'fin de siècle,' end of a century, old-age weariness suggests to the scientific mind! Is a century an animal, a living thing, which passes through all the stages of childhood, adolescence, manhood, until it becomes senile, idiotic, and feeble! Only a baby or a savage could entertain so primitive a notion!"

"Well, but what is the right explanation?" asked the Hostess.

"It can only be given by science — medical science," returned the Physician sententiously.

"Which is not a science, but only an extremely imperfect form of art," murmured the Philosopher softly.

But the doctor was not to be denied. "Take all the extraordinary phases of cerebral activity which we find to-day in the nations of Europe. In Russia Mysticism and Tolstoi; in France, the extravagance of the Symbolists, the Décadents, the Parnassiens, the Diabolists — and Mallarmé and Verlaine; in Belgium, Maeterlink; in Scandinavia, Ibsen and Björnson; in England, all of these influences filtered through our essentially bourgeois mind, and aggravated by a pre-Raphaelite mania, which we owe to Ruskin."[8]

---

[7] Theodicy: a vindication of the goodness and justice of God who, nevertheless, permits evil and suffering to exist.

[8] Tolstoy wrote about a quasi-mystical belief in Christian love, non-violence, and anti-materialism. Symbolists and Decadents are discussed in the introduction to this edition. The Parnassians were a group of nineteenth-century French poets who rejected romanticism in favour of highly-wrought form and emotional detachment; preceding the Symbolists and the Decadents, they were influenced by the philosophy of art for art's sake. Of the four terms, Diabolists is the most opaque, as it was a negative term — implying the worship of Satan — that was applied to artists and others who did not conform to normative canons of art and morality. Stéphane Mallarmé (1842–1898) and Paul Verlaine (1844–1896) were French Symbolist poets. Bjørnstjerne Bjørnson (1832–1910) was a Norwegian author and political reformer. The Pre-Raphaelites were a group of mid-nineteenth century painters and poets in England who rejected industrialization and materialism in favour of what they perceived to be the beauty and richness of the Middle Ages. Their style, however, was frequently highly ornate and mannered. One of the Pre-Raphaelites' main early supporters was the English scholar, critic, and social reformer John Ruskin (1819–1900).

"And in Germany, Max Nordau and his book on Degeneracy from which you are quoting," interrupted the Philosopher.[9]

"Yes, I know I am," answered the Physician, fiercely; "but that is because I believe in what Max Nordau says and in the Italian doctor, Lombroso, from whom he himself often quotes.[10] Max Nordau's great book on 'Degeneration,' which has for some time been known in a French version, is at last to be published in an English form, which will shortly appear."

"But what does this eminent gentleman say?" asked the Hostess. "You have not told me that yet."

"The Philosopher interrupted me," said the Physician, tartly, "because, being a philosopher, he likes abstract theories, about 'the tendencies of an age,' which explain nothing. Now medical science takes you into the heart of things and shows you that the real cause of all these contemporary phenomena is a diseased state of the nerves."

"Really," laughed the Hostess, "is the Yellow Book a disease?"

"Assuredly," said the Physician, "a very virulent form of jaundice, due to an imperfect digestion and a morbid condition of liver."

"Yes," continued the Philosopher, meditatively, "and 'Theodora' is a form of typhoid, due to ethical blood poisoning, 'Little Eyolf' and 'The Rat-Wife' are varieties of cerebral mania, Mr. Aubrey Beardsley's figures are salient examples of locomotor ataxy, and as for 'The House of Shame' and 'The Great God Pan' — well, there are some kinds of maladies which are not mentioned outside medical treatises!"[11]

"The Philosopher is pleased to laugh," said the Physician. "Of course all these books of yours" — he pointed vaguely and expressively to our hostess's extremely modern library — "are only symptoms of disease, not the disease itself, which is common alike to all of them."

"And what is that?" asked the Hostess, with a shade of alarm in her tones. She had a constitutional horror of sickness.

"Neurasthenia, hysteria, epilepsy — the thing has many names, but the form is the same.[12] All our heroes have weak nerves, all our heroines are neurotic;

---

[9]   Max Nordau (1849–1923) was a Hungarian physician who wrote *Degeneration* (1892–1893; English translation 1895). His ideas had a major impact on debates concerning cultural, social, and aesthetic Decadence.

[10] Cesare Lombroso (1835–1909) was an Italian physician and criminologist whose theory of criminal atavism — resemblance to remote ancestors — was highly influential in both society and art.

[11] Ibsen's play *Little Eyolf* (1894) is an intense psycho-emotional drama that includes the arrival of a mysterious character known as the Rat-Wife, a woman who can enchant rats and lead them away to drown them in the sea. In this play, however, a disabled boy named Eyolf instead follows the Rat-Wife and drowns. Locomotor ataxia is a painful syphilitic condition that leads to paralysis and loss of control of muscular movements (especially walking).

[12] Neurasthenia is a form of physical and mental debility (sometimes in the form of a

they are just on the confines of lunacy, they quiver on the balance between sanity and madness. What are the symptoms of the disease? Oh, that's easily answered — a love of obscurity, gloom, melancholy; a tendency to mysticism, a weakness for symbols; culture running to seed, refinement tottering on the edge of coarseness; an Art that has grown fantastic, a Literature that is occupied with form rather than matter, with expression rather than ideas — these are all early stages. Then the nerves break down altogether, the mind becomes unhinged, and when the tongue speaks or the pen writes — well, you remember how Ophelia talked and the subjects she became interested in when she lost her reason."

"Dear me, dear me," said the Hostess, with a shudder, "how very uncomfortable! And that is how medical science accounts for my literary tastes, I suppose. You are not very complimentary!"

"I am your medical man," said the Physician, with a bow.

"I think I prefer talking with you," she said, turning to the Philosopher. "Doctors are so unsympathetic sometimes. Why, if my favourite books are so full of microbes and other horrid things I might just as well have eaten oysters for dinner!"

"The modern world is his oyster, you see," said the Philosopher, gravely.

W. L. Courtney, 'Novels and Nerves', *Daily Telegraph* (1 February 1895), p. 7. William Leonard Courtney (1850–1928) was an English writer who edited the well-respected *Fortnightly Review* from 1894 until his death.

---

nervous breakdown) that lacks evident physical causes. On hysteria, see note 19 of *The Great God Pan*.

18

Arthur Sykes:
The Great Pan-Demon:
An Unspeakable Story (1895)

'Libet mihi efficere ut membra tua horreant' dixit Puer Pinguis.
DICKENSIUS[1]

[The following narrative was discovered among the manuscript papers of the late Dr. Frankenstein, the well-known symbolist and diabolist of Vigo Street.[2] It has been deciphered and translated with some little difficulty from the original chemist's-Latin, with which the author sought to veil his incredible experiences. The date 'Kal. Apr. 1895,' appears on the right-hand corner of the MS.[3] Below this is a barely legible motto, written in pencil, which may be read as *Cred. quant. suff.*][4]

I have grave doubts as to whether the scientific world is yet ready to accept my astonishing physiological discoveries. I prefer, therefore, to commit them to the obscurity of a dead language, an appropriate medium and repository for these secrets of the charnel-house.[5] It is possible, however, that my friend and literary executor, D., may at some future time consider that the psychologic moment has arrived to strike therewith a fresh keynote.[6] In that case, I beg to disclaim in

---

[1] Latin: '"I want to make your limbs creep", said Fat Boy. Dickens'. In Dickens's *Pickwick Papers*, the character Joe, the 'fat boy', tells an elderly woman, 'I wants to make your flesh creep'. In 1890, E. T. Reed (1860–1933) published a caricature of Wilde in which 'Oscar, the Fad Boy' startles Mrs Grundy with a copy of *The Picture of Dorian Gray* (1890, 1891), declaring 'I want to make your flesh creep!' ('Parallel', *Punch* (19 July 1890), p. 25). 'Mrs Grundy' is a common term for a prudish and conservative person or segment of society.

[2] In the 1890s, Vigo Street, in the London neighbourhood of Mayfair, was home to the Decadent publishing house The Bodley Head, which had published Machen's first two books.

[3] Kal. or Kalends (Latin): the first day of a month; in this instance, 1 April 1895, or April Fool's day.

[4] Latin: sufficiently (or moderately) believable.

[5] A structure in which the bones or bodies of the dead are placed.

[6] A keynote is the main idea or central principle of a text. Sykes is alluding to the publisher Lane's Decadent Keynote Series.

advance all responsibility for any mental alienation undergone by the reader, or any violence done to his sense of literary art and of verisimilitude.

For some years past I had been engaged on my *magnum opus* — the Demonic Origin and Properties of the Pineal Gland or Meridian Eye.[7] In the course of my laborious investigations I had made not a few perfectly appalling discoveries, which I hesitate to communicate, even in the language of symbols. But the functions of one particular brain-cell have always baffled my attempts at elucidation. This cell, which I found to be only present in persons of marked cataleptic tendencies, is of microscopic dimensions, rarely exceeding 1–1000th of a millimetre in diameter. None, even of the leading brain-surgeons, had hitherto noticed its existence. I was determined, therefore, not to be beaten, and, if necessary, to dedicate my whole life-work to research in this direction. I felt, from incidental scientific evidence (which I dare not specify or even hint at) that, under certain conditions, the reaction of this cell, situated in the exact centre of the pineal gland, to a cerebro-chemical stimulus would produce the effect I had so long striven to obtain. This result was simply the transformation of a corpse into a devil.

I was in my dissecting-room late one night, busily engaged, after a somewhat imprudent evening meal, in completing an experiment on a fairly fresh cadaver, that of a full-grown male idiot. I had obtained the required pineal cell from a hydrocephalous female subject, who had died of peripheral-epileptic dyscraniorrhagitis, and whose autopsy I had just attended.[8] This I treated in vain with a long series of acid and alkaline reagents, and was almost giving up in despair, when the thought flashed across my mind that I had not yet tried tetramyldiethylbenzoamidochloroxaltriphenylbromine. I rushed for the phial, and with a quivering hand poured a solution of this elixir mortis over the cell. On placing it immediately under my microscope, I began to notice an indescribable and mysterious organic change. Seizing a three-drain basanometer in one hand and a No. 2 Poupart's hodospore in the other, I rapidly transferred the already metabolising cell to the point of a compound Eastachian probe. I then inserted it behind the fifth antero-posterior convolution of the cadaver's cerebellum

---

[7]   In vertebrates that have a cranium, the 'pineal gland' is a region of the brain whose function is unknown; it may at one time have been a sense organ and Descartes believed it housed the soul. Sykes appears to have invented the term 'Meridian eye', although others had proposed the notion that humans have a third eye, sometimes called a pineal eye, that could see beyond regular perception. It is related to the parietal eye, a third eye found in some animal species.

[8]   The word 'hydrocephalous' means having an enlarged head caused by the accumulation of fluid inside the cranium, usually during infancy. Much of what follows in this paragraph is a comic-parodic listing of terms — some actual but most invented. The Latin term 'elixir mortis' (elixir of death) is a play on 'elixir vitae', which in alchemy was the term for a mystical substance (also known as the Philosopher's Stone) that had the ability to prolong life and to turn base metals into gold.

through an aperture previously trephined in the skull, and sank down in an operating chair, exhausted with excitement, to watch the effect.

I had not long to wait. As I gazed, I was hypnotised by the horror that slowly unfolded itself before my eyes. No haschish-vision, no ghoul-dream of Doré, could image the thing, or rather, the unnameable No-thing that was incarnated in my presence, the offspring of my own brain, the creation of my own hands.[9] I watched, with staring eye-balls and blanched lips, the gradual evolution of the inert mass into the embodiment of the Utter Diabolic. It shrank at first to a Devil-embryo, foul, repulsive, androgynous, abortional, a fœtus-product of the obscenest union of ægipans and hell-hags.[10] Thence the Devil-babe, *my* bantling, grew and grew, instinct with the very Negation of life, endued with the death-energy which causes the after-growth of a dead-woman's hair, or the gestation and coffin-birth of a corpse-mother's child. But I must not tell of all its hideous series of transfigurations, of its passage through the forms of satyr and sphinx and she-centaur, while in its cyclopean eye, directed towards myself, there gradually dawned a horrific light, a Satanic intelligence.[11]

Meanwhile, though my gaze was directed on the object before me and its awful adolescence, I was conscious of a horrible alteration in my surroundings. I was in the centre of the lost Pleiad, the abode of damned souls.[12] Possessed now of a sixth sense, that of molecular actinism, which superseded all the others, and of yet a seventh, the knowledge of all evil, I cast off the limits of time and space.[13] I heard and smelt and tasted with my eyes, and smelt and tasted and saw with my ears, and thought unthinkable thoughts.[14] I cannot record my impressions in this state, as my concepts were not reducible to the terms of any known or possible language. The totality of evil flashed in the millionth of an instant through my soul, which was yet not my own, but merged in the

---

[9] Paul Gustave Doré was a French visual artist renowned for his engravings created as illustrations within printed texts, including Poe's 'The Raven' (1845) and Dante's *Divine Comedy* (1320).

[10] Decadent artist Aubrey Beardsley was notorious for drawing foetus-like and androgynous characters, including the androgynous figure gracing the cover of Machen's novel *The Great God Pan*. Ægipans are male goat-like creatures, akin to satyrs and often associated with Pan. Hell-hags are diabolical women who practise black magic.

[11] Satyrs and sphinxes were established Decadent tropes; centaurs and the cyclops were not. On satyrs, see note 20 in *The Great God Pan*, and on the sphinx, see note 10 in 'The Ritual'. Centaurs, usually male, are humans with the legs of a horse. A cyclops is a giant with a single eye in the middle of the forehead.

[12] The Pleiades are Atlas's seven daughters who, to save them from Orion, were placed among the stars. One of the daughters — called the Lost Pleiad — hides from shame or grief.

[13] Actinism, from the Greek for ray, is a photo-chemical property that allows a chemical to be absorbed by a molecule, resulting in a photomechanical reaction (such as photosynthesis).

[14] Sykes is referencing the Symbolists' interest in synaesthesia, where one sensory stimulation results in the correlative experience in another sense. Machen himself represents synaesthesia in *The Hill of Dreams*.

universal Lost Soul, the multiplex occupant of chaos, of the annihilated limbo of the universe.[15]

I may not describe the entities which were the malevolent denizens of the lost Pleiad. They were existent and non-existent simultaneously, but are only comprehensible to the owners of a seventh sense. But I was actinically aware of an addition to their number — the result of my experiment. This was announced by audible letters of fire, burnt into my brain with inconceivably cold and foul-smelling sounds, and written in the language of Hell. What the actual words were I must not relate, but I give their Latin equivalents in the form of an inscription:

DIVO.M.PANJANDRO.
SEU.DIABOLO.ABSURDISSIMO.
HANC.CLAVIFORMEM.NOTAM.
POSUIT.BODLEIANUM.CAPUT.[16]

Whilst I considered over their point and application with what now appears to have been remarkable self-possession, the shape was executing an infinite medley of synchronous quick-turn changes, from Venus of the cross-roads with her *beauté du diable* to the most bestial Harpy or Tanith with the direst attractions of hellish repulsiveness.[17] He-she-it transfixed me with a lurid leer, with a cobra-glance of quenchless lubricity, and the octopus-tentacles of a noisome lust-fury wound themselves round my very soul. I felt myself drawn from out my vitals downwards, and ever downwards, under the influence of a malignant and monstrous Bodily-Head, and plunged for a million years into an unfathomable malebolge.[18] I fell from Hades to Hades, and underwent all the torments of Inferno in each. At last I reached the bottom of the Bottomless Pit.[19] I opened my eyes, and found myself on the floor of my dissecting room, at the foot of my operating chair.

---

[15] A 'lost soul' is one who is damned to hell for eternity, such as Satan after his rebellion against God. By adding the adjective 'universal' and presenting 'Lost Soul' with initial upper-case letters, Sykes figures a Platonic, essential, all-encompassing phenomenon into which an individual lost soul would be absorbed.

[16] Sykes is parodying the Latin inscription found on an ancient Roman pillar towards the end of *The Great God Pan*. A jumble of mangled Latin and Latin-seeming words, Syke's inscription roughly translates as 'This notorious club-shaped, self-important god or extremely absurd devil M[achen], I place with the Bodley Head'.

[17] Sykes alludes to George Meredith's novel *Diana of the Crossways* (1885), substituting the Roman goddess of chastity (Diana) with the Roman goddess of love (Venus). The phrase '*beauté du diable*' is French for devilish (or demonic) beauty. A harpy is a monstrous, ravenous creature having the head of a woman and the body of a bird. 'Tanith' is another spelling for Tanit, an ancient Phoenician goddess, predominantly a lunar deity.

[18] The term 'Bodily-Head' is a play on the publishing firm The Bodley Head, which published Machen's novel. The Malebolge is the eighth circle of Hell in Dante's *Inferno* (part of his *Divine Comedy*). It is where Deceivers spend eternity.

[19] An echo of the biblical 'bottomless pit' (Revelation 9. 1–2, 11), out of which emerge horse-shaped locusts bidden to torment humans who have not been claimed by God.

Well, I had learnt at any rate the secret of Death-Life, and had seen the Great Pan-demon in his own pandemonium. ...

[Here the MS. rather abruptly ends. It should perhaps be added that the writer finished his days in a private establishment for patients suffering from demonomania. — *Translator's note*.]

Arthur Sykes, 'The Great Pan-Demon: An Unspeakable Story', *National Observer* (4 May 1895), pp. 669–70. No definitive information on Sykes has been found.

Review of
The Three Impostors (1896)

The horrible is sweet to the taste of Mr. Machen. He plays with it a little frivolously at times, but now and then it does seriously take hold of him, and on some of these occasions it impresses us. A curious medley is this book of the sensational, the trivial, and the occult. Written on an old plan, some idea of its design and tone may be gathered from thinking of Stevenson's "Dynamiters," with the sprightliness and fun, but not the frivolity, left out, and with dark occult sin substituted for the grotesque.[1] Every now and again we are struck with admiration of the picturesque and suggestive writing, and sometimes we think the same overweights what had been a better story if more plainly and briskly told. We thought for a time that Mr. Machen was fooling us with his horrible hints. (We had forgotten the contents of the prologue.) The hunt of the gold Tiberius, the ingenious imagination of the three impostors, we had thought might end farcically. Perhaps his learning in the black arts would so have been wasted, but we wish he had some restraining qualities that would keep him from writing such horrors as those in his last chapter.

Anonymous review of *The Three Impostors*,
The Bookman (January 1896), p. 131.

---

[1] Robert Louis Stevenson wrote the collection of linked short stories *More New Arabian Nights: The Dynamiter* (1885) with his wife, Frances Van de Grift Osbourne Stevenson (1840–1914).

Alfred Egmont Hake,
Chapter IX: The Religion of Self,
from *Regeneration: A Reply to*
Max Nordau (1896)

The term egomania is a welcome present from the scientists, which enriches our language with a verbal representation of a psychological condition which is certainly characteristic of our time. We trust that Nordau's diagnosis of the disease will be carefully studied by its victims, especially by those who are in the stage where it appears as egoism, self-sufficiency, indifference to others, to society, to the State, and as that fashionable and superior pessimism which despairs of self as an excuse for despairing of others.[1] For, though Nordau goes very minutely into the psychological aspect of egomania without indicating its origin or the remedies against it, he evidently does not reject the theory, which seems constantly to be confirmed by actualities, that mental diseases may be fostered and aggravated both by those who suffer from them, as well as by surrounding circumstances.

Putting his opinion as a psychologist together with that of others, we seem authorized to hope that when our egotistical pessimists have learned that the aristocratic characteristic on which they pride themselves is the beginning of a mental disease, they will fly to such remedies as may be found in the study of useful science and healthy work.

Such authors as Théophile Gautier, Baudelaire, Rollinat, and others attract especially Nordau's attention; but he deals with them in order to show that they individually had degenerated into egomaniacs, and he does not once try to realize the relation between their so-called degeneracy and the general tendencies of our time.[2] Had he done so, he might have felt inclined to be less

---

[1]   On Max Nordau, see W. L. Courtney's 'Novels and Nerves', note 9.
[2]   Gautier's novel *Mademoiselle de Maupin* (1835) and Baudelaire's poetry collection *Les Fleurs du mal* (1857) were foundational works for the Decadent movement. Maurice Rollinat (1846–1903) was also a French Decadent poet (e.g. *Les Névroses* (1883)).

hard on these exponents of *fin de siècle* corruption. Speaking of the hints which this school of poets and writers sometimes throws out that they are not quite serious, Nordau comes very near to discovering their significance when he says about Baudelaire that perhaps "he sought to make himself believe that, with his Satanism, he was laughing at the Philistines." But Nordau does not follow up the cue he has thus accidentally dropped upon, but adds a sentence revealing the one-sidedness of his inquiry, when he says: "but such a tardy palliation does not deceive the psychologist, and it is of no importance for his judgment."

That may be so. But it is of the utmost importance to humanity. That the yielding to the promptings of "unconsciousness," to the dictates of instincts bad or good, was on the part of the so-called Parnassians an experimental plunge in the dark — a challenge to those who pretended to know better to show them that they were wrong — cannot be denied by any one who has read their writings with some knowledge of the French character.[3]

These men took up literature at a time when the world began to perceive that science could not satisfy its emotional aspirations, that it could not explain the mysteries of the Universe, or bring about that balance between our emotional and intellectual natures on which a healthy life depends. But this was not the only disillusion which humanity experienced at that time. All the hopes which the altruistic feeling had prompted us to base on democratic governments and scientific political economy had vanished. When the Utopias of the economists turned out to be *fata morgana*, instead of the solid ladder leading up to the material heaven promised by the religion of humanity of the scientists, a Babylonian confusion arose among the people who had first been told to worship at the shrine of religion, then at the shrine of science, and now stood without any shrine whatsoever.[4] In France, more than in any other country, we meet with people whose minds are too subtle and whose emotions are too genuine to permit them to dwell contented in that Philistinism which leans on the one side towards the scientific creed or absence of creed, in order to appear modern, and, on the other side, on religion, in order to be safe, but whose real shrine is the money-safe. These French people, mostly authors and artists, had studied both the religious and the scientific theories, and had found the causes of their miscarriage.

The Church had said: "Nature is vile, man is naturally bad, instincts are prompted by the devil, and knowledge is one of the snares of hell." But the Roman Church had not only failed in its mission to keep up the faith and render humanity virtuous and happy, but was responsible for great social troubles, superstitions, and obstacles to progress. It had good intentions, but the way in which it tried to carry them out rendered them valueless. It required power

---

[3]   On the Parnassians, see note 8 of W. L. Courtney's 'Novels and Nerves'.
[4]   The term '*fata morgana*' refers to a type of mirage.

first, much power, complete power over everything, and the acquisition of power did more harm than the Church could do good when ever so powerful. The Protestant Churches in France were gloomy, prudish, anti-artistic, and appealed with difficulty to any French character. Their dogmas seemed incompatible with scientific truth, and their mission appeared to be rather to persuade their members that they were perfect than to render them perfect. Besides, a great many minds throughout the world, accredited with scientific accomplishments, had mercilessly opposed dogmatic religion.

Science, in its turn, when asked, Where is truth? Where is the ideal? could only point to a pile of facts laboriously built up like a brick wall, and had to confess that what it wished to give instead of religion was mere speculations. The ultimate conclusion it pointed to was selfishness, personal irresponsibility, and a mere animal existence. It failed entirely to satisfy the great moving power in the scheme of humanity — emotions — and could not therefore satisfy human yearnings and aspirations.

The postulates of religion — the wickedness of nature and of man — were rejected as groundless, and the guidance of intellect and science was spurned because they were powerless to influence the emotions.

Finding themselves in the plight of a ship driving about in the ocean without compass or rudder, the Parnassians, the Decadents, and many others thought it was time to try a desperate course. Perhaps, after all, they thought, nature is good, perhaps human instincts may be trusted; let us be natural and follow our instincts. There was much to encourage the new departure. It had often been found that the purest joys were the most lasting, that the good was the most beautiful, that lives and actions prompted by the altruistic feelings best satisfied selfish yearnings, that vice was disappointing, unhealthy, degrading, and joy-killing; that virtue improved life, increased the capacity for enjoyment, and beautified mind and body. These observations encouraged the belief in the religion of self. The *Ego* was not bad; but it required freedom to develop itself.

Like all founders of systems and philosophies, the Parnassians and Decadents sought for confirmation of their theories in the possibility of a Utopia. In imagining a state of things under which the self should have unlimited latitude for self-realization, where man could satisfy his highest aspirations and enjoy the greatest possible happiness under the guidance of his altruistic promptings, where his instincts should be so sharpened and developed as to unfailingly select the greatest and the most lasting, and therefore the noblest, pleasures — in imagining such a state of things these experimentalists perceived that society, such as it was around them, offered thousands of obstacles to every attempt at practical realization of their theories. They thus came to look upon themselves as at war with society, its old standards, its prejudices, its religions, and its morals.

Their writings were at once weapons, challenges, rallying-cries. They were intended to deride, to shock, and to draw attention to the new philosophy. The distinction between good and bad was obliterated. The artist and the poet should henceforth express their true feelings and nought else. Instinct should take the place of principles. The devil might be worshipped as well as God. Art should have no other object than art.[5] Nature might be abhorred as well as loved. And so on.

From this moral chaos the self was to rise in all its glory. For the present it was distorted by surrounding circumstances. The ugliness and morbidness of the subjects they wrote about and the distortion of their own feelings were the proofs of the decayed state upon which humanity had entered. Characters such as Huysman's [sic] Duc des Esseintes were intended to illustrate what the present state of society was, and what its present tenets would lead to.[6] He is intended to represent the final result of our civilization, and to show that disgust of our race may be so great as to inspire a man with the belief that by fostering evil and creating criminals he does a good action in so far as he accelerates the destruction of society.

The Parnassians and the Decadents have no proclaimed creed or any programme, and their own opinion of their philosophy is of the haziest kind. We are therefore far from asserting that we have here interpreted them as they would interpret themselves. Whatever may be said of their style and their writings, they have, at least, the merit of being frank and unsophisticated, and we think it must be recognised that, whether they know it or not, they hold themselves up as the "frightful examples" of the chaotic state into which creeds, principles, morals, are falling at the end of this century. To us the moral, both of their existence and of their writing, is that the world, and especially France, stands in sore need of better churches, of a better system of philosophy, and better principles of government. These authors have rendered a great service in tearing away the hypocritical mask which society is so anxious to maintain, and thus demonstrating the great need of regenerating agencies.

Of late, England has been considerably influenced by France, and the æsthetic revolt just referred to naturally affected the English, but merely as a faint echo.

When Nordau, who correctly points out the connection between the Decadents in France and the extreme æsthetes in England, insinuates that the whole of English society is affected by it, he labours under a wrong impression.

---

[5]   Hake is translating Gautier's famous dictum 'l'art pour l'art', from his preface to *Mademoiselle de Maupin*, usually translated as 'art for art's sake', understood to mean that art is self-fulfilling and its worth is not based on external values, such as morality and politics.
[6]   The Duc des Esseintes is the main character in Huysmans's influential Decadent novel *A Rebours*.

We have had here — and we speak purposely in the past tense — a knot of people who have believed, as Nordau states, that a work of art is its own aim, that it may be immoral. But, as he himself has stated, the æsthetic awakening in England has forced art almost in the opposite direction. We have had poets who have imitated Baudelaire and other writers of the same class, but these imitators have, by imitating many others, displayed a weakness which debars them from any great influence. There was a time with us when a thoroughly immoral decadence had a spell of influence and created a sickly literature. But the influence of this sham æstheticism is fast vanishing, since its essence has been mercilessly exposed.[7]

While the influence of the Parnassians and Decadents in France was only small, in England the circumstances which produced them have been in existence among us and have produced effects to some extent similar. The struggle between science and religion, the distrust of both, the failure of social panaceas, and the irresistible pushing of the working class against old social barriers have produced in a great number of educated men a peculiar state of mind which we wish that Nordau had noticed. Whether he would have placed those thus affected among his degenerates as egomaniacs it is impossible for us to decide, but there can be little doubt that egoism is the chief characteristic of a new religion or a new mental disease, which has made large inroads among educated men. It becomes manifest in their pessimism and in their indifferentism. They believe that everything is bad, that the classes are bad, that the masses are bad, that the country is in a bad state, and that everything will finish badly. At the same time they do not care. They will do nothing to avert the coming evils. They hope that none will think them foolish enough to make themselves martyrs. They wish it to be clearly understood that they care only for themselves and that they take no heed of what happens to others. They loathe the working class, and affect a desire to crush them out of existence at one blow. They belong to the few Englishmen who suspect women of vile things, except of course their mothers, sisters, *fiancées*, and wives. They think life hardly worth living, and certainly not worth any special exertions, but their main preoccupation is the state of their health. They study nothing save their own inclinations and cravings and certain excrescences of the most modern literature. Their capacity for hatred is stupendous in its scope but meek in its expression. They claim to enjoy all the benefits of social life without considering themselves obliged to perform any of its duties. They manage to be spendthrifts without being generous, and to be mean without being economical.

But we are strongly averse to classing these social phenomena among the hopeless egomaniacs. They exaggerate their egotism to such an extent as to suggest that they are rather following a foolish fashion than undergoing

---

[7]   On Aestheticism, see the introduction.

moral decay, and that the existence of pinchbeck patriots, political charlatans, sham enthusiasts, and professional philanthropists has frightened them from showing their best side and using their best abilities, and causes them to flout their pessimism and selfishness in every one's face lest they should be taken for one of these.[8]

In spite of their infatuated posing as degenerate egomaniacs, we believe that many of them may be counted upon as part of those elements from which the future regeneration may spring, when the cloud of scepticism has cleared away, and a goal worthy to strive for is discernible.

Alfred Egmont Hake, 'Chapter IX: The Religion of Self', *Regeneration: A Reply to Max Nordau* (New York: G. P. Putnam's Sons, 1896), pp. 230–40. Hake (1849–1916) was an English author, editor, and social commentator. For the study of Decadence, *Regeneration* is his most important work.

---

[8] Pinchbeck is an alloy of zinc and copper that appears like gold; by extension, as an adjective it refers to things that are imitations or, more negatively, fakes. Thus, 'pinchbeck patriots' refers to people who merely pose as patriotic.

Review of
The Hill of Dreams

This is the study, rather than the story, of a morbid or exceptional temperament. Lucian Taylor is not a decadent morally, though he lives for the cult of style, and dies from an overdose of a drug. He is an instance of the crude ferment which is set up in some fine natures who find themselves born with a hopelessly Philistine environment, and often wreck themselves in the effort to get clear. Lucian's father is a poor, scholarly parson in the country, and Mr. Machen has drawn vividly, if unkindly, the conventional Anglican and rural surroundings of the youth's boyhood. He comes up to London, dreams his dream of a mystic city of love and beauty, and dies, with his name written in water. The framework of incident is slight. But Mr. Machen has trained round it a luxuriant growth of analytic reflection, displaying much insight and subtle reading of character. Poor Lucian, living for his ideal's sake in a London garret, is a sad spectacle. But the reader is left with the sense that his sorrows were not unrelieved. He chose such a life deliberately in preference to that of his metropolitan relatives. "He could conceive the fine odour of hot roast beef hanging about the decorous house on Sunday afternoons, papa asleep in the dining-room, mamma lying down, and the children quite good and happy with their 'Sunday' books. In the evening, after supper, one read the *Quiver* till bedtime. Such pictures as these were to Lucian a comfort and a help, a remedy against despair. Often when he felt overwhelmed by the difficulty of the work he had undertaken, he thought of the alternative career, and was strengthened." Mr. Machen, at some length, has sketched this splendid failure. His book is not exhilarating towards the close, but it has an interest all its own, and, as might be surmised, it is excellently written.

Anonymous review of *The Hill of Dreams*,
The Bookman (September 1907), p. 212.

MHRA Critical Texts
Jewelled Tortoise

The 'Jewelled Tortoise', named after J.-K. Huysmans's iconic image of Decadent taste in *A Rebours* (1884), is a series dedicated to Aesthetic and Decadent literature. Its scholarly editions, complete with critical introductions and accompanying materials, aim to make available to students and scholars alike works of literature and criticism which embody the intellectual daring, formal innovation, and cultural diversity of the British and European *fin de siècle*. The 'Jewelled Tortoise' is under the joint general editorship of Stefano Evangelista and Catherine Maxwell.

For a full listing of titles available in the series and details of how to order please visit our website at www.tortoise.mhra.org.uk

CPSIA information can be obtained
at www.ICGtesting.com
Printed in the USA
BVHW091143191118
533502BV00019B/1226/P